Dear Readers,

Okay, I'll admit it—authors have favorite books. I know, I know, books
are like children and we don't always want to admit to liking one better
than another, but it's true. The Goddess Summoning books are my favorite children.

As with my bestselling young adult series, the House of Night, my Goddess Summoning books celebrate the independence, intelligence and unique
beauty of modern women. My heroes all have one thing in common—they
appreciate powerful women and are wise enough to value brains as well
as beauty. Isn't respect and appreciation an excellent aphrodisiac?

Delving into mythology and reworking ancient myths is fun! In Goddess of the Sea, I retell the story of the mermaid Undine, who switches places
with a female U.S. Air Force sergeant who needs to do some escaping of her
own. In Goddess of Spring, I turn my attention to the Persephone and
Hades myth, and send a modern woman to Hell! Who knew Hell and its
brooding god could be hot in so many wonderful, seductive ways?

I hope you enjoy my worlds, and my wish for you is that you discover
a spark of goddess magic of your own!

P. C. Cast

Praise for the novels of P. C. Cast

"Sexy, charming and fun, *Goddess of Love* is the fantasy romance of the year! You will fall in love with this book. (I did!)"

—Susan Grant, *New York Times* bestselling author

"Ms. Cast has taken mythology, Cinderella, a bit of Shakespeare and a dash of Shaw and mixed them with her own style of comedy for a winning read that is as heart-warming as it is funny."

—*Huntress Book Reviews*

"Most innovative . . . From beginning to end, the surprises in P. C. Cast's new page-turner never stopped. Its poignancy resonates with both whimsy and fantasy . . . I loved it!"

—Sharon Sala, *New York Times* bestselling author

"An amusingly tongue-in-cheek take on the Trojan War featuring a modern-day heroine . . . Funny, irreverent and clever . . . You can't go wrong."

—*The Romance Reader*

"Outstanding . . . magic, myth and romance with a decidedly modern twist. Her imagination and storytelling abilities are true gifts to the genre." —*RT Book Reviews*

"Pure enjoyment . . . Anything can [happen] when gods and mortals mix."

—*Rendezvous*

"A fanciful mix of mythology and romance with a dash of humor for good measure . . . Engages and entertains . . . Lovely." —*Romance Reviews Today*

"One of the top romantic fantasy mythologists today." —*Midwest Book Review*

"Captivating—poignant, funny, erotic! Lovely characters, wonderful romance, constant action and a truly whimsical fantasy . . . Delightful. A great read."

—*The Best Reviews*

"A fun combination of myth, girl power and sweet romance [with] a bit of suspense. A must-read . . . A romance that celebrates the magic of being a woman."

—*Affaire de Coeur*

Berkley Sensation titles by P. C. Cast

GODDESS OF THE SEA
GODDESS OF SPRING
GODDESS OF LIGHT
GODDESS OF THE ROSE
GODDESS OF LOVE
WARRIOR RISING
GODDESS OF LEGEND

Anthologies

MYSTERIA
(with MaryJanice Davidson, Susan Grant and Gena Showalter)

MYSTERIA LANE
(with MaryJanice Davidson, Susan Grant and Gena Showalter)

MYSTERIA NIGHTS
(includes Mysteria *and* Mysteria Lane, *with MaryJanice Davidson,
Susan Grant and Gena Showalter)*

ACCIDENTAL MAGIC
(includes P. C. Cast's novellas from Mysteria, Mysteria Lane *and* Mysteria Nights*)*

THE GODDESS COLLECTION, VOLUME ONE
(includes Goddess of the Sea *and* Goddess of Spring*)*

THE
Goddess
Collection

·VOLUME ONE·

P. C. Cast

B
BERKLEY SENSATION, NEW YORK

THE BERKLEY PUBLISHING GROUP
Published by the Penguin Group
Penguin Group (USA) Inc.
375 Hudson Street, New York, New York 10014, USA
Penguin Group (Canada), 90 Eglinton Avenue East, Suite 700, Toronto, Ontario M4P 2Y3, Canada
(a division of Pearson Penguin Canada Inc.) • Penguin Books Ltd., 80 Strand, London WC2R 0RL,
England • Penguin Group Ireland, 25 St. Stephen's Green, Dublin 2, Ireland (a division of Penguin
Books Ltd.) • Penguin Group (Australia), 707 Collins Street, Melbourne, Victoria 3008, Australia
(a division of Pearson Australia Group Pty. Ltd.) • Penguin Books India Pvt. Ltd., 11 Community
Centre, Panchsheel Park, New Delhi—110 017, India • Penguin Group (NZ), 67 Apollo Drive,
Rosedale, Auckland 0632, New Zealand (a division of Pearson New Zealand Ltd.) • Penguin Books,
Rosebank Office Park, 181 Jan Smuts Avenue, Parktown North 2193, South Africa • Penguin China,
B7 Jiaming Center, 27 East Third Ring Road North, Chaoyang District, Beijing 100020, China

Penguin Books Ltd., Registered Offices: 80 Strand, London WC2R 0RL, England

This is a work of fiction. Names, characters, places, and incidents either are the product of the author's
imagination or are used fictitiously, and any resemblance to actual persons, living or dead, business
establishments, events, or locales is entirely coincidental. The publisher does not have any control over
and does not assume any responsibility for author or third-party websites or their content.

THE GODDESS COLLECTION VOLUME ONE

Goddess of the Sea copyright © 2003 by P. C. Cast.
Goddess of Spring copyright © 2004 by P. C. Cast.
Excerpt of "Candy Cox and the Big Bad (Were) Wolf" from *Accidental Magic* by
P. C. Cast copyright © 2006 by P. C. Cast.
Cover photo by Shutterstock. Cover design by SDG Concepts.
Interior text design by Tiffany Estreicher.

PUBLISHING HISTORY
Berkley Sensation trade paperback edition / January 2013

Berkley Sensation trade paperback edition ISBN: 978-0-425-26504-8
An application to register this book for cataloging has been submitted to the Library of Congress.
The Library of Congress has cataloged a prior edition of *Goddess of the Sea* under LCCN: 2004572953.
The Library of Congress has cataloged a prior edition of *Goddess of Spring* under LCCN: 2004718976.

PRINTED IN THE UNITED STATES OF AMERICA

10 9 8 7 6 5 4 3 2 1

Contents

GODDESS OF THE SEA
1

GODDESS OF SPRING
291

Goddess
of the
Sea

For Kim Doner,
muse and friend.
Thank you for being the perfect problem solver.

Acknowledgments

Thank you, Meredith Bernstein, for being a wonderful agent. Your support and belief in me are priceless.

Christine Zika, you are a pleasure to work with. Your insight is invaluable; you truly are the Goddess Editor.

Thanks, Mom, for letting me borrow your maiden name.

Rachael Ryan, thank you for your enthusiasm; you're a great first reader.

And a special thank-you to the students in my second-hour Creative Writing II class for the helpful brainstorming. Hope you like your cameos!

The Valley Spirit never dies.
It is named the Mysterious Feminine.
And the doorway of the Mysterious Feminine
Is the base from which Heaven and Earth sprang.
It is there within us all the while.
Draw upon it as you will, it never runs dry . . .

FROM THE TAO TE CHING

Part One

CHAPTER ONE

Arms filled with groceries, CC struggled to pull her key from the lock and push the door shut behind her with her foot. Automatically, she glanced up at the clock in the foyer of her spacious apartment. Seven thirty already. It had taken her an eternity to finish things up at the Communication Center and then stop by the package store and the commissary. After that, fighting the traffic from Tinker Air Force Base had been like driving through axle-deep mud. To add to her frustration, she had tried to take a shortcut home and had ended up taking a wrong turn. Soon she was hopelessly lost. A kind soul at a Quick Trip had given her directions, and she had felt compelled to explain to him that she was lost only because she had been stationed at Tinker for just three months, and she hadn't had time to learn her way around yet.

The man had patted her shoulder like she was a puppy and asked, "What is a young little thing like you doing in the air force?" CC had treated the question rhetorically, thanked him and driven away, face hot with embarrassment.

Understandably, her already harried nerves jumped at the insistent sound of her ringing phone.

"Hang on! I'm coming!" she yelled and rushed into the kitchen, plopping the bags unceremoniously onto the spotless counter and lunging for the phone.

"Hello," she panted into the dead sound of a dial tone that was broken only by the rhythmic bleat of her answering machine. "Well, at least they left a message." CC sighed and carried the phone with her back to the kitchen, punching in her message retrieval code. With one hand she held the phone to her ear, and with the other, she extracted twin bottles of champagne from one of the bags.

"You have two new messages," the mechanical voice proclaimed. "First new message, sent at five thirty p.m."

CC listened attentively as she picked at the metallic casing that covered the wire-imprisoned champagne cork.

"Hello, Christine, it's your parents!" Her mom's recorded voice, sounding a little unnatural and tinny, chirped through the phone.

"Hi there, Christine!" More distant, but similarly cheerful, Dad's voice echoed from an extension.

CC smiled indulgently. Of course it was her parents—they were the only two people on this earth who still insisted on calling her by her given name.

"Just wanted to say we didn't actually forget your big day."

Here her mom paused, and she could hear her dad chuckling in the background. Forget her birthday? She hadn't thought they had—until then.

Her mom's breathy voice continued. *"We've just been running ourselves ragged getting ready for our next cruise! You know how long it takes your father to pack."* This said in a conspiratorial whisper. *"But don't worry, honey, even though we didn't get your box off, we did manage to fix up a little surprise for our favorite twenty-five year old."*

"Twenty-five?" Her dad sounded honestly surprised. *"Well, good Lord. I thought she was only twenty-two."*

"Time sure flies, dear," Mom said sagely.

"Damn straight, honey," Dad agreed. *"That's one reason I told you we should spend more time traveling—but only one reason."* Dad chuckled suggestively.

"You certainly were right about that *reason, dear,"* Mom kidded back breathlessly, suddenly sounding decades younger.

"They're flirting with each other on my message," CC sputtered. "And they really did forget my birthday!"

"Anyway, we're getting ready to leave for the airport—"

Dad's voice, even more distant, broke in. *"Elinor! Say good-bye, the airport limo is here."*

"Well, have to go, Birthday Girl! Oh, and you have a nice time on your little air force trip. Aren't you leaving in a couple of days?"

Her little air force trip?! CC rolled her eyes. Her ninety-day deployment as noncommissioned officer in charge of Quality Control at the Communications Center at Riyadh Air Base in Saudi Arabia to support the war on terrorism was just a "little air force trip?"

"And, honey, don't you worry about flying wherever it is you're going. You're old enough to be over that silly fear by now. And, my goodness, you did join the air force!"

CC shuddered, wishing her mother hadn't mentioned her phobia—

airplanes—since she would soon be flying halfway around the world over oceans of water. It was the only part of the air force she didn't like.

"We love you! Bye now."

The message ended and CC, still shaking her head, hit the Off button and put the phone on the counter.

"I can't believe you guys forgot my birthday! You've always said that it's impossible to forget my birthday because I was born right before midnight on Halloween." She berated the phone while she reached into a cabinet for a champagne flute. "You didn't even remember my box." She continued to glare at the phone as she wrestled with the champagne cork.

For the seven years CC had been on active duty service in the United States Air Force, her parents had never forgotten her birthday box. Until now. Her twenty-fifth birthday—she had lived one-fourth a century. It really was a landmark year, and she was going to celebrate it with no birthday box from home.

"It's a family tradition!" she sputtered, popping the cork and holding the foaming bottle over the sink.

CC sighed and felt an unexpected twinge of homesickness.

No, she reminded herself sternly, she liked her life in the air force and had never been sorry for her impetuous decision to join the service right out of high school. After all, it had certainly gotten her away from her nice, ordinary, quiet, small town life. No, she hadn't exactly "seen the world," as the ads had promised. But she had lived in Texas, Mississippi, Nebraska, Colorado and now Oklahoma, which were five states more than the majority of the complacent people in her hometown of Homer, Illinois, would ever live in, or even visit.

"Apparently that doesn't include my parents!" CC poured the glass of champagne, sipped it and tapped her foot—still glaring at the phone. It seemed that during the past year her parents had gone on more Silver Adventure Tours than was humanly possible. "They must be trying to set some sort of record." CC remembered the flirty banter in their voices and closed her eyes quickly at that particular visual image.

Her eyes snapped back open, and her gaze fastened again on the phone.

"But Mom, none of your homemade chocolate chip cookies?" She sipped the champagne and discovered she needed a refill. "How am I supposed to cover all the food groups without my birthday box?" She reached into the other bag and pulled out the bucket of Kentucky Fried Chicken, original recipe, of course. Pointing from the chicken to the champagne, she continued her one-sided discourse. "I have the meat group—KFC—mixed with the all important grease group for proper digestion. Then I have the fruit group, champagne, my personal favorite. How am I supposed to complete the culinary birthday ensemble without the dairy/chocolate/sugar group?" She gestured in disgust at the phone.

Lifting the lid off the KFC, she snagged a drumstick and bit into it. Then, using it to punctuate her hand gestures, she continued.

"You know that you guys always send something totally useless that makes me laugh and remember home. No matter where I am. Like the year before last when you sent me the frog rain gauge. And I don't have a yard! And how about the god bless this house stepping stone, which I have to hang on the *wall* of my *apartment*, because I have no house!" CC's disgruntled look was broken by a smile as she recounted her parents' silly gifts.

"I suppose you're trying to tell me to get married, or at the very least, to become a homeowner."

She chewed thoughtfully and sighed again, a little annoyed to realize that she probably sounded fifteen instead of twenty-five. Then she brightened.

"Hey! I forgot about my *other* message," she told the phone as she scooped it back up, dialed her messages, and skipped past her parents' voices.

"Next new message. Sent at 6:32 p.m."

CC grinned around a mouth full of chicken. It was probably Sandy, her oldest friend—actually she was the only high school friend CC still kept in touch with. Sandy had known her since first grade, and she rarely forgot anything, let alone a birthday. The two of them loved to laugh long distance about how they had managed to "escape" small town Homer. Sandy had landed an excellent job working for a large hospital in the fun and fabulous city of Chicago. Her official title was Physician Affairs Liaison, which actually meant she was in charge of recruiting new doctors for the hospital, but she and Sandy loved the totally unrealistic, risqué-sounding title. It was especially amusing because Sandy had been happily and faithfully married for three years.

"Hi there, CC. Long time no call, girl!"

Instead of Sandy's familiar Midwestern accent, the voice had a long, fluid Southern drawl. *"It's me, Halley. Your favorite Georgia peach! Oh, my—I had such a hard time getting your new phone number. Naughty you forgot to give it to me when you shipped out."*

CC's grin slipped off her face like wax from a candle. Halley was one of the few things she hadn't missed about her last duty station.

"Just have a quick second to talk. I'm calling to remind you that my thirtieth

*birthday is just a month and a half away—December fifteenth, to be exact—and
I want you to mark your little ol' calendar."*

CC listened with disbelief. "This is like a train wreck. It just keeps getting
worse and worse."

*"I'm having the Party to End All Parties, and I expect your attendance. So put
in for leave ASAP. I'll send the formal invite in a week or so. And, yes, presents are
acceptable."* Halley giggled like a Southern Barbie doll. *"See y'all soon. Bye-bye
for now!"*

"I don't believe it." CC punched the Off button with decidedly more force
than was necessary. "First my parents forget my birthday. Then not only does it
look like my oldest friend has forgotten it, too, but I get a call from an annoying
non-friend inviting me to *her* party!" She dropped the phone back on the counter. "A month and a half in advance!"

CC shoved the unopened bottle of champagne into the fridge.

"Consider yourself on-deck," she told it grimly. Then she grabbed the open
bottle of champagne, her half-empty glass, the bucket of KFC and marched purposefully to the living room where she spread out her feast on the coffee table
before returning to the kitchen for a handful of napkins. Passing the deceptively
silent phone she halted and spun around.

"Oh, no. I'm not done with you; you're coming with me." She tossed the
phone next to her on the couch. "Just sit there. I'm keeping an eye on you."

CC picked out another piece of delightfully greasy chicken and clicked on
the TV—and groaned. The screen was nothing but static.

"Oh, no! The cable!" Because she would be out of the country for three
months, she had decided to have the cable temporarily disconnected and had
been proud of herself for being so money conscious. "Not tonight! I told them
effective the first of November, not the thirty-first of October." She glanced at
the silent phone. "You probably had something to do with this."

And she started to laugh, semihysterically.

"I'm talking to the telephone." She poured herself another glass of champagne, noting the bottle was now half empty. Sipping the bubbly liquid thoughtfully, CC spoke aloud, pointedly ignoring the phone. "This obviously calls for
emergency measures. Time to break out the Favorite Girl Movies."

Clutching the chicken thigh between her teeth, she wiped her hands on the
paper towel before opening the video cabinet that stood next to her television
set. Through a full mouth she mumbled the titles as she scanned her stash.

"Dirty Dancing, Shadowlands, West Side Story, Gone With the Wind." She

paused and chewed, considering. "Nope, too long—and it's really not birthday material. Humm . . ." She kept reading. "*Superman, Pride and Prejudice, Last of the Mohicans, The Accidental Tourist, The Color Purple, The Witches of Eastwick.*" She stopped.

"This is exactly what I need. Some Girl Power." She plunked the video in the VCR. "No," she corrected herself. "This is better than Girl Power—it's Women Power!" CC raised her glass to the screen, toasting each of the vibrant movie goddesses as they appeared. They were unique and fabulous.

Cher was mysterious and exotic, with a full, perfect mouth and a wealth of seductive ringlets that framed her face like the mane of a wild, dark lioness.

CC sighed. She couldn't really do anything about her own little lips—if she did, they would look like a science experiment. But everything else about her was so small. Maybe it was time to rethink her short, boyish haircut.

Michelle Pfeiffer—now there was a gorgeous woman. Even playing the role of Ms. Fertile Mom, she was still undeniably ethereal in her blond beauty.

No one would ever call *her* cute.

And Susan Sarandon. She couldn't look frumpy even when she was dressed like an old schoolmarm music teacher. She oozed sexuality.

No guy would ever think of her as *just a friend*. At least no heterosexual guy.

"To three amazing women who are everything I wish I could be!" She couldn't believe her glass was empty—and the bottle, too.

"It's a darn good thing we have another." She patted the phone affectionately before rescuing the other champagne bottle from a life of loneliness in the fridge.

Ignoring the fact that her steps seemed a little unsteady, she settled back, grabbed a fourth piece of chicken and slanted a glance at the ever-silent phone. "Bet it shocks you that someone who's so little can eat so much."

It answered with a shrill ring.

CC jumped, almost choking on the half-chewed piece of chicken. "Good Lord, you scared the bejeezes out of me!"

The phone bleated again.

"CC, it's a phone. Get it together, Sarg." She shook her head at her own foolishness.

The thing rang again before she had her hands wiped and her nerves settled enough to answer it.

"H-hello?" she said tentatively.

"May I speak with Christine Canady, please?" The woman's voice was unfamiliar, but pleasant sounding.

"This is she." CC clicked the remote and paused *The Witches of Eastwick.*

"Miss Canady, this is Jess Brown from Woodland Hills Resort in Branson, Missouri. I'm calling to tell you that your parents, Elinor and Herb, have given you a weekend in Branson at our beautiful resort for your twenty-second birthday! Happy Birthday, Miss Canady!" CC could almost see Jess Brown beaming in delight all the way from Branson. Wherever that was.

"Twenty-fifth," was all she could make her mouth say.

"Pardon?"

"It's my twenty-fifth birthday, not my twenty-second."

"No." Through the phone came the sound of papers being frantically rustled. "No, it says right here—Christine Canady, twenty-second birthday."

"But I'm not."

"Not Christine Canady?" Jess sounded worried.

"Not twenty-two!" CC eyed the newly opened second bottle of champagne. Maybe she was drunk and hallucinating.

"But you are Christine Canady?"

"Yes."

"And your parents are Elinor and Herb Canady?"

"Yes."

"Well, as long as you're really you, I suppose the rest doesn't matter." Jess was obviously relieved.

"I guess not." CC shrugged helplessly. She decided she might as well join the madness.

"Good!" Jess's perkiness was back in place. "Now, just a few little details you should know. You can plan your weekend anytime in the next year, but you will need to call to reserve your cabin . . ."

Cabin? CC's mind whirred. What had they done?

". . . at least one month ahead of time or we cannot guarantee availability. And, of course, this gift is just for your personal use, but if you would like to bring a friend, the resort would be willing to allow him or her to join you for a nominal fee—*or* for totally free if he or she would be willing to attend a short informational meeting about our time-share facility."

CC closed her eyes and rubbed her right temple where the echo of a headache was just beginning.

"And along with your wonderful Woodland weekend," Jess Brown alliterated, "your parents have generously reserved a ticket for you to the Andy Williams Moon River Theater, one of the most popular and long-running shows in Branson!"

CC couldn't stop the bleak groan that escaped her lips.

"Oh, I can well understand your excitement!" Jess gushed. "We'll be sending you the official information packet in the mail. Just let me double-check your address . . ."

CC heard herself woodenly confirming her address.

"Okay! I think that's all the information we need. You have a lovely evening, Miss Canady, and a very happy twenty-second birthday!" Jess Brown cheerfully clicked off the line.

"But where *is* Branson?" CC asked the dial tone.

CHAPTER TWO

"THAT'S right!" CC shouted at the TV, sloshing champagne onto the carpet as she raised her glass dramatically. "Click him off, girlfriends! Jack Nicholson wasn't cute, anyway—it was the three of you who really had the magic the whole time."

CC hardly noticed her unsteadiness as she got to her feet to dance the Woman's Magic Victory Dance while the movie credits rolled.

"Mr. Phone." She took a break from her Victory Dance to catch her breath. Fleetingly, she wondered just who had eaten all that KFC.

Mr. Phone seemed to be smiling at her from his place on the couch.

"Do you know that women have all the magic?"

He didn't answer.

"Of course you don't—you're a phone!" CC giggled. "You didn't even know I was twenty-five instead of twenty-two." She laughed until she snorted. "But you do now. And after watching that most excellent movie, you should know that women have magic, too."

Mr. Phone seemed skeptical.

"It's true! Didn't Cher and Michelle and Susan just prove it?" CC wobbled, but only a little. "Oh, I see what you mean. You think *they* have magic, but you don't really believe that an *ordinary* woman, like me, could have magic."

CC couldn't be entirely sure, but he appeared to be willing to listen.

"Okay. You may be right, but what if you're not? What if women really do have something within them, and we just have to find it? Like they did." CC felt the spark of an idea, and her brow wrinkled in an attempt at concentration. "They didn't believe it at first, either, but that didn't stop it from working. Maybe it doesn't matter if you're ordinary-looking, or if you're new somewhere and you don't have any friends yet." Or, CC's mind added, if your birthday has been forgotten. "Maybe all it takes is a leap of faith."

And a milky light flashed in the corner of her left eye, breaking her concentration.

What the . . . ? A little shiver of trepidation fingered its way down the nape of her neck.

The light was coming from behind the closed drapes that shrouded the patio doors leading to her balcony.

CC checked the VCR clock. The digital numbers read 10:05 p.m.

"Must be the streetlights," she told Mr. Phone, but her eyes remained riveted on the captivating glimpse of brightness. The sliver of light she could see had an odd quality, totally unlike the sterile brightness of streetlights.

"Could be headlights from a parked car." But as she said it she knew it couldn't be true. Not in her top floor apartment. Car headlights didn't shine *up*. They also didn't have a quality of warmth that made her want to bathe herself in them.

CC's feet took her to the drapes before she consciously told them to move.

"You asked for some magic," she whispered. Slowly, like she was moving through the sweet twilight between awake and asleep, she reached up and parted the curtains.

"Ohhhh . . ." The word came out on a breath. "It *is* magic."

The full moon hung perfect and luminous above her as if the goddess Diana herself had placed it there as a birthday offering. It bathed the riot of potted plants that crowded the balcony in a warm, opal-like glow. She quickly unlatched the glass doors and stepped out into the gentle warmth of a late October night.

CC's balcony was large, and it looked out on a greenbelt that divided the apartment complex and an upscale neighborhood. The amazing balcony was the reason she had decided to stretch her budget and afford the rent for the pricey apartment. She loved to sit there and let the comforting sounds of the greenery melt away the tension that relentlessly clung to her from work and could even stubbornly stay with her through her kick-boxing class and the warm bubble bath soak she so often took after class. She had spent many evenings there, as was evident by the comfortable wicker rocking chair and the matching whatnot table that was just the right size to hold a book and a glass of something cold. Nestled in the middle of the lush plants was her favorite piece of balcony furniture, a mini version of a chimenea.

Tonight the creamy color of the chimenea caught the moon's caress and reflected its light like moonlight off the sands of an exotic beach.

Suddenly, she tilted her head back and spread her arms, as if she could embrace the night. The full moon filled her vision and she felt her body flush, like she was being saturated in the light of another world.

And her head snapped up.

"It is true," she said to the listening night. "It must be true."

And an idea was born, conceived of champagne and moonlight. CC grinned and whirled back through the open glass doors. Practically skipping, she rushed to her bedroom, already unbuttoning her air force uniform. The dark blue skirt and light blue blouse pooled with her pantyhose and bra.

"Step one."

Naked, CC pulled open her pajama drawer and pawed through it until she found the long, silk nightgown that lay at the bottom, ignored for her more practical cotton nightshirts. A uniform is good for work, but not for magic, she told herself and pulled the pale gown over her head, loving the erotic feel of it as it slid down her naked body.

"I will wear this more often," she promised aloud.

"Step two." She moved resolutely to her spare room, which she had recently begun to set up as an office. So far she had only had the time and money to buy a computer desk and chair for her five-year-old computer. Her books were stacked neatly on the floor, waiting for the bookshelves that she had promised them. She flicked on the overhead light and started searching through the piles of old textbooks, accumulated over the past seven years while she haphazardly took college classes, never sure which field she wanted to major in. CC combed through texts that ranged from Anatomy and Physiology lab guides to Basic Business Accounting 101.

"Here you are!" She pulled out the medium-sized text that had been hidden under an enormous Humanities tome. It was entitled, *The Matriarchal Era—Myth and Legend.* CC fondly remembered her semester of Women's Studies and the witty Professor Teresa Miller who had made that class one of her all-time favorites. She could still hear Ms. Miller's expressive voice reading aloud words that had been authored in an ancient time when women had been revered and even worshipped.

"Where is it?" she mumbled to herself as she scanned the index, her finger lightly going down each row of names, finally stopping near the beginning of the *G*'s.

"Gaea!"

She sat back on her heels, turned to page eighty-six, and read aloud: "Gaea, or Gaia, was an Earth goddess, the Great Mother, known as the oldest of the divinities. She ruled magic, prophecy and motherhood. Although Zeus and other male gods took over her shrines during the emergence of the patriarchal insurgence, the gods swore all their oaths in her name, thus ultimately remaining subjected to her law."

CC nodded her head. This was exactly what she had been looking for. Gaea was the Mother of Magic. Flipping back to the index she turned pages till she found the *R*'s.

"Rituals! Earth Ritual page one-fifty-two." She shuffled through the slick, white pages and made a victorious exclamation when she found it. "Ha! I knew it!" Silently she read the ancient invocation, tugging on her bottom lip in concentration. When she had finished reading, she took the book to her desk and sat quietly for a moment, then with a satisfied smile she wrote a single sentence in blue ink on a piece of plain white Xerox paper and folded it once. Bending the page to mark her place in the text, she headed back to the living room, book and paper in hand.

This time when she stepped onto the balcony she brought with her the book, the piece of paper, a clean champagne flute filled with cold water, a box of long-handled matches and a determination that showed clearly in the square set of her shoulders.

The chimenea was just big enough to hold one block of fragrant pinyon wood. Deftly, she fed its small mouth and lit the dry pinyon. Then she moved to a long, thin planter that was hooked to the wrought iron balcony railing. She caressed the velvety leaves and bent to inhale the tangy fragrance of mint.

"It's a lucky thing that I have such a green thumb." She smiled.

Choosing carefully, she snapped off the tops of several of the larger plants.

The spicy scent of burning pinyon rose from the chimenea like mist. The smoke hovered around the balcony. Clearly visible in the moonlight, it twisted and lifted in the warm breeze like ocean waves. CC's breath caught in excitement as she hurried to position herself in front of the chimenea. She placed the cut mint on the little table next to the glass of water and the piece of paper, then she opened the book to the turned-down page. With a growing sense of excitement she cleared her throat and began to read.

"Great Mother, Gaea, ripe creatress of all that exists, I call upon you to be here with me now."

As she fell into the rhythm of the ancient ritual, the tentative quality left her voice and she felt an unexpected rush of feeling pass over the hair on her bare arms, almost like a spark of static electricity.

"I need your guidance as I strive for spiritual knowledge and growth. Help me also with . . ." CC paused. Here in the text there were the parenthesized words *priestess states her purpose*. She took a deep breath and closed her eyes, concentrating with all of her heart and soul, then she repeated, "Help me also with creating magic in my life."

Reopening her eyes, she continued to read. "I wish with all my heart to accomplish my desires in a positive way. Reveal to me the direction to take. I await your guidance and aid."

A breath of air touched the pages of the open book and for a moment it quivered and felt alive in her hands.

CC shivered in response. The night was hushed, like a lover waiting for her beloved's next words.

"I give my desires and dreams into your keeping."

With one hand she held open the book. She used her other hand to fan her fingers slowly through the drifting pinyon smoke.

"By air, I create the seed." The smoke swirled in lazy, dancing circles.

With the same hand she reached for the piece of folded paper, on which was written a single sentence in CC's compact cursive hand, "*I want magic in my life*." The wish filled her mind . . . Oh, please, she prayed.

"By fire, I warm it."

The paper went into the fire and caught instantly ablaze with a fierce, green flame.

Through her mind brushed the thought that it shouldn't have done that—it was just a simple piece of copy paper. Nothing about it could have made a wild green flame. CC's heartbeat increased erratically, but she forced her hand to be steady as she took the crystal glass filled with cold, clear water, and with delicate flicks of her fingers she scattered it in a small circle around the chimenea.

"By water, I nourish it."

CC stepped within the newly made circle. It glistened in the moonlight like lacework made of mercury. She bent back to the table and gathered the sprigs of mint in her hand.

"By Earth, I cause it to grow."

She tossed the delicate plants into the fire where they sizzled and glowed. She watched as they began to dissolve. For an instant CC thought they looked like some kind of exotic seaweed, and she could actually smell the salty tang of the ocean.

"From spirit, I draw the power to make all things possible as I join in the power of the goddess." With a burst of emotion CC dropped the text to the table and completed the words of the ritual as if they were written upon her heart. "Thank you, Gaea, Great Mother Goddess!"

As if in response to her invocation, the breeze shifted and cooled. The pinyon smoke spiraled up, diaphanous and glowing with the light of aquamarines. Transfixed, CC watched it disappear into the moon-drenched sky.

The breeze continued to increase, and CC impulsively raised her hands over her head, fingers outstretched as if she could capture the moon within them. Slowly she began to sway, letting the wind move her in time to the symphony of the night. Her bare feet found their own dance as they followed the circumference of the damp circle. The wind licked her body, drawing the silk of her nightgown against the warmth of her skin.

CC looked down at her body, and felt her eyes widen in surprise. Usually she thought of herself as too petite to be considered sexy, but tonight the moonlight mingled with silk, casting a spell on her body. Through the thin fabric her breasts were clearly visible and her small, perfect nipples felt sensitive and tight as they puckered against its softness. She swung her leg forward in a graceful dance step that had lain dormant within her since grade-school ballet lessons. The nightgown molded itself to her thighs, making her feel like she had just stepped from the canvas of a voluptuous Maxfield Parrish painting. The moonlight caught the ripples and folds of silk, giving life to the pale color and turning it into frothing sea foam. She laughed aloud at her unexpected beauty and twirled on feet that had wings.

"I have magic!" she proclaimed to the night.

Shadows flitted across the balcony, and she looked up to see wisps of clouds, like half-formed thoughts, beginning to obscure the face of the attendant moon. The wind increased, and CC's dance kept time with it, mirroring the tempo of the swaying trees.

The deafening crack of thunder should have frightened her, but instead CC felt like the coming storm had originated within her body. When the blue-white shard of lightning pierced the sky, it only fueled her appetite for the night, and she whooped, adding her own voice to the tempest.

Like a ripened fruit the sky burst apart, sending a rush of whimsical rain to join in her celebration. CC spun and twirled and laughed aloud. She reveled in every instant. She noticed how her plants seemed to move their leaves with her, and how the falling rain glistened amidst them like faceted jewels. Her eyes were drawn to the mundane stretch of blacktop parking lot below her, and she was amazed at how the rain had transformed it into the glasslike surface of a mysterious, shadow-covered ocean.

CC lifted her arms and pirouetted as the rain swathed her in damp majesty. She laughed aloud and believed she clearly heard the sound of another woman's musical laughter—and for a magically suspended moment their voices merged, filling the balcony with joy and love.

Then the sky exploded with another flash of light, and the rain roped down in a torrent. CC realized that her drapes were billowing wildly within her apartment and rain was drenching her living room carpet. Still laughing, she scrambled wetly through the open patio doors and pulled them securely closed behind her.

Shivering a little in a puddle of sopped carpet she should have felt melted; instead she felt invigorated. CC held her arms away from her body and watched as drops of water, sparkling like diamonds, slid down the soaked cloth of her nightgown.

"I have never been this alive." She was compelled to speak the words aloud. She shook her head, letting the water float around her, and ran her fingers through her short curls.

"I will let it grow," she promised.

And she realized her hair wasn't all she was ready to change. She was going to break her own mold.

Walking lightly, she made her way back to her bathroom and pulled a thick towel from the linen shelf. On the short dresser next to her bed she lit a candle that she had bought from a quaint little boutique aptly named the Secret

Garden. She breathed deeply, filling herself with the candle's delicious vanilla-rum fragrance. The sweet scent drifted around her as she flicked the thin, damp straps of the gown from her shoulders and let the fabric slither from her body. Standing in the candlelit room she began to towel-dry, rubbing her already sensitized skin with light, circular strokes. Her hair was almost dry when she slid naked between the coolness of the clean sheets. With fingertips that were on fire, she caressed herself. Closing her eyes she moaned and arched into her hand, delighted and surprised by the exquisitely electric sensations that cascaded through her body.

As velvet sleep swept her away, CC was sure she heard a woman's laughter, the same magical laughter she had heard while she danced in the rain on her balcony. CC's lips curved into a smile, and she slept.

And while she slept, CC dreamed that a man's voice called to her in deep, seductive tones. Her dreaming body responded to that call and strained forward, but she felt unusually sluggish. In her dream she opened her eyes. She was surrounded by a veil of liquid blue. I'm underwater, her sleeping mind acknowledged.

Come to me, my love.

The rich voice sounded within her mind, and CC's pulse jumped.

Yes! She tried to yell her answer, but in her dream she was mute.

A light shimmered over her head and she peered up, squinting into the brightness. Just above the surface of the water a shape appeared. CC floated up, and the shape took on form and became a man. He was dark and exotic. His hair fell around his wide, bronzed shoulders in a black wave and his eyes laughed down at her. Through the ripples of the crystal waves she could see his easy smile as his outstretched hand beckoned to her.

She tried to reach up and take his hand, but her arm felt leaden. It would not obey her desire to respond.

The man's handsome face saddened. He looked lost and the voice inside her head was filled with longing.

Please come to me . . .

CHAPTER THREE

A different kind of light played crimson shadows across her closed eyelids. What an odd dream, CC thought as she stretched luxuriously. The smooth feel of fresh sheets against her naked body mixed with the poignant, unfulfilled seduction of the dream. She still felt super-sensitized and her naked body tingled.

Naked?

She never slept in the nude. Why the heck was she naked? She flung her eyes open and cringed at the brightness of her bedroom, then quickly closed them again. It couldn't be later than 0730. Could it? Hadn't she set her alarm? Was she late for work? Her heart pounded.

Memories of the night came flooding back—the two bottles of champagne, the movie, the sudden brainstorm that led to the idea that led to the ritual. Here she cringed and tried to burrow down into her sheets, but her memory was relentless.

"You'd think I'd had enough champagne that I would have blacked it all out," she groaned.

She peeked over the side of the bed. The vanilla-rum candle had burned out. Well, at least she could be thankful she hadn't set her apartment on fire. She glanced down. Her nightgown made a rumpled, pale spot on her cream-colored carpet.

She shook her head and sighed. Two bottles of champagne—what had she been thinking?

"I forgot," she muttered. "The process of rational thought stops after bottle number one."

No wonder she'd had the weird dream; she'd been in a drunken stupor.

She glanced back at the nightstand and squinted at her bedside alarm clock, which read 11:42 a.m. CC's eyes widened. Panic banished the dream, and she sat bolt upright.

"It's almost noon!" She yelped, scrambling to her closet to frantically pull out a fresh uniform before she remembered that she didn't have to report for duty that day. She was flying out tomorrow, which meant that today would be dedicated to packing and tying up the loose ends being gone for three months created.

She took a shaky breath and ran her hand through her hair. Actually, the only reason she had to go on base at all that day was to stop by the orderly room and pick up her new set of dog tags. (She was still chagrined that she'd lost her old set during the move from Colorado.) Besides that, she just needed to buy some last minute toiletries for the trip, come back to the apartment and move her plants from the balcony to her living room so that her neighbor, Mrs. Runyan, could water them and finish her packing. And, of course, she had to remember to drop her key off with Mrs. Runyan before she left for the airport the next morning.

CC took a deep breath. What was wrong with her? She was usually so organized and logical about a deployment. She had planned to get up early that morning and finish her business on base, and then get her plants taken care of and her packing completed early so that she could spend the rest of the day relaxing. The trip to Saudi would be long and exhausting, and CC definitely was not looking forward to it—and that's not even considering how much she hated flying.

She shook her head. Instead she'd chosen to send herself off with an enormous hangover. CC marched into the bathroom and flipped on the shower. As the warm, soothing mist began to rise, she started searching through the cabinet for some aspirin for her tremendous headache. But before she found it, she stopped herself.

Headache? No, now that her heart wasn't yammering a mile a minute, and she wasn't afraid she'd been AWOL for half a day, she realized her head didn't actually hurt. At all. Actually, she felt fine. She closed the cabinet door and studied herself in the mirror.

Instead of the sallow, hollow-eyed look of a morning-after hangover, CC's chestnut-colored eyes were clear and bright. Her gaze traveled down her naked body. Her skin was healthy and vibrant; she glowed with a lovely pinkish flush. It was almost like she had spent the night being pampered in an exclusive spa instead of drinking two bottles of champagne, eating a ton of KFC and getting caught in a thunderstorm while she danced in the moonlight.

"Maybe . . ." she whispered to her reflection.

A thrill of delight traveled the length of her nakedness as she remembered the moonlight and the electric passion it had fueled within her body. She could almost feel the night against her skin again.

The warm mist from the shower crept around her in thick, lazy waves.

"Like the pinyon smoke," she gasped, and her heart leapt. "Remember," she told her reflection. "You promised to break your mold."

Tentatively, she raised her arms, trying to mimic her movements of the previous night and turned slowly in a sleepy pirouette. The fog swirled around her, licking her naked skin with a liquid warmth that reminded her of her sensuous, bittersweet dream. Thinking about the handsome stranger her sleeping mind had conjured, CC continued to spin, catching quick glimpses of herself in the mist-veiled mirror. Her petite body looked lithe and mysterious, as if she had trapped some of the moonlit magic within herself.

"You believed last night; believe today, too." As she spoke something deep within her seemed to move, like smooth water over river pebbles.

"Magic . . ." CC whispered.

Maybe the night and the dream had been signs of things to come—things that would change—in her life. Maybe she just had to be open to change and answer when it called.

"Magic . . ." CC repeated.

She danced and laughed her way into the shower, loving the warm fingers of water that rippled down her body.

She didn't stop smiling the entire time she dressed and applied just a touch of makeup. The feeling wouldn't go away. It was like someone had taken a key and opened up something inside her, and now that it was open, it refused to be locked away again.

She stepped into her favorite pair of button-up 501 jeans. After listening to the decidedly cooler weather forecast, she pulled on her thick gray sweatshirt with AIR FORCE written in block lettering across her chest. Her feet felt light as she grabbed a V8 Splash from the fridge and hurried out of her apartment.

The stairs that spiraled gracefully from her top-floor apartment were still damp from last night's storm, which made CC's smile widen. Everything looked preternaturally clear and beautiful. Her car was parked almost directly below her balcony, and as she unlocked it, she glanced up. Her lips rounded in a wordless *O* of delight. The light of the midday sun formed a halo over the rich green foliage that still sparkled with beads of rain, making her balcony appear more like something submerged in an ocean than something on land.

Magic is happening. The thought sprang unbidden into her mind, and instead of questioning it, CC took a deep breath and let the enticing idea settle.

The gate guard at Tinker's North Entrance was checking military IDs, and when her turn came, CC rolled down her window and beamed a cheery "Good morning!" to the serious-looking young airman.

The granite set of his face softened, and he returned her grin with an endearingly lopsided smile. "It's afternoon, ma'am," he corrected gently.

"Oops!" She grinned. "Well, everything's so bright and clear that it still seems like morning."

"Hadn't thought about it till now, but I guess you're right. It is real pretty today." He looked honestly surprised at the discovery. "You have a good day, ma'am." He waved her through the gate, but his eyes stayed fixed on her car and the lopsided smile was still painted on his face long after she'd disappeared.

The Communications Squadron's orderly room was located in the Personnel Building. It was a typical military structure, large and square and made of nondescript red brick. CC was pleased to see that a front row parking space was open. Usually the parking lot was ridiculously crowded, and she had to park far away down the street. The lawn surrounding the building and the hedges that bordered the entrance were meticulously manicured. The sense of obsessive neatness carried through to the interior of the building as well.

CC pulled open the door and was greeted by the familiar smell of military clean. Yes, ma'am. You *could* eat off the floors, walls, ceilings and desks . . . literally. Directly in front of her a full-length mirror showed CC her reflection. She automatically read the words printed across the top of the mirror: does your appearance reflect your professionalism? CC started to grin sheepishly at her jeans and sweatshirt, then she did a fast double take.

Had her eyes ever looked so big? Entranced, she stepped closer to the mirror's slick surface. Her mother had always described her eyes as "cute" or "doe-like." CC usually didn't give them much thought beyond being glad that she had twenty-twenty vision. But today they seemed to fill her face. Their ordinary hazel color sparkled with—

"May I help you, ma'am?"

The rough voice caused CC to jump guiltily. Her cheeks felt warm as she turned around to face a weathered-looking chief master sergeant.

"Uh, yeah. Can you tell me where I'd go to pick up my dog tags?"

"Sure can." As soon as she'd started speaking his gruff appearance softened, and he smiled warmly at her. "The office for tags and military IDs is on the third floor. You can take the elevator that's down this hall." He gestured to the right.

"Thank you, Chief," CC said and bolted to the elevator, face blazing.

The old chief stood for a moment looking after her.

"Now there's a pretty girl," he pronounced to the empty air.

The ID office wasn't hard to find—it was the busiest office in the building. CC sighed as she took a number and found a seat along the wall. Orderly rooms were always ultra-busy during the lunch hour. She should have known better. Trying to find an interesting article in an old *Air Force Times* newspaper, she wished she had remembered to bring a book with her.

The room was almost empty and the black hands of the government issue clock told her forty-five minutes had passed when her number was finally called and she retrieved her new set of dog tags. Finally! CC felt like she'd been set free. She punched the Down button on the elevator, and as the door glided open she ticked off her "To Do" list on her fingers.

One: go to the Base Exchange and get a few toiletries. Two: pick up some plant food—her stomach growled. And three: some people food. She'd eaten most of the KFC last night, and anyway she couldn't handle KFC two nights in a row. Or at least she shouldn't.

She had just begun to step forward into the elevator when a woman's commanding voice spoke a single word.

"Wait!"

CC hesitated and turned. The woman standing behind her was breathtakingly lovely.

"What?" CC asked stupidly, stunned by the woman's beauty. She was tall—she seemed to tower over CC's petite five foot one inch frame. And her hair was amazing; CC had never seen anything so beautiful. It was the color of rich earth and it cascaded to the curve of her waist. Her face was regal and her cheekbones were high and well formed. But it was her eyes that captured CC in their liquid blue depths.

"Wait, Daughter." The woman smiled, and CC felt the warmth of that smile envelop her. She wanted to ask why she should wait, and why the incredibly gorgeous woman would call her daughter, but her mouth didn't seem to want to work. All she could do was to stand there and grin inanely back at the woman like a nervous kindergarten child meeting her teacher.

"WAIT, MA'AM!"

The shout came from the far end of the hall, and she turned her head just in time to see a man dressed in a firefighter's uniform launching himself at her. The tackle carried them several feet from the elevator's open doors. As soon as they slid to a halt the firefighter jumped up.

"Are you okay, ma'am?" He was trying to help her to her feet while he brushed nonexistent dirt off her jeans.

CC couldn't believe it. The wind had been knocked out of her, so all she could do was gasp for air and glare at the man.

"Sorry, ma'am. Didn't mean to be so rough, but I had to stop you from getting in that elevator," he said.

"W-what," CC sucked air and wiped her tearing eyes, "are you t-talking about?"

"Well, the elevator, ma'am." He pointed at the still-open doors.

The doors must be stuck, CC concluded.

"You knocked me over because the doors were sticking?" Thankfully she was regaining her ability to breathe and speak at the same time.

"No, ma'am. Not 'cause the doors are stuck." As if on cue the doors closed. "Because the elevator is stuck." He paused, letting CC absorb his words. "On the first floor."

"That can't be," CC spoke woodenly. "I just rode it up here."

The firefighter made a scoffing sound. "Sure, and an hour ago it was working. It just stuck 'bout five minutes ago. We were running an exercise next door for some new recruits when the First Shirt asked us to give him a hand in posting the warning tape and being sure that everyone on this floor knew about the problem."

For the first time CC noticed that clutched in one hand he had a roll of yellow warning ribbon much like the tape civilian police used to secure crime scenes.

"I don't believe it," she said.

"Take a look for yourself. Just be careful." He stepped out of her way.

CC approached the elevator and pressed the Down button, just like she had only minutes before. The doors swung smoothly open and CC peered down into a dark shaft of nothingness. She felt dizzy.

"Good thing I saw you. I'd hate to think what would have happened if I'd been a second later." The firefighter shook his head and pursed his lips.

"But it wasn't you," CC said shakily. "I *was* getting ready to step into the elevator." CC looked wildly around the hall, ashamed it had taken her so long to acknowledge the woman. "It was the woman standing behind me. She warned me—that's why I hadn't already walked into the elevator."

CC felt a wave of nausea. She hadn't been paying attention to her surroundings; she'd been too busy tallying errands.

"Uh, ma'am," the firefighter said gently. "Are you sure you're feeling okay?"

"Of course. I'm fine." CC was still looking down the hallway, trying to catch a glimpse of the beautiful woman.

"Maybe you should sit down for a while."

"What are you talking about?" CC snapped. First the guy tackled her, then he was trying to analyze her. She checked the stripes on his arm. Yep. She even outranked him. "I just want to find the woman who warned me so that I can thank her."

"That's what I mean, ma'am. There was no one else in the hall with you."

A chill shivered through CC's body. She shook her head in disbelief. "Yes there was. She was standing right behind me. I was talking to her when you knocked me over."

"Ma'am," he took her arm and eased her down the hall away from the open shaft. "You weren't talking to anyone. You were just standing there getting ready to step into the elevator."

"She was right behind me," CC repeated.

"No one was there. No one is here now." His gesture took in the rest of the hall. "There's only one way out besides the elevator, and that's the stairwell, right there." He pointed at the doorway from which he had emerged. "She would have had to walk past me to get there, and she didn't."

"You didn't see her?" CC asked numbly.

"No, ma'am," he said quietly. "And people don't just appear and disappear like magic."

Magic . . . The word echoed in CC's head and she had to struggle to pay attention to the rest of what he was saying.

"Maybe you hit your head. You know you could have blacked out for a second. I knocked you down pretty hard. Our guys can take you to sick call at the clinic and have you checked out."

"No!" CC swallowed, regaining her wits. "See, I'm fine." She ran her fingers through her close-cropped curls and around her head, pushing and prodding without cringing to show there was no tenderness.

The door to the stairwell opened and another fireman appeared and yelled down the hall. "Hey, Steve! Got that tape run yet?"

"I'm working on it," CC's fireman answered.

"Well, hurry it up. We don't have all day to play with pretty girls." He smiled and tipped his helmet to CC.

Steve's face colored, and CC took the opportunity to make her retreat.

"I'll let you get back to work." She headed quickly for the door, which the second fireman held wide open for her. "And I do appreciate you saving me from a nasty fall."

She ducked into the stairwell and Steve's "Don't mention it, ma'am" drifted after her, but CC hardly heard him. She was too busy repeating a single sentence that she could see clearly in her memory. It was written in her concise cursive on blue ink against plain white paper.

I want magic in my life.

CHAPTER FOUR

CC drove quickly to the Base Exchange, glad it was situated between the Personnel Building and the base's north exit. She could run in, grab what she needed and get right out—and then she could hurry back to her apartment. She needed to be alone to sit and think about what had just happened.

She hadn't imagined the woman; she was certain of that. But that was all she was certain of.

She pulled into the crowded Base Exchange parking lot, and as she drove by the main entrance she noticed an empty parking spot—the closest spot to the front doors that wasn't reserved for high-ranking officers. CC parked with a growing sense of wonder.

"I am having some seriously good parking luck today," she murmured.

The Base Exchange, known by military personnel as the BX, reminded CC of a weird cross between an upscale department store and a flea market. Tinker's BX was no exception. Just inside the front doors, but before she entered the body of the Exchange itself, was scattered booth after booth of sales people hawking everything from deli sandwiches to "designer" handbags and jewelry. CC hurried past the colorful area and impatiently let the BX worker check her ID. She almost sprinted to the section of the store that sold toiletries and haphazardly chose the necessary travel items. Then she had to stop herself from screaming with impatience as the cashier seemed to take forever to ring up her purchases.

Rushing back out the door, the scent of food and the insistent growling in her stomach made her pause. Why not get something for dinner right there? That meant she wouldn't have to stop again on the way home. She followed her nose down the row of kiosks until she located the deli sandwich stand and ordered a hot Italian sub.

While she was waiting for her order to be filled, the back of her neck began to itch. Like someone was staring a hole into it. Brow wrinkled in irritation, CC turned to find the woman at the jewelry stand directly across from the sandwich booth smiling graciously at her. She was wearing a flowing dress made of sapphire velvet. She raised a well-manicured, bejeweled hand and gestured for CC to join her.

"Come!" she said.

CC opened her mouth to decline the odd invitation, but the woman spoke again.

"No. Do not think. Just come." Her thick accent rolled the words.

"That'll be five dollars," the sandwich man said.

CC paid him, and then she did something unusual, something outside her mold. Without thinking, she let her feet carry her across the aisle to the jewelry stand.

"Ah," the woman said, taking CC's right hand in both of hers and turning it over so she could study her palm. "I knew it. She has touched you."

"She?" CC asked.

"The Great Mother." The woman didn't look up from CC's palm, but kept speaking matter-of-factly in her richly accented voice. "Yes, I saw it in your aura, and I see it clearly here. You are beloved by her."

"How—" CC started to ask, but the woman wasn't finished.

"But your journey will be long and arduous." She squinted at CC's palm like she saw something disturbing there.

"Well, I am leaving for a ninety-day TDY to Saudi Arabia tomorrow," CC said.

The woman's gaze lifted from CC's palm.

"No, little daughter, I do not mean a journey of distance. I mean a journey of spirit." CC was struck by a sense of familiarity as their eyes met. Then the woman abruptly dropped her hand and turned.

"Where is it?" The woman muttered to herself as she searched through a nest of hanging necklaces. "Ah, here you are." Triumphantly she held the necklace out to CC.

It was lovely. The silver chain was long and delicate, and suspended from it by a latticework of silver ivy was a glistening cinnamon-colored stone. It was about the size of CC's thumb and shaped like a perfect teardrop.

"Amber," the woman said. "It was formed by resin fossilized in the bosom of the earth."

"I've never had any amber," CC said. "But I've always thought it beautiful."

"This piece is the same color as your eyes." The woman smiled.

CC thought she was doing one heck of a sales job. "How much is it?" CC asked, returning the exotic woman's smile.

"This necklace is not for sale."

CC frowned. Was the woman trying to get her to look at a more expensive piece?

"This necklace is a gift." In one motion the woman placed it over CC's head.

"But, I can't accept this!" CC sputtered.

"You must. It is meant to be yours," she said simply. "And I sense that there has been a recent event for which a gift is appropriate. No?"

"Well, it was my birthday yesterday," CC admitted.

"Ah, a Samhain child. How appropriate. So you see, it is already yours. Take it with you on your journey. Wear it always. Amber is an earth stone. Know that it has the power to absorb negative energy and turn it to positive." The woman's eyes were dark and serious. "You may have need of it, little daughter." Then her eyes lightened and she hugged CC. "Now go home and prepare." She cocked her head like she was listening to something and added, "Your plants are calling you."

"Thank you," CC said. Blinking in surprise, she let the woman turn her and give her a gentle push toward the front doors. The amber drop nestled heavy and warm between her breasts. CC touched the stone and her face broke into an amazed grin.

CHAPTER FIVE

Dear Mrs. Runyan,

Thank you for taking care of my plants while I'm gone. I put the plant food next to the watering can in the kitchen. Please remember to feed them every two weeks. And it would be really nice if you'd talk to them a little, too. I know it sounds silly, but I think they like it. Enclosed you'll find my key and a gift certificate to Luby's Cafeteria. I hope you and your girlfriends have fun. I'll be home in ninety days. If anything goes wrong you have the number of my first sergeant on Tinker.

Again, thank you so much.

CC

P.S. Yes, you can borrow any of my videos! Enjoy!

CC slipped the letter into the envelope with her key and the Luby's gift certificate, then she slid it under Mrs. Runyan's apartment door. Mrs. Runyan was sweet and about a thousand years old, and she flat refused to take any money for watering CC's plants and keeping an eye on her apartment while she was gone. But CC knew that she and her girlfriends loved to go to Luby's after church on Sundays—so she'd splurged on a one-hundred-dollar gift certificate for her. CC wished she didn't have to leave so early, and she could be there to see the expression on Mrs. Runyan's kind face when she found the gift certificate. The thought made her smile in the predawn light while she struggled to carry her duffel bag, suitcase and carry-on bag down the three flights of winding steps and stuff them in the trunk of her car.

It was so early that the traffic to Tinker was unusually light, and CC's thoughts drifted back to the events of the past twenty-four hours. After she'd left the base and gone home, the rest of her day had been spent moving her horde of plants and finishing her packing.

There certainly hadn't been any magical happenings in any of that. That night she had even stood on the balcony trying to recapture the moonlit magic of the night before, but clouds had rolled in and there was no moonlight, nor any magic.

Could she have imagined the lady by the elevator yesterday? She didn't think so. The weight of the amber tear between her breasts told her the lady at the BX hadn't been a figment of her imagination either. And why should she question and try to poke holes into what had happened? She wanted it to be true; she wanted magic in her life.

One hand crept up to rub the amber drop with restless fingers, and CC nervously checked the car clock. It was 0530, and she was almost to the base. The shuttle that would take her from Tinker to Will Rogers Airport left the base at 0615. Her flight departed Will Rogers for Baltimore at 0825. At Baltimore she would board a military charter that would take her to the U.S. Air Base in Italy. From there she would travel via an Air Force C-130 cargo plane to Riyadh, Saudi Arabia. The whole trip would total just over twenty-four hours, with about twenty of those hours spent in the air.

And she really didn't like to fly. Right now the sour feeling in her stomach was a silent testament to how much she was not looking forward to the long trip.

If her mom had been here she would berate her, for the thousandth time, for joining the *air* force.

"Well, honey," she would say, "why in the blue blazes would you join the flying branch of our armed forces when you're afraid to fly?"

CC's answer was always the same. "I researched it, Mom. The air force was the branch of the service that had the best overall package. And there are a lot of jobs in the air force that have nothing to do with flying. Mine, for one example."

Her mother would make a scoffing sound and shake her head. CC had to wonder if her parents really understood that her military job was much like a civilian position in a big multi-media corporation. She was in charge of quality assessment for the Base Communications Center. Did they think she was covertly flying fighter planes?

She usually had only one or two temporary duty assignments each year, and, yes, she had to fly to them, but that would be no different than what her schedule would be like if she had worked her way up in a civilian company. Many jobs required their employees to travel periodically.

Well, CC smiled to herself, civilian jobs didn't typically require their employees to travel periodically into war zones. Her smile tightened. She was good at her job, and she was well trained. And she believed in what she was doing. She didn't think of it as being a hero or particularly patriotic; she had simply chosen a career that gave her the opportunity to serve her country in a very visible way. And, she admitted to herself, she liked the adventure of the air force. There were always new people to meet and new places to go. CC thrived on change—she'd had enough stagnation in the first eighteen years of her small town life to last for the next fifty-eight.

She breathed deeply, trying to quiet her nerves. Actually, she realized that she was feeling more than the normal amount of her preflight jitters. Right now she'd rather face several members of the Taliban than a long airplane flight. Weird, she told herself, noting again the sick feeling in her stomach. Maybe she was having some kind of premonition of danger? Could she be ultranervous because her sixth sense was trying to tell her something?

Her stomach growled, startling her, then making her smile. No, it was more likely that her upset stomach had been caused by the fact that she had been in too much of a hurry to eat breakfast. She'd have to try and get something to eat on the plane. She laughed out loud. Now there was something really terrifying— airline food. . . .

CC reminded herself of that while her stomach continued to roll nervously as she made her way across America. The layover in Baltimore was brief, and she had to scramble to catch her shuttle to the military charter, which was actually a huge commercial 747 stuffed with military personnel of varying ranks. CC stuck her face in a book and tried desperately to ignore the fact that they were hurling forward at an obscene rate of speed entirely too far above the earth.

The captain of the flight announced via the intercom that they would be landing at the air base in Italy in twenty minutes. He informed them proudly that the weather was a beautiful seventy-five degrees, with clear skies and a local time of almost 10:00 a.m., even though CC's internal clock insisted it was almost 2:00 a.m. instead. She ran her fingers through her tousled hair and rubbed her sand-filled eyes, wishing desperately that she could have relaxed enough to sleep during the long flight.

Just one more leg of this trip, she told herself. CC took the file that held her orders and her itinerary out of her carry-on. Yes, she'd remembered correctly. She had a little over an hour and a half layover in Italy. Unfortunately, it was not enough time to see any of the country, but it would give her time to grab something to eat and to change from the civilian clothes she had been traveling in, to the desert cammo fatigues that were the accepted uniform for the last leg of her trip on the C-130.

The thought of the military cargo plane made her shudder and almost forget that the plane she was on was landing, the second most dangerous time in a flight—takeoff being the most dangerous time. CC had flown in a C-130 twice before; both times had been extremely uncomfortable. C-130s were huge cargo transport vehicles with bigger-than-human sized propellers, no real passenger seats and rough, loud rides. That's why they were called C-130s. The *C* stood for cargo, which is what they were built to carry, not passengers.

CC thought that it would probably be a futile quest to try and find a nice bottle of chilled champagne at 10:00 a.m. anywhere on the air base within walking distance of the flight line, but she decided that as soon as she changed clothes she would make the attempt. Food could wait. Champagne should be a travel necessity.

"SARG! Wake up, we're boarding now." A rotund master sergeant shook her shoulder.

CC looked blearily around and tried to remember where she was.

"Let's go—everyone else is already on board and we're closin' up the tail." The master sergeant continued. "Should be airborne in no time."

Reality caught up with CC, and she scrambled to follow the master sergeant out of the passenger waiting area and onto the flight line proper. She rubbed her fingers through her hair and struggled to wake up. She couldn't believe she'd fallen into such a deep sleep. Her mouth tasted stale and her mind was fuzzy, but she quickly pieced together the past hour and a half. She had changed out of her jeans and sweater into her desert fatigues, then she'd gone in search of libations. No, she hadn't found any champagne, just a semihot roast beef sandwich and a semicold beer. She guessed she should have never had that beer—it certainly hadn't agreed with her like champagne did.

And then all thoughts of food and drink scattered out of her head as she approached the C-130. The enormous plane crouched on the runway like a mutated insect. It was painted the typical military green, which did nothing to dispel its buglike appearance. Its opened tail end was facing her, and she could glimpse enough of the inside of the thing to see that it was crammed full of huge, plastic-draped pallets of cargo. CC mentally shook her head in disgust. It looked like some horrible bug that was getting ready to poop. The metallic sound of hydraulics being engaged clicked on, and CC watched the tail section begin to close.

The master sergeant motioned at her to catch up with him. "Don't worry about the butt end being closed. You can board through the door in the front."

He pointed to a tall, narrow open area in front of and below the left wing. Stairs were pulled down from somewhere within the plane, and it was just a few short steps up into the aircraft. CC walked a wide circle around the silent, evil-looking set of propellers that were on that side of the plane, all the while sending them nervous glances.

The master sergeant noticed her discomfort and laughed. "Hell, they can't hurt you when they're not turned on."

"But they are getting ready to be turned on, aren't they?" she responded.

"Right you are, Sarg. So you better get aboard." He took her elbow to steady her on the steps. "Watch your head," he added.

"Ouch!" Too late, CC thought, grabbing her forehead where she had smacked it into a ledge of low-hanging equipment that protruded from the ceiling just inside the entrance.

Rubbing her head, she turned to the right and stepped up into the cargo/passenger area of the plane. Her eyes were watering with pain, and she could already feel a knot swelling under her fingers. She sincerely wished she was better at cussing; this was certainly the proper time to let loose with several choice words.

"Well, that's a darn stupid place to put a—" CC stopped and blushed furiously.

Six male faces were turned in her direction. They belonged to men clad in traditional sand-colored desert-issue flight suits. Each man wore the same distinctive patches and wings that clearly identified him as an F-16 Viper pilot.

"Hey, Sleeping Beauty," called out one of the pilots, a young lieutenant with a face that looked like it should have been on the cover of an air force recruiting poster. "Nice of you to wake up and join us."

CC felt her blush deepen. She was exhausted. Her face was greasy. She had sleep-head hair, and she was wearing desert cammos that on the best of days made her look about twelve years old. Needless to say, that moment was far from the best of days. Her eyes were bloodshot and her breath had to smell like the bottom of a birdcage. And she had just walked into a whole group of handsome fighter pilots after smacking herself on the head like an idiot right in front of them. Not to mention she was inside of a plane that was getting ready to take off.

She was probably in hell.

"Ignore him, Sergeant . . ." said a colonel with just enough gray in his thick hair to make him look dignified. He hesitated as he read her nametag. ". . . Sergeant Canady. He's just pissed because he doesn't look as cute as you do when he sleeps."

"Yeah," a lanky-looking captain added. "He drools."

That got a laugh from the group, and CC hurried into the cargo bay, settling into the first seat that was available. She stowed her carry-on under her feet and busied herself with securely fastening her seat belt, which was the same red color as her fold-down seat and the meshed webbing that served as a backrest. CC wondered, as she did each time she flew in a C-130, why the seats and webbing were all bright red, when everything else about the plane was either military green or metallic gray. It made her feel vaguely uncomfortable, as did the open view of aircraft equipment and pipes and wires and such. At least civilian airplanes had all the "stuff" covered by smooth, white walls. Here the guts of the plane were showing.

Lashed to the floor at intervals of about six feet were the pallets of cargo CC had caught sight of from outside the plane. They filled the body of the cargo bay. Hesitantly, CC let her eyes travel to the other occupied seats, and she breathed a sigh of relief when she realized that she could only see three of the six pilots. The cargo blocked her view of the others. CC sighed. As usual the plane was outfitted with little thought to human comfort. Hers appeared to be the last available seat—the rest were either folded up or already occupied. A young captain was seated a little way to her right. He was listening to a CD through headphones, and he had his head propped comfortably back on a pillow, but nodded a brief hello to her. Across from her and about three folded seats to the left she could see the colonel, who was obviously the pilots' ranking officer. He was deep in a discussion with someone sitting to his right, but CC couldn't see him because a stack of plastic-covered equipment blocked her view.

The only other pilot she had a clear view of was sitting across the aisle from her and to her right. She glanced at him and caught him staring at her, and then was astounded to see a bright crimson blush rise into his well-defined cheeks.

Good Lord, she thought. Why is *he* blushing? The man looked like a gorgeous statue come to life. She quickly looked away, but the sound of his voice made her eyes snap back to his.

"Um, hello," he said. His voice was deep, but he didn't boom it at her like so many military men seemed to think they needed to. His eyes traveled up to the knot on her forehead.

Great. No wonder he was blushing. He had obviously seen her bonk her head like a moron, and he was probably embarrassed for her.

"I did the same thing on the way in," he said and pointed to his own head, where a faint pink splotch painted a raised bump in the middle of his forehead.

CC couldn't have been more surprised if he had sprouted wings and laid an egg.

"And I don't even have the excuse that I'd just woken up and was still groggy. Mine, Sergeant Canady, was the result of plain clumsiness."

CC felt a genuine giggle bubble from her lips. The handsome pilot echoed her laugh.

"Please," she said. "Call me CC."

"Okay CC. I'm Sean."

CC's grin sobered. "Don't you think I better call you Captain something?" It was fine for an officer to call an enlisted person by his or her first name, but the other way around was considered too familiar—and the air force sincerely frowned on too much familiarity between officers and sergeants. Even if the officers looked like living statues, CC thought regretfully.

But Sean's grin didn't fade. "Actually, no. Like the rest of these guys, I'm stationed at the Air National Guard Unit in Tulsa, Oklahoma." He leaned forward and glanced around like they were sharing a secret. "We do things a little differently in the Guard. So just plain Sean is okay with me."

CC didn't know what to say. Of course she knew there was an Air Guard Fighter Unit in Tulsa—her Comm Center had sent and received messages from them several times during the past three months. But she'd never met any of the pilots. Actually, the only fighter pilots she'd ever met had been stationed at her last duty assignment, Peterson AFB, Colorado. They had been arrogant and conceited and had not impressed CC or her girlfriends at all. She couldn't imagine any of them insisting she call them by their first names, at least not in daylight. Thankfully, she was saved from answering Sean by the appearance of the master sergeant who had herded her on to the plane.

"Okay gentlemen," he said, glancing at CC and adding, "and ladies. We're fixin' to get underway. I shouldn't have to tell such a distinguished group to buckle up and stow your carry-ons, but I thought I'd better remind you since you're not used to riding in the back seats." He chuckled at his lame joke as he made his way slowly through the cargo bay, checking the security of the pallets and the pilots. The pilots paid him about as much attention as did the pallets.

CC sighed as the numbing noise of the giant, rotating propellers started to vibrate through the plane. The sound made her realize that she had left her earplugs in her carry-on. CC unsnapped her seat belt and crouched down to pull her carry-on out from underneath the seat, and as she was feeling around in the side pocket her eyes traveled to the wall behind her seat. Her brow furrowed in confusion. That was odd; she hadn't noticed before that framing her seat were two thick, red stripes painted on the inside wall of the plane. Between these stripes were stenciled in bright red the words danger and propeller, over and over.

"Sarg, you need to stow that and take your seat." The master sergeant had made his way over to her.

CC grabbed her earplugs, shoved the bag back and regained her seat. But when the master sergeant tried to walk on down the bay, she called him back.

"Sergeant," she almost had to yell to be heard over the propeller noise. "What do those red lines and words mean?" She pointed over her shoulder.

"That's marking where the propeller would come through the aircraft if we was to throw one." He grinned, showing her a wealth of yellow teeth. "But that don't happen very often." He laughed and moved on.

CC wasn't sure if she should cry or scream—but her body had suddenly frozen solid, so she found she was only able to sit there, ramrod straight and perfectly still.

Across the aisle Sean had overheard the whole exchange. He grimaced to himself as he watched the little sergeant's face turn a ghostly shade of white, which only made her big amber eyes look more fawnlike and appealing. She was such a small, young thing. She'd already looked a little scared when she'd bumped her head and stumbled into the plane, and now she looked practically terrified. Something inside of him lurched insistently.

"CC," he called to her.

She didn't respond.

"CC," he repeated, noting the glazed look in her eyes when they finally met his. "Would you trade seats with me? I hate flying on this side of the plane." He thought for a second, then added. "It's one of those weird pilot superstitions." He shrugged helplessly, like he was ashamed to admit it.

"Trade seats with you?" she asked as if she hadn't heard him correctly.

"Yep. I'd sure appreciate it." He beamed his best nice-guy smile at her.

"I suppose so," she said slowly. "If you really want to."

"I really want to," he said.

"Okay then."

He unbuckled his seat belt and grabbed his flight bag from under the seat. Before she could get her own carry-on, he crossed the ten feet or so that separated them.

"I'll get that for you," he said, taking the bag from her.

CC looked up at him. This close he was even more gorgeous. And just how tall was he? His muscular body seemed to stretch on forever. His short, military cut hair was a medium shade of blond, shot with glistening streaks that looked like they had been dipped in the sun. Actually, his whole body, or at least what could be seen peeking out of his flight suit, looked like he had been blessed by the god of the sun. Unlike so many blonds, he wasn't washed-out looking. Instead he was an irresistible shade of golden tan. His face was made of strong, square lines, and his lips . . . CC felt herself staring and she jerked her gaze from those amazing lips to his soft, brown eyes, which were smiling down at her.

"Thank you," she managed to stammer.

"Not a problem. Actually, you're doing me a favor." He took her elbow and guided her to his seat.

"Always the gentleman, ain't ya, Apollo." The master sergeant scoffed as he passed back by the two of them. "Just get her in that seat, then get yourself into yours. We're ready to get the hell outta here."

CC hurried to sit down, then she sent a questioning glance up at Sean.

"Apollo?" she asked.

"That's my call sign." He made a dismissive gesture with his hand. "Believe me, it wasn't my idea."

"Oh," was all CC could make her mouth say. It might not have been his idea, but it was certainly appropriate. The man oozed Greek god.

"Don't forget to fasten your seat belt," he said before turning to cross to his new seat.

CC's eyes had a will of their own, and they definitely enjoyed Apollo's rear view. He was one spectacularly handsome man. Of course, when he turned around and took his seat, she made sure she was very busy checking her seat belt, trying to find a comfortable place in the webbing, doing anything but gawking at him. And anyway, why was she getting all moon-eyed over him? Men who looked like that, especially fighter pilot men who looked like that, weren't interested in little, ordinary-looking staff sergeants. Unless maybe they had some kind of kid sister complex. That was probably it, she told herself. He probably had a younger sister at home and that was why he was paying attention to her.

The propeller noise grew to a deafening level, and CC put in her earplugs. Then the C-130 lurched forward. It moved slowly at first, but soon picked up speed as it made its way down the flight line to their designated runway. CC felt her palms begin to moisten and her stomach knot. She closed her eyes and repeated over and over to herself: *military flights rarely crash; military flights rarely crash; military flights rarely crash.*

Too soon they were poised at the end of the runway, propellers gyrating at a crazed speed, plane quivering with the need to take off. Or, CC thought desperately, with the need to smack itself into the ground and engulf them in a ball of flame right *after* takeoff. She felt the brakes release, and the C-130 began its acceleration down the runway. CC's eyes popped open. She didn't want to die with her eyes closed.

A movement caught her panicked gaze and drew her eyes across the aisle to Sean. His long body was sprawled comfortably in its new location. He was giving her a thumb's-up sign, and he looked relaxed and calm. Sean grinned boyishly at her and mouthed the words, "Not a problem." Then he gave her a flirty wink.

Well! CC felt a rush of pleasure. She certainly didn't think he'd give a little sister a wink like that. And the way he continued to smile and stare at her . . . it just didn't look like the way a man looked at a woman he was only interested in because she reminded him of a little sister. Stunned, CC realized the butterflies in her stomach had nothing to do with her fear of flying.

When the plane lifted off a few seconds later, CC thought that she might have just experienced the most graceful, effortless takeoff in the history of the United States Air Force.

Actually, once the plane became airborne, CC's nervous stomach had completely disappeared. It was like the whole flight seemed to be charmed. They climbed to their cruising altitude so smoothly that CC found herself totally relaxing against the soft webbing, and she was surprised to feel her eyelids growing heavy. Struggling to stay awake, she glanced at Sean. He was reading a book, but the moment her eyes touched him he looked up. He studied her for a second, then an astounding thing happened. CC could hardly believe it when he mouthed the words, "Sleep—I'll keep watch." Then he gave her that flirtatious wink again.

CC felt a little thrill travel down her spine. He was going to stay awake and keep watch. Over her. And that wink said he wasn't thinking of her as a kid sister. CC's eyelids fluttered shut as her sleepy mind whispered that Sean's presence was certainly going to make the deployment more interesting.

Sean watched her as she fell asleep, a contented smile curving her sexy lips. He rubbed a hand over his brow and smiled quizzically at himself. What was it about that girl? Ever since he'd caught sight of her curled up in the waiting area sound asleep, he couldn't stop looking at her or thinking about her. It was totally unlike him. Women usually threw themselves at him because of how he looked, and while he didn't complain about that, he certainly didn't have to seek them out, or change seats with them because they looked scared, or reassure them because they were afraid of—of all things—flying. He rubbed his brow again and tried to force his attention to the novel in his hands, but instead of black words on white paper, he kept seeing amber eyes framed by thick, sandy-colored lashes.

CC dreamed that she was swaying gently in a hammock that hung between two giant palm trees on the shore of a crystalline ocean. Warm tropical breezes tickled her skin and kept the hammock moving hypnotically back and forth. Then, the wind shifted and icy gusts started blowing toward land over the white-capped waves. They reached her hammock, and it started to shake and pitch and . . .

CC's eyes flew open. She was instantly awake. It was no dream. The C-130 was shaking violently, like it was in the jaws of a giant animal. She swallowed a scream and her eyes immediately found Sean. His face was flat and expressionless, but CC could sense the tension that he was trying to mask. She began fumbling with the safety latch of her seat belt, her only thought that she needed to be next to him.

"No!" He shook his head.

She tore the earplugs from her ears.

"Don't get up. It's too dangerous." He shouted against the horribly sick sound of the engines.

"What's happening?!" she yelled.

Before he could answer, the shaking increased dramatically. CC couldn't believe the plane was still in one piece; it felt like it had to be shaking itself apart. Then everything happened very quickly. Over the noise of the engines came the shriek of a metallic scream. While CC watched in horror, a deadly blur sliced through the skin of the plane just a few feet to her right and arrowed its way directly across the aisle. Like an invisible missile, the broken propeller blade splintered and struck Sean before tearing through the skin on his side of the plane. Time suspended as the left side of Sean's head exploded in a spray of crimson and he slumped silently forward.

CC's scream was swallowed by the deafening sound of the plane decompressing, and she grasped on to the webbing, desperately trying to find an anchor in a world gone mad. Everything that wasn't strapped down went flying through the plane in a maelstrom of noise. CC couldn't get a clear sight of Sean—there was too much debris in the air between them. But she could see the widening trail of blood and fluids that blanketed the area around his seat.

His seat? It should have been her seat. CC felt a sob catch in the back of her throat.

Gradually, the debris settled, but the shaking was still violent, and the roar of the air rushing through the gaping holes in the sides of the airplane was deafening. With an amazing effort, the young captain who was sitting to Sean's right unbuckled his seat belt and crawled to his friend's still body. The captain had a square white piece of cloth in his hand, and as he wrapped it around Sean's head, CC realized that it must be the pillowcase off his pillow. With precise motions he unlatched the folded seat next to Sean. He loosened Sean's seat belt enough so that he could swivel his legs around and lay his torso horizontally along the seats. Then he managed to secure another belt around Sean's chest.

CC couldn't take her eyes from the pillowcase and the grotesque scarlet stain that was soaking methodically through it to pool against the matching red of the seat.

Suddenly, above the din CC could hear short bursts of a clanging bell. She counted six times. The next thing she knew the colonel had his seat belt unbuckled, and he lurched his way to her side, where he quickly pulled down a seat and resecured himself.

"They're ditching the plane," he yelled into her ear.

Her eyes widened. She didn't have to be a pilot to know that meant they were crashing into the ocean.

"It's okay. We're going to make it." He gave her a smile meant to reassure her. "The water's warm. Good thing we're in the Mediterranean and not the Atlantic."

CC wanted desperately to believe that.

"What do I do?" she shouted.

Before he answered her he twisted around and pulled two life vests free of their holding place behind the webbing. CC noticed the captain across the aisle had done the same and was struggling to strap one on Sean's unresponsive body.

"Put this on. You'll need to brace yourself and hold on. Everything will be thrown forward when we hit. Be ready to get out of here. Don't know how long this thing will stay afloat."

"Sean?" she asked.

The colonel's face was grim as he shook his head. CC's eyes filled with tears.

"He's beyond our help; worry about yourself now," he said gruffly. The plane dipped sickeningly forward. The colonel pointed toward the rear of the cargo bay. "Remember where the tail opens up?"

CC nodded.

"There are two escape doors on either side of the plane. That's where we'll exit. Life rafts are in slots up there." He pointed to an area above the wings.

CC hoped that he wasn't explaining those things to her because he planned on being dead. Just then the master sergeant burst from the crew door at the front of the plane.

"We're goin' down!" he yelled as he strapped himself into a seat to the right of CC and the colonel. "Be ready to get your feet wet!"

CC couldn't believe it, but he almost sounded gleeful.

The nose of the plane sank again, and the colonel squeezed her shoulder.

"Ready?" he yelled.

Over the past seven years CC had researched and prepared herself for an airplane emergency. She had watched PBS specials on airline safety. She always dressed sensibly when she flew—jeans and sneakers, never heels and bare legs. She counted the seatbacks to her nearest exit, and she paid attention to the flight attendants when they gave their safety spiels.

But she knew she wasn't ready. She was numb with terror. CC nodded at the colonel and tried to give him a brave smile. Through the ragged tears in the C-130's skin CC could see the bright blue of a clear morning. She closed her eyes and tried to pray, but her mind was a whirlwind of fear. All she could think of was how much she didn't want to die.

Then from between her breasts she felt a sudden warmth. Her first thought was that something must have struck her, and she was bleeding. She opened her eyes and frantically felt down the front of her uniform top. No, no rips and definitely no blood. Just a hard lump.

Oh! She realized the lump she was feeling was made by the amber teardrop that dangled from around her neck, just below her dog tags. On an impulse she had decided to keep wearing it, even after she had changed into her uniform, but of course wearing dangly jewelry wasn't within military regulations, and she had had to keep it hidden under her top. Now it felt warm, and that warmth was spreading throughout her chest.

If ever there was a perfect time for magic, she thought, it was now.

"Brace yourself!" the colonel yelled.

CC just had time to wrap her hands into the netting and brace her feet firmly against the floor when the world exploded. The plane slammed into the ocean with an obscene metallic scream, as if it knew its life were coming to an end. The white froth of ocean spray could be seen through the holes in the sides of the plane. But the C-130 didn't stay down. CC could feel it lift, a temporary respite, before they met the ocean again with an even worse grating jar. They skipped several times over the surface of the water, like a broken, bloated stone. Each time the plane met the ocean, passengers and cargo were flung forward. CC saw a major get hurled against the front bulkhead when his seat belt snapped loose. She watched as one of the huge cargo pallets pulled free at the same time and came crashing against him, pinning him to the metal wall.

CC glanced over at Sean and then looked quickly away. Rag doll-like, his body was still strapped against the seats. Like a puppet whose strings had been cut, his limbs flailed in limp response to the jarring of the plane.

Something sharp hit her left shoulder. She didn't feel any pain, but when she looked down she saw that her flesh gapped open and a line of blood had started to spill down her arm. Then there was a final wrenching, and the plane settled and did not rise again. CC could see the bright blue of ocean water through the holes in the plane.

The colonel was the first to react, but CC could see that all of the pilots except Sean and the major were struggling to their feet.

"Out! Out! Let's go!" he barked, making his way quickly to the area over the wings. Then he started shouting orders.

"Ace, T-Man, Kaz, get those rear doors open!" The two captains and one lieutenant scrambled around the loose cargo, hurrying to the rear of the plane.

"Sarg!" the colonel yelled at her. "Out—now!"

With shaking hands, CC unbuckled her own seat belt, amazed that she was able to stand. She noticed that already the plane was tilting down at the head.

"The major is dead!" the master sergeant yelled from the front of the bay. He was kneeling by the bloody body of the major, still trapped against the bulkhead.

"Leave him," the colonel said as he lifted a slot and pulled out a neatly folded bright orange thing that CC guessed must be a life raft.

"The door to the cockpit is blocked!" The master sergeant had moved from the major's body to the area that should open to the front-most area of the plane. But another cargo pallet was wedged within the opening, effectively blocking the door.

"There's an exit they can use in the cockpit," said the colonel. He motioned for the master sergeant to get to the back of the plane, then he caught sight of CC still standing there. "Move, Sergeant!" He turned and headed to the rear of the plane, expecting CC to follow him.

CC meant to go to the rear of the plane and toward safety, but instead she found herself climbing over equipment and cargo until she was standing next to Sean's body. CC swallowed, trying hard not to be sick. There was blood everywhere. The two seat belts had kept his body from being hurled forward by the impact, and the pillowcase, now totally soaked with blood, was still wrapped securely around his head. His face was turned away from her, and all she could see was the strong line of his chin and neck. His skin was no longer golden brown. It had turned the chalky color of ash. CC forced herself to place two fingers against the spot where his jugular vein was. No pulse. His skin was already cool beneath her fingertips.

The plane heaved even farther down at the head. Now CC could see that the ocean was lapping around the gaps in the side of the plane.

"Sergeant!" the colonel's voice bellowed from the rear of the plane. "Where the hell are you?"

"Here, colonel!" she answered, crawling on top of a mound of cargo so she could be seen. The rear of the plane appeared to be raised up, and CC could see that the officers had one of the doors open. While she watched, one of the captains attached a tether to the deflated life raft, pulled a cord on it and threw it out of the door. With a *whooshing* noise the raft inflated.

"Get over here, now! This thing is sinking fast."

She looked back at Sean's body. It should have been her. Because of his kindness, he had taken her place and now he was going to be entombed in a lonely, watery grave. The thought was unbearable.

"We have to take Sean with us," she called back to the men.

"No time. The boy's dead. There's nothing to be done for him," said the colonel. At a signal from him, the master sergeant jumped out of the plane.

"I'm not going without him," CC said, surprised at the calm sound of her voice. Her heart was pounding, and she felt her hands trembling, but knew with a certainty that defied logic that she had made the right decision.

"Get up here, Sergeant. That's an order."

"No, sir. I'm not leaving him here."

Suddenly there was the sound of metal ripping, and CC felt sun on her face. She looked up to see a clean tear slicing a gap in the ceiling almost directly above her. The nose dipped farther forward, and CC had to struggle to stay on her feet.

"Goddamnit! Damnit all to hell!" CC could hear the colonel approaching before she saw him. He was cussing like crazy and yelling orders. "Unbelt the boy and get ready to get the fuck out of here!"

CC rushed to get Sean's seat belts undone and had just finished when the colonel climbed around the last of the debris. Without looking at her, he grabbed Sean's body and hauled it across one shoulder in the traditional fireman's carry.

"Keep up with me!" he yelled at her. CC was only too happy to comply with that particular order.

They were almost to the door when the entire front section of the plane tore free and sank with amazing speed. The tail area had been high above the water, but now that the rear of the plane was freed of the dragging weight of the flooded front, it flopped heavily down to sea level. To CC it felt like she was standing in an elevator that had just dropped several stories. She and the colonel fell hard to the floor. Water started rushing in through the open door.

The colonel regained his feet quickly. He grabbed CC by the scruff of her uniform and Sean by his leg and pulled them to the door.

CC had no time to think. The colonel tossed her roughly out of the door. She hit the water and went under, but almost immediately her life vest brought her bobbing to the surface like a human cork. She sputtered and blinked, momentarily blinded by saltwater and sunlight. She heard two quick splashes next to her, and in another instant the colonel's head broke the surface not far from her, along with Sean's lifeless body.

"There." He pointed and CC could see the florescent orange of the life raft about forty feet in front of them. "Swim! We have to get away from the plane." He set off, sidestroking and kicking hard as he dragged Sean's body with him.

Wishing desperately that she was a better swimmer, CC kicked and began stroking awkwardly after him. A horrendous explosion burst behind her, and she spun around in the water in time to see a flash of light and flame. The plane was an enormous, gaping monster that seemed to be thrashing and fighting against its death. And she was too close to it.

Adrenaline rushed through her body, and CC began swimming with everything within her. She didn't look behind her again, she just swam.

Then she felt it. A piece of wreckage wrapped around her ankle like a mechanical tentacle. Terrified, she kicked and kicked, but it wouldn't come free. She tried to reach down to get it off, but she was pulled under the surface with such force that she thought her leg would wrench from its socket.

Water surrounded her and the pressure on her leg was unrelenting. She tried to fight against it, but it was impossible. Her ankle had been securely captured, and she was being pulled to the floor of the ocean by the weight of the sinking plane.

She was going to die.

Panic rippled through her and she reached both hands up towards the fading light of the surface, struggling to kick against the enormous weight dragging her to her death. She didn't want to die—not like this—not so young. In that moment, CC didn't see glimpses of her life passing before her eyes, she just felt the despair of knowing that she was dying too soon, before she had ever really lived. She would never know the love of a husband; she would never watch her children grow and marry. Her chest was burning, and she knew it was only seconds before she would be forced to breathe in the deadly water.

CC closed her eyes. Please help me, she prayed fervently. Someone please help me.

Miraculously, the weight that had been dragging her under evaporated, and she was filled with an indescribable peace. She opened her eyes to find herself floating in a bubble of soft blue light. And she wasn't alone in that bubble. Suspended in the water directly in front of her, so close CC had only to lift a hand to touch her, was an incredibly beautiful young woman. Her long hair floated around her like a shimmering veil. CC thought it would be the exact color of her mother's buttercups, if flowers could shine and sparkle. The woman's face was a study in perfection. She had sculpted cheekbones and lovely aquamarine eyes that looked somehow familiar to CC. Her skin had the flawless complexion of a china doll. CC's eyes traveled down the body of the woman, who was quite obviously naked from the waist up. CC could clearly see her large, well-formed breasts. But what was she wearing on the bottom half of her body? Whatever it was glistened like it had been beaded with glass and colored in iridescent shades of blue and turquoise and amethyst. It fit her shapely body snuggly and tapered down to . . . CC felt her own body jerk in surprise. A large set of fins! She was no woman; she was a mermaid!

CC stared at the incredible creature, knowing that what she was seeing, what she was feeling, couldn't possibly be real. Her lungs didn't burn anymore. But it wasn't that she was breathing, because she was still definitely underwater; it was more like she had been infused with oxygen. She decided she definitely must be dead, or so near death that she was experiencing some kind of amazing hallucination.

The mermaid smiled tentatively at her.

CC smiled back.

Do you desire to continue to live, no matter the cost? The words were spoken clearly into CC's mind. She knew they had to have come from the mermaid, but her sensuous lips had not moved.

Well, of course I do, CC thought automatically and nodded her head vigorously.

The mermaid's timid smile was gone, replaced by a dazzling look of relief and joy. Without hesitation, the creature reached out and wrapped her smooth arms around CC in an intimate embrace. CC didn't feel any desire to pull away. Instead of being frightened or repulsed, she was mesmerized. The mermaid pulled CC gently against her body, and CC could feel the creature's naked breasts press softly against her fatigue shirt. The mermaid's curtain of gossamer hair surrounded them, and her tail wrapped around CC's legs. CC had always been firmly heterosexual, so she surprised herself when she felt her body re-spond and her own arms wrap around the mermaid's bare shoulders.

Suddenly CC understood that what was happening to her wasn't anything as simple as a sexual experience; it was a magical infusion of the senses. Just as the moonlight had energized her on the night of her birthday, so now was this creature bringing her back to life. Every inch of CC's body felt flooded with electricity. She wanted to throw back her head and shout at the surge of fabulous sensations.

Then the mermaid began to lower her face to CC's. CC closed her eyes as their lips met in a deep, intimate kiss. A wave of vertigo crashed through CC, and when she finally reopened her eyes, she was looking directly into her own face.

Disorientated, CC blinked and shook her head, but the image of the petite, waterlogged sergeant didn't shift, it simply smiled back at her.

Back at her? How could that be? CC turned her head to look for the edges of a hidden mirror and noticed the wealth of blond hair that was floating around her. She reached up to stroke its slick mass.

We must part now.

The voice was back inside her head, and CC's fragmented attention refocused on her mirror image. CC watched as hands that should have been her own reached into the neck of her uniform top to pull the silver chain over her head. Then the CC look-alike draped it over "her" head.

Keep this. It is your talisman, a part of your magic, the internal voice said.

The woman that looked like CC raised her arms and tilted her head back so that she appeared to be reaching for the surface.

I wish you well. Blessed be, little sister.

The soft light that they had been floating within refracted into a fireworks of rebellious blue. The body that CC should have been inside of was bathed in an eerie aqua-white glow, and with an intense explosion of light it was propelled violently up to the waiting surface. Caught in a tremendous wave of backlash, CC felt herself hurl end over end away from the site of the plane wreck. Everything became confused and dreamlike. CC had no control over where she was being pulled. It felt like she had been caught in an underwater tornado. The whirlpool was pulling her farther and farther down into the depths of the ocean, and even though she was having no problem breathing, she was still terrified of the black nothingness beneath her. So she struggled, swimming around and through different levels of turbulent currents.

Finally she broke through the wall of swirling current and found herself in a tunnel of calm water. Exhausted, she allowed herself to float for a moment, trying to sift through her scattered thoughts. What had happened to her? Was she dead? What should she do next?

The water in her little tunnel of calm was comfortable, denim blue, but outside of it, the dark and tumultuous currents through which she had struggled still surrounded her. CC could see them seething and frothing dangerously. She peered behind her and saw nothing but darkness. Ahead, farther down the tunnel, there was a faint, flickering light. That way, she thought blearily and kicked hard to propel herself forward. Even as tired as she was, CC noted with surprise that she had never swam so strongly and effortlessly before—it was like she had been shot from a liquid cannon. The dark sides of her watery tunnel blurred as she streaked past.

Then the spot of light was just ahead of her and she burst up, breaking the surface to find herself in a luminous grotto. Her vision was blurred with fatigue, but she could just make out a ledge around which calm water lapped softly. She forced her leadened limbs to move, and with an effort that left her quivering and gasping, she hauled her body out of the water. Curling into a fetal position, CC finally gave into unconsciousness and slept.

Part Two

CHAPTER SIX

THE rhythmic sound of water lapping against rock woke her. CC opened her eyes slowly and was greeted by the sight of sparkling blue crystals. She shifted her body and stared around her, amazed at the beauty of the rocks. If laughter was a color, she thought, it would be this exact shade of blue. She reached out to touch the side of the cave with her perfectly shaped cream-colored hand . . . and stopped.

That wasn't her hand. Her gaze moved from her hand to her arm. It was long and graceful and looked like it had been carved from living marble. In shock, she sat up. A mass of luxurious blond hair was swept over one of her shoulders so that it cascaded down the front of her body, covering her torso like a silken shawl. She could just make out the mauve tips of her well-endowed breasts peeking through the blond curtain. With shaking hands, she pulled the gorgeous mane back out of her way and looked at the rest of "her" body.

The flawless skin tapered down to a voluptuously curved waist. Just where her hips started to swell, skin gave way to closely woven scales. Where legs and feet should have been, instead there was a tail that ended in an enormous, feathered fin.

"Holy fucking shit; I'm a fish!"

Unaccustomed to using such harsh language, CC's first impulse was to cover her mouth and look around frantically to make sure her mother hadn't heard her, but the jerky movement of her upper body caused her tail to flip in response. It felt kind of like she had just twitched her legs to keep her balance and they had responded—together.

"My language would be the least of the things I would have to explain if my mother was here," CC blurted. The sound of her voice wasn't even her own— instead it was perfect, complete with a sensuous accent and a soft, breathy tone. "And to think I've always wanted to be gorgeous like Marilyn Monroe." CC shook her head at the irony. "Now that I am, I'm a . . . I'm a . . ." Semihysterical giggles broke from her mouth.

Swallowing back her hysteria, she closed her eyes and forced herself to calm down. Breathe deeply, breathe deeply she told herself—it wouldn't help for her to lose it now. Another deep breath, then she reopened her eyes and looked at her body again. And she couldn't wrench her eyes from her tail. CC told her legs to kick, and the feathery fin lifted gracefully in response. The blue light of the grotto was reflected in the scales, and her tail glinted with a myriad of brilliant sequins. CC had to acknowledge that it really was very beautiful. With a shaking, hesitant hand she reached out and touched the shining surface of fishlike flesh and was instantly surprised by the soft warmth under her fingers. Now that she was touching it, she could tell that the tail wasn't actually made of fish scales at all, it was more like the skin of a dolphin, just colored with amazing shadings of blues and purples. She stroked herself, enjoying the slick smoothness of her new skin. It was like being wrapped in liquid silver, she thought, only instead of one color, it was countless fantastic colors.

And she felt incredibly powerful. She could actually feel the energy that simmered within her body. She cocked her head, as if listening to that newly found strength, and she realized that the water seemed to call to her. CC could almost hear its voice asking her to come frolic within its depths.

Maybe she was dreaming, or even dead, but the thought didn't hold any horror for her. Whatever had happened to her, she still had her own mind, and she most certainly was getting a bigger dose of magic than she could ever have imagined possible in her old life.

CC dipped the finned end of her tail down so that it broke the surface of the enticing water, and then with a ripple of muscle she flipped it up again. Warm seawater rained in a glistening arch around her; wherever it touched her body she felt it as a lover's caress.

Leaning forward, she gazed into the calm water of the grotto at her remarkably changed reflection. The only familiar thing she saw was the amber teardrop that dangled between her bare breasts.

"I'm her." The beautiful creature's lips moved as CC spoke. "Somehow I'm the mermaid now." She remembered watching her own body lift toward the faraway surface. "And she's me."

A tremor ran though her, and she raised a hand to touch the curve of one perfect cheek. Totally engrossed in studying her refection, CC didn't look up at the sound of a disturbance in the water.

"Undine, need I remind you of the lesson the gods taught Narcissus?"

A deep, mocking voice made CC gasp and jerk back in surprise. Not far from her ledge a huge man floated in the water. His torso was bare and he was powerfully built. His hair was so blond it was almost white, and it fell in a thick wave past his shoulders. He would have been handsome, had it not been for his sneering expression.

"But of course I must admit that you are truly spectacular." He dropped his voice to a seductive purr. Then, noting her expression, he added, "Are you surprised to see me, sister dear?" He floated a little nearer CC's ledge. His storm gray eyes were intense. "How could you doubt that I would pursue you?"

"Wh-what?" CC's lips felt numb, and she shrank back.

"Please, let us not play your tiresome games. Our father demands you return, and you know how angry Lir can get when his demands are not obeyed." Slowly he floated even closer to her.

CC was confused and frightened. What did this man want and who was Lir?

"When Lir noticed that you were missing again, I graciously volunteered to find you and bring you home."

He wasn't looking in her eyes, instead his gaze kept shifting from her breasts to the jointure in her tail at the place where her thighs would meet, if she had thighs. His hot stare made her feel intensely uncomfortable and completely naked. She scrambled back until she could go no farther and was pressed firmly against the side of the cave.

He reached CC's ledge and placed his hands on the edge of it. With a quick flex of his powerful arms, he raised himself partially out of the water, and CC gasped again.

His muscular torso tapered down to meet the glistening skin of a mer-creature. CC's eyes grew round with shock. Mer*man*, she amended as she watched the hard pulsing flesh surge from a slit in his tail where a human man's groin would be. This creature was quite obviously male.

"Now," his voice was low and ominous. "I am finished with chasing you. I have tried wooing you. I have tried reasoning with you. I have even tried begging you. Nothing works. You continue to spurn me. Your stubborn tricks have left me no choice. You force me to take what I desire."

His malevolent presence filled the cave. CC could feel her heart beating erratically. Her reaction was intense and immediate. He repulsed her.

"Stay away from me." CC was surprised by the power in her new voice.

"No, my darling. Not any more. I am finished with waiting." He reached forward and stroked a thick strand of hair that had fallen over her breast. "So lovely." His breathing deepened.

CC flinched from his touch, which enraged him.

"You will be mine!" he screamed in her face. Then, with an effort, he regained control of himself, shifting his tone to a more reasonable one. "Why do you pretend you do not understand? Our father is busy elsewhere, and he has grown weary of your little escapes. He is not listening for your cries." The merman grimaced. "And your landlocked goddess mother cannot hear you within my wonderful little cave; I made quite certain of that. Do you like the gift I created for you?" One powerful arm gestured to take in the grotto. "Be reasonable and this will be pleasant for us both. You must realize that Father will actually be pleased when we have mated. I believe he even plans on granting us a realm of our own."

CC's mind whirred. No wonder the beautiful mermaid had been so eager to exchange places with her! CC would much rather be a plain, ordinary human girl than a magical mermaid raped by her perverted brother.

The creature pulled himself all the way up on the ledge. His body was almost twice the size of CC's mermaid body. His chest and shoulders bulged, and his powerful tail was banded with thick stripes of crimson and dark green.

"Do you appreciate that I attempted to duplicate the color of your eyes in these crystals?" Again his voice was ingratiating and deceptively gentle. He leaned closer to her. "But nothing could match the beauty of your eyes."

He brushed the fall of hair off her chest, leaving her completely exposed. Then he reached forward and cupped her breasts in his huge hands, worrying her nipples painfully between his thumb and forefingers. Before CC could even attempt to push his hands away, his attention wavered.

"What is that thing?" he spat. "It reeks of human design." The merman freed her breasts to grasp the amber teardrop, which glowed softly where it dangled between them.

The instant his skin met amber, he shrieked in pain and dropped the pendant. Stunned, CC watched him curl over his hand, his entire body shaking violently. He was moaning and she could see spittle frothing around his lips.

The jewelry lady's words echoed through her mind. *Know that it has the power to absorb negative energy and turn it to positive. You may have need of it . . .*

She had to do something. The cave was a prison; she had to escape. CC heaved herself forward, squeezing around the merman's convulsed body and hurled herself headfirst into the water. As soon as she was immersed, she felt her panic subside. With an instinct of its own, her body took control and she dove swiftly down and away from the crystal prison.

Expecting to be caught in the swirling current of black water, she was surprised to see that tranquil blue surrounded her. There was no sign of the tunnel through which she had traveled. Still swimming with incredible swiftness, she glanced up and saw the lighter blue of daylight against the surface not far above her head. CC angled her body up, and with one powerful stroke of her tail propelled herself to the surface and broke through the liquid barrier.

She looked frantically around. On the horizon behind her she could see the dark outline of the grotto. She was amazed at how far she had traveled so quickly. In front of her, the ocean appeared to come to a halt. Confused, she rubbed her eyes clear and let herself drift forward. No, it wasn't that the ocean stopped. It was a huge coral shelf. On her side of it the water was the deep sapphire of the bottomless ocean. White-capped waves crashed against the barrier. CC flipped her tail and raised herself up farther out of the water. On the other side of the barrier she could see calm, turquoise water, which led to—her heart beat faster—a sandy shoreline.

That mer-creature had said that he was hiding from her "landlocked goddess mother." If he had felt the need to hide, then that must mean he was afraid. Could the mermaid's mother help her? If so, since she was "landlocked," perhaps she could be found near the shore.

A prickly feeling along her spine interrupted her thoughts. Her skin twitched somewhere on the back of her neck where it seemed eyes touched her.

She turned quickly, searching the ocean for signs of her pursuer. Nothing. As far as she could see the surface was disturbed by nothing except waves. Almost as if it was as natural a movement as stepping backwards, she waved her finned tail and submerged herself under the water. The blue depths were clear and visibility was good, but CC could see nothing more villainous than a drifting jellyfish. She resurfaced.

Maybe she had escaped and was safe for that moment, but one thing CC knew for sure, she couldn't just float there and wait for that creature to recapture her. Doing anything was better than that. With a powerful flick of her tail she leapt up and over the thick coral reef, splashing headfirst into the clear waters of the cove and straight into a school of huge, brightly-colored fish.

CC's first reaction was fear—they were really big fish—and she made shooing motions at them. But they refused to shoo. Instead they quivered and milled around her, a little like puppies. Curious, CC reached a hesitant hand out to touch one florescent-scaled side. The ecstatic fish went into very doglike spasms of glee. CC laughed, which caused the entire school to explode into joyous leaps of playful abandon.

She was just thinking that she didn't know how the day could get much weirder when she came face-to-face with a full-grown dolphin.

"Ah!" She jerked back, bubbles of surprise bursting from her mouth. The dolphin didn't look at all shocked by the appearance of a mermaid who was surrounded by a school of jubilant, silly-acting fish.

They have so little dignity.

The thought was placed gently within her mind. She stared at the dolphin. She had never seen a real one this close. Well, she had visited Sea World at San Antonio once, and there had been dolphins there that people could pay to swim with, but the price had been beyond her budget. And this creature was no tamed hothouse flower; it was stunning. Its sleek skin glowed with vitality and its expressive eyes telegraphed intelligence.

I ask you to forgive me, Princess Undine. I did not mean to startle you.

I, uh, just didn't expect you, CC thought automatically.

The dolphin dipped its head in graceful acknowledgment. *May I offer you my assistance, Princess?*

She could send her thoughts to this wonderful creature? What an incredible gift!

I need to find my mother. CC quickly decided it was worth a try to enlist all the help she could get. And the creatures seemed to know her—maybe they would know how to help her, too.

Of course, Princess Undine. CC was almost sure the dolphin grinned at her. *Gaea comes to these shores often, as you well know. It would be my honor.* The dolphin glanced at the school of waiting fish with what CC thought was an endearingly long-suffering look before adding, *And the honor of these small ones, to escort you to shore.*

Gaea! The goddess Gaea was the mermaid's mother! What a bizarre coincidence. CC thought about the elevator and the jewelry lady . . . perhaps coincidence was the wrong word.

She smiled her gratitude to the beautiful creature. *Yes, please take me to my mother!*

Together they swam through the clear, warm water. The ocean floor was not far below them, and CC could easily see hulks of coral clustered like mysterious rock castles against the white sand of the bottom. Brightly colored fish darted in and around delicate underwater fronds like autumn leaves in a windstorm. CC looked in wide-eyed wonder at the underwater world. She had never imagined such loveliness existed. Honestly, she had always been a little afraid of the water; she hadn't even ever snorkeled. Look at what I've been missing, she thought over and over to herself.

Just a few feet from the shoreline the dolphin surfaced beside a half-hollowed rock. Its flattened top jutted just above the waterline. As if she had done it so many times before, CC slid onto its smooth surface and studied the lush shore. Diamond waters lapped gently against the velvet sand of the beach so that land and ocean melted together harmoniously, like lovers embracing. Huge trees decorated with flowering vines surrounded the cove. A slight breeze brought to CC the sweet scent of flowers mixed with the tang of salt air. There was a definite aura of peacefulness about the cove. CC breathed deeply, enjoying the unexpected serenity. She felt like she could stay there forever, basking in the warm sun and the honey-scented air.

Princess? The dolphin was looking expectantly at her, returning her thoughts to her present situation.

And the terror of the merman's pursuit rushed back into her mind. Quickly she looked over her shoulder, but she could see nothing except the serenity of the ocean. But she didn't even know if he could be seen approaching. Except for the leap over the coral shelf, she'd traveled underwater to get there. She probably wouldn't know if he was streaking after her at that moment. She had been stupid to relax like she was on some kind of Caribbean vacation.

What was she supposed to do now?

She studied the land, this time not allowing herself to be distracted by its beauty. She certainly didn't see a goddess waiting anywhere. CC fiddled nervously with the amber pendent. This wasn't exactly like picking up the phone and calling her mom. But maybe moms everywhere had at least one common characteristic—they were accustomed to answering the cries of their children.

CC squared her shoulders and cleared her throat.

"Mother!" she shouted, enchanted by the way her melodic voice carried over the water. "Goddess Gaea! It's me. Your daughter, Undine." She looked nervously at the dolphin, who was floating quietly, still looking toward the shore. "I need your help." Please answer me, she prayed silently.

From the thickest nest of verdant ivy and hanging flowers a movement drew her gaze. CC's eyes widened in surprise. A beautiful woman was tucked gracefully amidst the vines. She was sitting on a makeshift swing made of living plant.

"Good morning, Daughter." The woman's voice rang over the water.

CC felt a shock of recognition. "You're the lady who saved me from the elevator!"

A familiar smile curved Gaea's lips. "Yes, I heard your unique call which you offered under the full moon. It pleased me, and I like to care for those who remember me." She paused and her smile widened. "Even if they are living in a far-off world." She pointed at the amber teardrop that dangled between CC's breasts. "I am pleased that you value my gift."

CC swallowed hard past the lump that had lodged in her throat, and her fingers wound themselves around the warm stone. She was speaking with a real goddess. Or she was dead. Either way, it was nerve-wracking.

"Yes, thank you. It's beautiful and magical." She cleared her throat. "Then you know that I'm not really Undine."

The Goddess's eyes filled with unshed tears, but her expression remained kind. "Of course I know it, young one. Undine is a daughter of my flesh. You, Christine Canady, staff sergeant in the United States Air Force, who prefers to be called CC, are a daughter of my spirit."

"How?" CC felt overwhelmed.

Gaea made a slight motion with one hand, and the vine swing dipped low enough to let her step down to the ground. Gracefully, she walked toward the waterline. CC couldn't take her eyes from the goddess. She realized that the glimpse she'd had of Gaea outside of the elevator had been just a shadow of the goddess's true visage. Today she was magnificent. Her hair was the deep brown of fertile earth, and it curled thickly around her waist. Woven within it were flowers and glistening jewels. CC thought her face looked like it could have served as a model for countless classic sculptures—which, she thought, it probably had. CC couldn't remember getting a clear view of what the goddess had been wearing when she had seen her that day at Tinker, but today her generous curves were draped in transparent green linen, which was the exact color of the ivy growing in profusion all around her.

"You're so beautiful!" CC embarrassed herself by blurting.

Gaea's laughter glittered between them. "Come, child," she said as she reached the water and sank to the sand, letting her bare feet play in the crystal surf. "Come closer to me."

The dolphin chattered joyfully, leaping around the cove as CC slid off the rock and swam to the goddess. Gaea was gazing steadily at her, and CC realized that the reason Undine's startlingly blue eyes had seemed familiar to her was that they were the exact image of the goddess's eyes. Awkwardly, she pulled herself up on the sandy shore until she rested within touching distance of the beautiful immortal.

CC ducked her head apologetically. "I'm sure Undine was much better than I am at navigating with this." She pointed at her tail.

"Do you dislike this body?" The goddess didn't sound judgmental or angry, only genuinely curious.

"Oh, no! I think it's amazing. It's just a lot different from having legs and feet," she said. "And she's so gorgeous, much more so than I am. Or was. Or . . ." CC trailed off, confused by the tenses as well as the situation.

"I think you underestimate yourself, little one. But I am glad you are pleased with this form." The goddess's expression became distant. "And I am sure that my daughter, Undine, is pleased with her new form as well."

"So she is me now?" CC asked, amazed at how easy it was to talk with Gaea.

"Yes. She has taken your place in that world."

"Am I dead?"

Gaea's laughter caused the tree boughs to sway in delighted response. "Oh, no. You are very much alive."

"Then I don't understand," CC said, feeling more lost than ever.

The goddess reached out and touched CC's cheek in a motherly caress. "This must be very difficult for you, poor child. I will try to explain. Undine is the child of my body, but she is also very much her father's daughter."

"Lir," CC said.

Gaea looked surprised at her knowledge, but nodded. "Yes."

"Um, who exactly is Lir?" she asked.

The goddess smiled. "Lir is the great God of the Seas. You might recognize him by one of his other titles. He has been known as Tethys, Pontos, Neptune, Barinthus, Enki, Poseidon and many others."

CC's eyes widened in surprise. "Poseidon is Undine's father?"

Gaea's eyes held a faraway expression as she gazed out at the waters. "We knew that the land and the sea were not meant to mate, but one day I was bathing here, in this very cove, and the Lord of the Sea cast his eyes upon me." Her face softened with remembrance. "For one brief night I allowed him to envelop me, and from that union Undine was conceived."

CC listened intently to the tale the goddess spun.

"Undine was born a mermaid, so it was destined that she live in her father's realm, but she was not content there. She longed for the land and for her mother." Gaea's face was shadowed by sadness, and CC felt her own eyes fill with tears in response. "I tried to coax Lir to allow me to gift our daughter with a human form so that she could live with me on land, but he adored the child and refused to be parted from her."

Gaea took CC's hand and squeezed it. "Do not think him cruel. Lir loved his daughter. And she wasn't always unhappy. She adored her father and the creatures of his realm, and she came here many times, sitting where you are now, telling me fantastic stories of the underwater crystal castle in which she lived and the wonders of the seas."

"It was only recently that she changed." The goddess's expression was haunted. "Sometimes I would find her weeping, there on that rock. Ceaselessly she begged me to gift her with a human form."

CC shivered. She thought she knew why Undine had become so desperate. "Did she tell you what was wrong?"

Gaea shook her head sadly. "No. I asked her, but she said only that she longed to be with me always."

Tears spilled from the goddess's eyes, yet Gaea didn't seem to notice.

"I was afraid she would do harm to herself. I am a goddess, but her father is also an immortal, and I could not cause her form to shift without his consent, as he could not have taken her from me if she had been born in human form." Her eyes glinted with determination. "But I am also a mother, and I could not allow my child to suffer. I wove a spell for her, giving Undine the ability to attain a human body, but only if she could find a human being who would be willing to exchange lives with her." Gaea stared into CC's eyes. "And I knew you would have need of her aid, as she had need of yours, little daughter."

"I don't understand," CC said.

"Your Samhain ritual was heartfelt, and I still heed the call of my children in other worlds, even a world in which I have been forgotten. You pleased me that night, and I touched you."

CC blushed, remembering the passionate feel of the moonlight on her skin.

The goddess put one perfect finger under CC's chin and lifted her face. "Do not ever be ashamed of a gift from a goddess." Before CC could respond she continued. "I asked the Fates to show me your future, and I saw your life's thread end too soon in a watery grave." She sighed sadly. "There was little I could do to aid you, as there was little I could do to aid the daughter of my flesh, but together you could help one another. Thus you are here and she is there."

"Where is here?" was the first of many questions that leapt to CC's mind.

"Here is a world where gods and goddesses still live."

CC's expression was puzzled.

Gaea tried to explain. "This cove is of my making, so it is like nothing that would be familiar to you, but beyond here you would find a land your world would call medieval Cymru." Her arm swept in a gesture meant to include all of the land behind them.

CC felt her face pale. "You're not talking about somewhere in southern California, are you?"

Gaea smiled at her. "Actually, I believe your books would tell you it is the Land of the Britons, or more specifically, ancient Wales."

"You mean I'm smack in the middle of medieval Europe!"

Gaea patted her hand reassuringly. "There is much that historians left out of your world's texts." The goddess winked one large blue eye at CC. "Like magic, my daughter."

"And how do I—"

The angry chattering of the dolphin interrupted CC's question. She looked over her shoulder and her body went numb. The merman had surfaced in the middle of the cove.

"Silence you meddling beast!" he snarled at the dolphin.

Automatically, CC scooted closer to Gaea.

"Goddess Gaea, what an unexpected privilege it is to see you." His voice had shifted to silk.

"And why would it be unexpected, Sarpedon?" Gaea smiled graciously at him. "This is my cove; it is well known that I come here often."

"*Your* cove?" The merman's instant sarcasm shocked CC. "I thought the water realm belonged to Lir."

"That would be true, young Sarpedon, had your father not gifted me with all the waters within this cove." Gaea's eyes narrowed. "You would do well to remember that water must flow over land, and where you find land, there you will always find my realm."

"I beg your pardon, Goddess Gaea. I did not mean to offend," he said, suddenly contrite. "I come to *your* cove on an errand for Lir himself."

When Gaea didn't respond, Sarpedon hurried on, taking the opportunity to drift closer to the two of them. "My father asks that I escort my sister back to him. Undine has been absent so frequently of late that she has been greatly missed," he said, and his intense gaze shifted briefly to CC.

"No."

The word slipped from CC's lips as a whisper. She glanced up at the goddess, who was studying her carefully. Bolstered by Gaea's presence, CC cleared her throat and repeated the word in a loud, firm voice.

"No!"

"You must obey our father," Sarpedon said between clenched teeth.

"Must she?" The goddess broke into the exchange. Gaea's eyes were wise as she looked from the mermaid to the merman.

"Yes!" Sarpedon struggled to control the anger in his voice. "Goddess, you know that Lir misses his daughter."

"I know that Lir loves his daughter and would not see her harried," Gaea snapped.

"I want only to do our father's bidding." Sarpedon raised his hands, palms open in a gesture of helplessness. CC could clearly see the angry red welts that dotted one palm where his skin had touched her amulet.

CC's head was whirling. She knew that Undine must have been trying to escape from this creature, but she also knew that the mermaid had not confided in her mother about her problem. Well, maybe Undine had spent her life being bullied and hounded by her half brother, but CC had spent the past seven years in the male-dominated United States Air Force. Even before the goddess touched her she knew how to stand up for herself. If this was going to be her world, she might as well get the rules straight right away. And she sure wasn't going to play by Sarpedon's rules. She raised her chin and looked straight in his almond-shaped gray eyes.

"You are a liar," she said.

"You have been too long away from your home." He had moved to within only a few feet of CC. His face darkened dangerously. "You have forgotten yourself."

"Really?" CC said sardonically. "I think I could be gone a lifetime and still know rape when I see it."

With an abrupt movement, Gaea stood. She spoke with deadly softness. "You dared to touch my child against her will?"

"He tried, but your amulet protected me," she said before Sarpedon could respond. For the goddess's ears alone she whispered, "I think he's what Undine was so afraid of."

"Leave my presence, Sarpedon!" The goddess's voice was amplified until it filled the small cove. "And I warn you to keep far from my daughter."

But instead of being admonished, the merman rose out of the water, balancing on his powerful tail until he towered over CC. Automatically, she shrank back.

"I will have her!" Spittle flew from his lips and his eyes flashed wildly. "My father is Lord of the Seas—you hold no power over me, *Land Goddess*." He spat the title like it was an oath.

"Foolish creature. Even the Lord of the Seas knows not to evoke the wrath of a goddess!"

Gaea pointed one slim finger at the sandy earth under her feet and made a small, circular motion. The sand stirred. With a flick of her wrist she gestured to the merman. The sand whirlpooled from its damp bed and flung itself into Sarpedon's face, causing him to choke and rub frantically at his eyes. He fell back into deeper water, sputtering and cursing. Then she stretched out her arms, as if she would embrace the cove. When she spoke her voice was seductive and rich with authority.

"Winds that play over my body, which is the living Earth herself, come to me now and blow this usurper from my presence."

The goddess pursed her full lips and blew a light burst of air at Sarpedon. Then something amazing happened to that light, almost playful bit of air. It seemed that all the winds in the cove suddenly rushed to join it. The gust struck Sarpedon like a fist, lifting him from the water and hurling him to the coral reef barrier.

"Trespass upon my realm again, and I will destroy you." The power in Gaea's voice lifted the hairs on the back of CC's neck. *"So have I spoken; so shall it be."* The air around the goddess shimmered, making her promise a tangible thing.

Awestruck, CC could only stare at Gaea. Her mind could hardly grasp what she was witnessing. The goddess loomed huge and powerful, and CC was overwhelmed by her majesty.

But Sarpedon seemed oblivious to Gaea's power. "Do not forget that Undine is a creature of the seas! She must exist in my realm, Land Goddess!" He shrieked at her before leaping over the coral reef and disappearing into the blue depths.

CC stared after him, shivering with an ominous foreboding.

CHAPTER SEVEN

"YOU were very brave." Gaea's voice had returned to that of a mother praising her child.

"I don't feel very brave right now," she said hesitantly, still awed by Gaea's power.

The goddess bent and stroked CC's soft hair. "I am proud of you. There is a strength in you that was lacking in Undine."

CC felt a rush of pleasure at her words.

The dolphin surfaced, blowing water on the two women and chattering like an upset nursemaid. Laughing, Gaea wiped the drops of seawater from her gown.

"You had better comfort her; she will not leave us in peace until she is assured of your safety."

Feeling a little shaky at first, CC slid from the shore. Again, she felt that prickle at the nape of her neck that made her think she was being watched.

No, she told herself firmly, Sarpedon is gone. He cannot come within Gaea's grove. She was just being paranoid—and who could blame her? Thankfully, as soon as she was immersed in the water, her fears began to subside. She glided up to the distraught dolphin and stroked the creature's smooth sides.

"Hey, I'm fine," she said aloud. "Gaea got rid of him. He can't hurt me here."

We feared for you, Princess. The dolphin nuzzled CC, then turned and bowed its head reverently at Gaea. *Thank you, great goddess, for protecting our Princess.*

Solemnly, Gaea inclined her head and acknowledged the dolphin's adoration.

CC could see the shapes of the smaller fish timidly hiding around the clumps of bright coral.

You can come out now. She coaxed and was delighted to see them respond by wriggling up to her. With one arm draped over the back of the dolphin, she petted and soothed the frightened fish.

"Sarpedon was correct about one thing," Gaea said.

"What?" CC's attention had been focused on the delightful fish, but the goddess's words sent a chill through her body.

"I cannot protect you there." The goddess pointed to the seemingly limitless expanse of ocean. "And you cannot live forever in this cove."

"But what am I going to do?" CC knew the goddess was right. How could she live her life in this small cove? It was the equivalent of being trapped forever in an apartment. No matter how luxurious or wonderful, she would still be trapped.

"We will do what we must to keep you safe," Gaea said.

"Which means what?"

Gaea studied the girl who inhabited her daughter's body. She had strength, yes. And she was outspoken and brave. But did she also have wisdom? Perhaps the child had a kind of wisdom that was foreign to this world; but perhaps that was the kind of wisdom that would be needed for her to survive the tests that were sure to be ahead of her. The goddess made her decision.

"There is only one answer. I must take you from the sea."

CC eyes widened in surprise. "But I thought that was the problem. You couldn't take Undine from the sea without Lir's permission." Then an idea came to CC. "So why can't we get Lir's permission now? You said he loves Undine. Doesn't that mean that he wouldn't want her own brother to rape her?"

"Sarpedon is Lir's child, too." Gaea's expression was grim. "Perhaps Lir has given his permission for your mating."

"Ugh, that's disgusting—brother and sister mating." Just the thought made CC feel sick.

"Gods and goddesses do not view these things the way humans do," Gaea said simply.

"You think it's okay that he wants me?" CC was shocked.

"Never," Gaea said firmly. "But only because you have rejected him; thus, he has no right to you. Understand that relationships are different between the gods."

"I'll take your word for it," CC muttered. "So we can't go to Lir. How do I get away from Sarpedon?"

"There is a way, but it may prove difficult."

"Is it worse than being raped by Sarpedon?" CC asked.

"Only you can answer that question, little one." The goddess began pacing back and forth along the shore as she explained to CC. "I can gift you with a human form, but it will not be permanent. You will still be tied to the seas." She gave CC an apologetic look. "Your body will long to return to the water; it may even be painful for you. And you must return to the waters and your mermaid form once each third night, or else you will sicken and die."

"Well, I suppose that's better than being trapped in this cove forever," CC said doubtfully.

The goddess stopped pacing and spoke earnestly to her. "But there is a way to make your human form permanent. You must find a man to love you and to accept with a full heart that you are a daughter of the sea, as well as that of the land. Then even Lir cannot break the bond of true love, and you will be gifted with your human form permanently."

"Oh, Gaea," CC groaned. "I'm not very experienced with men. Actually, they treat me like I'm a little sister." Then she added quickly, "And where I come from that didn't mean they wanted anything romantic to do with me."

"The handsome young pilot on your transport desired you."

Gaea's words cut into CC. Her eyes filled with tears as she remembered Sean's sweetness. "Yeah, and look what happened to him."

"He was living his destiny, child." Gaea's tone was soothing. "It was not your fault; he was fated to die on that journey. He did so heroically. You should honor his memory."

"He was going to die anyway?" CC asked.

"Yes. You did not cause his death. His life's thread had run out."

At Gaea's words CC felt a weight of guilt lift from her. She closed her eyes and said a silent prayer of thanksgiving for Sean's bravery. When she opened her eyes she met the Goddess's gaze with a clear conscience.

"Tell me what I need to do."

"I will cast the spell. You must simply find the man who can accept and love you."

"Wait! Shouldn't that be easy in this world? You said gods and goddesses live here. Aren't people used to magical things?" CC asked.

"At one time, perhaps." Gaea hesitated, as if weighing her words. "You have priests in your world."

Gaea hadn't made it sound like a question, but CC nodded anyway.

"They are here, too. And many of them are good men who serve their God with love and devotion." She paused, and when she spoke again her voice sounded disgusted. "But not all of them are honorable. There has begun a new sect of priest that has infected parts of their religion. They preach that all magic is evil, and that there is only one way to believe—their way. They believe beauty, especially that of the female body, is sinful and evil." Gaea's laugh was dry and humorless. "They are fools, afraid of their own desires. But of course they want people shut away from beauty. It is easier to control people who lack hope." She shook her head sadly. "Unfortunately, too many listen to their poison."

"I wouldn't want to be with a man who believed that anyway," CC said.

"Do not judge too harshly. Even good men can be misled. Be wise in your choice and all will be well in the end."

"Ha! My choice? I haven't even had a date in six months." CC felt her cheeks color at that admission.

"My daughter," the goddess smiled indulgently. "I promise you that men will desire you."

CC glanced down at her sexy curves. "Oh! I get to keep *her* body?"

Gaea's laughter rang throughout the cove. "What was hers is yours, *Undine*."

"Ooooh." CC's mouth rounded in wonder. She was going to be beautiful. Incredibly, amazingly, as-gorgeous-as-Marilyn-Monroe beautiful.

"You must appear to be a princess who has survived a shipwreck." Gaea's words were coming quickly now that the decision was made.

"But—"

Gaea held up her hand, cutting off CC's question. "I am afraid I must create a storm." She looked narrowly at CC. "You can swim?"

"Yes, but not very—"

Again, the goddess cut her off.

"Good." Gaea paced while she spoke to CC in a matter-of-fact, instructional tone. "Feign loss of memory. You should even appear desperate to find your family . . ."

CC wanted to ask how she was supposed to find true love based on lies, and amnesia, but there was no interrupting the goddess.

". . . that desperation is why you must insist on staying near the ocean—so that messages can be more easily sent and received. And I will be certain that you come to shore in a place surrounded by water." Gaea's gaze was piercing. "But do not forget that in truth you must stay near the water or you will perish."

Then the goddess softened. "But you will already know that, child. You will ache for the water. Just be wise when you change your form. Do not let yourself be seen, and always stay close to the shore where you will be under my protection. If Sarpedon traps you away from my shores, I cannot aid you."

"But you will be with me when I'm on the land?" CC's voice sounded panicky.

"I will be watching you." The goddess smiled softly. "Remember to wear your amulet. I will always be there when you truly have need of me, but you must choose your own path, Undine. Be sure to choose wisely."

Before doubts could overwhelm her, CC said, "I'll try my best."

"Are you ready, Undine?" the goddess asked.

CC fought back the nervousness that threatened to overwhelm her. She almost changed her mind and begged the goddess to let her stay in the protected cove where she knew she would be safe and loved. But she wasn't a fish in a bowl, and she'd already left one life that had been too small to contain her when she joined the air force. Was this really so different?

"I'm ready, Mother," she said resolutely.

"Then know my blessing as well as my love goes with you."

The goddess stepped away from the water and walked back to the greenery that lined the sandy shore. Once surrounded in living plants, she turned and faced the ocean. Lifting her arms over her head she began to speak, and CC shivered as the power of the goddess's words filled the cove.

"*I call upon the elements I command. Air—that blows over and through me, ever present and ever blessed. Fire—that is fed and brought to life by me, a true partner and respected friend. And Earth—my body and soul. It is through you that my child was born, and to you she shall someday return.*"

As the air around Gaea started to glow, CC could feel the lower half of her body begin to tingle.

"*With this Earth spell I protect my own. I command that only true love will complete it—and only death can break it. So have I spoken; so shall it be.*"

The glow that had been surrounding Gaea exploded, hurling its brightness outward and directly at CC. She closed her eyes and threw her hands over her face just before she was enveloped in a blinding flash of color and sensation. She could tell she was being pulled into the air, and her body felt as if it was on fire. CC could see nothing and she was deafened by a cacophony of shrieking wind.

Time had no meaning. She tried to scream Gaea's name, but the words were ripped from her mouth, lost in an unnatural gale of noise and light.

And then she was plunged back into the water. Only her body didn't obey her with the awesome power of a mermaid. This time she could feel her human legs kicking feebly against the angry current as she struggled for the surface. She couldn't breathe and her lungs screamed. Finally, she broke through the surface and gulped air.

The sky was black and bruised looking. Waves crashed over her head making her sputter and choke. The peaceful cove was nowhere in sight, nor was her dolphin friend or the goddess. She could see an unfamiliar shoreline a daunting distance away from her. Trying to keep a growing sense of panic at bay, she started swimming for land.

The skies opened and rain began to pelt her. A white-capped wave hit her, and CC was slammed under the water. She clawed for the surface and realized that in the liquid blackness she couldn't tell which direction was up. All rational thought fled her mind and panic surged through her as she flailed helplessly in the drowning darkness.

Strong hands gripped her by the waist and lifted her, holding her above the seething water so that she could suck air into her burning lungs. She coughed and gagged, vomiting the seawater she had been unable to keep herself from swallowing. Her body shook uncontrollably. She could feel hands holding her waist securely. Her naked back was pressed firmly against the hard muscles of a man's chest—she could feel his deep, even breathing. She thought that he had to be standing on firm ground to be able to support her so well. With shaking hands she rubbed her eyes clear of saltwater, expecting to see the shore close before her. Instead, it was still a too distant line of darkness.

Confused, CC twisted around to find that she was being held in the arms of an oddly familiar stranger. His wild black hair hung in runnels around his shoulders. He didn't speak, but his sable-colored eyes were fixed intently on her.

Questions surged through CC's mind. How could he look familiar to her? Hadn't Gaea sent her to a medieval world? Had the goddess made a mistake?

And then realization hit her with a rush of dizzy wonder. He looked familiar because he reminded her of the man from her dream! The one who had called to her so desperately the night she had summoned the goddess and danced in the rain.

Fascinated, CC stared at him. His broad chest was bare and smooth and felt hard and warm against her naked breasts. The corded muscles of his arms flexed with the effort of holding her above the surface. But instead of being able to feel the muscles of a man's legs against her own bare legs, the lower half of her body was pressed firmly against a single expanse of slick, warm flesh that flexed and beat steadily against the current. She glanced down. Even through the swirling water she could see the orange and gold brilliance of his thick, banded tail.

CHAPTER EIGHT

CC gasped with shock. The thought that flooded her mind was that she had to escape, and she pushed violently against his chest, kicking her way free of his arms. Instantly another wave battered her, pulling her under the water again. When she felt his hands on her, she forced herself to be calm and to quell the overwhelming urge to fight. She allowed him to lift her back to the surface.

This time, instead of holding her securely against his chest, he grasped her waist and held his arms straight out from his body, keeping her as far from him as he could. CC could see his thick tail beating hard against the water below, keeping them afloat.

"If you do not allow me to help you, you will drown." His deep voice sounded surprisingly gentle. "Your new body cannot breathe under the water."

"Who are you?" she asked breathlessly, pulling her water-soaked hair forward to cover her naked breasts.

"I am called Dylan."

"I won't go back to Sarpedon."

The merman's brows came together, and he shook his head. "I am no friend to the son of Lir."

"He didn't send you here?" She couldn't stop shivering.

"No." The word was clipped.

"Did Gaea?"

He shook his head.

"How—" she started to ask, but he broke in urgently.

"Undine, I must get you to land." He paused and looked deeply into her eyes. "It would be best if you would put your arms around my shoulders. I . . ."

He hesitated again, trying to catch his breath, then he continued with an apologetic shrug. "I do not have the strength to carry you to shore as I am holding you now."

And he obviously didn't. His breath was coming in gasps, and the muscles in his arms were tight and quivering. CC could see the effort it was costing him to keep them afloat in the choppy waters. She looked at him more carefully. If he had been human, he would have been a tall man. The merman's torso was well defined; his arms were powerful and his flat abdomen rippled with strength. But he didn't have the bulky cords of muscles that had packed Sarpedon's frame, nor did he have the other merman's overwhelming size. Obviously, mer-creatures came in different shapes and strengths, just like people.

"I give you my oath that I will not harm you, Undine." Dylan spoke the words slowly and clearly, enunciating carefully around his ragged breathing. "Look—" He shifted one hand from her waist, causing her to slip a little way down in the water. He grasped her arm, still keeping her head and shoulders above the water, and with his other hand, he reached toward her breasts.

"Stop!" CC jerked back.

"You misunderstand," he assured her quickly. "I wish only to touch the amulet of the goddess. If it does not burn me, you will see that I have no desire to harm you."

CC held very still as the merman's hand moved slowly between her breasts. He cupped the amber teardrop in his palm.

Nothing happened. Dylan let the amulet fall from his hand and held his palm open for her inspection. It was unmarked.

"Do you believe me now, Princess Undine?" he asked.

She nodded. "What do you want me to do?"

"Hold onto my shoulders and rest your body against my back. Then I can swim under the water while you remain above the surface."

"Okay," she said, fighting back her fear.

"Come, then."

Still holding her securely by the arm, he pulled her toward him and turned so that she was facing his broad back. His skin was tan and flawless. His hair fell thick and heavy past his shoulders. It was wet and it glistened like a raven's wing. He slipped down in the water so that she could easily reach his shoulders.

She hesitated, afraid to touch him. *He's just trying to help me,* she told herself and forced her hands to grasp the rounded tops of his shoulders.

"You must hold tightly." He turned his head and spoke over his shoulder.

"I'm trying," CC said. Her hands felt numb and they didn't seem to want to obey her. Her lips were cold and the skin on her arms looked unnaturally pale.

Dylan reached around and with his forearm held her firmly against him. The length of CC's naked body was pressed to the back of the merman. She could feel his muscles tensing against her. His breathing was rough, and his skin felt incredibly warm against her chilled flesh. He turned his head again and their eyes met. Hers were wide with shock; his were dark with unspoken emotion.

"You have nothing to fear. I will not let you fall," he said simply.

A strong thrust of his tail sent the merman forward. He ducked his head under the water and began swimming just below the surface. CC clung to his back, struggling to breathe as waves slapped her face. Against her body she could feel the rhythmic beat of the merman's tail as it propelled them toward the shoreline.

As they neared the shore, the rain stopped. The sky began to clear and the waves quieted. Within minutes it was as if there had never been a raging storm. Dylan swam around jutting clumps of coral and rocks until CC could see that the shoreline was just a few yards from them. With a graceful flick of his tail he lifted his torso out of the water. CC still clung, gasping, to his back. Hesitantly, as if he didn't want to stop touching her, he unwrapped his arm from around CC. Her feet found the sandy bottom, and she let go of his shoulders.

The instant her feet met land, she felt an electric tingling throughout her body, and there was a burst of incredible light. Threads of brightness obscured her vision, like she had been trapped in a glowing spider's web. Then, as abruptly as it had begun, the light show ended.

CC was standing in water that came just below her breasts, and her body felt somehow different. She looked down at herself and gasped. She was clothed in layers upon layers of cloth that created a beautiful dress, which sparkled and shimmered with the exact colors that had been in her mermaid's tail. The fabric was heavy and wet, but CC could still see the intricate needlework that covered almost every inch of it. Her fingers and wrists were covered with rings and bracelets. She shook her head in wonder and felt dangling earrings brush against her neck. Her hair, too, felt unnaturally heavy, and CC raised a hand to touch strands of jewels that had been magically woven within it and draped around her slender neck.

"The Goddess Gaea cares for her own," Dylan said. The merman's tail was curled under him so that it appeared that he was standing beside her. He had drifted a step away from her, as if to give the magic room to work, but he didn't seem surprised by the sudden manifestation of CC's new wardrobe.

"Thank you, Gaea," CC said aloud. She studied the thickly leafed trees lining the beach, but she didn't see any sign of the goddess. Then her gaze returned to the merman.

"And thank you," she said. "I think I owe you my life." The sun had come out and its rays were already warming her. She was exhausted and her body felt like it was made of lead, but her uncontrollable shivering had stopped, and now that she was dressed, she didn't feel nearly as helpless.

He shook off her thanks. "No, Undine. There is no debt between us. I only offered aid when it was needed."

"Well, thank you anyway." Automatically, she offered her hand to him, and with only a slight hesitation he took it. But instead of shaking it he lifted it slowly to his mouth and pressed it to his lips. CC stopped breathing. Dylan's lips were warm—and that warmth traveled through her body, making the fine hairs on her arm rise in response. His eyes met hers, and CC realized how darkly handsome he was.

She found herself wanting to whisper *I think I dreamed about you*, but his gaze mesmerized her into silent breathlessness.

He continued holding her hand in his, and she felt him stroke it gently with his thumb. Her skin tingled under his caress, and her breath came back in a rush. The smile on his full lips was reflected in his dark, expressive eyes. When he spoke his voice was rough with emotion.

"Undine, you are most wel—"

A shout from the shore startled them. In one blink, Dylan dropped her hand and plunged headfirst, disappearing instantly beneath the waves.

CC turned to the shore in time to see, surging from the line of trees, a man riding a huge black horse. She took a step forward and her feet became tangled in the thick skirts of her dress. She fell face first into the water, where she struggled and floundered impotently against the weight of her clothes. Before she could regain her feet she was pulled roughly to the surface, swept up into the man's arms and carried to the beach like a child. She coughed and wiped water from her eyes, thinking how extraordinarily tired she was of swallowing seawater.

"You are safe now, my lady," the man said earnestly. Placing her gently on the sand, he kneeled beside her.

"Th-thank you." CC coughed. She looked up at him and couldn't help staring. He was dressed like she imagined an ancient knight would have been dressed. He wore a pointed helmet made of silver metal that left most of his face open, except for a studded nosepiece. A long tunic of gray chain mail covered him from torso to knees, leaving his thickly muscled legs bare. He had a huge sword strapped to his waist and the scarlet cape that was tossed over his shoulders was held in place by a large pewter brooch in the shape of a roaring lion. Blond hair escaped from under the helmet and curled around his shoulders. He looked like a young war god.

But he wasn't looking at her. His attention was focused on the water. "My lady, were there no other survivors from your vessel?"

"No," she said quickly. Then she remembered Gaea's words and pressed her hand to her forehead, leaning heavily back as if she was on the edge of fainting. "I-I don't know. I can't remember." She felt her body quiver with shock and the sob that escaped her lips was suddenly very real. "I can't remember anything."

He turned his attention back to her and his eyes widened as his senses registered the beauty he held within his arms. "Forgive me, lady," he said hastily, patting her shoulder awkwardly. "You have been through a horrible ordeal. It is just that for a moment I thought I saw someone in the water with you."

Two men on horseback burst through the tree line. The warrior shouted orders to them.

"Marten, Gilbert—search the shore and the waters for other survivors. This lady is injured. I must get her to shelter."

The two men saluted him and instantly obeyed his orders, but CC couldn't help noticing the way their eyes kept snaking back to her. The way they looked at her made her feel like she was still naked. The man kneeling beside her seemed to notice their looks, too, because he shifted his body to block her from their view.

"Can you ride?" he asked gently.

CC glanced at the gigantic black beast and gulped. Slung over its odd-looking, curved pommel was a large silver shield that looked a little like a monstrous kite. The creature pawed dangerously. The only horse she'd ever ridden had been attached to a carousel, and that had been many years ago.

"Not without help." She definitely wasn't pretending when her voice shook.

In one motion he scooped her from the sand and strode to the waiting horse, who snorted and shied at the waterlogged body in his master's arms. Without any warning, he tossed CC into the saddle, then grabbed a handful of the stallion's thick, dark mane and vaulted up behind her. Leaning forward he gathered the reins, kicked his heels into the horse's sides and the stallion leapt forward.

"Wait!" CC felt a stab of panic as they headed into the forest and away from the ocean. Something inside of her wrenched, and a wave of dizziness washed over her. "Where are you taking me?"

"Do not fear, my lady. There is a monastery not far from here. The good monks will give you aid."

"But I can't leave the ocean," she said frantically. "My family—" she broke off with a frightened sob.

His arms tightened around her protectively as he thought of her lovely helplessness. He was unaccustomed to having a woman touch his emotions, but it felt as though this young woman's beauty had already cast a spell upon him. She most assuredly shook him. When he spoke his voice was gruff, making his words sound harsh.

"We are not leaving the ocean. Caldei Monastery is but a short distance up this coast." He forced himself to add a smile to his voice, trying to reassure her. "And it would be impossible for us to ride away from the ocean. Caldei Monastery is built on the island of Caldei. We are surrounded by the ocean."

The man's words didn't seem to register to her battered brain. She couldn't stop her body from shaking. What had she gotten herself into? Where was Gaea?

They broke through the trees onto a dirt-packed road and the warrior pointed his horse to the right. Clearing his throat and forcing himself to speak in a more soothing tone, he said, "My name is Sir Andras Ap Caer Llion, eldest son of the great Lord Caerleon. I am pleased to be of service to you, and I pledge that I will not allow any harm to befall you." His warm breath touched the side of her face. "May I be honored with your name?"

CC forced her eyes from the snatches of blue that she glimpsed through the trees. Her mind was in turmoil. She wanted nothing more than to shake free from the cage of the knight's arms and to hurl herself back into the ocean.

You will ache for the waters. Gaea's words drifted through her memory as she struggled against the primitive urge that engulfed her.

"Your name, lady?" the knight prompted.

CC breathed deeply, forcing herself to relax in his arms. The sun glinted through the trees that lined the dirt road, and as the stallion galloped forward, the play of light and shadow danced alluringly over the knight's silver helmet and golden hair. CC felt another wave of overwhelming emotion. She had been rescued first by a creature from her dreams and then by an authentic knight in shining armor.

And through it all, her body ached and cried for the sea.

"I am the Princess Undine, and I cannot leave the water," she whispered, closing her eyes and allowing her head to rest against the strength of his shoulder.

A safe distance from shore Dylan watched as the human man carried Undine away. His hands balled into fists, and he clenched his jaw until it ached. It didn't matter that he knew this was what she had always wanted. It didn't even matter that he knew the soul inside her body wasn't that of his childhood playmate, Undine. He still felt drawn to her. He remembered the look in her eyes when he had kissed her hand, and the hope that had filled him at her unexpected response to his touch. Watching her ride away, he felt like a piece of his body had been hacked from him.

Through the trees he could see that the horse had turned and was traveling parallel to the ocean. Ignoring his despair, he glided through the water, careful to keep her always within his sight.

She may still have need of him. He had failed her at the grotto; he would not fail her again.

CHAPTER NINE

"THIS princess has been shipwrecked!" The warrior shouted at the robed man standing nervously behind the barred doors. "I am Andras, son of Caerleon. I demand entrance and sanctuary for this lady."

"I must get the abbot." The little man scuttled quickly out of sight.

Andras made a derisive sound through his nose, and the black stallion pawed restlessly. CC closed her eyes on a wave of nausea. She could no longer see the ocean. The monastery had been built on the top of a cliff that dropped steeply to a rugged shoreline. Although out of sight, she could hear the waves crashing against the rocks below, and if she focused hard enough on the sound, it soothed her frayed nerves.

"Not much longer, Princess," Andras said. "Abbot William and my family are well acquainted. We will be admitted."

CC wanted to say that she thought monks were supposed to help people, whether they knew their families or not, but she couldn't summon the energy to speak. She wanted to get her drenched clothes off and sleep for days—and not necessarily in that order.

But most of all she wanted the sea to quit calling to her.

"Andras! Is that you, my son?" A soft voice with an accent that sounded vaguely British called from within the walls of the monastery.

"Yes, Father. I am in need of your aid."

"Of course, of course," the voice said hastily. "Brother, unlock this gate and allow our friend entrance."

Rusty hinges complained as the gate swung open. CC tried to sit straighter, ashamed of her bedraggled appearance. But before she could even smooth her hair, Andras slid from the horse's back and pulled her down beside him. CC was horrified to realize that she couldn't stand on her own. Her vision was blurred and everything went cloudy and gray as her knees buckled. Instantly the warrior lifted her into his arms.

"The princess needs rest and care. I found her washed ashore not far from here."

"Brother Peter, have the guest quarters readied for this lady and have one of the sculleries attend to her." CC could hear the scuffle of robes as the man hurried to do the abbot's bidding.

"Are there other survivors to follow, my son?"

CC could feel the warrior shaking his head.

"Poor child," the priest spoke quietly, but he made no attempt to mask the obvious curiosity in his voice. "And you say she is a princess?"

"She remembered her name, but I am afraid she has not been able to say much else," Andras said.

"What is her name?"

"She is the Princess Undine."

Silence greeted the knight's words, and CC wanted desperately to open her eyes and see the abbot's expression. But common sense warned her that it was best to keep up the pretense that she had fainted and was still unconscious.

"Undine?" The man enunciated the name carefully. "Are you quite certain she said Undine?"

"I believe so," Andras answered. "Yes, I am certain she told me her name was the Princess Undine. Do you recognize that name, Father?"

"I only know that in some tongues an *undine* is a spirit from the sea. How very odd."

"Abbot William." The first monk hurried back to them. "The guest room is ready for the lady and the scullery awaits."

"Let us get her safely within," Andras said. "There will be time to question names and such when she has recovered." CC could feel the warrior's eyes on her and when he spoke his lips were close to her ear. "Look at her, Abbot. It is most certain that she is a princess." Andras's arms tightened possessively around her.

"Let us not be deceived by beauty, my son." The abbot's voice was condescending. "But you are correct, she must rest before we can expect her to speak. Follow me to the guest quarters."

CC rested her head against Andras's shoulder, slitting her eyes to try and catch a glimpse of her surroundings. She saw the green of the grass as they crossed some kind of courtyard, and she was surprised to note the fading light. It was obviously dusk, but it had seemed like only minutes had passed since she had been pulled ashore by the merman. Her hand twitched in remembrance. Surely that wasn't his kiss that she still felt warming her skin?

When they entered the monastery, the heels of Andras's shoes rang against the stone of the floor, and all CC could see through her half-closed eyes was the gray of the stone walls in a dark, narrow corridor.

"Through that door, my son," the priest instructed. "Leave her on the bed. The maid will care for her."

Andras put her gently on a hard, cotlike bed and reluctantly released his hold on her. CC curled onto her side, careful to keep her eyes closed.

"Isabel!" Abbot William's voice was hard and cold when he addressed the maid. "Get her some water with which to wash and one of the good Brother's robes to wear until her own clothing can be cleaned and dried. If she can take sustenance, offer her some broth and watered wine. Then come report her progress to me."

"Yes, Abbot." CC could hear the rustle of the servant's skirts as she curtseyed and rushed out of the room.

"Let us have our own dinner, my son. There will be ample time to speak with the child tomorrow." The priest's voice lost its hard edge when he spoke to the knight. "Your princess is in excellent hands, and as you said, she must rest."

The door closed securely behind them. CC breathed a sigh of relief and opened her eyes. The room was small and barren. The walls were made of thick gray stone. CC hugged herself, feeling a chill that the newly lit fire did little to dispel. The room held only a small, hard bed that was covered with a scratchy brown blanket and a narrow dresser on which was placed a large, plain bowl made of brown pottery. Over the head of the bed hung the only decoration in the room—a wooden crucifix which was bare except for pointed splinters of wood resembling nails that had been driven into it where Christ's hands and feet would have hung.

She squinted and stepped closer to the crucifix. During her years in the air force she had attended church services on several bases for many different denominations, everything from Baptist to Methodist, Protestant to Catholic, but she had never seen anything like that nail- decorated cross. Something about the barren crucifix made her feel very alone.

A breath of fresh air blew into the small room and ruffled her hair. CC breathed deeply, savoring a scent that was at once magical and familiar. She took another deep breath. The air was filled with salt and water and life. Desire flooded her. As if she followed the sound of an imaginary Pied Piper, her face turned to the wall farthest from the door. High up on that wall was cut a narrow window slit, probably less than three feet wide. CC's body went still as she breathed in the odors of the sea. She could hear the rush of the waves against the shore. She could almost feel the warm fingers of water against her body.

An image came to her of Dylan pressing her hand to his lips. She touched the back of that hand, remembering the jolt of feeling his caress had caused.

The door opened and CC jumped guiltily. A small, stooped woman wearing a dress made of rough, nondescript brown wool limped into the room. Her face was so heavily wrinkled that it almost looked deformed; CC thought that she had to be the ugliest woman she had ever seen. In one skeletal hand, she balanced a tray, which held a pitcher, a goblet and a bowl. In the other, she clutched a folded piece of material. Her body jerked in surprise when she saw that CC was awake and instantly dropped into a nervous, lopsided curtsey, sloshing some of the red liquid out of the goblet.

"Oh! I am so sorry, Princess." She lurched over to the dresser, pushing the tray onto the top of it. In her haste she almost knocked over the bowl that was already sitting there. "I am afraid you startled me. I thought you would still be asleep."

Her voice was low and whispery and creaked with age.

"It's me who should be sorry," CC said quickly, covering her shock at the woman's appearance. "I didn't mean to frighten you."

The old woman ducked her head and wouldn't meet her eyes. She curtseyed awkwardly again, then stood nervously plucking at her skirt with her free hand. CC waited for her to say something, but she just stood, looking like she couldn't decide if she wanted to faint or run.

CC cleared her throat and gestured at the goblet that was still on the tray. In a gentle voice she said, "I really am very thirsty."

"Yes, of course, my lady!" In a shaky motion, the woman yanked the goblet from the tray and held it out to CC, who took it with a grateful smile and drank deeply. It was wine watered with cool water, and it was sweet and delicious.

"If the princess will allow me to help her disrobe, I will take her garments to be cleaned and dried." She shook out the material with her gnarled hands and it became a towel-sized cloth and a long robe. "I will help you wash the saltwater from your body, then you can wear this robe until your clothes have dried."

CC looked down at her dress, which was really several dresses, each layered over the top of the other. Even wet the skirts hung gracefully and the long, full sleeves ended in embroidered points that almost dragged the floor. The outfit was certainly beautiful, but she didn't see one zipper or one hook. She had no idea how she would get out of it without the woman's help, and she was honestly too tired to care.

"Please," CC said gratefully. "I would appreciate your help."

CC's legs felt shaky as she stood. The old woman moved quickly behind her. CC could feel her tugging and pulling at laces and ties as she stripped several layers of damp clothing from her body. When CC was left with only a white shift, made of almost translucent linen, the woman averted her eyes hastily.

"I give you my word that I will not look upon my lady's body. I will just hold and rinse the washing cloth for you if my lady would like to clean under her chemise."

CC was baffled. Clean under her chemise? But the thing was wet, salty and just plain disgusting. CC's tired brain felt foggy. How was she supposed to clean herself with her clothes on?

"I need to take this wet thing off, *then* I can clean myself and put the robe on," CC said, feeling stupid for having to say the obvious aloud.

The woman sounded shocked. "You would wear the robe with no underclothing?"

CC ran her hand down the front of the shift, where it was beginning to dry and crinkle with sea brine.

"What is your name?" CC asked.

The old woman gave her an owlish look, and her eyes almost disappeared in the wrinkled folds. "Isabel."

"Isabel," CC said calmly. "This shift needs to be cleaned. I need to be cleaned. Both things can't happen together. Now, we're both women, so it's fine with me if you see me naked." CC gave her a weary smile. "I really do appreciate your help, and I don't mean to offend you, but I'm afraid if I don't get this wet thing off and sit down pretty soon, I'm going to fall down."

Isabel's eyes widened even farther, and with jerky movements she turned around, poured the water from the pitcher into the bowl, dunked the cloth in the water and then, without looking at CC, she handed her the dripping cloth.

"Thank you," CC said.

What a ridiculous attitude, CC thought as she washed herself. The woman had literally looked horrified at the thought of seeing another woman's naked body. CC remembered the silky green gown the goddess had been wearing. It had done little to hide Gaea's erotic, voluptuous curves. And Undine's mermaid form had only been clothed in skin. What was it the goddess had said? Something about some priests being afraid of beauty. CC pulled over her head the robe of rough, undyed wool the color of parchment and grimaced as it scraped against her bare breasts. She looked down at her own lush body, now engulfed and almost completely sexless within the enshrouding robe. A sliver of unease pierced her. Didn't she remember reading in one of her college Humanities texts something about medieval people believing that the naked body, especially the naked female body, was sinful and inherently evil?

"Are you covered, my lady?" Isabel asked.

"Yes, completely," CC said, trying to keep the worry out of her voice.

Isabel turned around and studied her. "Shall I dress your hair back, Princess? It is most unseemly that it is left all"—here she paused and gestured helplessly with wizened hands to her own hair that was pulled severely back and covered with a plain white headdress— "free."

Automatically CC reached up, letting her hand skim through the thick length of the heavy tresses that reached to her waist. She could feel the jewels Gaea had magically twined throughout her hair. The thought of hiding that wondrous hair and the generous gifts from her goddess mother made CC's stomach tighten.

"No," she said. "I think I'll leave it as it is tonight."

Isabel gave her a dark look and opened her mouth to argue. Before she could speak, CC smiled sweetly at the old woman. "It is the way of my people for maidens to wear their hair free."

Now where had that come from? CC thought. But she was glad she had said it, even if the effort it had taken to stand up to Isabel had sapped all of her remaining strength. Her knees felt wobbly, and, all of a sudden, she found herself sitting down hard on the bed while the room spun around her.

"My lady," Isabel's voice was back to being kind and subservient. "You are exhausted. Here, this broth will help you to regain your strength."

Isabel put the bowl in her hands, and CC sipped the warm liquid, surprised at how wonderful it tasted.

When the bowl was empty, Isabel took it from her and gathered CC's damp clothing.

"Sleep now, my lady. You will feel better in the morning."

Without another word, the maid shuffled out. CC thought she heard a bolt being drawn on the door, but she was too tired to care. She fell asleep listening to the soothing sound of waves lapping against the distant shore.

CHAPTER TEN

THE clean scent of the sea teased her awake. Without opening her eyes, she breathed deeply. The room was very quiet. Somewhere in the distance CC could hear the bleating of sheep punctuated with the call of gulls and the crash of waves on rock. She felt her body tremble with need. That's where she should be. That's where she wanted to be. The ache was lodged deep within her, like an unbearable secret. She opened her eyes and her gaze was instantly drawn to the window. She rose unsteadily, as if her legs weren't exactly sure how they should work, and tottered to stand under the high, open window. Even with the height of her new body stretched as tall as it could, she couldn't quite see out.

CC looked around the barren room. There was a large chamber pot that had been placed next to the bed. Thankfully, it was empty. She dragged it over to the window and turned it upside-down. Grasping the window ledge for balance, she stepped up.

The wall of her room made up part of the outside wall of the monastery, and it faced directly out to the ocean. The view was breathtaking. Under her window there was only a few feet of open ground, then it looked like the earth fell away and a steep cliff dropped to give way to the majesty of the ocean. CC could see the rocky shoreline below and the frothy caps of the playful waves. Her knuckles whitened as she clung to the window ledge, forcing herself to ignore her body's insistent longing.

Two quick knocks against the door forced her attention away from the window, and she hurried clumsily to put the chamber pot back in its place.

"Yes?" she called as she sat on the bed.

"It is Isabel, my lady." The door opened slowly, and the woman limped into the room, giving CC a tentative smile. "I see you look well rested."

"I feel much better." CC was happy to see that Isabel carried a bundle of her newly cleaned and dried clothing.

"Abbot William asks that you join him for the evening meal if you are recovered enough."

CC's stomach growled, and she realized suddenly that she was starving. "Do I have to wait for evening to eat?"

Isabel looked surprised. "It is evening now."

CC felt a rush of foreboding. "How long have I been asleep?"

"You have slept for two nights and into evening of the second day," Isabel answered. "If you allow me to help you dress, you can join the abbot immediately."

Almost as if she was detached from her body, CC let Isabel help her into the gown. No wonder her body ached so badly. This was the third night. She had to find a way to get to the water tonight so she could change back into her mermaid form. Just the thought of that transformation made her heart hammer against her chest.

"There, my lady," Isabel said as she tied the last of the laces. "Please follow me."

They left the room and turned down the long, dark corridor that CC had glimpsed between half-closed eyes two days before. She was relieved that the more she walked, the stronger her legs felt, because even though Isabel moved with remarkable agility for an old, lame woman, CC had to struggle to keep up with her. They stepped out of the hall and headed across a grassy courtyard, at the far side of which was the closed gate through which CC had arrived. Directly in the middle of the courtyard was a large, round well, made of the same ponderous gray stone as was the rest of the monastery. As they walked by it, CC felt a rush of cold air, and she was overcome with dizziness.

"Princess Undine!" Isabel called in alarm when she noticed her charge was no longer beside her.

CC rubbed a hand over her eyes. "I feel strange."

Isabel's arm went around CC's waist. "You are still weak from your ordeal. Let me help you." The two women stumbled forward together.

After a few steps the dizziness passed and CC was able to walk on her own again. She thought she must be so hungry her glucose levels were messing with her equilibrium, and she sniffed the air hopefully, trying to catch a whiff of something cooking.

They left the courtyard through a low, arched doorway and entered a room that was filled with long wooden picnic tables. Seated at the tables were monks, all dressed in the same drab cream-colored woolen robes belted with huge wooden rosary beads. CC quickly estimated that there were probably twenty or thirty monks in the room, but it was unnaturally silent for a room filled with that many people. The only sound of conversation came from the head table, at which sat a slightly built man whose robes were brilliant crimson instead of cream, two monks in the more typical lightly colored robes, and the knight, Sir Andras.

The instant the knight saw her, he leapt to his feet and hurried to her side. CC was struck anew by his strong masculine features and his easy charm.

"Princess Undine," he said, taking her hand and kissing it gallantly. "I am pleased to see you looking so well." He linked her hand through his arm and led her to his table. "Princess, I am honored to present you to an old family friend, Abbot William. Caldei is his monastery."

Instead of greeting CC, the abbot ignored her and smiled warmly at Andras. "Sir Andras, truly Caldei belongs to you as well as to me. It was your great father who gifted it to our Holy Order. I would be pleased if you thought of

Caldei as your home while you visit us." Finally, his gaze shifted to CC and all traces of warmth instantly died.

Something about the coolness of the man's expression told CC not to offer him her hand. Instead, she decided it would be best to drop into a quick, impromptu curtsey.

"I'm pleased to meet you, Abbot William. Thank you so much for your hospitality."

The abbot was a short, slender man with well-defined features and a severely receding hairline. His hands were very white, small and soft looking, and CC noticed that he liked to use them to punctuate his gestures when he spoke. He wore a large, square ring on the middle finger of his right hand, which he tended to hold solicitously straight, like he was afraid it might slip off. The square, rust-colored stone that was set in the middle of the ring caught the dim light in the dining room and winked with a fierce brilliance. But the priest's most striking feature was his eyes, which were an unusual shade of brilliant blue. CC thought that he would have been considered a nice-looking man, had his expression not been so pinched and hard-looking.

"The pleasure is mine." The priest's smile was tight. "Please, join us." He gestured at an empty place setting across from him. "You must be hungry."

Andras returned to his seat next to Abbot William. The other two monks sitting at the table nodded briefly at her and then returned to their meal. An old woman hurried up and ladled a generous portion of aromatic stew onto CC's plate. When she smiled her thanks at her, the woman shot her a surprised look before she rushed away.

"There have been no other survivors found, Princess."

Abbot William's voice was soft and seemed gentle, but when CC met his eyes, his expression was flat and guarded. She forced herself to take a bite of the stew and chewed carefully, buying time as she tried to choose how best to respond to this intimidating-looking stranger.

She had never been a very good liar, and her seven years in the air force had only reinforced her dislike for lies. Dishonesty led to problems—usually career-ending problems. She had decided early on that it was better to tell the truth and deal with the consequences than to be a dishonorable person. Unfortunately, she thought, that lesson was not much help in her current situation. She glanced at Abbot William. She had a feeling that telling him the truth would probably get her burned at the stake.

The next best choice was to stick as close to the truth as she could.

Swallowing, she said, "I am sorry to hear that, Abbot. I was hoping another survivor could help me remember more about my past."

"Then you still have not regained your memory?" Sir Andras asked. Leaning forward he reached across the table and took her hand.

At Andras's gesture, CC saw a dark flicker in the priest's eyes. Now there was definitely a man who had issues with women—major issues. CC didn't want to antagonize the priest, but Gaea had made it clear to her that she had to find a man to love her. Right now Andras was her best, if not only, chance at that. And, she admitted to herself, the knight was certainly handsome and obviously interested in her.

In the back of her mind the memory of the merman's kiss lingered enticingly, but she pushed it away. Gaea had said *man*, not *merman*. And beside that, Dylan was long gone somewhere out at sea and could be of no help to her. Trying her best to ignore Abbot William's hateful look, she smiled warmly at the warrior and squeezed his hand before releasing it.

CC squinted, like she was trying hard to think. "No. I remember my name, but I can't remember much else." She bit her bottom lip. "I don't even know what year it is." She blinked innocently at them while her heart raced.

"It is the year of our Lord, one thousand and fourteen. You are on the island of Caldei near the mainland of Cymru." The abbot's voice was as hard as his eyes.

CC gulped. Trying not to show her shock at hearing it confirmed that she was, indeed, smack in the middle of the European Dark Age. She flashed the abbot a grateful smile. "Thank you. The more I know, the more I might be able to remember." She paused. "I do also remember a terrible storm and a giant wind." She let her eyes widen. "It picked me up and dropped me into the ocean. I remember I was drowning," CC said truthfully and reached for a goblet of wine with shaking hands.

"After such a horrible ordeal it is understandable that your memory has fled," Andras said quickly.

"Can you remember nothing more about your journey, Princess Undine?" Abbot William enunciated her name carefully. "Or perhaps why you were so near our island?"

CC could feel his eyes studying her, and she forced herself to meet them, while she shook her head sadly.

"No. I wish I could."

"And you can remember nothing about your family nor your home country?"

CC couldn't tell which irritated her more, his fluttery hand gestures or the cruel edge to his condescending tone. The modern woman in her wanted to snap at him to stop being such a jerk, but she quickly squelched that impulse. She wasn't in the modern world; she was in ancient Wales, and this man was providing her sanctuary. And wasn't it perfectly natural for him to be wary of her? She had literally washed up at his doorstep; he really knew nothing about her.

She met his cold blue eyes with a sweet, apologetic smile.

"I remember my name and that my parents love me very much. I truly wish I could remember more." Then she added, "I am sure that my family will be looking for me, and that they will reward anyone who has helped me."

The priest pressed his lips together. Their edges turned up in a parody of a smile. "Those of us who have chosen the priesthood seek a reward that cannot be found in this world."

"Of course not, Abbot," CC agreed quickly, stung again at the man's cold, disdainful tone. "I didn't mean to imply anything except that I'm sure my family will be very grateful to you for helping me."

"I will send inquiries to the nearby ports on the mainland. Perhaps there will be word of your family there," the knight said.

"You won't leave, will you?" CC asked. She definitely didn't want to be left alone with the abbot.

Sir Andras took her hand again and smiled. "I have pledged to be your protector. If you would have me stay, I will send my men in my stead."

Not looking at the priest, CC nodded. "I would like that."

"Yes." Abbot William's tone was ingratiating. "I would welcome your visit. I get so little news from inland. And you haven't told me, what brought you to our island?"

Andras shrugged nonchalantly. "My father was holding Tournament and, as a boon to a friend, I agreed to complete a quest to the sea." Then he smiled warmly at the abbot. "When my quest took me near Caldei, I knew I could not continue until I had ferried here and greeted my old teacher." Then he turned his gaze to CC. "And how was I to know that my sea quest would yield such a treasure?"

"Ah, the Caer Llion Tournament." Abbot William's eyes sparkled, and he pointedly ignored Andras's last comment. "How well I remember those fine games. You must tell me of all who attended."

While the priest monopolized Andras's conversation, CC concentrated on eating, glad that for the moment she didn't have to fabricate any more answers. As often as she could, without seeming ridiculously obvious, she sneaked looks at the warrior. He was definitely a gorgeous man. Today he wasn't wearing the chain mail or the silver helmet. Instead, a plain brown tunic made of fine linen draped over his strong body and belted at his waist. CC had a hard time stopping herself from staring. She just wasn't used to seeing such a blatant display of male muscles and strength. Yes, there were handsome, well-built men in the military, but they didn't just sit around partially bare and bulging, unless they were working out at the base gym. And this certainly wasn't a gym.

She also wasn't used to the way Andras kept looking at her. If she had been having a hard time remembering that the body in which her soul resided was a beautiful stranger's, this handsome knight's blatantly appreciative glances were all the reminder she needed. Their eyes met, and CC felt color heat her cheeks as she realized he had been speaking to her and she didn't have any idea what he was saying.

"I'm sorry, Sir Andras, my mind was elsewhere. What did you say?"

"I asked if you would consent to take a short walk with me before retiring to your chamber."

"Do you think that is wise?" Abbot William asked in a voice that CC thought was just a little too tinged with sarcasm to be considered concerned for her welfare. "The princess has yet to recover from her ordeal."

CC wiped her mouth on her napkin and stood. "Thank you for your concern, Abbot, but I think a walk would do me good. I believe in exercise."

"Does that mean that you are remembering more about your life, Princess?" the priest shot back.

"No," CC said, smiling energetically into his frozen eyes. "It means I'm healthy." Placing her hand on the arm Andras held out to her, she inclined her head graciously to the priest. "Thank you for the lovely meal." In a swirl of skirts, CC allowed the warrior to lead her from the dining room.

"Shall we walk around the courtyard, Princess?" Andras asked.

CC looked across the green expanse to the closed iron gate. The perfect lawn was broken only by the large stone well which sat in the middle of the courtyard. A breeze stirred the air around them, and CC breathed in the alluring scent of saltwater.

"Actually, Sir Andras, I would like to see the view." She looked determinedly toward the gate.

"Oh," he sounded surprised, but recovered quickly. "Certainly, Princess."

"I would like it if you called me Undine," CC said as they started across the courtyard.

"I would be honored, Undine." He looked intimately into her eyes as he repeated her name. "And it would please me if you did not address me formally, but simply called me by my Christian name, Andras."

"Then I will." They smiled at one another.

They were walking by the well when a sharp chill passed through CC. It was so intense that it was painful, and she felt the blood drain from her face. Her knees felt weak, and she tripped. If it hadn't been for Andras's strong arm she would have fallen.

"Undine! What is it?"

"I just need fresh air," she managed to whisper, and the knight helped her over to the gate.

After walking a few feet, the chill left her and she could feel the color coming back into her face. What was wrong with her? Was this part of her body longing for its true form? CC didn't think so. This feeling was different from the ache that seemed planted permanently within her.

"Perhaps Abbot William was right, you are not recovered enough for our walk." Andras's eyes were bright with worry.

"No, I'm better now. I was just feeling a little dizzy. I want to walk; the exercise will be good for me. And if I keep a hold of you, I'm sure I'll be fine." She smiled and squeezed his arm.

He placed a warm hand over hers. "Then I will simply have to be certain you do not release your hold on me."

Trying to shake off the creepy feeling that seemed to have rooted itself in her spine, she walked forward. Andras unbolted and opened the gate for her.

The road that led to the front gate was lined with tall, exotic-looking pines, and it looked vaguely familiar, like CC had visited it in a dream. But it wasn't the road or the trees that interested her. Like a homing pigeon, her feet found a little path that hugged the side of the monastery's outer wall. She pulled Andras with her.

"Undine, this path can be dangerous. It leads to the face of the cliff. The drop to the ocean is treacherous."

"I'll be careful," she promised breathlessly. She had to force herself to walk slowly when everything within her wanted to rush around the bend in the path and drink in the sight of the ocean.

Finally, they turned the corner and CC felt a thrill of pleasure. The endless ocean was swallowing a huge, shimmering sun, which painted the waters with gold and amber. Like giant teeth, rocks peppered the rugged shoreline, and even in the fading light CC could see the foamy caps of the crashing waves. She wanted to climb down the steep side of the cliff and let the water carry her body away. Then the never-ending aching inside of her would stop—she would be where she belonged.

"It is so beautiful," CC said, unable to hide the longing in her voice.

"Yes, I have never seen anything as beautiful."

Andras's voice had deepened, and she pulled her eyes from the ocean to see that he was staring intently at her. Something moved within his eyes, and his gaze flared with a heat that took CC completely by surprise. With a choked moan, he grasped the hand that she had wrapped through his arm and lifted it to his lips. Closing his eyes, he kissed her hand as if he was dying of thirst and her skin was water.

His lips were warm and soft, and CC appreciated the passion he was demonstrating. She studied the strong lines of his handsome face and enjoyed the way his chest flexed as his breathing deepened. But that was it. His touch awakened nothing inside of her except a detached appreciation for his masculine beauty.

Andras raised his face from her hand and his eyes captured hers. Lust flared so blatantly there that for a moment they glowed with an unnatural light. It even seemed his features shifted and darkened. His breath came in ragged gasps. CC felt a tremor of foreboding. This man wasn't the chivalrous knight who had rescued her and pledged his protection. He was a powerful stranger whose expression was filled with barely controlled lust. CC gasped at the change in him.

Instantly, a shadow lifted from the knight's eyes. He dropped CC's hand and took a step away from her, blinking in confusion.

"Forgive me, Princess," he said, mopping a hand across his brow like he had been sweating profusely. "I did not mean to take advantage of you."

"You didn't take advantage of me, you just kissed my hand," CC said nervously, trying to keep her tone light.

"If I frightened you—" he started to say, but CC interrupted him.

"No, you just surprised me." She was relieved that he appeared to be himself again, but she continued to watch him carefully. He looked dazed, like he had just awakened from a bad dream. Again, CC felt a tremor of warning shiver through her stomach.

"You are not angry with me?" the knight asked.

"No, I am not angry."

"Then you will forgive me? I assure you that my behavior is not usually so dishonorable."

"There is nothing to forgive. You only kissed my hand." But even as she said it, a part of her mind whispered that there had been more to the knight's actions than an impulsive kiss.

"Thank you, my Lady," Andras said, inclining his head in a small bow. "Would you care to continue our walk?" he asked hesitantly.

CC glanced down the path and then back at the knight. She really did need to continue their walk. It was the third night; she had to study the land around the monastery and figure out how she was going to get to the ocean. The knight appeared to be his normal, gallant self again, his eyes had quit flashing, and his breathing was back to normal. Maybe she had overreacted. After all, she hadn't had very many men react so passionately to her. Okay, she admitted, she had *never* had a man react so passionately to her.

And wasn't she supposed to be finding true love? How the heck was she going to do that if she ran from a man's desire? Get a grip on yourself, Sarg! CC took a deep, steadying breath.

"Yes, I would very much like to continue our walk."

Almost reluctantly, he offered her his arm and they continued walking down the path, which curved gently until they came to an area where the cliff-side dropped away almost directly under their feet. CC halted there, staring out at the beckoning sea.

Andras didn't speak, and CC pretended to watch the sunset, the knight's presence almost forgotten as her mind raced with possibilities. Behind them the monastery sat dark and silent. The view from where she was standing was familiar enough that CC was sure that one of the windows on the nearby wall must be the window to her room. Rocks and fallen logs rested against the side of the monastery. Climbing in and out of her window would not be impossible. She studied the face of the rocky cliff. From her room, it had looked too sheer and imposing to scale, but now that she was closer, she could see that it was riddled with little trails that crisscrossed down to the ocean. In the distance she could hear the ever-present sound of bleating sheep and silently thanked them for liking to climb rocky cliffs. If she was careful, she could use the trails to get down to the water. As if echoing her thoughts, in a last burst of light, the sun sank into the ocean.

"We should return, Undine," Andras said.

CC nodded reluctantly and let him lead her back the way they had come. She was so busy considering all that she would need to do that night that she was surprised when she and Andras had stopped in front of the door to her room.

"Thank you for the honor of your company this evening, Undine."

His motions were formal as he bowed to her. He turned to leave so quickly that she had to reach out and grab his arm to stop him. At her touch he stiffened, but he turned back to her.

"I haven't thanked you for saving me." She stretched up on her toes so that she could kiss his cheek softly. "Thank you."

His frozen look thawed a little, and he smiled at her. "I am only glad my actions have brought you into my life."

CC knew that then would be the right time to say something encouraging to the knight, but the memory of the change that had come over him earlier still seemed to hang in the air between them. When she spoke, all that she could make herself say was, "Good night, Andras. Could you please send Isabel to me? I am very tired."

"Of course. You must rest and regain your strength. I will see you tomorrow." This time his bow was accompanied by a warm smile. "Rest well, Undine."

"Thank you, Andras. You are very kind," she said before entering her room. She closed the door and leaned against it. What was wrong with her? Andras was handsome, sweet and obviously interested in her. Yes, for a moment he had been a little scary, but couldn't it have been her own inexperience that frightened her?

"But I didn't feel anything when he kissed me," she whispered. "At least nothing good." His kiss had been a little like visiting a museum and admiring a lovely statue. It had been nice enough to look at, but she certainly didn't want to get in bed with it.

"Well, Gaea didn't say anything about me having to love the man back. Maybe the spell will work if he just falls in love with me," CC said to the silent room, but she was afraid that it was a futile wish. Gaea had said Lir wouldn't break the bond of true love, and CC didn't think "true love" and "one-sided, infatuated lust" were anywhere near synonymous.

I'll try harder to care about him, she promised herself. Next time he kisses me, I'll make sure it's on my lips and not my hand. And I won't let his passion scare me. She shook her head at herself. She wasn't a skittish teenager. She was a sergeant in the United States Air Force, and she certainly wasn't afraid of men.

Unbidden, the memory of the merman's kiss burned through her mind. Just the memory caused her body to tingle in response.

CHAPTER ELEVEN

THIS time Isabel didn't argue with her about her hair. She seemed mollified that CC was willing to wear her shift under the coarse night robe, and CC solved the bathing problem by saying she was too tired to wash that night—she would do it in the morning. Isabel had even appeared concerned at CC's obvious exhaustion and nagged her good-naturedly about doing too much too soon. CC agreed readily with her and asked only that Isabel make sure she wasn't disturbed so that she could get a good night's rest. Isabel limped out, humming happily as her charge pretended to fall asleep before the scullery had finished folding her clothes and banking the fire.

As soon as the door was closed CC leapt out of bed, pulled the scratchy robe off and put on her shoes. The clank of her many bracelets sounded like alarm bells ringing in the quiet room, and she quickly took off all her jewelry, except, of course, Gaea's amulet, leaving the bangles and rings in a sparkling puddle in the center of her cot. Pressing her ear against the door, she listened intently. She could hear nothing—not even the sound of the monks' swooshing robes.

"They're probably all in church or something," CC muttered to herself.

She went to the narrow dresser and set the pitcher and bowl carefully on the floor. Then, very slowly, so that she didn't make any noise, she dragged the heavy piece of furniture over to the window. Using the bottom drawers as ladder rungs, she climbed to its smooth top. CC breathed a sigh of relief. It was the perfect height. All she had to do was sit in the narrow window frame and let her legs dangle down until she found a toehold. And she'd noticed on her walk that there was a lot of debris outside against the wall. She shouldn't have any trouble piling enough up so that she could easily climb back through the window.

She peered into the night. The moon had just risen. It was almost full, and it glistened off the waiting ocean like a beacon. When she looked at the water, the ache in her body twisted unbearably. Nothing moved outside her window. She slid onto the windowsill. With her soft, moccasinlike slippers, it was easy for her to find a toehold, balance and then drop quietly to the grassy ground. Her feet felt light as she picked her way carefully down the side of the cliff, following the well-worn sheep path. She could hear her own heartbeat echo the sound of the waves.

Then her feet sank into sand, and she was standing on the shore, quivering with need.

What am I supposed to do? CC's mind screamed. She was panting, and she felt disoriented.

"Simply call your true body to you, Daughter."

Smiling graciously at her, Gaea was sitting near the beach leaning comfortably against the trunk of an ancient tree.

"I don't know how," CC gasped.

"Your body does. Listen to it," the goddess reassured her.

CC tried to listen, but all she could hear was the call of the water.

"Then follow that call," Gaea said, as if she could read her mind.

CC started to walk forward, but paused when the goddess called, "Take off your chemise. You do not want them to have any evidence of where you have been."

Without any hesitation, CC pulled off her shift. Naked except for the goddess's sparkling amulet, she walked into the ocean's embrace. Stretching her arms over her head, she dove into the surf. *I want my true body back*, she thought desperately. The tingling began at her waist and spread quickly down her body, exploding in a burst of energy out through the feathered fins that replaced her feet. Her powerful tail sliced through the water, propelling her forward. Then, with a simple flick she changed directions and shot up through the surface with a joyous shout. CC shook the water from her head and looked for the goddess, but she had disappeared.

She was about to call a thank-you, or a good-bye, or something, after the absent goddess, when she felt the skin on the back of her neck twitch. Just like it felt at the cove, she thought. Someone had to be watching her.

A familiar chattering behind CC made her jump, but she turned with a happy cry of welcome.

"It is you! I'm so glad to see you." CC swam over to the dolphin and stroked her slick side.

I have missed you, Princess. The dolphin nuzzled her.

"I've missed you, too," CC said. "Swim with me—I want to be surrounded by the water."

Of course, Princess!

The dolphin butted CC playfully, then dove under the waves. Laughing, CC followed. Surprisingly, it wasn't dark under the moonlit surface. The crystal waters seemed to capture the light of the moon and the underwater world was illuminated with a silver glow. CC was thrilled by how easily she caught the dolphin and she reveled in the power of her body as the two of them played tag, swimming around the rocks that dotted the shallows, then over and through colorful masses of coral that grew in deeper water. CC wanted to swim on forever. The deeper within the water she swam, the more she wanted to immerse herself in the silken depths and never leave.

A strong hand grabbed her arm and jerked her to a stop. CC whirled, at once frightened and angry. Dylan floated in front of her, worry creasing his brow.

The goddess told you that you must stay near the shore. The words bored into her mind.

A shudder passed through CC. How could she have forgotten about Sarpedon? She looked frantically around.

Sarpedon is not here tonight, but he does search the waters for you, so you must have care where you go.

How do you know all of this? CC thought to him.

Come near the shore, and I will explain.

The dolphin swam back between them, clicking and whistling restlessly. CC watched the merman's face soften as he gently touched the creature's blue-gray side.

I will care for the princess now, faithful one.

The dolphin ducked her head, nuzzled briefly against CC's side and then disappeared into the depths.

Dylan gestured towards the shore, and CC nodded. She followed the merman, noticing how in the moonlit water the orange and gold of his tail glistened like it glowed magically from within.

They surfaced next to one of the huge rocks that lined the shallows. CC faced the merman. Tonight his thick dark hair was tied back. He floated next to her with his shoulders and most of his chest exposed above the water. The moonlight touched his bare chest and clearly illuminated muscular ridges and hollows. CC still felt a little uneasy at her own body's nakedness, and she was glad that her mass of hair covered her breasts.

"Okay, now tell me how you know so much," CC demanded, covering her nervousness with a no-nonsense military tone of voice.

"I followed you."

"After you just happened to be there to rescue me and bring me to shore?" CC shook her head. "That doesn't explain enough. You were there when I was drowning, and now you're here again tonight. Seems too coincidental for me."

"I followed you from the grotto," he admitted, looking away from her with a pained expression. "I did not know Sarpedon had you trapped in the cave. I knew something was very wrong when I could not find you for the length of an entire day. It was only after you escaped from him that I found you again. I followed you to the goddess's cove, and I watched your transformation. That is how I knew to help you when you were drowning."

"So you know that I'm not really Undine?"

"I know that the soul of another lives in Undine's body," he answered simply.

"You say that so easily, like it's a normal thing. You obviously knew Undine before. Doesn't this surprise you, or upset you, or make you angry? Why are you willing to help me when you know that I'm not her?"

"Undine and I were childhood playmates. We spent many years together," he explained, choosing his words carefully. "But she was not happy here. She longed for the land even before Sarpedon desired her."

"Did you love her?" CC asked, suddenly understanding the strained expression on the merman's face.

Dylan's jaw tightened, but he nodded his head. "Yes, but she would not allow herself to love a creature of the seas."

"But she was a mermaid—and that is definitely a creature of the sea."

"When you are on the land, your body is human, is it not?" Dylan asked.

"Yes, of course."

"But do you not long continually for the water?"

CC's memory of that horrible, empty ache was sharp. "Yes, constantly."

Dylan's smile was sad. "That is how Undine felt. I am glad for her. She has finally been granted her wish and her longing has ended."

"Then you're helping me out of love for her." CC was ashamed of the twinge of jealousy she felt.

"I could not very well let you drown." Dylan's sudden grin was boyishly endearing. He reached out to pluck a long piece of seaweed from CC's hair. "And you know nothing of how to be a creature of the sea."

CC surprised herself by batting playfully at his hand. "And you're going to teach me?"

He raised one eyebrow at her rakishly. "That I will, my princess."

CC's heart did a little skip beat at his expression. Did his words have a double meaning, or was she being too sensitive?

CC told herself firmly not to be ridiculous. He was being kind to her because he was in love with Undine. Well, she could certainly allow herself the pleasure of his company—and she truly had a lot to learn about his world. She spread her arms, meaning to encompass the entire ocean. "Good! I want to know everything."

"Everything?" He crossed his arms. CC thought if he'd had feet, he would have tapped one of them at her.

"How about everything in this little area around here—for starters."

"That can be easily accomplished." He held his hand out to her, enchanted by her innocent enthusiasm. "Come with me; I will show you the wonders of our world."

CC put her hand in his. At his touch, she felt a shiver of excitement, but she didn't have time to dwell on her reaction because immediately he dove, tugging her under the surface with him.

Hand-in-hand they swam around the shallows. Dylan seemed to know just where the most unusual fish were playing and where the most colorful coral grew. He showed CC long, orange tubes, bright red fans and purple rectangles— all of which he explained were types of sponges. He pointed out a large, flabby-nosed octopus that rested sedately on the sandy bed; CC laughed and thought it looked like a wrinkled old man. The octopus seemed to take offense and swam off in a jet of dark ink, which made both of them laugh. Like under- water angels, jellyfish floated silently past them, ethereal and translucent. Huge, bloblike sea anemones enchanted CC with their lilac coloring, and she was intrigued by their friends, the brightly colored clown fish.

And Dylan was intrigued by this new Undine. It had been true that at first he had watched over her because she had taken the form of the mermaid he had known and loved all his life, but her physical form was where any similarity between them ended. The mermaid Undine had been a beautiful, ethereal creature who was kind, but aloof. She had been his friend, but she had always yearned to be something else, somewhere else. This new Undine was so very different. She seemed to be bursting with energy and curiosity. She embraced the sea as if she couldn't get enough of it. Her endless questions were laced with humor and a sweetness that moved the merman more than he wanted to admit.

She, too, was a creature of the land, he reminded himself. She belonged there; he belonged to the seas.

Dylan had been so patient with her many questions that CC had thought that he was actually enjoying himself, so she was a little surprised when he pulled her away from a cluster of feathery starfish and back to the surface.

"What—" she started to ask, but the predawn lightening of the morning sky was explanation enough. "Oh. I hadn't realized so much time had passed."

"It is almost dawn," he said. His face, which had been so expressive and animated all night, was now neutral. "You must return to the land."

CC nodded, biting her lower lip. "You were the perfect teacher. Thank you."

His quick smiled warmed her. "In the oceans we say that the teacher is only as good as the student."

"Well, isn't that a coincidence?" CC grinned back at him. "We say the same thing on land."

Dylan's laughter, rich and deep, surrounded them. They were still holding hands, and she used her free hand to splash water at him.

"It's not very dignified for a teacher to laugh at his student."

Dylan tried to compose his face, but his eyes sparkled with good humor as he teasingly bowed his head to her. "Forgive me, my princess. It has been an honor to be your teacher."

Dylan lifted her hand, meaning only to give it a gallant, playful kiss, but when his lips met her skin all thoughts of jesting with her fled his brain. He breathed deeply, and her delicate, feminine scent filled him. Her skin was unbearably soft, and he couldn't stop himself from turning her hand over and pressing his lips to the pulse point at her wrist. He felt her tremble, and he lifted his face slowly, afraid he would see rejection in her eyes. She was staring at him, and in her eyes he thought he read passion, not disgust. His mind registered her expression, and even though he knew he should not touch her, should not allow himself to love her, he could not stop. The way she looked at him made him feel as if his heart would break from happiness.

"When you touch me," CC said softly, "you make me tremble."

Still holding her hand, Dylan drifted closer to her until their bodies almost touched. "Is that because I frighten you?" he asked. Maybe he had misread her eyes. His heart stopped beating as he waited for her answer.

"No," her voice sounded breathless.

Slowly, she reached up and touched the side of his face. She let her fingers trail down his neck and shoulder until they finally came to rest against his chest. He quivered under her caress.

"Is that because I frighten you?" she whispered his words back to him.

"No," he said quickly. Then he captured her eyes with his. "What is your name?"

The question surprised her, and, not knowing what he meant, she hesitated to answer him.

"I want to know your true name," he explained. "I do not want you to think I care for you only because I wish to be with Undine."

CC could feel her cheeks coloring. She hadn't been thinking that; she hadn't been thinking about anything except the way it felt when he touched her.

"My real name is Christine Canady, but almost everyone calls me by my initials, CC."

He raised one brow at her. "Almost? Who does not call you by these initials?"

"My family."

"Then I ask that I be awarded that privilege. May I call you Christine?"

"Yes." She thought her name had never sounded so beautiful.

"Christine, when will you return to the water?" Again, he tried to keep his face neutral, but she heard the longing in his voice.

"I have to come back every third night." Under the palm she still had pressed against his chest she could feel his heartbeat. "Will you be here?"

He was caressing her hand softly with his thumb, just like he had done on the day they had met.

"I will be here every third night until the end of eternity."

At his words her heart lurched, but the thought instantly went through her mind that even though she didn't want to leave the water or him, she didn't have a choice. She wasn't safe in the water. Dylan had said Sarpedon was searching for her—it was only a matter of time until he found her again. Could Dylan protect her? She remembered Sarpedon's size and incredible strength and blocked that thought from her mind. She wouldn't put Dylan in danger.

"I have to change back," she said aloud. As soon as she had spoken the words, she felt the already familiar tingling begin around her waist. Heat shot down her body and an instant later she was kicking her legs feebly and clutching Dylan's chest to keep from slipping under the water.

"I'm sorry," she said. "I didn't know it would be that easy to change back."

His strong arms wrapped around her waist and he held her securely against him.

His smile was sad. "I understand. You must go." But neither of them moved.

"I wish you would kiss me," CC said the words quickly, before she could take them back.

With a moan, he bent his head to hers and their lips touched, gently at first. CC shivered in response.

Against her lips Dylan again asked one last time, "Not frightened?"

For her answer CC lifted her chin and recaptured his lips. Winding her hands around his neck, she pressed herself against his body and opened her mouth to accept him. His hands caressed her back and then slid to her sides and up, so that his thumbs rubbed erotic circles across the edges of her breasts. CC was lost in the taste of him, which was salty and wild. Her body was on fire and his mouth consumed her.

The tolling of the bell that called the monks to early Mass splintered their world. Dylan broke the kiss and for a moment he rested his forehead against hers while he forced his breathing under control.

"I will take you to the shore."

He leaned back, pulling her up on his chest so that she lay more securely in his arms. With strong strokes of his tail, he swam slowly backwards, with CC nestled against him. When the water was shallow enough to allow her to stand, Dylan loosened his grip and she slid out of his arms.

"I want to kiss you again," he told her. "But I am afraid if I do so, I will never be able to let you go."

CC felt a silent cry burning in her throat and she nodded, not trusting herself to speak. She walked out of the water and back to where she'd left her crumpled shift and shoes. She couldn't look at the water. She didn't want to see him disappearing under the waves. Without looking back, CC pulled on her clothes and started toward the path.

"Christine." Dylan's voice carried easily over the water.

She turned. He was floating exactly where she'd left him.

"Remember that I will be here," he said resolutely. "For an eternity, Christine. I would wait for you for an eternity."

She nodded again and turned to begin her trip up the side of the cliff. This time the path wasn't obscured by darkness, but by her tears.

Dylan watched her go, keeping his eyes on her until she was only a light-colored smudge that climbed up and over the side of the cliff. His heart ached as she disappeared. Why was he doing this to himself? He raked his hand through his hair. Like his mother before him, was he forever fated to love the unattainable?

He could still feel the softness of her lips against his. He clenched his jaw. He wanted her, and not because she wore Undine's body. He wanted Christine, her sweet humor and her exuberance.

He thought about the innocent trust she had shown him as she had rested in his arms, and her passionate response to his touch. His heart made the decision for him. If he could only have her every third night, then so be it. He would love her, and, just perhaps, this time he would break the cycle and be loved in return.

CHAPTER TWELVE

CC awoke thinking about him. The internal ache that throbbed with its incessant reminder that her human body was only a borrowed shell mingled with her desire to see Dylan again until she couldn't tell where one began and the other ended. Just tonight, then tomorrow night—then she would be able to go to the water and to him. She sighed and touched her lips. They felt wonderfully bruised and sensitive.

She had dreamed of him. Somehow in another world, in another time, he had called to her, and now she wanted nothing more than to return to the ocean and answer his call.

Two quick knocks on the door made her jump. She cleared the sleep from her throat.

"Yes, I'm awake."

Isabel limped quickly into the room. CC was beginning to wonder if the woman ever slowed down.

"Good morning, Princess," she said in her raspy voice, exchanging the old pitcher of water for a new one. "Sir Andras has asked that you break your fast with him. I believe he has something special planned."

"Something special?" CC sat up and swept the hair back from her face.

"Yes, my lady. Here, let me help you into your dress." Isabel shook her head and clucked what was probably meant as a mild rebuke when she noticed what CC was, or rather wasn't, wearing. "It is unseemly for you to sleep only in that light chemise."

"Why?" She couldn't stop herself from asking as she stepped into the layers of soft fabric that made up her wonderful gown. "That other robe is hot and the material scratches. And the only person who could possibly see me in it is you."

Isabel worked the intricate laces, and her voice took on the tone of a schoolroom lecturer. "It is proper that the coarse fabric of the robe remind us of our sins, which we carry with us eternally, so that we are constantly aware of our need for absolution. To surround ourselves with luxuries is to give in to the temptation of the corporeal world."

CC felt suddenly very sad for Isabel. Had the old woman spent her entire life being deprived of beauty out of fear of damnation? CC was careful to keep her voice light and curious when she asked, "And from whom do we need absolution?"

"The good abbot, of course." Isabel sounded surprised that she should have to ask.

"Isabel, what if the beauty around us is meant as a reminder of the many gifts we have been given, and our need to give thanks for them?" CC asked slowly, as if she had just considered the idea herself.

Isabel made a scoffing noise in her throat, but when CC turned and their eyes met, the old woman was studying her with an openly curious expression.

"It was just a thought," CC said, smiling brightly at Isabel while she put on the jewelry that was a gift from a goddess. Isabel averted her eyes at the show of opulence. CC could only imagine what the old woman's reaction would be if she knew where the jewels really came from.

"Sir Andras is waiting in the dining hall. I can take you there in just a moment," Isabel said as she started to make the bed.

"There's no need—I remember the way. You go ahead and do whatever you need to do, Isabel. I know you must be very busy. Thank you for your help with my dress."

Ignoring Isabel's sullen expression, CC smiled cheerfully and walked quickly out of the room. Having Isabel around was like being shadowed by a brooding schoolmarm. The woman seemed to dislike her on sight. CC sighed. And no wonder. CC glanced down at her lush, richly clad body. Isabel had been raised to believe beauty and luxury were dangerous and sinful.

"To her I must be the embodiment of everything she's been taught is bad," CC muttered.

She realized the old woman's dislike really bothered her. People usually liked CC—a lot. Maybe not with the passionate response that Undine's body evoked, but CC had never had any problem making friends. Well, she was still the same person; she was just shelled in a different body. CC made a mental note to make sure she got up early enough the next day to make her own bed. She would show Isabel that she wasn't a spoiled, pampered princess. Sexy, incredible body or not, Christine Canady would win the old woman's friendship.

The hallway abruptly emptied out into the courtyard. The sun beaming into the open space was such a contrast to the dim interior that CC had to hold a hand up to shade her eyes from the sudden brightness. Squinting, she stepped out into the well-manicured lawn, heading toward the arched doorway that led to the dining hall. A movement at the well caught her eye, and she felt a shudder of fear pass through her body. Hovering over the middle of the open well was a dark shape, easily noticed in the otherwise brightly lit courtyard. The form was in the shape of a man's torso, but it was insubstantial. CC could clearly see the far wall of the courtyard through it. Its back was to CC, and there was something horribly familiar in the massive breadth of shoulder and in the thick length of ghostly hair that floated around the apparition as if it was underwater.

As she watched, it rotated slowly and shifted its glowing gaze until CC was staring into the spectral eyes of Sarpedon. The creature saw her, and his triumphant smile was terrible. She couldn't stop the scream that ripped from her throat.

Andras burst from the arched doorway and into the courtyard, followed closely by Abbot William. The moment the two men appeared, the image of Sarpedon wavered and dissipated back into the liquid depths of the well.

Andras rushed to her side. "Undine! What has happened? Are you ill?"

"I-I saw something." She pointed. "There, over the well."

Both men turned to look at the offending structure. Abbot William walked over to it. CC flinched as he bent over its open mouth and peered down.

"There is nothing here now," he called over his shoulder.

"Come." Andras put a strong arm around her waist. "Let me help you into the dining room and out of the sun."

Abbot William gave the well one last look before following them.

"Bring the princess some wine!" Andras ordered one of the servants, helping CC onto a bench.

The servant reappeared almost immediately. CC's hands were shaking so badly that she spilled some of the wine. Drinking deeply, she tried to steady herself, while she wondered how much, if anything, she could dare tell the two men.

"What exactly did you see?" Abbot William asked. He was studying her with an expression that verged on gleeful.

CC felt a tremor of foreboding. It was like he reveled in her fear. "I'm not sure," she said slowly. "I had just stepped into the courtyard, and I glanced at the well. There was something there, floating over the top of it. The figure was dark, like a shadow, but it seemed to be in the shape of a man."

"Could it not have been the shadow of an oddly shaped cloud?" Andras said. "The day is bright and you had just entered the courtyard. Perhaps your eyes misjudged."

CC summoned up a relieved laugh, glad the knight had given her an acceptable answer. "You're probably right, Andras. It just startled me. I think fear and my imagination must have temporarily caused me to see something."

"Of course." Andras patted her back awkwardly.

CC could still feel the priest's eyes on her, but he remained silent.

"I had planned a small surprise for you, Princess," Andras said. "You so enjoyed the view last night that I had a few things packed into a basket for us. I thought we could break our fast outside, near the ocean you find so intriguing. But perhaps now would not be a good time for such exertion."

"No!" she reassured him quickly. "I'm feeling much better. It was ridiculous of me to be so frightened of a little shadow. Fresh air and a view sound wonderful." Just the thought of being near the water again made CC's heart race—and if Sarpedon was close by, surely she would be safest away from the monastery's enclosing walls and near the lush land that was the domain of the goddess.

"If you are sure." Andras's face brightened at the prospect. "I will take care not to overtax your strength."

He called for the servant to bring a basket that had already been prepared, but before they could leave the dining hall, Abbot William spoke with a sly sharpness.

"Princess Undine, before you go, I must ask you about the interesting design that decorates your gown. Do you know what those symbols represent?"

CC looked down at the fabulous dress. It was made up of several layers of material that felt like an intriguing mixture of silk and gauze. She smiled at the familiar coloring that so accurately represented her mermaid's tail. The topmost layer of material was covered with silver needlework. CC had noticed the intricate embroidery before. It was a repeating pattern of symbols interwoven with birds and flowers. Now that she studied it, she could see that amidst the land creatures and symbols Gaea had woven dolphins and starfish. She ran a finger reverently down one long, silver-threaded sleeve.

"No, I don't know what they represent. I just know that they are beautiful."

"Let us not forget that beauty can hide many things," the priest said cryptically.

CC beamed a smile at him. "Well, wouldn't you say this dress hides much less than your robes?" She laughed and pointed at his voluminous skirts. "I think you could probably hide a small person under there."

"Undine!" Andras's voice had a hard edge to it CC had not heard before. "It is unseemly to say such a thing to Abbot William."

CC didn't allow her smile to falter, but as she studied Andras's handsome face, she felt a twinge of unease. For a moment she had forgotten where she was, which was definitely not twenty-first century America. Women in medieval Europe didn't kid around with uptight abbots, or if they did they probably ended up flayed or boiled or . . . She bit her lip.

"Oh, Andras, you're right. I guess I'm still a little nervous about what I thought I saw in the courtyard." She turned her set smile on the priest. "I do apologize, Abbot William; I certainly didn't mean to offend you."

Abbot William waved his hands dismissively. "There is no need to apologize, Princess. I understand that young women sometimes say things that are fraught with several meanings, even if they are unaware of it."

CC's eyes widened at the abbot's rudeness, but her smile didn't waver. "That is such an interesting observation, because I've noticed that men sometimes read double meanings into things that women say, even when none are intended. I think that could be why there seems to be such confusion between the sexes. I'll have to be more careful in the future so that there are no such misunderstandings between us." She turned back to Andras and took his arm. "Are you ready? All this excitement has made me very hungry."

Andras smiled and patted her hand. His façade of good-guy-boyfriend was securely back in place. "Of course, Undine." He bowed his head reverently to Abbot William. "I look forward to our evening game of chess, Father."

"I, too, my son," the priest said. Then he added, as if it was an afterthought, "Princess Undine, about the symbols on your gown. They remind me of runes that I have seen on pagan shrines." He made a dry sound in his throat that CC assumed was supposed to be a chuckle. "But, as you said, you would know nothing of that."

"That's correct," CC said truthfully. "I know nothing about runes or pagan shrines."

"Then you would have no objection to joining us for vespers this evening?" His eyes were bright, and he watched her reaction closely.

"I'm sure the princess would be happy to attend evening mass," Andras said quickly.

CC had to grit her teeth to keep from telling the knight that she preferred to speak for herself. Instead, she met the priest's probing gaze evenly. "That would be lovely; thank you for inviting me."

"I shall look forward to seeing you there," Abbot William said.

CHAPTER THIRTEEN

ANDRAS didn't choose the path they had taken the evening before; instead he followed the road. It angled steeply down, then took a sharp, right-handed turn before it wound back toward the sea. All the while they walked he talked about the history of the island and how there had been a monastery on this site for more than four hundred years. CC struggled to listen to him. Most of her attention was focused on the nearness of the sea and the call it had on her body. She did try to look attentive when he explained that he was so well acquainted with the monastery and Abbot William because the land had belonged to his mother's family for centuries. When his mother married his father, the land had passed to the Lord of Caer Llion, and, naturally, the most senior priest from his father's barony had to take over the running of Caldei Monastery.

"Oh, that's why you and the Abbot know each other so well," CC said, trying to appear interested.

"The Abbot taught me how to read and write. He is an exceptional teacher, unrelenting in his desire to instruct," Andras said with a definite tone of hero worship.

CC thought about the way Abbot William looked at Andras, and she wondered cynically if he would have been such an exceptional teacher if Andras had been less rich and handsome.

"It's nice that you had such a dedicated teacher," was all she said aloud.

Andras grinned at her. She couldn't help smiling back at him. He really was endearing in a chauvinistic, clichéd kind of a way.

Once they were at sea level, several small paths branched off from the main road. Andras turned onto one that led through a thick grove of tall, fragrant pine trees and spilled out onto the pristine sand of well-shaded beach.

The ocean was heartbreak blue that morning, and CC trembled at its beauty. She wanted to rip off her clothes and dive into the frothy waves.

"Do you like it?" Andras asked in a smug voice. "I chose this spot especially with you in mind."

CC tore her eyes from the allure of the waves and gave him a compulsory smile as she tried to cover the rush of resentment she suddenly felt towards the knight. He knew nothing about the ocean or about her.

"I hope it pleases you."

At her hesitation, Andras's voice had lost its smug edge, and he was once again only a man trying his best to impress a woman. CC sighed. It wasn't that he was doing anything wrong, she realized. It was just that he wasn't Dylan.

"It's perfect," she said, warming her smile. "I love the ocean. I feel at home when I'm near it."

He gave her an odd look and said, "I find that rather surprising, Undine. I would think that in light of your recent experience you would be frightened of it."

"I'm not frightened of it—or at least I'm not anymore." The water pulled her gaze, and her expression became dreamy. She wondered where Dylan was at that moment. He said he would stay there as long as she was there, too. Actually, she thought back, he had said he would wait for her for an eternity. But that didn't mean he was keeping a constant lookout for her; he wasn't expecting her to return to the ocean until the third night. Could he be out there, watching her now? She shivered at the thought of his possible closeness.

"Did I not tell you that you must be frightened?" Andras had unfolded a blanket that had been packed in the basket, and he paused to glance at her as he unloaded their brunch. "You are trembling."

He was bent over the basket and his shapely rear end was all too easy to see. She had a sudden, mischievous urge to lift her leg and kick him squarely in that oh-so-perfect butt, watch him fall flat on his oh-so-perfect face and then tell him that where she was from women didn't need men to think for them.

"I just shivered because the ocean and my recent accident remind me of the frailty of the human body—that no matter how strong or how wise humans think they are, the might of the ocean is even greater."

Andras gave her an appraising look, like she could possibly be more intelligent than he had originally anticipated, but the look was fleeting, and soon he went back to unpacking their food.

CC watched Andras unload their brunch. She understood that he really couldn't help his archaic attitude towards women—after all, he truly was archaic. And he wasn't a bad man, actually he was quite charming. It wasn't his fault that he was trying to woo a modern woman with his ancient ideals. He had hauled her from the water, she reminded herself, and he had pledged to protect her. For that he deserved to be treated courteously. She glanced at his handsome profile. Maybe they could even be friends.

She sat on the edge of the blanket. Picking up a hard-boiled egg and the leg of a grilled bird, she started eating both with genuine gusto. As close as she could figure, she had only slept for just a few hours, and she should have been very tired, but instead of fatigue she felt exhilarated, like she had exercised all day and slept soundly all night, and her body was demanding that she feed it. She finished the egg and started on a thick slice of tangy yellow cheese.

"This is really very good," she said through healthy bites.

"You seem to be enjoying it. I have rarely witnessed a lady eating with such vigor." His tone said that ladies either shouldn't eat with such *vigor*, or if they did, they should do so only when not in the company of gentlemen. How very Old South of him, she thought, and almost giggled.

"Where I come from, ladies enjoy their food," she said, thinking that sometimes they even eat entire buckets of fried chicken—especially when it's their birthday and they're under the influence of too much champagne.

"Undine, are you remembering more about your homeland?" Andras asked eagerly.

Oops—CC took another big bite of meat, forcing him to wait while she chewed and thought up an appropriate answer.

"Sometimes I remember little things during the course of conversations—and then I wonder, *Now how did I know that?* because then I can remember no more." She moved her shoulders. "Like when Isabel tried to pull my hair back and I told her, no, that maidens from my land wear their hair down. I remembered the fact that maidens in my land can let their hair be free, but nothing else." She chewed thoughtfully and hoped he'd be satisfied with her vague answer.

Reaching across the space that separated them, he captured one of her glistening locks and wrapped it around his finger.

"I am pleased that you remembered this custom of your people. I would not have your hair bound."

CC realized that she didn't need to be worried about him questioning her too much. Unlike Abbot William, Andras wasn't bent on interrogation; his interests were obviously elsewhere. CC pulled the strand of hair out of his finger and laughed with what she hoped was maidenly nervousness.

"Isn't memory a funny thing?" She clapped her hands together, then made a show of searching through the food. "Did you bring anything to drink? All this eating is making me very thirsty."

"Of course. I brought a wine skin we can share." Andras uncorked a floppy baglike thing before passing it to her. He let his fingers linger just a moment longer than was strictly necessary on hers before releasing it to her.

CC stifled the urge to slap him away like a mosquito. Courtesy, she reminded herself firmly. Treat him like he's a superior officer who is acting fresh.

"Thank you," she said, and smiled through a mouthful of food. His quick grimace at her unladylike behavior was worth the breach in manners. She felt the tension in her shoulders relax as he withdrew out of her personal space. The wine was thick and delicious, and she felt a satisfying warmth begin to build in the pit of her stomach.

They ate in silence, and CC took the opportunity to absorb the sight of the ocean. She had to admit that Andras had chosen well. That particular area of the shore was much tamer than the breakers below the monastery had been. Here the waves were still white-capped, but they met the beach with lazy strokes, rather than the violent crashing of water against rock. And the sea appeared more shallow, too. The water that lined the beach was turquoise, rather than the sapphire of deeper seas. There were a few bunches of coral that clustered here and there. Her full lips curved up in remembrance. Last night Dylan had introduced her to many of the colorful fish that made coral their home.

"You are so beautiful when you smile like that." Andras's voice broke into her daydream. "What are you thinking?"

"I was thinking about creatures of the sea and their beauty," she said.

Abruptly, he reached out and snatched her hand that was temporarily emptied of food. She jerked back in surprise, but he kept a firm hold on her.

"No beast of the sea could ever hope to match your beauty," he said fervently. He lifted her hand to his lips and kissed it passionately, leaving a wet spot in the middle of her skin.

CC's stomach jolted in a fluttery brush of fear, and she looked closely at his well-defined face, afraid she would see the frightening lust that had blanketed his features the first time he had kissed her. She drew in a shaky breath of relief when all she read in his expression was earnest and open adoration. Unfortunately for the knight, she felt nothing in response except an embarrassed sense of unease. The only urge she had to touch him was to pat his cheek and apologize for her lack of romantic interest.

"Andras," she said carefully. "I don't think it's proper for you to—"

A loud chattering interrupted her, and Andras dropped her hand in surprise. CC's attention swiveled to the water, and with a joyous laugh she jumped to her feet. Lifting her skirts, she ran to the edge of the shore.

"Hello, pretty girl," she called to the dolphin, who continued chattering while leaping and whirling in jubilant welcome. "Isn't this a beautiful day?" CC laughed again, and without thinking she did a little dance step and twirled around, loving the feel of her skirts twining around her legs.

The thunk of stone against flesh came hard and sharp, jarring CC's happiness. The dolphin's shrill cry of pain pierced the air, and the animal dove quickly beneath the waves and disappeared. CC spun around to see Andras testing the weight of another rock in his hand.

"What are you doing?" CC's voice had the sharp edge of command seven years in the air force had honed.

Andras blinked in surprise. "It is a wild beast; it could have caused you harm."

"Don't you know that wild is not synonymous with evil?" She forced her voice to be even. He had thought he was protecting her. "The dolphin wasn't going to hurt me. She was just a beautiful creature enjoying her freedom."

"Abbot William would remind us that many things are not as innocent as they appear, Undine, and that excessive beauty must be guarded against, for it can hide prurient intent," he countered.

CC could hardly believe she had heard him correctly. Prurient intent? A dolphin? She took a deep, cleansing breath and counted to ten before she spoke again.

"Andras, I really do appreciate the help you and the abbot have given me, and I don't mean to sound disrespectful, but did you ever consider that some people get power by convincing others they should constantly be fearful?" she asked.

"Abbot William gets his power from God," Andras said as if he was reciting a Sunday School lesson.

"I'm not saying that he doesn't; I'm only saying that just because something is beautiful or exotic or even wild, doesn't mean that it's dangerous or sinful," she said, forcing the knight to meet her gaze. He looked away quickly.

"I think you have become fatigued, and it is time we return," Andras said stonily. He was already busy repacking their leftovers.

"I think you're right. I am ready to return," CC said.

She stood looking out at sea like a breathing statue, ignoring the sounds the knight was making as he tossed their leftovers haphazardly into the basket. She felt displaced and alone. Her entire being ached to be a part of the waves. For an instant she thought she saw the glint of orange and gold, barely visible offshore just below the crystal surface, and she had to close her eyes. If she really saw him would she be able to stop herself from going to him? Then what would happen to them?

With her eyes still closed, she concentrated on sending two words out into the ocean. *I'm sorry*, she thought desperately. She wasn't sure if she was sending the message to the dolphin or to Dylan.

As she wearily accepted Andras's offered arm and trudged away from the water yet again, one thought was foremost in her mind. She had to talk to Gaea.

Chapter Fourteen

"SHALL I escort you back to your room? You just have time for a refreshing nap before evening vespers and dinner."

Andras turned to face her as they entered the front courtyard. They hadn't spoken on the walk back to the monastery, and the stiffness in the knight's voice matched his body language. CC knew that her behavior must baffle him, and she felt sorry for the tension between them, but her head was throbbing. She wanted relief from the stress of having to continually watch her words and actions around Andras, but she didn't want to be closed up in her little room.

"No, I think I'd rather explore the monastery." Andras opened his mouth and CC hurried on before he could insist on accompanying her. "And I think I need to spend some time alone in, uh, prayerful meditation before evening mass." She blinked innocently up at him.

"Of course. I would not want to intrude upon your need for prayer." His voice was smooth, but his eyes had hardened. CC was unexpectedly reminded of Abbot William.

"Didn't I see another courtyard and some gardens out past the dining room?" she asked.

"Yes. The entrance is through the hall on the other side of the monastery. You may enter it through the dining chamber. I need to take our basket back to the kitchens, so I can escort you to the entrance myself." He smiled at her, satisfied that she could not immediately escape him.

CC tried not to sigh when she took his arm. She knew the knight was well-meaning, but she could feel the pulse in her right temple beat in time with her headache. She truly needed some time alone. As they walked past the well, she was careful to keep Andras between it and her, but nothing unusual happened. She slanted a gaze at the silent rock structure. It looked innocent and mundane. Surely she hadn't imagined the image of Sarpedon?

The dining room was empty and Andras strode across it, leading her into another dimly lit hallway. At the far end of that hall there was an arched exit that opened to a large courtyard-like area. Andras pointed at the exit.

"Through there are the gardens and a pond. At the far end is the chapel." His gaze was searing as he raised her hand and pressed it firmly to his lips. "I look forward to escorting you to evening mass."

She pulled her hand free. "Thank you for lunch. I'm going to attend to my prayers now," she reminded him in case he was having second thoughts about letting her go. Then she beat a hasty retreat.

CC stepped briskly into the garden area and glanced around to make sure there was no one nearby. Without conscious thought, she wiped Andras's lip print off her hand. She needed to talk to Gaea. Perhaps tonight she should sneak out into the woods. Maybe she would be able to find the goddess there. Absently, she continued to rub the back of her hand. She sighed, wishing she had a couple of Tylenols.

CC began to walk slowly down a little trail that curved and looped through the monastery gardens. Ornamental trees and trellises laced with fragrant flowers dotted the area. Everything was meticulously cared for—not a leaf was out of place or a branch unpruned.

"No wildness, that's for sure," CC mumbled to herself.

Stone benches were arranged strategically amidst the greenery so that one could sit and meditate with the optimum of privacy. CC thought it felt wrong— too contrived, too well planned. Somehow its controlled beauty came across as stilted and forced.

A delicate breeze brought the tinkle of running water to her, and automatically she followed the sound, choosing a left-handed fork in the path that turned in the direction of the outer monastery wall. The path brought her all the way to the wall, which was lined with oaks that were decidedly older than those in the rest of the garden. CC smiled up at them. These were obviously too big for the monks to cut and reshape into their idea of proper foliage. Actually, that whole area looked more natural than the rest of the gardens. Wildflowers painted the grasses with splashes of orange, violet and lace, and honeysuckle vines covered the wall, filling the air with sweetness. A little brook ran along the wall, too. It bubbled noisily over smooth rocks, pooling in a rounded area before disappearing under the wall and out into the forest. There was no orchestrated sitting area, so CC brushed off the top of a large rock that rested near the pool and sat down. She watched a frog leap from the bank to a lily pad and let the sound of running water ease away her headache.

"What am I going to do?" she whispered.

"About what, Daughter?"

CC pressed a hand against her chest like she was trying to hold down her leaping heart. The clear, beautiful voice of the goddess came from above her. CC looked up to see Gaea reclining regally along a thick branch of the largest oak. Today her transparent robes were the color of bark, except that the browns and grays in the material shimmered magically like they had been sprinkled with gold dust.

"You're going to give me a heart attack someday," CC said.

Gaea's laughter made the water reeds and grasses sway in response. CC looked around quickly, worry creasing her brow.

"Do not worry, Undine," Gaea reassured her. "I choose who can see and hear me." A brief grimace marred her lovely face. "And none here will be allowed to hear me but you."

"I'm a little surprised to see you." CC gestured around at the monastery. "In here, anyway."

The corners of Gaea's eyes crinkled with her smile. "You might be surprised, Daughter, to learn that even here I have not been completely forgotten. But that is not why I have come." She sat up. The sparkling fabric of her gown drifted sensuously around her. "You look thirsty, Daughter." She clapped her manicured hands together and ordered, "Wine, please!"

Immediately a pewter goblet, decorated with vines and flowers, appeared in her hand. CC blinked in surprise and the goddess pointed to a spot on the ground in front of CC, where an identical goblet had appeared.

"I think you will enjoy the taste. Cernunnos gifted me with this particular vintage during the last fertility festival." She sipped and sighed happily. "He certainly knows wine."

CC took the goblet and lifted it to her lips. The wine was golden in color and so cold it hurt her teeth. As she took a drink the bubbles that broke the surface tickled her nose, and she almost sneezed. Then her eyes opened wide in amazement.

"It's champagne! The most delicious champagne I've ever tasted!" She grinned up at the goddess. "After the day I'm having, I can sure use some of this."

"I thought you would appreciate it. Now, child, tell me what has troubled you."

CC sipped and talked. "Andras can't be the one."

"Andras is that tall, handsome warrior who pulled you from the water?" Gaea inquired with a purr in her voice.

CC nodded and rolled her eyes. "Yeah, but he's not Mr. Hero. As a matter of fact, the more time I spend with him, the more he reminds me of Abbot William."

Gaea's face twisted in a frown. "Abbot William! That silly child. He is terrified of everything he cannot control or understand, which means he is filled with bitterness and rage, especially towards women. He is a eunuch." The goddess looked like she wanted to say more, but instead she took a deep drink from her goblet. Shaking her head as if to free her thoughts, she asked, "Are you certain the warrior and he are the same?"

"Well, I don't think Andras is exactly like him; actually sometimes he can be very charming. And I understand that it's a different world with different beliefs, but he sure doesn't respect women, and I've spent the last seven years working hard at being respected—so that's a major strike against him. The truth is, I'm just not interested in him, even if he is the classic knight in shining armor and I should swoon at the thought of him sweeping me off my feet." CC sighed and took another drink of the delicious champagne. "Is Abbot William really a eunuch?"

Gaea made a scoffing noise in the back of her throat. "Not physically—I refer to the way he has chosen to live his life. He hides behind the robes of priesthood and uses his position for selfish reasons. He is not fit to serve any God. Be wary of him. He is a desperate, lonely man, and he should be pitied, but always remember that unacknowledged despair can make men dangerous."

"I'll be careful. It was pretty easy to see that he didn't like me. And it's not that I think that Andras is the same kind of man as he is, it's just that the knight seems to parrot Abbot William's beliefs without thinking for himself."

Gaea's eyes narrowed thoughtfully. "I do not like the sound of that."

"So, does it have to be him?" CC blurted.

"Explain *it*," the goddess said.

"You know, that whole my true love thing. Does it have to be Andras—or if it does, is it enough for him to love me without me loving him back?"

The goddess tossed back her hair and laughed again, and even though she had assured CC that no one else could hear her, CC's eyes restlessly searched the clearing for listeners.

"Daughter, how you make me laugh! True love is not a potion one person can swallow and another refuse to drink. It happens only when the souls of two join together to form one."

"Well, I don't think I'm going to be joining my soul with Andras's. I don't even like it when he kisses my hand," CC said.

"That does not bode well for true love," the goddess agreed.

They drank together in thoughtful silence.

CC cleared her throat and glanced up at Gaea. "Um, speaking of kissing, do you know anything about a merman named Dylan?"

Gaea studied the young woman who inhabited her daughter's body. She was truly coming to care for this child and not just because she felt obligated to watch over her. She was special, this young one—curious and outspoken and witty. It would be a lovely thing, to have this remarkable child live beside her as her daughter forever. But Gaea recognized the longing the girl was trying hard to mask. The goddess smiled sadly at the irony. She finally had a daughter who could be gifted with the ability to exist on land, and the child was falling in love with the sea. Sometimes life was surprising, even for a goddess.

"I know Dylan well. He was Undine's playmate of old." Gaea raised her delicate eyebrows at the girl. "What is this about kissing?"

CC felt her cheeks warm. "Well, it's just that I feel different when Dylan kisses me." Now her cheeks were practically on fire. She never could talk to her mother about sex—apparently that meant *any* mother, even if she was a goddess.

"So, the merman has kissed you?"

CC could hear the smile in Gaea's voice, but she didn't look up at the goddess. Instead she busied herself with drinking the last drop of champagne.

"Too bad that's gone," she said, trying to avoid the kissing subject she had bumbled into. "It was delicious."

Gaea snapped her fingers and suddenly the goblet had refilled itself.

"Thank you!" CC took another long drink. This time she did sneeze at the bubbles.

"The merman kissed you?" Gaea repeated insistently.

CC nodded.

"And you found pleasure in his touch?" Gaea asked.

CC nodded again.

Lost in thought, the goddess remained silent until CC couldn't stand it any longer.

"Is that a bad thing?" she blurted, looking desperately up at Gaea.

"No, child," Gaea said. "But you must understand that Dylan is a lesser creature than Sarpedon."

The goddess held up her hand, silencing CC when she would have defended Dylan.

"I do not mean that Sarpedon is more honorable than Dylan—that is obviously not true. What I mean is Sarpedon holds a position of much greater power than Dylan. Sarpedon's father, as you know, is the great God, Lir. His mother is Morrigan, the Goddess of Battle. Dylan's mother was a simple water nymph named Okynos. Unfortunately, she committed suicide after her human lover, Dylan's father, rejected her." The goddess held her hand out to CC in a sympathetic gesture. "Dylan does not have the protection of a mother, or of a father. He is not helpless, but his gifts are much less than those of Lir's son. Dylan exists peacefully within the waters only because Lir is generous and because Sarpedon ignores him."

"But if Sarpedon thought I loved Dylan, he would destroy him," CC finished the unspoken thought.

Gaea's eyes were sharp. "Do you love him?"

CC considered the question while she stared into the little pond. She had never been in love before. She was technically not a virgin, but it was hard to count that one time, right after basic training when she had come home on leave and her high school boyfriend, Jerry Burton, had groped her in the back seat of his Impala. He had penetrated her. She vividly remembered the flash of pain, but it was over soon and everything had ended up on her inner thigh. The event had been awkward and unsatisfying—not an experience CC had been in a hurry to repeat—so she hadn't.

Since Jerry, she hadn't even come close to having a lover, let alone being in love. She thought about Dylan, and the way he made her smile. He had been so patient with her silly questions. And when he touched her he made the world dissolve into a pool of throbbing feelings.

But did that mean she loved him?

"I don't know," she told the goddess honestly. "I need to spend more time with him. I think I might, but it's just too soon to know for sure."

"A wise answer from one so young."

Gaea's look was tender and motherly, and CC felt a sudden rush of homesickness for her own mom.

"Then spend time with him, Daughter. Find the truth of your feelings," the goddess added. "But be kind to the warrior, too. Allow yourself the luxury of learning more about both males. Do not let lust make decisions of the heart. Do not mistake desire for true love. And remember, right now the seas are only safe for you if you stay near the shore and under my protection. Even if you decide you love the merman, you have to stay in your human body until I find a permanent solution for the problem of Sarpedon. That mer-creature is even more dangerous than the childish priest."

"Sarpedon!" CC slapped her forehead. "How could I have forgotten? I think I saw him, or at least some kind of ghostly vision of him, today."

The goddess's eyes widened at CC's words, but a shout kept her from responding.

"Princess Undine!" Isabel sounded out of breath as she limped up to CC. The instant the servant appeared both the goblet of delectable champagne and the goddess disappeared. "Well, there you are! I have been searching and searching these gardens. Sir Andras sent me to find you. Evening mass is beginning; you must come at once."

CC reluctantly allowed the maid to help her to her feet.

"Sir Andras does applaud your piety, but you certainly cannot miss vespers, even for prayerful meditation." Isabel looked sharply at CC. "At least you must not miss it *again*."

"I suppose I did get carried away with my prayers," CC said, following the old woman as she hurried down the path which would take them through the garden to the chapel that stood at its far end.

"I am sure you were in need of much prayer," Isabel rasped over her shoulder.

"If you only knew," CC muttered under her breath.

Isabel chose the most direct path across the garden area, which led to the wooden doors of a modest chapel. It was made with the same gray rock as was the rest of the monastery, but on this building the stones were carved into intricate renditions. CC squinted at the carvings and then her eyes opened in shock. All of the scenes were horrible. Horned demons were eating naked, writhing people. Stone flames burned full-fleshed women. Men who were half goat whipped human men, who were chained to each other, their tortured mouths open, frozen in eternally silent screams. CC shuddered and was glad that Isabel literally pulled her through the doors and into the dimly lit chapel.

The first thing CC noticed was the incense. It was thick and pungent and it curled in waves over the carved stone pews, which were filled with monks who were already kneeling and chanting in a dirgelike litany. Their cream-colored robes made them appear like spirits hovering in the dim, smoky light.

CC sneezed. At the sound, several of the heads turned briefly in her direction. One tall, blond-headed figure stood and moved quickly down the aisle and to her side. Andras took one look at her and shook his head like she had just flunked some kind of test.

"Why are you not prepared for mass?" he asked in a strained tone, making an obvious effort to keep his voice low.

CC blinked at him in confusion. She was here, wasn't she?

But before she could ask what he meant, Isabel sighed and gave her a severe look. "Princess, I am shocked that you did not think to bring a covering for your head." Clucking and shaking her head, Isabel dug into the depths of her apron pocket. "It is fortuitous that I thought to bring an extra scarf, although it is not so grand as the Princess is accustomed to, I am sure."

Isabel handed CC an ivory-colored scarf made of plain, serviceable linen. Her own head was already covered with a similar cloth.

"Thank you," CC said, draping the fabric over her head.

"It was very kind of you to think of the princess," Andras said formally.

"I only wish to serve. Sometimes those who are very young and very beautiful can also be very forgetful," Isabel said nonchalantly, but CC was sure she heard the hurt that hid in the old woman's gravely voice. Then the servant melted her way silently into a rear pew.

CC watched sadly as she disappeared into the gloom. She certainly wasn't making much headway in her quest to win Isabel over.

"I waited for you and was disturbed that you did not come," Andras whispered fiercely to her.

CC allowed her face to assume a shocked expression. "I was praying, Andras. Time seemed unimportant."

She watched as he brought his anger under control. "Of course. I was just concerned over your absence."

Oh, right, CC thought. That's why he looks like he'd love to shake me to death.

"Come, we are seated near the front. It is a great honor."

With a sigh CC followed him into the heart of the chapel, pausing briefly at the stone edifice that held the shallow pool of holy water. And she'd thought that those Sundays on base when she had mistakenly shown up for Catholic instead of Methodist services had just been pleasant little ceremonies she'd accidentally sat through. Without fear of making a fool of herself, she followed the correct motions of dipping her fingers in the holy water and genuflecting.

She had to hurry to catch up with Andras, who led her to the second row of pews. (The first row was unoccupied.) He motioned for her to go before him, and she slid down the empty pew, trying not to grimace at the coldness of the stone bench.

Evening mass was already under way, and CC was pretty sure that Abbot William had shot her a quick, contemptuous look, but it was so dark in the chapel that it was hard to be certain. His voice droned on and on, soft and rhythmic, in a language that CC decided must be Latin. The priest stood behind an ornately carved wooden table at the chapel's nave. The table was filled with gilded relics that glittered and sparkled, even in the dim light. There was an enormous golden chalice and a matching platter, which held a loaf of bread. Huge candelabrum stood on either end of the table, but even the light of their many candles did little to dispel the gloom of the chapel.

Suspended almost directly over Abbot William's head was a life-sized golden crucifix. CC squinted, trying to get a better look at it. As on the cross in her room, the only sign of Christ were the shards of wooden nails that pierced the cross where his hands and feet would have been. This time drops of blood were painted on the gold, the color of which reminded CC of Abbot William's robes, and she had to suppress a shudder of revulsion.

What had happened to Christ? Why was he conspicuously left off of the crucifix? The omission both saddened and angered CC.

The cross was suspended between two thick gray columns. At the base of each column were lit dozens of tall, white candles. Their soft flames seemed to be swallowed within the cross's shadow.

CC followed Andras's lead, kneeling and genuflecting when appropriate. She even managed to whisper what she thought were correct responses to the small portion of the service that was in an understandable language.

CC had just begun to think that her knees had fallen asleep when Abbot William turned his back to the congregation and raised the chalice to the bleeding cross, asking for the blessing on the wine. As he returned the chalice to the table and lifted the bread to be blessed similarly, a flickering movement to her left caught CC's gaze. The shadows that ringed the pews were thick, but she was sure she saw something in an alcove off to the side of the sanctuary. She concentrated, peering into the murky darkness, and an image formed out of the haze. Her breath caught and her heartbeat quickened.

"We will take communion next," Andras's voice spoke in her ear.

She looked around, startled at his words. The monks who had been seated in the row of pews directly across from them were standing and making their way slowly and reverently to take the blood and the flesh from Abbot William's hands.

CC's decision was quickly made. When Andras stood, she stood with him, but instead of following him like a good little lamb, she patted his hand and whispered, "Please excuse me, Andras. There is something I must do."

As she slipped out from the other side of the pew, the knight's face tightened in anger, but instead of following her, he moved out of the opposite end of their row and stood obediently in line behind the cream-robed monks. She ignored his irritation and headed with unerring certainty to a forgotten alcove in the side of the chapel.

The figure of the Virgin Mary was carved within the chapel wall. An arch made of ivory marble framed her. Intrigued, CC stepped closer. The statue was filthy, completely covered with dirt and spider webs, but an area around the base of the figure was worn smooth, as if hundreds upon hundreds of velvet knees had once rested there. CC's eyes traveled up the exquisite figure. Mary's robes swirled in graceful simplicity around her sandaled feet. Her hands were open and beckoning; CC found something very comforting in the gesture. CC's eyes continued up, and she sucked a breath in shock.

Mary's face! It was ethereal in its serene beauty and astonishingly familiar.

"Gaea!" CC gasped.

The statue had the goddess's face. Gaea's words came back to her: *You might be surprised, Daughter, to learn that even here I have not been completely forgotten.*

The shuffling of the monks to communion invaded her thoughts, drawing her attention back to the nave. The profusion of candles winked at her. Moving with swift silence, she tiptoed, sneaking through the foglike shadows to grab a lit candle in each hand and carry them back to the statue. She set them at Mary's feet, pleased that the flames seemed to burn suddenly brighter.

On impulse, she sank to her knees, clasped her hands and bowed her head.

"Great Mother," she prayed aloud. "Help me to be wise." She glanced up at the face she knew as that of the goddess, smiled brightly and let her voice drop to a whisper. "Please keep me safe from Sarpedon—I think I can handle the rest of this mess. Him, I'm not too sure about, though."

CC was so surprised when an answer rang in her head that she let out a little yip of shock.

Sarpedon is near and dangerous, but stay close to my realm, Daughter, and the merman cannot possess you. My blessings go with you . . .

"Undine! What are you—" The warrior's angry voice trailed off as he recognized the statue she was kneeling before.

CC closed her eyes tightly, gritting her teeth. Deliberately ignoring him, she kept her head bowed. Her lips moved silently as she recited to herself as much of the rosary as she knew. What she didn't know she ad-libbed, sending a silent plea for forgiveness to the Virgin/goddess for the unintentional blasphemy. She took her time finishing, before genuflecting deliberately and slowly. Then she glanced up at the knight who was still standing at her side and blinked her eyes in pretended surprise.

"Oh, Andras!" She held out her hand and automatically he helped her to her feet. "I'm sorry. I was so lost in prayer that I didn't even know you were there." She looked around at the empty chapel and painted a concerned frown on her face. "Is mass over? I wish I hadn't missed the end of it, but when I noticed this wonderful statue of the Virgin Mother, I felt compelled to come to her."

Andras's expression said he was torn between his desire to reprimand her for once again doing the unexpected and his pleasure at her decidedly Catholic piety.

"I am just surprised. I have never before noticed this statue of the Virgin."

"No wonder." CC didn't hide the irritation in her voice. "She looks like she's been abandoned!" CC leaned forward and pulled a cobweb from Mary's head. "It is disgraceful that the Blessed Mother is in such a state! I intend to speak with Abbot William about it."

Andras seemed to be having trouble forming his thoughts into words, but he finally cleared his throat and asked, "May I escort you to dinner, Princess?"

CC took his offered arm. "That would be nice. Thank you, Sir Andras."

CHAPTER FIFTEEN

DINNER was already being served when CC and Andras entered the dining room. CC tried to ignore the frowning looks the monks shot her, but she felt a little like an errant Catholic schoolgirl who was being sent to the headmaster's office. Obviously, she was in trouble for missing communion.

CC struggled to keep her expression neutral as Abbot William stood and greeted Andras with effusive warmth, offering the knight his ring, which Andras kissed without hesitation. Although he ignored her, CC curtseyed respectfully to the priest before taking her seat.

A servant hustled over and filled her plate with a steaming lamb stew that made CC's mouth water. Another servant topped off her goblet with sweet white wine. CC drank deeply, enjoying the cool liquid.

"I noticed you refused to take Holy Communion, Princess Undine." The priest's voice was a whip.

CC furrowed her brow in confusion. "Refused? Why would I refuse Holy Communion, Abbot?" She shook her head. "I'm sorry you misunderstand. I discovered a beautiful statue of the Holy Mother, and I was simply overcome with emotion when I noticed its state of disrepair." CC met his cold gaze evenly, and she made sure her voice carried. "I know how busy you must be, Abbot, so I am sure you had no idea that the Mother of God was being neglected."

The priest's face darkened, and his jaw clenched.

CC squeezed Andras's arm and smiled up at him. "I knew the abbot didn't realize the awful state of that statue."

"It was indeed fortuitous that you noticed it," Andras said.

CC brightened her face and laughed girlishly. "I have an idea! I will take special charge of the Blessed Mother's statue. While I'm here, it will be lovingly tended and restored to its original glory."

When Abbot William started to speak, her brilliant smile silenced him.

"There is no need to thank me." She beamed. Then CC deliberately mimicked the words he'd spoken to her the day before. "For this I seek a reward that cannot be found in this world."

The priest's eyes narrowed, but his lips smiled. "Of course, Princess. That is very"—he hesitated as if choosing his words carefully—"generous of you."

"I have noticed that there aren't many women here, so I suppose it's not surprising that the Holy Mother has been accidentally neglected." She looked at Andras and widened her eyes. "Maybe that's my purpose in coming here. Maybe the Holy Mother guided me to this shore, not just to save me, but to save her statue." And, she added silently, maybe if the knight believed she had been specially blessed by the Virgin, he would be less inclined to seduction and more inclined to respect.

Andras looked impressed. "Yes, Undine. I am quite certain the Holy Mother is watching over you."

The priest's voice sliced across the table. "It is good for a person to know one's purpose."

CC studied him over her goblet. "I agree completely with you, Abbot William."

The look the priest sent her was clearly adversarial. She met it with a forced smile.

"Father, I have been considering the move that led to my checkmate last evening . . ." Andras began, oblivious to the tension between his old teacher and the woman at his side.

As the abbot's attention shifted from her, CC suppressed a sigh of relief and concentrated on her second helping of stew. She needed food to ground her and to stop her head from reeling. So many things had happened in such a short amount of time. Despite the confidence Gaea showed in her, she felt a little like the Dutch boy who'd tried to stop the leak in the dike with his finger. And her medieval dike was feeling very, very leaky. Little wonder she was overwhelmed. She'd traveled a thousand years into a mythical past, exchanged bodies with a sea creature, met a goddess, kissed a merman . . . CC's stomach butterflied at the thought and she had to remind herself to chew.

Now she had to deal with the obvious hatred of a powerful abbot and the amorous attentions of an incredibly handsome, macho knight. And, of course, there was Sarpedon. CC thought about the goddess's words that day in the garden and again scolded herself that she hadn't thought to mention Sarpedon's manifestation earlier in their conversation. But she had received her answer in the chapel. Sarpedon couldn't possess her as long as she was under Gaea's protection. With one hand she absently fingered the amber amulet. She must be careful to stay near land, even when she reverted to her mermaid body, no matter how alluringly the sea called.

Her quiet contemplation was broken by the noisy clanging of boots against the floor of the dining hall. CC looked up to see one of Andras's men quickly approaching their table. He stopped and bowed sharply to the knight.

"Forgive me for interrupting you, Sir Andras."

"Gilbert, have you news of Princess Undine's family?" Andras asked.

CC held her breath.

"No, Sir Andras." The squire glanced around the room and lowered his voice, obviously reluctant to speak further. "I do have a message for you from the mainland."

Andras looked apologetically at Abbot William and CC.

"I regret I must ask you to excuse me."

"Of course, my son, we would not think of keeping you from your rightful duties." The abbot fluttered his fingers in the direction of the exit.

"I should not be long detained." Andras stood and bowed to them. He and the squire hurried from the room.

The knight's absence left a definite hole in the conversation, which the abbot filled with chilly indifference. Except for an occasional disdainful glance, he pretended CC didn't exist.

CC kept her eyes averted from him and tried to focus on finishing the delicious mutton stew. She wouldn't allow him the pleasure of seeing her bolt through her meal and rush from the room like a terrified child. She remembered his reaction to her fear when she had seen the specter of Sarpedon. Fear fed the priest.

She chewed slowly and sipped her wine. She had been in difficult situations before. Like the time she was a young two-striper and the noncommissioned officer in charge of the Comm Center had come down with a violent stomach flu, thirty minutes before he was to give an instructional briefing on changing procedures for their newly installed computer system. Between dry heaves he had ordered CC to give the briefing. Two hundred people had filled the base briefing room that day, and she was pretty sure that one hundred and ninety-seven of them had outranked her. She'd done fine. No, she'd done better than fine; she'd been awarded a commendation for her ability to perform under pressure.

She wasn't a shrinking flower easily intimidated by powerful men. She wouldn't let him see her fear. No, as before, she'd do better than that. She wouldn't let one mean-spirited priest intimidate her. Gaea had told her that he should be pitied, and it was ridiculous to be intimidated by someone she should feel sorry for.

Eventually her stew bowl was empty and her stomach was pleasantly full, and CC couldn't stifle a yawn. This time when she felt the priest's censoring gaze she met it.

"I'm going to have to ask you to excuse me, Abbot William. The day has exhausted me, and I'm afraid I won't be able to wait for Sir Andras to return. Could you please give him my apology and tell Isabel that there is no need for her to come to me until morning? I know how busy she is."

If CC could run a complex military communications system, she could certainly figure out how to untie the lacings of her dress herself, and she really didn't want to keep appearing to Isabel as selfish and bothersome.

"It is understandable that you are fatigued. Women were made as weaker vessels." His voice was laced with undisguised hostility, and his smile was a patronizing façade. "I will await the knight. I can assure you that he will not be concerned with your absence. He does so enjoy our chess matches."

Good lord, he made it sound like the two of them were rivals.

"I'm glad he does. I hope you two have a nice evening," CC said with as genuine a smile as she could force on her tired lips. "Good night, and, again, thank you for your hospitality." CC curtseyed and hurried from the room, aware that the priest's reptilian gaze followed her unblinkingly.

She paused under the arched exit. It was late evening, and high, winglike clouds obscured the fading light, casting the little courtyard that separated the dining hall and her wing of the monastery into shadowed darkness. CC stepped onto the soft grass and rolled her shoulders, determined to relax now that she was away from the priest's oppressive presence. She inhaled deeply the cool, moist air. It smelled like rain. The thought of water, even if it just came from the sky, lightened her spirits. She yawned and stretched, wishing she had a book she could curl up with for a little while before falling asleep.

She was halfway across the courtyard when a noise startled her. It was the deep sound of a man's chuckle, but it held no humor. Instead it vibrated with sarcasm. CC stopped. Blinking, she peered through the darkness, unable to distinguish between shadows and shapes.

"*Undine.*"

"Is that you, Andras?"

One of the shadows moved and became a man. He was standing near the well. As he spoke, he walked towards her.

"Did you think you could hide from me?" His voice had an unnaturally hollow sound, as if he were speaking to her from a great distance instead of mere feet.

Something was very wrong. Fear curled taut in her chest, and she had trouble breathing.

"Why would I hide from you?" She tried to keep her voice calm and matter-of-fact. "I just asked Father William to make my apologies to you. I'm afraid he was right about me doing too much too soon. I am very tired."

The knight stood directly in front of her; they were almost touching. His eyes flashed with the same eerie, silver light that she had seen within them the first time he had kissed her hand. Transfixed by a paralyzing sense of horror, she watched while his face seemed to shift, as if his well-defined features had suddenly become fluid and mutable. Power radiated from him with a palpable force. His lips twisted into an obscene leer.

"You will belong to me!" he snarled and lunged forward, grabbing her arms in an iron grip. He crushed her against his body, and CC could feel his huge erection pulsing through the silky layers of her gown.

Then a blast of heat shot with electric speed from her chest as the amulet of the goddess came into contact with the knight's body. His shriek was deafening, and he flung CC away from him so violently that she fell to the ground with a jarring thud.

"What is the meaning of this?" the abbot's voice cut through the night.

The breath knocked out of her, CC could only look up and gasp for air. The priest was silhouetted in the dining room doorway. Like a nest of baby birds, several shocked monks peered at her from behind him. How long had they been watching? She tried desperately to catch her breath and glanced at Andras. He stood near her, rubbing his chest and looking dazed.

"The well . . ." Andras began, sounding shaky. "There was something in the well." The knight was breathing hard, and CC could see that a sheen of sweat covered his pale face.

"Yes! It was scary!" CC's breath came back in a rush of words. She gave a jittery laugh and held out her hand. After only a slight hesitation Andras took it and helped her to her feet.

"What of the well?" the abbot asked sharply, striding into the courtyard and approaching Andras.

The knight hunched his shoulders and struggled to speak. His eyes were glassy and blank.

CC wasn't similarly confused. She knew who had emerged from the well. She also knew that it would be disastrous if the abbot realized what had really happened.

"Bats!" CC said suddenly and added a shiver she didn't have to fake. "I'd just begun to cross the courtyard when I noticed Andras standing by the well. He said he'd seen something, and after my experience earlier today he had, of course, felt the need to take a closer look." Thinking quickly she wove the fabrication. "All of a sudden a huge bat came flying up out of the well. It knocked Andras in the chest and then came straight at me. I screamed and fell to the ground." She shivered again and puckered her face. "I hate bats."

"That must have been what you saw this morning," Andras said slowly. The confusion was clearing from his face and he appeared willing to accept CC's story.

Relieved, CC nodded enthusiastically. "I think the well mystery has been solved. I feel like such a fool making a big fuss over nothing. Abbot William, please forgive me for interrupting you again."

The abbot's blue eyes narrowed at her, but he gave her a brief nod.

"We must speak, Father," Andras said suddenly. CC was pleased that he sounded coherent and in control once more. "I have had news from the mainland that is of concern to Caldei." As an afterthought, Andras turned to CC. "Undine, I—"

CC waved her hand. "I wouldn't think of taking you away from important business with the abbot. I'm fine now and can easily find my way to my room. Good night Andras, Abbot William."

"Come, my son. Let us retire to my chamber where we may speak in peace."

Without another glance at her, the Abbot and the knight hurried from the courtyard, and the monks returned to the dining hall. CC was left alone with the silent well.

She ran a shaking hand across her face. Her knees wobbled and she felt the sharp bite of bile in the back of her throat. Sarpedon had followed her, and he had found a way to reach beyond his realm. The thought of being trapped within the walls of the monastery with the merman's malevolent spirit overwhelmed her. She needed space. No, she acknowledged grimly to herself—she needed the ocean. She ached for its comfort and the sense of belonging she felt whenever she was submerged in its liquid embrace.

And Dylan, her heart reminded her. She needed Dylan. Could he be out there in the soothing water, waiting for her?

CC hesitated, chewing her bottom lip. Yes, the ocean was Sarpedon's realm, and she was vulnerable to him there, but apparently that vulnerability now extended to the monastery. CC felt a surge of anger. What right did he have to stalk her?

The gate to the monastery was open, and it was much easier to walk through it than it would have been to climb out of her window. She would only be gone a little while, she promised herself. She'd be back before anyone would notice her absence. Squaring her shoulders stubbornly, she followed the sound of the calling waves through the gate and out of the monastery.

Picking up her skirts, she jogged down the path that led around the outside wall of the monastery to the edge of the cliff. The sun was low in the sky, and blushing colors of mauve and saffron lit the sea. On the horizon cumulus clouds billowed like giant dust bunnies that had been dyed the colors of evening. Carefully, she chose the winding path she had followed the night before, forcing herself to slow down so that her dress wouldn't catch and rip on the scrubby brush that lined the little trail.

Unexpectedly, fog began to form over the water. CC watched it spread, surprised at the ease with which it covered the rich colors of the evening sky. Like the cloak of a giant, it billowed up the side of the cliff. Within just a few steps CC was totally surrounded and had to slow her descent even more, picking her way down a path that seemed to dissolve into fairylike mist. She waved her hand in front of her body and was intrigued at the way the tendrils of wetness curled around her. She had never seen fog like that before—it shimmered with a strange iridescence, as if it was made of opals and pearls. She probably should have been frightened; instead the soupy fog made her feel hidden and secure.

Her shoes sank into sand at the moment a small section of mist shifted and parted, allowing Gaea to step through its diaphanous curtain. Tonight her robes were the color of smoke sprinkled with starlight and diamonds.

"Good evening, Daughter." The goddess embraced CC, holding her within the maternal comfort of her arms. "I thought you would desire to be free of the monastery this evening."

CC stood with her head resting on the goddess's shoulder. Gaea smelled like summer grass and lilacs.

"It was Sarpedon, wasn't it?"

"Yes. He possessed the knight." Gaea stroked her hair.

"I was so scared!" CC sobbed, feeling her body begin to tremble again.

Keeping one arm around her daughter, Gaea motioned to a large moss-covered rock behind them, inviting her to sit.

"Sarpedon only intensified the desires which already exist within the young man." Gaea's lips tightened. "The knight is honorable, but Lir's son is very powerful. It is a simple thing for him to manipulate Andras's lust. The knight has no defenses against Sarpedon, and you cannot warn him. Andras is a man who has been fashioned to despise the supernatural and the unknown."

"He didn't seem to remember any of it. He just accepted the explanation I made up."

"No doubt Andras has only a vague, dreamlike memory of his actions while he is under Sarpedon's influence. He is not the kind of man who would admit weakness, and a loss of memory, or of control, would be something that he would refuse to acknowledge, so consciously he will cling to any excuse offered him. It is only unconsciously that he will be in tumult. The knight's will and soul are as a kingdom in civil war, and he does not have the ability to reach beyond what he has been taught to seek aid."

"Then what can I do?"

"I do not mean for you to fear Sarpedon, but I do want you to be wise. Right now he enjoys toying with Andras. It amuses him to use the warrior's desire while he searches for a way to possess you." The goddess's tone was businesslike, which was as much a comfort to CC as was her presence. "But as long as you stay under my protection he cannot possess you directly, nor do I believe he can force the knight to act so against his nature as to actually do you harm, even if that was his intention."

CC gave the goddess a dubious look.

"Remember, Sarpedon does not want you injured; he simply wants you returned to him." Gaea's frown was a gentle chide. "Do you not trust me, Daughter?"

"Of course I trust you," CC said quickly, feeling her fear begin to thaw.

"There . . ." Gaea cupped her daughter's chin in her hand. "All will be well, do not doubt it." The goddess kissed her forehead gently. "Now, I hear the waters calling to you. I know they will soothe you even better than I."

"Isn't Sarpedon still looking for me?" CC asked.

"My fog will hide you from his eyes tonight. And I believe you need to conduct a search of your own." Gaea raised her beautifully arched brows suggestively and nodded towards the sound of the waves. "Find what is in your own heart, Daughter."

"Is Dylan out there?" CC's voice had dropped almost to a whisper.

"Did he not say he would be waiting for you?"

"He thinks I won't be here until I need to change back to my mermaid form, and that's not for two more nights." CC brushed a hand through her heavy hair. "Can I even change tonight?" She felt the call of the water, as always, but it wasn't as intense as it had been the night before. Instead of an overwhelming desire, it was just an itch somewhere under her skin.

"You must wait for the third night to change into your mermaid form—if you change more often than that, you may not be able to overcome your desire to remain a creature of the water."

"And then Sarpedon would get me." And he would kill Dylan, CC added silently to herself.

"Do not concern yourself with Sarpedon tonight. Concentrate instead on knowing your heart."

"But if I can't change back into a mermaid . . ."

"If Dylan is your true love, he must accept the part of you that is human."

CC gestured at her layers of skirts. "I'm not exactly dressed for swimming."

Gaea's smile was mischievous. "I have always believed one should not be dressed at all when one finds herself embraced by the ocean." With a slender finger she touched the intricate laces at CC's back. Instantly they fell open and the cloth slipped from her shoulders as if twenty nimble-fingered servants had assisted her.

CC stood to step out of the dress and smoothed it across the rock. Before she pulled off the shift, she glanced at Gaea. "How am I going to get back into that thing?"

Gaea's smile widened, and she passed her elegantly shaped hand over the dress, speaking softly to it.

"*When she wills, your braids rebuild. So have I spoken; so shall it be.*" The air around the dress stirred, and CC could feel the spark of Gaea's magic.

CC grinned at the goddess. "Thank you." Then she lifted the chemise over her head and kicked off her shoes. Almost automatically she pulled her long hair forward, obscuring the view of her bare breasts.

"Are you ashamed of your body, Daughter?" Gaea asked.

"No. I think it's beautiful."

"Then perhaps living at the monastery has convinced you that beauty is something to be feared and hidden?" The smile in Gaea's voice softened the reprimand.

"Absolutely not," CC said firmly. In one quick motion she swept her hair back, leaving her breasts totally bared. Then, naked except for her jewelry, she started walking toward the sound of waves. But soon her steps faltered and she was suddenly unsure of herself.

"Call to him." Gaea's voice came from behind her.

"Just call?" CC asked, looking over her shoulder at the goddess.

"He will hear you." The mist started to close and thicken around Gaea, so that her last words were disembodied. "You cannot remain long tonight. There is a storm coming, and they will be looking for you. My blessing goes with you, Daughter."

"I'll remember," CC said to the mist before turning back to face the sound of water. She walked slowly forward, making her way carefully between the many rocks and shells that littered the sand. The fog surrounded her, brushing against her skin in a wet caress, forming tiny drops of dew which glistened to decorate her body like liquid jewels.

When her feet touched water she stopped, peering outward, but she could see nothing through the thick fog. Feeling a little foolish, she cupped her mouth with her hands and called to the merman.

"Dylan! Are you here?"

Only the sound of waves breaking against the rocky shore answered her. She sighed and cupped her mouth again.

"Dylan!"

CC felt him before she saw him. There was a tingling all along her skin that settled somewhere low in her stomach—and she knew he was there. Over the section of ocean that stretched in front of her the mist thinned.

Dylan broke the surface, sweeping his long dark hair from his sparkling eyes. His blood throbbed hot at the sight of her. She was so lovely, standing there in her exotic human body which was all soft curves and long, supple lines. Her beautiful face lit at the sight of him, and her full lips shaped a delighted grin that was solely Christine—his vibrant, joyous Christine.

There was laughter in his voice when he spoke. "You do not need to shout for me, Christine. You need only call me from here." He smiled and pointed to his own temple. "Simply send your thoughts to me, as we do under the water. I will hear you."

"Oh," CC said inanely. She was sure he could also hear the herd of butterflies that were pounding around in her stomach. "I didn't know. Gaea just told me you would come if I called."

His expression sobered. "Always, Christine. I will always answer your call." He glanced around at the fog. "Is this the doing of your goddess?"

CC nodded. "It seems Sarpedon is on the prowl. Gaea says he can't find me in this. And, anyway, I think he's busy at the monastery tonight."

"It almost makes me feel pity for the monks," Dylan said, trying to lighten his voice, but it was clear the mention of Sarpedon made the merman uncomfortable.

"Don't be too hasty with your sympathy. I think that monastery could use a little shaking up, or at least that abbot sure could." She dug her toes into the sand and looked down. She didn't want to tell Dylan about Sarpedon's possession of Andras. She could only imagine how it would make him feel—probably mad and jealous and frustrated that he couldn't do anything about it. And she didn't want the oppressive subject of Sarpedon to ruin her time with Dylan.

She glanced at the merman, and all thoughts of Sarpedon dissipated. Dylan's eyes were on her naked body. She could feel his gaze. It made her skin flush with a sensuous tingle.

He made her feel breathless and very nervous.

"I know it's not the third night, so I'm early, and, well, I can't *change* yet, but I'm glad you came."

He smiled at her. "I am glad you appeared early."

"Even if I can't, uh, be a mermaid tonight?" she stammered.

He raised one eyebrow, grinning at her boyishly. "Are you worried that I might let you drown?"

At his easy jest, CC felt her nerves loosen, and she smiled back at him. "Well, I do remember swallowing a lot of water the first time we met."

He laughed. "That is only because I was unprepared for your kicking and squirming." Drifting closer to shore he held one strong hand out to her and his voice deepened seductively. "Tonight I am prepared; come to me. I will not let you drown."

Without hesitation, CC walked into the water. When her feet no longer touched ground, she began to swim, but before she could finish a full stroke Dylan pulled her into his arms.

"I think it would be safer if you allowed me to do the swimming," he said with mock seriousness.

"And what will you do if I kick and squirm?" CC teased.

"I said that tonight I am prepared." His arms circled her naked body, pressing her firmly against his chest. CC could feel the rhythmic beat of his powerful tail as he tread water, easily keeping both of them afloat in the calm, fog-shrouded ocean. "I will simply hold you closer."

"That makes me want to kick and squirm," she said breathlessly, his touch making her feel a little light-headed.

"And I will be careful that you do not drown," Dylan murmured as he bent his head to her.

Their lips met in a rush of heat, and CC wrapped her arms around his shoulders, loving the mixture of hard muscle and slick, wet skin under her hands.

"Oh, Dylan," CC whispered against his lips. "I missed you today."

Dylan kissed her forehead softly. When he spoke his voice was rough with suppressed emotion. "I saw you."

CC blinked in surprise. "You mean when I came to the beach to eat brunch?"

"Yes. With the man."

CC touched his cheek gently, hating the haunted look in his eyes.

"I watched as he kissed you." The merman's jaw clenched. "I have never before wished to have legs, but today I wanted nothing more than to walk from the waters and take you from him."

A tingle of emotion flushed her body at his words. She took his face between her hands and looked into the deep brown of his eyes. "You need to know something." She felt him tense, as if readying himself for a blow, and she hurried on. "I'm not very good at this. I mean I'm not very experienced in relationships. I really haven't had much practice, so there's a lot I'm not sure about. But there is one thing I do know. I won't lie to you. I believe in truth and fidelity. And I'm giving you my word that I do not want Andras. He is not the man for me."

The tension in the merman's jaws relaxed under her hands, but his eyes were still shadowed.

"Man . . ." Dylan said, smiling sadly. "You say he is not the man for you, and I am glad of it. But I am also not a man."

"I didn't mean—"

Dylan's lips brushed gently against hers. "*Shssh.* I have something to show you."

Before CC could say more he flipped to his back, pulling her up so that she rested against him, safely out of the water. He propelled them backward, careful to keep her protected from the wash of waves while she lay securely within his arms.

"I did miss you," she whispered into his ear. He didn't answer her, but she felt him nod, and his hand caressed the curve of her back intimately.

After traveling down the shoreline, Dylan stopped in front of a large arrangement of stone and coral, part of which towered above the ground. It was vaguely cavelike, but the top was open to the sky. It was round and reminded CC of a corral.

"There is no other way to enter than from under the surface. You will have to hold your breath, but it will not be for long."

The sun had set, and it was almost totally dark, with the mist obscuring even the dim light left in the evening sky. CC looked nervously at the hulking structure that jutted imposingly out of the water. "Are you sure?"

Dylan smiled reassuringly at her. "Do you promise not to kick and squirm?"

"I'll be good," she said, trying to laugh off her trepidation.

Dylan kissed her forehead gently and cupped her chin with his hand. "I would never cause you harm."

His eyes were warm and she felt undeniably safe wrapped in his strong arms.

"I'm ready," she said.

Dylan shifted her so that she floated in front of him, then he turned her so that her back was to him. His hands cupped her waist, which left her own hands free.

"When you are ready, take a deep breath and dive. I will do the rest."

Before she could change her mind, she took a huge breath, nodded and stretching her arms over her head, she dove under the surface. Guiding and pushing her from behind, Dylan's power made CC feel slick and strong under the water—and she was almost disappointed at how quickly he angled them up so that their heads broke the surface together. CC shook the water from her face, laughing.

"Wow! That was almost like I had a tail of my own . . ." Her words trailed off as she registered the beauty that surrounded them.

They floated in the center of a ring of coral and rocks. As she had already observed from outside, the structure was open to the sky, and the circle formed a calm pool in the center, sheltering them from the rhythmic crashing of waves against rock. But that wasn't what was so spectacular about the structure. All around them hundreds, maybe even thousands, of phosphorescent blue fish the size of one of CC's thumbs, darted in schools of perfectly synchronized swimming. Their lights illuminated the ring of water with an otherworldly turquoise glow, giving their little section of the ocean the appearance of a swimming pool lit by magical, moving bulbs. It was an oasis of brilliance in their fog-shrouded world.

"Dylan," CC breathed. "I've never seen anything like this."

"That is not all." He pulled her with him to the side of the wall. Pointing down at a little pocket of coral under the water, he said, "Watch."

CC peered down into the clear, neon-lit water and gasped in wonder. Within the rocky pocket she could see two sea horses. The miniature equine replicas were about six inches long and colored mostly an amazing black-bronze, except for an area of their bodies that looked like waistcoats; there they were splashed with brilliant patches of pink, yellow, blue and white. As CC watched, the two creatures swam in delicate circles around each other, coming ever closer. Finally, they met in a trembling embrace, joining their bodies together.

"There are more." Dylan's lips moved against her ear and he pointed to another place within the coral wall. CC followed his gesture to see that another pair of sea horses were beginning their graceful mating dance.

CC leaned back against the merman, wrapping her arms around his. "I didn't know there was such beauty in the ocean. I never spent much time around it, and I didn't realize how incredible it could be." She turned fluidly in his arms. "You really are a wonderful teacher. Thank you for showing me."

"I cannot imagine you away from the water."

"It seems ridiculous now, but I used to be afraid of the water. As you may have noticed, I'm not even a very good swimmer."

"Then you did not know any of the mer-folk in your old world?" Dylan asked.

CC laughed. "There aren't any mermen or mermaids where I come from."

Dylan looked startled. "Are you certain?"

"Well, I'm pretty sure. They are considered mythological beings. People tell stories about them and draw pictures of them, but if they ever existed in my world they haven't been seen in more than a thousand years."

Dylan studied the woman in his arms with new eyes. He was struck by the realization that he loved a woman who was not simply a land creature, but from a strange world where none of his kind even existed. How could he hope to win her love in return? He knew she found him interesting and probably even exotic and appealing, but those were not emotions on which to base a lifetime of love—they were fleeting, transient and would vanish like mist with the rising sun of experience. He began to understand the despair that had destroyed his mother.

"I must seem very strange to you."

CC could hear the vulnerability in his voice and felt him pull away from her—not enough that she would be in danger of slipping under the surface, but the intimacy with which he had been holding her faltered, like he was suddenly afraid to be too close to her.

"Strange is not the word I would choose." She tightened her arms around him, so that he had to come back to her.

"Then what word would you choose?" Dylan asked, trying hard to keep his voice neutral and his tumultuous emotions controlled.

"Well, I don't think one word would do—I think I would have to use several." She kept one arm wrapped securely around his shoulder. With the other she let her hand trace a path down his face and over his chiseled cheekbone. "Beautiful," she said softly, moving her fingertips down the side of his neck and over the firm muscle of his shoulder. "Spectacular," she continued, stopping to caress his thick bicep before crossing over to his chest and continuing down. "Amazing." CC's hand moved over the side of his taut waist. When her fingers felt the flesh of his skin change from human to mer-being, she hesitated and her gaze shifted to his eyes. He was watching her intently, and his breathing had deepened.

"I have legs now and not a tail," CC said.

Her words made Dylan's lips curl up in a surprised ghost of a smile. "Yes, I did notice that," he said.

"Have you ever, uh, been with a human woman before?" she asked.

Now his surprise was complete. "No! I have never before known a human woman." He paused, trying to find the right words. ". . . in any way . . . What I mean is that I have not . . ."

CC nodded quickly. "So what you're telling me is that you've never been intimate with, or even known, a human woman, yet you don't seem to find me repulsive, even though right now my body is very definitely human."

"I could not find you repulsive," Dylan said as understanding lit his eyes. "Even though I have not known any other beings of your kind." *She* had been worried about *his* acceptance. She truly desired him! In part of his mind he allowed himself to begin to believe that perhaps he wasn't destined to repeat his mother's tragedy. Relief flooded his body and the ghost of a smile became real.

"Then I don't think you should worry about me not having known any other mermen. That is unless you want me to start worrying about you thinking my legs are disgusting."

CC could feel Dylan's body relax, and she floated easily against him once more. One of his hands traveled down her back and past her waist. CC sucked in a surprised breath when it skimmed over her butt to caress the length of her thigh.

"Your legs are soft and warm." His voice was deeply seductive. "And I admit to wanting to touch them—very much."

"I want to touch you, too," CC said, letting her hand move purposefully down from his waist to skim over the unique texture of the rest of him. She looked into his eyes. "But I would like to see you, too. A little more clearly. Do you mind?" She hurried on as his brow furrowed. "I mean, you've seen me—all of me—very naked. Just a little while ago I was standing on the shore with not much on except a smile. But, well, I haven't really been able to see . . ." She nodded her head toward the water and what shimmered gold and orange beneath it, "*you*."

Dylan made a muffled noise in the back of his throat, but he shook his head, holding her gaze with his own.

"No, I do not mind," he said.

Looking around the ring of rock, Dylan searched until he found what he needed. With CC still in his embrace, he floated them across the turquoise pool to a smooth ledge that protruded about a foot above the water. CC eyed it. It was easily seven or eight feet long, curving gently along the inside of the rocky corral. It looked wide enough that two people could lie next to each other on it, especially if they were lying on their sides and didn't mind being very close.

CC felt a thrill of nerves mixed with excitement as Dylan lifted her out of the water and sat her gently on the ledge. She moved to her side with her back against the rock and lay on one hip, watching him. In a powerful movement he grabbed the edge of the ledge and lifted himself out of the water, shifting his weight so that he lay on his side, too, facing CC.

The first thing CC noticed was his size—he seemed so much bigger out of the water. She felt dwarfed by him, even though Undine's human body was tall and voluptuous.

"You're really big," she blurted.

Dylan's chuckle helped to ease some of her tension. "Christine, I am the same as I was in the water."

His dark hair had fallen over his shoulder, and CC brushed it back from his face. He turned his head and caught her palm in a quick, playful kiss, making her smile.

Dylan's torso was strong and familiar, and CC let her hand rest briefly on his chest. Then, taking a deep breath, she looked down.

His bronze skin tapered to his well-muscled waist, where it joined with the merman's tail. The colors were unbelievable. What CC had thought was only orange banded with gold was really a convergence of many different shades of yellow and cream and rust and red, all combining to form a rainbow the color of sunlight and flames. The bands of gold were metallic in color, and they ran in thick horizontal stripes around his muscular tail, which ended in a huge feathered fin that glistened gold streaked with ebony.

CC leaned forward and let her fingers stroke the side of that amazing tail. As she had discovered with her own mer-body, the flesh wasn't actually scaled, it just caught the light in a swirling pattern that could be mistaken for scales. Under her fingers Dylan's flesh was warm and smooth. She let her hand explore him, enjoying the feel of the bunch and swell of his muscles as he quivered under her touch.

CC forced her gaze from his body to his eyes. "You are amazing, Dylan. I could explore you forever."

Dylan thought his heart would explode with joy. She was his! By some in-credible miracle, she wanted him as he wanted her. With a moan he wrapped CC in his arms and crushed her against him. His lips met hers and began their own exploration as they tasted each other. Intoxicated by the feel of her, Dylan's hands moved over CC's body, cupping her butt and stroking her legs.

CC's breath caught in her throat when she felt his hardness press against the center of her body. She shut out the mental picture of Sarpedon's throbbing maleness as it had emerged, engorged and demanding from his pelvic slit. No! She would not allow memories of Sarpedon to taint her. This was Dylan; she welcomed his touch—and he would never hurt her.

She slid her hand between their bodies and cupped him, wishing suddenly that she had more experience with men. He felt much like she had remembered Jerry feeling, with that wonderful combination of hardness wrapped in a shaft of velvet softness that she had found arousing, despite Jerry's awkward attempt at lovemaking.

Tentatively, at first, CC stroked him, allowing herself to become accus-tomed to him. He's just a man, she thought. Just a different, incredible type of man. Dylan's skin was hot and his body was becoming slick with sweat. The scent of him filled her senses with its uniqueness. He was sea and man melded together and she wanted to drown in him.

His breathing was ragged as he suddenly broke their kiss.

"Slowly, Christine." His hand shook when it brushed her cheek. "Your touch enflames me."

She pulled her hand abruptly from between their bodies. "I'm sorry. I told you I wasn't very experienced with men—or males—or . . ." She looked away, embarrassed.

He took her chin in his hand, forcing CC to meet his eyes. "You misunderstand. It is I who am having an experience," he raised one eyebrow and gave her his boyish grin, "or rather I should say, *control* problem. You are making it very right for me, but I would have it be so for you, too, my love."

"Oh, I didn't know," CC said, feeling a rush of joy at his endearment.

"Let me learn your wonderful human body. Perhaps I will find a way to give us both pleasure."

Then he began his own exploration. At first CC closed her eyes as his mouth moved from her lips to her neck, and on to kiss the swell of her breasts, where they lingered. But soon she found she preferred to keep her eyes open. She liked watching him as he bent over her, his eyes dark and his face taut with desire. His lips kissed the curve of her waist and his hand moved over her rounded hip to her legs. He bent one of her legs and kissed the inside of her knee. Lingering there he nuzzled and nipped gently.

"They are so soft that they cry for my touch," Dylan murmured, his lips still exploring her legs. He loved the distinctly female scent of her. The smooth heat of her body filled his senses, and he fought to control his desire to bury himself within her. He would not allow himself to rush. He inhaled deeply and let his tongue taste her thigh. "Your skin is a silk finer than any even your goddess could wear."

CC bit her bottom lip to stifle a moan.

"Do you like that, my love?" Dylan asked.

"I like it when you touch me," CC said breathlessly. "Anywhere—everywhere."

Dylan's hands caressed her inner thighs, moving toward her core. When he finally touched her wetness she couldn't stop herself from arching up into his hand and moaning aloud.

"Show me," he pleaded. "I want to know how to please you."

With trembling hands she guided his, until his fingers found the right rhythm. When she cried his name in release, he covered her mouth in fierce joy and held her against him, so that when the world stopped spinning she was lying on top of him. She could feel the tension in his muscles as his heart beat wildly against her bare breast. Sitting up, she moved his hands to her waist as she straddled his golden flesh. His eyes widened in surprise when she lifted herself and reached between them once again, this time guiding his hardness to the center of her.

She set her teeth against the pain she remembered experiencing with Jerry, and in one swift motion, sheathed him within her own slick heat. But instead of pain, she echoed his cry of pleasure as he fit perfectly within her.

Dylan spoke her name, murmuring wordless sounds of passion as he held her hips tightly while she arched her back and rocked against him. Now it was his turn to guide her and they moved together over and over, their rhythm increasing until the wave of pleasure crested and pulled first CC, then Dylan over into fulfillment. She collapsed against him, and they held onto each other while their bodies stopped trembling. CC fell asleep cradled within Dylan's arms.

THE sound of annoyed chattering woke her. She was snuggled securely against Dylan. His eyes were closed, but his lips were tilted up in a satisfied smile, and he was stroking her hair.

"She sounds angry with you," he said.

Lifting herself up on one elbow, CC peeked up over his shoulder at the fluorescent water. The dolphin's head bobbed in the middle of the calm pool.

The goddess sent me for you, Princess.

CC felt a stab of fear. "I didn't realize! How late is it?"

Do not worry, the dolphin soothed. *You have time.*

Dylan sat abruptly and pulled her into his lap. "What is it?"

"I have to get back. Gaea warned me not to be gone too long. She said they would be looking for me."

Dylan's jaw tightened, but he nodded and slid both of them easily into the waiting water. In an absentminded gesture of kindness, he reached out to stroke the squirming dolphin.

"Thank you, loyal one. Assure the goddess that I will return your princess to land now."

The dolphin chattered at him, nuzzled CC and disappeared under the surface.

Dylan kissed the side of CC's neck. "Are you ready?" he asked. "Just like before."

She nodded and took a deep breath, diving down with the power of her lover steering her to safety.

They didn't speak as Dylan backstroked to shore. CC clung to him, trying not to think about the separation that had to come next.

"You can stand now," the merman said reluctantly.

CC stood, but stayed close to him, still wrapped in his arms. She could hear the surf breaking against the nearby shoreline, but fog and darkness prevented her from seeing it.

"I have to go back," she said, not able to look at him.

"I know." His arms tightened around her. "Will you return tomorrow night?"

"I don't know," she said. "I'll try. But if not tomorrow, the next will be the third night, and I have to return and change back to mermaid form."

He loosened his grip on her so that he could look into her eyes. "I will be here. Always. You need only call me."

CC tapped her head, trying to smile. "In here?"

Dylan kissed her forehead. "Yes, and I will hear your call in here." He took her hand and placed it on his chest over his heart.

CC tilted her face to his and they came together with desperate urgency. The kiss was deep and frantic.

"You are a part of me now!" Dylan broke the kiss to grip her shoulders and force her to meet his gaze. "We belong together. There will be a way." Then he kissed her one last time.

Fighting back tears, she stepped away from him. He brought her hand to his lips before releasing her. She turned and forced herself to walk out of the water. As she stepped onto dry land, she glanced over her shoulder, but the fog had already hidden him from her view.

"Christine?" His disembodied voice found her.

"I'm still here," she said.

"You know how you feel when you are separated from the sea? How your body aches for it?"

"Yes. I know the feeling," she said to the fog.

"That is how I feel when you are not with me. If you ever doubt that I will be here, or doubt that I will wait for you, remember that feeling, and know that I can do nothing else. For an eternity, Christine. I will wait for you for an eternity . . ." His voice faded as he returned to the sea.

"I'll remember," she called after him, biting her bottom lip to keep from crying.

In front of her the fog thinned, and she could see the rock where she had left her clothes. Hurrying, she used the shift to dry herself, grimacing as she pulled the damp cloth over her head. Then she stepped into the layered gown. As soon as she put her arms within the sleeves, CC felt a tugging at her back and the intricate laces magically rebraided themselves together.

"Thank you, Gaea," she said to the silent, misty night.

This time the goddess didn't answer, but to her left the fog swirled and parted, providing a little pathway of clarity in the darkness. She followed it unquestioningly, trying to ignore the pang of loss she felt as each step took her farther from the water and from Dylan. Soon it was obvious that the path she was taking was not any of the ones that led up the cliff. This one wrapped over and around rocks and sandy dunes, and at first it appeared to be taking her away from the monastery. Just as she was beginning to worry about where the goddess was leading her, the fog shifted and opened at a sudden right angle and CC found herself following a familiar trail, which she recognized as being the path she and Andras had taken earlier that day. It led up past tall trees and emptied into the well-packed road. CC turned to her right and sighed in relief when she saw the lights of the monastery glowing dimly in the murky distance. She hadn't realized before how exhausted she was, but two nights of very little sleep had caught up with her. She smiled grimly to herself. Even her hard, narrow bed would be welcome that night. She lifted up her skirts and tried to coax her tired feet to move more quickly.

"Let's get going, girls, before they send out a posse."

"To whom do you speak, Undine?"

CC let out a little shriek of surprise as the knight materialized out of the fog before her.

"Andras! You scared me." She felt like her heart might beat its way out of her chest.

But Andras wasn't looking at her. Instead he was walking a tight circle around her, obviously searching the area.

"To whom do you speak, Undine?" he repeated the question more forcefully.

"No one except my feet. I'm afraid you caught me talking to myself." She smiled and fluttered her hand in front of her face like she was trying to fan away the heat of embarrassment, but her mouth went dry when he turned to her. Had Sarpedon possessed him again? She swallowed down her fear and studied him. His face was a mask of barely contained fury, but no manic silver light glowed from his eyes and his features remained his own. CC felt a surge of relief. She was just dealing with an angry man, not a malevolent spirit.

Automatically, CC took a little half step away from him, but the knight moved forward and roughly took her shoulders in his callused hands.

"Where have you been?" he demanded.

"Nowhere. I just went for a walk." CC forced herself to meet his furious gaze calmly.

"Alone, as night was falling? Why would you do such a thing?"

CC's thoughts raced as she fabricated an answer. "The bat that came out of the well scared me more than I realized." She allowed her voice to shake. "You were busy with the abbot, and I really didn't want to interrupt either of you again with my silly fears, but I couldn't stand to be in my room alone, so I thought I would go back to the beautiful beach you showed me today." She gestured with her head back down the road, and she saw the knight's eyes widen as he recognized the entrance to the path they had taken earlier. CC sent a quick, silent thank-you to Gaea for putting her in a place that lent itself to a ready excuse for being gone so long. "Then this fog came in and I got lost." She let a little half sob escape her lips. "And it got dark and I didn't think I would ever find my way back."

Andras studied her face, noticing for the first time the circles that darkened the area under her lovely eyes. She did look exhausted and disconcerted. The princess needed his protection—that was very apparent. And, of course, he wanted very much to protect her. He almost pulled her into his arms, until he noticed that her thick mass of hair was soaking wet, yet it seemed that under his hands her gown was dry. His eyes narrowed.

"How did your hair get so wet?"

Before his sentence was completed the darkened sky opened and a cold rain began to fall, effectively dissipating the fog.

"All of me is wet!" CC said, unable to keep the exasperation from her voice. "It's been a foggy, rainy night." She wiggled her shoulders. "Andras, you're hurting me."

Slowly, Andras dropped his hands from her shoulders.

CC hugged herself and shivered. "I'm cold and wet and tired. I've been lost and afraid most of the night, and my feet—who you already heard me talking to—are aching. Now would you like to escort me back to the monastery, or do I have to walk back by myself?"

Silently, the knight held his arm out for her. His look told her that he didn't like what she had said, or the tone in which she had said it, but as she took his arm he didn't comment on her rudeness or reprimand her. Instead he appeared to be deep in thought. CC was glad he wasn't questioning her, but she didn't like the idea of him thinking too much either—at least not about her or her fabrications.

It was raining steadily as they entered the deserted courtyard. CC was careful not to even glance at the well, but she didn't need to look at it to feel its ominous presence. They were almost to her room when the abbot stepped out of the shadows in the dimly lit hall.

"I see you found her, Andras." He smiled warmly at the knight, but when he turned to face CC, his expression changed to a sneer. "The good knight was worried about you, Princess, as well he should have been. I cannot imagine why you would choose to leave the monastery alone at night."

Courtesy, she reminded herself. She forced the annoyed sarcasm from her voice.

"I didn't think I was doing anything out of the ordinary. Maybe where I'm from women don't have to worry about being safe if they want to take a walk." Before either man could press the issue she added. "No! That does not mean that I've remembered anything else about where I'm from—unfortunately. Now if you will excuse me, I need sleep. Please have Isabel come help me get out of this wet dress."

She started to turn to open her door, but the abbot's voice stopped her.

"Isabel is already within. She is the reason we knew you were missing. When she came to your chamber to assist you, as you had requested, you were not there. She, too, was very worried, and she immediately reported your absence to me."

CC couldn't believe what she was hearing. She had specifically asked this jerk *not* to send for Isabel. Obviously, he was letting her know that he would be sure she was being watched, no matter what.

"I thought I asked that Isabel not be bothered to wait on me tonight. Perhaps it is because I'm so tired that my memory is not clear. I will apologize to Isabel for having worried her. I'm usually not so inconsiderate." She gave Andras a tight smile. "Good night, Andras. I am sorry that I worried you, too."

Her gaze shifted to the abbot and hardened. "I will be more careful in the future."

This time she had the door partially open when the priest's question stopped her.

"Princess Undine, what does the name *Wyking* mean to you?"

Wearily, she looked over her shoulder at him. The priest's glittering eyes were locked on her, but CC noticed that Andras wasn't looking at her at all, instead he was staring at Abbot William, and his expression said that the priest's question had come as quite a shock.

The word he had said sounded very much like *Viking*—which made sense, she realized. This was an island and the Vikings had done a lot of raiding during the Middle Ages along the coast of Europe, or at least she thought she remembered that they had. She opened her mouth to quip a fast answer, denying any knowledge of anything, even if the word sounded familiar, but an idea came to her.

Slowly and distinctly CC raised her chin and squared her shoulders, forcing the weariness out of her stance and replacing it with what she hoped was the regal bearing of a princess. She smiled cordially at the priest and said, "If you mean *Viking*"—she enunciated the word carefully—"to me it means tall, blond, vengeful warriors who do not like it when something that belongs to them is mistreated by another. Good night, gentlemen. Even a princess can get tired of answering questions."

Tall and blond, she stepped gracefully into her room, closing the door securely behind her.

CHAPTER SIXTEEN

THE unrelenting ache in CC's body caused her to wake early the next morning. It started in the pit of her stomach and traveled through her in a wave of pain. The distant sounds of the ocean spilled through her window, enticing and tormenting her at the same time. She lay with her eyes closed, breathing deeply and trying to quell her internal torment. Just one more night, she told herself, then she could rest in her natural form—and she could be with Dylan again.

"Dylan." She whispered the merman's name. Just the sound of it made her stomach flutter.

Last night she hadn't had the opportunity to think about what had happened between them. After her confrontation with Andras and the abbot, she had only been able to keep her eyes open long enough to apologize to a silent, sulking Isabel, get undressed and fall into bed. She thought she might have been asleep before her head had hit the hard, narrow cot.

But this morning she was completely awake. The soft gray of dawn filled her room with a hazy, slate-colored light, reminding her of last night's fog. CC smiled and stretched like a cat, the ache in her body suddenly secondary to the memory of pleasure. She longed to be with him again and not just so that they could make love—although she admitted to herself that she was eager to do that again, too. She wanted to hear his deep, caring voice as he explained the fascinating world beneath the seas to her. And she wanted to make him laugh. She wanted *him*, all of him.

"I love him." She spoke the words quickly, then covered her mouth like she had betrayed a secret. "Oh, Gaea," she breathed. "What are we going to do?"

Sitting up, she kicked her legs free from the scratchy blanket. The air force had trained her to act when there was a problem to be solved, not to sit around and worry. That morning she said a silent thank-you for her early crises training. She needed Gaea's help, and a plan to get it was already forming in her military brain. Not wanting to wait until Isabel decided to assist her, she rejected the multi-layered gown. Instead, she pulled on the raw wool robe that Isabel had left in her room and took off all of her jewelry except for Gaea's amulet. Then she rolled up the sleeves of the robe and used one of several long-stranded pearl necklaces as a belt. Satisfied with the results, CC remembered to make her bed before she quietly pulled open the heavy wooden door.

Peering into the hall, she listened intently. Nothing was moving, and no one was making any noise. She tiptoed silently down the hall, glad the soles of her slippers were soft and soundless. When she came to the entrance to the courtyard, she hesitated. No, she thought sternly. She absolutely did not want to chance facing Sarpedon. But she needed to get to the kitchen, and the entrance to the kitchen was on the other side of the dining room, which was on the other side of the courtyard. She closed her eyes and visualized the dining room. There had been, she counted in her head, the entrance from the courtyard, the entrance the servants used that had to lead to and from the kitchen and two others. Opening her eyes she looked down the shadowy hall that led away from the courtyard. It was, after all, a main hallway. It must lead to something that would eventually take her to the kitchen, she decided quickly. She'd definitely rather get lost and bumble into some lecherous monk's bedroom than come face-to-face with Sarpedon.

When the hall came to a T, CC chose the left-handed fork and breathed a sigh of relief when the smell of hot porridge drifted to her. Ahead she could see that the hall turned to the left again, and she thought that from there it would probably empty out into somewhere near the area of the dining room. Happily, she picked up her robe, ready to rush ahead, when she heard the sound of two familiar voices. She slowed, creeping noiselessly forward until she could make out their words, then she stopped, listening intently.

"But a Wyking?" Andras sounded as shocked as he had looked the night before when the priest had mentioned the word. "I would not have thought so."

"After the news you received last night, how can you doubt it? The heathen have been raiding the shores of the mainland anew. It is simply too coincidental that she was discovered at the same time. She was quite possibly involved in the raiding herself. It is known that the Wykings educate their women, so why not involve them in their plundering, too?"

"It is so difficult for me to believe. Are you certain, Father? She attended mass. And look at her tie to the Blessed Mother—how could one of the heathen be touched so?"

"She is a princess. She could easily have been nursed by a slave who had been captured from our shores. The poor woman probably tried her best to instill within Undine the true religion. You must remember, though, that she refused to take Holy Communion," he said, self-satisfied and smug. "My son, it was her beauty that deceived you." The abbot's voice turned warm and fatherly. "From the first I knew that she was evil. Look at the garish show of wealth in which she is swathed, and her unusually tall stature. And remember how outspoken and willful she became last night?"

CC pulled at her bottom lip, sorry she hadn't kept a better hold on her temper the night before.

"And I simply thought of her as exotic and beautiful."

Even though CC didn't love the knight, she felt stung at the betrayal in his words.

"The heathen mean to entice us to forget ourselves," came the priest's answer.

"Then my time here has been wasted, and my quest to find a wife who could dower Caer Llion back to its original state of glory has failed."

CC blinked in shock. Andras was on a wife hunt and her jewels and her title had made Undine look like the perfect prey. She shook her head in self disgust. Why should she be so surprised? Noblemen had been allying themselves with wealth and land for centuries. Actually, arranged marriages were probably the norm for ancient Wales. What would be unusual would be to marry for love. And she had to admit she did feel a sense of relief. The knight didn't love her. Sure, he desired her body, but at least she didn't have to feel guilty for breaking his heart.

"Let us not discard the princess's possibilities too hastily," continued Abbot William.

"You would have me ally Caer Llion with Norsemen?"

"Perhaps." CC could hear Andras begin to sputter a response, but the abbot interrupted. "True, the Wyking are heathen murderers, thieves and black-guards, but they have wealth. Caer Llion is far enough inland that you need not worry that her family could appear at your gate, so the alliance would be tenu-ous at best."

In other words, CC thought angrily, Andras should just take the money and the girl and run.

"Remember, once she is your wife, she is your property to do with as you so desire." The abbot's voice was sly. "And she would be beyond the reach of her heathen people. Of course, you would immediately have to correct her willful spirit and be sure that her religious training is completed."

"I had already decided that if she became my wife she would have to curb her tongue and end her unacceptable behavior." He made a sarcastic scoffing sound. "Walking alone at night is not the behavior of a good Christian wife!"

"Just remember the Rule of Thumb, my son." The priest's voice sounded pleased. "You may not strike her with anything thicker than your thumb, no matter how much she vexes you, or how deserving she is of harsher discipline."

CC's mouth dropped open in shock.

"It would not please me to strike her at all, but I do understand that it is my duty," Andras said.

"I have no doubt that you would do your duty."

CC thought the abbot sounded almost giddy at the prospect, but his tone shifted and became more serious as he continued.

"There is one thing that concerns me very much. I am not certain that her walking alone at night is entirely innocent."

CC tried to still her heart from beating as she strained to catch every word.

"She may have been attempting to contact her people."

CC blinked in surprise. How was she supposed to have done that?

"How could she, Abbot?" Andras echoed her question.

"For all of her supposed ties to the Holy Mother, I believe that she is heathen, and perhaps even a sorceress."

She clearly heard the knight's sharp intake of breath.

"She could have been casting a spell in an attempt to contact the Norsemen. Did you not notice how mysteriously the fog suddenly surrounded Caldei? It could have been her conjuration in an attempt to cover her use of the black arts. Since Undine's arrival, Caldei has been filled with a sense of unease." The abbot paused, and neither man spoke for several breaths.

"I, too, have felt something." Andras's voice was almost a whisper, but it carried to CC's listening ears like a church bell. "I have not wanted to speak of it, but I have felt discord within these good walls."

"I cannot help but agree with you, my son. The woman's presence here in some way is causing evil."

CC thought that the abbot sounded more pleased than upset at the prospect.

"And knowing this, you still think I should consider marriage with her?"

"The Rule of Thumb, my son. Do not forget the Rule of Thumb. And do not underestimate the power of a strong, God-fearing husband. I believe once she is away from the sea, and the possibility of contact with other heathen, she will be able to be controlled. Of course, you may choose not to marry her at all."

"Then what of Caer Llion?" Andras asked.

"The princess could be ransomed. True, a dowry would probably be more profitable than a single ransom payment, and the Wykings are notoriously difficult traders, but then you would be free of the problems she could create, and you would have at least a portion of the money needed for Caer Llion."

The priest sounded like he was considering trading an animal or buying a piece of property.

"I shall decide upon my course with the princess soon. It is not honorable to give the impression of courting her, when I am, in truth, only willing to ransom her."

CC was pleased to hear that the knight did sound sincere in his desire not to mislead her. He wasn't evil; he was just a man of his times.

"Do not fret, my son. There is no need for a hasty decision. If her powers were great enough to truly call forth the heathen, she certainly would not have allowed herself to be lost at all, and it will take some time for your squires to spread the news of her rescue so that it can reach her people. Perhaps their response will illuminate the path you need to take."

"As always, Father, I look to you for guidance."

"You were wise as a child, and you have grown into a fine man." The priest's voice was wistful. "I often wished that you were not your father's firstborn son, so that you could have entered the priesthood. But Caer Llion needs you, and my desire was not to be."

CC's eyebrows raised. She thought she knew just exactly what Abbot William's true desire was for the knight, even if Andras refused to read between William's very suggestive lines.

"You flatter me, Abbot."

"And you please me, my son . . ."

CC's mouth twisted in a grimace as she silently retraced her steps. She didn't need to listen to the conversation deteriorate into a "You're so great—No, *you're* so great" contest. And anyway, she'd heard what she needed. They believed that she was a heathen Viking who had magical powers.

Well, she thought, her grimace changing into a grin, one out of three wasn't too bad. She had magic. That she knew for sure. She also knew that she wasn't going to be anyone's chattel, whether that anyone was Andras or Sarpedon.

She walked several yards back down the hall before she turned and began making her way very noisily to the entrance to the dining room. Smiling, she began to loudly hum the USAF theme song, hearing the *"Off we go, into the wild blue yonder . . ."* singing in her head. She pretended not to notice the knight and the abbot until Andras cleared his throat, then she jumped and giggled girlishly.

"Oh, you frightened me! I didn't realize anyone else was in the room. Good morning, Andras, Abbot Williams. Isn't dawn a lovely time?"

"Good morning, Undine." The knight's voice sounded strained and unnatural.

"I am surprised by your attire, Princess Undine." The priest fluttered his fingers at the monastic robe she was wearing. "I would have thought our simple robes much too plain for your august tastes."

CC sighed and painted her face with a long-suffering expression. "So many people believe that princesses have to be constantly swathed in jewels and silk. It's simply not true. How would we get any work done?"

The priest raised a single, haughty eyebrow at her. "And what work could there be here for you to do, Princess?"

"I pledged that I would restore the statue of the Holy Mother," she admonished him. "It surprises me that you have forgotten such an important task."

For once the priest didn't have a glib comment waiting. CC realized that he really had forgotten and pressed her advantage, heading quickly for the servant's exit.

"I'll just go to the kitchen and have the servants lend me some cleaning supplies."

Andras finally found his tongue. Speaking quickly he said, "Undine, I can help you with collecting and carrying your supplies."

"No, Andras, this is something I need to do alone. I feel a special connection with the Virgin Mother, and I think it is important to her that she is cared for by another woman, but thank you. You always seem to be looking out for my welfare. I do appreciate your consideration very much." She smiled warmly at him and was pleased to see the knight shift guiltily in his seat.

"Princess Undine, will we be seeing you at evening mass today?" the abbot asked.

"Yes, Abbot William, I am pleased to say that you will be seeing a lot of me in the chapel. The statue of the Blessed Mother is in a sad state of disrepair, and it will take much work to be restored," she said over her shoulder as she disappeared into the servants' hall.

Ugh, what an awful man!

Chapter Seventeen

T HE hall did open into the kitchen area, which was a huge room, immaculately clean and lively. Hanging from the low-beamed ceiling were dozens of different types of herbs, many of which CC was pleased that she recognized. The walls of the kitchen were lined with hearths, both big and small. Isabel and three women whom CC had not seen before were busy preparing what would probably be the midmorning meal. None of them noticed CC in the shadowed doorway, and she took the opportunity to study them. It was easy to see a trend in the women chosen to be servants at the monastery. Each of them was old and in some way disfigured. The right side of the face of the woman kneading an impressive mound of bread dough was drooped and slack, giving her a partially melted appearance. The woman who was chopping potatoes and onions did so with one hand, holding her uselessly curled left hand tightly against her body. The third woman, who was plucking the feathers from a fat hen, did so hunched at an awkward angle caused by a large hump on her back.

CC felt the slow burn of anger in the back of her throat. The abbot might as well have had a huge sign hung around each woman's neck which read: i'm allowed here because men don't find me attractive. No wonder Isabel had disliked her on sight.

Over one low-burning fire was suspended a huge blackened kettle in which Isabel, her back to CC, was slowly adding crushed garlic and leaves of basil.

"It smells wonderful," CC said. Each woman jumped in surprise at the sound of her voice. CC smiled warmly at Isabel. "I didn't know you made the stew. If I had, I would have told you sooner how delicious it is. You're a magnificent cook."

CC couldn't be sure, but she thought the sudden flush on Isabel's shriveled cheeks might have been from pleasure at the unexpected compliment. She turned and included the other women in her smile.

"Good morning! It's sure nice to see female faces. I've felt kind of outnumbered lately." She nodded her head back toward the rest of the monastery. When the women didn't speak, but continued to stare, she just widened her smile. "My name is Undine."

This seemed to thaw them to action, and the three women dropped quick, awkward curtseys and mumbled hellos in her general direction. Isabel limped to her side.

"Princess, are you lost?"

"No, I came looking for the kitchen."

"I did not think you would awaken this early or I would have been there to help you dress."

"Oh, that's not why I was looking for the kitchen. I need to get some cleaning supplies to take to the chapel. I thought the kitchen would be a good place to find a bucket and some rags, as well as soap and water. Did I guess right?"

"Yes, Princess, but all you need do is to tell me what you wish cleaned; you need not supervise the details." The shock of CC's sudden appearance had passed and Isabel's tone had returned to being edged with thinly veiled sarcasm.

"Oh, I don't want you to do the cleaning—I will." CC was pleased when Isabel's eyes widened in surprise. "All I need is for you to show me where I can get the supplies." She looked at each woman as she continued speaking. "Did you know that there is a beautiful statue of the Virgin Mother in the chapel?" All of the women remained silent, but CC nodded her head at the group as if they had answered her. "Apparently, no one knew about it. It's such a tragedy. It's obviously been ignored and neglected for years. I found it yesterday during mass and I pledged to the Mother that I would restore it." She turned her smile back on Isabel, who was staring at her like she had totally lost her mind.

"You will clean it yourself?" Isabel asked, unsure she had heard CC correctly.

"Yes. I'm not afraid to get my hands wet," CC said, loving her own little private joke. "So, if you'll just point me to a bucket and some soap, I'll get to work."

Numbly, Isabel pointed to an area next to the humpbacked woman who had been plucking the chicken.

"Thank you!" CC said. Purposefully, she walked across the room and picked up an empty bucket.

"There is water in the barrel and rags and soap there, Princess." The humpbacked woman pointed to a cupboard near one of the smaller, oven-looking hearths.

CC smiled her thanks and grabbed a bucket. There was a large ladle hanging from the side of the freshwater barrel, and CC quickly filled her bucket, then she picked several clean rags and a crude bar of pungent-smelling soap from the cupboard.

"Which way to the chapel?" she asked Isabel.

"That hallway will take you to the gardens. Can you find your way from there, Princess?"

CC nodded. The bucket was heavy, and she was glad that Undine's body was tall and strong. Before she left the room she turned, speaking to all four women.

"I appreciate your help. And, please, you don't need to call me Princess. My name is Undine—and I'm just another woman in a place filled with men."

Pleased with her parting comment, her smile didn't waver even as she struggled her way across the perfect gardens, occasionally sloshing water onto her robes and pointedly ignoring the shocked stares from monks already busy with their morning chores.

"They act like they've never seen a woman work before," she mumbled. Climbing the steps up to the chapel she tried not to look at the horrific renditions of hell carved around the entrance, but her eyes couldn't help lingering on them. For some reason they were even more disturbing the second time she saw them, even though this time she was ready for them. She hesitated, searching the stone for some glimpse of hope or salvation, but every scene mirrored only desperation and despair—eternal damnation and pain.

"It's like an awful car wreck I can't look away from," she whispered. Shaking herself, she forced her eyes away from the macabre artwork and entered the dim, incense-saturated building. Even the soft gray light of dawn was bright compared to the darkness within, and CC stood still for a moment, blinking to accustom herself to the gloom.

The chapel was deserted except for two monks who knelt before the mound of flickering candles that were to the right of the nave. When they glanced back at her, she smiled a greeting to them. They acknowledged her with brief nods before returning to their monotonous chanting.

As if a magnet was drawing her, CC made her way along the rear of the chapel to the deeply shadowed left side. Two brightly burning candles beckoned her back to the forgotten statue. She paused in front of it, taking a moment after setting down the bucket to catch her breath. She hadn't been wrong. The lovely statue had Gaea's unmistakable face.

First, she thought, she must have more light. Without hesitation she strode to the table at the front of the nave. It was laden with unlit candles and long, dry pieces of twig that were obviously used for lighting them. Gathering as many as her voluminous robe could hold, she clanked her way back to the statue. Then she worked at placing the candles all around the statue and lighting them. As her little corner of the chapel blazed with light, she felt the eyes of the monks on her back. Glancing quickly over her shoulder she caught them looking at her.

"Brothers, please add to your prayers those for the renovation of the Virgin's statue. It is long overdue." Without waiting for their answer she turned back to the job before her.

It was worse than she had realized the day before. The statue was flaky and filthy, but that wasn't all. That entire side of the chapel appeared to have been ignored. Filth and spiders ruled supreme. When CC dipped the first cloth into the bucket she was sure she heard something slither into the shadows.

Gritting her teeth, she swiped the bar of soap against the damp cloth, telling herself over and over again that crawly things were more afraid of her than she was of them—even though she sincerely didn't know how that could possibly be true.

While she worked she thought and prayed. She asked Gaea for guidance and tried to sort through the tangle of her own feelings. It didn't take long for her to realize that understanding she was in love wasn't the answer to everything—instead it was the beginning of many more questions.

Soon she fell into a cleaning rhythm. She had always been fond of keeping things neat and in their proper places—that was one of the reasons the air force had been such a nice fit for her. Military clean was a good thing, not passionless and contrived like the gardens of the monastery; just everything in the place in which it belonged and everything in the best shape possible. CC tore one of the rags in half horizontally and used it to tie her thick hair back out of her way. Three times she made the trek through the garden to the kitchen for clean water. The women still didn't speak to her unless she spoke to them first, but Isabel had a mug of herbal tea and a hunk of bread ready for her after the second trip, and on her last trip the woman with the shriveled hand smiled shyly at her.

She did notice that the sun was well overhead and that the day was pleasantly warm, but she was too busy cleaning to pay attention to much else—until she straightened up, groaning and rubbing at a kink in her back. Stretching, she stepped back and studied her work.

"Oh!" she gasped, struck by the sudden beauty of the statue. The newly cleansed Virgin seemed to glow with life. The warm light of the many candles illuminated the blue of her dress and the deep gold of her hair, and it seemed like she was surrounded with a halo of soft color.

"You are doing a wonderful job, Daughter." Gaea's voice came from behind her, and CC turned to find the goddess perched on the edge of a nearby pew. Today she was wearing a gown made of silk so white and ethereal that it looked like the goddess had found a way to capture a cloud and wrap herself within it.

CC glanced around the chapel. She had no idea when the two monks had left, but she was relieved to see that the building was deserted.

"I'm glad you think so." She wiped her wet hands on the dirt-smudged robe and walked over to Gaea. With a sigh she sank down to the floor at the goddess's feet. Leaning against the pew, she smiled up at Gaea. "It's tiring work, cleaning all that gunk away."

Gaea's eyes drifted back to the statue. "She has been forgotten for years. I want you to know that you are washing away more than simple dirt. You are washing away hatred and neglect."

"How could I do that? I don't understand."

"You will, Daughter. You will." The goddess reached out and smoothed a strand of hair back from CC's face. At her touch, CC felt some of the weariness leave her. "Now, I sense that you have come to a decision. Are you ready to tell me?"

CC nodded. Looking into the goddess's eyes she said, "I'm in love with Dylan, and I want to spend my life with him."

For an instant CC thought she saw an incredible sadness pass over Gaea's face, but the emotion was gone so quickly that she wondered if it had just been her imagination.

"Dylan is a wise choice," Gaea said, touching CC's cheek in a motherly caress.

"You mean except for the fact that I can't live in the sea without Sarpedon killing him and raping me?" CC put her chin in her hands and rested her elbows on her drawn-up knees.

"I must simply petition Lir on your behalf."

CC glanced sideways at her, not fooled by the lightness in the goddess's voice.

"If it was really that simple you would have done it before now," CC said.

"You did not know you loved Dylan until now," Gaea countered.

"Do you think Lir will listen to you?" CC asked tentatively, almost afraid to hope.

Gaea's smile was one of a seductress. "He has before. You are proof of that."

CC almost rolled her eyes and said she didn't want to hear the details, but she caught herself in time. Then she looked up to see the goddess watching her with sparkling eyes, and they both began to laugh.

"There are some things all daughters do not want to know," Gaea said, wiping mirthful tears from her eyes.

"You're right about that," CC said, then added, "Actually, you're right about most things. So, I'd like to know, do you think I'm making the right decision in choosing Dylan?"

"Before I answer you, I would like you to answer one question for me, Daughter. And do not ponder your answer; I want to know the first thought that comes to your mind." The question shot out. "What do you love most about the merman?"

Without hesitation CC answered, "His kindness."

"Ah," the goddess breathed. "I see. Then, yes, I believe you have made a wise choice, for when the thrill of his body fades or changes, and the difficulties of pledging yourself to only one person surface, kindness will be the balm that soothes the wounds of life."

"Thank you, Mother," CC said softly, her eyes filled with tears.

Unexpectedly, Gaea found that she, too, had to blink back tears, and she cleared her throat delicately before she could speak again.

"I will call to Lir tonight. Perhaps I will have news for you as soon as tomorrow night."

CC felt her heart skip. "Then maybe I won't have to change back into human form at all!"

Gaea returned the young woman's smile, careful to keep any sadness from showing on her face. "Perhaps," she repeated. "But remember, child, the immortals have their own timetable, and gods, particularly, do not like to be rushed. Lir may take some persuading." Gaea waggled her eyebrows suggestively.

CC pulled a face at her, and they sat together in compatible silence, each woman lost in dreams of the future, as the goddess slowly stroked her daughter's hair.

After several minutes CC said, "You know, it's not just the statue that is in bad shape over here." With a flick of her wrist she gestured, encompassing that entire side of the chapel. "This whole area is a mess. It's like someone purposely wanted this part of the chapel to repel people. You wouldn't believe all the filth I've found, and all I've focused on so far has been the statue." She pointed into the thickly shadowed corners. "I haven't started cleaning over there, yet, but it smells like some animal has used this place as a toilet. It's disgusting."

Gaea shook her head sadly. "It is what William has allowed, even encouraged. Having the statue of the Mother forgotten was not enough for him. He wanted it fouled and desecrated."

"Why? What's wrong with him?" CC asked.

"William is a complicated soul, and an excellent example of what happens to a man when he embraces all the negative aspects of power. He controls through fear and manipulation, preying on the weakness of others so that his own weaknesses will not be discovered. That is a particularly dangerous path for a man who has chosen the priesthood. Instead of embracing love, he encourages his followers to turn to fear and denial for salvation. In truth, he is a very passionate man, who at one time had a great deal of love to give." Gaea sighed. "Now he is a sad, twisted man. I pity him, but I am relieved that you will not have to stay near him for much longer." The goddess shook back her hair like she was flinging away a bad habit. "Enough of such morose thoughts! I must ready myself to call Lir, but first I believe I should give my hardworking daughter a little aid with her task."

The goddess approached the statue. Surprised, CC stood and followed her. Gaea stopped in front of the newly cleaned Virgin.

"Yes, I remember well that the devoted young sculptor wanted to add a little something to the hair, but the abbot who commissioned the work could not afford it. . . ." Gaea's words faded as she smiled secretly to herself.

"You knew the man who sculpted this?" CC asked, intrigued with the idea.

"Of course! How do you think he copied my features so well?" She smiled mischievously at CC. "I pretended to be a shepherdess who just happened to cross his path as he was praying for inspiration for the Virgin's statue. It was a pleasure to grant the prayers of such a talented artist." Her playful smile widened. "I have always believed art should not be controlled by one's purse. Do you agree, Daughter?"

Grinning, CC nodded.

"Good! Then I shall complete the sculptor's work."

CC watched as the goddess held open her left hand, palm up. With her right hand she swirled the air above her palm until CC could clearly see a little tornado of sparkles that looked like floating gold dust. Speaking to the swirling dust, the goddess intoned, *"Complete what the artist began. So have I spoken; so shall it be."* Then she blew gently on the little spiral and it burst apart. In a shower of golden waterfall, it rained down on the statue, settling like a fairy cloud into Mary's hair. For an instant more it twinkled and glistened magically, then Gaea made a little clucking sound, tongue against teeth.

"Not so brightly, beautiful ones," she said, and the twinkling died to the more earthly shine of plain, pressed gold.

"It's so lovely!" CC exclaimed, then she sobered. "But won't this cause Abbot William to ask me a lot of difficult-to-answer questions, like 'How did you cast a spell on the statue, Princess?'" CC scowled, imitating the abbot's simpering tone.

Gaea laughed lightly. "No, child, then he would have to admit that he knew what the holy statue looked like in its glory, thus proving that he purposefully allowed it to be forgotten and misused." She shook her head. "That would open too many difficult-to-answer questions for him. There are still good people left at Caldei, people who would be upset by the intentional desecration of the Virgin's image. William does not want to do anything to awaken them from their apathy." She took her daughter's hand. "But know that even though he will not mention its gilding, he will recognize that it has been added to the statue, and he will know that you are responsible. Beware of him, especially tonight and tomorrow when I may be otherwise occupied and unable to come quickly if you have need of me."

"I'll be care—" she started to say, but the sound of someone entering the chapel interrupted them.

CC glanced at the doors to see the distinctive shape of Isabel's limping body framed against the outside light. Suddenly the goddess was gone. CC sighed, but put on a happy face as Isabel approached.

Isabel looked around the sanctuary. "I thought I heard you talking to someone, Princess."

"I was just talking to the Holy Mother, telling her how wonderful she looks."

The old woman turned her questioning gaze to the statue and her eyes widened, instantly filling with tears. Trembling, she approached the Virgin and dropped to her knees in front of her with a grace that surprised CC.

"Look at her! I have never seen anything so beautiful. It is as if the Holy Mother glows with life." Isabel bowed her head and clasped her hands. When she was finished praying she genuflected and rose unsteadily to her feet. Then she turned to face CC.

"You did this. You brought her back to life. Thank you," Isabel said simply.

"There's no need to thank me, Isabel. And anyway, in a place filled with men, women need to stick together. Don't you think so?"

"Yes, Princess."

This time when Isabel used the title she did so with a smile, changing it from a formality to a term of endearment. CC could hardly believe how that genuine smile transformed the old woman's face. For the first time CC glimpsed the more youthful Isabel that hid behind the old woman's mask of bitterness.

"You must be hungry, Undine. You have worked through the day. It is almost time for vespers."

CC was surprised that so much time had passed. "It seems like it shouldn't even be midday yet." She looked down at her grimy robe. "Much as I would like to stay and watch the monks' reactions when they first see our statue, I don't think I'm dressed appropriately for vespers."

Isabel's face had split into another happy grin when CC used the word *our*, to describe the statue, and CC felt a rush of pleasure at the old woman's obvious joy.

"Let us change this soiled robe for clean clothes," Isabel said.

"Clean clothes sound wonderful," CC said.

She emptied the bucket of filthy water outside, and she and Isabel walked slowly through the garden, chattering about what cleaning supplies CC would need the next morning to continue the renovation.

They took a little turn in the path and walked through an area of the gardens that CC didn't recognize. That part of the gardens lacked flowers, but on either side of the path were sectioned off row after row of small, neat-looking plants. CC paused to take a closer look at the greenery.

"Oh!" she said with a delighted gasp. "Herbs! Isabel, look." CC tiptoed carefully between the rows, then she bent and brushed her hand over the nearest plant. It had dark green leaves with slightly jagged edges. She inhaled deeply the wonderful scent. "Mint." Her gaze shifted and she caressed other leaves. "And basil, cilantro and parsley." She laughed. "No, I mean parsley and cilantro. It's easy to get the two mixed up." She smiled up at Isabel who was staring at her in open surprise.

"You have knowledge of herbs?"

CC nodded. "Not as much as I wish I did, but I've always grown things. I love digging in the dirt and knowing that it was from my own efforts that the mint in my tea tastes so wonderful. Actually," she paused, choosing her words carefully so that she wouldn't offend the old woman. "Have you ever thought about adding mint to your amazing stew? I think it would compliment the mutton very well."

The old woman blinked owlishly.

"I didn't mean to offend you," CC said quickly, worried at Isabel's silence. "Your stew is already the best I've ever tasted."

"You have not offended me. You have surprised me. I believe I have been mistaken in my judgment of you, Undine, and when I am mistaken I do not dawdle about making corrections. I must ask that you forgive me."

"There's nothing to forgive." CC's smile reflected her pleasure at the old woman's words. "You didn't know me, and I didn't know you. Let's just call it a misunderstanding."

"A misunderstanding," the old woman repeated. "I like that. I also like your idea for adding mint to my stew. Shall we harvest some?"

"Together." CC grinned.

"Yes. Together." Isabel returned the grin and the two women began breaking off the tops of the fragrant herb.

Isabel's apron was filled with mint, and she and CC were talking amiably about the many uses of cilantro when they entered the kitchen. The other three women looked up, surprise clearly showing on their aged faces.

Isabel dumped the mint on the nearest counter. Several tendrils of silver hair had escaped from her bun and they curled wildly around her face. She pushed them behind her ears and grinned, suddenly reminding CC of a young girl.

"Undine has given me a wonderful idea for the evening stew." Isabel looked at each of the other women. "The princess is wise in the way of herbs."

"Well, I wouldn't call it wise. I just like working with plants, and I like to use them in my own cooking," CC said, a little embarrassed at Isabel's unexpectedly effusive praise.

"It is a wise woman who understands the ways of herbs." The humpbacked lady spoke softly.

CC smiled at the old woman. "I like to work with my hands. It makes me feel good when I've finished something, and I know that it's a job well done."

"Oh, you must see the Holy Mother!" Isabel exclaimed. "It is a miracle!"

"It is not a miracle," the woman with the shriveled hand grumped. "It is plain to see that the princess simply took the filth from the Mother and placed it on herself!" Then she cackled uproariously at her own joke.

The other women were silent, looking at CC to see if she took offense.

"I still think it can be classified as a miracle," CC said seriously. "Have you ever known any reason for a *princess* to get this dirty, I mean, unless she was terribly clumsy and she fell off her knight's charger as he was whisking her away to their golden castle?" She placed the back of her mint-stained hand against her smudged forehead and attempted her own rendition of a princessly swoon.

Isabel chuckled. "Princess, I think you need to practice your swoon. It does not seem very . . ." She searched for a word.

". . . believable," the slack-faced woman finished for her, slurring the word slightly.

"Not believable!" CC pretended offense, pressing her hand against her heart. "You've wounded me!"

"Oh, posh," the woman with the shriveled hand said. "You are too tough to be wounded so easily."

CC smiled at them. "Well, perhaps the four of you would care to demonstrate for me a believable swoon?"

Four pairs of sparkling eyes looked at her, then at one another. Then mayhem broke loose as each old woman, amidst much laughter and sighing, staggered around the kitchen, demonstrating her own version of a believable swoon.

CC couldn't remember when she'd laughed so hard. She'd just fallen into a chair, holding her side and begging the women to stop, when a monk CC recognized as Brother Peter burst into the kitchen.

"What is happening in this room?" he yelled. Then he came to an abrupt halt when he noticed CC.

The women sobered instantly, and CC clearly saw fear flash in their eyes.

She stood quickly, addressing the monk in what she hoped was the snotty, imperious tone of royal command. "You are Brother Peter, aren't you?"

The monk nodded. "Yes, Princess."

"As you can see by the filthy state of my garment, I have been cleaning the Virgin Mother's statue all day. It is tiresome, tedious work, and I needed some levity. Of course I didn't want to trouble any of the Holy Brothers, so I came looking for Isabel. I commanded that she and these other servants amuse me." She wafted her hand absently in the direction of the frozen women. "I am finished being amused now." She smiled graciously at the confused-looking monk. "Thank you for coming to check on me. Please give the abbot my regrets that I must miss mass this evening, but as you can see I am not dressed for vespers." She turned her back on him dismissively.

"Yes, Princess," he said and hurried from the room.

When she was sure he was gone she said to the women, "The monks don't have much fun, do they?"

The women slowly thawed, making scoffing sounds in their throats.

"It doesn't mean we can't," CC said. The women threw her doubtful looks.

"Abbot William says mirth is sinful," Isabel said, only this time her voice didn't sound smug, as it had the other times she had repeated the abbot's dictums to CC; this time she sounded tired and sad.

"How about what Jesus said?" CC asked, and all four pairs of eyes were instantly attentive. "He said, 'Suffer the little children to come unto me.' Well, children, especially little children, laugh and play and have fun all the time. You'd think if happiness was some big sin, then Christ would have said something like, 'Suffer the little children to shut up or I'll beat them and oppress them into heaven.' Wouldn't he?"

"You make an excellent point, Undine," the woman with the shriveled hand said.

"What is your name?" Undine asked her.

"Lynelle," she answered with a bright smile, showing lots of big, yellow teeth.

"And yours?" Undine asked the woman with the partially paralyzed face.

"Bronwyn," she slurred.

"My name is Gwenyth," the lady with the humpback volunteered before CC could ask.

"Ladies, it is a great honor to meet you. I am the Princess Undine Who Can't Remember Anymore Than Her Name," CC said in her best imitation of a British queen. Her audience cackled appreciatively. Then she dropped into the bow of a prima ballerina—and almost fell face first onto the floor when her back foot caught in the hem of her robe.

Laughing, Isabel caught her. "Perhaps I should help you out of this robe."

CC smiled at her. "And into something more queenly?"

"Of course," Isabel said, mimicking CC's royal imitation. "After you, my lady."

Both of them backed from the kitchen, waving royally at their laughing "subjects."

"Is there any possible way I could take a bath?" CC asked as they made their way through the deserted dining room.

Isabel patted her hand. "Go to your room. I will get the tub. If you stand in it, I will pour the water over you."

"Can I be naked?"

Isabel tried unsuccessfully to stifle a smile. "If you insist."

"I insist," CC said firmly.

"I do not actually leave my chemise on while I bathe," the old woman admitted.

"I knew that," CC said.

Isabel wrinkled her heavily lined forehead in surprise. "How did you know?"

CC sniffed in her direction. "You don't smell bad."

CC could hear the old woman's chuckles long after she disappeared to fetch the tub.

CHAPTER EIGHTEEN

Cc's stomach let out a very unladylike growl as Isabel finished lacing up her outer gown.

"Forgotten to eat, have you?" Isabel laughed.

"Please tell me there's some of your wonderful stew left."

"For you, yes. After all, you are the one who thought of adding the mint."

"It was good?"

"It was wonderful. I think Bronwyn was so impressed that she may even have saved you a loaf of her excellent bread."

"That sounds great," CC said as they hurried down the hall. "Do you think the monks will still be at evening mass? I'm really tired, and I'd rather not have to make conversation with the abbot and Andras." The hard physical labor of cleaning and scrubbing all day coupled with the ever-present ache for the water had exhausted her, and the last thing CC needed was to spar with the abbot or fend off Andras's attempts at courtship.

CC could feel Isabel's gaze. When she spoke, the old woman's voice sounded wise. "It is obvious that you and the abbot dislike one another, which is certainly no surprise. Abbot William disapproves of beauty, and you are beauty personified. Even I judged you harshly because of your appearance."

CC started to say something, but Isabel shook her head, not wanting to be interrupted. "No, do not excuse me. I am old enough to recognize when my behavior is foolish. So that explains why you would have hard feelings for the abbot, but I do not understand why you are not pleased by the attentions of Sir Andras. It seemed at first as if you enjoyed his company, but I have been observing the two of you. Of late it appears you are more often annoyed or distracted when you are with him than not."

"I didn't think I was being so obvious."

"It is only apparent when you are very tired." Isabel smiled at her. "And perhaps only then to another woman."

They began walking across the courtyard, and CC chewed her bottom lip, not sure how much she should admit to Isabel. She glanced at the silent well, but it looked like an ordinary pile of stone. Well, she thought, at least she's not asking me about that.

"Forgive me, Undine, if I have asked too personal a question," Isabel said.

"No," CC assured her. "I don't mind that you asked. I was just trying to figure out how best to answer you." She sighed, and decided on telling her the truth—or at least as much of the truth as she could. Liars didn't make good friends, and CC very much wanted to be the old woman's friend. "You're right. At first I thought I might be able to care about him, maybe even love him. He seemed nice, and he's certainly handsome enough."

Isabel made an appreciative noise and nodded.

"But the more time I've spent with him, and the better I've come to know him, the more obvious it is that he's not the man for me. It's not that he's a horrible guy or anything like that. It's not even really his fault. The truth is that he and I are mismatched." CC bent her head to Isabel's and lowered her voice. "And this morning I overheard him talking to the abbot about me. They were discuss-

ing whether or not he should marry me and it sounded like they were considering buying a brood mare or a piece of property."

Isabel raised her eyebrows. "And this surprised you, Undine?"

"Not really." CC sighed. "But I would never marry a man who thought of
me as his property."

Isabel blinked slowly at her. "You must be from a land far away."

"That's one thing we know for certain," CC said firmly. "Another thing is
that I'm sure that not all males think of women as property. Some of them are
kind and respectful and consider us partners in life." CC's voice softened as she
thought of Dylan.

"So you love another?" The old woman's eyes twinkled, and CC couldn't
help but smile in return.

"Whore!" The word hissed through the air behind them.

Both women gasped and spun around to face Andras. The knight was
wide-eyed and so unnaturally pale that he looked ghostly. His blond hair was
in wild disarray, and his eyes flamed with an ominous silver light.

"Whore!" he hissed. *"Do not think you have fooled us. We know what you
really are. We know you are not pure. You have whored yourself and you will pay
the price for your betrayal!"*

CC shivered at the eerie sound of his words. They echoed from his mouth
with an otherworldly force. *We?* Who was he talking about? Her thoughts raced
through her mind as she glanced at the well. Hovering above it CC could see
inky waves, like heat rising from the top of a sun-baked blacktop road.

"Go get help!" CC whispered frantically to Isabel.

"No! I will not leave you," she whispered back. Then she made a shooing
gesture at the knight and spoke sharply in the confident voice of an irritated
grandmother, "Go on, Sir Andras, leave the Princess be. If the two of you have
had a misunderstanding, there are other ways to solve it. I do not think the
abbot would approve of your ungentlemanly words."

The knight's eyes slitted as he answered Isabel. *"Yes, we have had a misunderstanding."* Snakelike, his glowing eyes shifted to Undine. *"One that can only
be righted when we have been joined together. I will have what is mine by right!"*

Before CC could move, Andras lunged forward and grabbed her wrist in a
vicelike grip.

At his touch, the amulet of the goddess began to radiate heat. CC could feel
its power building swiftly.

"*Stop this foolish charade,*" the disembodied voice whispered hot words into her ear. "*You cannot alter the ending. You will be mine.*"

She met the silver eyes and spoke directly to the spirit which possessed the knight. "Never! I will never be yours, Sarpedon." CC concentrated on the power of the goddess that burned within the stone hanging between her breasts. She could feel it like she felt the ebb and flow of the tide. The power was fluid, and she knew it was hers to claim. In a blindingly swift motion, CC cast the power of the amulet down her and struck the knight a stinging blow across his cheek.

Andras shrieked as the might of the goddess knocked him away from CC. He doubled over and fell to his knees. From where she stood, CC watched the dark fumes dissolve down into the well.

Except for the sounds of the knight's ragged breathing, the courtyard was silent. CC felt weak, like the blow she had delivered had drained her of all her strength. She stumbled back a little, and Isabel rushed to give her a steadying hand.

"My son! What is it?"

The abbot strode into the courtyard, his red robe flapping behind him like a crimson flag. Several monks hurried after him, looking like confused white mice. The priest closed the space between them and helped Andras to his feet.

"Abbot William, the knight—" Isabel began with a shaking voice, but CC cut her off.

"He must have fainted." CC finished for her, squeezing her hand to keep her quiet. "Isabel was escorting me to dinner, and we found Andras lying here in the courtyard. He wasn't moving. It was quite a shock."

"Yes," Isabel added. "I would have gone immediately for help, but the princess was so distraught that I didn't feel I could leave her."

CC sent her a grateful look.

"Then Andras started to move, which is when you came into the courtyard."

Everyone turned to the knight. The glow in his eyes had completely extinguished, and his features had returned to normal. His expression was dazed. Sweat plastered his hair to his head and darkened wet circles under his tunic.

"I-I remember hearing Undine's voice." He shook his head in an attempt to clear the confusion from his mind. "And the amulet. I remember the amulet." He raked a trembling hand through his wet hair. "Then I remember nothing more until I heard your voice, Father."

"Do not fear, my son. We will discover what it is that has clouded your mind." His voice was gentle and fatherly. "Since its influence fled from my presence, whatever has affected you must be of the darkness because it flees the light of God."

The priest wasn't looking at the knight as he spoke; instead he studied CC. She could feel it when his gaze found the amber teardrop that hung on its long, silver chain. In the evening light it looked darker than its usual golden brown. Automatically, CC touched the amulet. The warmth that still radiated there comforted her. The abbot stepped closer to CC, narrowing his eyes as he peered at the pendant.

"What is this heathen talisman?" His voice lost its gentle charm when he addressed CC. "Take it off and let me examine it."

CC shook her head. "It is not heathen, and I can't take it off. It's a gift from my mother."

The priest's eyes were slits. "Now you have memory of a mother?"

"I remember her love and I remember her gift," CC said defiantly.

"I shall examine this gift," he sneered.

He walked toward her in slow motion, and all CC could think was that she knew the amulet *would* burn him. It had not failed to turn negative energy away from her, and the priest was one large ball of negative energy. His little piglike eyes glared at her, and she felt like she was going to hyperventilate.

That's it! she thought. And with a sigh that would have made Lynelle, Bronwyn and Gwenyth proud, CC swooned dramatically.

Thankfully, Isabel's strong arms were there to catch her, and both women tumbled to the ground. CC lay half in the servant's lap as Isabel rocked her like a child. Gulping air, she fluttered her eyelashes, pretending partial consciousness.

"Poor thing!" Isabel said. "She has had almost nothing to eat today. The child has been toiling since dawn for the Holy Mother." Out of the corner of her vision, CC could see several of the monks cross themselves reverently at the mention of the statue. "Here!" CC felt a tug as Isabel grasped the amulet firmly in her callused palm. "It does not burn. It is but a gift from a loving mother. Sir Andras has had an unfortunate apoplectic attack. The good knight is not in his right mind. He obviously needs your aid, as the princess needs mine." Isabel spoke with a firmness that appeared to shock the abbot into silence.

"Oh, Isabel, I feel so weak," CC gasped. "What happened?"

Isabel smoothed back CC's hair. "Hush, lamb, all is well. You will recover when you have eaten."

Struggling to her feet, the old woman pulled CC up with her. "Now I beg you to excuse us, Abbot. I will see that the princess is cared for and then retires for the night."

Isabel began limping towards the door to the dining room, one arm wrapped protectively around CC's waist. The sea of silent monks parted for them.

"Until we understand exactly what caused the attack on Sir Andras, I will post one of the Brothers outside the princess's door—to keep her from *harm*." The whiplike sound of the abbot's voice caused the women to pause.

CC kept a tight hold on Isabel as she half-turned to face the priest. He had moved back to the knight's side and his hand was resting protectively on Andras's shoulder.

"Thank you for your concern for my safety," CC said, allowing her voice to sound weak and shaky.

"I have concern for all of the lost . . ." The abbot's voice drifted after them as the women left the courtyard.

"I don't want to eat in the dining room," CC whispered to Isabel in the hall. Isabel nodded in understanding, and they headed for the servant's entrance to the kitchen.

Lynelle was the first to notice them. Her look of welcome shifted instantly to one of concern.

"Sir Andras attacked her," Isabel said grimly, leading CC over to a roughly carved stool that sat near the center workstation. "She needs food and drink."

The four women went to work like a well-oiled machine, and soon CC was eating a steaming bowl of Isabel's excellent mint-flavored stew and taking turns sipping from a mug of herbal tea and a goblet of rich red wine.

"Drink all of the tea," Bronwyn slurred as she and the other women hovered henlike around CC. "It is chamomile and rosehips. It will help to soothe your upset stomach."

"And drink all of the wine," Lynelle rasped in her grumpy voice. "It will help with everything else."

CC smiled weakly at the old women.

Isabel offered her a second helping of the stew, which CC enthusiastically accepted. As Isabel placed the steaming bowl in front of her, she asked, "Have you recovered enough to explain?"

The other women paused in their chores, their interest piqued. CC nodded slowly.

"The knight was not himself?"

"No, he wasn't," CC answered, meeting Isabel's gaze squarely.

"He seemed to be possessed," Isabel said.

CC heard the shocked gasps from the old women, but she kept her eyes on Isabel.

"Yes. Andras was possessed by a creature named Sarpedon. I was escaping from him when the knight found me washed up on the shore."

Isabel nodded. "I knew it. I could clearly see the change in the knight, and that was the name you used when you spoke to him." The old woman took a deep breath before she asked her next question. "You did not want the abbot to touch your amulet. Why?"

The room fell silent waiting for the answer.

"Because I didn't know what he would feel if he touched it. What did you feel?"

"Warmth," Isabel said simply.

CC nodded. "Because you don't wish me harm. Sarpedon did, and the amulet protects me. I think the abbot wishes me harm, too. I didn't know what would happen if he touched it."

"Are you a sorceress?" Isabel asked.

Still meeting her eyes, CC shook her head. "No, I'm not."

"But how do you know?" Gwenyth broke in breathlessly. "You cannot remember your past."

"I remember more about my past than I can admit to you right now, and I'm sorry about that. I can assure you, though, that I am not a sorceress." CC looked at each woman as she spoke. "But I do believe that women have magic. I don't mean anything dark and sinful. I just mean that I think that there is something special inside of us, and it's a part of what makes us women. I don't think you have to be young or beautiful or a princess to have it—you just have to be female and willing to listen within and to believe."

The room was silent as CC continued eating, but the silence didn't feel tense, instead it felt thoughtful.

"I had no idea I would be putting to use what you taught me this afternoon so quickly," CC said, breaking the silence with a smile.

CC was surrounded by looks of confusion until Isabel threw back her head and laughed.

"It was a ruse! The swoon was a ruse," Isabel said gleefully, nudging the two women nearest her. "You should have seen our princess. Like a delicate flower folding, she crumpled into my arms." Isabel did a rough imitation of CC's faint and the women cackled happily.

"Probably not as believable as my swoon," Lynelle grumbled before winking at CC and refilling her wine.

CC drank the last of the wine, grateful for the warm buzz in her stomach that helped offset the ache within her that seemed to be getting stronger by the minute. Now that work or talk wasn't distracting her, desire for the sea rolled through her and coupled with the longing she felt for Dylan, almost caused her to wince with the pain. Tomorrow night, she reminded herself. Then maybe she would never have to leave the water or Dylan again.

"You are tired, Undine. Come, let me take you to your chamber," Isabel said gently.

"Thank you, ladies. I appreciate all of you. Dinner was delicious—almost as good as the company. And thank you for trusting me."

A medley of "Sleep well, Princess" followed CC and Isabel from the room.

In the middle of the dining room, CC paused. "I don't want to walk back through the courtyard. Can we go the other way?"

"Certainly," Isabel said, changing direction for the doorway at the far end of the room through which CC had entered that morning.

"The creature's spirit comes from the well, doesn't it?" Isabel asked in a low voice.

CC glanced at the old woman. Then she nodded. "He is using the well to enter the monastery."

Isabel looked sharply at CC. "Can this thing harm you?"

CC shook her head slowly. "Not directly, but he can cause all kinds of problems for me, like he did this evening. And I worry what would happen if the abbot or even Sir Andras realize what is happening." CC turned to Isabel and grasped the old woman's gnarled hands. "Thank you so much for not betraying me to the abbot."

Isabel's smile was motherly. "As you have already said, women must stick together."

"And we certainly did stick together."

The women shared a satisfied smile that was decidedly feminine. They continued down the dim hall, swinging their joined hands.

"I am relieved to hear that the evil spirit cannot harm you. But I would also be relieved to know . . ." Isabel said haltingly.

"No, I don't think he is able to possess you and the other ladies." CC cocked her head to the side and grinned at her. "That is unless any of you are harboring hidden lusts for my body."

Isabel cackled and it took several moments for her to answer CC. "I feel confident that I speak truly for the other women when I say we feel no such desires for you."

"I'm glad to hear it."

Isabel snorted, and CC laughed.

They walked on a little way before CC spoke again. "I have to stay at the monastery for a little while longer."

Isabel flashed her a look of understanding. "You are safe here."

"Yes, and my family is helping me."

"As is the Holy Mother," Isabel said with certainty.

CC squeezed her hand. "Yes, the Great Mother is helping me."

They turned the corner. A plump little monk knelt near the door to CC's room. He appeared to be deep in prayer.

"Your guard," Isabel whispered.

"More like a jailer," CC whispered back.

The women exchanged grim looks as they entered CC's room, ignoring the kneeling monk.

CHAPTER NINETEEN

CC warred with herself. She wanted to climb through the window, rush down the path to the sea and hurl herself into its wet comfort. She missed Dylan, and, of course, she worried for him, too. She knew he waited for her, just as surely as she knew Sarpedon hunted for a way to possess her.

Her skin crawled at the memory of his glowing eyes and the touch of his hand on her skin. Gaea had told her not to be afraid of the merman's spirit, but

Andras's use of the word *we* had frightened her. He had said *we* know that you are not pure. Did that mean Sarpedon knew she loved Dylan? Or was he talking about an imagined affair with Andras? If Sarpedon had access to Andras's mind when he possessed the knight, he would know that Andras and Undine were not lovers, which gave the *we* an ominous meaning. He probably knew about Dylan. Wouldn't she just endanger Dylan if she went to him again?

And then, of course, she had to worry about the abbot. Before the incident in the courtyard, he already believed Undine was a Viking witch. The events of the day had done nothing but support his belief, and that definitely made CC uneasy.

Tossing fretfully in her narrow bed she wanted desperately to call to Gaea, but she knew she couldn't. Gaea would be busy with Lir, and CC couldn't interrupt her just to ask her a string of self-serving questions. CC sighed. She needed Dylan. She ached to have the comfort of his arms wash away the poison of Sarpedon's lust, and the pain of being separated from the sea, but tonight the answer had to be that she stay safely in her room and try to sleep. She closed her eyes. She'd dreamed of Dylan once before, maybe tonight she would again. . . .

DYLAN swam restlessly back and forth along the shore. He could feel Christine's need as clearly as he had felt her fear earlier that night—a fear that had to have been caused by Sarpedon. The merman must have found her in the monastery and discovered some way to accost her. Dylan's jaw clenched. He could feel it when she used the power of the goddess to thwart Sarpedon's attack. If only he could be there beside her!

A school of giant angelfish fled from his path as his rage caused the surrounding waters to froth and boil. He felt another surge of frustration as Christine struggled alone on land against her need.

"By Lir's trident, there must be something I can do!" Dylan raged.

"To begin with, you could change your curses. Evoking the power of Lir will not aid you at all if what you desire is on land." Gaea's lilting voice was a song as it carried clearly over the waves.

"Gaea!" Dylan exclaimed.

With powerful strokes, he propelled himself to the shoreline. The goddess was sitting on an old piece of driftwood, dangling her feet in the surf. She was clothed in a dress the color of night, but it shimmered with the reflection of the water as if it was made of liquid velvet.

"Your daughter needs me, Great Mother," Dylan said respectfully. His chest heaved as he tried to catch his breath.

The goddess's gaze was sharp. "Are you saying that you feel her need, merman?"

Dylan's fist closed over his heart. "As if it were my own."

Gaea's eyes warmed. "Yes, I can see that. You and Christine are linked. Your souls have found their match. It is a rare and wondrous thing, but it is a double-edged sword. Her pain is yours, as yours is hers."

"I would have it no other way."

"What is it you wish of me, Dylan?" she asked so softly that the merman had to strain to hear her.

"Grant me human form!" he said in a rush of words. "Allow me to go to her and comfort her."

Gaea tapped one slender finger against the driftwood as she considered the merman's request.

"My father was of the land. That must bind me to you in some way," Dylan beseeched. "I ask only for a temporary form. Allow me the remainder of this one brief night as a human man."

"It is true that you have a tie to the Earth. But this bond is mortal, as was your father. If I gift you with the form of a human, it will strengthen the part of you that is mortal. The cost could be high, Dylan. You may age. You certainly will become more vulnerable to injury, especially if you are wounded by an immortal." Gaea's beautiful voice was sad.

"Christine needs me."

The goddess sought and held the merman's steady gaze. She read clearly there his love for Christine. And she could feel Christine's soul, too, as it yearned for the respite only her lover's arms could provide.

"I am ever weak when faced with true love." Gaea spoke more to herself than to Dylan, but her words made his face blaze with joy. The goddess held up her hand in a gesture of restraint. "Listen well, Dylan. The spell will last only a short length of time. You must return to the waters before the light of the new day touches the land. If you do not"—she added power to her words which raised the hair on the nape of Dylan's neck—"you will be trapped. You will belong to neither realm—the land or the sea. You will perish, and your soul will roam without rest for eternity."

The merman nodded gravely. "I will not forget, Great Goddess."

"See that you do not. My daughter would be most displeased."

Dylan smiled. "As would I."

Gaea tried unsuccessfully to keep her lips from turning up. "I am beginning to understand why my daughter chose you, merman."

"She simply showed the discerning wisdom of her Great Mother." Dylan bowed gallantly.

The goddess's laughter glittered around her as she motioned for the merman to swim closer so that she could begin casting her spell.

CC decided the night was never going to end. Her body ached and her mind wouldn't shut up.

"Wine," she said to the silent room as she lit the candle next to her bed. "That monk outside my room has to be good for something. I'll just act all regal and send him off to get me some wine." She spoke to the sputtering wick. "A couple cups of that thick red stuff I had the other night should do the trick."

Isabel had left her a fresh woolen robe, and CC wrapped it around her like a cloak. Satisfied the transparent chemise was well covered she walked quickly to the door, wincing at the cold of the stone floor against her bare feet. Mentally she made a note to stoke the fire to take the chill from the room.

She opened the door slowly, not wanting to startle the Brother. He was sitting with his back resting against the wall beside her door. His cowl was pulled up, and she couldn't see his face.

CC cleared her throat.

The monk didn't move.

"Um, excuse me, Brother," she said.

"He sleeps." The deep voice came from the shadows. The sound of it made her heart leap in response.

"Who's there?" CC asked.

"Do you need to ask, my love?" Dylan said as he stepped toward her.

"Oh!" CC pressed her hand against her mouth, sure that she was hallucinating, or that Sarpedon was playing a horrible trick on her.

Dylan touched her face. "Am I so very different, Christine?"

Her eyes darted from the strong lines of his familiar face down his body. He was wearing a monk's robe, but peeking from beneath it were two very human, very bare feet.

"I . . . you . . . but how?" Had she dreamed him?

"Let us call it a gift from a goddess."

His smile convinced her. He couldn't be a trick. Sarpedon wasn't capable of using such joy as a masquerade. She grabbed his hand and pulled him into her room, closing the door carefully behind them.

"The monk will not awaken. Gaea has seen to that." Dylan's eyes were sparkling. Then he looked around with open curiosity. "This is where you spend your days?"

"Well, not exactly," she said, surprised at her sudden nervousness. "I mean, I change my clothes here, and I sleep here, but I spend most of my day out there." She jerked her thumb in the direction of the door and ordered her mouth to quit babbling.

"It is . . ." Dylan hesitated. ". . . very gray," he finally concluded. Then he nodded at the narrow bed. "And that is where you rest your body at night?"

"In theory," CC sighed. "I don't seem to be having much success with resting lately."

Dylan turned to her and took her face in his hands. He noticed the dark circles under her eyes and the sallow tinge of her skin. He kissed her forehead and then gently kissed her lips. Her eyes fluttered shut.

"I have come to help you rest," he said.

Keeping her eyes closed, she leaned into him. "Now that you're here, I'm not tired at all."

She could feel the chuckle rumble through his chest.

"Then perhaps you would be willing to teach me something of this human body. It is an odd thing to have legs."

His kiss cut off her laughter. When they broke apart Dylan's eyes had darkened with desire. CC took his hand and led him to her bed. First, she dropped the robe from around her shoulders. Then she let the chemise fall from her body. She tugged on his robe, and he bent so that she could pull the rough woolen fabric over his head.

"Look at you," she said breathlessly. He was tall and had the build of an athlete. "Thank you, Gaea."

Dylan smiled. "I make an adequate man?"

CC raised one eyebrow as her gaze flicked down to the flesh that already stood erect between his long, muscular legs.

Her face warmed as her cheeks flushed pink. "Oh, yes. You make more than an adequate man."

Dylan pulled her into his arms. "Teach me how to love you as a human man loves a woman."

CC looked up at him and felt the restless pain within her loosen its stranglehold. "It's the same, my love. In any form you and I were made to fit perfectly together."

They sank down onto the bed, lost in one another.

Dylan knew that he hadn't banished the ache within her, but he had soothed it and made it bearable. She had needed him, and he had responded. No price was too great to pay to be with her. They would belong to each other for an eternity.

CHAPTER TWENTY

THE screech of a seagull woke him. It was such a normal sound, a sound he heard every day of his life. He had almost drifted back to sleep when the gull screeched again.

"Make it go away," CC mumbled, and snuggled more securely against his chest.

Dylan's eyes shot open, and he was instantly awake. His heart pounded painfully in his chest until his mind registered that the room was still cast in the darkness of predawn. He forced his panic to subside.

The gull screeched again.

CC's eyes cracked open. The bird was perched on the window ledge.

"What is it doing?" she grumbled. Then she kissed Dylan's chest and nuzzled him.

"I believe it is a messenger from your mother, reminding me that my time is limited."

"Do you have to go?" she asked sleepily.

Dylan kissed the top of her head. "If I do not, I will not live," he said simply.

"What?" CC's eyes sprang open. She read the truth on her lover's face. "You should have told me!" She lunged out of bed, pulling him after her. "When do you have to return?"

"Before light touches the land."

CC ran to the window. Dylan moved behind her, looking over her shoulder.

Predawn was already beginning to gray the night-darkened ocean. His stomach contracted.

"You can't take the time to leave through the monastery." Her eyes darted to his masculine body, gauging his size. "I think you can fit if you squeeze."

He lifted his brows in a question.

"Through the window," she said, pointing. "The cliffside is right outside there. Hurry!"

Dylan nodded and bent to kiss her quickly. Then he hoisted his naked body up to the windowsill. It was a tight fit, and rock scraped his skin painfully, but it took him only a moment to pop through like a cork to the surface of a pool of water. On her toes, CC peered out the window. His smile flashed in the darkness.

"I have enjoyed being a man, Christine." His grin was endearingly male.

Even through her worry, CC smiled. "Hurry, silly."

"I will wait for you tonight," Dylan said. "And for all of eternity."

Then he turned and sprinted towards the cliff. CC's mouth opened in a soundless scream when she saw his naked muscles bunch powerfully. Before she could shout a warning, he reached the edge of the cliff and leapt from its impossibly steep side. His body arched in a spectacular dive, and in the moment before the sun touched the land CC saw the flash of fire that signaled his change from human to merman. She stood at the window for a very long time, struggling against the painful desire to follow him.

Dawn had shifted from gray to mauve when she finally turned from the window. All sight of Dylan was gone. Slowly, with movements that might have belonged to a woman Isabel's age, she pulled on her robe and belted it. Rolling up the sleeves she pushed open the door, almost causing the monk who knelt outside in the hall to fall over.

"Good morning, I didn't mean to startle you," CC said.

The monk stood. CC noticed that his face was flushed and he looked woozy, like he had just awakened from a delicious, goddess-induced dream.

"The abbot asked that I bring you to him upon your waking." The monk's voice cracked with sleep.

CC shook her head. Dylan's absence was a raw wound, and it left her in no mood to deal with Abbot William's sly questioning. "Please tell the abbot that I am honored by his invitation, but that I must get to work immediately on my restoration of the Holy Mother."

The monk's mouth opened and closed compulsively. CC thought it made him look like a bizarre species of land flounder.

"I'm sure the abbot will understand. He, of all people, knows the importance of honoring the Holy Mother. Have a blessed day, Brother, and thank you for watching over me last night."

CC hurried down the hall. When she glanced over her shoulder at the monk, he was still standing in front of her door. And his mouth was still open.

The way through the dining room which led to the servant's entrance to the kitchen felt like a familiar friend, and CC's leather slippers made soft little padding noises as she circumvented the courtyard and the silently watching well. Peeking into the dining room she let out a relieved breath. It was empty except for Isabel, who was clearing the last of the dishes from one of the tables.

"Good morning," CC said.

"That stubborn look tells me that no matter how weary you are, you will still be about the Virgin's business," Isabel stated with frustrated concern.

"Stubborn? I'm not stubborn."

Isabel's answer was a rude noise in the back of her throat, which almost made CC laugh.

They both headed into the kitchen, which was a wonderful mixture of busy women and delicious smells. Each woman greeted CC with a smile and a warm hello.

"Already had your bucket and such taken to the chapel," Lynelle said in her gruff voice.

"Thank you, but you didn't need to go to any trouble for me. You already have enough to do," CC said.

"We did not do it," Gwenyth said. "We asked some of the Brothers to gather and carry the things."

CC blinked in surprise.

"There are those among the Brothers who are pleased that the Holy Mother is being restored," Isabel explained.

"And a little water fetching does not take them long from tending their precious sheep and gardens," Lynelle grumbled.

"I made this for you," Bronwyn slurred softly, handing CC a mug of warm tea.

"Eat this on the way to the chapel. You must not allow yourself to weaken. The Holy Mother needs you strong and healthy." Gwenyth gave her a hard roll with a hunk of cheese and meat inside of it.

"You have no idea how much this means to me this morning," CC said, suddenly feeling near tears. "Thank you. I appreciate all of you."

The four women made scoffing noises, waving off her thanks, but CC could see the pleasure that flushed their wizened faces.

"Go on with you," Isabel said. "Today we will make certain that you eat."

On impulse, CC leaned down and kissed the old woman's cheek before hurrying out the door.

It must have rained sometime during the night, because the gardens were still wet and sparkling. CC breathed deeply, enjoying the damp smells of grass and flower as they mixed with the ever-present salt tang of the nearby ocean. Chewing the last of the breakfast roll, she strolled slowly through the twisting paths, taking the long way to the chapel. She passed several monks already busy pruning and weeding and was pleasantly surprised when two of them met her gaze and nodded shy good mornings.

The chapel was dim and still filled with an oppressive layer of incense from dawn mass, but as CC made her way to the Virgin's statue, she felt her spirit lighten. The Blessed Mother was lit by dozens of white candles, and the statue glowed like a golden beacon of hope. Yesterday, CC had left six candles burning around the base of the statue. Someone, perhaps even several someones, had already begun visiting the Virgin.

Placed in a neat row to one side of the niche that held the statue were three buckets of clean water, a hunk of soap, a pile of clean rags and a large straw broom.

"Time to get to work," she told Gaea's serene face.

"UGH!" CC scooped up another pile of rancid-smelling mess while she muttered to herself. "I have no way of being certain, but I think that this is poo from a giant squirrel."

"Actually, it is from a raccoon, but a giant squirrel is an excellent guess." Gaea had materialized in front of the statue, her blue and gold silk wrap mirroring the soft colors in the Virgin's robes.

"I should have known that even a giant squirrel wouldn't be giant enough to make this nasty mess." CC smiled at the goddess. "Good morning, it's nice to see a clean face."

"Good *afternoon* to you, daughter. You have worked the morning away." Gaea returned her smile and clicked her fingers. In a shower of silver sparks a wet towel appeared in one hand and a goblet appeared in the other. She gestured for CC to join her.

"Come, sit and refresh yourself. I have news."

CC sat next to the goddess and gratefully accepted the damp towel, wiping the dirt from her face and hands with a sigh of pleasure. When she was at least semiclean, Gaea handed her the goblet. It was filled with a thick, honey-colored liquid. CC sipped.

"Yum! This is delicious. What is it?"

With a gentle wave of her wrist Gaea produced her own goblet.

"It is Viking mead. I thought it the appropriate drink since you have been mistaken for a Norse sorceress."

"Very appropriate," she agreed. "I want to thank you for the gift you gave Dylan and me last night." She felt heat spring to her cheeks as Gaea's sparkling eyes smiled knowingly at her.

"He did make a spectacular man," the goddess said wistfully.

"As usual, you are correct. Last night was . . ." She sighed dreamily. ". . . exactly what I needed. Thank you, Mother."

Gaea nodded graciously and sipped her mead. She would not share with her daughter the cost of last night's passion. It had been Dylan's choice, and he had made it willingly. She would not taint his sacrifice by telling Christine news that would surely cause her guilt and pain. And, if fate was kind, the price Dylan would have to pay would be no more than a few wrinkles or an attractive graying of his ebony-colored hair.

Gaea cleared her throat. Without preamble she said, "Lir is preoccupied. I called to him from our private cove, and he sent a selkie as his messenger." The goddess flipped back her thick hair and crossed her legs, obviously annoyed. "There is some problem with Pele, the Hawaiian fire goddess. Mano is causing some mischief with her local priestesses, and Pele has threatened to erupt an underwater volcano in retribution. Mano has appealed to Lir. And, of course, Lir has never minded interceding when the passion of a goddess is involved."

"Who is Mano?"

"The Hawaiian shark god—and a rather nasty fellow." Gaea shook her head in disgust. "Island immortals are all so petty. Too little land to ground them and to provide them the depth they need for real wisdom."

"So you didn't get to talk to Lir at all?"

"No, his message said he would come to me as soon as he has resolved the Hawaiian problem."

"And he didn't say when that would be."

"No, but I will not allow him to put me off for long. I am a goddess and I will not be trifled with." Gaea's eyes flashed with suppressed power.

"Speaking of being trifled with, Sarpedon has become more annoying," CC said. "Yesterday he possessed Andras again. Your amulet reminded him that wasn't a smart move, but while he was possessed Andras made some comments about knowing that I'm not pure."

Gaea's eyes narrowed. "The merman is troublesome, but now that he has found you it seems that he is focusing his attention on the monastery. I know from your dolphin friends that he has been distinctly absent from the waters near Caldei." Gaea's expression lightened and she smiled playfully at CC. "That is especially fortunate because the dolphins report news of another merman, who is spending all of his time in the waters surrounding this island."

"Dylan?"

"Of course it is Dylan. Who else?"

CC smiled sheepishly. "I know it's silly, but I just wanted to hear you say it."

"This silliness, as you call it, is part of the magic of love. And remember love is the strongest magic in the world. It even has the ability to tame a goddess."

"I want to be with him, Mother. Always."

Gaea smoothed back CC's hair. "I know, Daughter, and tonight you shall be with your lover again. Feign exhaustion and retire early to your bed. I will summon storm clouds to obscure the sun so that you need not wait for full dark to go to Dylan." Gaea's look turned sly. "It is my turn to use Sarpedon's connection with the young knight. I will whisper dreams to Andras in which you figure predominately. Sarpedon will be kept very busy tonight trying to decide what is real, and what is fantasy. He will be much too busy chasing the ghosts of dreams to haunt the waters looking for you."

CC hugged Gaea in gratitude, and the goddess's laughter filled the chapel.

"All will be well, Daughter. With just a little more patience, all will be well. Do not forget, you must return to the monastery when the bell tolls for morning mass."

"I won't forget. Will you be at the shore tonight?" CC asked.

"Tonight I will leave you to your lover. You see, I, too, will be concentrating on calling a lover. Lir will not long be able to resist."

CC wondered how Lir could resist the goddess at all. Even in the dimness of the chapel, Gaea's beauty was awe-inspiring, and when she mentioned her lover the light that always shone within her intensified until CC almost felt the need to avert her eyes.

CC grinned at Gaea. "Lir's a goner, and he doesn't even know it—yet."

"Oh, he knows, Daughter. He knows."

The cheery yellow glow of the candles that surrounded Mary's statue blinked and quivered in response to the women's laughter, filling CC with a sense of well-being. How could anything go wrong as long as Gaea was beside her?

Suddenly, the expression on Gaea's face sobered and before CC could speak the goddess's body dissipated into hundreds of tiny golden lights, which pulsed once and then faded. Her disappearance was followed by the sound of a deep, male voice.

"Good afternoon, Undine," Andras said.

CC looked warily at the knight, half expecting his eyes to begin to glow, but there was no sign of anything unusual in his appearance.

"Hello, Andras." She took a breath and decided there was no way she could avoid the subject. "You look like you feel better today. Did you and the abbot figure out what happened yesterday in the courtyard?"

The knight's welcoming expression flattened. "Abbot William is diligently praying about the event. He remains confident that an answer will be found."

"Well, I'm just glad to see that you've recovered. I'm sure the abbot's prayers will be helpful." She kept her voice light.

Instead of meeting her eyes, the knight's gaze slid away and lit on the statue. "You have done an excellent job here. It is good to see that you are taking such an interest in religion. A woman needs to be grounded in the structure of the church so that she can know her proper place as wife and mother."

His face had relaxed and his smile was genuine, even if the words were patronizing.

"I'm not restoring the Holy Mother's statue out of religious zealousness or piety; I'm restoring it out of love," she said, reminding herself that it wasn't his fault that he was a medieval man. He probably thought he had just paid her an enormous compliment.

"Exactly." Andras sounded pleased. "Love of the church."

"No," she automatically corrected him. "Love of the Mother."

Confusion spread over his face. "Is there a difference?"

"I think so. I think there is a world of difference between devotion to man and devotion to the divine."

"Do you not believe that man can be divine?" Andras's chuckle said that he found it amusing that he was discussing theology with a woman.

"Truthfully, I haven't found much evidence of it."

Andras squinted his eyes at her, as if he wasn't sure he'd heard her correctly. Then he smiled indulgently. "Undine, I find your sense of humor refreshing, but the reason I need to speak with you requires us to be serious. My squires have relayed to me several reports of an unusual nature."

"Unusual reports?" she prompted when he just stared at her and didn't continue speaking.

"Creatures have been seen in the waters off the coast."

She forced her expression to be one of mild curiosity.

"Creatures? You mean like whales and dolphins? That doesn't seem very unusual to me. You and I saw a dolphin very close to shore just a couple of days ago."

"I do not mean creatures that were fashioned by God. The fishermen talk of abnormal beings, half man and half fish, that have been seen inhabiting the waters surrounding this island."

"And you believed the fantasies of those poor people? That surprises me, Andras. They are, after all, peasants." She hoped that she was using the right buzz words. Andras was a knight, which meant he was a part of the nobility. Hadn't he been raised to look down on the working classes? At that moment she fervently hoped so.

"You are correct. They are peasants. I simply find their sightings interesting, especially because they seem to coincide with your appearance on our shores."

CC laughed. "Are you saying that you think that I am half fish?"

"Of course not."

"Then what are you saying?" she asked. At the mention of the sea, the longing within her sprang painfully alive, wearing away at her ability to be cordial to the overbearing knight.

"I know of your love for the sea. I am saying that you should be content with observing it from afar, and save excursions to the shoreline for quieter times."

CC squeezed a tight smile on her lips. "As always, I appreciate the concern you show for my welfare, but I'm sure it is nothing but foolish superstitions worrying the fishermen. After all, I was blown ashore by a storm. It's only logical that other sea creatures were blown off course, too."

"Other sea creatures?" Andras pounced. "You sound like you are saying you are a creature of the sea, too."

"Do I look like a creature of the sea?" she asked with a teasing smile.

"I ask that you give me your word that you will not walk by the shoreline alone again."

Andras's voice had an unmistakably hard edge to it, and CC's ability to be polite was rapidly unraveling when Isabel's grainy voice quivered across the chapel.

"It is well after midday and you have forgotten to eat again, Undine." The old woman limped toward them. She paused when she neared the statue of Mary, crossed herself and curtseyed reverently. Then she nodded respectfully to the knight.

"Thank you for reminding me, Isabel. Now that I think of it, I am very hungry."

"The mutton stew that will be served for this evening's meal is ready. Just this morning I harvested a fresh crop of mint," Isabel croaked happily.

"I promised to meet with the abbot and share with him the news I received from my men, but if you can wait I would be pleased to have an early evening meal with you, Undine," Andras said.

"I wish I could wait, but I think I should hurry and eat so that I can get back to work before the chapel is needed for vespers. I wouldn't want to create an inconvenience for the abbot."

Before he could argue Isabel chimed in. "Princess, I think it wise that you eat immediately." She shared a conspirators' look with Andras. "We must be certain the princess takes care with her health."

"Of course I would not put the princess's health in jeopardy. Perhaps we can take in the air this evening, Undine?"

Andras reached for her hand to kiss. Laughing nervously CC pulled it out of his reach.

"Oh, you don't want to do that. My hand is filthy." She made a big show of wiping her hands on her dirty robe. "A walk would be nice, if I'm not too tired."

"I will come to your chamber this evening after vespers, where I will pray that you are not too tired." His look was intense.

CC felt her face flush. Could he not just leave her alone? Thankfully, Isabel spoke up.

"Sir Andras, you need not trouble yourself. I know how you enjoy your chess games with the abbot. If the princess is not too fatigued, I will come with word from her." She looked quickly at CC. "If that is agreeable to the princess."

CC hurried over to Isabel. "Yes! There's no need for you to interrupt your time with Abbot William if I'm asleep on my feet. Thank you, Isabel. That was a wonderfully considerate idea." She linked her arm through the servant's and began walking with her toward the door. "I hope you have a good evening,

Andras, and if I don't see you tonight I'm sure we'll be able to spend some time together tomorrow."

Andras stood silently in the shadowy church, watching the women disappear into the gardens. His expression was introspective and his full lips were turned down in irritation. Had she begun to avoid him, or was it only maidenly shyness coupled with her newly discovered devotion to the Holy Mother that seemed to be keeping her from him? The knight felt a stirring of anger as he pondered the question. His anger coupled with something else, something that whispered hypnotically deep within his mind. Andras's hands trembled, and he balled them into fists. Images flashed through his mind. Undine naked and slick with sweat . . . Undine on her knees before him . . . Undine crying his name aloud as his seed exploded within her . . .

Overwhelmed by the visions, Andras felt himself harden. His breath was ragged. He raked a hand through his hair. What was happening to him? He had never before experienced anything like his growing obsession with the princess. Perhaps the abbot was correct. His eyes narrowed so that the silver glow that stained them was almost undetectable. Sorceress or not, she was only a woman. When she belonged to him, he would purge the pagan taint from her soul, then he would satisfy his desire for her. She had no choice.

"THANK you," CC whispered as soon as they were out of range of Andras's hearing. "He doesn't seem to be able to take no for an answer."

"You are most welcome, but you must realize that few women would tell Sir Andras no," Isabel whispered back. "Are you quite certain that is your desire?"

"Absolutely. I don't want a husband who has to rule over and control me."

"So you have said before, but I still believe that there are few men of any other kind." Isabel looked closely at her. "At least not in this world."

"If there's not, I won't have any husband at all. I'm a human being, not a piece of property."

"So young and headstrong," Isabel clucked.

"Where I'm from we call it having good sense and a backbone."

Isabel's look was clearly disbelieving.

They were halfway across the voluminous gardens before CC noticed how murky the day had become.

"Is it really that late? It looks like the sun is setting already."

"It is late for your midday meal, but the sun is not yet setting. There is a storm coming." Isabel squinted up at the rolling clouds. "It is odd, normally my leg warns me of a storm long before I see clouds. Today it did not. It is almost as if the change of weather was suddenly conjured."

Not wanting to travel down that line of thinking, CC asked, "What happened to your leg?"

Isabel looked surprised at the question, but she answered without hesitation. "I was born with a twisted limb. My father wanted to dispose of me on the hillside, but I was the only girl child my mother had born, and she was quite old. She would not part with me."

CC was shocked at the matter-of-fact way Isabel spoke of something so horrifying.

"That's awful."

"A girl child with a twisted limb is of no use. My father knew no man would marry me." Isabel shrugged. "It is a blessing that I have a certain skill with cooking. When my youngest brother's beautiful wife gave birth to their fifth healthy child, she said there was no room for a crippled sister in their home. My other brothers felt the same. It was fortuitous that the monastery needed a cook. They took me in. I have been here since."

"Do you ever see your family?"

Isabel shook her head. "My mother and father are long dead, and my brothers do not visit. My family is here."

"The monks?" CC asked.

Isabel cackled and patted her hand. "Goodness no! The other women. We are all each other's only family now."

"I don't really have any family here, either," CC said.

Isabel paused on the threshold to the kitchen, where homey smells and sounds enveloped them. She turned to CC and smiled warmly at the younger woman.

"You do now, Princess."

CC paced and paced and paced. She had already pulled the dresser under the window. For what felt like the zillionth time she hitched up her chemise and climbed on top of it. She studied the fading evening. Gaea's clouds were rolling in from the west, directly over the tumultuous ocean. They were low-hanging and reminded CC of a giant gray comforter being pulled over the sky. The setting sun was certainly obscured, but was it dark enough yet? She didn't think so.

She could still see most of the way down the side of the cliff, which meant if anyone happened to be looking seaward, they would be able to see her if she was making her way down the side of that cliff. And she couldn't be sure that Andras wouldn't be looking seaward after the fishermen had aroused suspicion in him.

CC sighed and rubbed her temples. It seemed her heart pounded there in time with the distant crashing of the surf. Her body was a throbbing shell of need; she ached for the waters and for her lover. *Dylan.* Just thinking his name sent a shiver of anticipation low in her stomach.

Patience, she told herself firmly. Just a few more minutes and it'll be dark enough. She turned and sat on top of the dresser, resting her head against the windowsill. She'd lasted this long, she could certainly wait a little longer.

At first the day had felt like it would never end, so CC had been shocked when the Brothers began filling the chapel for vespers, and she realized that it must be late evening. Quietly, she had piled her cleaning supplies in a shadowed corner, wiped her hands on her very grimy robes and slipped out the side entrance before Abbot William or Andras could accost her.

She had stopped at the kitchen long enough to grab another bowl of Isabel's excellent stew and a goblet of wine. The ladies were at their busiest, cleaning up the evening meal and beginning preparations for the next day. It took some doing, but she persuaded Isabel that she really didn't need any help bathing and undressing. The old woman obviously didn't like it, but when CC promised that she really just wanted to get out of her dirty clothes and crawl into bed, Isabel acquiesced, assuring CC that she would make her excuses to Andras.

CC knew that the circles under her eyes had darkened to bruises; the need inside her was making her feel weak and nauseous. But after she had washed the filth from her body, she forced herself to eat all of the stew and drink the entire goblet of wine. The wrenching ache was still there, but a full stomach made her feel less nauseous and dizzy.

A sound turned her attention back to the view outside the window. CC smiled. "Thank you, Gaea," she said.

Rain was falling in the comforting patter of a gentle mist, swallowing the last of the evening light. Quickly, CC sat on the windowsill, found her toehold, and dropped quietly to the soft grass below the window. Gaea's rain was a cool caress against her feverish skin, and for a moment she stood on the edge of the cliff with her arms held straight out and her head thrown back, letting the water of the goddess soothe her body and soul. Keeping the image of Dylan's dive from the side of the cliff in her mind, she balled up her chemise with one hand so that her long legs were free to run, then she moved with unerring certainty down the winding sheep path.

Dylan! She used all of her mental strength to call to him. *I'm coming! Please be there!*

Rocky ground gave way to sand and she ran to her familiar log, pulling off her shift with shaking hands. She kicked off her slippers and hurried to the shoreline. When her feet touched the water she paused, suddenly unsure.

"Do not make me wait, my love." Dylan's voice carried over the waves, surreal and disembodied.

"I can't see you." At the sound of his voice, CC's breath caught and her stomach tightened.

"But I can see you. You are a white goddess of beauty, fashioned of long, curving lines and softness. Come to me, my goddess," Dylan said.

With two quick steps CC ran and leapt, diving into the surf. Before her outstretched hands touched the water she felt the exquisite burning begin at her waist and shoot down through her legs. A rush of power followed the burning as the inhuman strength of her tail propelled her forward and then up. She broke the surface laughing.

The merman materialized out of the mist in front of her. Tonight his long, dark hair was free, and it fell in a thick, damp wave around his shoulders. Dylan's exotic beauty and the erotic sense of maleness that surrounded him struck her, and she felt a thrill of excitement at his nearness. He drifted close.

"I have missed you, Christine."

"You were just with me last night," she teased.

"I have discovered that the more I am near you, the more I want you. You belong at my side, and I at yours." His voice reminded her of dark chocolate—rich and sensual.

She reached up and wound her arms around his neck, loving the way his boyish smile made his lips curve when he took her in his arms.

"I don't think I could have stayed away from you another second," she said as his face tilted down to hers.

Their lips touched in a gentle kiss as they became reacquainted with the taste and touch of one another.

"Not a moment went by today when I did not wish that you were here beside me," Dylan said as he rested his forehead against hers while his hands caressed the long, smooth line of her back.

"I tried not to think about you. I was afraid if I thought about you too much, I would throw myself off the side of the cliff and into the ocean like you did." She snuggled against him, wanting to get as close as possible.

CC could feel the tremor of emotion that ran down his body. Then the merman tightened his grip on her and she opened her mouth to him. Their tongues met and teased. CC couldn't stop the hum of desire that escaped from the back of her throat. She felt Dylan's muscles quiver in response and the kiss deepened. CC ran her hands down his shoulders, skimming over his firmly muscled arms and chest. He was slick and warm, soft skin and hard muscle all wrapped enticingly together.

CC pressed her body against his and jerked back in surprise when she felt their tails entwine.

Dylan looked down at her questioningly.

"I . . ." CC hesitated, feeling a little foolish. She cleared her throat. "I've never . . ." She trailed off, pointing down at the part of their bodies that was submerged under the water.

Understanding cleared Dylan's questioning look. He touched her face. "Remember last night? I was afraid, too."

"You were afraid?" she asked, incredulous. "It certainly didn't seem like it."

His smile was gentle. "Making love to you as a human man was an experience I will remember always."

CC pressed her face into his palm. "I want you now as badly as I did in my human body. I'm just nervous." She took a breath and met his eyes. "The truth is, even though I said that we fit together perfectly in any form, I'm really not sure what to do."

He smiled at her and brushed her lips lightly with his. "Will you trust me tonight, as I trusted you last night, Christine?"

Without hesitation she nodded.

"Then let me teach you."

This time she was able to smile at him. "Well, I already know you're an excellent teacher."

He took her hand in his. "Then let me teach you how mer-folk make love."

CC nodded again, this time breathlessly.

Dylan pulled her under the waves and they swam side by side into deeper water. Before they surfaced, the merman stopped and turned to her, but, instead of taking her in his arms, he held her out, almost half an arm's length away from his body. First, he kissed the palm of her hand. Then he touched her cheek, letting his hand slide down her long neck to her shoulder, then on down to gently cup her breast. Teasingly, he ran his palm over her nipple, which puckered under his caress. But his hand didn't stay at her breast, instead it moved down over her rib cage to the curve of her waist. When his hand met her mer-flesh, his caress changed. Instead of his palm, he used his fingertips to touch her with featherlike strokes, which swirled enticingly down and around her hips.

His fingers were fire. Dylan's touch was like nothing she had ever experienced—it was so incredibly different from having her legs caressed by a man. When he stroked that soft, glowing skin, his touch was magnified. It carried through every part of her mer-body, like his fingertips were superconductors for erotic sensation, and she was his conduit. As the newness of unexplored sensations surged the length of her body, CC felt weak and powerful at the same time. She closed her eyes, overwhelmed by the intensity of the feeling.

No, Christine. Dylan's voice came gently into her mind. *Do not close your eyes. Watch me touching you. Look how incredibly beautiful you are.*

CC opened her eyes. Dylan kissed her gently again, then he let his body drift down, so that his hands and his mouth could explore the rest of her. His mouth traveled from her breasts to the softness of her belly. When the warm heat of his mouth slid to her mer-flesh she had to hold tightly to his shoulders to steady herself.

Amazed, she felt herself open to him as his tongue moved down her body, coaxing and teasing alive sensations that she hadn't even imagined possible. She watched him love her and the last of her trepidation died under the heat of his touch. She gazed at her body and at the astonishing creature who held her so intimately, and she realized that it truly didn't matter what form their bodies reflected—it was love that anchored her to him, not a body or a time or place.

Dylan's mouth and hands continued to work their magic, and CC's ability for rational thought splintered. All she could do was to hold tightly to Dylan and experience the sensations that surged through her body. His touch merged with the soft pressure of the water that surrounded them until it seemed to CC that even the ocean was making love to her. Suddenly, her mind fragmented as an orgasmic rush of electricity rippled through her body.

Dylan cradled her within his arms and pulled her to the surface. He kissed her deeply. CC felt so liquid that she almost believed that her body could dissipate and become a part of the seas, and only Dylan's touch kept her connected to the physical world. They drifted in the ocean, hidden by the loving caress of the goddess's rain.

"Did that please you, my love?" he whispered against her lips.

"You please me, Dylan, more than I could ever tell you. It was a good thing that we were underwater; I think if air had touched me I might have combusted."

Dylan laughed. "Your nervousness must be gone."

"Forever." She grinned, then playfully took his bottom lip between her teeth and pulled gently. His moan of response brought to her a rush of new pleasure. "Now I want to please you," CC said.

She reached between them and took his already hard flesh in her hand. Stroking his shaft, she felt him throb and pulse with need. His breathing deepened sharply and his eyes closed.

"No," she said, her voice thick with the power of seduction. "Don't close your eyes. I want you to watch me touch you, too."

Dylan's gaze was hot as he watched her hand slide up and down his length. She kissed him again, then let her body drift down under the water until she took his golden flesh in her mouth. She felt him quiver as she let her tongue and lips work together. When she took him deeply into her mouth, his gasp of pleasure sent a thrill of desire through her. She loved the taste of him. He was salt and sea and the musky tang of an aroused man. And he was beautiful.

Abruptly, she felt him tug at her shoulders and she allowed him to pull her up. She found his mouth, and heat exploded within her at the ragged intensity of their kiss. She felt his hardness against her. Instinctively, she reached down to guide him within her, but Dylan stopped her.

"Wait, love. There is more," he said between broken breaths as she kissed the firm line of his jaw and slid her tongue teasingly down his neck.

"How could there be more than this?" She pressed against him.

"Watch," he said, his eyes dark with passion and promise.

Dylan unwound one hand from where it had been buried in her hair. Raising his arm he drew a circle in the air above them. CC's eyes widened in surprise as the ocean around them started to swirl in response.

"I command a bed in which to love our princess!"

Dylan's voice was filled with power, and it echoed against the misty night. As he spoke the seething water changed. It bubbled and frothed and somehow hardened until the two mer-creatures were buoyed up on a bed of aqua sea foam where they lay in each other's arms. It was as if they were resting inside a crested wave where Dylan had somehow halted time and the elements.

"You have magic," CC gasped.

"My magic is you, Christine."

Dylan kissed her, letting his hands move down her body to cup her breasts and then stroke her glowing flesh until CC moaned in response.

"Now, please," she panted. "Don't make me wait anymore."

Dylan shifted his weight until he lay over her, holding himself up on his forearms. When she reached down to guide him into her, he was powerless to resist.

"Christine!" he gasped her name as her heat tightened slickly around him.

They moved together easily, finding a rhythm that was at first slow and gentle. CC marveled at how well they fit. His body pressed against hers, and everywhere they touched sparks of sensation tingled through her skin. She ran her hands over the taut muscles of his arms, amazed at his power and how he trembled under her touch. Then their rhythm quickened, and CC strained upward to meet his thrusts. Her hands found the hard ridges of his back, and she let her fingernails tease, before she locked her arms around him, pressing him more firmly against her.

"I cannot wait," Dylan moaned.

"Then don't. Please, Dylan!" she urged.

With a last, powerful thrust CC felt Dylan begin to throb within her, and when he shouted her name she felt her own body explode in response. As her sense of reality fragmented into the realm of sensation she held tightly to Dylan, trusting him to bring her safely back to earth.

CHAPTER TWENTY-ONE

"I love you, Christine."

She must have fallen asleep, because Dylan's voice woke her. At first CC thought they were still lying on the bed of sea foam, but the sound of waves breaking against the shore around them and the velvet feel of sand under her hip made her realize that she and Dylan had drifted to shore. She was still nestled against his chest and he lay semireclining, with his back against one of the many smooth rocks that peppered the shore.

"I'm so glad," she said and stretched languidly. Then she laughed.

"What?" he asked.

"I was just thinking that I feel like a satisfied cat, which seemed kind of funny under the circumstances." She gestured at their entwined tails. Then she raised her eyebrows at him. "You do know what a cat is, don't you?"

He tugged a wet strand of her hair playfully. "It is a feline creature that is closely allied to human women." He looked introspective for a moment, like he was remembering something, then he added, "They are fond of eating fish." His face split, and he laughed, too.

"Not that we're fish," CC said between giggles.

"Certainly not. You are Goddess of the Seas," he amended good-naturedly.

"That must make you," she finished with a flourish, "God of the Seas!"

Dylan's face instantly changed. It took on a guarded expression that caused CC a pang of anxiety. He hesitated before he spoke, and when he did his words sounded heavy, as if they were weighed down by the sadness of painful memories.

"No, Christine. We are different. My mother was a simple water nymph who preferred rivers and streams to the ocean. My father was a human. When my mother became pregnant she went to Lir and asked that she be granted a human form so that she could spend her life with her human lover. Lir agreed, but when my mother left the waters my father rejected her." Dylan's jaw tightened, and he looked away from her. "He already had a wife and a family. He had no use for a sea creature and her bastard offspring. My mother returned to the waters, which is where I was born. But she never found contentment. She was forever returning to the river where she had met and mated with my father. When he failed to return she killed herself. Lir allowed me to stay in his crystal palace while I was young out of love for Undine, who was my playmate. When I grew to adulthood he granted me the responsibility of overseeing the waters where they merged, river and sea. I think the great sea god hoped that under my watchfulness no other river nymphs would be lost to the lust of humans. But I am not the son of immortals; I am not as you are. Perhaps you did not realize that. Forgive me for not explaining our differences to you earlier." He wouldn't meet her eyes.

"Dylan." She took his chin in her hand, forcing him to look at her. His face was tight and withdrawn, but she could see the pain reflected in his eyes. "I'm sorry about your mother, and it makes me sad about your father, but it could never change what I feel for you. How could you believe that could matter to me?"

"You are Goddess of the Sea. I do not have even a palace or a realm to offer you."

"Yeah, I know all about being offered a realm—Sarpedon already did that," she said fiercely. "And I'm not interested." She nodded her head toward the monastery. "And there's a knight up there who has a castle to offer me," she scoffed. "I'd rather be trapped on land than accept their kind of love. Or, better yet, I'd rather have no lover at all than what they offer."

At the mention of the other two males Dylan's jaw clenched, and she could feel his body tense against her.

"I want what you offer me," she said.

"But I have nothing to offer you," he said miserably.

CC splayed her open hand on his chest over his heart. "You have this."

"No," Dylan's voice was thick with emotion. "I do not even have a heart. It was lost to you lifetimes ago."

"Don't ever think it's lost, Dylan. I'll keep it safe. Always." She pulled him down to her and their kiss was filled with the tenderness of true love.

"For an eternity," he said.

"Yes, for eternity," she agreed. "And I want to stay with you. Here, in the water, in this form, forever."

Dylan's look of joy was quickly shadowed by worry. When he spoke his voice was calm and filled with the hardness of purpose.

"I will protect you from Sarpedon," he said. "I will not allow him to harm you."

Remembering the raging, insane power of the gigantic merman, CC felt a stab of fear. "No! You won't have to. Gaea is going to Lir. She'll work everything out; she just asks that we be a little patient. She said Lir has some problem with another goddess who's taking his attention right now."

"I am not God of the Sea, but I do have some power of my own, Christine." Dylan's expression had darkened, and CC felt the deep, constant strength that rested beneath the merman's kind exterior.

"I know you do! But Sarpedon is crazy, and he's getting more and more bizarre. He scares me, Dylan. Please let Gaea handle it. I couldn't bear it if anything happened to you."

Dylan opened his mouth to argue, but CC silenced him by pressing a finger against his lips.

"Promise me you'll stay away from him."

When he didn't answer her, the stab of fear turned to panic. Her mind whirred while she searched for something she could say to convince him. Then she knew.

"If something happened to you I would be forced to marry the knight so that I could stay on land, away from Sarpedon's realm," she said simply. She hated that her words caused the flash of pain that crossed the merman's face, but fear for his life overrode her desire to protect his feelings.

"I promise you I will not seek out Sarpedon. But I also promise you I will not allow him to take you from me."

She smiled at him, trying to lighten his mood. "Do you really think it would be so easy to take me?"

Begrudgingly, Dylan's face relaxed, and he smiled back at her.

"No, I believe you would be very difficult to capture." He kissed her quickly. "You must have been a goddess in your old world, too."

CC's laughter sparkled.

"Well, I was a sergeant. I guess that's pretty close to a goddess, at least in some circles."

"What is this, *ser-geant?*" He pronounced the foreign word slowly, which made CC want to laugh again. "Where was your realm?"

"The Comm Center." She grinned. Then she sighed at his confused expression and tried to explain. "I was in the USAF, the United States Air Force. My, uh, I guess you'd call it my realm, was the United States. The air force is a branch of the armed forces that protects my realm's freedoms. I worked in the communications part of the USAF—making sure different people and countries got the information they needed to make wise decisions."

Dylan nodded his head. "A messenger goddess protecting her realm. Yes, that suites you. I would have guessed as much."

CC opened her mouth to try and explain that there really were no goddesses in the USAF, but she sighed again and stayed silent. Hadn't she just been trying to convince Isabel that there was magic inside of each woman? So why couldn't she take that belief one step further and claim the goddess within every woman?

A wonderful thrill swept through her as her thoughts touched upon a belief so ancient that she could feel the depths of her soul leap in response. That was it! Each woman must hold some part of the Divine Feminine deep within her. CC wanted to shout with the discovery.

"Yes," she said joyously. "You're right. I am a goddess."

Dylan didn't look surprised at all. "I wish I could visit your realm of the United States Air Force."

CC almost choked as a mental image of Dylan in Oklahoma flashed into her mind.

"Well," she said quickly. "It's in the middle of a land that's far from the ocean. There's really no way to swim there." Even if we were in the same century, she finished the sentence silently.

"I would have to have legs again," Dylan said thoughtfully. "Having legs was such an unusual experience."

CC tried not to laugh.

"I do not think we can ever go back," Dylan said.

CC shook her head. "I seriously doubt it."

The merman studied her. "Will you miss it? What of your family there?"

CC took a deep breath. She had been avoiding thinking about her parents. Now homesickness filled her. Yes. She would miss them. She loved them. But . . . her gaze traveled out over the fog-covered water. The soft fingers of the surf caressed her body.

The realization came swiftly to her mind. She belonged here.

She had left home when she was so young because she had never felt like she really belonged, and she had been traveling all of her adult life trying to find someplace where she truly fit in. The air force had been satisfying, she realized, not just because she enjoyed her work, but because she never stayed in one place long enough to begin to feel the discomfort of not belonging. While her peers were settling down, getting married and having children, she had been living the nomadic life of a woman searching for home. Deep within her she knew she had finally found that home.

She touched Dylan's cheek. "Yes, I'll miss my parents, but it's time for me to grow up and move on." She remembered their Silver Cruise schedule with a poignant smile. "They'll be fine. They have each other. And this is where I belong."

The monastery bells began their lazy morning toll. CC felt each clang as if it was a physical thing.

"I wish you would stay," Dylan said, his voice sounding strained.

CC pressed her head against his chest. "There's nothing I want more." Except to keep you safe, she thought. "But I promised Gaea that I would be patient and wait for her to fix things with Lir."

"You must keep your word to the goddess." Dylan's voice was muffled as he buried his face in her hair.

"It can't be too much longer. You should have seen Gaea today; she was magnificent. There's just no way Lir will be able to resist her. Soon she'll come to me and tell me that everything's fine, and I'll run down that cliff and swim to you, and whatever human is watching can just go straight to hell if they don't like it!"

"Do not place yourself in danger," Dylan said sharply. "You are right. We can be patient."

CC kissed the corner of his mouth. "You'll be waiting here in case I can slip away?"

Dylan cupped her chin in his hand. "For an eternity, Christine. I will wait for you for an eternity. Never forget that."

"I couldn't, Dylan," she whispered.

They kissed—a long, gentle kiss that held the sweet promise of more to come.

"I have to go." When she spoke the words aloud she felt the morphing burn begin at her waist, and in an instant the sand gave way under her naked legs.

Dylan smiled sadly and ran a hand caressingly down the length of one of her newly re-formed legs.

"You know I do love to touch your legs."

"Apparently men don't change much, no matter their form." She smiled, trying to keep her tone light. She kissed him quickly before she stood.

"I love you, Dylan," CC said. Then she turned and walked slowly to the log that held her clothes.

"And I love you, Christine. Always." Dylan's voice echoed around her. She heard the wet slap of his body against the water as the ocean reclaimed him.

The goddess's rain had finally stopped, and the lightening of the sky told CC that she should hurry, but her steps were slow and leaden. Her feet felt awkward after the powerful grace of her mermaid body. And each step took her away from Dylan. She forced herself to navigate the final twists of the path. As she climbed up onto the grassy space outside the monastery wall, she spoke a prayer aloud to her goddess.

"Please hurry. I can't stand this separation much longer."

"The abbot was wise when he told me to beware your beauty. I see now that it clouded my mind into believing you were simply an innocent maid." Andras's voice was hard and angry as he and his two squires stepped from the shadows of the monastery wall.

CC jumped, and her hands automatically splayed to cover her breasts, which were clearly visible through the sheer, damp chemise.

"Andras! You startled me," CC blurted, her heart pounding painfully.

"Yes, I imagine being caught would startle you."

"Caught?" She straightened her spin, irritated at the arrogant tone of his voice. The way the three men leered at her overrode her rush of fear at the possibility of arousing the spirit of Sarpedon. "At what do you think you've caught me?"

"Innocent maidens do not cavort at night naked and alone."

She noticed that his eyes maintained their normal color, but he squinted and peered around her like he expected to discover a busload of sailors she had been entertaining.

"Cavort? I was climbing up from the cliffside path. There was very little cavorting involved. And I'm certainly not naked."

"It is improper for you to be seen in your chemise, and it is obvious from the state of your chamber that you escaped through your window," Andras challenged.

"I didn't want to ruin my dress," CC said reasonably. "And I didn't *escape*. I used my window because I didn't want to wake any of the Brothers."

"Enough talk!" Andras snapped, grabbing her arm painfully. "You shall return to your chamber now. We will speak of this with the abbot after he has completed morning mass and when you are properly clothed." He started to pull her toward the front entrance of the monastery.

CC dug in her heels and wrenched her arm back. Andras whirled to face her. His face was flushed with anger and the hand that didn't hold her arm was closed in a fist as if he wanted to strike her. CC swallowed her fear and pulled strength from deep within her. As she spoke she felt the protective warmth of the amber amulet against her breast.

"Don't ever touch me without my permission. I am still a princess and even though this is not my realm I am not totally without power here. I will not tolerate such treatment," she hissed at him. Her body felt hot and her head tingled like energy was rushing into her from above.

The fierce look on the knight's face faltered as he watched Undine transform. Seconds before she had been a wet, nearly naked woman, who looked scared and alone. Now she stood with her back straight and her chin held high. Her drying hair crackled around her and she seemed to glow with radiant power. Unexpectedly, a little shiver of foreboding crawled the length of his spine. *Sorceress!* The word whispered through his mind and he loosened her arm as if it burned his hand.

"That's better," she said. "Now I will be pleased to return to my chamber; I was already on my way there when you interrupted me." CC turned and strode confidently down the path to the monastery gate. The three men followed silently behind her.

The gate was unbarred, and CC pushed it open without waiting for the knight. Expecting the courtyard to be deserted, she was surprised to see Isabel, Lynelle, Bronwyn and Gwenyth huddled nervously against the wall near the gate.

"Oh, Undine!" Isabel's words came out in a rush of air.

But before she could say any more, Andras broke in. "You were right to report her absence. Your diligence and loyalty will be rewarded."

His words stabbed her heart. Isabel had betrayed her? She remembered how cold and judgmental Isabel had been when they had first met, but CC had thought those days were over, that Isabel and the other women had begun to care for her as she had them. She forced her face to remain expressionless as she continued woodenly across the courtyard to the entrance of the hallway that led to her room. She wanted to rush back to the group of women and yell, *Why? I thought we were friends—family even!* But she refused to give Andras the satisfaction of seeing her pain.

At the door to her room Andras spoke belligerently to her. "The abbot will expect to see you as soon as mass is finished. I will send for you then." He paused before adding, "I assume you will not be making any further lone trips today, but for your own safety my men will see that you remain in your chamber until you are summoned."

CC met his eyes with her own hard gaze. "For my protection, is it? It sounds to me like you're appointing jailers."

Without waiting for a reply, she entered her room, giving the door a resounding slam behind her.

CHAPTER TWENTY-TWO

Cc sat on her narrow cot and hugged her legs against her chest. Her anger was gone, and it had taken with it most of her princessly bravado. Andras had stationed one of his men outside her door and another outside her window.

"It's a jail," she muttered, fighting down a sudden sense of panic. What would happen if she was still being watched this closely in three days? Her stomach fluttered nervously. Gaea had said if she didn't return to her mermaid form that she would die, and after experiencing the throbbing ache that filled her body every third day as she waited impatiently to change, she knew all too well the truth of the goddess's warning. Trapped, alone in this room, she would die a horrid, painful death. And she would never see Dylan again. She shuddered. No wonder the monks called it a cell.

A hesitant knock sounded against her door, and before CC could call out, the guard opened it for Isabel. The old woman was carrying a tray that held a goblet of wine and a hunk of fresh bread and fragrant white cheese. She nodded to the surly guard, who gave CC a sharp look before backing from the room and closing the door. Isabel limped to the dresser, where she placed the tray.

In an abnormally loud voice she said, "Princess, I brought you something to break your fast. And it is time you readied yourself to meet with the good abbot." Isabel brought the goblet over to CC, who took it and drank the sweet white liquid, grateful for the soothing effect it had on her throat and her nerves.

"I did not mean to betray you, Undine," Isabel whispered urgently, almost causing CC to choke on a swallow of wine. The old woman leaned closer to CC, her voice low and soft. "I was worried about you—you looked so tired and wan yesterday. When my duties in the kitchen were complete, I came to check on you. I knocked, and when there was no answer I was afraid that you were not simply sleeping deeply, but that you were truly ill. When I found the room empty I could only think that you were somewhere alone and perhaps you were very sick. I rushed from your room to check the chapel, hoping that you had returned to the Virgin Mother's statue for comfort, but on the way there Sir Andras discovered me. He saw that I was troubled, and asked if he could aid me." Isabel tightened her lips and shook her head in obvious disgust. "I should have remembered your misgivings about the knight. Instead, I explained my worry. When you were not in the chapel, he became incensed. His anger was terrible." Isabel's eyes were bright with unshed tears. "Forgive me, Undine."

CC took one of the old woman's gnarled hands. "There's nothing to forgive," she whispered. "It's my fault. I should have confided in you, then you would have known not to worry."

The sound of a man's sudden cough from outside her window caused both women to narrow their eyes.

"Here now, eat some of this bread and cheese while I comb through your hair, Princess," Isabel croaked, raising her voice so that it carried easily through the window.

"Please do," CC said in a loud, imperious tone. "I expected you some time ago. I have been sitting here waiting. It seems I am to be treated with disrespect, even by servants." CC curled her nose and made a face at the window. Isabel covered her mouth to stifle a laugh.

"Disrespect was not my intention, Princess," Isabel blared.

"Oh, do stop speaking. I want to enjoy my breakfast and my coiffure in silence!" CC commanded.

"As you wish, Princess," Isabel shouted.

The two women rolled their eyes at each other.

CC chewed the bread and cheese as Isabel brushed gently through the tangles in her long hair. She felt relieved at the knowledge that Isabel and the other women had not betrayed her, and her mind whirled with possibilities. Abruptly, she turned her head, interrupting Isabel's grooming. The old woman looked questioningly at the princess.

"Do you think that I am evil, Isabel?" CC asked, being careful to keep her voice low enough that it wouldn't be overheard by her guards.

Isabel's furrowed brow raised. "No," she answered quietly. "Some of your beliefs are rather odd, but your heart is kind and your love for the Mother is true."

CC nodded. "If I asked you to trust me, even if what I tell you will seem unbelievable and maybe even a little frightening, would you?"

Isabel's eyes widened until she looked like an ancient bird, but she nodded her head and whispered a single word. "Yes."

"Then listen, and I'll tell you everything."

CC began with the night of her birthday and worked forward from there. She was amused to hear that Isabel found the idea of an inanimate creation that flew through the skies more disturbing than learning about Sarpedon or the fact that CC was really Undine who was really a mermaid, although CC told her she agreed completely with her terrified reaction to the airplane. When CC described her love for Dylan, Isabel nodded and smiled thoughtfully. The only thing CC was not completely honest about was Gaea. She was afraid that the old woman would not be able to accept the goddess. CC didn't leave her out of the story, she simply changed the goddess's name. When she spoke of Gaea, she called her the Holy Mother. Isabel believed totally in the power of the Virgin, and she didn't question CC's bond with her.

"So you must claim sanctuary here until the Holy Mother can be certain that Sarpedon is no longer a threat. Then you can be united with your Dylan," Isabel said after CC had finally stopped talking. The old woman's hands were clasped firmly together in her lap as if to keep them from trembling, but her gaze was bright and steady.

"And I have to have the freedom to be able to get to the ocean," CC added.

"I think the other women and I can aid you with your freedom," Isabel said thoughtfully. She smiled mischievously at CC. "The men are much too busy and important to spend their time watching a lowly woman, even if she is a princess. It is a task better performed by women."

CC felt a rush of gratitude and relief. "Thank you, Isabel. I know how difficult this must be for you to believe. It means so much that you trust me."

Isabel squeezed the young woman's shoulder. "Do not think on it. Women must help one another." Then her face twisted with worry. "But I am concerned about your safety."

"Sarpedon can't hurt me as long as I'm on land, well, at least not directly."

Isabel shook her head. "It is not his evil spirit that I fear most. I have heard rumors. Some of the Brothers are saying that you are a sorceress, and that it is your connection with the devil that caused Sir Andras's apoplexy. Now that you can no longer trust the protection of the knight, I am afraid of what could happen if the abbot thinks he has enough evidence to take you to trial for witchcraft."

A chill moved down CC's spine, and she searched frantically through her memory. Did they burn supposed witches in A.D. 1014? Isabel's grim expression said that it was very likely that they did. CC swallowed hard.

"Evidence?" CC's whisper came out as a croak.

"Yesterday he sent several Brothers to scour the surrounding countryside to see if there have been any unexplained illnesses or deaths."

CC's eyes widened in horror. "I don't mean any offense to your time, Isabel, but aren't most illnesses or deaths hard to explain or linked with superstitious beliefs?"

"Yes, and it does not end there. The Brothers are also to look for evidence of cows or goats that have gone dry, babies that will not stop crying once the sun sets, and the appearance of more than three black cats."

"But any of those things would be easy to find—or easy to fabricate." CC felt the blood leave her face.

"Then we must fabricate evidence that says you must not be harmed," Isabel said firmly.

CC chewed her bottom lip. Think! she told herself. She was an intelligent, independent woman from the modern world. Surely she could figure out a way to stay safe. She just needed to think of it as a puzzle that had to be solved—then put the pieces together . . .

And a wonderfully simple plan came to her. She sat up straight and smiled at the confused-looking Isabel.

"Isabel, what do you know about the Wykings?"

CHAPTER TWENTY-THREE

A hard fist knocked brusquely on the door.

"The abbot summons Princess Undine," the guard's voice rasped from the hall.

CC and Isabel looked at each other. Isabel nodded.

"Tell him I am coming," CC snapped. Then she whispered to Isabel. "Isn't it ironic? I'm supposed to be royalty, yet he's summoning me. Talk about princess envy."

"You are a princess." Isabel smoothed an invisible wrinkle from the front of CC's dress. "I do not think I have ever told you how lovely you are, and that loveliness comes from more than these jewels or your beautiful gown."

CC felt her eyes fill. "Thank you, Isabel." She hugged the old woman, breathing in her comforting scent, which was a mixture of stew and freshly baked bread. "Your friendship means so much to me."

"As yours does to me, child. You have breathed life into this dreary place, and into me again; do not ever forget that."

CC nodded at her. "Let's get this over with. It's show time."

Isabel looked confused.

"It means it's time for us to start performing." CC grinned, and almost told her to "break a leg," too, but she didn't think they had time for more explanations.

Isabel's face hardened with resolve. "Show time," she whispered in perfect agreement, and both women stepped into the hall.

"Follow me to the abbot," said the stone-faced squire. "He and Sir Andras will receive you in his antechamber."

CC had no idea what an antechamber was, but she gave the man a curt nod and followed him. Isabel limped behind them. The squire led them through a maze of halls that threaded through a part of the monastery on the opposite side from which CC's little room was located. Just when she was thinking how hopelessly lost she was, the squire stopped in front of a large wooden door. He knocked quickly twice.

"Enter!" The abbot's high-pitched voice carried easily through the door.

CC hesitated only a moment, and then she strode into the room. It was a large chamber, and CC was surprised by how comfortable it appeared at first glance. A fire was burning cheerfully in a hearth that was large enough that four or five men could have stood at full height inside of it. There were several metal candleholders scattered around the room, mostly between groupings of well-upholstered chairs and polished side tables. Something about the walls of the room caught her attention and CC's gaze slid to them, then her eyes widened in disgust. Carved into the rock walls around the circumference of the room were intricate scenes of suffering, much like the carvings that decorated the exterior walls of the chapel. CC forced her eyes from them.

"You may approach, Princess Undine." The abbot made a delicate gesture with one hand.

He sat on a dais in an ornate chair, thronelike in its intricate design. It was placed at the far side of the room, so that it faced the other chairs and the entryway. Andras stood at his right hand, smug and silent. To his left were four monks. Only Abbot William met her eyes.

Ready for battle, CC walked purposefully forward. Isabel stayed inside the room, near the door.

"I was just admiring your lovely furnishings." CC swept a graceful finger at the chairs and sconces. "It pleases me to see such sumptuous things, even if it is a surprise to see them in a monastery."

The abbot's spine straightened at CC's words, and his pale cheeks flushed suddenly red, reflecting the crimson of his robe.

"They are gifts from my benefactor, and though I would be comfortable with less opulent furnishings, it would be rude to refuse them."

"Benefa*ctor*?" CC's brows came together in confusion. "I understood that this monastery belonged to Sir Andras's mother, so wouldn't that make her a benefa*ctress*?"

The knight spoke up quickly. "The monastery belonged to my mother's family and passed through her to my father at the time of their marriage." His handsome face twisted into a superior sneer. "Women cannot own property. What is a wife's is, by right and by law, always her husband's."

"How very convenient for the husband," CC said without glancing at Andras.

"We are not here to discuss the role of husbands and wives, no matter how badly you are in need of such instruction." Abbot William's voice was sharp. "We are here to solve the problem of your behavior, Princess Undine."

"Then this will be a short visit. I know of no problem with my behavior." CC inclined her head regally. "I hope you have a nice day, Abbot William."

But before she could turn to leave the abbot's voice shot out. The hatred in it chilled CC's blood.

"You will not leave until you have my permission to do so!"

CC froze, her eyes riveted on the abbot's florid face. She thought she could actually see the veins at his temples throbbing in anger. When he continued to speak, he did so through clenched teeth.

"Your behavior has been indiscreet and inappropriate. I believe evidence will come to light that you are a danger to this monastery and to those within it."

"How could that be? By your own standards, I am nothing more than a woman, and even though I am a princess, my function ultimately will be to belong to a man. What possible danger could I represent?" CC spoke quickly, her heart hammering so loudly that she was sure everyone could hear it.

The abbot smiled slyly, like she had just unknowingly stepped into the loop of a trap.

"You are correct that alone a woman is a helpless creature, fashioned only to serve man and to bear his body and his children. But it is that very weak and seductive nature that man must guard against. Remember, it was Eve's original sin that destroyed the paradise that God had created for man!" His voice had risen until the word *man* came out as a shriek. The monks at his side began to glance nervously around the room, as if looking for an escape or a hiding place. Andras was nodding his head in agreement, completely ignoring his mentor's crazed tone.

The outrage that had been simmering inside of CC for days finally boiled, and she slipped the noose of cordiality, allowing herself to truly speak her mind.

"Where I come from many of us look a little deeper into that particular Biblical story. If I remember correctly, Lucifer, who was described as God's most beautiful creation, tempted Eve. She resisted, but eventually gave in." CC shrugged her shoulders nonchalantly, but her eyes challenged the priest. "I think even the strongest among us has something by which he can be tempted, don't you Abbot? Anyway, Eve gave in to Lucifer's temptation. Then she went to Adam and offered him the fruit. And Adam basically said, *'Okay!'* He chose the forbidden—with no supernatural temptation, and without much resistance; he just automatically did what a woman told him to do. When you look at it logically, as I would think a *man* would, you come up with a much different conclusion about who committed the greater sin. At least I think most—"

"Silence!" The priest's shriek echoed off the disfigured stone walls. This time the monks literally cringed, and even Andras's eyes widened in surprise at the abbot's loss of control.

"You will not dare to speak such blasphemy in my presence. Your words are proof that you are in league with the Evil One. Since you first passed through our gates, you have brought darkness within. You shall be purged from this holy place, and by thus purging you from our midst, evil will be defeated once more."

He pointed a shaking finger at the squire who hovered behind her. "Take her to her room to await her punishment."

Terror turned her stomach, but she held her chin high and in her most imperious voice she spoke for the first time directly to the knight.

"Sir Andras, please explain to the abbot that harming me would not be your most profitable course of action."

When the abbot started to speak, Andras lay a calming hand on his arm.

"Father," he soothed. "Let us hear her out."

"I have remembered my birthright. Harm me and know that you trifle with the only daughter of King Canute, conqueror and Lord of Vikings." Her voice was strong and filled with pride.

At her proclamation, Andras's body went very still, and the florid color of the abbot's face drained away like dripping wax.

CC's smile was arrogant. "I have already sent my own message to him. The fishermen were right in part of their reports; it's too bad that they were so clouded by superstition that they did not recognize that what they sighted were my people searching for the daughter of their beloved king. Last night they found me, and it was then that my memory returned. You know yourself that you accosted me as I finished my climb from the beach." Her laughter was sharp. "Why else would I be so drawn to the waters? They are my birthright. Soon my father will come for me." The anger in CC's voice filled the room. "If you harm me, he will loose his Berserkirs and they will destroy you."

The room was silent. Andras and the abbot exchanged furtive glances.

"If your father is King Canute and his men did come for you last night, why is it you remain here?" Andras shot the question at her.

CC scoffed indignantly. "A Viking princess does not steal away in the night like a lowly servant. I sent word to my father that I had been rescued and was uninjured. I knew he would want to come for me himself so that he could reward those who treated me well."

And punish those who did not . . .

The unspoken words seemed to hang powerfully in the electric air around CC.

"If you don't believe me your solution is simple. Just wait. If I'm telling the truth, my father will appear to claim me, and you will be rewarded. If I'm lying, and I don't have a powerful family, no one will come for me and you can *punish* me to your heart's content." CC raised one eyebrow at the knight. "And something tells me that you very much need my father's reward money."

The knight and the abbot exchanged another look, and CC was relieved to observe that the priest seemed to have brought himself under control.

"We would, of course, not wish to harm the daughter of a king," Abbot William said. He glanced again at Sir Andras, who nodded briefly. "We will continue to provide you sanctuary for the amount of time it should require your father to come for you."

"No more than a fortnight," Sir Andras added.

The abbot nodded solemnly. "A fortnight it is. If King Canute has not claimed you as his own within that time, I will have no choice but to put you on trial for heresy and witchcraft."

"I agree," CC retorted.

"Until King Canute comes to Caldei, you will remain in your chamber under guard. We must be certain that no harm befalls such a *valuable* lady," the priest said.

CC felt panic like a brand. She was going to be locked in her room? Her heart skittered in her chest.

She met the abbot's reptilian gaze. "I am a Viking princess—I demand more freedom than that. If you lock me in my room I will tell my father that you treated me like a prisoner and not a guest. He does not reward jailers."

"Undine." Andras's tone had lost its anger and had returned to being patronizing. "Surely you will agree that your safety is of the utmost concern to us, especially in light of the proclamation of your noble blood."

"Yes—"

Andras cut her off. "Good. Then you will understand that if you choose to leave your chamber you will be accompanied at all times by an armed guard."

CC raised her chin. "Am I so dangerous?"

"You are so protected."

"Oh, do not think that I'm without protection." She narrowed her eyes to slits and was pleased to see Andras's eyes widen in response.

"Enough, witch!" the priest spat. "We may have to tolerate your presence until your heathen father claims you, but we will not tolerate your blasphemous threats."

CC shook her head slowly side to side and gave the abbot a pitying look. "Why do you automatically assume a strong woman is evil? What happened to you to twist you into this?"

Abbot William held up a shaking hand, palm forward like he could ward off her words. "Escort the princess back to her chamber. Now!" he snarled.

Without waiting for the squire, CC turned and strode across the room. As she neared the door, Isabel made a spectacular show of cringing away from her and crossing herself. CC scoffed and made a dismissive wave in her direction. As the squire closed the door behind them, CC could hear Isabel's distinctive voice croaking, "Evil! I knew it from the first day I laid eyes on her! Evil!"

Isabel's performance made CC bite the inside of her cheek to keep from laughing as the nervous young squire led the way back to her chamber.

CHAPTER TWENTY-FOUR

C C wrenched open her door, startling the squire who stood guard outside. "I want to go to the chapel, and I need help changing my clothes. Get that old servant, whatever her name is."

The squire blinked balefully at her, suddenly reminding her of a calf. She sighed. "Now! I don't have all the rest of the day to waste!" She slammed the door in his face.

"This princess stuff just gets easier and easier," she muttered to herself. His boots clinked smartly against the stone floor as he hurried down the hall, rushing to obey her command.

She paced while she waited for Isabel. She had been back in her room for hours, alone, under guard, with absolutely nothing to do except worry. She couldn't stand it anymore. Maybe if she spent time cleaning the chapel she could work off some of her tension, and if she got really lucky Gaea might even show up. The goddess certainly had been quiet lately, which was making CC more than a little uneasy.

Two theatrically hesitant knocks sounded on her door.

"Come in!" CC didn't have to pretend the frustration in her voice.

"You summoned me, Princess?" Isabel said as she limped with obvious reluctance into the room.

"Yes, yes, yes," CC said. "Hurry up and close the door. I'm going to go work in the chapel, and I need help changing."

CC saw the old woman give the squire a frightened look before she closed the door.

As soon as they were alone Isabel hurried over to her and the women embraced.

"You were spectacular!" Isabel spoke into CC's ear as she worked loose the intricate set of laces at the back of CC's outer garment.

"You weren't half bad yourself," CC whispered back, and the two women shared a grin. "But I can't sit here any longer. I have to stay busy, and cleaning the chapel will definitely keep me busy."

"I will bring your food to the chapel. It is well past midday." Isabel shook CC's shoulders. "You have missed another meal. How will you stay strong for your lover if you do not eat?"

"You're always so wise," CC said.

"And well it is that you remember it," Isabel scolded her fondly.

"What happened after I left?" CC whispered.

Isabel's hands stilled for a moment as she collected her thoughts. "The abbot wants to destroy you. That has not changed," she spoke grimly. "It is only the knight's influence, and the fear of retribution from the Vikings that keeps him from harming you."

"It seemed like Andras believed my story."

CC could feel the old woman's nod. "He covets King Canute's money, and he still desires you, but he is not a fool. He is sending for reinforcements from Caer Llion. He worries that even if you are returned safely to the Vikings, the king will decide to sack the monastery."

"Doesn't seem that there's much here to sack," CC muttered.

"Oh, you are wrong, Undine. The monks are well known for their fine wool and their fat, tasty lamb. Also, Abbot William has several ancient manuscripts that Brothers, specially chosen by him, meticulously copy."

"I didn't realize all that," CC said thoughtfully.

"The knight is acting wisely."

"Well, I never thought Andras was stupid, just narrow-minded."

"I agree with you," Isabel said.

"It's about time."

The old woman snorted.

"Do you *have* to follow me into the chapel, too?" CC asked the guard, who was walking a little behind her, carrying two buckets brimming with clean water. "I'm going to be in there working."

"I must stay with you at all times, Princess," the squire said mechanically.

"While I work I like to pray. Your presence will be interfering with my prayer time." She shot him a knowing look. "Are you married?"

Caught off guard by her question, he was too surprised not to answer. "Yes."

"Do you have any children?"

"Not yet, Princess."

"Well, in my country there is a belief that the Holy Mother can gift couples with children and can make men especially potent." She paused pointedly and let her glance drift briefly down his body before continuing. "*If* they please her. And, of course, she can do the opposite if they don't. I can't believe that the Holy Mother will be very pleased by you interrupting my prayer time."

"I would never want to interfere with the piety of one so devout. I will await you outside this door." The squire suddenly looked very pale.

"Thank you. I'm sure your sensitivity will be rewarded," CC said sweetly. Taking the buckets from him, she entered the dim sanctuary and breathed a sigh of relief when the door closed firmly behind her.

The laughter of the goddess greeted her.

"Oh, Daughter! Threatening that poor man with impotency. Really, I think that was somewhat harsh."

Gaea lounged on the floor in front of her statue, looking radiant in a long gown of sheer, sparkling silk the color of ripe green olives. Her hair curled around her waist and seemed to pool in a glistening carpet all around her.

The enormous sense of relief CC felt at the sight of the goddess didn't stop the sharp edge in her voice.

"I'm tired of being followed and watched and kept under guard."

Instantly, the weight of the buckets disappeared as invisible hands took them from her. They floated inches off the floor until they came to rest just where CC would have placed them herself. She smiled her gratitude at Gaea and felt her mood lighten, too.

"Thank you, Mother. That helps. And I'm sorry I snapped at you."

"It is understandable, young one," Gaea said indulgently. "So the abbot has you under guard? What has happened?"

Quickly, CC brought Gaea up-to-date on the events of the day. By the time she finished speaking the goddess's eyes were glowing with pride.

"You have done well, Daughter. You have found your way by using your own wits. I am pleased with you."

CC felt a wonderful rush of warmth at the goddess's praise.

"And I have news for you. Lir will be in these waters on the third night. There he will hear your petition and render judgment."

"But how did he sound? Did you tell him about Sarpedon and Dylan?"

"I have not spoken with the God of the Seas." Gaea tossed her hair back in irritation. "He is still embroiled in the problems of the Hawaiian deities."

"Then how do you know he's coming?" CC asked.

"I sent my messenger to him with my request that he come to us. His own messenger brought his reply just this morning." A shadow passed over the goddess's face, clouding her lovely features.

"But something's bothering you. Are you worried about what he'll decide?" CC asked nervously.

"No," Gaea said quickly. "I do not fear his judgment. Lir's wish has always been for Undine to love the waters and for her to choose to live there happily. Now he will have his wish. I do not believe that your rejection of Sarpedon's suit will change his feelings, especially after he understands that you have my full support."

"So you think Lir will keep Sarpedon from going after Dylan?"

Gaea patted her hand reassuringly. "Lir knows Dylan. He knows that the merman is honorable and kind. I believe that he will honor your choice. It will, undeniably, be an uncomfortable scene when he explains to Sarpedon that you have chosen another, but the word of the God of the Seas will be obeyed—and there are many willing nymphs from which young Sarpedon may choose."

"Then why the worried look?" CC pushed.

"You begin to know me too well, Daughter," Gaea said affectionately. Then she squinted her eyes thoughtfully. "Lir's choice of messenger was unusual. I have never known him to use any messenger but one of his handpicked dolphins or selkies, and this time he chose to send a sea eel. The creature did not even appear to be very intelligent." Gaea shrugged her shoulders. "Perhaps the trouble with those barbarous island gods has been more of a strain on him than I imagined."

"So it wasn't meant as a slight to us or a sign that he's mad or anything?"

"The Lord of the Seas would not slight the Mother of the Earth or her daughter." Gaea's eyes sparkled.

"I should have known better," CC said, giving the goddess a knowing look.

"Yes, you should have." Gaea winked back at her. Then her voice sobered. "In two days this part of your life will be over, and you will forever be a creature of the sea, mated with a merman. I will only ask you once more, Daughter. Are you certain of your choice? You need not think that the only human from which you have to choose is the knight. If you ask me to intercede, I will send forth a call that many men will answer. You could have your pick of them."

CC spoke slowly when she answered the goddess, but her words were firm and her decision was clear. "I know it should seem scary to me to leave the land forever, but the water calls me, Gaea. And, yes, I know that a lot of that is because this body's true form is not human, so it continually longs for the water." CC gazed steadily into Gaea's eyes, willing her to understand. "But I don't want to give that up. I love who and what I am when I'm a mermaid. And I love Dylan. It's like I've finally found the perfect mixture of magic in my life." CC pointed in the direction of the sea. "And it's out there."

The goddess's smile was bittersweet. "I will honor your choice, my daughter, as well as take pride in your strength."

"But, it's not like I'll be gone forever. I'll still get to see you!" CC exclaimed.

"Yes, Daughter. My cove will be waiting to welcome you, and I will always answer your call." She raised one brow and smiled mischievously. "Perhaps one day you will gift me with a land-loving granddaughter."

"How about several of them?" CC laughed.

Before Gaea could answer they were interrupted by Isabel's distinctly gravelly voice coming from the entrance of the chapel.

"Yes! If I need your protection from her witchcraft, I shall certainly call. But I must bring her food. If she weakens and dies it will not go well for us when her father, the king, appears." Isabel's gruff voice easily traveled the length of the chapel. She sighed theatrically before the guard closed the door behind her.

CC giggled and winked at Gaea. "She really should have been an actress; she's enjoying this a little too much."

Expecting the goddess to disappear as usual, CC turned to greet the old woman and took several steps toward her, intending to take the heavy tray from her. Isabel was limping down the side aisle, scanning all of the pews to be certain they were alone. When she saw there were no monks lurking around praying, her disgruntled expression shifted into a wide grin.

"I brought you a new kind of st—" The old woman stopped speaking. She was staring at something behind CC.

Confused, CC glanced over her shoulder to see what had startled Isabel. There stood Gaea, next to the statue of Mary. And yet it wasn't Gaea. The woman was very pretty, but she was most definitely mortal. Delicate wrinkles gave her face a comfortable, lived-in look, and laugh lines betrayed her good humor. She was clothed in simple robes of undyed linen. A brown shawl was draped over her head, hiding most of her coffee-colored hair, but what escaped the shawl was just beginning to show a fine weaving of silver. Despite the evidence of age, her face had a timeless look. She could have been twenty or forty, it was impossible to tell. She smiled at Isabel.

"Excuse me, Princess Undine. I did not realize that you were not alone." Isabel set the tray on a nearby pew and turned hastily to leave.

"Please, there is no need for you to go." Gaea's voice was melodic and accented much like Andras's. "My name is Galena. I came to Caldei to barter ewes for my father's flock. I heard word of the restoration of the Holy Mother, and I could not leave without visiting her shrine."

Isabel was studying Gaea with an intent expression of open curiosity. "Forgive me for saying so, but it is unusual that a father would allow a daughter to tend to his business."

"My father has no sons, and I have no husband. In his old age he is wise enough to trust me."

"See, I told you some men respect women," CC said, recovering her voice.

"You are correct, Princess, some men do," Gaea said with a soft smile. "But no matter the beliefs of men, women will always have a special power within themselves." Her gaze touched the gleaming statue. "I believe Mary would agree with me."

"You sound much like the princess," Isabel said.

Gaea's smile widened. "What a lovely coincidence, as is my visit today."

Isabel's eyes hadn't left Gaea's face. Suddenly, they widened in discovery. "Forgive me for staring, but you bear a striking resemblance to the statue of the Holy Mother."

Gaea's laughter was a musical sound. CC hoped that Isabel wouldn't notice that the flames of the candles surrounding the statue leapt and danced in response.

"Is that so surprising?" the goddess said. "Do you not believe that every woman carries the spark of the Divine Feminine within her?"

"I . . ." Isabel cleared her throat. "I have never heard it spoken so."

Gaea's voice was filled with compassion. "Come close. I have something to show the two of you."

On unsure feet Isabel let CC lead her to the disguised goddess's side.

Gaea held one hand out in front of her, palm down. "Place your hands beside mine."

Without hesitation, CC put her hand next to Gaea's, and Isabel followed suit.

"Look at how amazing we are, we three, as we reflect the three aspects of the Divine Feminine," Gaea said. She pointed to each of the women's hands in turn, beginning with CC's, which were shapely and unlined. "The maiden, lovely and young, with her life stretching before her, magical and new. She is vibrant and fresh, drawing the power of springtime to her."

Then she pointed at her own hand. It was stronger and the knuckles were already beginning to show lines. It was a hand that could do a full day's work and then comfort a sick child. "The mother, full and ripe, filled with the power of summer and autumn. She is life-giver and nurturer. She is the heart of her hearth and home. Without honoring the mother, the family cannot thrive."

Then, with an infinitely gentle gesture, she touched Isabel's gnarled hand. "And the crone, although I prefer her matriarchal title, the wise woman. She is rich with wisdom and experience, a leader to those who will someday take her place when she is gone, and a comfort to those who are at the end of their life's journey. Her power is of great depth. It is that of the experience of ages forged with the strength of winter." Gaea spoke solemnly, clasping their hands in hers. "Alone, each is important and unique. But joined together, they form a three-fold link that is soldered by the Divine Feminine. We need each other—that is how we are fashioned. To deny this is to live a life less than fulfilled."

"Women need to stick together," CC agreed. "Even if we are different."

"Isn't that what woman is, a magical, complex blending of differences?" Gaea said.

"I am ashamed that it has taken me a lifetime to know this," Isabel said.

Gaea's smile was filled with unending love. "So you see, it should be of no surprise when you recognize the reflection of the divine within another woman."

"You are very wise, Galena," Isabel said, still holding Gaea's hand.

"I am a shepherdess who has had long hours of solitude in which to think and pray," she said simply. Then she squeezed Isabel's and CC's hands before slipping loose from them. "And now I can hear my flock calling me. They are impatient for my return. I must bid you good day, ladies."

"May the blessing of the Holy Mother go with you," Isabel said.

"Yes, have a safe journey home," CC added quickly.

Gaea nodded to each of them, then she bowed briefly before the statue of the Holy Virgin. When she raised her head, CC caught the sparkle in her eyes. The disguised goddess called a farewell to them as she walked toward the chapel's exit. The ever-present mist of incense seemed to swallow her as she faded into the shadows.

"A very interesting woman," Isabel said thoughtfully.

"She sure is."

"I will consider her words. They are new thoughts for me, but they touched my heart in a way that I have never before felt . . ." Her words faded as the squire threw open the door.

"Is all well here?" he asked, blinking quickly like a nervous bird as his eyes became accustomed to the dark. "I heard something odd."

"Everything is fine. I'm just going to keep this old woman in here to help me with the rest of the heavy cleaning. You should probably send word to the kitchen that she's going to be busy for the remainder of the afternoon." CC made a shooing gesture at him.

He looked doubtful, but CC's impotency threat still weighed heavily on his mind. "I am only a short distance away," he told the silent Isabel as he backed out the door.

CC and Isabel looked at each other.

"I thought maybe you'd want to stay here for a while," CC said simply.

"Thank you. I would like nothing more than to aid you in restoring the Mother's chapel. And I do so enjoy spending time with you."

CC grinned. "I like it, too."

Isabel took a deep breath and asked the question that had been haunting her mind. "When must you leave us?"

CC felt a pang of regret. "I must leave on the third night. But it doesn't have to be forever. I'll still be here—I'll just, well, live in the water and look a little different, that is, from my waist down."

Isabel blinked in surprise. "Then we could still visit with one another?"

"If I wouldn't frighten you," CC said slowly.

Isabel touched her cheek in an infinitely tender gesture. "You could never frighten me, my dear friend. Differences do not matter between us."

Relief flooded through CC. "I'm so glad, Isabel."

"As am I, sweet girl." Then she squared her shoulders and began rolling up her sleeves. "If we only have two more days, we had better get to work."

"My thoughts exactly," CC said.

Isabel took the closest broom and began attacking a nest of spider webs in a dark corner. "You know, you may be a wise woman yourself some day," she said.

"Make that a wise mer-woman, and I'll take you up on it."

As they worked together to restore what was rightfully the Mother's, their laughter joined and painted the walls with the joy of women working together in perfect harmony.

CHAPTER TWENTY-FIVE

ISABEL had just finished combing through CC's thick hair when a sharp knock interrupted their quiet conversation. She limped to the door and cracked it open.

"I have come to see the princess," Andras's deep voice commanded.

"Please tell Sir Andras that I have already dressed for bed. The events of the day have tired me so much that I have to retire early." CC let her voice carry to the listening knight.

"Sir Andras, the princess—" Isabel began, but the knight cut her off.

"Perhaps the princess would not be so fatigued if she had not felt the need to cavort about the countryside last night."

CC sighed and yanked a robe over her head. Ignoring Isabel's silent look that counseled temperance, she shoved open the door. Andras stood with his hands planted on his waist, face flushed with irritation. He had obviously taken great care with his appearance. He was freshly scrubbed and wearing the same dashing outfit he had worn the first day she had met him. Appalled, CC realized that he must have come to her door to court her.

Wasn't she his prisoner and possibly a dangerous witch?

Then CC understood and blinked in surprise. Andras had told the abbot that he would make his decision soon about whether he was going to marry or ransom her. Obviously, he had decided on marriage, so he was simply behaving honorably and beginning his courtship in earnest. It seemed the Rule of Thumb had outweighed her heathen tendencies and her outspoken mouth. CC supposed she should have been flattered. Instead she was annoyed. He didn't want her, he wanted a medieval Barbie doll.

"Sir Andras, I am exhausted because over the course of one short day I have remembered my birthright, defended myself against a charge of witchcraft and worked hard to restore a chapel that looks like it has been neglected for decades. I think that even a man would find a day like that tiring," she finished, trying to keep the sarcasm out of her voice.

Almost as if he couldn't help himself, Andras's eyes studied her face, lingering on the high, graceful planes of her cheeks and the full, sensual sweep of her lips. Then they traveled down her long, shapely neck and stared hotly at the glimpse of skin where the chemise gaped open. He wet his lips.

CC watched him closely. Just how far had Sarpedon's influence spread? His eyes appeared normal, and his facial features were his own, but his look was one of raw desire, and that was unusual for the knight. Until Sarpedon began possessing him, Andras had treated her carefully—he had not seemed like the kind of man who would think it was proper behavior to leer at the lady he was trying to woo.

"True, Undine, you have had a difficult day. But I remember that not long ago you proclaimed that you found the exercise of walking especially gratifying, even when you are fatigued," he persuaded. "I ask that you walk with me, Princess Undine." He held a muscular arm out to her as if he expected no other response than for her to happily accept his proposal.

"Not tonight, but thank you for asking."

Isabel stirred restlessly at her side as Andras's face darkened with anger at her rejection.

"I ask as a knight and a gentleman that you come walking with me, and you spurn me?" he said incredulously.

"I was under the impression that when a lady is asked a question, she has the right to answer yes *or* no," CC said impatiently. She hadn't been lying to the knight. She was tired and wanted nothing more than to finish her glass of wine and to fall into bed. "I didn't spurn you, I simply exercised my right."

"Then as a gentleman I choose to exercise my right to protect you from your own excesses so that you will be less exhausted and able to walk with me. Tonight and every night hereafter there will be a guard stationed at your door and your window to insure that you do not exhaust yourself with further needless forays to the shore," he said with cruel finality. "Tomorrow, then, Princess Undine. May I find you in more lively spirits, or perhaps I will have to be assured of your health and rest by confining you to your room for the daylight hours, too."

He closed the door with a solid slam.

"I should have just walked with him." CC sighed.

Isabel nodded her head. "I was afraid your refusal would bait the knight. His behavior has been unusual of late."

"Yes, I can see that now, and we both know why."

"Sarpedon." Isabel whispered the name.

CC nodded, rubbing her face wearily. "All this time I've been more worried about Abbot William. I guess I underestimated Sarpedon's effect on Andras."

"You underestimated the effect of your beauty," Isabel said as she helped CC off with the robe.

CC laughed sardonically. "I'm not used to it. My other body was nothing like this one. Men pretty much ignored me."

Isabel gave her a skeptical look and made a rude noise in her throat.

"What?" CC asked.

"Did you not tell me that a woman's beauty is more complex than her physical appearance? That applies to you as well as to me."

When CC started to argue Isabel held her hand up to silence her.

"Take this wise woman's words for truth. There is more to you than physical beauty. The knight knows that and desires to possess you—all of you. Sarpedon's evil influence has simply intensified that desire." Isabel turned down the covers of the narrow bed and gestured for CC to climb in. "Rest, Undine. Your eyes have that dark, haunted look. Sleep will strengthen you."

CC pulled the coarse blanket up under her arms and leaned against the hard wooden headboard as she watched Isabel tidy the small room. Outside her window she could hear the sounds of a guard settling in for the night. What would happen in two nights? How would she get out of her room? Her stomach churned. Isabel's weight caused the bed to sag.

"Do not fear," she whispered reassuringly while she fussed with CC's bed sheets. "Remember, we are one, the maiden, the mother and the wise woman. Together we will find a way to return you to the seas."

"And to Dylan," CC murmured, her eyes suddenly bright with tears.

Isabel cupped CC's chin gently. "And to your lover. We are stronger than they know. All will be well."

CC curled onto her side and Isabel stroked her hair, soothing her into a deep sleep by humming a lilting lullaby that somehow reminded CC of the sound of waves.

CHAPTER TWENTY-SIX

THE next day, flanked by two guards, CC managed to stay unavailable to Andras through a hasty breakfast in the kitchen, and a midday meal, even though it took her only a few crowning polishes to complete her work in the chapel. To avoid the knight, she kept herself busy weeding the herb garden and harvesting a long list of fresh plants for Isabel. She was pleasantly surprised when, from time to time, a passing monk would stop to compliment her on the beauty of Mary's restoration. She had just returned to her room to scrub something sticky from her hands and change her soiled robe for a new one when a knock sounded against her door.

She cracked the door. The knight was dressed as he had been the evening before, and his expression was strained.

"Good afternoon, Sir Andras," CC said formally, feeling especially uncomfortable without Isabel at her side.

Andras inclined his head. "Princess Undine, I trust today you are recovered and able to walk with me."

"I would be happy to, but as you can see I'm really not dressed for it." She pointed at her dirty robe.

"I will send for the servant, Isabel, to aid you. I await you in the courtyard," he said firmly, then executed an abrupt military about-face and strode away.

CC sighed and closed the door. She didn't have to wait long for Isabel to arrive.

"Come, let me help you into your beautiful gown," she said, lifting the shining material from where it was draped across the bed.

"I don't want to walk with him," CC said.

"You must, or you chance being locked away."

At that reminder, CC shivered in fear.

"Smile at Sir Andras. Stroke his ego," Isabel said.

"I'm worried about what Sarpedon could make him do." CC chewed her bottom lip.

Isabel frowned. "You must take care not to arouse the knight's anger, then perhaps the evil spirit's influence will sleep. Think of Andras as the dashing knight who rushed to rescue you from the seas. And remember, this is the last night you will spend as a human. Tomorrow you return to the water. Can you not play the pretty princess for such a short time?" Isabel finished lacing her outer garment and began clasping the long strands of jewels around CC's neck. "Perhaps you can persuade the knight to walk with you by the sea. Could you not tolerate him in exchange for the chance at a glimpse of your Dylan?"

"I hadn't even thought of that!" CC said, her heart racing.

As had become her habit during the time that she could not spend with him, CC had tried to stay busy and not think too much of Dylan. She had found that if she dwelled on how much she missed him, the ache of her longing for him and for the sea merged into one painful force, which came dangerously close to overwhelming her. Now she felt herself tremble with suppressed desire as thoughts of her lover filled her mind.

"Hurry!" she told Isabel.

"Child"—the old woman took CC's shoulders in her hands, forcing her to look into her eyes—"you may catch sight of him, but you must control your reaction to his nearness. Do not display your emotions and reveal yourself to the knight. Remember, you must wait on the timing of the Holy Mother. Promise me you will use caution."

"Yes, yes! I promise," she said quickly, wanting to reassure Isabel and bolt from the room. But the old woman wouldn't release her.

"Remember Sarpedon. Do not put yourself or your lover in danger because you mistakenly allow passion to rule your actions."

At the mention of Sarpedon, CC felt her head clear. "You're right. I promise to be careful."

"Go, child. And luck be with you as well as the blessings of the Holy Virgin."

CC turned in the doorway. "Thank you, my wise friend." Then she hurried to the courtyard.

Andras was pacing restlessly back and forth in front of the arched entryway that led from the hall. His two squires were flanking him a little way inside the courtyard.

"I'm ready for our walk," CC said.

The three men looked at her, and the heat of their stares was a tangible force against CC's body. Their eyes seemed to bore into her, and she felt the exposed skin on her chest, neck, face and arms burn with an electric shock of discomfort.

Her hand went automatically to her neck. "Is something wrong?" she asked.

Andras blinked and pulled his gaze from her body to meet her eyes. He approached her with a feral glide that reminded CC of an animal stalking its prey. When he reached her side he took her unresponsive hand and raised it to his lips. CC wanted to pull her hand from his possessive grasp and bolt back down the hallway.

"I had forgotten how lovely you are in your gown. It is unfortunate that you have been spending so much time in the coarse robes of the Brothers." He slid her hand through his arm proprietarily and together they moved across the courtyard. "A woman of your beauty and breeding should spend all of her time in glittering gowns surrounded by luxurious things."

With an effort, CC didn't sigh. "Then I would be no more than a pretty doll or a piece of art. Those things are nice to look at, but they have no real purpose."

The knight's laugh was condescending. "Is not a woman's purpose in life to be a thing of grace and beauty, a true asset to her husband and family?"

"As I am not yet a wife, I believe I am being an asset to my family by working to restore the area of the chapel that is devoted to Mary. Do you not agree that my work for the Great Mother is important?"

Andras nodded quickly. "Of course—piety is always important, especially in a woman."

CC ground her teeth together to keep her retort inside her mouth.

Just then they passed the well, and CC felt her attention and her gaze drawn to it. During the past few days, she had successfully avoided coming near this area of the courtyard. Until now. At the sight of the well her stomach fluttered nervously. The stone structure stood silently in the middle of the courtyard, looking perfectly normal. There was no vapor escaping from it, no ghostly shape hovering above it. CC didn't even detect any of the feelings of dread she had experienced around the time Sarpedon began manifesting.

CC wasn't sure why, but her lack of any reaction to the well made her feel very uneasy.

"How have you been feeling lately?" she asked abruptly.

"Much improved," Andras said.

"No more"—she struggled for an appropriate word—"dizziness, or falling or anything?"

"None. During the midday meal Abbot William even mentioned how pleased he is that I have recovered and returned to myself. His prayers on my behalf were obviously successful."

"And no one else has been acting, um, *strangely*?" CC asked.

"No." His voice had a suspicious edge to it. "Why do you ask?"

She shrugged nonchalantly. "No reason in particular." She could feel that the knight was still studying her, so she added what she thought he wanted to hear. "The whole thing scared me. It's a relief to know that you are well."

Andras patted her hand indulgently. "Of course it would frighten you, but you may rest easy. I am fully recovered, and you must know that under my protection you have nothing to fear."

CC gave him a tight grimace masquerading as a smile, and he patted her hand again. At least he seemed to be acting like himself.

They exited through the monastery gates, and it was then that CC noticed that the squires were following them. And they, like Andras, were well armed.

Raising her eyebrows at the knight she asked, "Is there something out here that you're afraid of?"

"Of course not," Andras said, drawing himself up to his full, imposing height, blond mane shimmering in the early afternoon sunlight.

He really was incredibly handsome, the perfect knight in shining armor.

"Oh, then those guards must be for me." She fluttered her eyelashes at him coquettishly. "Silly me, I thought I just heard you say that I didn't need to be afraid of anything while I was under your protection. Or is that just while we're within the walls of the monastery?"

The knight's jaw tightened. "Marten! Gilbert! Remain here. I will escort the princess alone."

The two squires sent hot looks in CC's direction, but they did as they were ordered.

"Come," Andras said, his voice gentled from the tone of command he used with his men. "We shall walk down the road. It branches not far from here and the eastern fork winds through a rather nice meadow. I thought that you should visit some of the *inland* parts of Caldei," he said, putting an emphasis on the word.

CC wanted to tell him that she could care less about what was inland—she just wanted to go to the seashore! Instead she swallowed her frustration and strolled casually beside him, careful to keep her expression neutral.

"Anywhere you would like to go is fine with me. You were right; I do enjoy the exercise."

Andras smiled at her compliment, and CC couldn't help returning his smile. He did seem to have shaken Sarpedon's influence and was his usual, macho self again. The thought made her smile turn into a grin, and even though they weren't near the water, CC found that she was actually enjoying the walk. Soon they came to what CC recognized as the little path that branched from the road and meandered down to the shore. CC pointed to the trail.

"Isn't that the path that we took before?" she asked.

"Yes."

CC sighed dramatically.

"Are you well, Undine? Perhaps you would like to rest before we continue?" Andras asked.

"No, I'm fine. I was just remembering what a wonderful lunch you had packed for us and what a nice time we had that day."

Andras's eyes widened. "I am pleased to hear you say so, Undine."

CC took a deep breath, steeling herself. Then she turned to face the knight. "Andras, I have been thinking about us." She paused, letting the word *us* linger in the air between them. "We have had some unfortunate misunderstandings, and I am sorry for that. After all, you did save me, and I should be more appreciative than I have been." Purposefully she looked down at her feet, pretending maidenly shyness. Then, glancing up at him through thick lashes she said, "Maybe we could start over."

CC watched a fierce look of triumph pass quickly over the knight's face.

"Yes, let us begin anew," he said passionately.

CC plastered a wide smile on her face. When the knight began to lean toward her as if he wanted to kiss her, she pulled her hand from his arm and clapped girlishly.

"Oh, good!" CC chirped, waggling her fingers in the direction of the trail and brightening her face, as if an idea had just occurred to her. "And what better way to start over than for us to follow the same path we did before all of our misunderstandings started!"

The knight hesitated only a moment before responding. "If it would make you happy, Undine."

CC sighed in relief as they stepped off the road and began following the twisting trail. It took very little time for them to break through the trees and come to the sandy shoreline. CC breathed deeply, washing herself in the aroma of the salt breeze. Her spirit, dressed in her human body, quivered and strained with its desire to rejoin the waters. The ocean was sweet-laughter blue, and the whimsical waves played tag with the shore, calling to her in a voice that echoed through her blood.

"You always become even more beautiful when you are near the sea." Andras's voice was raw with lust. "I wonder why that is."

CC wrenched her thoughts from the water to focus on the knight. His features were tight, locked in the intense expression of a man determined to possess a woman. CC felt a shiver of apprehension. She had been a fool to believe that Sarpedon's influence could be so easily shaken. She realized that she had to distract him. Struggling to calm the fear within her, she formed her lips into a friendly smile.

"Well, it must be because I love the sea so much. Being near it makes me feel like I'm home." She took another deep breath, schooling her face into an aspect of polite interest. "But enough about me. You've hardly told me anything about your childhood. I would love to hear about Caer Llion."

The mention of his home seemed to break through his fog of lust, and Andras blinked like a man surfacing after a long dive.

"Caer Llion is a place of great beauty," he said solemnly. "It is not wild, as is this coastline. It is well-ordered and civilized." Andras stepped closer to her. "You could find there everything your heart desires."

CC summoned up a delighted laugh and skipped a step away from him, as if she could hardly contain her glee at the thought of learning more about his home.

"Oh, it sounds wonderful! Please, tell me more," she said as she wandered girlishly down the shoreline, picking up an occasional seashell or piece of discarded coral, while she moved ever closer to the water.

"Well," Andras said thoughtfully as he followed CC. "The first thing you should know about Caer Llion is that it is a well-ordered castle . . ."

Andras loved his home, and his voice was warm and animated as he enumerated the wonders of Caer Llion. All CC had to do was to make an occasional, interested noise and smile encouragingly. He was so intent on his description of Caer Llion's stables that he didn't even notice when CC slipped off her shoes. It was only when she hiked up her skirts and actually stepped into the water that he paused in his recitation.

"You should have care. The water can cause a chill."

CC noticed that his gaze was riveted on the glimpse of knee and calf she was exposing.

"I'll be careful," she said, cheerfully ignoring the heat in his eyes. "Go on, you haven't described the main hall of the castle yet."

CC breathed a sigh of relief as he continued his dissertation. Nodding and smiling, she half turned away from him and continued walking down the shoreline. Hungrily, her eyes scanned the water. There was no flash of orange and gold, no sign of Dylan's sleek body.

She wanted to call to Dylan. She had planned to—until she had stepped onto the beach. What would Dylan think when he saw her with Andras? Would he trust her, or would he be angry and jealous? Or worse, would he feel hurt and betrayed? Questions filled her mind as she made polite noises at the knight to keep him talking.

The shoreline bent to the east, then it curved back abruptly to the west. In the middle of the bend was formed a shallow cove that was littered with large, smooth rocks. The water there was more tamed than the wild waves that jarred the shore beneath the monastery. CC pulled her skirts up a little higher and walked out into the cove, climbing easily up on the rounded top of the nearest rock.

"Undine, those rocks are slick with sea water," Andras said.

"Oh, they're really not very slick. See?" She tapped the sand-colored rock with her toe. "The tide is out and the top is dry." She smiled at him. "Andras, would you say that the stones from which Caer Llion was constructed are the same color as this rock, or do they look more like the gray stones of the monastery?"

Andras rubbed his chin, pondering rock colors and shades of his beloved Caer Llion. CC stepped to the next rock. By skipping from rock to rock she had traveled well out into the cove and was four stony mounds away from the knight before he finished the description of the wall surrounding Caer Llion.

"Undine, perhaps you should return to shore now."

CC glanced over her shoulder at him. He had walked closer to the waves and was nervously watching the water. This time CC didn't stifle her grin.

"Andras, can't you swim?" she asked.

The knight stuck out his well-defined chin. "No. I cannot."

CC's laughter danced across the water. "You really should learn—it's a lot of fun, not to mention excellent exercise."

"I have no desire to engage in such barbaric behavior." He took one step closer to the water. "You should return now, Undine."

Before she could answer him, a flash of brilliance caught the corner of her gaze. Her heart thumped wildly as she saw a familiar golden shadow just below the surface of the water. It was gliding toward her rock.

"I think I'll sit out here a little while," CC said quickly. Gathering her skirts she sat on the smooth, cool surface of the rock. Her legs dangled down into the water, which covered her feet and calves. "I think I am a little tired. I should rest before I try to climb back to shore." She gave him an apologetic look. "I guess you were right, again."

"I will come to you." Andras's voice was curt as he put one booted foot into the edge of the waterline.

"No!" she shouted. The knight paused, and CC continued in a more controlled voice. "I'll be fine in a few minutes, and I wouldn't want you to fall into the water. I'm pretty sure that it's well over your head out here."

Andras gave the waves a distasteful look.

A few yards from her rock the water flashed golden.

"I'll just sit here," she said. Then she looked down at her legs. Widening her eyes, as if noticing for the first time that she was showing so much skin, she squeaked a little gasp of shock. With what she hoped was maidenly modesty, CC shifted her seat until her legs were facing seaward, their partial nudity hidden by the bulk of the rock. She twisted at the waist to look back at the knight. "How foolish of me to get into this situation. And I certainly didn't realize I was being so immodest."

"It is just the two of us, Undine." Andras's voice deepened suggestively.

"And what a relief that is to me!" CC said, filling her voice with naiveté. "I'd be mortified if anyone else knew. I hope I can trust you not to mention this to my father."

"Your honor is safe with me, Undine." The look Andras sent her was long and intimate.

"Thank you. Now, I'm going to sit here and rest for a little while. Why don't you continue with your description of Caer Llion? You haven't told me yet about your personal chambers."

"I would rather that you visited those chambers yourself someday, Undine," Andras said.

"Why don't you whet my curiosity with a description?" she said quickly.

As Andras launched into another lengthy description, Dylan's head broke the surface of the water near her feet. His body was shadowed by the rock, and as long as he remained on the seaward side of it he would be shielded from the knight's vision.

"Is all well, Christine?" The merman's whisper was strained and his eyes were dark with worry.

"Yes. But don't let him know you're here." CC glanced nervously over her shoulder and nodded attentively at the knight's description of the tapestries that covered the walls of his bedchamber.

He holds you prisoner? Even inside her head the words sounded fierce.

Not really. He is just escorting me on a walk. CC sent her thoughts to him, pouring all the love she felt for him through her eyes. *Lir has sent word to Gaea that he will be in these waters tomorrow night. She is sure that he will bless our union and tell Sarpedon to back off. Tomorrow night I can return to the water and to you. Forever.*

Dylan reached out and with one strong hand he stroked her right calf with a slow, sensuous touch. CC shivered at the current of desire that traveled up her leg to nestle, pulsing with heat, deep within her.

It seems an eternity from now till then. Within her mind his voice was a seductive lure.

You did say you would wait for me for an eternity, she teased.

And I shall, Christine. I shall, my love.

"Undine, have you recovered your strength enough yet?" Andras's voice cut into their thoughts.

Dylan's jaw clenched.

He is nothing to us. CC sent the thought to Dylan before calling over her shoulder to the knight.

"Almost. Just another few minutes. Your chamber sounds lovely. Why don't you tell me what a normal day is like at Caer Llion."

"For whom? Caer Llion and its grounds are home for hundreds of people," he said with easy arrogance.

When CC turned her head and answered the knight her face was a mask of innocent curiosity. "Start by telling me what you do. Then I would love to hear what the ladies of the castle do to keep themselves busy during the day."

Andras's chest swelled. "Being the eldest son, my duties are extensive and they begin at daybreak . . ."

"The warrior wants you to belong to him." The softness of Dylan's voice did nothing to disguise his anger.

"It doesn't matter what he wants. I could never belong to him," she whispered urgently. "Please believe me, Dylan. I want no one except you."

"Did you say something, Undine?" Andras shouted.

CC swiveled at the waist. "I was just commenting on how interesting all this is becoming to me. I'm sorry to interrupt, please continue." She turned back to Dylan as Andras resumed his description of castle life.

I hate that you must endure him. Dylan's thought entered her mind.

He's really not that bad; he's just not the man for me. And anyway, it won't be much longer now.

One moment without you is too long, my love. The merman pulled her leg to him and gently kissed her calf. *Your legs are such soft, wonderful things.* With light kisses his mouth moved down the shapely swell of her calf, burning a trail of erotic heat. *I admit that I shall miss them.*

His lips found the delicate arch of her instep. While his mouth possessed her, his hands caressed the sensitive area behind her knees, then moved down to her ankle and back. When he moved to her other leg CC couldn't hold back the moan of pleasure that escaped her parted lips.

"Undine! What is it?" CC could hear the splash of the knight's boots as he plodded awkwardly into the water.

"Nothing! Nothing!" she yelled, looking back in time to see him floundering up to his knees in the surf. "No need to come out. I'm rested and ready to leave. Just let me make sure that I am presentable," she said, fussing with her skirt.

She turned back to Dylan, sending her thoughts to him. *Tomorrow night, my love. Wait for me tomorrow night.*

Reluctantly, the merman took his hands from her leg and began to sink beneath the shimmering surface.

For an eternity, Christine. I will wait for you for an eternity.

Then he was gone. CC swallowed hard, fighting against an almost overwhelming desire to leap into the water and swim after him.

No, she told herself firmly. I have to wait on the timing of the goddess. I've come too far to mess it up now. It's just one more day.

But as she stood and began her rock-skipping trip back to the restlessly waiting knight she felt empty, like her soul had followed Dylan out to sea, and she had been left with only the shell of her body.

Reacting to the bereft expression on her face, and her sad, lethargic movements, Andras began his lecture as soon as he had helped her down from the last rock.

"Perhaps next time you will remember that it is wise to listen to me, especially in matters of your safety."

Dylan's absence filled her with sadness, and her shoulders slumped as she muttered a quick, "You're right, next time I'll be more careful."

Andras gave her a self-satisfied smile. "I am pleased to hear you say so, Undine. I understand that you are a princess, but even a princess must take counsel from those who are wiser and more experienced. But please, there is no need for you to look so sad. I am here for you."

Andras took a step closer to her. Before she could protest, he took her hand in his and raised it to his lips. Thankfully, the kiss was short, but he didn't let go of her hand when he had finished. Instead he stepped even closer to her and placed his hands on her shoulders. They were rough and heavy, and CC felt their weight as if they were shackles. A tremor of fear mixed with loathing traveled through her, and she tried to pull away from him.

"Do not be frightened." His voice was husky. "You must know my intentions are honorable. I plan on speaking to your father as soon as he arrives."

"About my ransom?" she asked, still trying to pull away.

"It is little wonder you tremble if that is what you believe!" Andras said heatedly. "You may be assured, Undine, that I am not the type of man who would use a maiden lady and then send her back to her father soiled. Your honor is safe with me."

"So are you saying you'd only use a woman who you didn't consider a lady?"

Andras's brow furrowed as if he couldn't decide if her question was naive or impertinent. Remembering her reaction to discovering she was displaying an immodest glimpse of her legs, the knight realized that Undine must have meant the question in simple naiveté. He smiled indulgently at her, and his voice took on a fatherly tone.

"What I am saying, my beautiful one, is that I intend to ask your father for your hand in marriage."

"But I thought you said that beauty needs to be guarded against," she blurted, scanning his face for the telltale signs of Sarpedon.

Believing her breathlessness was a result of joy at his announced intentions, Andras freed one of her shoulders so that he could cup her chin within his hand.

"Not if the beauty has proper guidance. As your husband, I will provide you with that guidance." His voice deepened and his eyes gleamed with a light that caused her stomach to clench. "Consider us betrothed, my beauty. You belong to me."

The knight's grip on her tightened, and he bent his head down to her. CC couldn't breath. She was trapped, overwhelmed by his size and strength. What would happen if he kissed her lips? Intuition told her Sarpedon's influence would flare to an uncontrollable level. She had to do something that would break his desire for her without making him angry. Fighting panic, she forced herself to think rationally. And a single idea came to her, ironically born from something Andras had said. Suddenly she wanted to laugh aloud in glee.

Instead she drew in a deep breath, as if she was readying herself for an underwater dive, and the instant before Andras's lips touched hers, CC sneezed. Violently.

The knight jerked back from her.

"Oh, my goodness!" CC covered her nose with her hands and sniffed. "I'm so sorry."

When she lowered her hands from her face, Andras took her forcefully back into his arms.

"It is of no matter, my beauty," he murmured, bending again to her lips.

"*Ahhh, chew!*" This time CC opened her mouth and managed to actually rain spittle onto the knight's face.

He let loose of her so quickly that she staggered forward, causing him to back away from her.

"*Ahhh, ahhh . . .*" CC gasped, waving her hands in front of her face. "*Chew!*"

CC rubbed at her nose. She was pleased to feel it getting hot and red under her rough handling. Andras was looking at her as if he was afraid she might begin to indiscriminately release any number of bodily functions. All traces of glowing silver had left his eyes.

"It looks like you were right, again," she said, giving her voice a nasally twinge. "I must have caught a chill out there on that wet rock."

"We should return," Andras said.

"You are so wise," CC said, ending her sentence in a barking cough.

As she followed the knight up the path that led from the beach, CC was sure she heard Dylan's deep, male laughter mixed with the rhythmic music of the surf. She disguised her answering giggle in a phlegmy cough.

REENTERING the monastery grounds, CC was relieved to see Isabel's silhouette in a nearby hall, obviously keeping watch for CC's return.

CC coughed and sneezed almost simultaneously.

"You, there!" Andras yelled at Isabel. "The princess has taken a chill. What herbal remedies have you?"

Isabel hurried over to the knight, clucking her tongue like a ruffled hen.

"It seems I should have listened to Sir Andras's advice. He warned that I could catch a chill from the water, and I think I—ha . . . ha . . . ha . . . chew!— have," CC said wetly.

Isabel took the shawl from her shoulders and wrapped it around CC while she muttered under her breath about foolish young women and ushered her toward the hall that led to her bedchamber. Andras began to follow them, then he stopped, looking as if he wasn't sure what he should do.

"Sir Andras, I will care for the princess. It would be wise if you had one of the servants pour you a strong draft of the Brothers' special vintage. We certainly would not want you to become ill, too." She lowered her voice ominously, then said, "The princess may be contagious."

The knight's eyes widened, and he automatically backed a step farther away from CC.

"I will be in the dining hall if you have need of me, Undine." Andras gave her a neat little bow. Then he told Isabel, "Care for my betrothed well. I hold you personally responsible for her health." The knight turned and retreated quickly across the courtyard.

"Betrothed?" Isabel whispered as they hurried down the hall to CC's room.

CC grimaced and whispered back. "Somehow Andras managed to get engaged to me today without me saying yes." CC paused to add a sneeze and a couple of loud coughs, just in case any of the Brothers were lurking around.

The door to her room looked like a sanctuary. As soon as it was firmly closed behind them CC nodded to the window and asked in a low voice, "Is the guard still out there?"

"No," Isabel answered in a normal voice. "The squires are busy scanning the coast for any sign of Vikings." Isabel looked closely at her. "This illness is only a pretense?"

CC nodded and grinned. "Absolutely. Do you honestly believe that water could make *me* sick?"

As her laughter joined Isabel's, CC felt her spirits lift, and she sent a silent thank-you to the goddess for the gift of the old woman's friendship.

"It is a ruse to keep the knight away from you?" Isabel asked.

CC nodded. "He scared me out there. It's like Sarpedon is with him all the time, even when Andras appears perfectly himself, but any little thing I do or say can cause him to surface."

"Little wonder you looked ill," Isabel said.

"I'm glad this will be over soon. I don't know how much longer I can avoid Andras."

"The chapel is certainly clean, and the kitchen has become a forest of drying herbs," Isabel said.

"I can promise you that there are no weeds in the herb garden."

"Then it is best if an illness renders you indisposed," Isabel said thoughtfully.

CC grinned mischievously. "So what kind of remedies do you have in mind for me?"

"Oh, I think we should begin with mulled wine laced with healing herbs, and perhaps a mustard poultice for your chest to relieve that raking cough."

CC wrinkled her nose, and Isabel laughed.

"I'm fine with the wine, but the poultice sounds kind of scary. What are you going to put in it? Frog poop and lizard tongues?"

"Would you rather have Andras or a poultice on your chest?"

"I'll take the frog poop," CC assured her.

Isabel cackled cheerfully as she gathered up the pitcher and cup from CC's dresser. "It will be necessary to make you as aromatic as possible to ensure that the knight will want to stay well away from you."

"I suppose that means that I'll have to stay confined to my room tonight and tomorrow," CC sighed.

"I imagine that if you appear well enough to walk about, Andras will devote himself to personally overseeing his betrothed's recovery."

"*Ugh*," CC groaned.

"Exactly," Isabel said, walking to the door. "I shall prepare your remedies and return shortly."

"Don't be gone too long."

"Only as long as it takes to gather the frogs and lizards." The door closed on Isabel's cackling laughter.

CHAPTER TWENTY-SEVEN

"UCK! I thought you were kidding about the frog poop. That stuff smells horrible. What the heck is in it?" CC asked, backing away from Isabel who was holding a jar that she had just uncovered. CC could almost see the waves of stench emanating from its open mouth.

"Ground mustard, garlic, lard and sheep urine," Isabel said, smiling evilly. "It is an ancient remedy for a wet cough."

"I don't have a wet cough," CC said, being sure to keep her bed between the two of them.

"The knight needs to believe you do."

"Can't we just smear it around the door? I'm sure he'll be able to smell it even through six inches of wood."

Isabel laughed. "I suppose we could dab it on some rags and waft them about. That should keep the knight away."

"It'll keep Andras, his friends, the Brothers and every creature known to man away," CC said, glancing nervously at the jar even after Isabel placed it on the dresser. "And do you think you could wait to start the wafting until after I've eaten my dinner?"

"You are very demanding for a woman who is supposed to be so ill," Isabel teased.

"Well, I am a princess."

"Obviously."

They grinned at each other, and CC nodded a grateful thank-you to Isabel, then began eating the thick stew with gusto.

"Funny that this illness hasn't affected my appetite," CC said through bites of fresh bread.

"I already considered that." Isabel pointed to the heavily laden tray she had carried into the chamber.

"Seems like a lot of jars of poultice. I don't think anyone can be *that* sick." CC scowled. "Not and still live."

"Yes, it would seem like I am rather overdoing it with the poultice, but it is understandable. I have never before treated a sick princess."

She lifted the cloth covering from one of the jars, and CC flinched, but instead of the rank odor of sheep urine, all she could smell was more of the wonderful stew.

Isabel grinned conspiratorially. "This, I believe, is more than even you can eat. I will refill your bowl, and it will appear that your appetite is suffering."

"You are a genius, Isabel."

"Just a wise woman, Princess," Isabel said smugly.

CC reached for her goblet of wine and hesitated. "Is there anything awful in the wine?"

"Just some mild herbs. Nothing that will do anything more than cause you to relax."

CC sniffed at the wine. "It doesn't smell bad."

Isabel took her own goblet and drank deeply.

CC smiled in relief and took a healthy drink. "It's good!"

"Do not be so surprised," Isabel grumped. "I made it."

"You made the poultice, too," CC pointed out.

"No, Bronwyn and Gwenyth made the poultice," Isabel said smugly. "They are renowned for their healing poultices. They send with it their love."

"Well, it's only their love and my loathing for Sarpedon that could get me to let that stuff anywhere near my body," CC said, giving the jar a squeamish glance.

Isabel cackled. "They are all too aware of that. You should have heard them preparing it. *Add a little more urine, shall we? The princess should only have the best.*" Isabel mimicked the two ladies' voices so accurately that CC laughed so hard she almost spilled her wine.

"While I'm sequestered do you think there's any chance that the other women could visit?" CC asked. "It may be the last time . . ."

"They will come," Isabel said brusquely, pouring both of them more wine. "And that is quite enough of talk like that. We will see you again."

CC nodded firmly. "You're right, of course. It's not like I'm going back to my own time, I'm just going—well—some place wetter."

They smiled at each other and sipped their wine.

"Undine, would you tell me of your time?"

CC shrugged. "Sure." Then she realized she didn't have any idea how to start explaining the twenty-first century to a medieval woman who had never been more than a day's walk away from her home. "Is there something in particular you'd like to know?" CC asked, hoping for some direction.

"I would like to know how food is prepared in your time," Isabel said without hesitation.

CC grinned. "You'll love this. Wait till you hear about supermarkets and microwaves."

CC had just finished explaining to an open-mouthed Isabel about fast food restaurants, when two quick knocks sounded on the door.

CC barked several loud coughs before calling in a raspy voice, "Who is it?"

"Andras."

CC sneezed. "Just a moment."

Isabel was already unveiling the foul-smelling pot. "Time for wafting," she whispered and ladled a generous amount of the yellowish goop onto a linen rag, which she began waving around the room. CC added to the effect by coughing loudly.

Turning her head upside-down CC vigorously snarled her hair into a twisted mess and rubbed at her already much-abused nose. Then she wrapped the blanket from the bed around her shoulders and shuffled to the door.

"Wait!" Isabel whispered urgently. Before she could protest Isabel took the poultice-encrusted rag and hung it around her neck. CC gagged and didn't have to pretend the sneeze that rocked her body.

When CC cracked the door her nose was running. She smelled like a vat of old urine and she looked disheveled and pale. In the hall Andras and Abbot William had their heads bent together speaking in low voices. At the sound of the door opening they broke off their discussion and turned their attention to her. CC was pleased to see the shocked expression on Andras's face and the look of disgust on the abbot's. Emboldened, CC took a half step out into the hall. Both men moved quickly back.

"Andras! Abbot William!" CC said in a thick, nasally voice. "It's so nice to see both of you. Would you like to come in?"

"No!" the knight said hastily. "We would not think of tiring you."

"It would be most improper for Sir Andras to enter your bedchamber, even chaperoned by me," the priest said, fluttering his fingers effeminately in front of him, as if he was trying to ward off her contagion.

"Oh," CC said sadly. The poultice was causing her nose to run and she paused to wipe it on the back of her hand. "Are you sure? After all, Andras and I are betrothed."

"Not officially until your father arrives and blesses the union," Abbot William said. "That is what Andras and I have been discussing."

"I'm sure my father will—*ahh . . . ahh . . . ahhh . . . chew!*—approve," CC said, pleased beyond words that her latest sneeze had caused the two men to retreat another step from her.

"I, too, am certain of his approval," Andras spoke rapidly. "Now you must rest and regain your strength."

"Yes," Abbot William said, his nose curled in distaste as he caught another whiff of the foul poultice. "Have the servant Isabel bring you anything you wish." The two men were already moving away from her door. "We bid you good night and a hasty recovery."

"Pray for me," CC called after them. She could barely make out their mumbled replies.

As soon as the door was closed she took the stinking rag from around her neck. Laughing, she handed it back to Isabel.

"They didn't want to come in for a visit. Imagine that."

"It certainly does not seem very caring of them," Isabel said, and her cackles joined CC's melodic laughter.

"They did say you could bring me anything I wish." CC picked up her empty goblet and said dramatically, "I wish for more of this excellent wine. It's medicinal. And company. Do you think the other women would be willing to brave possible contagion to visit me?"

"Certainly. It is only right for a princess to have several nurses." Isabel performed a graceful curtsey that made CC laugh. "And I shall leap to obey you, my lady." Grabbing the empty pitcher, Isabel hurried to the door with the energy of a girl one-third her age.

Chapter Twenty-eight

Several hours later the four old women and CC lay in heaps around the floor amidst scattered bedding and pallets. Isabel had returned to CC's room accompanied by the three "nursemaids." On her trip from the kitchen, Isabel had interrupted Sir Andras and the abbot at their nightly game of chess. She had explained that the Princess needed more care than she alone could provide, and that she would need that care all during the night. The two men readily agreed, both visibly relieved that the responsibility for Undine's nurse-maiding would not be their own. Isabel had mimicked the abbot's simpering voice as she repeated how he had ordered her and as many other women as were necessary to spend the night in the princess's chamber. Isabel had invited the men to look in on her patient during the night. The abbot had explained that his time would be better spent in prayer. Although Andras had appeared honestly concerned about her, he had hastily agreed that Undine must be allowed to rest, and that she certainly could not do so if he insisted on visiting her.

And, of course, the guards stationed outside the princess's door and window would not be needed. Even if the princess was well enough to sneak out—which Isabel assured them she was not—the all-night presence of the old women would ensure that she would have to stay in her chamber.

CC felt a wonderful sense of freedom as she sipped Isabel's excellent mulled wine. The five women had been laughing and talking well into the night. Isabel had confided in them the truth about CC, and the women couldn't seem to learn enough about modern customs and conveniences. Now their weathered faces were flushed with excitement as well as wine.

"I did so enjoy learning the Poultry Dance," Gwenyth said, waving a hand in front of her heated face.

"Chicken Dance," CC corrected with a giggle.

"Chicken Dance," Gwenyth repeated. The old woman's eyes sparkled.

CC grinned at her. "Just let me catch my breath, and I'll teach you another dance." CC waggled her eyebrows suggestively. "And how about a song to go with it?"

The four old women squealed in delight. It was like a slumber party, CC thought. The year didn't matter—the comradery of women joined together to celebrate life and friendship was eternal. While the women chattered excitedly about what they were going to learn next, CC hummed softly to herself, trying to remember all the words to Aretha Franklin's classic, "Respect." When they were cheerleaders, she and her best friend, Sandy, had made up a funky dance to the song for a high school pep rally, and she was pretty sure she could remember most of the moves. CC eyed her backup singers. They were going to love this one. . . .

"No, Bronwyn, you have to flick the tips of your fingers on both hands in time with the words—just a . . . just a . . . just a—before you do the side-to-side head toss and sing the *just a little bit* part," CC explained again to the old woman.

"Undine, is it then that we begin thrusting our hips?" Gwenyth asked.

Isabel spoke up before she could answer. "Yes. We thrust our hips in time with our head tosses."

CC had to stifle her grin. The ladies had attacked learning the motions and words to "Respect" with a vengeance. And she had to admit the four old women had decent voices and natural senses of rhythm.

"Okay!" CC said, and the room fell to an attentive silence. "Think we're ready to try it again from the beginning?"

In the candlelight the four gray heads seemed to glow as they nodded enthusiastically in response.

"Bronwyn, you cannot dance with that wine goblet in your hand," Isabel pointed out.

Bronwyn's smile showed two missing teeth as she winked at CC before gulping the last drop from the goblet and sliding it out of the way on the floor.

"Backup singers take your places," CC said officially, and the women hurried to form a horizontal line behind her. "Are you ready?"

"Ready, Undine!" the four answered.

With a huge grin CC turned around and started shimmying and humming in time to the beat of an imaginary band, and with a *Whoop!* her backup singers joined her in a rousing medieval version of Aretha's classic, after which the five of them collapsed in breathless laughter across CC's bed.

"In your old world women must have such fun," Lynelle said wistfully.

"Yes, they do. But I can't remember a time when I was happier there then I am here, at this moment."

The women beamed smiles at one another. Bronwyn hiccupped a little drunkenly, and they all laughed.

"Tell us of your lover," Lynelle said.

CC blinked at her in surprise. Until then they had confined their questions to CC's past—her human life. She had assumed that the thought of her mermaid life made the women uncomfortable. Now Bronwyn and Gwenyth echoed Lynelle's request. Isabel nodded encouragingly. CC's heart swelled at their acceptance.

"Well," she said softly. "Dylan is different from the men here."

Lynelle snorted. "Of course he is, child."

"Yes," Bronwyn blurted. "He is a fish."

Isabel elbowed her and made a *shush*ing noise. Bronwyn looked chagrined.

"Actually," CC said, smiling at her, "he's a mammal, like a dolphin or a whale. But when I said he's different, I wasn't talking about his body." CC touched her temple with one finger. "He's different in here." Then she moved that finger to rest briefly on her breast over her heart. "And here. He is kind and good. He doesn't see me as a thing to be possessed or used. He sees me as his equal, as even more than his equal."

"He loves you," Lynelle said.

"Yes, and to him that doesn't mean that he has to control me or destroy what is unique about me so that he can remake me into some kind of twisted image of what he sees as female perfection."

"That would be Sir Andras," Isabel said.

"And many other men of our world," Bronwyn added. Isabel and Gwenyth nodded in agreement, but Lynelle looked thoughtful.

"My husband was not like Sir Andras. I believe his love was more like your merman's," Lynelle said.

CC's eyes widened in surprise and Lynelle's smile was bittersweet.

"No, I have not always been as such." Her good hand pointed at the shriveled appendage that she held limply against her side. "This happened shortly after we were married. He could have cast me aside, but he did not . . ." The old woman's eyes filled with tears and she took a gulp of wine and cleared her throat before she could continue speaking. "He was a good man. And it was my great joy to be his wife."

"And you will find joy in being Dylan's wife," Isabel said.

"To love!" Lynelle said brightly, raising her goblet.

"To love!" the women toasted, beaming at each other.

They drank in compatible silence, each lost in memories, until Lynelle's voice interrupted the stillness with another question.

"Does . . ." she hesitated and glanced quickly at the other women as if for support. Then she rushed on. "Does his touch please you?"

CC felt her cheeks growing warm from more than the wine. "His touch makes me feel like I'm on fire."

The four women sighed happily.

"Undine!" Lynelle's voice was filled with excitement. "Why don't you go to him tonight?"

"I have to wait until tomorrow. Then Sarpedon will be dealt with," CC said.

"Yes, to join him permanently you must wait until tomorrow," Lynelle said quickly. "But can you not visit him before then?"

CC felt a rush of exhilaration. "I-I think I can, but I would have to be very careful."

"We have taken care—neither the abbot nor the knight will be looking for you tonight," Isabel said.

"But the squires have been posted to watch for Vikings," Bronwyn reminded them.

"True," said Isabel. "But they will be looking out to sea for the invaders. They will not be watching for one fleet-footed girl who knows how to disappear into the waves."

"Will your merman be there tonight?" Gwenyth asked.

CC nodded. "All I have to do is call him."

Gwenyth's aged face crinkled with worry. "You must not call loudly."

CC laughed and stood up, spinning in a little improvised dance step of happiness. "I don't have to call him with my voice; I call him with my heart." An eternity, CC thought. He would answer for an eternity.

"Go to him," Lynelle said.

"Yes," Bronwyn and Gwenyth said together.

CC turned to Isabel.

With the gentle hands of a mother, the old woman brushed a blond curl from CC's face.

"We will be here. If the abbot or Sir Andras call for you, we will simply tell them that the drugged wine and the illness have left you senseless. Then we will waft more poultices under their noses. Go to your lover."

"Then help me pull that dresser under the window," CC said eagerly. "Could someone find my shoes?"

The room exploded into female motion. In one sweep the clutter was removed from the top of the dresser, the dresser was wrestled to its position under the window and CC's two doeskin slippers were located and placed quickly on her feet. She was already wearing only her chemise, so she didn't have to wait impatiently for Isabel to unlace her from the bondage of her ornate gown.

Before she climbed atop the dresser, she hugged each of the women.

"It is so romantic," Lynelle whispered into her ear.

"And wonderful," Bronwyn agreed.

"Exciting," Gwenyth added.

"Go with the blessing of the Holy Mother." Isabel's hug was strong.

CC kissed the old woman's cheek. "I'll be careful."

"You must return before dawn so that the lightening of the sky does not betray you to the knight's men."

"I will. Don't worry." She gave Isabel another quick hug and started to turn, then, changing her mind, she stopped. On a sudden impulse CC lifted the silver chain from around her neck. The amber teardrop swung lazily as she placed the pendant over the old woman's head.

"Keep it for me while I'm gone," she said to Isabel, whose eyes were filling with tears as her hand lovingly cupped the goddess's amber.

Unable to speak, the old woman nodded and watched as CC climbed nimbly up the dresser, using the partially opened drawers as stair steps.

Slowly, CC peered out the window. The night was dark; the richness of the late hour cloaked the monastery in a veil of black velvet. The moon was a thin, glowing scythe that cast just enough light to turn trees into shadows and paths into ribbons of pale light.

"Do you see any of the men?" Isabel's whisper carried in the still room.

CC shook her head.

"Then go quickly," Isabel urged.

Holding her breath, CC shifted her seat to the windowsill, then she turned, found her toehold and dropped silently to the soft ground. She heard a grunt from inside the room, followed by a glimpse of Isabel's face framed by the window. A flash of moonlight reflected off the silver chain.

"What are you doing?" CC hissed.

"Keeping watch for you." The old woman whispered. "Now go to your lover."

CC smiled and blew Isabel a kiss before scurrying across the little patch of ground that separated the monastery from the rocky cliff. With feet that felt light and swift, CC navigated the familiar path. Often she glanced up at the cliff's edge above her, worried that she would see the silhouetted shape of one of Andras's squires, but the cliff remained empty and soon her feet sank into the sand of the beach.

Dylan! Her heart called as she stepped out of her slippers and slid the chemise from her naked body. *I'm here! Please come to me.*

The cool fingers of the waves washing against her legs felt like a wonderful, erotic dream, and as she walked into the surf the almost uncontrollable desire to change into her mermaid form and disappear into its inviting depths tugged at her will. She forced the desire down, trembling with the effort it cost her.

Tomorrow, she promised herself. I only have to wait until tomorrow, then I will never have to be parted from my mermaid form.

Or from me. Dylan's voice sounded within her mind an instant before he surfaced a few feet in front of her.

"Have I dreamed you here, my love?" the merman asked.

"Well, let's see. If you touch me, and I can feel it, then it's not a dream," CC said.

Her feet ran out of firm ground, but before she could swim two full strokes, Dylan pulled her into the warmth of his arms. Greedily, their bodies met. CC felt a shiver of pleasure as she tasted his slick, hot mouth.

"Can you feel that?" Dylan's breath was warm against her parted lips.

"I can feel everything," CC said.

"Then I did not dream you here; I wished you here."

"I don't have long tonight." CC's breath caught as the merman's mouth explored the hollow of her neck. "Andras thinks I'm sick, so he's not looking for me, but his men are keeping watch for Vikings."

Dylan's laughter was muffled against her skin, and his teeth pulled playfully at her earlobe before he spoke.

"I did enjoy your performance on the beach."

"Well, I couldn't very well let him kiss me," CC said. She would not mention Sarpedon's possession of the knight to him. She would not spoil their short time together and cause him needless worry.

Dylan cupped her face in his hand. "No, you could not let him kiss you." And the merman pressed his lips to hers, effectively erasing the image of Andras's thwarted kiss from their minds.

"I'll have to leave before dawn this time," CC said, arching her body against his, loving the intensely erotic sensation of his exotic body pressed against hers.

"I want to feel myself within you." Dylan's voice was rough with passion.

"Yes!" CC said, pulling on his bottom lip with her teeth.

The merman moaned, and CC felt his hard shaft as it pulsed against the softness of her thigh. She shifted so that he could easily slide within her, but Dylan shook his head.

"Not here. Not like this. This is the last time you will make love as a human. It should not be something done in the haste of thoughtless passion. It should be savored."

CC nibbled on his neck. "I am savoring it."

Dylan's laughter mixed with a groan of desire. "Come with me, siren; I will teach you of savoring."

"Well, there's certainly no doubt that you're my favorite teacher," CC said as she settled against his chest, letting the powerful strokes of his tail propel them down the beach. CC closed her eyes, enjoying the mingled sensations of the water and her lover against her naked skin. When she felt sand against her body her eyes opened in surprise.

They were laying half out of the water in the little rock-dotted cove CC had found earlier that day. The curved moon cast a subdued, magical light, which reflected off the lazy water around them. Dylan's body pressed against hers, and he stroked the length of her with sea-slick hands.

CC felt hot and cold and liquid all at the same time.

"I think you're the siren," she said, caressing the flame-colored flesh that swelled erect against her.

Dylan made a choked noise and shifted his weight so that they were on their sides, facing each other, and she could touch him more easily.

"I cannot be. It is *I* who am under *your* spell," Dylan said.

The merman drew his hand up the length of her thigh, rubbing enticing circles over the silken skin of her legs. Then he bent to her and his mouth replaced his hand and he lavished her skin with kisses and teasing pretend bites until he found the wet center of her. There he devoured her, his tongue continuing his circular caresses, increasing in movement and rhythm until CC gripped his shoulders and shuddered with the intensity of her climax.

Again he shifted his weight and pulled her into his arms. She felt alive with sensation, and enfolded within his strength, CC explored his mouth, letting her hands roam down his body as if they had a will of their own.

"Your body amazes me," CC told him as her mouth and hands discovered new ridges of muscle.

Remembering the sensitivity of her own mer-body, she caressed his fiery flesh with teasing fingertips. Dylan's breath quickened and CC could feel the tension humming through his body, which was now slick with sweat as well as the salty water that lapped against him. When her mouth began tracing the line low on his torso where mer-flesh met human skin, his body trembled and he called her name between ragged breaths.

In one swift movement, he pulled her up. Then he was above her, resting his weight on his forearms. The night sky outlined his powerful body, and CC could see his dark eyes flash with unleashed desire. She opened herself to him, and, wrapping her legs around him, she arched, wordlessly urging him on. Dylan buried himself within her, and CC met his thrusts with equal intensity. He devoured her mouth and their tempo increased. CC felt the delicious tension build within her again, and when the merman's body began to shudder in orgasm, her own climax met his as the night fragmented into an explosion of sensation.

Afterward, CC nestled securely against Dylan's chest. The merman brushed sand from her shoulders with gentle hands that tended to linger at the long, graceful curve of her back.

"Now I see what you mean about savoring," she murmured.

Dylan's chest rumbled with his deep chuckle. "I would like to have attempted more savoring." CC felt him shrug his shoulders. "But I could not resist you, siren."

CC looked up at him. "Are sirens mermaids?"

His chuckle turned into laughter, and he hugged her. "No. Sirens are water nymphs."

"Not mermaids?"

"Definitely not mermaids." He kissed her forehead. "But they are alluring creatures filled with erotic intent." He gave her a meaningful look.

"Are you sure they're females? They sound a lot like you," CC teased.

Dylan smiled at her. "There are no male sirens."

"You could have fooled me," CC said, pulling his mouth down to hers. She kissed him, pressing her body so closely against his that she could feel his heartbeat increasing against her breast.

"If you keep kissing me like that, you will not be back at the monastery before dawn." Dylan's voice had already deepened with his growing desire.

CC sighed and nibbled at his full bottom lip. "One more day."

"One more day," he repeated, kissing her gently.

They didn't speak as they floated away from the shore and back toward the cliffs that held the monastery. CC rested against her lover's chest, watching the night sky begin to unveil its layers of darkness as it climbed steadily toward dawn. A thought tickled the edges of her mind as CC pulled her attention from the sky to look around her.

"You know, I haven't seen my dolphin friend the last couple times I've come to the water. Have you seen her?" she asked Dylan.

Dylan considered the question, then shook his head.

"No, I have not encountered the little creature."

"I guess I don't blame her for staying away, especially after Andras hit her with that rock," CC said.

"She never stays away from Undine for long. I am certain she is there,"— Dylan gestured out to sea—"awaiting the return of her princess."

"I'm sure you're right," CC said, trying not to worry.

The water around them became choppier and the sound of the waves crashing against the beach told her that they were near the monastery even before Dylan changed direction and swam slowly to the shore.

"You can stand now," Dylan said.

CC put her feet against the sandy bottom, but she kept her arms wrapped around the merman.

"The sky lightens," he said and kissed the top of her head.

"I wish it wouldn't," CC spoke into his chest.

Dylan cupped her face in his hands. "Then this last day would not pass. Remember, my love, with its passing comes the night."

"And that's when I'll come to you . . . forever," she finished for him.

Their kiss was a sweet promise. Before she began walking away from him she linked her fingers through his and said, "Tell me once more how long you would wait for me."

"For an eternity, Christine. I would wait for you for an eternity."

He brought her hand to his lips and kissed her palm. Reluctantly, he released her and she turned to the beach.

The lightening of the sky was becoming more pronounced and her discarded chemise was easy to find. She was shaking the sand from it when a sharp voice cut across the beach.

"Behold the whore!"

CHAPTER TWENTY-NINE

THE abbot stepped triumphantly from the cover of the trees that grew in dwarflike tufts at the base of the cliff. Several confused-looking monks milled nervously there, too. Andras stood beside the abbot, so close that in the dim light their bodies appeared to be joined. The knight's face was a pale disk broken only by his eyes, which were bright silver slits of hatred, and he was dragging with him a weeping Isabel.

"They broke into your room," Isabel sobbed. "We could not stop them. They said they must have proof that you were within."

Andras's voice echoed with Sarpedon's demonic amplification. *"I knew the whore was with her lover. I knew it! Take her."* His command was like ice, and one of the squires leapt to obey him.

CC felt as if their appearance had turned her to stone. She held the chemise to her chest, trying to cover her nakedness. She wanted to run back into the sea, but her feet would not obey her. The squire quickly covered the few yards that separated them and grabbed her arm, purposely digging his fingers into her delicate flesh.

"Maybe we will have a little fun before they burn you," he sneered, his eyes ravishing CC's naked body. The foul cloud of his rotting breath made her gag.

"Touch her again and you will not leave this island alive," Dylan's voice carried across the waves with such force that CC saw the squire cringe—then he stared open-mouthed at the sight of the merman.

Dylan had raised himself well out of the water, so that his powerful tail seemed to glisten and ripple as if he was on fire.

"The demon!" Abbot William's voice held an edge of hysteria. "The witch has a demon lover!"

"Kill it!" Sir Andras barked the order, and almost instantly the chilling sound of an arrow whistled from the other squire's position behind them on the beach.

As the arrow flew toward the water, CC felt a rush of power within her, and her body unfroze. The squire who held her arm was still gazing slack-jawed at the merman, and it was with surprising ease that CC rammed her knee into his groin and wrenched her arm from his grasp. Spinning around she ran for the waterline.

"Stop her, you fool!" Andras yelled.

"Quickly, Christine!" Dylan called, dodging another arrow.

She could hear the sounds of the squire as he grunted and scrambled to his feet behind her. She glanced over her shoulder to see Andras sprinting across the sand, longbow held forward and eyes flashing as he took aim at Dylan. As the arrow twanged free, CC reached the water. Thrusting her arms over her head as if she was an Olympic diver, she leapt forward, calling the power of her mermaid body alive. The delicious heat of transformation sizzled down her body, and she hit the water flying. CC's sleek mermaid form skimmed just below the surface, and then with one stroke of her tail she swam up, angling herself at Dylan's body. She broke through the waves like she had been shot from a cannon.

And the arrow meant for Dylan sliced neatly through the muscle of her left shoulder blade. The pain was white hot, and she crumbled forward into her lover's arms. Dylan's agonized cry was echoed on the shore. Through a haze of pain Christine looked back to the beach.

Andras was standing unnaturally still and straight. His mouth was stretched impossibly wide by a horrible shriek of rage.

"No!" The voice no longer made any pretense of belonging to the knight. *"Not her! You were not to harm her!"*

Andras fell to his knees, his body writhing grotesquely like there were hundreds of worms beneath his skin. Then, with a ripping sound a liquid cloud of darkness vomited from his mouth. It shimmered and pooled in hideous wetness and seemed to crawl toward the surf. When it touched the water the darkness shifted and reformed, drawing substance from the saltwater. With a roar, Sarpedon rose, fully formed and glistening with power.

He faced the humans, swollen with anger and disdain.

"Puny creatures. You dare to harm a child of Lir! Know that your fate has been sealed."

Sarpedon swirled one massive hand into the water next to him until it boiled and seethed with activity. In horror, the humans watched as a many-tentacled monster erupted from the sea. It engulfed the shrieking body of a monk who had drifted too close to the sea, and in one motion snapped his spine and hurled his lifeless body against the cliff. Then it turned its awful attention to the knight. Preparing for battle, Sir Andras planted his feet and brandished his sword. Shouting, his squires scrambled to reach his side.

Suddenly, a wall of flesh obscured CC's view of the battle, and Sarpedon towered above them.

"The game is ended, Undine. It is time you took your rightful place as my mate." Sarpedon's voice was deceptively calm.

CC felt light-headed. Dylan still held her within his arms, and CC noted with detached curiosity that the water surrounding them was tainted scarlet. That must be my blood, the thought played slowly through her mind and she struggled against the urge to close her eyes and sink beneath the waves.

"Stay away from her, Sarpedon." Dylan spoke with iron in his voice. He shifted his grip on CC so that he placed his body protectively between Sarpedon and the mermaid.

Sarpedon's laughter was a roar. "Does the son of a human believe he can stand against the power of the gods?"

Blinking to clear the bright spots from her vision, CC forced herself to move to Dylan's side.

"He and I stand together against you, Sarpedon. And when Lir gets here tonight he will stand with us, too." CC's voice surprised her by sounding strong and clear.

Sarpedon's lip curled in a sneer. "Oh, I seem to remember there was a message sent to our father. Tragic that the little dolphin messenger met with such an untimely end, *before* she could relay the Earth goddess's request. But, no matter. I was gracious enough to answer for our father. So you see that I stand ready to render judgment in his stead."

A tremor of fear passed through CC. "No. You can't."

The enormous merman moved closer to them. "You have been wrong about many things, Undine. And you are wrong yet again."

A scream from the beach interrupted them. Sarpedon turned, laughing evilly as the creature he had called to the surface squeezed the life out of the squire who had grabbed CC.

"See how I punish those who would do you harm?" Sarpedon said.

"Make it stop," CC cried. Her voice was hoarse with emotion.

Sarpedon's eyes widened in surprise. "But they would have killed you. Why would you ask to spare them?"

"Because to use your power like this is wrong."

"It is justice," Sarpedon scoffed.

"It's not justice—it's vengeance. Vengeance meted out by a creature bloated with his own imagined importance. You are a disgusting toad. I loathe you, and I will never belong to you."

Sarpedon seemed to swell with rage. "Never is a very long time. Perhaps you will change your mind when you see your pathetic human friend in my grasp." The merman shouted a command in a garbled language that CC was shocked to realize she could understand.

"Kill the old one!"

Instantly the sea monster snaked out a tentacle around Isabel's neck, but the amulet of the goddess sparked and glowed, causing the creature's grip to falter. As the old woman tried to scramble out of reach, Sarpedon shouted another command, and the monster wrapped a tentacle around her ankle. Isabel lost her balance and fell hard onto the sand. The creature began to pull her toward the water.

"No!" CC screamed.

"Never, you said!" Sarpedon bellowed. "We shall see how long never is as you watch your lover and your friend die!"

Sarpedon closed his hand around a froth of wave and instantly it solidified into the foam-colored blade of a stiletto. The huge merman lunged forward and CC struggled painfully not to slide under the surface as Dylan lost his protective hold on her and surged forward to meet the giant. The two mermen met with a sound that cracked and reverberated like thunder.

"Undine!" Isabel's voice was a sob of terror. The sea creature appeared to be toying with the old woman as it slowly pulled her to the edge of the water where its beak-shaped head glistened with daggerlike teeth. The remaining squire and

Sir Andras sent arrow after arrow into its pulsating body, but the creature seemed impervious to their weapons.

The sound of wailing came from the cliff, and CC glanced up. Lynelle, Bronwyn and Gwenyth were clinging to each other and crying with terror. Around them milled several of the monks. Some of them were on their knees praying, but most of them stood in impotent silence. There was no sign of Abbot William.

Dylan hissed in pain, and CC's eyes snapped back to her lover as Sarpedon's blade sliced a trail down the muscles of his chest.

"That is just a taste of what is to come, son of a human. My Undine will watch as I carve you into pieces," Sarpedon said.

Dylan circled him warily. When he spoke his voice was calm. "You may kill me, Sarpedon, but you will not win her love. She will loathe you forever."

Sarpedon's laughter was sharp. "An eternity is a long time. She will forget you."

An eternity. The words echoed within CC's mind. It was Dylan's promise to her. And there was only one way she wanted to spend eternity—next to Dylan's side.

Ignoring the pain in her shoulder, she beat against the water with powerful strokes of her tail, so that she rose up, lifting her entire torso from the waves.

I am the daughter of a goddess, she told herself, and I claim my birthright. With a voice that filled the morning air, she called to her mother.

"Gaea! Your daughter needs you! Help me, Mother!"

Then, using the sea magic that sang within her true mermaid body, CC reached out and cupped some of the bubblelike foam that surrounded her.

"Make me a weapon," she commanded the waters. Instantly, the handle of a knife formed against her palm. Her blade wasn't the color of foam—it was the crimson of her newly shed blood.

"Dylan!" she called to her lover, and both mermen paused in their battle to turn to her. "Catch," she said and tossed him the dagger.

Dylan caught the knife deftly and sent her a tight smile of thanks. Then his attention shifted back to Sarpedon.

"That will not help you," Sarpedon snarled, and they continued circling each other, blades flashing in the morning light.

CC felt the change in the air the moment before the goddess materialized. She strode from the foliage at the base of the cliff. Her anger was terrible; the air around her crackled and sparked with it. The knight and the squire dropped their weapons and cringed before her on the beach. She spared no glance for them. Her attention was riveted on the sea monster that had dragged Isabel to within inches of its gaping maw.

The goddess stretched out her hand and in a burst of green light a leaf-colored spear appeared. Gaea plucked it from the air and hurled it straight into the monster's open mouth. The force of the spear was so great that it traveled through the creature's body and exploded out the rear of it, followed by a slick fountain of blood and entrails.

"Return to the dark depths from whence you were born!" Gaea commanded.

The monster writhed spasmodically. Losing its grip on Isabel, it sank below the surface in a muddy cloud. Isabel scrambled to her feet, but she wasn't able to walk and she stumbled, falling in a heap at Gaea's feet. The goddess knelt and passed her shining hands over the old woman's body.

"There, the pain is gone, my Isabel."

Isabel's eyes widened in recognition as she gazed upon Gaea. The old woman crossed herself reverently.

"Thank you, Holy Mother!"

Gaea touched Isabel gently. Then she stood, facing the sea. Her silver cloak billowed behind her and the white silk of her transparent gown shimmered with the goddess's might. She walked to the water's edge, and the sand surged forward, hardening under her delicate feet until she stood on a bridge of earth that jutted out into the sea.

Mere feet from the goddess, the mermen were locked together in silent combat, each straining to end the battle with a killing slash. Dylan was bleeding heavily from several gaping wounds. His body looked like it was clothed in scarlet.

"ENOUGH!"

The power of the word was a tangible thing, lifting the hairs on CC's neck and ringing through her blood. A wall of white light exploded between the mermen, knocking them apart. CC swam quickly to Dylan's side.

Sarpedon spun on the goddess, raising himself out of the water until he levitated over her bridge.

"This is not your battle, Land Goddess," he spat. "I preside here in my father's absence."

"Foolish child," the goddess's voice held pity. "I have tolerated your interference out of love for your father. But your hatred has gone too far."

Gaea lifted her graceful arms to the sky, crossing them at the wrist. Above her materialized a cloud of power that spun and sparked like the dust of diamonds.

"LIR! THE EARTH DEMANDS YOUR PRESENCE AS SHE RENDERS JUDGMENT UPON YOUR SON!"

As Gaea spoke the command she brought her arms down in a sweeping arch, fingers pointing at the surrounding water. Like fireworks, the cloud exploded, raining power and energy, and the echo of the goddess's words into the sea.

Sarpedon's face had paled, but when he spoke his voice was still filled with arrogance.

"My father will not answer your summons. He is not an Earth child to jump at your bidding." His laughter sounded hollow and forced. "And he is much too busy presiding over the problems of the islands. The Shark God and I have made quite certain of that."

Gaea shook her head sadly at the merman. "Lir's absence stank of your interference. I knew it, and I should have interceded. The deaths that have happened today were needless. Your hatred caused them, son of Lir, but I could have prevented them. That guilt will be my sadness to bear. But with or without the presence of your father, I will cast judgment upon you—and fulfill your punishment."

"You have no right to punish me, Earth creature!" Sarpedon growled. "I am a sea god. In the realm of water my desires are fulfilled, and my commands obeyed. I will have Undine as my mate, and the rest of these pathetic creatures will stand aside or face my wrath!"

Before the goddess could respond, the water surrounding them began to seethe and bubble. Then a pillar of brilliant seawater geysered into the sky. The thick column swirled, morphing in color from the clarity of glass to the turquoise of shallow water, which refracted and changed in shade to the blue-black of the ocean's depths. The center of the pillar suddenly split, as if a bolt of lightning had cleft it apart, and from within that split appeared a giant of a man, carrying a massive trident made of deadly looking ebony. On his head was a crown of golden shells speckled with the iridescent white of perfect pearls. His silver hair was the color of moonlight on water and it curled in a thick cascade around his shoulders, mingling with the luxurious length of his beard. His togalike robe, the exact color of waves, was draped across his body. It left much of his powerful chest exposed, and as he stepped free of the pillar and strode to

Gaea, walking as if the water was solid ground, CC couldn't help but marvel at his majesty.

Gaea spoke first, offering him one slender hand, which the giant took and bowed over, kissing it with an easy intimacy.

"Lir, the Earth welcomes you." The goddess's voice was warm and intimate.

"The sea responds in kind," the giant said. "It has been much too long since we two have met." Lir spoke with obvious affection. Then his attention shifted to the scene surrounding them and a frown creased his brow. "What have we here, Earth Mother—errant children?"

"Father, this Earth goddess interferes in matters of the sea. There is no trouble here that is not of her making," Sarpedon blurted.

"Sarpedon, your tone is offensive. Gaea does not meddle in the affairs of others. Be wary that you do not make the Earth your enemy." Lir's face tightened and though his voice remained calm, his reprimand was sharp. He glanced around the restless water and the sea god's eyes narrowed in anger as he noticed Undine's injury.

"Who dared to harm my child?"

The waves trembled at Lir's words, and CC's tongue felt thick and awkward. But Dylan's answer was swift, and he met the sea god's eyes unflinchingly.

"The arrow that wounded your daughter was meant for me. Although Sarpedon did not loose the arrow, it was his jealousy that caused the humans to try and destroy me."

"Undine." Lir turned to her. "What has happened here?"

CC took a deep breath, swallowing her fear and the pain that radiated in cruel fingers from her shoulder. When she spoke her voice sounded tinny and strange, like it belonged to someone else.

"First of all, you need to know that I'm not really Undine. My soul is human. Your daughter and I exchanged places because she hated it here and because—"

Lir's roar stopped her words. "Deceit and deception!" He whirled on Gaea. "Did you do this?"

Calmly, Gaea touched the sea god's arm. "Allow the child to finish, Lir. Her soul may not have been born as your daughter, but she is tied to you through her body and, unlike Undine, she has a deep, abiding love of the sea."

Lir narrowed his eyes, but he nodded tightly and turned his attention back to the mermaid.

"I will listen."

CC tried to smile her appreciation, but her lips could only form a brief grimace of pain. Then Dylan's hand linked with hers. She clung to him and drew strength from his touch.

"Undine's desire to exchange places with a human wasn't just because she longed for the land; a big part of it was because she wanted to escape from Sarpedon."

"She lies, Father!" Sarpedon shouted.

"Silence!" Lir commanded his son. Then he gentled his voice and said, "Continue, child."

"I know all too well what Undine felt. The first thing that happened to me when I found myself in her body was that I had to escape from an attempted rape—by him." CC tossed her head in Sarpedon's direction.

"More lies, Father!" Sarpedon exploded. "There was no need to force myself on her; she wanted me. Then she decided to dally with this pathetic son of a human, and I have simply tired of waiting for her to finish her little game. Now I claim what has always been mine."

"Love is not something that can be possessed and ordered," Gaea broke in, her voice filled with scorn. "And the only lies spoken here have come from your mouth, Sarpedon." Gaea raised her hand, palm up, and drew a glistening oval in the air before them. "Behold the truth, God of the Seas." The goddess pursed her shapely lips and blew a delicate breath of air onto the shining mirror. Instantly, images flashed across its surface like a movie playing in a darkened theater.

First there was an image of the plane wreck, and CC watched herself being pulled beneath the waves and exchanging souls with the beautiful mermaid. Then the scene flashed to Sarpedon's attempted rape, and CC's magical transformation into a temporarily human body. The mirror showed Dylan's rescue of her and Andras's subsequent discovery of her as he pulled her from the sea. Glimpses of scenes from CC's days at the monastery included Gaea's various calls for Lir's aid, and the death of the loyal dolphin messenger at the hands of Sarpedon. Included in the images was the discovery of the Mother's statue in the chapel and her growing friendship with the women, as well as her hard treatment at the hands of Abbot William.

Then the images shifted again, and Sarpedon's presence was clearly seen drifting, oil-like, out of the well. The mirror reflected the events that unfolded when the merman inhabited the knight's body, and it clearly displayed the havoc Sarpedon's influence caused among the humans.

CC felt her head spin as she watched the mirror's image of herself being shown the wonders of the sea by Dylan. She experienced again the magic of their love as it was born and reveled in hearing the mirror image of her lover repeat his promise of waiting an eternity for her.

Again, the scene changed to show the humans' discovery of CC and her lover, and Sarpedon's materialization from the body of Andras. The last vision exposed through the glassy surface was of Gaea calling forth Lir to preside over the punishment of his son. Then the glistening surface went blank, and Gaea blew on it again, causing it to dissipate into a puff of shining smoke, leaving a shroud of silence that hung over the water.

Lir spoke first to the goddess. "I did not hear any of your calls." He shook his head sadly. "Sarpedon should not have been able to keep them from me. I allowed myself to be distracted."

Gaea nodded in understanding. "I knew Sarpedon was involved in your absence, but I was loath to act against your child. We share the responsibility of our errors."

"Yes. And too many have paid for them in our stead." The sea god faced the beach.

Andras and his squire were still crouched in the sand, eyes glassy with shock at what they were witnessing. Bronwyn, Lynelle and Gwenyth had joined Isabel on the beach and the four women stood together, their hands linked. Most of the monks had fled from the cliffside, but the few who remained were kneeling as if in prayer. The abbot was nowhere to be seen.

Lir glanced at Gaea and asked, "Are you willing to exchange roles, so that justice will truly be served?"

The goddess lifted her brows questioningly. "What do you propose?"

"I propose that I render judgment in your realm, as you will in mine."

Gaea hesitated only a moment. "Agreed."

Lir turned his attention to the humans on shore. First he focused his hard gaze on Andras and his man. "My judgment is thus—the knight and his squire shall return to their kingdom of land unharmed." Lir paused, and his eyes took on a sly glint, then he added, "Sir Andras, you shall learn the value of women. Henceforth you will be able to father only daughters, and your daughters will bear only female children. You would be wise to remember that the goddess of the Earth will be watching closely that you treat your daughters well." The knight's face drained of all its color, and he seemed to shrink in upon himself; then the two men scurried off the beach.

Lir spoke to the women next. "Wise women, because I am grateful for the friendship you have shown my daughter, I gift you with this monastery." Lir swept his arm in a grand gesture that encompassed the rocky walls above them, and suddenly the bland, gray color was washed away, replaced by stones that seemed to shine with the color of pearls. The four women on the beach gasped in pleasure.

"You will find I have made some *changes* within, too, as is befitting your new home." Lir smiled fondly at the women. Then he raised his head and his voice carried to the few monks who were still kneeling on the cliff. "You males may stay, but know that these women are no longer your servants. Live and worship peacefully with them, as equals, or flee their island and the wrath of the God of the Seas."

Then Lir's sharp gaze searched the beach until he found a quivering mound of flesh hiding behind a fallen log.

"Abbot! You cannot hide from the gods. Stand and receive your judgment."

Trembling, Abbot William raised his head and struggled to his feet. His face was streaked with tears and vomit soaked the front of his blood-colored robe.

Gaea touched Lir's arm again. Her voice was gentle. "Perhaps we should judge him together. He is, after all, our child."

The abbot's eyes widened in horror, and he shook his head from side to side in jerky, panic-filled denial.

Lir scowled. "Stop sniveling, William. *Remember!*" he commanded as he flicked his wrist, raining a spray of seawater across the beach and onto the abbot.

Instantly, a change came over William's face, and he blinked several times, rubbing his eyes as if he was just awakening from a bad dream.

"I told you we should have left him with his memories," Gaea said.

Lir sighed. "He always was our most difficult child. He could not abide the seas, yet he did not belong on the land. What do you propose we do with him now?"

Gaea tapped her chin thoughtfully with one slim finger. Then her eyes widened, and her smile was glorious. "I propose he spend the next century with Cernunnos helping him guard the Gateway to the Underworld. Perhaps one hundred years with the dead will teach our son to appreciate the beauty of life, and to be more accepting of himself and of others."

"Excellent!" Lir said, and he struck his trident three times against the water. At the third strike the beach at William's feet split open and swallowed him, closing quickly on his high-pitched cry for help.

"Now it is your turn, Earth Mother," Lir said.

"I will try to be as wise and just as the Lord of the Seas," the goddess said with a magnanimous smile.

Gaea and Lir faced the mer-beings. Gaea turned first to the two lovers. When she spoke, the goddess's words were filled with the warmth of a mother.

"Undine and Dylan—your love is strong and true. Though it causes me sadness to have my favorite daughter live apart from the land, your union brings me great joy. I bless your lives and smile upon your joining. May an eternity not diminish your love."

CC felt the goddess's blessing settle over her, and her soul swelled with happiness as Dylan took her gently into his battered arms.

Then she faced Sarpedon, whose face had already darkened in a rage of disbelief, and her expression hardened. His eyes flicked nervously from Lir to Gaea, as if he expected his father to step in and prevent the goddess from continuing.

"Sarpedon, you have been an overindulged child, and your punishment is long overdue. Since you misused the well that nourished the monastery, and you thought that through violence and entrapment you could cage love, your punishment shall reflect your misdeeds. I sentence you to be trapped within a well for the next century. And your jail will not be near the seas so that you can draw power from them to cause evil among those who would use your well. You will be caged far inland, deep in the center of a castle known for its well-ordered discipline. In the land of Caer Llion, the people banished magic decades ago. There you will neither be acknowledged nor feared. My wish for you is that this punishment teaches you to appreciate your freedom enough to allow others their own."

Gaea raised her hand to call forth her judgment, but with a snakelike movement Sarpedon's arm struck out, and he used his supernatural strength to shatter the bridge of land on which the goddess stood. The sand dissolved under her feet and, with a cry of shocked surprise, Gaea fell into the water. Whipping his thick tail, Sarpedon caused the water to whirlpool and boil as it closed over the goddess's head.

Roaring in disbelief, Lir parted the seething blue liquid and grasped Gaea's hand, pulling her up into his arms.

Quickly, Sarpedon spread his hands out into the water, as if he was searching for a hidden treasure within the waves. His voice was the sound of madness.

"If I cannot have her, no one will have her!"

The crazed merman raised his mighty arm from the waves. In his fist he clutched the spear Gaea had fashioned to kill the sea monster. In a movement blurred with speed, Sarpedon hurled the spear at CC.

Dylan saw the spear coming and the world seemed to slow around him. He could not let Sarpedon kill her. She needed him; the cost did not matter.

An instant before the weapon would have penetrated CC's body, Dylan twisted, throwing himself in front of the mermaid. CC felt her lover spasm as the spear embedded itself in his back, and she watched in horror as its tip blossomed out of the merman's chest like a terrible crimson flower.

Her cry of despair joined with Lir's roar of rage. The sea god's reaction was swift. He hurled his trident at his son, striking him full in the chest. Sarpedon's eyes widened in shock an instant before his lifeless body began to liquefy and lose substance, until he no longer held the form of a merman, but became part of the waters from which he had been born.

In two enormous strides the sea god was at Dylan's side. He barked a word of command and the water hardened so that it held Gaea aloft, above its frothing wetness. Both deities knelt before the wounded merman.

Dylan focused his remaining power and sent one simple thought to Gaea.

Do not let her know. It is a cost I willingly paid.

Gaea knew that his transformation into a human had weakened him too much. Now, not even the power of the Gods could save him. The goddess closed her eyes on tears and nodded.

My daughter shall not know.

Dylan's body slumped in CC's arms. His eyes were closed and his breathing was shallow and rapid. Blood poured from the flesh that gaped around the spearhead. Lir grasped the handle of the spear protruding from the merman's back, as if to pull it from Dylan's body, but Gaea's restraining hand halted him.

"It will only cause him more pain." The goddess's words were rich with sorrow.

"What do you mean?" CC's voice was tinged with growing hysteria. "Of course you have to pull it out! How else are you going to save him?"

In a gesture infinitely gentle, Gaea touched the mermaid's tear-drenched cheek.

"I cannot save him, Christine."

"You have to!" CC sobbed. "You're a goddess. You have to be able to save him."

The goddess's eyes filled with tears. As she spoke they spilled down her cheeks, leaving trails of glistening diamonds in their wake.

"He has been pierced with my own spear, a weapon fashioned by my hand as a device of destruction. I cannot heal a wound caused by my own hand."

"But you didn't throw it!"

"I wrought it, and that is enough. I did not have to wield it, too," Gaea said sadly.

CC looked desperately at Lir. "Then you save him. You're a god."

The sea god exchanged a look with Gaea. When he spoke, his voice held the weight of centuries. "I cannot undo the destruction brought about by the Earth goddess. Even gods and goddesses are bound by the rules of the universe."

"Then turn back time! Do something!" CC screamed.

"Christine." Dylan's voice was a choked whisper. His body twitched as he struggled to turn his face up to hers. "They cannot help me." He coughed and blood gushed in a new torrent from his wound.

"*Shhh.*" CC pressed her hand to his lips. "Don't talk. Save your strength. We'll figure out something."

With an almost imperceptible movement, Dylan shook his head. "I knew the choice I was making when I moved within the path of the spear. I made it freely"—he paused to pant for breath—"and I would make it again." The merman closed his eyes, struggling against a wave of pain.

"Dylan, no!" CC kissed him frantically. "You can't die. You can't leave me. Remember," she sobbed, "you promised me an eternity."

The merman's lips tilted briefly in a smile, and he opened his eyes. "I still await you. For an eternity, Christine."

In one last heave, the merman's chest rose and his shaking hand brushed CC's tear-soaked cheek.

"For an eternity . . ."

With those last words, Dylan's life fled his body, and CC was left clutching the shell of her beloved until it, like Sarpedon's body, began to fade and liquefy, returning to the water of his creation.

As if sifting sand through a colander, CC's hands tried to recapture the scattered brilliance of the colors of flame that floated briefly atop the water.

"Come, child," Gaea said, grasping CC's hands so that their frantic motion was stilled.

Gaea opened her arms to her daughter, but even the embrace of a goddess could not soothe the pain of loss within CC, and the mermaid sobbed so desperately that she felt as if her soul had dissolved around her like Dylan's body.

Then other arms joined the goddess. They were softer, more aged arms, arms that were weathered and worn and had born witness to a lifetime of hardship and sorrows.

"I know, child. I know."

CC looked up into Isabel's tear-stained face. Then she felt more arms around her. Standing chest deep in water, Lynelle, Bronwyn and Gwenyth had joined Isabel. The four women completed the circle around CC, lending her their strength and filling her with their love. CC sobbed out her pain and loss, secure in the knowledge that the women who held her would not let her go.

In the midst of despair, Gaea reached her hand out to her daughter, motioning to the path that the arrow had carved through the mermaid's flesh.

"Let me heal you of this wound, Daughter," Gaea said. But before the goddess touched the bloody furrow, she hesitated. Slowly she withdrew her hand. "I must wait. The judgment is not complete." Gaea looked at Lir. "Events have changed, and so must my judgment."

Wearily, the sea god nodded.

"This judgment will differ from those of the past, because today's events have forever changed me." Gaea's audience was hushed; even Lir seemed to be holding his breath in anticipation of the goddess's next words. "For the bravery and loyalty you have shown, my beloved daughter, my judgment is that you may choose your future path." CC's tear-ravaged face brightened, and Gaea was quick to continue. "I cannot change your lover's death, and for that I will be eternally sorry, but I can offer you two choices."

"What are they?" CC asked in a voice that shook.

"You may choose to stay here, in this world and this time, either as a mermaid and Goddess of the Seas, or as Earth's beloved daughter and a goddess in my realm. You will reign beside either parent, and your days will be filled with the duties of a deity."

"Forever?" CC asked.

"Forever," Gaea assured her.

"What is my other choice?"

"I will return you to your old world and your old time—to the site of your accident, the moment before the wreckage pulled you under the waves. You will survive the accident and continue with your human life."

"But what will happen to Undine if I choose to return to my world?" CC asked.

Lir's voice sounded ancient with grief. "My son exists no more. That is as unchanging as the death of Dylan. If Undine returns to me, she will be allowed her own choice. Whether she decides to remain in the seas with me, or joins her mother on land, she has my blessing. I shall no longer try to control the lives of my children."

"There is one more thing you should know before you make your choice," Gaea spoke into the silence that surrounded the god's words. "It is within our power"—here she glanced at Lir and he nodded slowly in agreement—"to wipe clean the slate of your memory."

"You mean you can send me back to the instant that I was being pulled under by the wreckage, and you can make me forget everything that has happened here? It'd be like I was never gone, like Undine and I had never changed places?" CC asked.

"Yes," the goddess said.

CC felt herself become very still. She closed her eyes and, against the background of her darkened lids, she replayed the days and nights she had spent on Caldei. And her eyes snapped open.

"I know what I want," she said firmly.

"Tell me, Daughter; complete your own judgment."

"I have loved being in this world; I thought that I had finally found a place where I could belong, a place I could call my true home. But I understand now that a sense of belonging is not physical. We can't find it by changing where we live or what we do. We have to carry it within us." CC took a deep breath. "Forgive me, Mother." Her gaze included both Gaea and Isabel. "I can't spend an eternity without him, even if it is as a goddess. And I've learned that I carry my true home within me. So I want to be sent back to my old world. And I want to remember—all of you and him." Her words ended in a whisper.

"Very well," the goddess said.

"We will miss you, Undine." Isabel spoke for the women, who nodded and wiped tears from their streaming eyes.

CC hugged each of them.

"Take care of each other and other women, too," CC said through her tears.

"Take this back with you." Isabel tried to return to her the amber amulet, but CC shook her head.

"No, keep it and remember me."

"We will never forget," Isabel promised.

Then CC turned to Lir. She touched his arm gently, in a gesture that mimicked that of the goddess.

"I would have liked to have known you."

"As I would have you, child." His voice rumbled with feeling. "You no longer have your mother's amulet. Allow me to gift you with one of my own." The sea god reached into the waves and when he pulled his hand up, a delicate golden chain glittered from one of his fingers. From the end of the chain hung an exquisite baroque pearl, gleaming all the colors of sunrise. He placed it around her neck and kissed her lightly on her forehead. "Remember me," he said sadly. "And know that if you ever desire solace, all you need do is to find the water. In any world it will welcome you with a father's embrace."

At last CC faced the goddess. With the loss of Dylan she had thought her heart unable to ache anymore, but as Gaea smoothed back her hair and wiped the tears from her face, CC felt a new wound open within her.

"No, child." Gaea cupped CC's face in her hands. "Do not let this parting cause you more grief; I could not bear it. You must know that even in your distant world, I will be watching you. You can find me in the trees and flowers and plants you so love. And whenever the moon is at its most full, look there and you will see the reflection of my face."

CC choked back a sob, wondering if she would die of sadness.

As if reading her mind the goddess spoke quickly with knowing finality. "You will survive. You are a child of my spirit and your strength is great."

CC nodded, feeling fresh tears warm her cheeks.

Gaea kissed her gently on the lips. "Go with my blessing, Daughter. Always remember that you are much loved by a goddess, and that you hold within you the magic of the Divine Feminine."

Then Lir moved to stand beside Gaea and, as one, the immortals raised their arms to the sky.

"*I call upon the power at my command. I am Earth, body and soul.*" Gaea's voice was filled with strength. In response to her call, the air around the goddess began to shimmer with energy.

"*I call upon the power at my command. I am sea, breath and life.*" Lir's voice followed Gaea's and as he spoke the water around them began to glow.

"*Once we joined to create a child,*" Gaea intoned.

"*Now we join to send a child back whence she came,*" Lir continued.

"*Return to the world of man,*" Gaea said.

"*Carrying blessings from the world of gods,*" Lir said.

"*SO HAVE WE SPOKEN; SO SHALL IT BE.*"

The immortals intoned the final command together, and CC felt a great funnel of power settle over her, as if she had been swallowed by a current of electricity. Blinding light engulfed her, and she squeezed her eyes shut. Her body was being pulled backward with such force that she was unable to breathe. On and on the sensation went, like she was caught on a giant roller coaster that only ran in reverse. Panicking, CC wrenched open her mouth to scream, and it filled with saltwater as her head broke through the surface of the water, and she choked and sputtered, struggling to breathe and stay afloat.

She heard two quick splashes, and, in an instant, a head broke the surface not far from her, along with a lifeless body clad in a flight suit and strapped within a life jacket.

The sense of déjà vu was so overwhelming that she had to struggle to concentrate past blinding dizziness.

"There."

Blinking wildly, CC watched as the colonel pointed at the fluorescent orange life raft that drifted about forty feet in front of them.

"Swim! We have to get away from the plane." He set off, sidestroking and kicking hard as he dragged the lifeless body with him.

CC's numbed thoughts told her that those were the same words the colonel had spoken to her before. And the body was Sean. Another man who had died for her. She choked again, this time on a sob instead of seawater. Her mind felt stuck in a labyrinth of pain and remembrance.

A horrendously familiar explosion burst behind her, and she spun around in the water in time to bear witness a second time to the death of the plane. It was an enormous, gaping beast, and, in its death throes, it eerily reminded her of Sarpedon's sea monster.

With a sense of increasing detachment CC realized the same thing she had understood all those days before—the sinking plane was too close to her.

And this time she didn't care. There had been so much death. Why shouldn't she just relax and give in to it? At least this time she wouldn't be filled with fear of the water. She felt cold and unbearably tired. CC closed her eyes and quit struggling as she waited for the mechanical tentacle to wrap around her ankle.

When she felt the first bump against her body she was mildly surprised. She hadn't remembered getting thrown around before the thing had dragged her under.

The bump turned into an insistent, jetlike force, and soon she was sputtering, gasping for air, and flailing her arms desperately around for balance as she was firmly propelled up and forward by two somethings that felt slick and muscular and very familiar against her swiftly moving body.

This isn't happening, she thought. It can't be real.

"I'll be! Will you look at that?" A dark-haired captain holding a flat yellow paddle pointed in her direction.

Even the colonel, who was dragging Sean's lifeless body aboard the raft, paused to stare.

The pressure against CC released, and she came to a halt as she knocked against the side of the orange raft. The pointing captain grabbed her arm and pulled her aboard. At the rough handling, newly awakened pain raked through her body, and CC shivered violently as a warm rush of blood poured from her wounded shoulder.

"It's the same shoulder," she said, looking down at the red stain that was blending with the desert brown of her sodden fatigue shirt. "Different body, but same shoulder." The words were coming out of her mouth, but CC didn't feel very connected to them, just as she didn't feel very connected to her body. Somewhere through the layers of grief and shock, the laughter of hysteria began to bubble inside her throat.

"Shit, yes, your shoulder's hurt. We know that. But what the hell were those things?" the master sergeant asked, pointing at the sleek gray shapes that were streaking away from them.

"Dolphins," CC said, erupting into uncontrollable giggles. "They're dolphins."

"Well, kiss my ass and call me Santa Claus! I've never seen nothing like that. Those damn fish just saved your life," the master sergeant said, slapping his thick thigh.

"Actually, they're mammals, not fish," CC said between giggles and gulps for air. "And I guess they still think I'm a princess."

Except for her unnaturally shrill giggles, the raft was quiet while the men stared at her.

"Uh, sarg," the colonel said gently. "You better let me take a look at that shoulder."

The pain of having her shoulder handled killed CC's hysteria.

"This will hurt like hell," the colonel told her. "But I have to pack it and get the bleeding stopped or you're going to be in bad shape."

CC wanted to tell him that she didn't care, that she'd rather just die, but he had turned away and was busy searching through the first aid kit for packets of gauze.

"Looks like a fuckin' arrow sliced through her," the master sergeant said before the colonel told him to shut the hell up.

"Here, bite this." The colonel handed her a wooden tongue depressor, and she clamped her teeth down on it. "You try and think of someplace you'd rather be, and I'll try and be quick," he told her.

"Ready?"

She nodded weakly and closed her eyes, thinking of a moonlit night when neon-colored fish were candles and the world was filled with the newness of love. She could see Dylan's face as he bent to kiss her and, for an instant, she could almost taste his wild, salty flavor.

Pain exploded, splintering her concentration as flecks of light dotted her closed lids. And then the sweetness of unconsciousness claimed her.

"HANG on, sarg! We've got ya!"

The steady *twap, twap, twap* of the helicopter and the pain in her shoulder wrenched CC back into screaming consciousness. She opened her eyes to find a Search and Rescue Trooper working over her, murmuring encouragement while he unsnapped the lid of a syringe filled with clear liquid and jabbed it into her thigh. The medicine's sharp burn was almost unnoticeable compared to the agony that was her shoulder.

"It'll be better now. Just relax, and we'll have you in the chopper in no time."

He spoke to her soothingly as he finished strapping her into the harness. Then he gave the thumb's up sign to the air above him, and CC felt a sickening lurch as she was lifted from the raft to the hovering helicopter.

She was the first to be rescued, but the others weren't far behind. CC watched through a morphine haze as Sean's body was pulled into the helicopter, followed quickly by the master sergeant, then the lieutenant, the captains, and finally the colonel.

As they flew away from the crash site, CC locked her gaze on the glimpse of sapphire water she could still see through the helicopter's open door. With all her soul she wished she would catch a flash of fiery orange streaking under the surface, shadowing the path of the aircraft and eternally waiting for her return.

Her vision of the glistening water blurred as her eyes filled and spilled over with tears.

"You'll be all right now, sarg," said the medic who was starting an IV in her arm. "We'll get you home and get you all fixed up."

CC opened her mouth to say that it would never be all right again, but a cry from the other side of the chopper bay interrupted her.

"Oh, shit! Johnson! Get over here; I need another set of hands! This man is alive."

The medic working on CC gave her IV sack a quick adjustment before he rushed to help his colleague.

Somewhere in the back of her mind CC understood that the frantically working medics were surrounding Sean's body, but her thoughts weren't working properly, and she couldn't seem to focus her mind.

And she thought she knew why. It had nothing to do with the loss of blood, or the pain, or the morphine. It was because even though her body was alive, her heart was dead. It died in another world and dissipated to nothingness within the seas.

The blue of the ocean crystallized through her tears, and then began to fade as gray unconsciousness folded over the edges of her vision, and, like a favorite blanket, lulled her into a deep, dreamless sleep.

Part Three

CHAPTER THIRTY

Nine months later

"OH, please! That's nothing but a big pile of poo!" CC yelled and threw the book across the room, narrowly missing decapitating the lilac-colored orchid that was in magnificent bloom on her coffee table. "Hans Christian Andersen, T.S. Eliot, Lucretius, Tennyson, and now this horrible de la Motte Fouqué person. Uh! None of them were even close to getting it right!"

CC sighed and retrieved the book, all the more irritated that she had to reach under the couch for it. Finally grabbing it, she made straight for the wastebasket in the kitchen, rolling her eyes at the title.

"*Romantic Fairy Tales*," she scoffed, and lifted the lid of the wastebasket. But, as usual, she couldn't make herself actually throw the book away. Shaking her head and mumbling, she marched to her spare room.

"There's not one thing romantic about that stupid story. As usual, the mermaid doesn't even have a soul unless she can get some mule-headed guy to marry her. And in this particular version, he betrays her for another woman and she still pines away for him."

In her spare room she searched through her new bookshelves, trying to find a place for the slim book. Finally she slipped it between a lavishly illustrated copy of *Mermaids: Nymphs of the Sea*, and Oscar Wilde's *The Fisherman and His Soul*. Then she put her hands on her hips and glared at her ever-expanding collection.

"All those words and you couldn't manage to capture more than a fraction of the truth. And none of you so much as hinted at the magic of his smile."

CC didn't say his name aloud; she didn't even think it. She couldn't. Even after nine months, she still felt too hollow and fragile. If she allowed herself to think too much about the empty place inside of her, she was sure that the shell of normalcy she had tried to glue together around her life would shatter. And then she didn't know how she would go on.

So instead, she haunted the bookstores and the Internet, always searching for everything and anything that pertained to mermaids. Then she devoured the pages as if they were her lifeline. Maybe they were. They kept her anger and frustration alive, which felt easier to live with than emptiness and despair.

She had gone on the Web and searched Amazon once using the term "merman." Two responses had popped up—an audio collection of Ethel Merman's greatest hits, and some kind of toy called Masters of the Universe Evil Enemies: Mer-men. After that, she had confined her searches to mer*maids* and mythology in general.

When she discovered her newest acquisition, the *Romantic Fairy Tales* book, she had been filled with an almost unbearable sense of anticipation as she opened its pages. The blurb on Amazon had said that de la Motte Fouqué's classic tale was written about the mermaid Undine. It proclaimed that the story was about "a water nymph who falls in love, acquires a soul and so discovers the reality of human suffering." But, as usual, her reading had left her disappointed and irritated.

"It was nothing but another preachy allegory written by some old dead white guy," CC said miserably.

Then she sighed again and rubbed at the pink, puckered scar that furrowed across her shoulder, cringing at the dull ache that radiated down her arm. CC glanced at her watch. It was almost 9:00 p.m. on a Friday night. Even on a hot August night, the opulent, Olympic-sized pool at her apartment complex would be deserted, which was just the way she liked it.

As she changed into her one-piece racing style Speedo and hastily pulled her shoulder length brown curls up into a tight ponytail she could almost hear her mother's voice echoing through her apartment.

"Dear, a pretty girl like you shouldn't be alone on a Friday night. It's just not good for the soul."

The bathroom light glinted on the golden chain that always hung around her neck, and CC's lips curved into a bittersweet smile. With one finger she stroked the smooth, iridescent surface of the huge pearl. Then she looked at herself in the mirror, pretending she was speaking to her mother.

"My soul's fine, Mom. It's just not all here."

Imagining the shocked reaction on her mother's face made her lips tighten. She didn't like to think about the pain her accident had caused her parents.

They had never left her side throughout her month-long hospital stay, and when CC was released to return to Tinker AFB, her mom had come with her and had stayed another two months, helping her with the painful rehabilitation exercise routine. She certainly would never say anything to her mother that would make her worry any more about her than she already did, which meant she could never tell her mother that she longed to be in another world and another time.

CC shook her head. No, she wouldn't let depression win—she refused to live as a morose shadow. She felt like she had spent the past nine months trying to give birth to a new self, and she had to keep reminding herself that the birthing process always involved pain. It was just another part of life.

CC forced herself to smile as she pulled on her terrycloth cover-up, grabbed a towel and her swim bag and hurried out her apartment door. The water would make her feel better. It always did.

Mrs. Runyan was just coming up the stairs, and she waved a cheerful greeting.

"Going for your nightly swim, dear?" she asked.

"Yes, ma'am." CC smiled warmly at her. CC and her neighbor had grown very close in the months of her recovery. She felt honored to have been gifted with the friendship of another wise woman.

"Well, it's a lovely night for it. The moon is full and the sky is clear."

CC glanced up in surprise. The butter-colored moon was just rising, full and lustrous, over the greenbelt that backed their apartment complex.

"You're right. I hadn't remembered that it would be a full moon tonight."

At work CC had been preparing for another of the Communication Center's endless inspections. She had only been back full-time for three months, and she was so busy that she had completely lost track of the phases of the moon. Now she felt an unexpected rush of pleasure at the thought of swimming her laps beneath the beauty of the full moon.

Mrs. Runyan smiled mischievously at CC and tapped her on the nose. "Better keep your eyes open tonight. Wonderful things happen during the full moon."

"I'll remember, Mrs. Runyan. And I'll also remember our date tomorrow night to watch *An Affair to Remember*," CC said as she hurried past her friend.

"You had better, young lady. You're bringing the champagne!" the old woman called good-naturedly after her.

CC was still smiling as she swung through the wrought-iron gate to the pool. She sighed happily. As she had hoped, the pool was totally unoccupied. It never failed to surprise CC how quickly the residents of the pricey complex lost interest in their beautiful facility.

The pool was magnificent. It was a huge rectangle made of aqua-colored tile, hand painted around the rim with images of frolicking fish. To one side of the pool was a built-in Jacuzzi, complete with a fountain and cascading waterfall. Expensive deck chairs were clustered in neat circles around glass-topped, canopied tables. Thickly cushioned lounge chairs dotted the edge of the pool.

CC shrugged off her cover-up and fished her goggles out of the bag, then she left both bag and wrap in a heap on the nearest lounge chair. Eagerly, she approached the deep end of the pool.

Tonight the turquoise water was illuminated from above as well as below. Like hidden lanterns, the recessed lighting cast a magical turquoise glow through the calm water, while on its surface the moonlight danced and played, breathing life into the water's stillness and temporarily lending it the appearance of ocean waves.

The last time she had seen the moonlight reflecting off the ocean she had been in the arms of . . .

CC's breath caught in her throat, and hastily she reined in her thoughts. She hadn't been prepared for the sudden powerful image or for the painful memory it had evoked. In the past nine months she had discovered that memory was a tricky thing, and to keep from being dragged into its vortex of pain she had to stay vigilant, only allowing certain memories to sift into her consciousness, one at a time, and only when she was well prepared for them. Tonight she hadn't been prepared, and her desire for Dylan was a sharp yearning.

CC rubbed at her eyes, reminding herself firmly that she was finished crying. She was getting on with her life. Then she turned her face up to the moon.

"I hope you can see me," she said. "You were right; I did make it. I am strong."

A little breeze whispered around CC's body, ruffling the fine hairs on the back of her neck before it blew across the pool, causing the surface of the water to ripple in response.

CC smiled. "Thank you, Mother, for not allowing me to forget the magic that I still hold within me."

Feeling her soul lighten, CC fitted the goggles on her face and took several deep breaths. Then she sprang in a graceful arc into the water. Kicking, she angled to the surface where she started the steady, measured strokes that would carry her lap after lap across the pool.

As she counted laps, CC thought about what a shock her sudden love of swimming had been to her friends and family. Her first real request as she was recovering from her shoulder injury was to be taken to the water—any water— and allowed to swim.

"But dear, you've never liked the water," CC's mother had said, clearly confused by her daughter's unusual request.

"You aren't even a very good swimmer," her dad had added.

But CC had insisted, and, along with the blessing of her doctor, she had begun working in a pool with her physical therapist.

Now CC could say with confidence that she was an excellent swimmer, as a matter-of-fact; her physical therapist had said she showed a special aptitude for swimming. That had made CC laugh, and then, much later when she had been alone in her bed, it had made her cry.

Continuing to count laps as she kicked away from the side of the pool, she felt the tension in her body begin to relax. In the water, CC always felt secure. Lir had been right; it welcomed her with a father's touch—even if it she was only swimming in a man-made pool. And she ached for the sanctuary the water provided. The C-130 crash had been big news, especially after word of CC's dolphin saviors and Sean's resurrection had leaked to the civilian media. To CC's horror, reporters from all over the world had descended on her, all vying for a "personal angle to the tragedy." Apparently, *leave me alone* was a phrase that was not taught in journalism school.

CC only hoped that they hadn't been as tenacious about bothering Sean. She hadn't seen him since the rescue helicopter. She had been taken to the military hospital at Navy Siganella in Italy and rushed into surgery. Sean had ended up in Ramstein Air Base, Germany. She had only heard snatches of reports about him, but from them she had discovered that he had recovered, and that the doctors were calling it a miracle.

All she knew for sure was that she had nearly been responsible for his death, and that was a guilt she carried around with her every day. She had sent him a card—once. She'd addressed it to him in care of his fighter unit in Tulsa. She still cringed when she remembered her bumbling attempt at thanking him for exchanging places with her and her inept apology. He hadn't replied—and she hadn't expected him to.

Her stroke faltered, and she pushed thoughts of the accident from her mind. The moon was full, and she was alone, surrounded by the security of the water. All she had to do tonight was to stroke, kick and breathe—stroke, kick and breathe.

When she tilted her head up for her next breath, she thought she saw a shape pass over the moon. Clouds, she thought, and disappointment washed through her. She hadn't remembered the weatherman saying there was a chance of rain, but Oklahoma in the summer meant changing weather. With a burst of energy, she redoubled her efforts. If she was going to have to cut her swim short, at least she would be sure she got in a decent workout.

The shout came through the waves of water as more vibration than sound, and at first CC ignored it, thinking it was just the distant rumble of approaching thunder. At her next breath, though, the vibration turned into words.

"Sergeant Canady!"

CC ground her teeth together and came to an abrupt halt, treading water near the edge of the lap end of the pool. A man was standing several yards away from her. Through the blur of her goggles he looked tall and lean, but indistinct. She didn't bother to remove them.

"What?" she snapped.

"Are you Sergeant Canady? Sergeant Christine Canady?"

The man's voice was vaguely familiar, which told CC that he was probably one of the reporters who had been calling her for the past several months, whining for a story.

"Look, you shouldn't be here."

"I only ask if you are Christine Canady. The Christine Canady who was in the accident."

Irritation sliced through CC. She pulled her goggles off her face and brushed her escaping curls from her eyes.

"I don't want to talk to—"

Her words stopped as her vision cleared and she got a good look at him. She had been right, he was tall and lean, almost too thin. He was wearing faded jeans and a polo-style shirt. Over the upper right chest pocket of the shirt there was an embroidered emblem. The moonlight touched it, illuminating clearly the head of an Indian chieftain in the distinct pattern that was the well-known logo of Tulsa's F-16 Unit.

CC's eyes snapped to the man's face. His hair was military short, and he was clean-shaven. The raised pink ridge of scar tissue ran from the hairline over his left eye and down, marking a path over his well-defined cheekbone before disappearing into the shadows behind his ear.

"Sean?" CC's stomach heaved in a nauseating flutter.

His brow furrowed, and he hesitated before answering. CC thought that he looked nervous.

"Yes, but I . . ." Here he gestured abstractly and sighed, as if at a loss for words.

CC stared at him, and then, ashamed of herself she looked quickly away. He'd had part of his head sliced off. It was a miracle that he was walking and talking, so it shouldn't be surprising that he got words mixed up, or that he seemed confused about what he was trying to say. When CC met his gaze again she gave him a tentative smile.

"How about I get out of this pool so we can talk?"

Sean nodded and CC swam away from him to the ladder. As she started to climb out of the water she called to him over her shoulder.

"Can you wait a second while I get my cover-up and dry off a little?"

"I would wait an eternity for you, Christine."

Sean's words filled the night.

Like she had been hit in the stomach, CC's body jerked in response. She missed the next rung of the ladder and tumbled back into the water. Gasping, she kicked for surface, but, before she reached air, strong hands grabbed her arms and pulled, lifting her up to the side of the pool where she sat in a heap, coughing the water she'd swallowed and staring at the pale man who crouched beside her.

"I would never let you drown," he said softly.

"Why?" CC shook her head, pulling back from him. "Why are you saying these things?"

"Christine, I . . ." Sean reached for her and she lunged away from him.

"Please stop!" Her whisper sounded like a hiss of angry steam. "I know you've been hurt, and I know I'm responsible. But you have to stop talking like this."

Sean's face twisted in sadness. When he spoke, he kept his tone kind, like he was trying to reason with an upset child. "I told you once that I made my choice freely, and that I would make it again. That has not changed. You did not cause it, my love."

"There!" CC exploded to her feet. She wrapped her arms around herself as if she was afraid she would break into pieces. "That's what I mean. Stop saying those things."

Sean stood slowly and took a tentative half step toward her, but when she backed away from him, he stopped, holding his hand out like a peace offering.

"I cannot stop speaking thus to you. My words are truth," he said.

"Why are you doing this? *How* are you doing this?" She felt herself begin to shake uncontrollably.

"Christine, do you not know me?" he asked gently.

"I know who you sound like, but he's dead. I watched him die in another world." CC covered her face with her hands and sobbed.

Sean crossed the space between them and took her into his arms. At first she struggled, but soon she just stood there, rigid with pain in the cocoon of his unfamiliar embrace.

"I see that I must convince you." She felt the warmth of his breath against her wet hair. "Then let me describe for you a place. It is a place you would easily recognize, for there is none other like it. A ring of stone stands proudly in the middle of clear waters; its dome is open to the sky."

As he spoke, CC lifted her face so that she could look into the hazel depths of his eyes.

"The waters there are lit by luminous fish and filled with the magic of sea horses moving together in a dance of mating." He smiled tenderly at her. "It was there that you first loved me, but I believe that I have loved you forever—that you were a part of me even before we met in the storm that was your mother's creation. And I will continue to love you for an eternity, Christine."

Hesitantly, as if she were afraid he would disappear if she moved too quickly, Christine reached up and touched his cheek.

"How?" she asked.

He turned his head so he could kiss her palm. "I do not know, but I like to think of it as a gift from a goddess. I am sorry it took me so long to come to you. Being human is a very odd thing." He paused and laughed with a sound so familiar that CC's heart quivered in response. "When they die their bodies do not return to water. They stay intact, as if waiting for another's soul to fill them, but this body was . . ." He paused, shrugging his wide shoulders. "It was very badly damaged, and it has taken me longer to heal than I would have thought possible. Many said I would not heal at all, but they did not know the promise I had to fulfill."

"Dylan." CC breathed the word.

"Yes, my love," Dylan said.

CC felt the pain within her shatter and dissolve. In its place she was filled with an overwhelming sense of joy. Then her eyes widened in wonder.

"It's the opposite of all those mermaid stories that humans have written!" she exclaimed.

He gave her a quizzical look.

"In those stories the mermaid is saved by the love of a human man—and if he doesn't love her, she dies."

Dylan's smile mirrored her own. "It appears the humans had it wrong. It is the *woman's* love that saves the *merman's* soul."

"Or maybe they just save each other," she said.

"And so we shall, Christine."

"For an eternity."

"For an eternity," he assured her.

And as he claimed her lips, their ears were filled with the magical sound of a goddess's delighted laughter.

Goddess
of
Spring

To the other three parts of the Core Four—
Kim, Robin and Teresa.
I cherish the blessing of our friendship.

ACKNOWLEDGMENTS

I am thankful for the continued magic of my editor, Christine Zika, and for the brilliance of my agent, Meredith Bernstein. What a fabulous team we make!

I am profoundly grateful to my friend Lola Palazzo for her expertise. Thank you for helping me to create a dream bakery and for educating me about baking in general. Lola—you would be doing Tulsa (and your friends) a great service if you opened another restaurant!

Thank you, Sean Georges, for your research help. Once again, we work very well together.

I appreciate Pamela Chew for taking the time to answer my questions about the Italian language. Any inaccuracies in translation are my own.

PROLOGUE

"Even amidst the lovely Dryads your daughter shines, my Lady," Eirene said. She wasn't looking at me as she spoke. Instead she was smiling at Persephone in a proud, motherly fashion, and she did not notice that my lips tightened into a thin line at her words.

"She is Spring personified and even the beauty of the nymphs cannot begin to compete with her splendor."

At the sound of my words, Eirene's sharp gaze immediately shifted to my face. My faithful nursemaid had known me too long not to recognize my tone.

"The child troubles you, Demeter?" she asked gently.

"How could she not!" I snapped.

Only Eirene's silence betrayed her hurt. I shifted my golden scepter from my right hand to my left, and leaned forward so that I could touch her arm in a wordless apology. As usual, she stood near my throne, always ready to serve me. But she was, of course, much more to me than a simple nursemaid or servant. She was my confidant and one of my most loyal advisors. As such she deserved to be treated with respect, and my harsh tone toward her was a sign of how distracted I had become.

Her distinctive gray eyes softened with understanding at my touch.

"Would you like wine, Great Goddess?" she asked.

"For us both." I did not smile; it was not my way. But she understood me and my moods so completely that often only a look or a word was needed between us.

I studied my daughter as Eirene called for wine. The little Nysaian meadow had been the perfect choice in which to spend the unseasonably warm afternoon. Persephone and her wood nymph companions complemented the beauty that surrounded us. Though the day was pleasant, the trees that ringed the meadow were already beginning to shed their summer clothes. I watched

Persephone twirl gracefully under one ancient oak, making a game of trying to catch the brilliantly colored falling leaves. The nymphs aided the young goddess by dancing on the limbs to assure a steady waterfall of orange and scarlet and rust.

As usual, Eirene was correct. The woodland Dryads were ethereal and delicate. Each of them was a breathing masterpiece. It was easy to understand why mortals found them irresistible. But when compared to Persephone, their beauty turned mundane. In her presence they became common house slaves.

My daughter's hair shone with a rich mahogany luster, the color of which never ceased to amaze me because I am so fair. It does not curl, either, as do my grain-colored tresses. Instead her hair was a ripple of thick, brilliant waves that lapped around the soft curve of her waist.

Obviously feeling my scrutiny, she waved joyously at me before capturing another watercolored leaf. Her face tilted in my direction. It was a perfect heart. Enormous violet-colored eyes were framed by arched brows and thick, ebony lashes. Her lips were lush and inviting. Her body was lithe. I felt my own lips turn down.

"Your wine, my Lady." Eirene offered me a golden goblet filled with chilled wine the color of sunlight.

I sipped thoughtfully, speaking my thoughts aloud, secure in the knowledge that they were safe with Eirene. "Of course Persephone is supple and lovely. Why would she not be? She spends all her time frolicking with nymphs and picking flowers."

"She also creates glorious feasts."

I made a very ungoddess-like noise through my nose. "I am quite aware that she produces culinary masterpieces, and then lolls about feasting to all hours with"—I wafted my hand in the direction of the Dryads—"semi-deities."

"She is much beloved," Eirene reminded me patiently.

"She is frivolous," I countered.

Suddenly, I closed my eyes and cringed as another voice rose from the multitudes and rang with the insistence of a clarion bell throughout my mind. *Lover, somber Goddess of the Fields and Fruits and Flowers, strong and just, please aid our mother's spirit as she roams restless through the Darkened Realm without the comfort of a goddess . . .*

"Demeter, are you well?" Eirene's concern broke through the supplication, effectively causing the voice to dissipate like windblown dust.

Opening my eyes I met her gaze. "It has become never-ending." Even as I spoke more voices crowded my mind. *O Demeter, we do call upon thee, that our sister who has passed Beyond be accorded the comfort of a goddess . . . and . . . O gracious goddess who gives life through the harvest, I do ask your indulgence for my beloved wife who has passed through the Gates of the Underworld and dwells evermore beyond the comfort of a goddess . . .*

With a mighty effort I blocked the teeming throng from my mind.

"Something must be done about Hades." My voice was stone. "I understand the mortals. Their entreaties are valid. It is fact that there is no Goddess of the Underworld." I leapt up and began to pace back and forth in frustration. "But what am I to do? The Goddess of the Riches of the Field cannot abandon her realm and descend into the Land of the Dead."

"But the dead do require the touch of a goddess," Eirene agreed firmly.

"They need more than just the touch of a goddess. They need light and care and . . ." My words faded away as Persephone's bright laughter filled the meadow. "They need the breath of Spring."

Eirene's eyes widened. "You cannot mean your daughter!"

"And why can I not! Light and life follow the child. She is exactly what is needed within that shadowy realm."

"But she is so young."

I felt my gaze soften as I watched Persephone leap over a narrow stream, allowing her hand to trail over the dried remains of the season's last wildflowers. Instantly the stalks filled and straightened and burst into brilliant bloom. Despite her faults, she was so precious, so filled with the joy of life. There was no doubt that I loved her dearly. I often wondered if my fierce devotion had kept her from growing into a goddess of her own realm. I straightened my shoulders. It was past time that I taught my daughter how to fly.

"She is a goddess."

"She will not like it."

I set my already firm jaw. "Persephone will obey my command."

Eirene opened her mouth as if she wished to speak, then seemed to change her mind and instead drank deeply of her wine.

I sighed. "You know you may speak your mind to me."

"I was just thinking that it would not be a matter of Persephone obeying your command, but rather . . ." She hesitated.

"Oh, come! Tell me your thoughts."

Eirene looked decidedly uncomfortable. "Demeter, you know that I love Persephone as if she were my own child."

l nodded impatiently. "Yes, yes. Of course."

"She is delightful and full of life, but she has little depth. I do not think she has enough maturity to be Goddess of the Underworld."

A hot retort came to my mind, but wisdom held my tongue. Eirene was correct. Persephone was a lovely young goddess, but her life had been too easy, too filled with cosseted pleasures. And I was at fault. My frivolous daughter was proof that even a goddess could make mistakes as a parent.

"I agree, my old friend. Before Persephone can become Goddess of the Underworld, she must mature."

"Perhaps she should spend some time with Athena," Eirene said.

"No, that would only teach her to pry into the affairs of others."

"Diana?" Eirene offered.

I scowled. "I think not. I would someday like to be blessed with grandchildren." I narrowed my eyes. "No, my daughter must grow up and see that life is not always filled with Olympian pleasures and luxury. She needs to learn responsibility, but as long as she can draw upon the power of a goddess, as long as she can be recognized as my daughter, she will never learn—" Suddenly I knew what I must do.

"My Lady?"

"There is only one place where Persephone will truly learn to be a goddess. It is a place where she must first learn to be a woman."

Eirene drew back, her face taking on a horrified expression as she began to understand.

"You will not send her there!"

"Oh, yes. *There* is exactly where I shall send her."

"But they will not know her; they do not even know you." Eirene's deeply lined brow furrowed in agitation.

I felt my lips turning up in one of my rare smiles. "Exactly, my friend. Exactly."

CHAPTER ONE

Oklahoma, Present Day

"NO, it's not that I don't 'get it,' it's that I don't understand how you could have let it happen." Lina spoke slowly and distinctly through clenched teeth.

"Ms. Santoro, I have already explained that we had no idea until the IRS contacted us yesterday that there had been any error at all."

"Did you not have any checks and balances? The reason I pay you to manage the taxes for my business is because I need an expert." She glanced down at the obscene number typed in neat, no-nonsense black and white across the bottom of the government form. "I understand accidents and mistakes, but I don't understand how something this *large* could have escaped your notice."

Frank Rayburn cleared his throat before answering. Lina had always thought he looked a little like a gangster-wannabe. Today his black pinstriped suit and his slippery demeanor did nothing to dispel the image.

"Your bakery did very well last year, Ms. Santoro. Actually, you more than doubled your income from the previous year. When we're talking about a major increase in figures, it is easy for mistakes to happen. I think that what would be more productive for us now is to focus on how you can pay what you owe the government instead of casting blame." Before she could speak he hurried on, "I have drawn up several suggestions." He pulled out another sheet of paper filled with bulleted columns and numbers and handed it to her. "Suggestion number one is to borrow the money. Interest rates are very reasonable right now."

Lina felt her jaw clench. She hated the idea of borrowing money, especially that much money. She knew it would make her feel exposed and vulnerable until the loan was repaid. *If* the loan could be repaid. Yes, she had been doing well, but a bakery wasn't exactly a necessity to a community, and times were hard.

"What are your other suggestions?"

"Well, you could introduce a newer, more glitzy line of foods. Maybe add a little something for the lunch crowd, more than those . . ." He hesitated, making little circles in the air with one thick forefinger. "Baby pizza things."

"Pizette Fiorentine." She bit the words at him. "They are mini-pizzas that originated in Florence, and they are not meant to be a meal, they are meant to be a mid-afternoon snack served with cheese and wine."

He shrugged. "Whatever. All I'm saying is that it doesn't draw you a very big lunch crowd."

"You mean like a fried chicken buffet would? Or maybe I could even crank up the grill and churn out some burgers and fries?"

"Now there's an idea," he said, totally missing the sarcasm in her tone. "Suggestion number three would be to cut your staff."

Lina drummed her fingers on the top of the conference table. "Go on," she said, keeping her voice deceptively pleasant.

"Number four would be to consider bankruptcy." He held up a hand to stop her from speaking, even though she hadn't uttered a sound. "I know it sounds drastic, but after those expensive renovations you just completed, you really don't have any reserves left to fall back on."

"I only commissioned those expensive renovations because you assured me that Pani Del Goddess could afford them." Lina's hands twitched with the desire to wrap themselves around his neck.

"Be that as it may, your reserves are gone," he said condescendingly. "But bankruptcy is only one option, and not the one I would recommend. Actually, I would recommend option number five—sell to that big chain that offered to buy you out a couple months ago. They just want your name and your location. Give it to 'em. You'll have enough money to pay your debt and start over with a new name and place."

"But I've spent twenty years building up the Pani Del Goddess name, and I have no desire to move." If Frank Rayburn had been the least bit intuitive, he would have recognized the storm that brewed in Lina's expressive eyes, even though it had not yet reached her mouth.

Frank Rayburn was not intuitive.

"Well, I just tell ya the options." Frank leaned back in the plush chair and crossed his arms while he gave Lina what he liked to think of as his stern, fatherly look. "You're the boss. It's your job to decide from there."

"No, you're wrong." Lina's voice was still calm and soft, but it was edged with steel. "You see, I am not your boss anymore. You are fired. You have proven yourself to be as incompetent with my business as you are with your choice of attire. My lawyer will be in contact with you. I'll make sure that she has several *options* drawn up for you to consider. Maybe one of them will keep you out of court. Now, good day, Mr. Rayburn, and as my dear, sainted grandmother would say, '*Tu sei un pezzo di merda. Fongule e tuo capra!*'" Lina stood, smoothed her skirt and snapped shut her leather briefcase. "Oh, how rude of me. You don't speak Italian. Allow me to translate my grandmother's sage words: 'You are a piece of shit. Fuck you and your goat!' Arrivederci."

Lina turned and strode through the professionally decorated office grinning wickedly at the well-rouged receptionist.

CHAPTER TWO

GUT instinct, she reminded herself as she gunned her BMW and almost flew over the Highway 51 overpass, heading away from Tulsa's downtown business area to the trendy Cherry Street location of her bakery. Next time she was going to listen to her gut, and when it told her to run screaming in the opposite direction she wouldn't be stupid enough to hire another jerk. What in the hell had she been thinking?

Lina sighed. She knew what she'd been thinking. She'd needed help. The money management end of her business had never been one of her strengths. Her father had always taken care of that for her, but three years ago he and her mother had joined her grandmother in a Florida retirement community. Dad had been so sure she could handle her business finances herself that she hadn't wanted to admit it to him last year when she had finally given up and hired an accountant. So instead of asking for his advice in who she should hire, she'd bumbled ahead and, in a stressed-out rush, chosen Frank Rayburn, Mr. Sleazy Non-Personality.

"It's what you deserve for allowing your pride to get the best of you," Lina muttered to herself as she turned east onto 15th Street—the street that would, within a couple of blocks, morph into the area known as Cherry Street, and lead her to the door of her wonderful, incredible, beautiful, and now completely broke, bakery.

The pit of her stomach ached. There must be a way to pay her debt and keep her two long-time employees as well as her name and location. She gripped the steering wheel with one hand and twirled a short strand of hair around and around her finger. She would not sell her name. She couldn't.

Pani Del Goddess, or Breads of the Goddess—the name sang like magic. It was indelibly tied to all the most wonderful memories of her childhood. *Pani del goddess* is what she and her beloved grandmother used to create on long winter afternoons as they watched old black-and-white movies and drank fragrant, honey-sweetened tea.

"Carolina Francesca, you bake like a little goddess!"

Lina could still hear the echo of her grandmother's voice from her childhood, encouraging her to experiment with classic recipes from the Old Country, her beloved Italia.

"Si, *bambina,* first learn the recipe as it was written, test it and try it, then begin to add *un poco*—a little here, and a little there. That is how to make the breads your own."

And Lina had made them her own, with a talent and a flare that had even impressed her grandmother, who was renowned as an exceptional cook. It had been her grandmother who had bragged so much to her friends that they began asking Lina to bake "something special" for them on the occasion of birthdays or anniversaries. By the time Lina graduated from high school, she had a steady stream of customers, mostly retired widows and widowers who appreciated the taste of quality homemade breads.

When her grandmother had offered to send her to Florence to study at the famous school of baking, Apicius, she had begun shaping the design of her dream—the dream of owning her own bakery. When she was a child, her grandmother had whispered to her that Italy and baking were in her blood. After she graduated from Apicius, Lina followed the whispers of her childhood back to Tulsa. With her she brought a little piece of Italy, its style and its romance—as well as its amazingly rich assortment of breads and pastries. Again her grandmother helped her. Together they discovered a worn-down old building smack in the middle of the artsy area of Tulsa known as Cherry Street. They'd bought it and slowly turned it into a shining sliver of Florence.

Lina shook her head and flipped off the radio. She couldn't let Pani Del Goddess fail. It wouldn't just break her own heart; it would cut her grandmother to the bone. And what about her customers? Her bakery was the meeting place for a delightfully eclectic group of regulars, made up mostly of local eccentrics, celebrities and retirees. It was more than a bakery. It was a unique social hub.

And what would Anton and Dolores do? The two had been working for her for ten and fifteen years. She knew it was a cliché, but they were more than employees; they were family to her, especially since she had no children of her own.

Lina sighed again, and then she inhaled deeply. Despite the horrors of the day, her lips curved up. Pinyon smoke drifted through the BMW's partially rolled down windows. She was passing Grumpy's Garden, the little shop that signaled the beginning of the Cherry Street District, and, as usual, "Grumpy," who was actually a very nice lady named Shaun and not grumpy at all, had several of her huge chimeneas perpetually burning, perfuming the neighborhood with the distinctive smell of southwest pine.

She felt the knot in her stomach loosen as she downshifted and slowed her car, careful of the pedestrians crossing the streets while they moved back and forth from antique shops, to new-age bookstores, to posh interior design studios and unique restaurants. And finally, in the heart of the street, nestled between a trendy little spa and a vintage jewelry store, sat Pani Del Goddess.

As usual, there were few parking spaces available on the street, and Lina turned into the alley to park in one of the reserved spaces behind her building. She had barely stepped out of her car when she felt an all too familiar tug at her mind. The feeling was always the same, though it varied in degree and intensity. Today it was like someone far away had spoken her name, and the wind had carried the echo of the sound to her mind without having to reach her ears first. She closed her eyes. She really didn't have time for this . . . not today.

Almost instantly Lina regretted the thought. Mentally she shook herself. No, she wouldn't let financial troubles change who she was—and part of who she was, was this. It was her gift.

Glancing around her, Lina peered into the shadows at the edges of the building.

"Where are you, little one?" she coaxed. Then she focused her mind and a vague image came to her. Lina smiled. "Come on, kitty, kitty, kitty," she called. "I know you're there. You don't have to be afraid."

With a pathetic mew, a skinny orange tabby stepped hesitantly from behind the garbage receptacle.

"Well, look at you. You're nothing more than a delicate flower. Come here, baby girl. Everything will be fine now."

Mesmerized, the small orange cat walked straight into Lina's outstretched arms. Ignoring what the cat's matted, dirty fur could do to her very clean, very expensive silk suit, Lina cuddled the mangy animal. Staring up at her rescuer, eyes filled with adoration, the cat rewarded Lina with thunderous purring.

Lina could not remember a time when she hadn't felt a special affinity for animals. As a small child, she had only to sit quietly in her backyard and soon she would be visited by rabbits and squirrels and even nervous little field mice. Dogs and cats loved her. Horses followed her like giant puppies. Even cows, who Lina knew had big, mushy brains, lowed lovingly at her if she got too close to where they pastured. Animals had always adored her, but it hadn't been until Lina had become a teenager that she had really realized the extent of her gift.

She could understand animals. Sort of. She wasn't Dr. Doolittle or anything ridiculous like that; she couldn't carry on conversations with animals. She liked to think of herself as if she were a horse whisperer, only her abilities weren't limited to horses. And she had an extra "thing" that most people didn't have. Sometimes the "thing" told her that there was a cat that needed her help. The "thing" was something that went off in her mind, like a connection she could plug into.

She knew it was weird.

For a brief time in high school she had considered becoming a veterinarian. She'd even volunteered at a veterinary clinic during the summer between her sophomore and junior years—a summer that had taught her that while blood and parasites were definitely not a part of her special animal "thing," they certainly were two things that were a consistent part of veterinarian work. Just remembering it made Lina shudder in revulsion and want to scratch her scalp.

"In a bakery, you never, ever have to deal with blood *or* parasites," she told the little orange cat as she stepped out of the alley, turned left and inhaled deeply.

"*Magnifico*," she murmured in her grandmother's voice.

The enticing aroma of freshly baked bread soothed her senses. She sniffed appreciatively, expertly identifying the subtle differences in the fragrance of olives, rosemary and cheese, wedded to the sweet smells of the butter, cinnamon, nuts, raisins and the liqueurs that went into the creation of the bakery's specialty bread, gubana, which was the sweetbread of Friuli, a small region east of Venice.

Lina paused in front of the large glass window that fronted her bakery. She nodded appreciatively at the beautifully arranged crystal platters that were displayed on tiers and filled with a fresh assortment of Italian pastries and cookies. Pride filled Lina. As always, everything was perfect.

She glanced beyond the window display to see that about half of the dozen little mosaic-topped café tables were occupied. Not bad, she thought, for late Friday afternoon. She shifted the cat in her arms and checked her watch. It was almost 4:00 p.m. and they closed at 5:00 p.m.; usually the hour or so before closing was a quiet, winding-down time.

Maybe that was one answer. Maybe she should extend her hours. But wouldn't she have to hire more help then? Anton and Dolores already worked full-time shifts, and Lina herself was rarely absent from the bakery. Wouldn't the additional cost of another employee cancel out any revenue generated by staying open longer?

Lina could feel the beginnings of a serious tension headache.

Forcing herself to relax, Lina squinted past the glare of the highly polished picture window. She could see the newly painted frescoes that decorated the walls—part of the expensive renovation that had just been completed. But the price had been worth it. Lina had commissioned Kimberlei Doner, a well-known local artist and illustrator, to fill the walls of Pani Del Goddess with authentic scenes from ancient Florence. The paintings, coupled with the vintage light fixtures and café tables, created an atmosphere that made her patrons feel like they had stepped off the streets of Tulsa and had been temporarily transported to magical, earthy Italy.

"Let's go in and see what we can do about you," she told the cat, who was still purring contentedly in her arms. "First I'll take care of you, then I'll figure out what to do about the money," she said, wishing desperately that money was as easy to come by as cats.

The wind chime over the door tinkled happily as Lina entered Pani Del Goddess. She stood there for a moment, basking in the familiar scene. Anton was fiddling with the cappuccino machine and humming the chorus of the song "All That Jazz" from *Chicago*. Dolores was explaining the difference between panettones and colombe to a middle-aged couple Lina didn't recognize. They were the only people in the shop that she didn't recognize.

Anton glanced up as several customers called hellos to her. His full lips began a grin when he saw Lina, but then they pursed into a resigned pout when he noticed the cat in her arms.

"Oh, look, it's our fearless leader—the Cat Savior." Anton fluttered his fingers in Lina's direction.

"Don't start with me, Anton, or I'll take back the DVD of *Chicago* that I got you for your birthday," Lina said with mock severity.

Anton's pout turned into a gasp, and he clasped his hands over his heart as if she had just stabbed him. "You're wounding me!"

Dolores giggled as she rang up the couple's order. "He's been tapping to 'All That Jazz' all day. It's worse than his *Moulin Rouge* phase."

"Musicals are not a phase with me; they're my passion," Anton said.

"Then you should understand me perfectly. Helping animals is my passion," Lina said.

Anton rolled his eyes and sighed dramatically. "I think it's more than slightly disturbing that I have the number to the Street Cats Rescue Line memorized."

"Just make the call," Lina told him, but Anton was already dialing the number. She winked her thanks to him.

"Well, Lina! I was hoping to see you today."

Lina smiled and walked over to the table closest to the picture window. But instead of speaking to the dark-haired woman who had waved her over, first she greeted the miniature schnauzer who sat ramrod stiff on a scarlet-colored cushion at his mistress's feet.

"Dash, you are certainly looking handsome today." The cat stirred in her arms, but Lina soothed it with an absentminded caress.

"He should. He just came from the groomers."

Lina grinned at the well-mannered little dog. "A day of beauty, huh? Honey, it's what we all need." She turned her attention to Dash's mistress. "How is the olive bread today, Tess?"

"Excellent. Simply excellent as usual." Tess's distinctive Tahlequah drawl was lazy and melodic. "And this San Angelo Pinot Grigio that Anton recommended is absolutely perfect with it."

"I'm glad you think so. We aim to please."

"Which is why I wanted to talk with you. The Poets and Writers Association has chosen their Oklahoma Author of the Year, and we'll be having several functions to honor her next week. I want to make sure we have a selection of your excellent breads for the dinner."

Lina's mind raced ahead. Tess Miller was the director of Oklahoma's Poets and Writers Association, as well as the host of a very popular regional talk show—and one of Pani Del Goddess's most loyal customers. For years she and Dash had been stopping in the bakery during their daily walks; Lina had even had a doggie cushion made for the little schnauzer, which she kept in a special cubby underneath the cash register. There would certainly be no one better with which to begin her expansion. Even if she wasn't sure exactly what that expansion was yet.

"Uh, Tess," Lina cleared her throat. "Of course I would be happy to provide any breads you might need, but I would also like to talk with you about our new expanded menu. Perhaps we could cater the whole meal for you."

"Well, that would be just splendid! I'm sure anything you come up with will be perfect. Why don't I call you Monday? You can give me my menu choices and I'll fill you in on the details?"

Lina felt herself nodding and smiling as she turned away from the table. She kept the tight smile plastered on her face while she made her way to the counter, speaking to each of her patrons as she passed them. It was only when she reached the counter and ran into the blank expressions of shock that had taken up residence on Anton's and Dolores's faces that she faltered.

"Did I hear you say the word *cater*?" Anton whispered.

"And *whole meal*?" Dolores squeaked.

Lina jerked her head toward the back of the bakery before stepping through the cream-colored swinging doors that divided the kitchen, the storeroom and her office from the rest of the bakery. Her two employees scurried after her. Lina spoke quickly as she pushed the startled orange cat into the carrier she retrieved from the coat closet.

"You know the appointment I had with my accountant today? It wasn't good news. I owe money. Big money. To the IRS."

Anton blanched and sucked in air.

"Oh, Lina. Is it really bad?" Dolores sounded twelve years old.

"Yes." She looked carefully at each of them. "It is really bad. We're going to have to make some changes." Lina registered the twin looks of horror on their faces. Instantly Anton's eyes began to fill with tears. Dolores's already pale face drained of even the pretense of color. "No, no, no! Not that! There will be none of that—you'll be keeping your jobs. We'll all be keeping our jobs."

"Oh, God. I need to sit down." Anton fanned himself with his fingers.

"My office. Quickly. And there will be absolutely no fainting." She picked up the cat carrier and clucked at the ruffled tabby as she headed to her office. Over her shoulder she said, "And no crying either. Remember—"

Anton finished the sentence for her. "—There's no crying in baking."

Dolores nodded vigorous agreement.

Lina set the cat carrier next to her desk before taking a seat behind it. Anton and Dolores sank into the two plushly upholstered antique chairs that faced her. No one spoke.

Hesitating, Anton made a vague gesture in the direction of the cat. "Patricia from Street Cats said that she'd stay a little past closing today, so if you want me to, I can drop off that little orange thing on my way home. It's really not out of my way." He finished with a weak smile.

"Thank you, Anton, even though you called her a little orange thing, I'll take you up on your kind offer."

"Well, I meant little orange beast, but I was trying to be nice," Anton said, sounding more like himself and looking less likely to hyperventilate.

"What are we going to do?" Dolores asked.

True to form, Dolores was ready for the bottom line. Though only twenty-eight, she had been working for Lina for ten years. The reason Lina had hired her was not just because she had a flair for baking pastries and a way with old people, but Lina appreciated her no-nonsense personality. And she was the perfect balance for Anton, who was—Lina glanced at her other employee who sat with his legs crossed delicately, the sheen of almost-tears still pooled in his eyes—decidedly more dramatic. They fit together well, the three of them, and Lina intended that they stay that way.

"We expand our menu," Lina said firmly.

Dolores nodded her head thoughtfully. "Okay, we can do that."

Anton gnawed on the side of his thumb. "Do you mean, like, add sandwiches or something?"

"I'm not exactly sure yet," Lina said slowly. "I haven't had time to think it through. I just know that we have to make more money, which means we need to bring in more customers. It only makes sense that if we expanded our menu, we would appeal to a larger group of people."

Anton and Dolores nodded in unison.

"Catering Tess Miller's dinner is a good place to start," Dolores said.

"Catering," Anton whined. "It sounds so, I don't know, *banal.*"

"As banal as bankruptcy?" Lina asked.

"No!" The word burst from his mouth.

"My thoughts exactly," Lina said.

"So what are we going to serve?" Dolores asked.

Lina ran her fingers through her neatly cropped hair. She had absolutely no idea.

"We're going to serve selections from our expanded menu. That way we'll get practice as well as publicity."

"And that expanded menu would be what exactly?" Dolores prompted.

"I have absolutely no idea," Lina admitted.

"And to think I didn't bring even one tiny Xanax with me to work today." Anton was gnawing at his thumb again.

"Quit biting your finger," Dolores told him. "We'll figure this out." She shifted her gaze to Lina. "Right?"

Lina's heart squeezed. They looked like baby birds gaping up at her expectantly.

"Right," she said, painting her voice with confidence. "All I need to do is to . . ." she faltered. Her nestlings blinked big, round eyes, waiting for her next words. "Is to . . . um . . . brainstorm." She finally finished.

"Brainstorm? As in the step before writing a paper?" Anton, who was perpetually a sporadic night school student at Tulsa Community College, clutched onto a familiar idea.

"Of course," Dolores added brightly. "Lina probably has about a zillion and a half cookbooks at home. All she needs to do is to go through them and pick out a few great recipes for wonderful meals."

"Then she'll share them with us, and we'll begin our new creations!" Anton gushed. "How ab fab! I can hardly wait!" Then he reached over and squeezed Dolores's hand. "I feel just awful that I was so negative in the beginning. I almost forgot our Baker's Motto."

Dolores and Anton grinned at each other, and then as if they were getting ready to say the Pledge of Allegiance, they covered their hearts with their hands and spoke solemnly in unison:

"In baking we must always rise to the occasion."

Lina thought that she very well might have been in baker's hell, but she kept nodding and smiling. Dolores was partially correct, she did have a wonderful collection of cookbooks at home—all filled with fabulous recipes for breads and pastries. She had very few cookbooks that contained recipes for meals. Actually, she didn't even cook many full meals herself. A little pasta here, a little salad there, and a nice glass of Chianti was her idea of cooking a full meal. Baking was her specialty and her love. Meals were, well, banal.

Out of her element, she admitted to herself. This whole thing was totally out of her element. So, feeling a little like a sparrow struggling to feed the cuckoos in her nest, Lina kept smiling and nodding at her chicks.

"Well, I think we've been absent from the front long enough. Now that we've got a plan, why don't you two handle it for the next hour and close up for me? I'll go home and begin brainstorming."

"Tess said she'd call you on Monday about the menu for the dinner, didn't she?" Dolores asked.

"That's what she said, all right." Lina focused on keeping the panic out of her voice.

"Oooh, this really is exciting. You know, I'll bet there will be lots of local celebs at that dinner." Anton waggled his well-maintained eyebrows. "Not to mention media coverage."

"I imagine there will be." Lina walked briskly from her office.

As she called quick good-byes to her customers and hastily retreated out the door, she could hear Anton telling Dolores that he would certainly need several new, exciting outfits to go with their new, exciting menu.

Her grandmother had told her many times that swearing was common, unladylike behavior reserved only for peasants and men who were not gentlemen. On the other hand, she totally endorsed a well-accented, well-chosen Italian curse as simply showing one's creativity. Standing in front of her bakery Lina let loose with a string of Italian that began with telling the IRS they could *va al diavolo,* or go to hell, and ending with saying they were nothing more than a chronic, flaming *rompicoglioni,* or pain in the ass. Just to cover all bases in between she strung together several "shits" and "damns," in Italian, of course. She felt sure Grandma would have been proud.

When people began staring she shut her mouth and told herself to breathe slowly and deeply. She was an intelligent, successful businesswoman. Hell, she could even curse eloquently in Italian and English, but she tried to keep the English to a minimum—Grandma had been right, it just didn't sound as well-bred (and yes, Grandma would also have appreciated the pun). How difficult could it be for her to come up with a few new menu choices? Even if they were meals and not breads.

She started to twirl a strand of her hair, but caught herself and forced her hand to stay at her side. The problem wasn't that she couldn't come up with some new recipes. The problem, she realized, was that through Pani Del Goddess she had established a solid reputation for preparing breads that were unique and delicious. She couldn't just slap some pesto over pasta and toss a salad on the side of the plate. She wouldn't do it at all if she couldn't do it well. The name Pani Del Goddess meant excellence, and Lina was determined that it would never stand for anything less.

She should call her grandmother; she'd have a stack of ideas that she'd be thrilled to share with her beloved *bambina*. Again.

"But as Anton would say, I'm *sooo* not a baby," Lina muttered to herself. "Good God, I'm forty-three. It's about time I quit running to Grandma."

Lina's dialogue with herself was interrupted by the sound of carefree laughter coming from two women who had just emerged from the used bookstore across the street. She scowled and wished that all she had to worry about was shopping with a friend for the perfect book.

The scowl shifted as her expression turned thoughtful. The Book Place was a wonderful used bookstore with a vast selection of fiction and nonfiction. Lina had spent many satisfied hours lost in their maze of shelves. Surely she could find a fabulous old cookbook in the stacks, something that had been hidden in out-of-print obscurity for years, and within its pages there would be a recipe that was the perfect blend of Italy and magic and ingredients.

Yes, she thought as she dodged cars and crossed the street, The Book Place was the perfect place to begin brainstorming.

CHAPTER THREE

THE pile of used books was daunting. She'd found ten of them. Ten old, interesting looking, out-of-print Italian cookbooks. While she was choosing them they hadn't seemed so thick—and ten certainly hadn't seemed to be so many. But now that they were home with her, piled in a neat stack on the glass top of the wrought iron sculpture she used as a coffee table, they appeared to have multiplied.

Couldn't she have narrowed her choices down by a few less books before she'd left the bookstore?

"In baking we must always rise to the occasion," she reminded the enormous, longhaired black-and-white tomcat that perched in the middle of the black-and-white toile chaise. The perfect match made Lina grin. She enjoyed purchasing furniture that properly accessorized her pets, even if the cat didn't deign to notice. Lina did receive a brief look of boredom from his side of the room and a quick swish of his tail in response to the proclamation of her bakery motto.

"Patchy Poo the Pud Santoro," she addressed him formally by his full name. "You are a handsome beast, but you know nothing about baking."

At her feet, the half-sleeping old English bulldog snorted as if in agreement with her.

"Don't be rude, Edith Anne," Lina scolded the dog halfheartedly. "You know considerably more about eating than you know about baking."

Edith sighed contentedly as Lina scratched her behind her right ear. With the hand that wasn't busy, Lina picked up the first book. It was a thick tome entitled *Discovering Historical Italy*. She let it fall open and began reading a long, complex paragraph about the proper preparation of veal. She blanched and snapped the book shut. Veal was a popular dish in Italy, but to her veal meant baby cows. Mush-brained, adorable, wide-eyed baby cows.

"Perhaps it's not possible to rise to a very difficult occasion without the proper preparation," she said to the now snoring Bulldog. "In baking or otherwise." She closed the book, setting it gently back on the table a little like it was a bomb that might very well explode if not treated carefully.

"I think this particular preparation calls for a nice glass of Italian red," she told Patchy Poo the Pud Santoro. He glanced at her through slitted eyes and yawned.

"You two are no help at all."

Shaking her head, Lina walked away from the table and headed directly to her wine closet. In her opinion, a Monte Antico Rosso Sangiovese was the perfect preparation tool for any difficult situation—baking or otherwise.

"Maybe I can serve enough wonderful Italian wine with my new menu that my customers will get too soused to pay much attention to what they eat." She spoke over her shoulder to her animals as she poured herself a ruby-colored glass of wine, but she didn't need a non-response from her pets to know that her last statement was ridiculous. Then she'd be running a bar and not a bakery, which would give Anton an apoplectic fit. Lina straightened her spine, snagged a bag of double-dipped chocolate-covered peanuts, the perfect accompaniment for the Sangiovese, and marched back into her living room. Planting herself on the couch, she opened her notebook and chose the next book in the pile, *Cooking With Italy.*

The dog and cat lifted their heads and gave her identically quizzical looks.

"Let the games begin," she told them grimly.

THREE hours later she had finished combing through nine of the ten books, and she had a list of four possible main course recipes: chicken picatta, puttanesca on spaghetti, eggplant parmigiana, and a lovely aioli platter, complete with artichokes, olives, tomatoes, poached salmon and carpaccio.

Lina felt a little thrill of accomplishment as she looked over her list. She was actually enjoying herself. Delving through the musty old books had become an exercise in Italian history and culture—two things that had been a constant part of her upbringing.

Only one more cookbook was left. Lina picked up the slim hardback. She had purposefully saved this one for last. In the bookstore she had been intrigued by the cover, which was a deep, royal blue etched with a gold embossed design. The title, *The Italian Goddess Cookbook,* rested over the golden illustration of a stern looking goddess who sat on a massive throne. She was dressed in a long robe and her hair was wrapped around the crown of her head in intricate braids. In one hand she held a scepter topped with a ripe ear of corn, in the other she held a flaming torch. Underneath the illustration the words, *Recipes and Spells for the Goddess in Every Woman,* flowed in beautiful gold script. The author's name, Filomena, was branded into the cover underneath the embossed print.

"Just one more recipe. Help me to find just one more, and I'll call it a night," Lina said as she ran her fingers over the raised embossing.

Her fingertips tingled.

Lina rested the book on her lap and rubbed her hands together. She must be getting tired. She glanced at the clock. It was only a little past nine o'clock, but it had been a long day.

Lina looked back down at the cover. The gold print caught the lamplight, causing the words *Recipes and Spells for the Goddess in Every Woman* to seem to flicker and glow.

What an unusual coincidence that the woman who baked like an Italian goddess had found an old, discarded copy of *The Italian Goddess Cookbook.* Her grandmother would have called it *la magia dell' Italia,* the magic of Italy. On impulse, Lina closed her eyes. She believed in the magic of Italy. She'd experienced it in the multicolored marble of Florence's Duomo, the geranium-filled window boxes of Assisi, and the eerie wonder of the Roman Forum at night. She focused her mind on her love for her grandmother's homeland, then she opened the book that rested on her lap, allowing the pages to fall where they chose.

Lina opened her eyes and began reading:

> *Pizza alla Romana, or Pizza by the Meter. This extraordinary recipe comes from Rome. It is proper to allow the soft, supple dough a very long rest—up to eight hours, the longer the better—then place it on a baker's peel two and a half feet long, while rhythmically pounding it with such vigor that it literally dances beneath your fingers.*

Lina blinked in surprise and grinned. A baker's peel! The long, wooden paddle that was used to drop bread into and scoop it out of the oven. Of course Pani Del Goddess had several of them. She kept reading:

> *. . . when the dough has finished dancing, you paint it with oil and then set the peel in the oven where the totally unforeseen occurs: you slowly, slowly*

withdraw the peel, stretching the remarkably elastic dough to a thin, incredibly light dough of up to an astonishing six foot length—depending upon the size of each individual goddess's oven.

Well, Pani Del Goddess had several very long ovens. She could stretch the dough to its full six feet! She scanned the rest of the recipe. Included in the book were several different toppings, everything from a light Pizza Bianca, made simply with olive oil, garlic, rosemary, salt and pepper, to Pizza Pugliese, which was a plethora of Italian favorites—eggplant, provolone, anchovies, olives . . . the list went on and on.

"This may be the answer. Why mess with a bunch of different recipes? Why not have one basic specialty, Pizza alla Romana, with several variations? And it's still baking!"

Reacting to the excitement in her voice, Edith Anne woke long enough to offer a muffled woof of support. Patchy Poo the Pud exercised the innate initiative of a cat and ignored her completely.

Lina patted the dog's head while she studied the dough recipe.

. . . because this dough uses so little yeast and wants a long rising, a goddess can work its preparation into her busy American schedule by making the dough at night with cool water and refrigerating it immediately after it is mixed. Next morning, place it in a cool spot to rise slowly at room temperature all day. Then simply shape and bake it for dinner . . .

Lina ran her eyes down the list of ingredients. Dry yeast, water, flour, salt, olive oil—yes, of course she had everything on the list. She could make the dough that night, let it sit all the next day, then she and the "baby birds" could sample it tomorrow night. Delighted, she began reading the preparation directions.

Before beginning, you will need a green candle, to represent the Earth. The goddess we honor with this recipe is She who breathes life into the flour with which we create our dough, Demeter, Great Goddess of the Harvest, and of Fruits and the Riches of the Earth.

Lina's eyes widened.

As you start preparation, light the green candle and focus your thoughts on Demeter. Then you may begin.

Lina's eyes scanned the recipe. Sure enough, interspersed between instructions for stirring the yeast, and mixing the flour and salt, were otherworldly instructions.

Lina read a line and her brow furrowed.

Was it a spell?

Lina read another line.

It seemed to be more of an invocation, or maybe a prayer. But whatever she called it, the supernatural directions were definitely a part of the recipe. Lina couldn't help but smile. *La magia dell' Italia.* Her grandmother would approve.

Humming to herself, she went in search of a green candle.

CHAPTER FOUR

LINA looked around the counter and nodded in satisfaction. She had assembled all of the ingredients and kitchenwares she would need to make the dough. She had even found a small green candle that gave off a vaguely piney scent. It was a relic from the previous Christmas, and she'd had to dig through two boxes of ornaments before she discovered it. Lina opened the cookbook and set it on the counter next to her favorite stainless steel mixing bowl. Then she began:

> *First, light the green candle and focus your thoughts on Demeter, Mother of the Harvest.*

Ever the consummate chef, Lina followed the directions precisely. She lit the candle and let her thoughts drift to the long-forgotten Harvest Goddess. She wondered briefly what lovely, eccentric cooking rituals had been forgotten along with the goddess.

Lina continued reading:

Stir the yeast into the warm water in a small bowl; let stand until creamy, about 10 minutes.

Lina felt relaxed and happy as her experienced hands stirred and mixed.

While the yeast is standing, center your thoughts and take three deep cleansing breaths. Imagine power filtering up the center of your body and traveling along the path of your spine all the way through your head and then pouring out in a waterfall around you to be reabsorbed into your core again. When you feel invigorated, you may begin Demeter's Invocation.

The directions reminded her a little of a new-age relaxation class she had taken once. With a self-amused smile, she set the kitchen timer for ten minutes before beginning the steps of the centering exercise.

She had to admit that in no time she was feeling . . . well . . . if not invigorated, at least very awake and self-aware. Lina went back to the recipe.

When you feel ready, please read the following aloud.
"O most gracious and magnificent Demeter, goddess of all that is harvested and grown, I ask that some portion of Your presence be here with me now. I summon You to enrich the bounty You have already so plentifully provided. I ask also that You breathe a breath of magic and wonder into this kitchen."

The timer chimed and Lina jumped, surprised that ten minutes had passed so quickly.

Mix the flour and salt in a large wide-mouthed bowl while invoking,
"Come, Demeter, I summon you with this salt and flour, which are the riches of Your Earth."

The rhythm of the invocation melded harmoniously with the recipe, and Lina found herself eager to read the next lines.

Make a well in the center of the flour; then pour the dissolved yeast, 1¾ cups plus 1 tablespoon water, 1 tablespoon oil, and the lard into the well. Speak to the goddess as you gradually stir the flour into the liquid and work to a soft dough that can be gathered into a ball. "I call upon You, O Goddess of the Harvest, and bid You welcome here in the midst of that which You created."

Then knead on a floured surface until soft, smooth, and elastic, 10 to 15 minutes, sprinkling with additional flour as needed. As the dough takes form, recite the following to Demeter: "Power be drawn, and power come, and make me one with thee, O Goddess of the Harvest. Make me greater, make me better, grant me strength and grant me power."

Lina's hands fell into a rhythm as she effortlessly plied the dough against the floured countertop. Her eyes were locked on the words that seemed to come as easily to her lips as the familiar kneading motion came to her hands.

"O Demeter, who is my guardian and sister, I give You thanks. May my summons fall lightly on Your ears, and may Your wisdom and strength remain with me, growing ever finer, as grains ripe for the harvest."

Lina kneaded the dough while her mind drifted. What an incredibly intriguing thought—to couple the magic of an ancient goddess with the perfection of a recipe that had been passed down from mothers to daughters and preserved for generations. It was such a wonderful, natural idea. To call upon the strength of a goddess through baking! Whether it actually worked, whether or not a goddess really listened, was beside the point. It was a lovely, empowering ritual—one that, if nothing else, could serve to focus her thoughts on the positive and remind her that she should take a moment to enjoy the rich femininity of her chosen career.

The sweet scent of the pine candle mixed with the more earthy smells of yeast and flour. The aroma was delicious and heady. Unexpectedly, Lina felt a wave of sensation, fueled by scent, rush through her body. For a moment she was dizzy and disoriented, as if she had been suddenly displaced from her kitchen and transported, dough and all, to the middle of a pine-filled forest. She rubbed the back of a flour-crusted hand across her forehead. Her head felt unnaturally warm, but the touch of her hand re-grounded her and the dizziness dissipated.

It had been a tough day. She shouldn't be surprised that it was wearing on her. She rolled her shoulders and let her head fall forward and backward, causing tired, overstressed muscles to stretch and relax. She would certainly sleep well tonight.

Lina glanced down at the conclusion of the dough recipe. It contained the usual mundane instructions about covering it in a bowl and letting it rise for at least eight hours. Impatiently, she scanned past the recipe to the completion of the invocation ritual.

> *Pinch out a small portion of the dough. Choose a special place—out of doors—where you can leave your offering. Sprinkle it with wine and offer it to Demeter, saying "O goddess of the plentiful harvest, of strength and power and wisdom, I give You greeting, and honor, and thanks. Blessed Be!"*
> *Note: You might choose to add your own personal request or praise before concluding the ritual. May blessings rain upon you and may you never go hungry!*

Lina's smile tilted sardonic. The fullness of her hips said that she might consider going hungry once in a while. Not that she was fat, she amended quickly, she was just voluptuous. And voluptuous wasn't particularly "in" today. She huffed under her breath. She would never understand the current generation's obsession with waif-like women who starved and puked everything feminine from their bodies. She was all softness and curves, and she preferred herself that way.

"I'm goddess-like," she said firmly.

With no more hesitation, she pinched off a small piece of the newly-kneaded dough and set it aside while she reshaped and then covered the rest of the large ball. She'd already performed the invocation, it was only right that she should follow through to its conclusion. After all, no good cook ever left a recipe incomplete.

It didn't take long to tidy up her already immaculate kitchen and load her dishwasher. After drying her hands, Lina poured a fresh glass of wine and wrapped the small piece of dough in a paper towel before hurrying from the kitchen. Balancing the glass and dough in one hand, she opened the door to the closet in the hall. Before she had her jacket pulled on she heard the tell-tale slap of Edith's paws on the tiled hallway. Smiling, Lina took the bulldog's leash from its hook.

"It doesn't matter how soundly asleep you are, when this door opens, here you are." Lina laughed as she snapped the leash onto Edith's collar.

The bulldog yawned then snorted at her.

"I know it's late, but I have something I need to finish, and I know the perfect spot."

Far from complaining, Edith was the first one to the door of the condo, and Lina had to juggle to balance the wine without spilling it.

"Easy there, big girl!"

Shifting the ball of dough to her jacket pocket, Lina locked the door behind them. It was early March, and the Oklahoma night was unseasonably warm. The air felt rich and heavy with the promise of spring. Lina let Edith lead her into the heart of the well-kept courtyard. A shadow flitted overhead calling Lina's attention upward. A full moon sat high in the sky, round and bright and the color of whipped butter. She stared at it. What an odd shade of yellow. It lent the familiar surroundings of her English Tudor–style condo complex an ethereal glow, casting mundane hedges and sidewalk edges into new and slightly sinister roles.

"Oh, please. I must be having a *Lord of the Rings* moment," Lina admonished herself. "Dolores was right. I've taken too many trips to the IMAX to drool over Aragorn."

The ritual and the dough-making frenzy had obviously gone to her head if she was imagining sinister shapes around her well-kept condo complex.

"I'll have to tell Anton all about this," she mumbled to herself. "Maybe I can finally convince him to share his Xanax with me."

Actually, now that she was outside and the spell/recipe book was neatly stacked with the other cookbooks in her living room, she was beginning to feel a little foolish.

"Maybe I should have had more wine before this part of the recipe," she told Edith, who flicked her ears back at her and huffed, but kept on winding her way along their familiar path. "Or maybe I'm just exhausted and I need to go to bed."

They were coming to her favorite part of the complex—the grand marble fountain that sat squarely in the middle of the cobblestone courtyard. Year-round it spouted water in an impressive geyser that cascaded down three delicately curved, bowl-like tiers. Actually, it was the fountain that had convinced Lina to purchase the condo. During the summer Lina found the area around the fountain, with its cool cobblestones and old oak shade trees, even more refreshing than the pool, and a good deal less crowded. In the winter months the fountain, like the pool, was heated, and Lina had enjoyed many an Oklahoma winter afternoon swathed in blankets, feet tucked under her, while she read to the musical sound of falling water.

"This is it. The perfect special place," Lina told Edith Anne, who was snuffling around an azalea bush. "Stay there, this won't take long."

She dropped the bulldog's leash. Obediently, Edith planted her wide bottom on the ground, then seemed to reconsider and, with a doggy sigh, relaxed into a full, stretched-out recline, her half-closed eyes watching Lina with sleepy semi-interest.

The nearest oak was also the biggest. Lina approached it carefully in the buttermilk moonlight, careful not to trip over the intricate knots of exposed roots that proliferated the area around the base of the tree. Unexpectedly, they seemed ominous, calling to life visions of grasping tentacles and writhing snakes.

"Stop being ridiculous," Lina said in the tone she reserved for generic perfume solicitors. The sound of her voice dispelled the disturbing vision, and the oak shifted back to its familiar, solid self.

Lina extracted the small lump of dough from her pocket. She looked around the courtyard. No one was stirring; even Edith Anne had stopped watching her and was snoring softly. Lina crouched down and placed the dough ball in the vertex of two especially thick roots that intersected at the base of the tree.

Lina looked around her again. Certain that except for the snoring bulldog she was alone, she dipped her fingers into the glass of wine and flicked red drops over the dough.

It felt good. Lina smiled. It felt right. Still smiling, she wet her fingers again and playfully rained the excellent Chianti Classico all over the base of the ancient tree. Stifling girlish giggles, she continued splattering wine on the gnarled roots until the crystal goblet was empty. Then she squared her shoulders and cleared her throat.

"I would like to say something before closing this remarkable recipe ritual."

Lina grinned at her intentional alliteration, but she quickly schooled her features to appear more sober. She certainly hadn't meant any disrespect, but grinning and giggling at the end of a goddess invocation ritual would probably be considered a faux pas. Lina began her speech again.

"Demeter!" The word came from Lina's mouth with such power that the sound of the goddess's name carried across the courtyard, making Edith stir and flutter her eyes before resituating her stocky body and continuing her nap. Lina swallowed hard and softened her voice. "My name is Carolina Francesca Santoro, and I want you to know that I have enjoyed your ritual very much. I think the dough will make excellent pizza, and I'm looking forward to trying it."

Her impromptu speech reminded her of the reason why she had felt the need to experiment with the recipe, and while remembering Lina was amazed that she had ever forgotten. The lines on her forehead deepened and her shoulders slumped.

"I hope it's good. No, I more than hope it's good—I *need* it to be good. I can't lose my bakery. It's my responsibility; too many people depend on me. Demeter, if you're listening, please send me some help. In return I'll . . . I'll . . ." Lina stuttered and then blurted, "Well, damnit, I don't know what the hell I could possibly do for you in return." She shrugged her shoulders. "And I apologize for my use of common English swear words. How about if I just say, one mature woman to another, that I would really appreciate your help and I would return the favor if I could."

Satisfied, Lina closed her eyes, visualizing the final words of the ritual.

"O goddess of the plentiful harvest, of strength and power and wisdom, I give You greeting, and honor, and thanks. Blessed Be!"

At the words, *blessed be*, Lina felt an overwhelming sense of release, as if—Lina's lips twitched—as if her prayer had been heard and answered. Logically, she knew that wasn't really possible, but she did believe in the power of positive thinking . . . self-fulfilling prophecies . . . feng shui. Her lips tilted upward. She believed in the power of *la magia dell' Italia.*

Lina drew in a deep, cleansing breath, and her eyes sprang open in surprise. Enticing sweetness filled her nose. What was that smell? Lina took another deep breath. It was wonderful! Scenting the soft wind like a wary deer, she sniffed her way around the oak. And came to an abrupt halt. In between a tangle of roots halfway around the tree grew one perfect flower. Its stem was thick and long, the width of a garden hose, and it stretched up almost two feet until it morphed into a huge bell-shaped cup with scalloped edges.

"Oh! Aren't you lovely. It's too early for a daffodil." Lina shook her head and automatically corrected herself. "I mean narcissus." She could hear her grandmother scolding her, *not by their common name*, bambina, *call the* bei fiora— *beautiful flowers—by their formal name, narcissus.*

But by whatever name she called it, the flower was certainly unusual, and for more reasons than just its early blooming. Transfixed, Lina squatted in front of it. The blossom was a luminous, creamy yellow color, as if a piece of the moon had fallen to earth and bloomed that night. She couldn't remember ever seeing a narcissus of that size. If she balled up her fist it would fit neatly inside the cupped bloom. And its perfume! Lina leaned forward and took a long sniff. She hadn't remembered any of her grandmother's flowers smelling like this one. What was that scent? It was illusively familiar, but she couldn't quite name it.

Lina took another deep breath. The fragrance made her heart beat and the blood rush through her body. There was something about that fanciful aroma that filled her with a youthful yearning, and suddenly she remembered her first kiss. It had been many years, but she easily recalled that the kiss had contained this same sweetness. She sighed. The blossom smelled like what would happen if moonlight and the innocence of spring had mated to create a flower.

Lina blinked in surprise and huffed through her nose, sounding a little like her dog. She was certainly waxing poetic and romantic. How bizarre and unlike herself—well, unlike herself at forty-three anyway. She used to be romantic and dewy-eyed and blah, blah, love, blah, blah. Until life and experience and men had cured her naïveté. Lina narrowed her eyes at the flower. Romance? Why was she thinking about *that*? She'd sworn off romance on her fortieth birthday. Finished. Through. Ka-put. And she hadn't regretted her decision.

A vision of her last date flashed back through her mind—Mr. Fifty-Something Successful Businessman: divorced twice, four dysfunctional kids— two from each marriage. The best thing that she could say about him was that he was consistent. During their entire very expensive dinner at one of Lina's favorite restaurants he had whined and complained about how much child support and alimony he had to pay his two hateful, money-grubbing ex-wives, who had never understood or appreciated him. Before the main course had been served Lina had found herself empathizing with the ex-wives.

And that experience summed up men in her age range. It was a cliché that was, unfortunately, true. The good ones were taken—or gay. The rest of them were balding has-beens who spent their dates complaining about past choices. Or, like her ex-husband, had chosen newer, more perfect women as their mates. Women who were able to nurture more than stray pets. Women who were able to bear children . . .

Stop it! Lina scolded herself. Why was she thinking about *that*? Her ex-husband was ancient history, as was her desire to date and play the game. Quite frankly Lina would rather stay home and bake a cake. Or walk her dog. Or pet her cat (if he decided he was in the mood for petting).

No, she hadn't regretted giving up on romance. Her eyes refocused on the unusual narcissus. It was just a flower, just a beautiful, early-blooming flower. And she had just had a very long, weird day, which explained why she was feeling odd. Maybe she was hormonal. She made a mental note to ask her mom about *the change* next time they talked.

A teasing breeze stirred the narcissus, bringing another wave of its sweet aroma to Lina. Just one more little sniff. She'd take one more smell, then she'd collect Edith Anne and take herself off to bed where she belonged. Balancing on the balls of her feet, she leaned forward, cupping the heavy blossom in her hands. As she brought her face closer to the flower, the area within the bell-shaped bloom rippled.

Lina blinked. What the hell? She leaned closer and peered into the open cup.

Like water down a sluiceway, shock caused all feeling to drain from her body. She was staring, not into the center of the narcissus, but straight into the face of an amazingly beautiful young woman. The woman's large violet-colored eyes were opened wide, her hair was in wild disarray, and her lovely lips were rounded as if she had been caught in the middle of uttering a terrified *Oh!*

Lina tried to move, but her body refused to obey her. She was frozen, transformed into a living statue. Fear pulsed through her and she felt her heart leap painfully in response, and then it was as if she was being pulled from her body by a giant vacuum cleaner. For a moment she was actually able to look back at the immobile shell that was her physical self before she was yanked forward and into the blindingly brilliant light that pulsed at the center of the expanding narcissus blossom. Lina's mind rebelled as her consciousness whirled down the circular shaft.

She tried to cry out. She tried to stop. She tried to breathe, but there was nothing except the sense of motion and a wrenching feeling of displacement. Just as she was sure she would go mad, Lina felt an enormous tug and she popped from the shaft and slammed into something. Tears swamped her eyes, making it impossible for her to see more than vague, blurred images.

Automatically, she gasped for air. Drenched in vertigo, her arms flailed around until they collided with the grassy earth against which her butt was resting. Struggling to anchor herself, she let her body collapse, arms spread wide as if she was embracing the ground. Lina pressed her face into the grass. She was shaking and panting, and she seemed to be trapped in some kind of silken netting.

"Get it off me! Get it off!" Still panicking she tore at what was entrapping her. "Ouch! *Merda!*"

The distinctive pain of roughly pulled hair penetrated her frenzy at the same instant her vision cleared. She was, indeed, lying against the grass-covered ground. Her hands were tangled in a thick mass of rich mahogany-colored hair that was so long that it fell to her waist.

Her waist. Blinking away tears, Lina gazed down at "herself."

Sucking in a deep breath Lina opened her mouth and screamed her best slasher-horror-movie-girl scream.

CHAPTER FIVE

"CALM yourself! There is nothing here for you to fear."

Lina tore her eyes from the body that was decidedly *not* hers. A few feet from where she lay were two women. The one who had spoken was tall, thin and had gray hair that was pulled back into a severe knot. She stood beside the silent one. The silent one sat on—Lina blinked rapidly, her mind not wanting to believe what her eyes reported—an enormous throne. She was draped in cream-colored linen. Her blond hair was wrapped around her head in a series of complicated braids, and an intricate crown of delicately carved golden—Lina blinked again, but the image remained the same—golden ears of corn rested regally atop her head. In one hand she held a long scepter, in the other she had a gilded goblet. The seated woman was beautiful, but her beauty was fierce and serious, what history described as a "handsome" woman. She was watching Lina intently.

"Welcome to my realm, Carolina Francesca Santoro, daughter of man."

Questions warred in Lina's brain and she struggled to shift through the teeming confusion and the lingering sense of physical displacement. She was breathing in short, panicked gulps. Lina glanced down. Through the silky shift she was wearing she could clearly see the mauve-colored nipples of her perfectly shaped breasts thrusting against the thin material barrier.

Even twenty years ago her breasts had never looked like those. Those breasts looked like they belonged on the pages of an airbrushed magazine. Real flesh couldn't be that perfect.

"Oh, God! I think I'm going to throw up," Lina said. Then she pressed her hand against her mouth. That wasn't her voice. Where was the soft mixture of

Oklahoma twang and her grandmother's Italian influence? "What has happened to me?" she gasped.

"As Eirene has said, there is nothing here for you to fear."

The queenly woman's voice was deep and comforting. Lina clung to it and willed herself to slow her breathing. Puking wouldn't help things. As her hyperventilation ceased, her mind began working again, and the woman's words registered.

"You said your 'realm.' What did you mean? Where am I?"

Demeter took her time before answering the human. Already she mourned the absence of her daughter's soul. She wanted nothing so much as to call Persephone back and know her child was close to her, protected and safe. But that was the problem. She had kept her daughter too protected. It was time Demeter allowed, or in this case, insisted, that she grow. And the goddess had made a decision; she was bound by her word—even if it had only been given to herself.

"My realm is never-ending—from the smallest garden plot to the vastness of the great fields as they grow ready for the harvest, there you will find what is mine. As to where you are . . ." She hesitated, considering. "Is Olympus a name you recognize?"

In short, jerky movements Lina nodded. "Yes. In mythology it's where the gods lived."

"Why is it that mortal daughters always say gods and leave out goddesses?" The woman who stood beside the throne asked the other.

"That I cannot answer." She shrugged her broad shoulders. "Mortals do not always make sense, especially mortals from Forgotten Earth."

"Wait, stop." Lina brushed the thick hair out of her face, forcing herself to ignore the fact that it was the wrong color, length and texture to be hers. "I need to know where I am, who you are, and what is going on."

In unison the women's heads turned to her.

"Mortal, do you not know to whom you speak?" The gray-haired woman whose name was Eirene bowed her head in the queen's direction. When Lina didn't answer, she frowned, but continued speaking. "You are in the presence of Demeter, Great Goddess of the Harvest."

Demeter did not smile, but her blue eyes softened. "How could you not know me? Was it not my assistance you invoked?"

Dumbfounded, Lina felt her jaw unhinge. It had to be a dream—a horrible, amazing, realistic dream. When she woke up she'd have to remember not to eat whatever she'd eaten before she'd gone to bed. Or maybe it was hormones. Again. She really needed to have a long talk with her mom.

"Carolina Francesca Santoro," Demeter said, sounding disturbingly like her grandmother. "You are not dreaming, nor do you hallucinate."

"Can you read my mind?"

"I am a goddess, and your expression is quite transparent." She gestured at a spot in front of her. Instantly a gilded chair materialized. "Come closer. We have much about which we must speak, and our time is limited."

Unsteadily, Lina stood. Her steps should have been halting and awkward, but her body seemed to have a rhythm of its own. On delicate feet she stepped forward and then sank gracefully into the offered chair.

Demeter gestured, speaking softly to Eirene. "She needs wine."

Lina watched, wide-eyed, as the gray-haired Eirene nodded, turned and seemed to disappear into a fold in the air behind her. Within two breaths, she returned, carrying a goblet that matched the one Demeter held, and a crystal bottle of golden liquid. First Eirene refreshed the goddess's cup, then she filled the goblet and brought it to Lina.

The hammered metal was cold in her hand and the wine was icy and incredibly delicious. Its taste filled her, instantly soothing her harried senses.

"It's wine, yet it's not. It's like drinking sunshine," Lina whispered.

"It is ambrosia. Drink deeply. It will quiet the trembling within you," Demeter said.

Lina obeyed the goddess, letting the cold liquid flash through her body. As she drank she could feel the last of the sense of displacement vanish, leaving her mind clear and surprisingly calm.

Lina met Demeter's steady gaze.

"I'm in Olympus."

Demeter nodded.

Lina glanced down at the stranger's body. "But this isn't me."

"No, you inhabit my daughter's body," Demeter said simply.

Lina took another long drink of the ambrosia. Her daughter's body? Her mind flipped through dusty mental files of leftover useless knowledge from school. Demeter's daughter? Who was she? A name came to her.

"Persephone?" Lina asked. There was something else that came with the name, some vague remembrance of a myth, but the goddess's quick response gave Lina little time to ponder the elusive thought.

"Yes. My daughter is the Goddess Persephone." Demeter nodded solemnly.

"If I'm here"—Lina pointed at herself—"then where is she?" But the chill of dread that shivered through her body answered the question before she heard the goddess's voice form the words.

"You are she, and she has become you."

"Why?" She croaked the question.

"You invoked my aid. My daughter is fulfilling that request."

"Your daughter? But what does your daughter trading places with me have to do with saving my bakery?" Totally confused, Lina struggled to stay calm.

"Foolish child!" Eirene snapped. "Enough of your questions. There is no better way to breathe new life into your insignificant little bakery than for it to be blessed by the personification of Spring."

Lina looked sharply at Eirene. She was confused and out of her element, but she was certainly not going to tolerate that woman's offensive words.

"First of all, I'm not a child. Don't call me one." Eirene's eyes widened at Lina's words. "Second, it might be an 'insignificant little bakery' to you, but you're talking about my life's work, and the livelihood of my employees. I have every right to ask questions and to expect them to be answered."

"How dare you . . ." Eirene sputtered, but Demeter's upheld hand silenced her.

"Enough." Though the goddess's tone was commanding, her expression was open and thoughtful as she studied Lina. "Your points are valid."

Eirene huffed and Demeter tilted her head in her friend's direction.

"Carolina Francesca is only demonstrating her maturity and sense of responsibility."

Eirene's mouth tightened into a thin line, but she didn't speak.

"Lina," Lina corrected, drawing the goddess's attention back to her. "My friends call me Lina."

Demeter's brows rose.

"I would be honored if you would call me Lina, too," she said, holding her breath. Had she overstepped herself?

"Then I shall," Demeter said.

"And you shall call her Great Goddess—"

"Or Demeter," the goddess interrupted, flashing an amused look at her friend.

"Demeter," Lina said, "please explain to me why Persephone and I have exchanged places."

"I heard your invocation. It moved me. No one from your world has called to me with such earnest hope in many ages. I chose to answer you."

With her free hand, Lina rubbed her forehead. "But why exchange your daughter and me? Couldn't you have just, I don't know, zapped some new life into my business?"

Demeter's lips almost smiled. "I did. I gave it my daughter."

"I don't mean any disrespect, Demeter, but what does your daughter know about the baking business?"

"My daughter has the wisdom of a goddess." Demeter's face hardened and her tone brought gooseflesh to Lina's arms. "And she is the embodiment of Spring. She will honor your bakery by breathing the freshness of new life into it." The goddess's expression softened. "Have no fear, Lina. You have my word that your business will thrive and prosper. In six months the money you owe the tax collectors will be repaid threefold."

"Six months?" Lina felt like she'd been hit in the stomach. "She's going to take my place for six months? What am I supposed to do while she is being me?"

Demeter appeared to consider the question. "There is a small task you could perform for me. For a woman of your maturity and experience it should be easily accomplished." Demeter's eyes captured Lina's gaze as she mirrored the final words of her invocation. "Let us just say that you are returning my favor."

Lina had offered the deal. The goddess had accepted. And Lina the businesswoman would keep her word.

She nodded stiffly. "Okay. What can I do for you?"

CHAPTER SIX

"YOU want me to go to Hell!" Lina's head was beginning to throb.

"Do not think of it in your limited, mortal terms," Demeter explained. "Hades is the Underworld. A place where souls spend eternity. There are many realms within the Underworld—most of which are places that hold both beauty and magic."

"And the rest of it is Hell," Lina said. She glanced at Eirene, who was impatiently listening to her exchange with Demeter. If the old woman had had a watch she would have been checking it every minute or so. "I'd like some more wine, please."

Eirene huffed, but she refilled her goblet.

Lina took a long drink.

"You still misunderstand," Demeter said patiently. "There is no 'Hell' in the Underworld. There are just differing levels of reward or punishment."

"Which are all filled with dead people," Lina blurted.

Demeter shook her head sadly.

"Okay, not dead people—the ghosts of dead people."

"Souls, Lina. Hades is filled with souls."

"Just exactly what is the difference?"

"You of all mortals should well understand that difference. Does your soul not quicken within my daughter's body? Does that make you one of the unnumbered dead? Or, as you would call it, a ghost? No, you are simply displaced. That is all that has happened to those who rest in the Underworld. They, too, have been displaced. Some of them will spend eternity amidst the wonders of the Elysian Fields; some will pay for their sins in Tartarus. Others will drink from Lethe, the River of Forgetfulness, and be allowed to be reborn within another mortal body. Some souls will languish beside Cocytus, the River of Lamentation, never able to cease mourning for their lost mortality. Still others—"

"Wait!" Lina blurted. "You've completely lost me. I don't know anything about those rivers or the levels of Hell . . . ur . . . I mean the Underworld. How am I supposed to manage these . . . these . . . dead, displaced souls if I don't even know where they should be or what they should be doing? It seems to me that you have the wrong woman for the job."

Demeter waved off her doubts. "That is all easily understood. Just listen to the voice within your body. There is enough of Persephone's essence left within you to guide you through any difficulty you might have in understanding."

Lina looked dubious.

This time Demeter's lips did turn slightly upward. "Try it, child of mortals. Listen within."

Lina narrowed her eyes and concentrated. Demeter had said there were rivers down there. She'd only remembered ever hearing about one. Styx. As soon as she thought the word, the whisper of a response, like a half-forgotten memory, came to her mind.

The River Styx is the River of Hate. Do not drink from it, it will cause no good end.

Lina yelped in surprise. It wasn't that there was another person inside her head, it was more like she could tap into an information source that was the ghost of a shelf of ancient encyclopedias buried somewhere in her medulla oblongata. Lina appreciated the irony of her analogy and smiled askance at the goddess, who was nodding in understanding.

"And does Persephone have this ability while she's in my body, too? Can she get information from—I don't know how to put it—from the echo of me?"

"The echo of you. That is an excellent description. Yes, she has the same ability. Though she will be mortal, she will not be lost in your world."

"And she's really mortal while she's in my body?" Lina asked.

"Of course. Just as you become a goddess while your soul inhabits my daughter's physical form."

Demeter's words caught Lina in the middle of swallowing a sip of wine, and she choked, almost causing ambrosia to spew from her nose.

"I'm—I'm a goddess?" she sputtered.

"Yes," Demeter said. "As long as you inhabit Persephone's body you are invested with her powers."

"Powers?" Lina repeated stupidly.

"Even in your foolish mortal world you must know goddesses wield many powers," Eirene snapped.

"Merda!" Lina swore in exasperation. Why did Eirene dislike her so intensely? "Could you give me just a little break here? How would you like it if you were suddenly sucked out of your world and plunked down in the middle of Tulsa, Oklahoma, circa the year 2000-something"—she glanced at Demeter and added—"a.d., with a stranger telling you that you had a six-month job to do in a place you thought only existed in fairy tales and bedtime stories. You wouldn't necessarily have to be in Hell to feel like you might just be visiting there."

Eirene blinked in confusion.

"See, it's not so easy, is it?" Lina turned back to Demeter. "What kind of powers?"

"Persephone is Goddess of Spring. She carries life and light with her, and she can share her gifts as she wills," Demeter said.

Lina's eyes widened. "You're sending me down to Hell and I can resurrect people?"

"Not people. Persephone cannot return life to dead mortals. I share my realm with my daughter, so she has dominion over growing things: flowers and trees, the wheat of the field and the grass beneath you. They all respond to Persephone's touch," Demeter explained. "She also can create light. Do not ever fear that the Underworld will be a dark, cheerless place. Persephone's presence evokes light."

"So I can make flowers grow and I light things up. What else?"

"Everything you need know is within you. Look deeply, and you will find the powers you seek," Demeter said cryptically.

Lina met the goddess's gaze. She knew evasion when she heard it. Okay, so Demeter didn't want her to know the extent of the powers within her new body.

"I guess I'll just have to discover some things on my own," she said carefully.

"You have a quick mind. You will have little trouble accomplishing your goal," Demeter said.

"Then why six months? That seems like a long time if I'm going to have 'little trouble' accomplishing my goal," Lina said.

"The six months is needed for your bakery to thrive. But do not be concerned about the passage of time—it is measured differently by the gods." Demeter made a vague, dismissive gesture with her hands. "Six hours, six months, six years—it is all the same. Focus on accomplishing your goal, and all will be well."

"And that goal is managing the Underworld?"

Demeter nodded. "That is one way to put it."

"I'm assuming there is some kind of problem down there right now."

"Think of it as a problem with morale." Demeter shrugged nonchalantly. "The Underworld needs the touch of a goddess. It has too long been a place devoid of feminine influence. It is simple. Allow yourself to been seen by the dead. They need to believe that their eternal rest will not be without the love and attention of a goddess. Think of yourself as a figurehead, a symbol of female strength and wisdom. Mortal souls crave the love and attention of an immortal mother. Your very presence will begin to set things to right."

Lina rubbed her forehead again. What was going on down there? Was there the equivalent of a bunch of male spirits sitting around scratching and farting as they watched the mythological version of the Super Bowl while forcing ghostly women to cook tacky, fattening foods for them?

Demeter's no-nonsense voice continued over Lina's mental turmoil.

"Think of it as a large bakery that is in disarray because its proprietress has long been absent. Use your wisdom and experience to put it to order. And know that as you do so, you are returning the favor of a goddess."

"Demeter, the time is short. She must begin her journey," Eirene spoke urgently.

"You are correct, as usual, my friend." Demeter smiled at Eirene and stood, gesturing for Lina to follow her. "Come, I will take you to the entrance of the Underworld."

"That's it?" Lina asked breathlessly. "Those are all the instructions you're going to give me?"

"Are you a child who needs to be led about by the hand?" Eirene asked sarcastically.

"You know, if you touched up some of that gray in your hair your attitude would probably get better. It always works for me," Lina quipped.

Eirene's mouth opened and closed. Once.

Demeter covered her bark of surprised laughter with a small cough. This human woman certainly had a will of her own. She cleared her throat delicately before addressing Lina.

"I have not left you bereft of aid. I have arranged for one of the recent dead to guide you to the Palace of Hades. She will help you with the questions your inner voice does not answer." As the goddess spoke, she was striding quickly through the grassy meadow and Lina had to scramble to keep up with her. "But you must understand that you cannot allow anyone to know that you are not truly Persephone."

"What! But how will I—" Lina gasped.

"It would be an insult," Demeter interrupted her. "The dead deserve more respect than to believe that they cannot be afforded the touch of a true goddess."

"But I'm *not* a true Goddess!"

"You are!" Demeter's intense gaze captured Lina. "I have granted you my daughter's powers. Believe you are a goddess and behave accordingly. And remember, in your world Persephone abides by the same rule. No one will know she is not truly Carolina Francesca Santoro. Now you must give me your word that you will not betray your true identity."

"I promise I'll keep who I am a secret," she agreed after only a brief hesitation. What choice did she have?

Demeter inclined her head in regal acknowledgment of Lina's oath before she continued her trek, leaving behind the grassy meadow and entering a wooded area.

Lina barely had time to wonder what it was she had somehow gotten herself into as she hurried after the goddess's departing form.

They were making their way through a grove of thick trees. The breeze was light and still touched with summer's warmth, but it caused dried leaves to rain from the sturdy branches that formed a canopy of fall colors over their heads.

"It's not spring here," Lina said suddenly.

Demeter glanced over her shoulder at the woman who wore her daughter's body.

"No, as I already explained, time runs differently here, Carolina. Spring has departed from this world, and the resting seasons of fall and winter are upon us, which is why my daughter could visit your world where the growth of spring has just begun."

Lina pressed her lips together. Well, didn't that just figure. It was appropriate that it was spring in the Oklahoma she'd just left, especially since Persephone had just arrived. It reminded her of an old myth. . . .

And Lina turned to stone.

Eirene stumbled and almost bumped into her from behind.

"You must hurry," the old woman said in irritation. "We have no time to—"

She was silenced by the expression on Lina's face. Sensing trouble, Demeter had already turned when Lina's next words sliced through the air between them.

"The Rape of Persephone." Lina crossed her arms, hugging herself defensively. "I remember the myth now. Hades, the King of Hell, abducts the maiden goddess, Persephone. He rapes her and tricks her into staying down there with him by getting her to eat six pieces of fruit." She searched her memory and came up with the name. "Six pieces of pomegranate. That's why for six months there's fall and winter—because her mother, that would be you, Demeter, went into such mourning at the loss of her daughter that she refused to let anything bloom until she returned."

Lina gulped for air, fighting down her fear. She wasn't an innocent young virgin. She was a mature, middle-aged woman, and she would not be led docilely into a trap. "You're setting me up. You want me to take your daughter's place so that it's not actually Persephone who is raped."

Lina could hear Eirene's shocked gasp at Lina's words, and before she could say more, Demeter covered the space that separated them so quickly that Lina's vision blurred. The goddess took Lina firmly by the shoulders and met her gaze unblinkingly. "You must not believe this lie, Lina," Demeter said.

"I've read the story; it's how it goes."

"Not here, Lina, not in this world." Demeter could feel the girl's body trembling under her hands. She focused the power of her will on Lina's eyes. She had to make this mortal daughter believe she was telling her truth. "I would not allow such a thing to happen. Not to my own daughter, and not to you."

"But I remember it. That's what happens," she insisted stubbornly.

"The stories you know of this realm are only the shadows of truth. Think of them as tales too long repeated by too many gossips. Truth has been twisted and changed and used to explain away mysteries. Think logically, daughter of mortals. Do you honestly believe that I would allow anyone to steal my daughter from me?"

Lina met Demeter's eyes. The goddess filled her vision. Her power was a tangible thing. Suddenly Lina was reminded of her mother, and her grandmother. She recognized in Demeter the protective, earnest tone of another mother who would do anything to ensure that her daughter wasn't harmed. And Demeter had the strength of an immortal to support her maternal instincts.

"When you put it like that it doesn't seem very logical that a goddess would allow her only daughter to be abused," Lina said slowly. "But then again, I'm not really your daughter."

A genuine smile softened the goddess's expression so that Lina saw clearly the love Demeter had for Persephone. "You stand in my daughter's stead. You speak through her lips; you are housed in her form. I would not allow harm to come to you, child."

"And the King of Hell doesn't want to rape me—or Persephone?"

"No, Lina. Hades is a reclusive, somber god. He does not cavort with nymphs; he has no mate, nor has he shown amorous interest in any goddess in"—Demeter scoffed, her handsome face twisted in disdain—"longer than I can remember. His dour existence is consumed with the workings of the Underworld. He cares nothing for love or life. And always remember that you are under my protection. All of the gods and goddesses know it. No one, mortal or immortal, would dare abuse my daughter."

Demeter's words felt logical. The goddess who stood before her exuded power and authority. It didn't seem likely that she would allow her beloved daughter to be harmed. Lina looked deeply into Demeter's clear, guileless eyes and realized with a start that she trusted the goddess.

"Does he know you're sending Persephone down there?"

"Hades will be pleased to have your assistance. Do not worry so, all will be well." Demeter squeezed her shoulders firmly before resuming her trek through the trees. She gestured impatiently at Lina to catch up with her. "It is time for you to meet your spirit guide."

When Lina still didn't move, Demeter turned and raised her distinctive brows questioningly.

"Saying that Hades will be pleased to have my assistance doesn't mean that you've told him I'm coming." Lina knew business rhetoric when she heard it. She'd just fired an accountant who specialized in it. "In other words, he has no idea I'm coming and not a clue that I'm there to mess around with the management of his realm. Right?"

Demeter's expression was wry. "You are experienced enough to understand that not everything can be spoken outright. Especially when dealing with men."

"You're right. I do understand what you're saying. So here's my request. I'd like you to send him word that your daughter is coming for a"—Lina gestured vaguely—"a little vacation. From a purely business standpoint it's always a good idea to keep the lines of communication within management as open as possible."

Demeter considered her request. Perhaps the mortal was correct. Hades should be told of Persephone's coming; even if the dour god didn't deign to bestir himself to welcome her. Still, it was only polite for one god to contact the other when entering another deity's realm.

The goddess raised one hand and pursed her lips, letting loose a series of melodic birdsong. Before the lovely sound had died on the wind, a flutter of wings burst overhead and an enormous raven circled Demeter once before gliding down to perch on her outstretched arm.

"Take the news of my daughter's arrival in the Underworld to Hades," Demeter said to the bird. "Tell him that the Goddess of the Harvest appreciates his hospitality and his protection as Spring visits the Land of the Dead." Demeter threw up her arm and the raven lifted gracefully into the wind, disappearing amidst the trees.

"Does that satisfy your sense of responsibility?" Demeter asked Lina.

"Yes, thank you," Lina said as she hurried after the stern goddess.

Demeter came to a rise in the land that signaled the end of the tree line. There she waited for Lina and Eirene to join her, but Lina's eyes were not on the goddess. They were focused on the incredible sight before them.

"Oh!" The breath left her in such a rush she felt dizzy. "I've never seen . . . this is . . . is . . ."

"It is Lake Avernus." For once Eirene's voice had lost its caustic edge. "Beyond it is the Bay of Naples."

"It's so beautiful," Lina said, at a loss for words to describe the awesome view. The lake stretched before them like a vast liquid mirror the color of sapphires. Light glittered and danced magically over its surface, breathing life to its face so that its perfect, glassy cover sparkled playfully. There were no trees near the lake's edge, but lacy ferns framed it with the soft touch of earthy green. Beyond the lake waited the ocean, its lighter shades of aqua and turquoise making it appear like it was the feminine complement to the darker, land-bound body of water.

"You have only begun to know the wonders of this world, Lina," Demeter said.

CHAPTER SEVEN

THE goddess's knowing steps found a small dirt path that appeared to circle the lake. Demeter turned to her right and followed the path around a gentle bend, which led directly to the mouth of a tunnel-like opening within a large rock formation mounded near the edge of the lake. As they approached the tunnel, Lina could see that its stone walls had been smoothed and painted with fabulous frescoes depicting gods and goddesses feasting, laughing and loving. But soon the frescoes were swallowed by the darkness within.

Lina's throat felt dry. The darkness was like a tomb.

Demeter's steps didn't falter. She marched into the tunnel. When Lina hesitated, she spoke gruffly to her.

"Well, you must come, too. How else will our way be lighted?" the goddess coaxed.

"Lighted?" Lina repeated, realizing she sounded like an idiot.

Eirene sighed. "You are the Goddess of Spring. Use your powers."

Lina's brow knotted.

"Listen within, *Persephone*." Demeter enunciated the name carefully. "Your body knows."

Ignoring her mounting frustration, Lina concentrated. Light. If she could make light, how would she do it? *Think!* she told herself. A half-formed idea flitted through her mind. She lifted her right hand to the level of her eyes. It was a lovely hand. The color of new cream, it was smooth and unlined—unlike her own, well-worn forty-something- year-old hand. If she could create light, she would do it like she had done so many other important things in her life—with her hands. And suddenly she knew. She turned her hand, palm up and cast a simple thought down her arm.

I'd like light, please.

With a perky snapping sound, a little globe of brilliance popped from her palm to hover inches above her hand. Enormously pleased with herself, she smiled past the light and into Demeter's eyes.

"That's how I'd make light."

"Well done, Persephone," Demeter said. The goddess nodded in the direction of the seemingly bottomless tunnel.

Squaring her shoulders, Lina stepped forward, leaving the ball of light hovering in the tunnel behind them.

"You must command it to stay with you," Demeter said.

The goddess was standing within the edge of darkness, so Lina couldn't tell for sure, but she thought Demeter might actually be laughing.

"Well, come on! Keep up with me," Lina told the light. Immediately it burst forward, almost hitting her head. Lina jerked back, squinting at its brightness. "With me, not on me." She whispered to the glowing ball, and it settled into a spot just above her right shoulder. "Up higher, you're blinding my eye."

The ball rose a few inches.

"Right there. Good job." The light seemed to wriggle in pleasure at her compliment, which made Lina grin at it. "Okay, we're ready," she told Demeter.

The three of them started forward, this time with Lina and her light leading the way. The tunnel was large and its downward grade was steep, but the walls around them changed very little. The colorful frescoes decorated the dim expanse, appearing incongruous with their bright cheer in the midst of such utter darkness. Lina was just about to ask Demeter who had painted the scenes when the walls around them fell away, leaving only unending darkness in their place. Directly in front of them a grove of trees materialized from the blackness. Lina stared at them.

"Ghost trees," she whispered in awe. That's what they looked like. Though their branches were thick and filled with leaves that appeared to be thriving and healthy, they were white—trunks, limbs, leaves—all the color of milk. They fascinated Lina. Their beauty was unearthly and delicate, and they appealed to her senses at a deep and elemental level.

"It is through this grove that you will find the entrance to the Underworld." Then Demeter raised her voice, calling into the grove. "Eurydice, come forth!"

Lina felt her stomach tighten with nerves. She was just about to meet her first dead person. No! She had to quit thinking about them as "dead," that would only creep her out. She needed to remember Demeter's words—they were just displaced souls, much like her.

Within the grove movement flickered and Lina forced herself to remember to breathe as a slender figure stepped from the tree line and moved purposefully toward them. Lina twirled one long strand of hair around and around her finger while she strained to get a clear image of the figure, but all she could see was a blurred sense of long hair and the flow of a diaphanous garment. Then Eurydice stepped within Lina's circle of light, and she felt the nervousness leave her in a rush of relief. This was no walking specter or *Dawn of the Dead*-like zombie. It was just a pale, frightened looking girl. If Lina had been able to give birth to a daughter, this child would have been her age—probably eighteen or nineteen.

She approached Demeter hesitantly and curtsied low. It was only then that Lina noticed that her body was not as substantial as it had at first appeared. Upon closer inspection, Lina could see that the light actually passed through the girl's body and the silky, toga-like robe she wore. She wasn't quite a shadow or a ghost; she was more like an unfinished watercolor painting that had come to life. Lina felt a rush of maternal sympathy for her. She was so young. What had happened to her?

"Great Goddess, I have awaited your presence as you commanded." Her voice was melodic and sweet.

"You have done well, child. This is the final task I require of you. I ask that you serve as guide to my daughter, who wishes to visit the Underworld," Demeter said.

"I am pleased to serve you in any way, Demeter," Eurydice said. She turned to Lina and inclined her head respectfully. "It is a great honor for me that the Goddess of Spring will join me on my journey to Elysia."

"Thank you for helping me, Eurydice." Lina smiled warmly at the girl. "I've never been to He"—she caught herself just in time and switched words, hoping the child didn't notice her slip—"Hades before."

"Neither have I, Goddess."

Eurydice's voice was shadowed with sadness, and Lina wanted to smack herself in the head for her insensitive comment, but before she could apologize, Demeter spoke to Eurydice.

"Though you have not yet experienced the wonders of Elysium, your soul knows the way and seeks to take you to your eternal destination. As your soul guides you, so you will guide my daughter, and I entrust her to your care," Demeter said, her voice gentle, her expression maternal.

Eurydice bowed her head, obviously humbled by the goddess's trust. Then Demeter turned to Lina.

"It is here I must take my leave of you, Persephone."

Demeter embraced her and Lina was enveloped in the rich, summer scent of ripe corn and windblown fields of wheat.

"May your sojourn in the Underworld bring Spring to Hades' realm, and comfort to those who have felt the absence of a goddess. Fare you well, daughter, my blessings go with you."

Demeter kissed her softly on the forehead, then she turned to go.

"Wait—wait—wait!" Lina stuttered. The goddess was leaving already? Just like that?

Demeter glanced back over her shoulder. "Listen within, Persephone. Your instincts will not fail you."

Lina took a step toward the goddess and dropped her voice. "What if I need more help than that?"

"Trust yourself. Draw upon your inner knowledge, as well as your *other* experiences," Demeter said pointedly. "Your life has prepared you well for this endeavor."

Lina's whisper was for Demeter's ears only. "How do I reach you if something comes up that I can't handle?"

Demeter nodded thoughtfully. "Perhaps it would be best." The goddess gestured toward the tunnel from which they had descended. "I will leave my oracle for you at the mouth of this entrance. You only have to look into it to see my face."

"But how can I be sure to find my way back there?"

"You are the daughter of the Harvest. Turn your face upward, and your steps will always lead you to your home," Eirene snapped in her usual, caustic manner. Then she met Lina's clear gaze and Eirene felt herself soften. This woman was, after all, housed against her will in Persephone's body. "Believe in yourself, child. Your strength rests within."

Lina was almost as surprised by the gentleness of the old woman's words as she was by her smile.

"I'll remember, thank you, Eirene," Lina said.

Demeter stepped forward and kissed her lightly on the forehead again. "May you be blessed with joy and magic, daughter."

The goddess turned away with a finality that told Lina not to call her back, even though her heart was fluttering nervously at the thought of what lay ahead. Lina watched the darkness swallow the two women, and she had just begun to think about whether she should send a little of her light to help lead Demeter to the surface when the goddess's staff began to glow with the brilliant golden light of a summer day.

"And she needed me to light the way for her?" Lina muttered. "Not hardly."

"I beg your pardon, Goddess, but we must begin our journey."

Lina turned back to Eurydice. The girl was plucking at the transparent folds of her garment. She gave Lina a shy, apologetic smile.

"I feel compelled to continue. My soul tells me that I have waited as long as I am able."

"Oh! Of course," Lina said, feeling instantly ashamed of herself. Here she was, fretting about Demeter leaving her alone to get started on a temporary job that she had been assured she could complete with no problem, and little, dead Eurydice was . . . well . . . dead. Poor kid. "I'm ready. Let's go."

Instantly, the young spirit re-entered the grove of white trees with Lina following close behind. The little ball of light enveloped them in a soft, clear glow, and as it touched the trees that surrounded them the light caught in the branches and sparkled between the leaves making them shine like they were faceted jewels.

"They're so beautiful," Lina said quietly.

"I think it is your light that makes them appear so, Goddess," Eurydice said in the timid voice of a child.

"Oh, I don't know, I'll bet they have always been beautiful." As soon as she had spoken the words, the limbs above Lina began to ripple, as if in response to her compliment, and more faceted leaves shimmered and glistened in her light. She smiled at her guide and pointed up into the forest of diamonds. "They were here a long time before I came. My light is just allowing them to be seen as they really are."

"Forgive me, Goddess. I did not mean to speak out of turn."

Lina pulled her gaze from the shining leaves. Eurydice had ducked her head, as if she was waiting for some kind of chastisement.

"You didn't speak out of turn. You just made an observation. I want you to feel free to talk to me. Honestly, I'm already missing my"—Lina paused. She'd almost said "life" or "bakery" or "world,"—"mother," she amended, "and I'd really appreciate some conversation to get my mind off her."

"I miss my mother, too," Eurydice whispered.

"I'm sorry. I didn't mean to remind you of . . ." Lina's words failed.

"It is not so terrible, Goddess," Eurydice said quickly. "Though I have been dead but a little while, I think I am already beginning to understand."

When the girl quit speaking, Lina prompted her to continue. "Go on, I'd like to know what you've come to understand."

"The pains of the living world are already fading away. I miss my mother and . . . well . . . others, but I know that I will eventually be reunited with them. I am, after all, still myself." Eurydice held out her arm so that Lina's light shined clearly through her delicate limb. "My body has changed a little, but my mind and heart are the same, which is a great relief to me. What I mean to say is that I have found that the terror of death is worse than death itself." The young spirit finished in a rush.

Lina smiled at Eurydice. "You are very wise."

"Oh, no," Eurydice said, shaking her head quickly from side to side and causing her transparent blond hair to float around her in gossamer wisps. "If I were truly wise I would have avoided my mistakes."

Before Lina could question the girl further, they stepped from the grove of white trees to find themselves standing in front of an enormous ivory gate. Beyond the gate Lina could see a smooth, black path that wound off into the eternal darkness like a thin ribbon of night.

"We must enter here and follow that path," Eurydice said. "It will take us to Charon."

Lina didn't need to pull from Persephone's knowledge; she recognized the name of the Ferryman of the Underworld. She nodded at Eurydice and had just reached up to push open the gate when the ivory wall swung away from her touch. At the same instant, a whir of sound caused the darkness before them to ripple, and a river of mist spewed from the other side of the gate, engulfing Lina in cold, gray vapor. Fear flowed from it like a raging river. Nightmare sounds assailed her senses, reminding Lina of every bad dream she had ever experienced. Her first response was to cover her ears and run away screaming, but the calm core within her took hold and spoke reassuringly into her frightened mind.

They are nothing but false dreams, the harmless mist of nightmare remembrances. You are a goddess; they hold no terror for you. Order them away and they will obey.

Forcing her hands to her sides, Lina stood tall and shook herself like a cat ridding itself of hated water.

"Get away, bad dreams!" she commanded, and breathed a sigh of relief when the mist responded by dissipating into nothingness.

"You made them leave. Oh, thank you, Goddess."

Eurydice had moved close to her side, and now the young girl stood almost touching her. Lina could see the fear in her pale eyes.

"They couldn't have hurt you, Eurydice. They were just the mist of nightmares," she reassured the girl with a quick smile. "Unpleasant, sure, but not dangerous."

"I have never liked nightmares," Eurydice said, looking around fearfully.

"Honey, no one does. That's why they're called *bad* dreams. Don't give them another thought—they're history." The ivory gate had remained open, and Lina pointed at the dark road. "Didn't you say this was the way we had to go?"

"Yes, Goddess."

"Well, then, off we go." Lina stepped through the gate and onto the road with Eurydice following closely behind. Under the soft leather slippers that adorned Persephone's dainty feet, the road felt cool and hard. She crouched down to touch it.

"Marble," she murmured. Lina peered into the distance. "It's made of what looks like a single slab of black marble." She stood up and grinned at Eurydice. "It's not the yellow brick road, but it's sure easy to follow."

"Goddess?" Eurydice looked confused.

"Oh, it's just a saying. It means our way is clearly marked." Lina started walking, Eurydice at her side and the ball of light floating between them. "And I would really like it if you would call me by my name."

"But you are a goddess." She sounded shocked at Lina's request.

"And I have a name. Anyway, goddess sounds so stiff and formal. After all, I am the Goddess of Spring, and spring is anything but stiff and formal." Lina listened within as she spoke and it seemed that the echo of Persephone was pleased by what she had said. Suddenly Lina wondered about the woman whose body she inhabited. What was she like? Lina glanced down at herself. That she was beautiful was obvious, but was she also arrogant and selfish? Or was she a benevolent goddess who treated others kindly?

"Then I will consider it an honor to call you Persephone."

Eurydice's voice broke into Lina's thoughts, but she smiled encouragement to the girl. "Good!" At least it was a start.

They walked on in companionable silence and Lina studied the land around them. She was beginning to distinguish between the levels of darkness on either side of the road. At first glance, it seemed that everything was wreathed in the black of a starless night, but as Lina's eyes grew more accustomed to the lack of light, she could see that there were shadows and shapes within the black. The land that stretched away on either side of them reminded Lina of a dark moor; she could even make out the feather-like shapes of gray-toned foliage and clumps of thick grasses that waved unerringly in the non-wind.

Then a shape flitted past, catching Lina's eye as it swam into focus. It was an old man, bent almost in two with age. He took one limping step toward the road, but his next step was backward, then he took another forward. His rheumy eyes blinked sightlessly at Lina. Just as she was wondering if she should help him, another shape took form out of the darkness. It was a woman. She looked to be about Lina's age and she was crouched on the shadowy grass, cringing in terror from an invisible attacker. Lina's first instinct was to go to her, but the voice within echoed throughout her mind.

You cannot help them. They are Old Age and Fear. Look about you. Grief, Anxiety, Hunger, Disease and Agony will join them.

As Lina watched other spectral forms took shape alongside the first two. They were wretched and horrible. The sight of them made Lina's stomach clench.

They are all a part of mortal existence. They cannot be helped. They can only be overcome. Do not tarry here.

Lina realized that she had slowed almost to a stop and Eurydice was staring fearfully around them.

"I think we need to speed up. You have a date with eternity, and I hate to be late for anything, don't you? I think it's rude," Lina said brightly as she stepped up their pace so that Eurydice almost had to jog to keep up with her. She heard

Grief wailing behind them and she shuddered, refusing to look back. Instead she focused her attention on several softly glowing shapes that hovered down the path in front of them. Even though she couldn't see them clearly yet, Lina didn't feel any danger or animosity from them, and her inner voice was quiet, which she took as a positive sign.

"Wonder what those are up there?" Lina asked, making light conversation with the silent girl at her side.

"I think they are others like me," Eurydice said slowly.

Lina stifled the instant trepidation she felt. She was, after all, in the Land of the Dead. Did she actually think that she wouldn't come across any dead people? That was a little like thinking she wouldn't find yeast in a bakery, she told herself sternly.

"Well, then we know we're heading in the right direction." She smiled at Eurydice.

"You knew we were on the right path," Eurydice said, smiling shyly back at her.

"That's because I have such a good guide," Lina said, which made Eurydice's smile widen, flushing her pale face with pleasure. Lina kept the warmth of the young spirit's smile foremost in her mind as they overtook the first of the ghostly forms.

It was a young woman, and again Lina found herself thinking that this girl, too, was young enough to have been her daughter. The spirit carried a bundle which she kept hidden and pressed close to her breast, but Lina could tell by its shape that it was an infant. The woman's blank gaze moved from the dark landscape before her and touched on Eurydice without changing expression, but when she noticed Lina, her shadowed eyes widened and her face suddenly became animated.

"Is it truly the Goddess of Spring who walks amidst the dead?" Her voice was thick with emotion.

With only a slight hesitation, Lina answered, "Yes, I am Persephone."

"Oh!" The newly dead woman pressed a transparent hand against her mouth as if to contain her emotions. She took a deep, steadying breath and said, "Then this dark journey is not so hopeless. Not if we walk in the presence of a goddess."

Out of the corner of her eye Lina could see Eurydice smiling and nodding. The whisper of her name passed like a gentle wave through the cluster of glowing spirits that suddenly surrounded them.

"Persephone!"

"It is the Goddess of Spring!"

"She has come to light our dreary journey!"

One by one the spirits turned to Lina. They came in all ages and forms, from old men stooped with age to youngsters who flitted between the shapes of the older dead with the exuberance of youth. Some spirits showed evidence of their wounds, with obvious sword slashes painting their otherwise pale bodies in crimson. Some, like Eurydice and the young mother, were unmarked, but no matter the state of what remained of their physical forms, all of them had one thing in common—the look of delight and newly rekindled hope at the sight of Persephone.

Lina was surprised at her reaction to being surrounded by spirits of the dead. It wasn't scary at all. She could even stand the sight of death wounds, as long as she didn't stare too long and instead focused on the person's eyes. There Lina could see the light that ignited within each soul as she smiled and greeted them with what she hoped was a proper display of caring.

As Lina and Eurydice followed the dark path, the number of dead surrounding them continued to grow. Lina could see that Demeter hadn't exaggerated. The spirits obviously needed her. They reacted to her presence like she was rain and they were a desert plain. Parched, they drank in her smiles and greetings. Voices whispered endlessly around her, murmuring words in languages she shouldn't understand, but did. Feeling a little overwhelmed, Lina tried not to think about the multitude of spirits. Take them one at a time, she chanted over and over to herself. Think of them as eager customers and not as the unnumbered dead.

As if sensing her growing unease, Eurydice stayed close beside her, making sure that she kept the goddess moving forward.

"I can see the marsh just ahead," Eurydice whispered to Persephone. "There we will board Charon's boat and he will take us across the lake to the path that leads to the Elysian Fields. The palace of Hades is at the edge of those fields. It cannot be much farther till we reach it."

Lina was just thanking Eurydice for the bolstering information when the pathway in front of them shuddered, and with a deafening crack, the black marble broke open, exposing an opening in the ground that gaped like a giant's mouth. With gasps of fear, the souls of the dead scattered, leaving only Lina and Eurydice to face the dark maw.

CHAPTER EIGHT

"DAMNIT! Damnit! Damnit!" Lina yelled, too shocked to remember to switch to Italian as the earth at her feet opened. She windmilled her arms to keep from tumbling forward, then hastily grabbed Eurydice by one cool, transparent hand and began to scramble back, pulling the girl with her. She'd only retreated a couple feet when four ebony-colored stallions surged from the opening. Snorting fire in an awesome display of power they converged on Lina and Eurydice.

"Goddess, help me!" Eurydice shrieked.

The girl's terrified voice snapped Lina out of her slack-jawed stupor. She dropped Eurydice's small, pale hand and stepped forward to meet the horses. The lead stallion challenged her with a piercing squeal, his ears turned flat against his massive skull. He was the first horse she approached.

Mentally crossing her fingers that her gift hadn't been left behind in her body, Lina dropped her voice to a playful level and held her hand out to his dangerous looking muzzle.

"Well, hello there you handsome boy."

The horse faltered, mid-fiery snort. His ears pricked forward so that he could be certain to catch every sound she uttered.

Lina smiled. Obviously, her gift belonged to her soul and not to her body. She breathed a sigh of relief. No matter how large or fierce, they were just horses, and like all animals, horses adored her. Lina made soothing clucking sounds with her tongue against her teeth as she caressed the magnificent animal's velvet muzzle.

"You certainly are a big boy," Lina cooed.

"Who dares to disturb the souls of the dead and to touch the dread steeds of Hades!"

The voice broke like a whip over her, and Lina jerked her hands away from the smooth muzzle, glancing guiltily up in the direction from which the deep voice originated.

Lina swallowed hard. She was such an idiot! She'd been so entranced by the horses that she hadn't even thought to look behind them.

The man stood in a brilliant silver chariot the color of moonbeams, holding a large, two-pronged spear in one hand and thick leather reins in his other hand. His massive body was swathed from neck to ankle in night-colored robes. A cloak rippled around him and Lina's little light illuminated its folds so that it shone with shades of deep purple and royal blue. His long hair was tied back in a thick queue. It, too, was black and the light showed its slick sheen. Lina's eyes moved to his face. His coloring was dark and exotic; his skin was a mixture of gold and bronze that gave him the intimidating look of a statue that had come alive. He was staring at her with eyes that blazed above high cheekbones and a strong, well-defined chin. His nose was hawkish. He was stern and angry and . . . magnificent.

God, she thought numbly, he's like an ancient Batman—minus the mask and the Batmobile.

"I'm sorry," Lina said nervously. "I-I didn't mean to disturb anything. The dead were just, well, glad to see me and—"

One of the "dread steeds," obviously annoyed at the lack of attention, blew in her face, obscuring her view of the man. Automatically, Lina clucked reassuringly to him and stroked the muzzle he offered.

"Again, you dare to touch a dread steed." This time the deep voice sounded more confused than angry.

Lina had to shove the stallion's head aside so that she could peer at him from under the horse's neck. "Apparently, he doesn't realize he's a dread steed." She smiled fondly at the horse and it lipped her shoulder. The other three animals had begun to stretch their heads toward her, too, eager for their share of the attention. "Well, that's not totally true. It's just that I have this *thing* with animals. They like me. A lot." She reached another muzzle and gave it a quick caress. "So I'm sure that they're still dread steeds, just not at this particular moment."

And then the man's words really registered in her mind. He'd said "the dread steeds of Hades." Lina ducked her head behind the nearest horse. *Merda!* That meant that Batman was really Hades. She closed her eyes and counted to three, took a deep breath and stepped back from the knot of horsy affection.

"I'm sorry, it's rude of me not to introduce myself. I'm Persephone, Demeter's daughter. I think she sent word that I was coming for a visit." The man's eyes widened, but he didn't respond. Lina barreled on. "I really didn't mean to disturb the dead. I apologize if I've done something I shouldn't have." Still the god remained silent. Lina's stomach fluttered. "You must be Hades. I hope I haven't come at an inconvenient time."

"I recognize you now, Goddess," Hades said. "And I did receive word of your coming."

Lina felt a little start of surprise. He recognized her? She hadn't expected Hades to know Persephone. Demeter certainly hadn't mentioned anything about the two of them knowing each other.

"You did no harm. It is just that the Underworld is not usually visited by immortals. The dead are not used to the presence of other gods," he said stonily.

Lina tried to smile. His hard gaze made her want to squirm uncomfortably.

"It was my mother's idea," Lina said, and was instantly sorry. She sounded like an insecure teenager. Quickly, she added, "And I thought it would be nice to get away."

Hades raised one dark brow, just as Lina imagined Batman would have done.

"Demeter told me that the Underworld is filled with magic and beauty," Lina repeated truthfully. "I'd like to see for myself."

"There are many wonders in my realm that go unnoticed by the immortals above," Hades said slowly.

"Then you don't mind if I visit?"

Hades studied her with dark, unreadable eyes. But before he could answer the stallion nearest to Lina suddenly laid his ears flat against his head, and with a squeal he bared his teeth dangerously at the small, pale form that had been silently approaching Lina.

With a terrified cry, Eurydice leapt back. Instantly, Lina stepped into the stallion's path, causing the huge animal to pull up short in his attack.

Hands on hips she scolded the massive beast. "That was a very mean thing to do! Eurydice was just coming to me. She wasn't doing anything wrong. I'm ashamed of you. You four have already scared away the rest of the souls. I'd think you'd know better."

Chagrined, the horse hung his head and blinked at Lina with the sad, calf eyes.

Incredulous, Hades watched as the young goddess chastised his steed. What had she done to the horse? Had she cast a spell over him? Hades' gaze took in the other three stallions, each of whom was hanging his head and looking lovingly at Persephone. What kind of magic did the Goddess of Spring possess? He had glimpsed her only a few times in his infrequent forays to the surface. What he had observed was a beautiful, but frivolous, fun-loving young goddess, and he had given her as little thought as he gave the rest of the immortals. Yet the woman before him appeared calm and carried herself with a definite air of maturity. And she had enchanted his steeds. Hades shook his head in disbelief. What was this feeling she had awakened within him? Curiosity? It had been eons since he had felt even mildly curious about another living being. How intriguing . . . the very thought of him finding the Goddess of Spring interesting made him want to laugh aloud. He abruptly made his decision and forced himself to speak before he could change his mind.

"You are welcome in the Underworld, Persephone," Hades said.

Lina looked up in surprise. The god's voice had changed, as had his somber expression. He was looking at her with an intensity that made his gaze feel almost tangible. His eyes were no longer remote and unreadable, they glistened with what she would almost swear was curiosity and, if she hadn't known he was God of the Underworld, something she recognized as good humor.

Batman—sexy, sexy Batman—on a good day when the Joker wasn't bugging him, and so damn male that he radiated power. Demeter's hasty description of Hades had definitely not prepared her for the reality of the god's presence.

"Well, thank you, Hades. I appreciate your hospitality," she said a little breathlessly.

"Come, then. I will show you to my palace." Hades gestured magnanimously to the open space next to him in the chariot.

Lina glanced back at the silent horses. "First, I better make things right with them."

Hades watched as without any hesitation or sign of fear, the goddess stepped into the middle of the massive stallions so that she was surrounded by living horseflesh. An odd little ball of light followed her, causing the animals' slick, black coats to glisten and shine while encasing the goddess in an illuminated globe so that her face was clearly visible and Hades could see her grinning girlishly as she patted each horse in turn. Where was the flighty, self-absorbed Goddess of Spring? This well-composed, horse-loving Persephone was not what he had expected.

"Oh, you're all good boys. Don't be sad. I'm not mad at you."

Hades still found it hard to believe, but his dread steeds nuzzled her and whickered softly. Like they were tame ponies.

Finally, laughing, she emerged from the nest of horseflesh. She felt his eyes on her again, and smiled up at him. "I love horses, don't you?"

The radiant expression on her face caused his stomach to tighten. Had a goddess ever looked at him like that before? His mouth felt dry. He swallowed hard.

"Yes."

Lina thought she could get lost in that one simple word spoken in Hades' rich, deep voice. For some ridiculous reason, she felt her cheeks warm with a blush, and she turned hastily back to stroke the stallion's slick neck. What the hell was wrong with her? She seriously needed to get a grip on herself. She was a grown woman. There was no reason for her to get all limp-kneed and goo-goo eyed just because Hades hadn't turned out to be a bore or a troll. She glanced at him. Jeesh, he made her nervous. "Reclusive and somber," *merda!* Demeter had failed to add gorgeous.

She needed to start thinking of him as nothing more than an upper-level executive. An incredibly powerful upper-level executive. Business—this trip was meant to be business. Remember that, she told herself firmly.

"I'm ready now." She straightened her shoulders, gave the stallion a final pat, started to join Hades and then stopped. She had just been scolding the horses for their bad behavior, and here she was, reacting to the presence of a handsome man like a silly schoolgirl and forgetting all of her own manners.

"Eurydice," she called, stepping away from the chariot so that she could see the spirit who was standing nervously a little way down the path. "Come on. Hades is going to give us a ride."

Eurydice's eyes were wide and frightened. "Oh, no, Goddess. I could not go with . . ." The young spirit's words ran out, leaving her silent and helpless.

Lina thought she looked like a pale, frightened little fawn.

"Honey, I wouldn't think of going on without you. You've been a wonderful guide and a good friend." Lina turned to Hades. "Isn't your palace on the way to the Elysian Fields?"

Hades nodded.

"So it would be fine for Eurydice to ride there with us?" she asked the god.

Instead of answering her, Hades shifted his attention to the little spirit and spoke directly to Eurydice.

"Do not fear, child. You may join your goddess."

His voice had changed again. Lina thought that now he sounded like a father coaxing a shy child to his side. His expression had softened, too, and gone was the intense look with which he had been studying her. In exchange his face was kind, and he looked suddenly approachable and understanding—and somehow older than he had originally appeared.

"As you wish, my Lord." Eurydice's sweet voice answered Hades. She even managed the shadow of a smile as she skirted around the four stallions to join Lina. "You don't have to worry about them now," Lina told her, forcing her eyes from Hades' shifting face and nodding her head at the horses. "They'll behave."

Eurydice sent the four beasts a nervous glance, and she was careful to keep the goddess between herself and them, even though they gave no sign of striking out at her. They were too busy whickering at Persephone and sending her adoring looks.

The lip of the chariot sat well above the ground, and Lina gratefully accepted Hades' help to climb aboard. His large hand engulfed hers in instant warmth, and Lina was surprised to feel the roughness of well-worn calluses against Persephone's smooth palm. She wondered what work Hades did with his hands, but she didn't have time to ponder the god's habits long because as soon as she pulled Eurydice up next to her, Hades barked a command and the chariot lurched forward, whipped around in a tight circle and plunged back through the jagged opening in the earth. Glancing over her shoulder, Lina caught sight of the crevice closing behind them. She gulped and drew Eurydice in front of her and grasped the smooth ridge that ran along the top of the chariot, effectively locking her within the circle of her arms so that she could be sure the girl didn't tumble off.

Lina's ball of light kept pace with them, hovering just above her right shoulder, but its illumination wasn't needed. Torches blazed from silver wall sconces, lighting the smooth, high sides of the dark tunnel through which they flew.

"It is like the Bat Cave."

Lina realized she'd spoken her thoughts aloud when Hades' head tilted down in her direction and he gave her a questioning glance.

"I was just wondering if there were bats in this cave," Lina said sheepishly.

"Yes, often there are," Hades said.

Lina watched his cape billow behind him. "I'll bet they're big bats," she said wryly.

Hades snorted, sounding much like one of his dread steeds. "Do you fear bats, Goddess?"

"I've never thought about it," she said honestly. "Actually, I don't know much about them."

"It is normal to fear that which you do not know," Hades said.

His tone was still fatherly, and, Lina thought, slightly patronizing. She raised an eyebrow at him. If she'd adhered to that belief system, the events of the past day would have paralyzed her.

"I don't think it's normal; I think it's a sign of immaturity," Lina said.

Hades snorted again, irritating Lina with his condescension. "Thus says a very young goddess."

"Maturity cannot always be measured by years," she retorted. He might be Mr. Tall Dark and Batman, but he was certainly going to be in for a surprise if he tried to treat her like she was young and stupid.

Hades' only comment was a piercing look. He shouted another command to his horses and they increased their speed, making further talking impossible. Lina focused on holding onto the chariot and making sure she didn't lose Eurydice's little spirit body during one of their blindingly fast turns.

Just as she was beginning to think that her hands might have formed permanently into claws from clutching the railing so tightly, Hades raised the two-pronged spear to the roof. A flash of light exploded from the spear's points, causing the tunnel to open and the floor to twist upward. With a thunderous roar the chariot shot from the newly exposed exit and, in a rain of impressive sparks from the hooves of the dread steeds, they slid to a halt.

Lina gazed around her in wordless awe. The first thought that struck her was that it wasn't dark anymore. The sky above them was bright and cheerful. Though there was no sun to be seen, it glowed a palette of luscious pastels—colors that ranged from the softest of violets to Caribbean turquoise and buttercup yellow. She could hear the lyrical calling of songbirds, and the breeze that caressed her face brought with it a sweet, familiar scent. Lina inhaled deeply. Where had she smelled that wonderful fragrance before? Her eyes moved from the subtle beauty of the sunless sky and her question was answered.

Tall, stately trees Lina thought she recognized as cypress lined the path on either side of them, but instead of growing out of marshy land, the area beneath them was carpeted, not in moss or swamp, but in flowers. Huge, moonlight colored flowers, the likes of which Lina had only seen one other time.

"They're narcissus flowers!" Lina exclaimed in surprise.

Hades glanced down at her. "Yes, the narcissus is the flower of the Underworld." The god drew in a deep breath. "I never tire of their sweet scent."

Lina clamped her mouth shut and said no more, but her mind kept circling around the irony of Demeter using the flower of the Underworld to exchange her soul with Persephone's. So, the Goddess of the Harvest had simply answered her invocation? She had just wanted to help out Lina's bakery as if she were performing a divine Good Samaritan act? Demeter had no hidden agenda, like . . . perhaps . . . a send-Lina-to-Hell-in-Persephone's-place plan? She glanced surreptitiously at the god who stood beside her. He didn't seem apt to leap on her and rape her. But he also wasn't the wooden god Demeter had described. In a very short time he had been intense, sexy, intimidating and kind. Definitely *not* a boring, asexual, disinterested god of the dead. What was Demeter really up to? Well, Lina wasn't some foolish young girl who had just fallen off the damn turnip truck. She'd keep her eyes open and her guard up. She had a job to do. She'd do it and then she'd go home.

Hades snapped the reins and the chariot started forward again. This time, Lina was relieved to note, at a more sedate speed. The woods on either side of them were thick and ancient looking. Exotic birds flitted playfully within their boughs and called to one another with melodic voices. The cypress roots were mantled in deep tapestries of the distinctive narcissus flowers, and occasionally Lina would hear the liquid whispering of a stream and catch sight of a crystal pool reflecting the watercolor sky. From time to time Lina thought she saw the flickering shapes of spirits, but when she tried to focus on the elusive images they disappeared, and no other souls traversed the road with them.

"It is so very beautiful," Eurydice said in the hushed voice of a child in church.

"It certainly is," Lina agreed. Then she glanced at the globe of light that hovered above her shoulder. Opening her hand, she held it, palm up, in the direction of the little light. "It doesn't look like we need you now." Instantly, the light reacted by diving into her palm, and with a popping noise it disappeared back into Lina's skin. Her palm tingled, and she had to force herself not to wipe it against her robe. Instead, she smiled brightly at Eurydice and pretended that it was normal for semi-sentient balls of light to pop into her skin.

"See," she told the girl, "you were right not to be afraid. There's nothing horrible or scary here."

The dark god beside them nodded in agreement and smiled kindly at the little spirit. "For such as you, child, death need hold no terrors. You shall spend eternity enjoying the delights of the Elysian Fields, or, if you so choose, you may drink from Lethe, the River of Forgetfulness, and be reborn to live another mortal life."

Lina tried to hide her surprise. Souls could choose to be reborn? She looked at the girl who stood quietly within the protection of her arms. She'd died so young; surely she would want the chance to be reborn and to live a long, full life.

"That sounds wonderful, Eurydice. You could rest for awhile. Maybe loll about the Fields like you're on a mini-vacation—like I am!" Lina grinned at her. "Then drink from the forgetful river and have a whole new life to live."

Lina's grin faded as she watched Eurydice's already pale face blanch to an almost colorless white. Her eyes clearly reflected an inner terror.

"What is it, honey?" Lina asked.

"Why can I not stay with you, Persephone?" Eurydice pleaded desperately. "I don't want to be reborn. I don't want to, even if I forget my past life I might make the same mistakes, might choose the same—" Her voice broke off with a sob and she buried her face in her hands.

Lina looked helplessly at Hades as she wrapped the girl in her arms. The god was studying the young spirit with knowing eyes.

"Be at ease, child," Hades said. "As long as your goddess remains in the Underworld, you will have access to her. Hush now, your tears are not necessary. Elysia is different for each mortal spirit—your Elysia will simply be found at Persephone's side."

Lina smiled her thanks to Hades. Eurydice was just young and frightened. If Hades allowed the girl to stay with her, that would give Eurydice six months to become settled. By the time Lina had to leave, the girl would be so used to the Underworld that she wouldn't be bothered by the absence of her goddess. Maybe Lina could even talk her into being reborn once she relaxed and gained some confidence. Lina wondered what had happened in her short life to cause the girl such pain, and made a mental note to talk with her about it when the little spirit was feeling more secure.

Eurydice raised her face. "Truly? I may stay with Persephone?" she asked Hades.

"Truly. You have the word of the God of the Underworld," Hades replied solemnly.

Eurydice's face blossomed with joy. "Oh, thank you, Hades! I promise to serve my goddess well."

Lina chucked the girl under her chin. "Friends don't serve one another, Eurydice."

The girl thought for a moment before speaking. "If you will not allow me to serve you, will you allow me to look after you and be certain that you are well cared for?"

Lina opened her mouth to assure the girl that she was more than capable of taking care of herself, but Eurydice's desperate expression stopped her words. The girl obviously needed someone on which to focus her attention. Maybe it would be best, at least for a little while, that she be kept busy.

"I'd be honored to have you look after me, Eurydice," Lina said, returning the girl's enthusiastic hug of thanks. "My mother has often told me that I need a keeper." Actually, it was her grandmother who had made the comment on the occasion of the zillionth time she had spilled some kind of food on herself— and she had made the comment in Italian, but Lina refrained from sharing the rest of the sentiment with Eurydice.

"As you will see, child, my palace has many rooms. You shall have one near your goddess." With a flourish, Hades swept his arm ahead of them and the two women looked up. "Behold, the Palace of Hades."

They had come to a place where the road made an abrupt T. The left-handed fork disappeared quickly into the thick forest, but it was the right-handed branch to which Hades drew their attention. It curved gracefully, circling a magnificent castle.

Lina's jaw dropped open. She told herself to close her mouth, but she couldn't keep from gawking like a bumpkin. The castle was built of the same black marble as was the path they had been following. It rose above them, stretching impressive, peaked towers and sweeping, balustraded roofs up into the violet sky. It, too, appeared to be made of a single piece of stone. Tall, arched mullioned windows were gaily lighted from within, giving the huge structure an inviting appearance. From the top of the tallest of the circular towers flew a great, black flag. Lina squinted and shielded her eyes with her hand so that she could see the coat of arms depicted in flashing silver. On one side of the flag was an ornate helmet; on the other was the figure of a rearing stallion. Lina smiled. The stallion looked very familiar.

"One of the dread steeds?" she asked Hades, pointing to the flag.

"Yes, it is Orion." Hades nodded in the direction of the lead horse, who turned his head and pricked his ears at the sound of his name. "He is, indeed, one of my steeds, though today he was only dread in theory."

"I think he is very dread," Eurydice said.

"There you have it," Lina called to the black stallion. Orion tossed his head and nickered in response. "Your reputation is safe."

Hades made a sound of disgust, which Lina ignored.

"Your palace is amazing. I can't wait to see inside," she said.

"It is a wonder that few immortals have experienced."

Hades sounded like a fond parent speaking with pride about a favored child, and it was easy to understand why. Lina had certainly never seen its like. Not in the old oil mansions of Tulsa, and not in the magnificent ancient structures of Florence.

The god pointed the chariot down the road that wrapped around the palace and as they turned the corner Lina gasped. Beautifully manicured gardens stretched in tier after tier behind the palace. Lovely fountains bubbled in happy voices. Hedges were trimmed to form perfect geometrical shapes. Flowers bloomed in profusion. Lina saw many she recognized, orchids, lilies, roses, and, of course, the ever-present narcissus, as well as several plants that were totally unfamiliar, but they all had one thing in common.

"All the flowers are white," Lina said.

Not that they were all the same. She hadn't realized until then how many different shades of white there could be, but all of them blazed before her—from the pure, bright white of newly fallen snow to the subtle iridescence of pearls—each with its own unique pigment range within the lightest of colors.

"It is the color of the Underworld," Hades explained. "White represents the purity of death."

"I thought black was your color."

"And so it is. Each black animal owes allegiance to me. The black of night and shadows were birthed in my realm, as is the black of that little death known as sleep. White and black—the most perfect of colors. They both belong to the Underworld."

"White for the purity of death. When you explain it like that, it makes perfect sense, but until now I wouldn't have associated white with He"—Lina caught herself, cleared her throat delicately as if she'd experienced a tickle, and continued—"the Underworld."

Hades looked pleased as he guided the chariot along a section of the path that branched from the main road. It angled around behind the palace and led to a long, narrow building made of the same black marble, obviously an opulent stable. They halted before it, and four spectral men emerged from the building, each wearing black livery garments bearing the same silver devices as the flag, and each took charge of one of the stallions.

"Treat them well," Hades commanded the ghostly men as he helped Lina and Eurydice from the chariot and gestured for them to precede him to the palace. "They have had an"—he paused, glancing at Lina and raised his dark eyebrows—"unusual day."

Lina blinked, surprised by his teasing tone. Then she said, in a voice staged loud enough for the stablemen to hear, "Well, they certainly scared me. Boy, they aren't called the Dread Steeds of Hades for nothing." She elbowed Eurydice. "Right?"

The girl stifled her smile and nodded vigorously. "Yes, Goddess!"

Hades snorted.

One of the dread steeds nickered like a colt at Lina, causing his stableman to send the goddess a bewildered look. Lina covered her laugh with a cough and quickened her steps to keep the dread steeds from embarrassing themselves.

CHAPTER NINE

"IT's even more beautiful on the inside," Lina said, so fascinated she couldn't stop staring around her.

They entered the palace from the rear, going through an intricately carved wrought iron gate and then crossing a wide hall that led to an impressive courtyard that seemed to have been built in the center of the palace. In the middle of the courtyard there was a huge fountain, as intimidating as Rome's Fontana di Trevi, except that the god depicted rising from the waters in the back of the chariot wasn't Neptune, it was Hades in all of his grim splendor, pulled, of course, by the famous steeds of dread. White flowers grew in clumps around marble benches— the ever-present narcissus, as well as a delicate blossom Lina didn't recognize.

"What is that flower?" she asked the god.

"Asphodel," he said, giving her an odd look. "It surprises me that you did not recognize it, Persephone."

Oops. Lina avoided his keen gaze by bending down and pretending to study the little plant. The Goddess of Spring should know her flowers.

She laughed nervously. "Of course, I recognize it now. It must be the unusual light here that made it appear strange to me." She held out one arm so that the soft, blush-like light glowed off the alabaster of Persephone's skin. "It's so different from sunlight. It makes everything seem somehow changed, even things that should be familiar." She smiled at the irony of implying that the arm she held out was anything like familiar.

"The light in my realm was created by me, and it is as different from Apollo's orb as I am from the God of Light." Hades' voice sharpened and he became instantly defensive.

"Oh . . . well . . ." Lina said uncomfortably. "I didn't mean to imply that I didn't like it. On the contrary, I think it's beautiful. It's just different, that's all."

Hades didn't reply, he just watched her steadily with those intense, expressive eyes. Lina thought it was little wonder that he didn't get many visitors; his moods were like an amusement park ride. Up and down, they changed with dizzying speed. Maybe she'd talk to him about that before she left. She might as well help Hades out while she was there, as well as whatever she needed to do for the dead. Actually, the thought was satisfying. What little she had already seen of the Underworld was far too beautiful to be buried in superstition and misinformation. And Hades was nothing like the uninteresting god Demeter had described. Lina looked slantwise at him. He was a sleek panther of a man, volatile and intriguing. What Hades needed was a good marketing campaign to bring about a change in image. Lina couldn't help smiling secretly to herself. She had always been excellent at marketing.

The three of them walked slowly across the large courtyard. Soon, Lina found herself completely engrossed in her surroundings. Beautiful statuary of nude gods and goddesses dotted the area. They were crafted so expertly from cream-colored marble that they appeared to be living flesh. Lina hoped that her temporary job wouldn't keep her too busy to enjoy the garden. It would be the perfect place to sit, sip wine and daydream.

"After your journey I imagine you would enjoy some refreshments," Hades said suddenly. "I would be pleased if you would join me." Then he added hastily, as if he expected her to refuse him and he wanted to provide her a credible excuse, "Unless you are too fatigued, which would be understandable."

"I'm not tired at all, and I am very hungry." Lina smiled at the somber god, wanting to put him at ease.

"Very well then," Hades said, his expression relaxing a little. "I will have you shown to your room." He nodded at Eurydice. "And you to yours, child, which you can be certain will be near your goddess."

The little spirit grinned happily and Lina felt a rush of warmth for Hades and the compassion he was showing Eurydice. As they continued through the courtyard Lina searched her memory. What did she know about Hades? She couldn't remember reading much about him. He was the King of Hell who had abducted the young Persephone. What else? Persephone's reservoir of knowledge stirred and whispered: *Hades . . . somber, reclusive, stern . . . the gloomy god enriches himself with mortal tears.*

Lina tried not to frown as she listened to her inner voice. He certainly didn't act like Eurydice's tears would in any way enrich him. Actually, it seemed as though the opposite were true. Confused, she shut her mind to Persephone's echo and smiled distractedly at Eurydice who was chattering merrily about the beauty of the white flowers.

The massive courtyard finally ended and they came to two large glass doors, which swung open without Hades touching them.

Magic, Lina thought, trying not to appear startled. She couldn't allow herself to be surprised at magic. She was supposed to be a goddess . . . she was supposed to be a goddess . . . she was supposed to be a goddess. . . . Reminding herself, she kept up the silent mantra. While Lina chanted to herself, Hades stepped aside and motioned for her to enter the palace.

She stepped into a dream.

The floor was the same smooth, seamless black that made up the road and the exterior of the palace, but the inner walls were miraculously changed. They were ebony veined with the palest of white; day and night merged harmoniously together. Silver wall sconces held torches which burned joyously. From tall ceilings hung chandeliers—Lina's eyes were riveted upward—made of faceted stones and candlelight. The flames caught the jewels and sparkled like the sun on water. Directly above their heads was a waterfall of amethyst. A little way down the hall hung another, which looked to be crafted from topaz. Farther on another chandelier winked with the pure green of perfect emeralds.

"Jewels!" Lina shook her head in wonder. "Are the chandeliers really made of jewels?"

"They are. Do not be so surprised, Goddess. Are precious stones not found deep within the earth? And is not the innermost realm of the earth the Under-world?" Hades sounded amused.

"I didn't realize you were God of Jewels, too," Lina breathed, still unable to tear her eyes from the wondrous sight.

"There is much the other immortals do not know of me," Hades said.

"Lord, forgive me for being late. I expected you to arrive at the front of the palace."

The new voice enabled Lina to pull her eyes from the jeweled chandeliers. A man was hurrying down the hall to them. He was wearing a white, toga-like robe, much like the one Hades wore, only less voluminous. He approached the god and bowed deferentially.

"It is no matter, Iapis. I thought the goddess would enjoy entering the palace through the courtyard."

"Certainly, Lord." He bowed again to Hades before turning to Lina. "Goddess Persephone, it is truly a pleasure to welcome Spring to the Underworld."

His bow was precise, but his smile was sincere, and Lina's first impression of him was of an oh-so-perfect British valet, like Anthony Hopkins in *The Remains of the Day*, except that he wore a toga, had more hair and was dead. She smiled graciously, trying to remember to forget the part about him being dead.

"Thank you. From what little I've seen of the Underworld I am already very impressed."

"Goddess, the trunks that your great mother sent have already been un-packed and arranged in your chamber. If you follow me I will show you the way and see that you are settled in." He glanced at Hades. "If that suits you, Lord."

"Yes, yes," he waved his hand dismissively. "You know best in these matters, Iapis. Oh, and find a room near her goddess for this little spirit. She has chosen to stay by Persephone's side."

Iapis nodded solemnly in acknowledgment.

Hades turned to Persephone. "You have only to call Iapis when you are ready for refreshment, and he will show you the way to me." The god inclined his head slightly, spun neatly on his heel and strode quickly away, cloak billow-ing in his wake.

Lina felt her eyes being drawn after his retreating form. She watched as he disappeared around a corner. The last thing she saw was his cloak. Batman. She couldn't help it. He really reminded her of Batman. And she had to admit that she'd always been ridiculously attracted to Batman, especially the one played by pouting, angst-ridden Val Kilmer. He and Hades had the most sensual lips. . . .

"Goddess?" Iapis said.

"Oh, I'm sorry. I was just so intrigued with the gorgeous . . . uh . . . chandeliers." Lina realized she was babbling, but she couldn't seem to make her mouth stop. "They're so unusual. My breath has been taken away by the beauty of the palace."

Iapis inclined his head in acknowledgment of her compliment, neatly ignoring the fact that her cheeks had suddenly become flushed.

"Hades designed the chandeliers himself."

"Really?" Now she was intrigued.

Iapis motioned for her to precede him down the long hall to their right. Lina walked slowly, and Eurydice stayed close to her side. The servant's voice took on a professorial tone as he walked and talked.

"Indeed. Hades has overseen each aspect of the creation of his palace and the surrounding grounds. There was no detail too minute for my Lord's attention; nothing that was beneath his notice. He has an artist's eye for color and surface, and a fine sense of design. The Palace of Hades is a monument to the God of the Underworld."

Lina pondered Iapis' words. So the stern, brooding, nonsexual, mortal-tear-loving God of the Underworld had fashioned the marvels that surrounded her. He had an artist's eye and a fine sense of design. Could a passionless, boring god have created such exquisite beauty with loving attention to detail? She didn't know about immortals, but she did have a mature woman's knowledge of mortal men, and she couldn't imagine a passionless man being capable of such an amazing creation.

"I like the flowers that are carved into the walls," Eurydice said, shyly pointing to the crown molding that framed each window and arched doorway under which they passed.

"Yes, Hades is quite fond of the narcissus flower, and has added it to much of the palace detailing." Iapis smiled at the little spirit.

"I'm sorry, seems I've forgotten all my manners today," Lina said. "Iapis, this is my friend"—she paused at the girl's sharp intake of breath when she used the word *friend* and gave her a fond look—"Eurydice."

Iapis stopped to bow to the girl. Eurydice responded with a graceful curtsy.

"I will be taking care of Persephone," Eurydice said, surprising Lina with the determination in her voice.

"I am quite sure that you will do an admirable job," Iapis said patiently.

"Perhaps we should meet daily so that you can keep me informed of your goddess's needs."

"Yes, I like that idea," Eurydice said.

Lina kept quiet. She didn't want to tarnish the happy expression on Eurydice's face. Like it or not, she had definitely acquired a keeper.

"Shall we go on, Goddess?"

Lina nodded and continued down the spacious hall. On her right, the wall of windows afforded a wonderful view of the palace's courtyard. She'd already lost count of the number of rooms that branched off to her left, but she had caught glimpses of ornately appointed chambers and an occasional semi-transparent form as it glided around a corner.

Yes, the beautiful Palace of Hades would certainly qualify as a haunted castle. Lina thought about all of the A&E Specials she'd watched over the years: "Haunted Hotels of Europe," "The Top 10 Most Haunted Mansions," "A&E's Haunted Bed and Breakfast List." Another spirit-like figure flitted past the edge of her vision. The Arts & Entertainment Channel would truly love this place.

Iapis guided them down the seemingly endless hall. They made several turns, and Lina felt totally lost. Finally, they came to a halt in front of a large door that was covered with silver overlay fashioned in the form of a blooming narcissus.

"Persephone, this will be your chamber," Iapis announced.

As with Hades, the door opened without the need for Iapis to touch the silver handle.

The sweet smell of blooming flowers welcomed Lina as she stepped into the chamber. Large arrangements of moon-colored bouquets standing in crystal vases dotted the opulent room. One wall had floor-to-ceiling windows which opened out onto a spacious marble balcony. Cream- colored velvet drapes were tied back with thick silver ropes so that the view of the rear grounds was spectacular. A fire crackled cheerfully in a man-sized fireplace. Several wardrobes of dark wood stood against another wall, divided by an impressive dressing table, which was laden with all sorts of women's toilette items. But what drew Lina's attention was the huge canopied bed. It was the most magnificent piece of furniture she had ever seen. The linens matched the velvet drapes and were exquisitely decorated with silver embroidery. The curtains of the canopy were a pale color that reminded Lina of fog—almost insubstantial in their diaphanous delicacy.

"Your bathing chamber is through that door, Goddess." Iapis said, pointing to another, smaller version, of the silver-encrusted entry door. "I have had your clothing and other items put away. Please let me know if all is not to your liking."

"I'm sure everything will be wonderful. Thank you, Iapis. This is an amazing room."

Iapis bowed. "I simply followed my Lord's instructions. When he received word from Demeter that you would be sojourning within his realm he ordered this chamber be prepared for you."

"But if there is something the goddess needs, she will inform me and I will pass that along to you," Eurydice interposed quickly.

"Of course, Eurydice. I will always defer to your knowledge of Persephone's needs."

Lina noticed how neatly Iapis covered his chuckle, clearing his throat and making his voice sound sincere and serious. He really was very kind, Lina realized. She smiled her thanks to him and he inclined his head discreetly in acknowledgment.

"Goddess, will you need assistance in dressing?" Iapis asked.

"Oh, no!" Lina answered hastily, aware of the fact that Eurydice's mouth had already opened. "I can manage just fine on my own. At least this one time," she added, noting Eurydice's disappointed look.

"Very well, Goddess. When you have freshened, you need only speak my name and I will escort you to Hades."

Lina nodded and smiled like that was how she usually summoned people.

"Until then, Goddess, I will leave you to your privacy." He bowed neatly to Lina. "Eurydice, your chamber is just down the hall. Shall I show you there?"

The girl looked nervous and Lina patted her arm reassuringly.

"Go on. I'll be fine. If I need you I can call you," Lina said, without thinking.

"Of course, if your goddess requires your aid, she need only summon you with a word," Iapis said.

Lina breathed a sigh of relief that her slip in wording hadn't been obvious. She'd meant *call* her, like with a cell phone.

"Well, if you are sure you do not need me," Eurydice said.

"Yes, yes, I'll be fine. You go settle into your room," Lina assured her.

"You will summon me if you have need?"

"Yes, child, yes," Lina said, trying to be patient. All she really wanted was a chance to be alone and to collect her thoughts.

"Come, Eurydice," Iapis told the girl, which was the final push she needed to make her leave the room.

Lina could hear them discussing "Persephone's needs" as the thick door swung closed of its own accord. She almost said "I need a drink" aloud, but she was afraid either or both of them would rush back to complete her request.

CHAPTER TEN

THE wardrobes were filled with clothes—gorgeous, expensive, silky robes in every color imaginable—but all of a similar style. Loose, long skirts, some slit up the side and some not, high waistlines and form-fitting bodices designed by wrapping lengths of fabulous material around and draping the folds over her chest. They were all beautiful and exceedingly feminine, which was in direct contrast to how Lina usually dressed. At home she usually chose comfortable velour sweat suits or shorts and T-shirts, depending on the weather. For work she had several well-tailored, professional looking suits, some with slacks, some with skirts. She tended to choose neutral colors, so that she could mix and match and expand her wardrobe. She let her hand slide across the silky material, enjoying the feel of the fabric as well as the bright, contrasting mixture of colors. When had she started dressing like a corporate matron? Probably about the time she had given up on romance. The thought was an unpleasant realization, and she pushed it aside, refocusing her concentration on the wardrobes.

In the wide, deep drawers there was a plethora of filmy undergarments, as well as delicate leather slippers and long, feminine nightgowns that reminded Lina of something an old-time movie star would have worn.

"Well, they did call them goddesses of the silver screen," Lina whispered as she fingered a particularly beautiful wrap.

The vanity had been stocked with more makeup and hair paraphernalia than a beauty supply store.

"So this is Hell. I've got to remember to be a really bad girl when I get back," Lina muttered, picking through a glittering pool of eye shadows.

The bathroom was another marvel. The bathtub was more like a bathpool, and someone had already filled it to brimming with steaming water that beckoned, making Lina realize just how grubby her journey had made her feel. She'd take a quick bath, change her clothes, freshen her makeup, then she'd call Iapis or Eurydice or both of them, Lina sighed, and be escorted to have refreshments with Hades. What did one eat in Hell, she wondered as she wandered around the huge bathroom.

"Hope it involves more ambrosia," she told a collection of colorful glass bottles of various shapes and sizes covering a marble ledge. Lina pulled the stoppers off each of them, sniffing appreciatively at their oily scents until she found one that she particularly liked, which smelled of lilies, then she poured it into the pool. From another ledge she grabbed a comb and used it to secure the mass of hair she piled atop her head. Undressing quickly she slid into the gloriously hot water and settled gingerly against the bottom with a long sigh of satisfaction.

She could have stayed there forever, but she reminded herself that Hades was waiting for her, and she certainly didn't want Iapis bursting in on her. She hurried through the wonderful bathing experience, promising herself that very soon she would pamper herself with a really long soak.

Rising out of the water she searched for a towel, which she quickly located on a shelf near the huge mirror.

And Lina froze, transfixed by her reflection. No, it wasn't *her* reflection, she reminded herself. It was Persephone, and she truly was a goddess. Of course she had realized before then that her body was different. Of course she'd known that her soul possessed a younger, prettier woman's body. But she'd had no idea . . .

Her slender hand reached up to trace a path along one of Persephone's perfect cheekbones. Her face was stunning. Luminous eyes, a remarkable shade of violet, were framed by thick, black lashes and arching brows. Her lips—Lina touched them—were full and the color of a blush. Lina knew, because as her eyes traveled down the rest of her naked body her cheeks flushed to that same lovely tint. Persephone was lush. Her breasts were high and round, as perfect as the rest of her. Her hand moved lightly over one smooth mound. When the pink nipple hardened instantly in response, sending a sweet, tingling sensation through her body, Lina watched the lovely lips open in surprise as she uttered a little gasp. Was this body ultra-sensitive, or had it just been so long since Lina had allowed herself to have sexual feelings that she had forgotten the thrill of arousal?

And what about Persephone's love life? Was the goddess a virgin? Or did she have many lovers? Lina's gaze continued to study her new body while she considered the questions. The goddess was slender without being gaunt. Her waist curved in gracefully, but her hips swelled, full and sexy. Her legs were long and beautifully shaped; the area between them was covered with a V of soft, dark curls. Her hand moved to touch that inviting triangle.

Lina's eyes snapped guiltily up. She shook her head, laughing nervously at her reflection.

"Oh, for heaven's sake. I have to live with this body. I can't be embarrassed to look at it." Lina grabbed a towel and began to vigorously dry herself, purposefully going intimately over every part of "her" body. "Or anything else." But as she chose a new dress and absently combed through the tangle of her long hair, questions kept circling around her thoughts.

What kind of life had Persephone lived? She must have had a lover—at least one. With this body, how could she have been celibate? Was that really why Demeter had made this exchange? Maybe she wanted to get her daughter away from an undesirable boyfriend. Lina sighed and rubbed her forehead. Too much had happened too quickly. She had no idea if the gods required sleep, but she certainly felt exhausted. She needed to get the refreshments over with so she could come back to her room and really relax and refresh.

Clearing her throat she called aloud, "Iapis! I'm ready for refreshments now."

Within two breaths there was a firm knock at her door.

"Come in," she said.

The door swung open and Iapis bowed to her. "Goddess, please follow me this way." He motioned down the hall the direction in which they had come.

"Thank you, Iapis. I am very hungry."

"I believe you will be pleased with the delicacies Hades has chosen to honor you."

Lina raised her eyebrows. "Hades cooks, too?"

Iapis laughed. "You shall see, Goddess."

Lina bit her lip and followed him from the room. What was she thinking? There was probably no cooking in Hell. Like spirits would need to eat? She remembered Eirene pulling wine from an invisible fold in the air. Goddess of Morons, that's what she was. She needed to keep her mouth closed and her eyes open until she learned the ropes of her new job.

Iapis interrupted her self-chastisement. "Goddess, shall we include Eurydice? I would not want the little spirit to think I am attempting to usurp her position."

"Yes, that's very thoughtful of you, Iapis." Lina raised her voice. "Eurydice! I need you."

Almost instantly a door down the hall opened and Eurydice burst out, rushing to her goddess's side in a flutter of wispy clothing and flying hair.

"Oh, Persephone! I am so glad you called," she gushed, hugging Lina.

"Your goddess thought that you might wish to accompany us so that you could find your way back easily if she called for refreshment at an odd hour."

Once again, Lina was impressed by Iapis' kind treatment of the girl.

"Thank you, Iapis, for putting it so nicely," Lina said.

"Of course." Eurydice nodded her head several times, reminding Lina of an exuberant puppy trying its best to be obedient. "I need to know many things so that I can properly care for Persephone."

With an effort, Lina kept from sighing aloud.

"Persephone, Eurydice, if you follow me, I will be pleased to escort you to my Lord."

Iapis led them through a maze of corridors, all the while explaining, mostly to Eurydice, that even though the palace was large, it was really not difficult to remember one's way around it. Hades had designed it in sections. The frontmost part of it was designated as the Great Hall of Hades, where he held court and heard the petitions of the dead. There was a smaller central meeting area, which was where they were headed. It was linked to the guest wing—where Persephone and Eurydice were staying—complete with two ballrooms. Lina wondered briefly why Hades had bothered to build an entire wing for guests and two rooms for dancing, when he obviously wasn't used to receiving visitors, but she kept her thoughts to herself and let Iapis speak uninterrupted.

"There is an entire wing of the palace designated as Hades' personal chambers. So, as you can see, Eurydice, you need only become familiar with the positions of the different wings of the palace to know where you are."

"Yes, I understand. Perhaps I could be allowed some material with which to draw, so that I might sketch myself a simple map," Eurydice said, looking expectantly at Lina.

"Absolutely. I think that's a great idea. Maybe it could help me find my way around, too. I'm terrible with directions," Lina said. "Iapis, do you think you could find some drawing materials for Eurydice."

"Of course, Goddess. It will be my personal pleasure to be sure your friend has all that she requires," Iapis said.

"Thank you," Lina and Eurydice said together, grinning at each other as their words mixed harmoniously.

Iapis turned another corner and stopped between a huge set of double doors, which, of course, opened without his touch into a large room in which there was one focal point—an enormous black marble dining table. Directly over the table were suspended three massive crystal chandeliers. Lina squinted her eyes against their bright, faceted beauty and suddenly understood that the glittering stones were probably not crystals at all.

"Diamonds," Eurydice said in a hushed voice.

"Yes," Iapis said. "My Lord chose to hang the diamond chandeliers in this room because they cast such perfectly clear light over the dining table and complement the chrysocolla candelabrum."

Lina dropped her stunned gaze from the diamonds to the half dozen multi-titiered candelabrums neatly arranged across the vast length of the table. They were made of an unusual blue-green stone into which blazing snow-white candles fitted neatly.

"Chrysocolla?" Lina asked. "I don't think I'm familiar with that stone."

"Chrysocolla hides itself well within the earth." Hades' deep voice made Lina jump. She hadn't heard him come into the room. "I enjoy its unique blending of the colors of turquoise, jade, and lapis lazuli, but the reason I chose to display the chrysocolla candelabrums on the dining table is because of the stone's properties." He paused, as if deep in thought.

"What are the stone's properties?" Eurydice asked, her voice barely above a whisper.

Hades smiled warmly at her. "Chrysocolla is a stone of peace. It soothes the emotions."

Eurydice's eyes widened. "I think it is the perfect choice for a dining chamber."

"I agree with you, little one," Iapis said, causing the girl to blush. Then he bowed to Hades and Persephone and gestured to the table. "If you wish to be seated, I will inform the servants that you are ready to be served."

Hades nodded curtly and strode to the table. He pulled out a high-backed chair that sat in front of one of the two place settings near the end of the massive marble expanse, and motioned for Lina to take her seat.

"Thank you," Lina said, smoothing the silky folds of her skirt as she sat. She'd been so entranced by the chandeliers and the candelabrums that she hadn't even noticed the beautiful china and crystal dishware.

Eurydice had followed Iapis from the room, leaving Lina alone with the god. She smiled nervously at him and tried not to fidget. Hades had changed his clothes. His robes were as expansive, and just as black as the toga-like attire, but these were trimmed in an intricate silver-edged design. His hair was still tied back in the same thick queue, but he was minus the cape. Any other man would have looked ridiculous and probably even effeminate in such an Errol Flynn–meets-Zorro-meets-*Gladiator* outfit.

Hades did not.

"I hope your chamber is to your liking."

Good, Lina thought. She'd just make conversation with him. Like he was a normal man.

"It's lovely—just like the rest of your palace," Lina said. "Iapis tells me that I have you to thank for the warm welcome of fresh flowers and a newly drawn bath. Thank you, everything was just perfect. It's like I was an invited guest instead of one who barged in all on her own." She gave him a chagrined smile.

Hades thought he had never seen anything as beautiful as the embarrassed flush that warmed her cheeks, and he suddenly felt himself doing something he hadn't done in centuries. He smiled, leaned forward, captured Persephone's hand and raised it to his lips.

"You are most welcome here, Goddess of Spring."

Lina thought she might fall off her chair. In forty-three years she had never had a man kiss her hand. She wasn't sure of the correct protocol. Did she leave her hand in his? Did she pull it out? Hell! What she really wanted to do was to kiss him back. Instead, she felt her mouth form what was probably a goofy smile.

"Th-thank you," she stuttered.

Hades dropped her hand and looked away from her. Impulsive! He was acting like an impulsive fool. She was a goddess; he could never allow himself to forget that.

Lina watched his expression change and a hardness settle on his features. What was wrong? It wasn't logical, but Lina had a sudden thought that this aspect of Hades—this stern, expressionless god—was a facade he drew over himself as a cover. But why?

Merda, just listening to her thoughts made her want to slap her own face and tell herself to snap out of it! When had her disciplined, well-ordered mind begun having such delusions of romance? She knew the answer already. It had been that damn narcissus. . . .

Uncomfortable silence crouched between them.

Think of something to say, she ordered herself. She took a deep breath and tried again.

"It's interesting what you said about chrysocolla. I don't know very much about the properties of stones." She glanced up at the brilliantly lighted chandeliers. "For instance, I think diamonds are beautiful, but I have no idea about their properties."

"Diamonds are complex gems." Hades' gaze turned upward, too, and as he warmed to the subject of precious stones his voice began to lose its hard edge. "They promote courage and healing and strength. When worn by warriors they can actually increase physical strength, which is why some mortal cultures go to war wearing them set within arm-bands of platinum or silver."

"And all this time I've only thought of them as a girl's best friend," Lina quipped.

"Are they the gem you prefer?" Hades asked.

Lina opened her mouth to give him an automatic *yes!*, but his penetrating gaze stopped her. Something in his eyes said she should think about her answer more carefully. She closed her mouth and reconsidered.

She didn't have many diamonds. Actually, the only diamonds she'd ever worn had been gifts from her ex-husband. She frowned, remembering how her beautiful, expensive wedding ring, with its large center diamond surrounded by a wealth of glittering baguettes, had become a symbol of bondage rather than of fidelity. Her diamond earrings had been a guilt-induced gift given to her after one of his drunken tirades because he found the growing success of her bakery intimidating. The diamond necklace and gaudy cocktail ring had belonged to his mother—a shallow, manipulative woman who had never liked Lina. Every time she'd worn either of the pieces she had felt shackled to her husband's cold, aloof family. Consequently, she'd stopped wearing them long before she'd stopped being his wife.

When she bought jewelry for herself, she never even considered diamonds.

She smiled as she thought about the lovely, dangling earrings she'd gifted herself on her last birthday. Yes, they would definitely qualify as her favorite stone.

"Amethyst," she said firmly. "My favorite gemstone is amethyst. What are its properties?"

Hades looked surprised, but not displeased. "Amethyst is a spiritual stone, with absolutely no negative side effects or associations with violence or anger. It is the stone of peace. It calms fears and raises hopes. Amethyst soothes emotional storms. Even in situations of potential danger it can come to your aid. It is a wise choice as your talisman."

"I'm so glad to know that." She grinned at him. "No wonder I've always loved it."

The goddess's beauty stunned Hades. When she smiled, she shined brighter than the diamonds over their heads. His stomach tightened. He had forgotten the power of a goddess's beauty and its overwhelming allure. His response to her was basic, his need raw. He felt his buried passion stir, and desires he thought he had entombed eons ago began to stretch and breathe. Hades felt powerless in the wake of the surge of foreign emotions.

"Amethyst matches your eyes perfectly."

His voice was rough and dangerously sexy. Lina's borrowed body responded to it as quickly as her soul and she looked deeply into the god's eyes.

"Thank you, Hades." This time experience took over and she didn't stutter or blush, she purred.

Hades was overwhelmed by the rush of heat that coursed through his blood. Persephone couldn't possibly know what a temptation she was to him. She was a goddess. She was accustomed to commanding the attention of males, mortals and immortals alike, but she was not accustomed to the Lord of the Underworld. She could not know how painful it was for him to see her there before him, so young and beautiful and desirable. With the return of passion, the old emptiness reared alive within him as the ancient difference between Hades and the other immortals reawakened. He forced his gaze from the velvet trap of her eyes.

"Would you like wine?" he blurted.

"Yes, please," Lina said, confused as he suddenly lurched from the table, shouting for wine like he was in the middle of a fish market. What had just happened? He had complimented her eyes, and she had thanked him. Electricity had passed between them. Even a young woman would not have had trouble recognizing that spark, and Lina was no young woman. She had even thought he was leaning toward her, then pain had flashed over his face and the attraction had been shattered. Lina felt like someone had thrown cold water on them.

Two servants rushed into the room, each carrying a pitcher of wine. Hades glowered, pointing to Persephone.

"Do you desire red or white, Goddess?" one of the servants asked.

"Red, please," Lina answered automatically, not caring whether Hades was serving fish, fowl, beef or pasta for dinner. She just hoped that the red was dark and rich and strong. She took a long drink. Thankfully, it was all of the three.

"Leave this wine and bring more," Hades ordered the servant after he had filled the god's goblet. The two immortals drank without speaking.

Hades studied his empty plate, wishing that he were different . . . wishing that her very presence didn't remind him of why he must remain withdrawn from the rest of the immortals.

"The wine is excellent," Lina broke into the silence.

Hades made a sound somewhere in his throat that might have been a grunt of agreement.

"I like red wine best," Lina said. Now that she had started speaking she didn't seem to be able to stop. She held up the crystal goblet and let the diamond light sparkle through it. "This wine reminds me of rubies."

Hades cleared his throat and allowed his eyes to meet hers again.

"Rubies," he repeated her last word, pouncing on a harmless subject. "Did you know that jewelry set with rubies can be worn to banish sadness and negative thoughts?"

"No, I didn't," Lina said, studying the blood-colored wine. "What else can it do?"

"Ruby-set jewelry can also produce joy, strengthen willpower and confidence as well as dispel fear." Hades noted the irony of his words. Perhaps while Persephone visited his realm he should take to wearing rubies.

"I had no idea jewels could be so fascinating," Lina muttered, looking from the diamond chandeliers to the gleaming chrysocolla candelabrum and then back to her ruby-colored wine. "Actually, I haven't given jewels much thought at all, especially lately."

Hades quirked one dark eyebrow up at her. "A goddess who hasn't given jewels much thought. That would make you a unique goddess indeed."

Lina felt a prickle of warning. Had she said too much? She had been so involved in what Hades was saying she had forgotten to remember that she wasn't herself—as confusing as that seemed.

A stream of semitransparent servants carrying trays laden with food, followed by Iapis and Eurydice, entered the room. Lina breathed a sigh of relief at the distraction. "Oh, Persephone, wait until you see what has been prepared for you!" Eurydice gushed. "I've never seen such delicacies."

Lina was already staring at the trays, and she couldn't agree more with the little spirit.

"It smells fantastic," Lina said, and watched in hungry anticipation as trays filled with color and scent and texture were laid reverently before her. There were clusters of white delicacies that Lina realized were several different kinds of flower petals, all of which had been sugared, crystallized, and frozen in perfect bloom. Olives, ranging in color from light green to black crowded against blocks of cheese that were thick and almost as fragrant as the slabs of warm bread that rested beside them. But it was the fruit that kept drawing Lina's eye. It commanded one tray by itself. Its dark pink skin had been broken open, and fat, red beads spilled forth, begging to be consumed.

"Pomegranates." Her lips felt numb.

"Do you not like pomegranates, Persephone?" Hades frowned at her troubled expression. "I can have them taken away."

Lina glanced up to see the covey of servants peering at her with large, pale faces filled with concern.

Don't be paranoid, she told herself, *it's just a silly coincidence.* "I love them. Everything looks absolutely perfect." She purposefully scooped up several of the drops of red fruit and popped them into her mouth. Flavor burst against her tongue and she sighed with delight. "They're wonderful!" She slurred through the sweet juice.

The servants let out a collective breath of happiness.

"All appears to be to my liking, too," Hades said sardonically. Persephone seemed to have cast the same spell over his servants as she had over his horses. "You may leave the platters. If we need more, I will call for you."

The servants scurried back to the kitchen.

"Aren't you going to join us?" Lina asked Iapis, looking from him to Eurydice. Did the dead eat? She had no idea, but it seemed rude not to ask.

"No, Goddess," Iapis said.

"Iapis and I have much to discuss," Eurydice added eagerly. "We are going to get the drawing supplies."

Lina smiled at the girl, glad that she appeared to be so at ease.

"Go ahead. I'll see you tomorrow," Lina said around another mouthful of pomegranate seeds.

"Oh, but you must call for me when you retire tonight so that I may help you ready yourself for bed!" The panicky edge had crept back into her voice.

"I'll be sure I do," Lina said quickly, not wanting to disappoint the child.

Satisfied with her goddess's reassurance, Eurydice was smiling happily as she curtsied to Persephone and Hades before following Iapis from the room.

"She will become more secure with time," Hades reassured her.

"I hope so. She's going to wear me out." Lina sighed.

"The dead require a great deal of care."

Lina nodded in agreement. "It's like the jewels—I had no idea until now."

Hades smiled, charming and relaxed again. "Which is why I have had the food of the Underworld set before you. Refresh yourself, Persephone, so that the little spirit need not be concerned that her goddess is wasting away here below the world of mortals."

"Ha!" Lina began heaping her plate full. "It's not likely that could happen, not surrounded by"—she gestured with the long silver spoon—"all of this."

"It pleases me that you appreciate the beauty of the Underworld," Hades said, helping himself to the olives.

"Who wouldn't?" she said between bites, and was instantly sorry when she saw his expression begin to change again. She thought suddenly that it was as if he placed a blank mask over his face so that he could cloak his emotions at will. She kept glancing nonchalantly at him, waiting for him to discard the mask and become approachable once more. For the next several minutes they ate in silence, until she noticed that the tension in his shoulders seemed to be easing and his features had begun to thaw. She took a sip of wine, considering. Yes, he definitely appeared more at ease with his fork full. Her lips twisted. He was a god, but he was still male.

"Do you mind if I ask you some questions about the dead?" Lina asked.

His eyes shifted from his plate to her and back to his plate again. He chewed and swallowed. "I do not mind," he finally said.

Lina hurried on. "It's just that I don't know simple things, and I don't want to say something that would embarrass Eurydice, or upset her again, like when I mentioned her drinking from that river, um . . ." She floundered.

"Lethe," Hades provided.

"Right, Lethe. See, that's exactly what I mean. I don't know enough about the Underworld."

"Ask as many questions as you desire," he said.

"Okay, well, the delicious food that we're eating makes me wonder if the dead can eat."

"No, the dead do not thirst and hunger as do the living, but their souls do retain the essence of their mortal life, so they carry with them into eternity their unique needs and desires. You have witnessed some of that with your little Eurydice. She carries with her fears and insecurities from the World of the Living, even though the things that troubled her there cannot touch her here," Hades replied, trying to hide his surprise at her question. Persephone was certainly not what he had expected. Unlike any other immortal he had ever known, she appeared to be honestly interested in his realm and the spirits of the dead.

"That makes sense." She frowned as she nibbled on a sugared white petal. "It's obvious that memories from her life are definitely bothering Eurydice. Poor kid. I wish there was something I could do."

"There is, Persephone, and you are already doing it. The little spirit needs to feel security and a sense of belonging. She would have eventually found those things in Elysia, but you have brought them to her by giving her a place at your side. She feels comfortable now and useful, and much less apt to obsess about lost chances and what might have been."

Hades smiled encouragement to the young goddess. She had done well by the little spirit. Too many immortals would have believed that noticing Eurydice's distress was beneath them. She was no longer among the living; therefore, she could no longer worship them. So the spirit was no longer of interest to them. Persephone's actions thus far told him that she did not adhere to that type of cavalier belief system. Hades watched Persephone ponder his words as she sipped her wine. The goddess was a mystery to him. She had the beauty of an immortal, but she seemed so different.

"That makes me feel better," Lina said, telling herself firmly that she was talking about Eurydice and not about the warmth of Hades' smile. She was quickly becoming fascinated with the dead—and not just with their god. "Do they sleep, too?"

Hades' eyes crinkled at the edges in amused reaction to her unusual questions. He had never had a conversation like this before, and he was surprised to realize how much he enjoyed talking with the young goddess about his realm.

"They do not sleep exactly as we do, or as do living mortals, but they require rest."

"Are your servants like Eurydice? I mean, did they choose to stay here with you rather than go on to Elysia?"

"Some did, but not out of love for me, as has your Eurydice. For most it is simply that they find comfort in holding fast to the echo of their mortal lives. Others are performing duties as a part of penance for past deeds."

Hades helped himself to the fruit of the Underworld while he awaited her next question. He could almost see her teeming thoughts. She had stopped eating and was twirling a strand of her long hair around one finger, an action that he found strangely endearing.

"So, Iapis must be one of the dead who stays because he loves you."

This time Hades could not help laughing aloud. "Iapis is not one of the dead, Persephone, he is a daimon. But, yes, he has chosen to remain forever by my side."

Lina didn't know what stunned her most—hearing that Iapis was a demon and/or the effect Hades' laughter had on her.

She reacted first to the least volatile of the two.

"Iapis is a demon?" she squeaked.

At the second burst of Hades' laughter the servant's door swung open and several startled heads peeked into the dining room then retreated quickly, but not before Lina registered their shocked expressions.

"I said he is a daimon, not a demon." Hades shook his head at the young goddess.

"Oh, well, of course," Lina sputtered while her mind screamed WHAT THE HELL IS A DAIMON? Thankfully, her inner voice provided an answer. *Daimon—a spirit of a lower divinity than the Olympian gods. They are guardians and semi-deities. They are immortal.*

"Young Persephone, how sheltered you must be not to recognize Iapis as a daimon," he said, still chuckling.

The damn man was laughing at her and looking at her with the same benevolent, fatherly expression he'd used on Eurydice. And he'd just called her "young Persephone!" Like she was a silly little girl! He had no idea he was dealing with a grown woman. One who definitely did not like being the butt of male jokes. Her irritation made her forget that he was God of the Underworld and she was visiting his realm. In that moment he was just another man who had pissed her off. Without stopping to consider the consequences, she narrowed her eyes at him and edged Persephone's soft voice with her own flint.

"I suppose in some ways I have been sheltered. I've been taught to believe that one's guests should not be used as a source of comedic fodder."

Hades sobered instantly as he recognized within her eyes the coldness of a goddess's wrath. He was a fool. He had allowed himself to relax around her and had stumbled into the snare of his own fantasies. Persephone was of Olympus—he must never forget that. He inclined his head in stiff acknowledgment of her reprimand. "I ask your forgiveness, Goddess. There is no excuse for my rudeness."

Without speaking further, he stood, bowed again, and walked from the room, leaving Lina to stare after him and curse sincerely and fluently in Italian.

CHAPTER ELEVEN

"IAPIS!" Hades' voice echoed through his vast chamber.

"My Lord." The daimon materialized within two breaths after his name had been spoken.

"Go to her. When she has finished her meal, show her the way back to her chamber. Be certain she has everything she desires." Hades paced restlessly as he talked. "I insulted her."

Iapis stayed silent, but he raised one brow.

"Then I left her there. She had not even finished her meal." Hades raked a hand through his hair, causing some of the shorter strands to come loose. He looked at his loyal friend. "You know I have never been able to do this."

"This?" Iapis asked.

"This! This! This mixing with them. This insane ritual of feint and stab they require to maintain their interest."

"Perhaps you mean conversing with a goddess?"

"Of course that is what I mean!" Hades exploded.

Nonplussed by the god's show of temper, Iapis kept his voice calm and inquisitive. "And was Persephone requiring much, as you call it, feint and stab before you insulted her?"

Hades stopped his pacing and rubbed his brow, considering Iapis' question. "No," he said truthfully.

"So you had been conversing with her?"

"Yes, yes, yes," he admitted and then reality caught up with him. He had been enjoying himself. She had shown such interest in his realm, and she had been so easy to talk to—so unlike Aphrodite or Athena or . . . his lips curled in a sneer as he thought of the other young goddesses he had known. They were spoiled, manipulative beauties who rarely thought beyond their own needs and desires. When Persephone's voice had hardened at what she had taken as an insult, he had instantly been reminded of those other lovely immortals and his reaction had been automatic. He had absented himself from her presence.

"Did you mean to insult her?" Iapis asked.

"Of course not!" He started pacing again. "I thought what she said was amusing." He gave Iapis a dark look. "She had mistaken you for one of the dead."

Iapis' lips twitched as he tried not to smile.

"I laughed at her and then I spoke to her as if she were a child. That insulted her. She reacted as any goddess would have." Hades hunched his shoulders.

"You say she reacted as any goddess would have. Then may I assume the dining room has been destroyed and she has departed the Underworld?" Iapis said.

"No, she . . . no. She remains and she destroyed nothing." He stopped his pacing and met the daimon's inquiring gaze.

"Then it appears she did not react as any other insulted goddess," Iapis said logically. "What exactly was her reaction?"

"She said that she was not accustomed to being used as comedic fodder," Hades said.

"And what did you say in return?"

"I apologized and left."

"Might I suggest that the next time you apologize and stay, my Lord?" Iapis said.

"The next time?"

Hades could feel the all-too-familiar burning sensation building in his chest. He knew that soon it would spread to the back of his throat and he would spend another miserable, sleepless night. Too choleric. That is what Hermes said was wrong with him.

Iapis nodded. "The next time."

"She is different." Hades' voice had deepened and he spoke with a quiet, controlled intensity.

"She is, indeed."

"She does not shun the spirits. She . . ." Hades broke off, remembering her flushed reaction to him, the curiosity in her voice and the warmth in her eyes. His jaw clenched. "I should stay far from her for the rest of her visit."

"My friend"—Iapis rested his hand on the god's shoulder—"why not let yourself enjoy her presence?"

"To what end?" Hades rubbed his chest and shrugged off the daimon's hand. "So that I can taste life, and then when she leaves or loses interest in dallying with me—as she must—I am left with what? It is not enough, Iapis. It has never been enough."

And there it was, Hades thought as he began pacing again, the thing that separated him from the rest of the immortals. Unlike the other gods and goddesses, he longed for something that he had witnessed over and over again between the souls of mortals, but he had not glimpsed once, not even briefly, between immortals.

"My Lord," Iapis said softly, "is it not better to experience even a small amount of happiness, than none at all?"

"I was not fashioned as the rest of them. I do not know how to treat love as a plaything."

Iapis looked into the god's haunted eyes and saw there the loneliness that Hades had kept at bay for countless ages. His spirit ached for his friend. The daimon thought about Persephone. There was something about the young goddess that was unique, something besides her much-lauded beauty and her ability to breathe light into darkness. Hades must not shut out Persephone. If he did, he was afraid that the God of the Underworld would forever be closing the door to any chance of relieving the dark loneliness of his existence.

But how was he to coax Hades out of his instinctive reaction to withdraw from the goddess until her visit was complete? His Lord was not used to visitors. His existence was planned and orderly and set, not at all conducive to disturbances from the other immortals. And the Goddess of Spring was a definite disturbance.

She was also beautiful and vivacious and intriguing.

If only Hades could feel as easy with her as he did with the unnumbered dead. Iapis' eyes widened as an idea took root and grew.

"Perhaps that is the answer, Lord."

Hades gestured impatiently for him to continue.

"Imagine that Persephone is simply one of the unnumbered dead."

"Iapis, that is ridiculous."

"Why?" The daimon threw his hands up in frustration. "You're at war within yourself, Hades! You say you should withdraw from her, yet when you speak of her I see in your eyes a spark that has been absent for an eternity. What if the Fates have been kind and there has been another immortal fashioned as you have been? How will you ever know if you remain sealed from everything that is living? Give the goddess a chance, my Lord."

Before Hades could comment, Iapis cocked his head, as if he were listening to an internal voice.

"She has just called my name."

"Go to her!" Hades commanded. But the moment after Iapis vanished the god shouted his name again.

"My Lord?" Iapis asked, rematerializing.

"Invite the Goddess of Spring to join me in the Great Hall tomorrow. Tell her if she is still interested in learning about the Underworld, hearing the petitions of the dead should provide an excellent source of information for her." Hades spoke the words quickly, as if he wanted to get them out of his mouth before he could change his mind.

Iapis smiled enigmatically. "Very good, my Lord."

"Tomorrow, then, Goddess," Iapis said.

He had almost bowed his way from Lina's bedchamber when Eurydice rushed through the open door and ran straight into his backside.

"Uhf!" He staggered forward, tripped over his own feet, and fell head first onto the floor.

Lina and Eurydice stared openmouthed at each other. Lina smiled. She couldn't help it. Iapis usually looked so dignified and there he was, sprawled on the floor with his toga in the air. A choked laugh slipped from her lips.

A small sound escaped from Eurydice. It was soft and fluid and delightful. It was also most definitely a giggle. And it destroyed the last of Lina's self-control.

Iapis stood, struggling to regain his bruised pride, but the musical sound of feminine laughter more than atoned for any ruffling of his dignity, and he found himself joining them.

How he wished Hades could be there. The god so needed laughter in his life.

"I seem to have found a slight"—still chuckling, he glanced down at the smooth expanse of marble at his feet—"something in the floor which tripped me."

"I think its name is Eurydice," Lina chortled.

Eurydice tried unsuccessfully to stifle her giggles with her hand.

"Then I will have to see that I pay special attention to that slight something."

Iapis' eyes were warm with good humor, and, Lina thought as she watched Eurydice's pale cheeks pinken, perhaps something else. She gazed thoughtfully after the daimon as he bowed to her, and this time successfully left the room.

"Oh, Persephone, I have had such a day!" Eurydice skipped over to the nearest wardrobe. She hummed a lively tune and pulled open drawers until she found the goddess's nightdresses. "Iapis found some wonderful parchment and charcoals and I have already begun a preliminary sketch of the palace."

"That's nice, Eurydice," Lina said. Still considering the warmth she had seen in the daimon's eyes, she wasn't really listening as she absentmindedly nodded and allowed the girl to unwrap her robe and help her step out of it. She held out her arms and Eurydice slipped the long nightie over her head. Lina ran her hand down the length of the material. It was white satin that had been intricately embroidered with narcissus blossoms. It felt like water against her skin.

"Come over to the table and sit down while I brush out your hair. You look exhausted," Eurydice said. She had been studying her goddess and she hadn't failed to notice the dark smudges under her violet eyes.

Lina sank into the padded vanity chair, breathing a sigh of pleasure as Eurydice began brushing her hair with long, even strokes. She hadn't realized how tired she had become. The girl chattered happily about the process of mapping the palace while she worked. The sound of her young voice was almost as soothing as the touch of her hands. Lina felt her shoulders relax and her mind wander.

After Hades had stormed out of the dining room, she had finished her meal and the rest of the bottle of wine. No. The truth was first she had cursed and grumbled about men in general, *then* she had decided that she wasn't going to let another man's lapse in good manners ruin a perfectly good dinner. When she finished the scrumptious meal and the excellent bottle of wine, she had simply said Iapis' name aloud. In what seemed like seconds he answered her call, ready to escort her back to her bedroom. During their walk he had made vague, nonspecific references to the lack of visitors in the Underworld and to how little practice he had in entertaining and conversing with guests. He had said that he hoped she wouldn't judge him, or the Underworld, too harshly or too hastily.

Lina heard the real message loud and clear. The "he" was, of course, not Iapis but Hades. He was obviously apologizing for the god's behavior. The wine she had finished by herself and her riled temper had made Lina want to tell Iapis to take a particularly colorful message (in Italian) back to Hades, but the remnants of her good sense had, thankfully, kept her mouth shut.

Hades was a god and she was staying within his realm. It was not smart to antagonize him and now that she was out of his presence and had time to think about the evening, Lina was regretting her little temper tantrum. Hades wasn't a middle-aged divorcé with sweaty palms who had asked her to dinner so he could whine about his exes and then grope her for dessert. He was a powerful immortal, a being she knew little about.

And, just exactly why had she been so pissed off at him? Okay, he had been moody and unpredictable at dinner, but he had also been interesting and sexy. Iapis' explanation about his god's lack of manners made sense. He wasn't used to visitors. Obviously, his social skills were a little rusty. As an immortal being, just how polite did he *have* to be? She thought about Demeter's imperious manner and Eirene's rudeness. Actually, Hades' temperamental behavior seemed to fit right in with those two.

Eurydice finished brushing her hair, but the little spirit obviously felt Lina's tension because her soft, cool hands began gently massaging her shoulders. Lina sighed happily and closed her eyes, letting the girl's touch soothe her nerves and clear her mind.

She'd really had no reason to snap at Hades. He hadn't been making her the butt of his joke, he'd simply been treating her like the naïve young goddess she was masquerading as, and her silly show of temper had done little to prove his opinion of her wrong. If she wanted him to treat her like a mature adult, she really should try acting like one.

Merda! She'd been there less than a day and she was already messing up. Had she completely lost her mind? She was, after all, in the Underworld to do a job. At least she'd had sense enough to say yes when Iapis had extended the invitation to join Hades the next morning to hear the petitions of the dead. She needed to get her head on straight and think of it as nothing more than just another part of the job Demeter had sent her there to do. She needed to be visible to the dead so that her presence could bring them comfort. It had nothing to do with the fact that she wanted to spend more time with Hades because the dark god intrigued her, which was really ridiculous . . . silly . . . foolish.

Yet undeniably true.

She knew it. As Eurydice soothed her frazzled nerves she could even admit it to herself. Hades fascinated her, but so did everything about the Underworld. She felt drawn to him, but it was probably because she had been displaced and everything in that incredible world was so new and unique. How could she not feel curious fascination about the magic that surrounded her? And that magic naturally included the god in charge. It was a perfectly normal reaction for her to feel compelled to find out more about him.

At least that's what she told herself.

"Persephone, you're almost asleep," Eurydice said. She tugged on her goddess's arm, pulling her toward the canopied bed. "Lie down. I will sing to you. Just as my mother used to sing to me."

Too tired to protest, Lina allowed the young spirit to tuck her into the voluptuous, down-filled bed. Eurydice nestled next to her. Still stroking the goddess's hair, she began to sing a soft lullaby about a child who rode on the back of the wind to a many-colored land of dreams.

"Eurydice," Lina said sleepily.

"Yes, Goddess."

"Thank you for taking care of me."

"You are welcome, Persephone," Eurydice said.

Sleep closed gently around Lina, bringing her dreams of riding the wind while she chased Batman's shadow.

CHAPTER TWELVE

THE Great Hall lived up to its name. Lina had thought the dining chamber and her bedroom extravagant, but they paled in comparison to Hades' throne room. The room was enormous, even when judged on the scale of the huge palace. Three colors dominated it—black, white and purple. The floor, walls and cathedral ceiling were all made of the unblemished black of the exterior of the palace, as was the raised dais on which stood a massive throne-like chair, which seemed to have been carved from a single piece of an ethereally white stone Lina did not recognize. On the dais next to the throne there was a tall, narrow table made of the same milky stone. On the table rested a silver helmet which looked oddly familiar to Lina. She stared at it and realized where she had seen it before. It was the same helmet that was emblazoned on the flag that hung over the palace and adorned the uniforms of the stablemen. It winked and sparkled in the candlelight with an otherworldly beauty. She forced her eyes from the helmet to the other color in the room, purple. It came from dozens of chandeliers and wall fixtures, all made of a pure sparkling stone Lina did recognize—amethyst.

Lina hesitated on the threshold of the room, intimidated by its austere grandeur. She felt suddenly small and insignificant and very, very mortal.

"Is something the matter, Persephone?" Eurydice asked.

Lina took a deep breath. She was a goddess, she reminded herself. Yes, it was only temporary, but she was a goddess nonetheless.

"No, honey, nothing's wrong. I'm just admiring the room." She smiled at the little spirit.

"Ah, Hades comes," Iapis said.

Hades entered the Great Hall from a doorway on the opposite side of the room. His gilded sandals rang against the smooth marble floor, and as Lina watched him she felt her heartbeat increase with each of his steps. He was wearing the cape again. It swirled behind him, accentuating his body's long, powerful lines. His toga-like robes at first appeared black, but as the light from the chandeliers touched him, the material shone like a raven's wing with glints of purple and royal blue. His hair was loose and it fell in a thick black curtain around his shoulders. His chiseled jaw was set and his face was dark, his expression somber. He exuded raw, masculine power.

Lina's stomach fizzed. She had to force herself not to twirl her hair nervously.

Hades took the steps of the dais in one stride. He turned and was about to sit when he noticed the three figures standing just inside the entrance across the chamber. His eyes met Lina's and held.

"Persephone," he said, inclining his head slightly, not breaking their gaze. "I am honored to welcome Spring into my Great Hall."

Lina swallowed, wishing her mouth wasn't so dry.

"Thank you, Hades," she said, pleased that her voice sounded strong and clear. "I appreciate your invitation."

"Please, join me," Hades said. Then, breaking the spell that had locked her eyes to his, he shifted his attention to the daimon. "Iapis, have a chair brought for the goddess."

"Of course, my Lord," Iapis called over his shoulder, and a flutter of activity ensued. Within moments spectral servants carried a delicately carved silver chair to join Hades on the dais.

Lina walked into the room. She could feel the god's eyes on her, and she lifted her chin with pride. Eurydice had helped her dress, and Lina was especially pleased that the violet silk she had chosen reflected the color of the amethyst chandeliers blazing over her head as well as her eyes. But she knew the lovely material that draped her body was incidental. That morning as she had been dressing, she had been struck anew by Persephone's immortal beauty. Lina knew that no matter what turmoil was going on within her mind, she crossed the room with all the beauty and grace of a goddess.

When she reached the dais Hades hesitated, then with a sidelong glance at Iapis he met her as she took the first of the dais steps. He offered her his hand, just as he had when he had helped her into his chariot the previous day. When Lina placed her hand within his, the dark god lifted it slowly to his lips.

"I hope you slept well last night, Goddess."

"Yes, thank you, I did," Lina said, trying to ignore the way her skin tingled at his touch.

"It pleases me to hear you say so," Hades said.

Lina smiled foolishly and nodded. Hades was different today—more powerful and more sure of himself. And there was something else about him, too, a magnetism that today he seemed to have focused on her. Standing so close to him she could feel the strength of his presence, and she found it a little intimidating, as well as very, very sexy.

Admittedly, it had been a long time since she had been around such a tall, virile man. She snuck a look at him as he helped her up the steps and led her to her chair. Okay, so she had quite possibly never been around any man like him before. She watched the cape wrap enticingly around his body as he turned and sat beside her. He definitely looked the part of God of the Underworld.

"Eurydice, you need not remain behind. You may stay with your goddess," Hades called to the girl, who was still standing in the doorway.

Ashamed that she had forgotten about the spirit, Lina whispered a quick thank-you to Hades as Eurydice scampered across the room and up the dais steps to take her place next to Lina's chair.

"Carry on as usual, Iapis," Hades said.

Iapis nodded to the god before disappearing from the room.

"Iapis is going to the front of the palace. There he will announce that I will hear petitions. It will not be long before the first begin to arrive," he explained.

"Do you do this every day?" Lina asked.

"No." Hades shook his head.

"Oh," Lina said. "How often do you hear their petitions?"

"As often as I feel it necessary."

"Oh," she said again, feeling uncomfortable at the shortness of his answers.

Hades watched Persephone brush nervously at her hair, and the little gesture of discomfort made him realize that he had fallen back into acting like he was made of stone. *Give the goddess a chance.* His friend's words rang in his memory. Hades cleared his throat and leaned close to Persephone.

"I can sense the needs of the dead. It is not that I can hear their feelings and desires; it is more like I become aware of their increasing restlessness. I can sense when they need me, and that is when I open the Great Hall to hear their petitions."

"That's an incredible gift—to be able to respond to the needs of mortal souls."

Hades turned his head so that he could look into the goddess's violet eyes. Their faces were very close, and he could smell the sweet, feminine scent that clung to her body.

"It does not repulse you that I am linked so strongly to the dead?"

"Of course not," she said. He suddenly looked so vulnerable that Lina had an overwhelming urge to brush her fingers down his face, to soothe the lines of worry that creased his handsome brow. Instead she reached out and took Eurydice's hand. She squeezed it and smiled up at the spirit, who grinned back at her. "Some of my best friends are dead."

Hades looked from the spirit to the goddess and all at once hope blossomed within his chest with such bittersweet intensity that he made a show of calling for wine to cover his heart-wrenching response.

The servants instantly settled a small table beside them and Hades was able to collect himself as they poured golden liquid into two goblets.

Lina nodded her thanks, sipped, and her face broke into a beatific smile.

"Oh, it's ambrosia! This is so delicious. Thank you for thinking of it."

Fascinated, Hades watched her. Why was she so different? She wasn't repulsed by the dead. She obviously cared a great deal about Eurydice; she even called her "friend." And things that most immortals took for granted, like ambrosia and the opulence of the gods, Persephone delighted in, as if everything was new and interesting to her. She was a puzzle, an intriguing puzzle he was beginning to yearn to solve.

"If it pleases you so much, I will have to remember to serve it often," Hades said. He raised his goblet to her.

Stomach fluttering, Lina tapped her goblet against his. The stilted, wooden Hades who had abruptly left their dinner last night appeared to have been banished. He had been replaced by a charming, powerful god. Her cheeks felt flushed and her body was incredibly warm. His dark, magnetic eyes were mesmerizing. Feeling a little lost, she forced her gaze from his and looked around the Great Hall, reminding herself to breathe.

The light from the chandeliers glinted off the silver helmet that sat on the table on the other side of Hades. It winked with an eerie glow that somehow made it hard to focus on. She felt the god's eyes on her and she looked back at him.

"The helmet is beautiful. I've never seen one like it," she said.

"Thank you. It was a gift from the Cyclops," Hades said, smiling in obvious pleasure at the compliment.

Cyclops? Wasn't that the guy with one eye? *Cyclops, a one-eyed monster who gifted Zeus with thunder and lightning, Poseidon with his trident, and Hades with the helmet—*

Okay! Lina broke into her internal encyclopedic monologue. Whoever he was, she certainly didn't want to get into a discussion about mythological creatures with Hades. So she did what any calm, collected, mature woman would do—she changed the subject. Quickly.

"Your throne is very unusual, too. I don't recognize the stone from which it is made."

"It is white chalcedony," he said.

"Does it have special properties, too?" Lina asked.

"Yes, it banishes fear, hysteria, depression and sadness. I thought it a good choice for this particular room."

"I agree with your choice."

Hades turned his head and leaned toward her again, bringing their faces close together again. "Do you recognize the colored stone in this room?"

"It's amethyst."

"It is the same color as your eyes, Persephone," Eurydice said in a happy voice of discovery.

"Yes, I have noticed that, too," Hades said slowly without releasing Lina's gaze.

His voice had deepened so that it was an audible caress, and Lina felt an answering flutter low in her stomach.

"The dead ask to speak to their god!" Iapis' voice carried his words with formal authority across the Great Hall.

Hades' attention shifted reluctantly away from her, and Lina mentally shook herself. How in the hell was she supposed to think about business with Hades beside her oozing Sex God? She almost wished he'd turn back into Mr. Wooden and Withdrawn. Almost.

She could only hope that Persephone was having better luck staying focused back in Tulsa.

"The dead may enter," Hades' powerful voice commanded.

Lina saw that Iapis was holding the two-pronged silver spear Hades had carried the day before, and with a sound like a crack of thunder, he banged it against the marble floor. One of the shadows from just outside the arched entryway quivered, and then moved into the Great Hall. Lina watched intently as the spirit approached the dais. She was a middle-aged woman. Lina couldn't see any obvious wounds on her semitransparent form. She was, Lina thought, quite attractive. Her hair was piled in intricate braids atop her head, giving the illusion that she was wearing a crown. She was swathed in layer upon layer of draped fabric that fluttered wispily around her as she glided to a halt at the foot of the dais. She dropped into a deep curtsy, which she held until Hades spoke.

"Stheneboia, you may arise."

The woman straightened, but as soon as her eyes widened in recognition of Persephone, she fell back into another deep curtsy.

"I am honored by the presence of Demeter's daughter."

The spirit's breathy voice reminded Lina of a bad Marilyn Monroe impersonator. "Please rise," Lina said quickly, wondering why she felt such an instant dislike for the spirit.

Stheneboia straightened again. Having paid proper respect to the goddess, she ignored Persephone and focused her large, kohl-ringed eyes on Hades.

"I have come, Great God, to ask that I be allowed to drink of the River Lethe and be reborn to the mortal world."

Hades studied her carefully. When he spoke, Lina noted that his voice was filled with the confidence and authority of a god, so much so that the fine hairs on her arms tingled and rose in response to his tangible power.

"It is an unusual request you make of me, Stheneboia. You know that the spirits of suicides are rarely allowed to drink of Lethe."

Lina felt a jolt of shock. The woman had killed herself? Why?

Stheneboia lowered her eyes demurely. "And you know, Great God, that I did not truly mean to die."

She said the title "Great God" like a verbal caress. Lina felt her jaw set. She was actually flirting with Hades!

The spirit's tone turned pouty. "It was a tragic accident. Must I pay for it for all eternity?"

"What have you learned as you have roamed the banks of Acheron?" Hades asked abruptly.

Stheneboia paused, as if carefully arranging her thoughts. When she spoke her words were a slow purr.

"I have learned that I chose unwisely. I will not do so again, Lord of the Underworld."

Hades' eyes narrowed and his deep voice was laced with disgust. "Then you have learned little. You lusted after Bellerophon, a youth half your age. When he rejected your desires, you told your husband the lie that he had tried to rape you. Thankfully, Athena thwarted his attempt to have the youth killed. The goddess was wise to give Bellerophon to your youngest sister. She was more deserving."

"That timid mouse did not deserve Bellerophon!" Stheneboia's sudden rage twisted her attractive features so that her face became hard and cruel.

Hades continued on as if she hadn't spoken. "You did not intend to kill yourself, this I know. You only intended to scare your family and cause them such pain and sorrow that they would reject Athena's matchmaking and send Bellerophon away in disgrace. It was your misfortune that your maid overslept and did not discover you until you had bled beyond saving."

Stheneboia's eyes slid away from the god's penetrating gaze and she pressed one cool, white hand against her brow as if his words had upset her.

"I will choose more wisely in my next life," she said breathily.

"Where is your remorse, Stheneboia?" Hades asked in a stone voice. "You tried to command love with lies and seduction. Love cannot survive such poison."

"But you do not understand." The spirit was beginning to sound desperate. "I wanted him so much. He should have wanted me. I was still beautiful and desirable."

"Love cannot survive such poison," Hades repeated. "Lust and desire are only a small part of love, but that is another ideal you have yet to learn." Then he shook his head sadly. "I deny your request, Stheneboia. Instead I command that you return to the banks of Acheron, the River of Woe. Perhaps spending more time there will enable you to open your heart to more than your own selfish desires. Do not ask to come before me until another century has passed."

Stheneboia's mouth opened in a wordless scream as a great wind rushed into the chamber and swirled around her like a miniature tornado before picking her up and sweeping her from their sight.

Iapis lifted the spear to signal another spirit forward, but Hades' raised hand halted him mid-gesture. The god turned his attention to Lina.

"What do you think of my judgment?" he asked.

"I thought you were wise," she answered without hesitation. "I don't know the whole story, but from what I heard she did an awful thing, and she certainly wasn't sorry about it. She did make me wonder something, though."

Hades nodded for her to continue.

"If she drank of Lethe she would forget all of her past life?"

"Yes," Hades said.

"But would she still be the same type of person? I mean, is it like wiping everything clean, or is there still a residue of the old self left behind?"

"An excellent question," Hades said with obvious appreciation. "When a spirit drinks of Lethe, memories are wiped completely away and the soul is reborn within an infant's body. But the soul can not help but to retain some elements of personality. Ultimately, the body is just a shell; it is the soul which defines the man or woman, god or goddess."

"Then that just reinforces the fact that you made a wise decision. Stheneboia would have been reborn to make someone else miserable."

"She based her life on lies—most of which she told herself about her true nature. It was not riches or luxury for which her soul yearned; it was love. And love cannot exist with lies and deceit," Hades said.

"You're very insightful about love," Lina said thoughtfully.

Hades paused before he spoke his next words, and as he paused he felt hope stir once again within him. "I have spent eons studying the souls of the dead, and I have come to understand that love is one emotion that mortals know infinitely better than the gods."

Lina blinked in surprise. Mortals knew love better than the gods? For a woman who had been divorced and hadn't had a decent date in years, his words came as quite a shock.

"Do you really think so?" she asked incredulously.

Hades felt the flicker of hope falter. "Yes, I know it as truth," he said with grim finality before he nodded to Iapis, who cracked the spear against the floor again.

Lina had little time to ponder Hades' reaction to her question. At Iapis' command, another shadowy figure detached from the waiting doorway and Lina watched a pale woman make her way hesitantly across the Great Hall. She was dressed in much more somber robes than Stheneboia had been, but her attire looked just as rich and her dark hair was intricately dressed in a similar fashion. A small coronet circled her head. As she drew closer, Lina could see that she was a plump but attractive woman who looked to be thirty-ish. Then she felt a jolt as she realized that the splash of scarlet on the front of her robes was an open wound, which still seeped blood.

The spirit curtsied deeply.

"Persephone and Hades, I am honored to bow before the Goddess of Spring as well as the Lord of the Underworld."

The woman's voice was strong and regal. Lina smiled and inclined her own head in welcome.

"Greetings, Dido. What petition does the Queen of Carthage have to set before me today?" Hades asked.

"Hades, I beseech your blessing that I may depart the Region of Lamentation beside the River Cocytus and pass into Elysia."

The god studied the spirit thoughtfully. "Have you overcome the grief of your unrequited love, Dido?"

The woman lowered her eyes, not coyly as had Stheneboia, but in a manner that Lina recognized too well from her own past. She lowered them to hide the pain that was still reflected there.

"Yes, Great God. I am finished pining for that which I cannot have."

Lina shifted restlessly in her chair and glanced at Hades. Surely he wouldn't believe Dido.

Hades rubbed his chin and considered the dead queen. "What have you learned from your time of lamentation?"

"That I should have believed more firmly in the strength of love. I should have known that Aeneas just needed time. He was ordered by Zeus to leave me, what else could he do? He was a pious man, a warrior of great faith. It was not his fault. I should have been more understanding, more willing to—" Her words broke on a sob and she covered her face with her hands.

"Dido, you have not overcome your lamentation." The god's voice was gentle.

"But I have!" Dido raised her chin and wiped her face. "It is simply that I am filled with the awe of a child at being in the presence of immortals, and it has made my emotions tremulous." Her shining eyes shifted to Lina frantically, looking for aid from the goddess.

Lina returned the desperate woman's gaze with sympathy. She knew too well how it felt to be abandoned and left to blame only oneself.

"I grant your request, Dido. You may enter Elysia with my blessing."

Hades' words shocked Lina to the core. She found herself staring blankly at the god as the exuberant Dido rushed from the Great Hall.

Again, Iapis moved to raise the god's spear and Hades' motion prevented him.

"You do not agree with my decision, Persephone?" He turned in his throne so that he was facing the goddess.

Lina straightened her spine and met his gaze. You're a goddess . . . you're a goddess . . . you're—no. She stopped the litany. More importantly, she was a woman who had, in real life, loved and been rejected and she understood exactly what Dido was feeling.

"No. I do not agree with your decision."

Surprised by her answer he said, "Could you explain?"

"Dido's not over Aeneas. She's deep in the trenches of hurting and blaming herself. She's still a victim. Whatever lesson the River of Lamentation was supposed to teach her, it hasn't taken hold yet."

Hades felt his anger rise. What did Persephone know of love and loss? She was a young goddess who had always been given everything she desired.

"And how would you know that?"

Lina's eyes narrowed at his condescending tone, but she caught herself before she spat a snide answer at him. To Hades she was only a young goddess. He had no way of knowing her true past and her heartaches. She took deep, slow breaths and got a firm grip on her temper before she began her explanation.

"Well, there were a couple major hints. First, looking away and crying was a dead giveaway. Pardon the bad pun. Second, did you listen to what she said?" Lina barreled on, without giving him a chance to reply. "Her whole little speech was filled with I, I, I and poor me, me, me. Add that to the 'it's not his fault, it's my fault,' and you have one huge victim complex. She doesn't need to go to paradise, she needs to go to the gym, or maybe to a shrink, and work out some of that self-hatred." Lina abruptly shut up, wondering if Hades had any idea what a shrink was.

He cocked his head sideways and looked at her as if she was a very interesting science experiment. Then he did something that really pissed her off. He smiled. And chuckled.

She set her jaw and dug deep, trying to find her own voice somewhere in Persephone's youthful sweetness, and she was rewarded by a steely tone with a satisfyingly sarcastic edge.

"Check into one thing, Hades. This Aeneas guy. I'll bet you one of your diamond chandeliers against one of Demeter's golden crowns that he's in Elysia. And that would be the same Elysia Dido just manipulated her way into. I'll also bet that he's a new arrival, which is what has instigated her sudden interest in moving into Elysia."

Hades' chuckle died and his eyes flattened. "Perhaps the young Goddess of Spring would like an opportunity to do more than observe and comment. The next judgment is yours, Persephone. Fate will, in turn, judge how well you choose."

Lina nodded tightly. Two words passed through her mind. *Oh* and *shit*.

Iapis struck the god's spear against the marble floor, and it rang its somber knell like it was heralding the end of the earth.

This time not one, but several shadows disengaged from the entryway and approached the dais. Lina counted almost a dozen spirits. Her heart pounded and her sweaty hands gripped the armrest of her chair. This wasn't one or two lonely petitioners, it was an entire herd. They were all women, but were of various ages, and their spirit bodies were in varying states. Some of them were almost as substantial in form as was Eurydice, and some were so transparent, they were practically nonexistent. They moved as a group like frightened sheep, at first hesitant and unsure, then they caught sight of Lina in her chair next to Hades, and a definite change came over them. They lost their timidity. As one they walked purposefully forward, their steps becoming more eager the closer they drew to the dais. When they were at the foot of the stairs they stood silently, gazing in open fascination at her. Then one spirit, a woman who was obviously the oldest of the group, dropped to her knees and bowed her head. The rest of the women followed her example.

For what seemed to Lina to be a long time, no one spoke, then Hades' strong voice cut the silence.

"What petition have you brought forth today?"

The oldest woman raised her head. She spoke her response to Hades, but her shining eyes never left Lina.

"We have no petition, Great God. We have come in supplication to the Goddess of Spring, thanking her for answering our orisons. We have been too long without the presence of a goddess." The old woman motioned with her hand, and several of the younger women stood and moved forward. They carried within their skirts bunches of freshly cut flowers, which they placed at Lina's feet.

Hades was looking at Lina with one brow quirked upward. He remained silent, apparently remaining true to his word and allowing her to handle the situation.

She cleared her throat and forced her hand to stay clamped to the arm of the chair when it really wanted to twirl frantically at her hair. She was a goddess, she reminded herself for the zillionth time, and goddesses didn't pull nervously at their hair—at least not in public.

"Well, this is certainly a surprise. I do appreciate you coming, and the flowers are lovely." She tilted her head toward the little spirit who stood by her side. "Eurydice will put them in water for me, and I will cherish them."

The women smiled and made happy, breathless sounds. Lina began to relax. They seemed like nothing more than happy well-wishers. Even a baker from Tulsa couldn't mess this up.

"You will not be leaving the Underworld soon, will you Persephone?" the old woman asked.

"No," Lina said firmly. "I will not be leaving soon." Six months was certainly not "soon."

The spirits whispered together in happy relief.

"We are so pleased, Goddess . . ." The old woman began, but her words trailed off as an amazing sound floated through the chamber.

Lina blinked in surprise. The sound surrounded her. Music. It was incredibly beautiful music. Entranced, she listened to notes that rose and fell like an impossibly complex birdsong. As the sound moved closer it became musical water. Some of it glided smoothly over pebbles in a clear brook, some tumbled along the slick bank of her hearing and still other notes cascaded powerfully over a rhythmic waterfall of tinkling sound.

"Iapis?" Hades' voice intruded on the music, causing Lina to frown and wish he would just be still.

"My Lord I do not—"

The daimon was interrupted as the musician entered the Great Hall. He walked toward the god's dais and the women parted to let him through. Lina studied him, still amazed at the beautiful music he produced. He was an average, normal looking young man and he was playing a small wooden harp that was gilded with gold. The gold was reflected in his hair and in the fine cloth that draped over his body leaving one tanned, muscular shoulder bare. He continued to pluck magic from the harp as he approached the dais. He was humming a lilting melody, and Lina was surprised when she noticed that his attention was not directed at Hades or at her. Instead his eyes blazed at a spot directly to her left.

"Why does a living man dare enter the Underworld?" Hades' voice sliced through the music, instantly silencing it.

Lina felt a shock of recognition. No wonder he looked so normal to her. He was alive.

"Who are you?" Hades thundered.

The answer came from the little spirit standing to the left of Lina.

"He is Orpheus. My husband."

CHAPTER THIRTEEN

EURYDICE'S voice was brittle with shock. Lina's eyes flew to her face. The girl was staring at her husband. Her eyes had gone huge and round. Her face was completely devoid of color.

"By what right do you enter the realm of the dead?" Hades demanded.

Orpheus tore his eyes from his wife. He bowed low, first to Hades and then to Lina. Then he ran his fingers lightly across the lyre, as if testing its readiness. When he spoke his words were accompanied by gossamer notes, and his voice was the magic that held them together:

O Hades, who rules the dark and silent world,
to you all born of a woman must come.
All lovely things at last return to you.
You are the debtor always paid.
A little while we tarry upon earth.
Then we are yours forever and ever,
but I seek one who came to you too soon.
This bud was plucked before the flower bloomed.
I tried to bear my loss, but oh, oh, I do love her so
and the pain of her loss is killing me slowly.

Love is too strong, a too tempting god.
I beg you return to me what was mine.
Then weave again her sweet life's refrain,
which ended too quickly,
I ask this small thing.
That you will lend her back to me.
Yours again when her life's span is full she shall be.

Because oh, oh, I do love her so
and the pain of her loss is killing me slowly.

Orpheus' words ended, but his fingers kept plucking a soft, sweet version of the melody of his song. Lina felt her heart ache and break. His music moved her like she had never before been moved. Her cheeks felt wet and she touched her face, wiping off the tears she hadn't realized she was shedding.

She looked at the silent god sitting beside her. His face, too, reflected the grief of the mortal's song. Hades began to speak, and then he stopped. His head turned slowly until his dark gaze met Lina's tear-filled eyes.

"The choice is yours. I gifted you with the next judgment, but even if I had not, Eurydice has pledged herself to your service. Only you can release her; therefore, twice over you are granted the power to decide her fate. Choose wisely, Goddess of Spring," Hades said in a voice that mirrored the emotion in Orpheus' song.

Lina drew in a shaky breath, feeling for the first time the awesome responsibility that went with being a goddess. Eurydice's future rested on her decision. She turned in her chair so that she faced the girl.

Eurydice's slender body had gone very still. The only movement that came from the girl was from the tears that washed wet trails down her colorless face and dripped steadily onto the gauzy fabric of her gown.

"How did you die?" Lina asked softly.

But Eurydice didn't answer her. Instead the tune Orpheus played changed to a darker melody, underscoring his words.

"Only one month after our wedding day we were taking a moonlit walk. She became separated from me, lost in a sudden fog. She chose the wrong path. Instead of leading her back to me, her loving husband, it led her to a nest of vipers where she met her untimely death."

Although Orpheus didn't sing, his words still sounded lyrical. Lina felt them create a spell of sadness around her. She wept anew over the tragedy of Eurydice's death. So that was the wrong choice the girl had made, and the loss of her young husband was the price she had paid for that choice—a price that still weighed heavily on her soul. So heavily, Lina noted, that Eurydice had been struck speechless with grief at Orpheus' appearance.

Lina reached out and grasped the little spirit's hand. Eurydice's hand was cold and Lina could feel the silent tremors that shook her body.

"I free you," Lina said through her tears. "You may return to your life with your husband. Now I understand your sadness, and I am so happy I can do this for you."

Eurydice gasped in surprise. Her body trembled visibly and her mouth twisted in grief.

"Oh, honey! Don't worry about me. I'll be just fine. Iapis will take good care of me, as will Hades." Lina squeezed the girl's hand, glancing at Hades for support.

The dark god was watching Eurydice closely.

"Persephone has spoken. I bow to her decision. I have but one condition." Hades' gaze speared Orpheus. "Eurydice may return to the Land of the Living only if you do not look back at her; you must trust that she follows you. When you turn from this palace you may not gaze upon her again until she has departed my realm and stands firmly once more in the mortal world."

"I will adhere to your will. She will follow me, of that I have no doubt." Orpheus bowed low to Hades and Lina. "Hereafter I will sing praises to you extolling your benevolence." His eyes captured Eurydice and his words turned to liquid music:

Follow me, follow me . . .
Together forever we shall be . . .
You belong to me, you belong to me . . .
Together forever we shall be . . .

Orpheus strummed magic from his lyre. With one last piercing look at his wife, he turned, and, singing his Siren's song, he walked from the Great Hall. Eurydice began to follow him as if he held her on an invisible tether. She stumbled down the stairs from the dais, righted herself and continued with jerky steps after her husband. She glanced once over her shoulder. Lina was shocked at the glazed expression in the girl's eyes. Eurydice looked as if she were in agony.

Orpheus, his music and Eurydice drifted from the Palace of Hades.

Hades spoke into the sudden silence. "Petitions are closed for today."

Iapis stuck the spear against the marble floor and the group of women bowed to Lina once more before they faded out of the entryway, leaving her alone with Hades and Iapis.

None of them spoke.

Lina couldn't get out of her mind the expression on Eurydice's face as she followed her husband from the room. The girl had looked—Lina wrapped a strand of hair around and around her finger—trapped. Eurydice had looked trapped. Now that Orpheus and his seductive music were gone, and Lina was replaying the scene in her head, it felt wrong. Her intuition was screaming that something was very wrong.

"I'm going to go back to my room now," Lina said, trying to sound nonchalant. She smiled briefly at Hades. "Thank you for inviting me. I found it very interesting." She hurried down the dais steps, holding her breath and hoping that Hades didn't stop her. She called to Iapis, who was still standing in the entrance to the Hall. "Could you show me back to my room? I think I'm going to take a nap. The excitement of the petitions has worn me out."

Lina saw Iapis' eyes travel questioningly over her shoulder, but he must have received the go ahead from Hades, because he nodded convivially to Lina and led her from the Great Hall. When they were out of Hades' hearing, Lina stopped and pulled at the daimon's sleeve so that he had to face her.

"Something's wrong with Eurydice. I can feel it. Well, I didn't while Orpheus was playing his music, but as soon as he was gone everything changed," Lina said.

"What is it you wish, Goddess?" Iapis asked, lowering his voice.

"I need to follow them." Lina didn't realize what she was going to say until she had spoken, but the words felt right. "I have to watch and make sure that I made the right decision by letting her go back to him."

Iapis nodded solemnly. "We would not want her to be hurt."

"No, we wouldn't."

"Come this way," Iapis said decisively. He led Lina quickly to the front of the palace. "There is the pathway." He pointed to the path of black marble. "She is not far ahead of you."

"Thank you, Iapis." Lina hugged him impulsively before she hurried down the path.

"The Underworld is opened to you, Goddess," Iapis called after her. "You may come and go at will. Eurydice belongs here. She, too, has access to this realm. But Orpheus is a living mortal. Once he passes through the Gates, he may not return as long as he is living."

"I'll remember," she called over her shoulder.

"PERSEPHONE follows Eurydice?" Hades asked the daimon.

"Yes."

Hades paced the empty Great Hall restlessly. "Orpheus was hiding something. His music spun a web of seduction, but his words were false. The little spirit did not want to follow him."

"I agree, Lord," Iapis said fiercely.

Hades stopped his pacing. "You care for Eurydice." It was not a question.

"I do," Iapis said.

"Are you certain?"

"Eurydice makes me laugh. I have not laughed in eons."

"Do you know her heart?" Hades asked softly.

"There has not yet been time, and she is so young," Iapis said helplessly.

Hades nodded. "Women are difficult."

"They are indeed."

"Bring me the Helmet of Invisibility. I will follow Persephone. It may take my intercession to right this error."

Relief flooded the daimon's face. "Thank you, Lord."

Hades' eyes warmed and he grasped Iapis' hand. "You need not thank me, my friend."

Iapis rushed to the pillar that held the Helmet of Invisibility. He grasped it firmly in his hands. As always, its weight was a surprise to the daimon. It appeared so lightly wrought, yet it was, indeed, a heavy burden to bear. He brought the Helmet to the Lord of the Underworld.

Hades took it from the daimon. Then he paused, considering.

"Iapis, I need you to look into something."

"Of course, Lord."

"See if Aeneas has recently entered Elysia."

"It shall be done, Hades."

The god nodded. Then in one swift motion, he placed the Helmet of Invisibility over his head. The pain that lanced through his body was excruciating. He pressed his lips together and refused to give in to the agony. It would pass, he reminded himself—nothing worthwhile comes without a price. He breathed deeply against the pain until his senses were his own again.

Iapis watched the god's body ripple and then disappear. He spoke to the empty space before him, "Bring them back, Lord."

Hades' answer floated to the daimon from across the room. "I shall. . . ."

CHAPTER FOURTEEN

LINA fell into a rhythm of hurry up and slow down. She managed to keep Eurydice's back just at the edge of her sight, while staying out of the reach of Orpheus' music.

"Doesn't he ever get tired?" she muttered to herself. When she considered the situation with a clear head, versus one filled with the compelling notes formed by a magician masquerading as a musician, it hadn't been difficult to see the drug-like effect Orpheus' music had on everyone and everything that heard it. The dead paused in their pilgrimages to Elysia as he passed. Flowers and trees swayed toward him. Even Lina found herself smiling ridiculously if she got too close to his voice.

"Ugh. He reminds me of too-sweet candy. He seems great at first, but pretty soon he'll just make me want to puke." Lina talked to herself, taking comfort in the nonhypnotic sound of her own voice while nodding briefly to the surprised spirits that curtsied and bowed as she hurried past them. "I should have been wiser. I should have paid more attention to Eurydice than to that singing boy. And I shouldn't have been so damn cocky after that whole Dido thing." She bit her lip in frustration.

The sky ahead of her was changing and a chill of trepidation shivered through her. She knew all too well that the fading light signaled the end of the bright, cheery part of the Underworld. She was retracing the path she and Eurydice had traveled from the upper world.

Lina ordered herself not to think about the bad dreams and the darkness. If Eurydice was going through it again, so would she.

Ahead of her she heard maniacal barking. Then the faraway music grew louder and the fierce barks changed to puppy-like grunts and whimpers. Lina shook her head. What the hell—she cringed at the unintentional bad pun—was Orpheus doing? Steeling herself against his compelling song, she picked up her pace until she was jogging at a steady beat. Persephone's long legs carried her swiftly forward. Her breathing was deep and even. She smiled in satisfaction. Persephone's body wasn't just young, it was also in great shape.

The road angled abruptly to her left and she stagger-stepped down to a walk. Blocking the pathway directly in front of her was a humongous dog.

The creature raised its head and growled a menacing warning. Lina blinked, trying to clear her vision, but the image remained.

"The damn thing has three heads," she gasped.

The "damn thing" growled.

Lina tightened her jaw. It was just a dog. Sure, the biggest dog she had ever seen. And it had—*merda!*—three heads.

The creature snarled a warning. Saliva dripped from its triple jowls.

Jowls?

Lina's face split into a relieved grin as soon as her stunned mind processed what she was seeing. The dog was nothing more than a giant version of Edith Anne, complete with slobber and under bite—times three.

Her laughter caused three sets of stubby ears to perk in her direction.

Lina hurried forward, speaking in what she liked to think of as her "doggie voice," (which was *much* different than her "cat voice"—cats didn't tolerate baby talk of any sort).

"Hey there you big, adorable thing!" she cooed.

Three tails wagged tentatively.

"Aren't you a wonderful surprise. And to think I was just missing my Edith Anne. Well, I guess I'll just have to make you my big, bad Doggie From Hell while I'm here." She was within touching distance of the multiheaded creature.

"Arrwoo?" said the beast.

"Edith always liked her ears scratched. Bend down here and let's give it a try." She reached her slender hand up toward one of the six ears. The creature tilted its nearest head in her direction.

Lina scratched.

One of the beast's heads sighed and leaned into her hand, almost knocking Lina over. The other two heads whined piteously.

"There's a good doggie." Lina grinned, patting the middle head's slobbery nose, causing the third dog to yelp like a needy puppy. "Oh, come here. How about a scratch under that chin?"

While Lina cooed and petted and cajoled she searched her mind for a name.

Cerberus—Watchdog of the Underworld—his job is to eat souls that attempt to escape and stop living people who attempt to enter Hades' realm.

"Well, you're falling down on the job, big boy," Lina said.

The dog whined and all three heads gave her pitiful, big-eyed doggie looks.

"Don't feel bad, Orpheus fooled me, too."

Three tails beat the air.

"Okay, here's the deal. I'm going to follow the shyster musician and Eurydice. You just be sure that Mr. Goldentongue doesn't get past you again." Lina tried to meet all three sets of eyes. "Understand?"

Cerberus squirmed and woofed.

"I've seen enough Lassie reruns to know a doggie 'yes' when I hear one. Be a good boy, ur, boys. I'll see you on my way back." With a final ear scratch Lina left the Guardian of the Underworld wriggling and yapping like a happy puppy(s). She hurried so that she was soon jogging with a quick, but steady pace.

"I should cease being surprised by her actions," Hades murmured to himself. He watched Persephone bespell Cerberus as she had his steeds. Safe within the Helmet of Invisibility, he had followed the goddess closely enough to hear her berate herself about allowing Orpheus' music to sway her judgment. She was much wiser than she knew. Hadn't he felt the pull of the mortal's words, too? And he was a mature god, experienced in commanding his realm.

True, she was a goddess, but she was really just a child. Even so, she continued to show amazing insight and maturity. For instance, his instinct was telling him that Iapis would report that Aeneas had indeed just entered Elysia. How had Persephone recognized Dido's deception when all he had observed was a lovely feminine soul unaccustomed to being in the presence of immortals? And then she had stood up to him, not with the blinding temper of an irate goddess, but with logic and insight and, he chuckled remembering the bet she had proposed, wit. Before she had come to his realm, he would have never believed it of Persephone, but there was definitely more to her than a shallow young goddess.

Persephone fondled Cerberus and Hades felt a sudden surge of jealousy for the attention she was lavishing on the slobbering, three-headed creature. The God ground his teeth. He wanted her to touch him. It shocked him, but he could not deny it. He was beginning to wonder if what Iapis had said was true, that perhaps it was better to experience even a small bit of happiness than none at all.

The very thought made his hands sweat.

As she jogged down the road, Lina decided that she'd have to come back and visit the three-headed dog. Maybe she'd bring him a treat. Edith Anne loved Bacos. Surely Hell's kitchen could fry her up a little bacon snack. She thought about the creature's size—okay, maybe she'd have them fry up a *big* bacon snack.

The road took another abrupt turn and Lina slid to a halt, scrambling back from the edge of a lake that seemed to want to swallow her feet. Its waters were thick and black, almost oily. She looked to either side. Darkness surrounded the lake so that the water seemed to stretch endlessly before and beside her.

Lina shivered.

She was a goddess. She thought each word carefully.

Light the recesses, her mind whispered.

With a gasp of relief she raised her hand and commanded, "I need light!"

The ball of brilliance popped from her palm and hovered expectantly above her.

"What is your desire, Goddess?"

Lina jumped and made a squeaky sound she was sure wouldn't qualify as goddess-like. Out of the darkness beside her a skeletal man materialized. He was wearing gray robes that dragged on the ground. He carried a long, hooked staff that reminded Lina of the rods gondoliers used to push their boats down the Grand Canal. But that's where his resemblance to anything mortal or romantic ended. This man was a grim being whose large, amber-colored eyes glowed with a strange luminescence. Lina did not have to delve into her memory to give him a name. He could be none other than Charon, the Ferryman of Hades.

"I want to follow Orpheus and Eurydice. Did you take them across the lake?"

"Yes, Goddess."

"Then I want to go, too."

"As you command, Goddess." He made a sweeping gesture and suddenly a boat appeared nudging the bank at their feet.

Telling herself not to think about sinking boats, bottomless lakes or the scary stuff that might be lurking just below the surface, Lina climbed into the little craft, taking a seat near the middle of it. Charon stepped into the boat and leaned forward to touch his staff against the bank, but he stopped mid-motion and stood very still as if he were listening to whispered words. He nodded his head with the briefest of motions, paused and then he finally pushed them away from the shore.

"The passage is not long, Goddess."

Lina nodded and tried unsuccessfully to relax. She kept her eyes focused on the distant shoreline. She didn't look down at the water. Unbidden, a memory came to her from the scene in *Lord of the Rings* when Frodo and Sam crossed the Dead Marshes. She shivered, afraid if she looked into the water she would see reflected faces of the dead. Her only consolation was the ball of light that hovered loyally close to her shoulder.

She looked afraid, so afraid that he almost tore the Helmet off his head and betrayed his presence. Then he remembered her reaction when he had chided her for being young and sheltered. Likely she would not look kindly upon his interference and the subterfuge of the Helmet. Persephone would not be pleased that he had hidden himself and followed her. But his heart whispered for him to take her in his arms and protect her from her fears. As always, Hades listened to his mind, but for the first time in his existence, he yearned to follow his heart.

Charon felt his god's presence. He knew when Hades boarded the boat. Charon also knew that Hades wished to keep his presence hidden from the goddess. The Ferryman was nothing if not discreet. So Hades stood at the opposite end of the small craft, his eyes never leaving Persephone. He saw how she clutched the seat on which she sat so tightly that her delicate knuckles whitened. She held her spine rigid, as if she could brace herself against her fear. Her little light illuminated the space surrounding her so that she appeared to be floating in a halo of brightness that was almost as brilliant as her beauty.

The boat hit a wave, causing it to rock dangerously. Persephone's body shuddered in response.

Carefully and quickly! Hades' anger burst through his thoughts to Charon. The Ferryman bowed his head in acknowledgment and shivered at the force of the god's fury. With the Lord of the Underworld standing vigilant attendance, the remainder of the passage was smooth and swift.

*   *   *

"FOLLOW the path that leads there, Goddess." Charon pointed ahead into the darkness. Lina stepped from the boat to the shore. "The Gates of Hades are just beyond. Through them you will find the entrance to the world above."

Lina realized she didn't really need his direction. Demeter had been right, it was as if her body felt the way to the world above. But she smiled politely at the Ferryman.

"Thank you, Charon. I know my way from here." She took a couple of steps, stopped, and turned back to the tall man. "You will be here when I come back, won't you?"

Charon almost smiled. "Yes, Goddess."

"Good."

Lina and her circle of light moved away from the lake. Under the shroud of invisibility Hades followed.

The ivory gates loomed before Lina. Thankfully, there was no sign of the eerie fog of a bad dream. Jogging through the gates she narrowed her eyes, trying to catch sight of Eurydice's ghostly form, but she saw nothing except velvet layers of darkness. Lina stopped and strained to listen. She could hear music, but it sounded far away and indistinct.

Please, please don't let me be too late, she prayed silently as she broke into a sprinter's run.

Lina passed through the grove of opaque trees in a blur. Then she spotted the tunnel, and, she breathed a sigh of relief, within it she could clearly see the silhouettes of two figures. One was several yards ahead of the other.

Lina ran silently and swiftly, covering the distance that separated her from Eurydice in a single breath.

The music was so sweet. Lina felt her shoulders begin to relax and her steps falter. She should just rest awhile and then . . .

Do not listen to his music! The words shouted within her mind, and with the power of a goddess they chased away the cloying notes of Orpheus' song. Suddenly clear-minded, Lina was able to hear something that had been hidden beneath the spell of music until that moment—the sound of Eurydice's sobs.

As if sensing her presence, the girl looked over her shoulder. When she saw Lina her face grimaced with the strength of her emotion. Lina could see that Eurydice was still struggling against the lure of Orpheus's song. Even though they were almost to the lip of the tunnel, the little spirit still stumbled and dragged her feet, pulling back with everything inside of her against the magical lure of her husband's music. With a powerful effort, Eurydice silently mouthed two words to her goddess, *help me.*

Orpheus stepped into the sunlight of the World of the Living.

Hades raised his hands to pull off the Helmet of Invisibility and do something he had never before done: he would revoke his word by refusing to allow Eurydice to leave the Underworld.

But before he could act, Persephone moved. She grabbed Eurydice's hand and held it in such a tight grasp that the little spirit was able to keep from stepping from the edge of the Underworld and into the light. Then, in a voice pitched to impersonate Eurydice's naïveté, she called to the musician who stood with his back resolutely facing them.

"Oh, my goodness! Orpheus, look! This sunlight makes my robe completely see through! And I have absolutely nothing on underneath it."

With a victorious shout, the arrogant young musician spun around, but the look of triumph vanished when he realized that he was staring at his wife and the Goddess Persephone. Both women were still safely within the dark mouth of the Underworld.

"NOOOOOO!" His shriek of rage echoed through the tunnel. He lunged forward.

Unseen, Hades threw his hand up and issued a silent command.

When the musician's living body tried to pass into the shadowy entrance of Hades' realm, the air surrounding him seemed to solidify. Orpheus set his square jaw and kept trying to move forward, but the invisible barrier prevented him. The harder he struggled, the more firm the barrier became.

"You belong to me!" His words were no longer seductive or magical; instead they had become hard and cruel.

Eurydice shrank back from him as if she was afraid he would strike her. Lina was filled with a wave of righteous anger.

"You sound like a spoiled brat. You can't own another person's soul. Go back to your world. Leave Eurydice at peace in hers," Lina said.

"Never! She will always be mine!" Orpheus shouted.

Lina shook her head. She had known his type of man. He would never be content with simply loving a woman. His kind had to control and bully and subjugate. She felt the anger expand within her, lending power to the words she hurled at Orpheus. "Go away, boy!"

The command slammed into the musician, lifting him off his feet and tossing him end-over-end away from the tunnel, carrying him back farther and farther until he disappeared completely from sight.

Apparently she'd discovered another one of Persephone's goddess powers. Lina smiled grimly. One shouldn't piss off a goddess.

Unaware that she was being shadowed by the invisible God of the Underworld, Lina wrapped an arm around Eurydice, who was sobbing quietly. Supporting her slight weight, Lina turned away from the World of the Living and led Eurydice through the welcoming darkness of the tunnel and into the glade of white trees. Once within their shielding canopy, Eurydice collapsed onto the soft, dark ground. The girl had quit crying, but she was panting like she had just run a marathon.

"You c-c-came for m-me!" She struggled to talk while she fought to bring her breathing under control.

Lina sat beside her and hugged her fiercely. "Of course I did. I knew something was wrong. I'm sorry I let you go—it was his music. At first I couldn't think clearly because of it, but as soon as Orpheus left with you, I understood that you didn't want to go with him."

"N-no!" She shivered, but drew strength from the embrace of her goddess. "I did not want to go with him."

"That wrong choice you said that you made. It wasn't taking the path that led to your death, was it?" Lina asked.

"No!" Eurydice said. The strength of her voice grew as she continued to speak. "It was him! He was the wrong choice I made. I was so incredibly wrong. I met him one day and the next I pledged myself to him. I was blinded by the magic of his music. I did not look into his heart." She trembled, but forced herself under control. She needed to say it. She had been silent too long. "If I had looked into his heart, I would have seen that it was filled with cruelty. I did not understand until it was too late. It began with little things. He did not like my hair when I wore it a certain way. He asked me to change it. I did." Eurydice's words came faster and faster. "Then it was my clothes. Then my friends. I tried to tell my family, but they could only hear his music. They gave me to him willingly, believing that my hesitation was simple, maidenly reserve. After we were married he would not even allow me to visit my family. He could not bear it if I was not always by his side. He wanted to consume me. When I tried to get away from him, even if it was just to have a moment of privacy, he struck me. He struck me again and again. Life with him was a prison." Eurydice's eyes were bright, but her tears had stopped. "When the fog separated us, I simply ran from him. I did not know about the nest of vipers. But I was glad of their bite. I welcomed the release."

"You are so brave." Lina touched the girl's damp cheek.

"Do you really think so, Persephone?"

"I know so. On that you have the word of a goddess."

Eurydice's smile flashed. "Then I must believe it." Her expression changed, and became introspective.

"What is it, honey?" Lina asked.

The girl was staring down the path that led back to the Underworld. "I have to go. I don't belong this close to the World of the Living. It does not feel right."

Lina nodded understanding. She could see the need in the little spirit's eyes. This time Eurydice's steps were confident as she hurried through the grove of milk-colored trees. Lina followed her more slowly. When they broke through the trees, Eurydice glanced over her shoulder at Lina, who had stopped.

"Will you not return with me?" Eurydice's voice had become frightened again.

"Yes, don't worry. I'm coming"—she hesitated—"but, honey, would you mind going on ahead of me?" Lina pointed behind her. "I need to do something first, and I don't want to ask you to wait for me."

"But you will return to the Palace of Hades?"

Under the Helmet of Invisibility, Hades held his breath, waiting for Persephone's answer.

"Of course! I just need to have a quick talk with Demeter."

Hades and Eurydice breathed sighs of relief.

The girl understood Persephone's need to speak with her mother. In many ways the goddess had taken the place of her living mother. She nodded and smiled. "I can return ahead of you to the palace."

"You won't be afraid to go by yourself?"

"No. I belong here. I am not afraid."

Lina hugged her again. "I won't be long."

Eurydice grinned and skipped through the ivory gates. As Lina re-entered the grove of trees, she heard the girl's voice echoing through the limbs. "I will see that a meal is made ready for you. You will be hungry when you return and I must make certain that . . ."

Lina smiled wryly. Eurydice would be fine.

*   *   *

FEELING like a voyeur, Hades shadowed the unsuspecting Persephone. He should not continue to follow the goddess. Eurydice was free; she was returning safely to his palace. That had been his reason for donning the Helmet of Invisibility and going after them. And it had been a credible reason. Now he should return to his palace. His task was completed.

But he didn't turn back. He couldn't. Not yet. He wanted to watch her as she hurried so gracefully through the trees. The ball of light touched her lovely features like a bright caress. He envied that light.

She passed through the tunnel quickly, barely pausing before raising her hand and calling the light back within her. Then she stepped from the entrance to the Underworld and into the soft glow of a beautiful pre-dawn morning. Hades followed her.

Persephone looked around quizzically. Hades wondered if she was worried that Orpheus might still be lurking near. No, he reminded himself. The musician had been cast away by the power of the goddess's righteous anger. Persephone would know that he would be far from there. But she was obviously searching for something. She walked away from the tunnel and down the little path that was lined in frothy ferns. Occasionally, the goddess stopped and peered amidst the greenery as if looking for a lost trinket. Then she would sigh, mumble something unintelligible, and move on.

The path tilted gradually up and soon Persephone stood near the high bank of Lake Avernus. The goddess smiled and breathed in deeply, obviously appreciating the view.

Hades wanted to shout that Avernus would seem as nothing when compared with the wonders of Elysia. There were beauties in his realm that were far more spectacular than an ordinary lake in the simple, mundane light before dawn. He ground his teeth together. He wanted to show the magnificence of his realm to her and to watch her face brighten with the discovery.

"There you are!"

Persephone's voice sounded relieved and she rushed over to a pillared marble basin which stood to one side of the path. Resting within the basin was a large glass ball. Its interior was murky, like it had been filled with thickened cream. Hades recognized it instantly as the oracle of a goddess.

Persephone stood in front of the oracle. She hesitated. To Hades it seemed that she was almost uncertain of what to do next. Then she closed her eyes, as if she needed to concentrate very hard. When she opened them a moment later her full lips lifted in the briefest of smiles. With no more hesitation, she passed her hands over the crystal three times, causing the inside of the globe to begin to swirl.

"Demeter," Persephone spoke to the oracle. "I almost messed up. Badly."

The face of the Goddess of the Harvest materialized within her oracle.

"You use the word almost, which must mean that you righted your error," Demeter said, her voice sounding a little hollow and unnatural as it echoed from the oracle.

Persephone sighed. "Yes, but if I hadn't, my mistake would have cost a lovely young girl a lifetime of misery."

"Being a goddess does not mean perfection. We must each use our best judgment. Sometimes mistakes are made."

Persephone pulled at a long strand of her hair and twirled it around her finger.

"I don't want to make mistakes that cause others pain."

Hades forced himself to turn away. He strode quickly back through the tunnel. He had intruded upon the goddess's privacy too long. His conscience would not allow him to continue to listen to Persephone's conversation with her mother. Hades yanked off the Helmet of Invisibility. It was not meant as an eavesdropping device. It was to be used with discernment, not selfishness. He was ashamed of himself. Had he not just berated Stheneboia for selfishness and deception?

He had never before behaved in such a manner. He was not a callow youth. He understood that sneaking and spying would not win a goddess's heart.

Hades stopped.

Was that what he desired, to win Persephone's heart?

He raked a hand through his hair. He wanted her. His body had begun to ache for her. For eons he had thought that his difference had in some way hermetically sealed him from the common lusts of the gods. He avoided women, be they mortal or immortal, because his very nature had been fashioned so that meaningless passion and brief dalliance was not enough for him. Age after countless age he had witnessed in the spirits of the dead that which mortals knew so well, the eternal bond forged by soul mates. Bearing witness to that unique, unforgettable depth of joining had soldered the difference that had already been imprinted into his nature. Anything less than mating for eternity would never satisfy him.

Oh, he had tried—centuries ago. His stomach still tightened when he thought of his one brief mortal lover, Minthe. He had come upon the maiden during one of his rare visits to the World of the Living. She had been gathering flowers for her first fertility ritual and his appearance had seemed an answer to her prayers. He had made her his, there in that fragrant meadow, and there he had visited her often until she vowed that she loved him and that she would leave her home and cleave only to him.

Looking back, he was amazed by his own naïveté. He still shrank away from the memory of her hysterics when he had finally revealed himself to her as Lord of the Dead. In his mind he could see it all happening again. Minthe's blind flight from him as she hurled herself over the cliff, and how he had snatched her from the air before she could end her own life. Instead of condemning her to an eternity of lamentation within his realm, Hades had called forth his immortal power and changed her form into the sweet scented, ever-growing herb that retained her delicate beauty, as well as her name.

Unlike mortal women, goddesses did not fear him, but they also did not understand him. They scorned him, thinking him somber and stern because he ruled the Underworld. Until Persephone, no goddess had ever bothered to visit his realm. He scoffed. Truly, he had never had any desire to offer an invitation. Goddesses had no real loyalty, no real ability to love. Look at Athena, she even betrayed her precious Odysseus by allowing him to be led astray for twenty years before returning home to his faithful wife.

It had been easy to convince himself that there was no mate for him. Mortal women must die to reign forever beside him, so they feared him and shrank from his love. Goddesses were immortal; therefore, they could never truly belong to him.

He had been content to rule his realm and live surrounded by the beauty of the Elysian Fields and the wonders of his palace.

But no longer.

Hades' lips twisted in self-mockery. The God of the Dead desired the Goddess of Spring.

Even within his head it sounded impossible.

Then he remembered the goddess's brilliant smile and the childlike wonder with which she responded to his realm. Yet she consistently displayed a maturity that belied her youthful appearance. She was different from the other goddesses—that she had proven. But was she different enough to love him?

How to woo Persephone? He paced back and forth across the black path while he considered. Then a sudden idea halted him. His smile was fierce with victory. Hades brought his fingers to his lips. His whistle pierced the blackness, traveling with mystical speed all the way back to his palace.

CHAPTER FIFTEEN

"IN other words, there is no magic wand, or whatever, that you can wave over me that will guarantee that I make the right decisions. Even if it means my mistakes might cause others a lot of misery." Lina knew she sounded exasperated. What was the use of being a goddess if she was still fallible?

Demeter's expression was kind. "Wisdom does not come with immortality, *Daughter*." The goddess emphasized the word to reinforce to Lina the role she must play. "It comes with experience. And you have had many years of excellent experience in your life. Listen to your intuition. Use your mind. Believe in yourself. If you do make a mistake, learn from it." The glass began filling with murky wisps of cloud-like tendrils, obscuring the goddess's face. "Return to Hades with my blessings, Daughter." Her voice faded and her image disappeared.

Lina sighed. Basically, she was on her own.

"I hope Persephone's having an easier time at Pani Del Goddess," Lina grumbled.

The instant she spoke, the vapor within the glass ball began to swirl again. Then, as Lina watched in amazement, the cloudiness cleared to reveal a scene that caused her stomach to tighten with an unexpected wave of homesickness.

Lina bent closer to the oracle, totally engrossed in what she was seeing.

Pani Del Goddess was definitely having a good day. The little bakery was filled with customers. Actually, Lina blinked in surprise, it was packed. She peered through the magical orb, counting the familiar faces and realizing that they were in the minority. She didn't recognize most of the customers.

They certainly looked happy. There was a lot of talking and laughing going on along with—Lina blinked again, then her face broke into a pleased smile— they were eating what she was sure she recognized as Pizza alla Romana, the pizza that had summoned Demeter.

There were also several new signs placed along the wall behind the pastry cases. In bold script one read pizza del giorno—*Pizza of the Day*—quattro stagioni—*Four Seasons, with all your favorites: tomatoes, artichokes, mushrooms, olives, three cheeses and prosciutto.* Another proclaimed the vino del giorno—*wine of the day*—peppoli, chianti classico riserva. It was the third sign that confused Lina. All it said was tubs of ambrosia cream cheese limited to three per customer.

Ambrosia cream cheese? What was that?

Then Lina gasped and felt her face flush hot as she watched herself saunter through the swinging doors from the kitchen and enter the bakery. Lina shook her head back and forth, back and forth, back and forth in a repeated motion of denial.

What had Persephone done to her? She wasn't wearing one of her well-tailored business suits. She had on a little silk wraparound skirt that was bright fuchsia and a flowy short sleeved shell the color of honeydew melons. The skirt was short. Very short. And fuchsia! She didn't even own anything fuchsia! The shell veed dangerously low to expose Lina's deep cleavage. Openmouthed, Lina stared at her own body. The long length of leg that the skirt revealed was tanned, as was the rest of her body—which, in her opinion, Lina could see entirely too much of. And she had lost weight.

Lina narrowed her eyes and studied herself. No, maybe she hadn't actually lost weight. She looked toned and healthy. Her curves were all still there. They were just tighter and more well-defined. And her hair was different. It was longer—a couple of inches longer. How could that be? Hadn't she only been gone a day or so? Lina looked again. Yes, it was definitely longer. It rested on her shoulders in messy, indistinct curls, giving her a naughty, windblown look.

A man waved at Lina's body and she responded with a saucy smile and a toss of her hair. The man—*merda!* He wasn't just a man, he was an incredibly young man—hurried over to the object of his attention. Lina gaped as she watched herself flirt outrageously with a young, handsome, young, muscular, *young* man who was quite obviously very well acquainted with her. He couldn't have been much older than twenty-five.

The young handsome man bent and kissed Lina's body's mouth. Right in the middle of the bakery. Right in front of everyone.

"I don't F-ing believe it." She was too shocked to curse correctly in Italian or English.

Persephone laughed and spun playfully away from her suitor. For a split second she looked up and winked. Right at Lina.

Lina gasped and jerked back like she'd been slapped. At once the glass began to swirl and become cloudy. The image of Pani Del Goddess dissipated like smoke.

"Problems with the oracle, Goddess?" A deep voice spoke from behind her.

Lina whirled around to find that she was facing a man. An amazingly beautiful man.

"Persephone! I did not realize it was you."

"Hello," Lina said breathlessly, her shaking hand covering her pounding heart. Who was this gorgeous man?

A name drifted enticingly through her mind like an erotic whisper—*Apollo.*

Lina fanned her hot face and tried to pull herself together.

"You startled me, uh, Apollo."

The god lounged against the side of a large boulder. He was wearing a short leather tunic that was carved with a chest plate that met an unusual looking skirt-like wrap slung low around his muscular hips. But the "skirt" in no way made him appear effeminate. Except for a pair of sandals the rest of his body was bare. Very bare. Apollo was made of long, golden lines of muscle. His smile was smooth and attractive. Lina couldn't help staring. Actually, she thought staring was probably required in her particular situation.

The god nodded his head at the oracle. "Talking to Demeter?"

"Um, yes."

"She is visiting Hera. I think the two of them are planning something new with which to plague Zeus." He dropped his voice to a conspirator's level and his eyes gleamed. "Gossip has it that the Thunder God is besmitten with a mortal maiden . . . again." Apollo scratched his strong chin in consideration. "I believe the hapless girl's name is Io." He shook his head and laughed, making his brilliant blue eyes sparkle mischievously. "I will never understand Hera's temper. We all know Zeus has an appetite for beauty, yet he has chosen only one wife. She should not waste her time on frivolous jealousies."

Lina lifted one perfect eyebrow. "You don't consider fidelity in marriage important?"

"I believe finding pleasure is important, as you know very well, Persephone." His look was intimate as well as seductive.

Ohmygod. Had Apollo been Persephone's lover?

"I would be honored to remind you of any number of pleasurable delights, Goddess of Spring."

He pushed himself from the bank and moved with a feral grace toward her.

Lina's mouth went dry. He looked like he was going to take her in his arms. Lina lifted one hand out in front of her like a stop sign. Yes, he was the most handsome man she had ever seen, but she wasn't the type of woman who would kiss a stranger—despite what Persephone might be doing in her world.

Apollo watched her body stiffen and her jaw clench. He was well-versed in seduction and he knew how to get past a goddess who was dabbling in coy flirtation. In a fluid motion he changed his intent. Instead of taking her luscious young body in his arms he captured her outstretched hand and bowed gallantly over it. Like the consummate gentleman he was not, he kissed her hand lightly. Still holding her hand, Apollo looked deep within her eyes.

"I have watched you frolic in the meadows as I have driven my chariot through the sky. Your body moves with more grace than the flowers that bend delicately in the morning breeze. We would make a good match, you and I—the God of Light and the Goddess of Spring."

Lina almost laughed aloud with relief. Now here was something she was used to dealing with—a slick guy with a ready line. She batted her long lashes at the handsome god and sighed with an excess of maidenly delight. For good measure she even added a little Oklahoma twang to her breathless response.

"Oh, Apollo, I'm so glad you finally asked."

The god's lips began to turn up in victory, but her next words caused his expression to freeze.

"Imagine—marriage to the God of Light! I simply couldn't be more thrilled! Just wait until I tell Mother," she gushed, squeezing his hand and bouncing up and down like a giddy school girl.

"Marriage?" His deep voice had gone suddenly hoarse.

Lina beamed an innocent smile into his sapphire-colored eyes.

He dropped the goddess's hand like it was a flaming torch and took a step back, retreating from her bubble of personal space.

"It is not wise to rush hastily into marriage." He cleared his throat as if the word *marriage* was stuck there.

She told her face to frown prettily.

A flash of gold over Apollo's right shoulder caught her attention and interrupted the pithy reply she'd planned. She glanced behind him and felt her mouth round in pleasure.

"Oh! They're amazing." Forgetting about the suave god she turned her full attention to the four horses that had just trotted into view. They were harnessed to a golden chariot that blazed with such a brilliant light that it made her eyes tear. And the horses! They were the same blinding golden color with manes and tails of silver-white. The four slid to a halt, snorting and stamping their delicate hooves.

Apollo glanced over his shoulder. His consternation at the goddess's mention of marriage vanished as he saw his escape.

"Yes, Hadar, yes. I come!" He returned his gaze to Persephone. He had meant to rush away, and considered himself lucky that he had such a ready excuse. Marriage? What had Persephone been thinking! But the rapturous expression that filled her beautiful face gave him pause. She was truly spectacular. Apollo felt a familiar heavy tightening in his loins. "I did not realize you were interested in horses, Persephone."

"I love them," she said without looking at him.

"Come, I will introduce you." He held out his hand to her. Absentmindedly, she took it and hurried eagerly toward the horses, pulling him with her. Apollo's brow wrinkled. It was as if she had forgotten about him. An odd feeling passed through the god. Never before had a goddess forgotten about him—especially not a young goddess who had just tried to snare him in marriage.

The four mares pawed the ground and blew through their noses restlessly. With a flourish, Apollo presented them to Persephone.

"Persephone, Goddess of Spring, I am honored to present to you the mares that draw the light of the sun across the sky. They are Hadar, Aquila, Carina and Deneb," he said, pointing in turn to each horse.

Persephone dropped into a prima ballerina's graceful curtsy. "I am so pleased to meet each of you. Your coats are the most amazing color! You take my breath away."

The effect of her voice on the horses was immediate. Four pairs of ears pricked forward. Hooves ceased their restless pawing. The mare who stood nearest to the goddess stretched her muzzle tentatively in her direction, whickering like a colt.

"Oh, you beauty," Persephone laughed and caressed her.

Apollo felt stunned. He watched the goddess move from horse to horse, clucking and murmuring and whispering strange endearments to each of them. His mares, who were usually aloof and proud, reacted to her with true warmth. They lipped her face and pressed close for her caresses. They all but wriggled and wagged their tails for her attention.

The mares' reactions amazed him, but he was equally surprised at Persephone. He had never seen this side of her. She had been a goddess with whom he had flirted and had even enjoyed an occasional tryst—always begun and ended at his discretion. He had thought she had no interests beyond growing flowers, frolicking with nymphs and hosting sumptuous feasts. Today she was different. She had not fallen willingly into his arms. His eyes narrowed as he thought about her actions. *She* had actually toyed with *him*. She hadn't truly been interested in marriage. And now she appeared completely enamored with his mares.

She was magnificent.

Apollo was still watching Persephone and trying to decide what could have caused the change in the young goddess when a shrill scream of rage split the air. His mares reacted instantly. They bowed their necks and shook their heads, answering the scream with squeals of anger. The God of Light spun around, ready for battle.

A huge black stallion reared and pawed the air above him. Apollo recognized the wrath-filled creature as one of the dread steeds of Hades. His teeth were bared and his eyes blazed fire. Apollo's horses answered with their own show of rage.

"Stop it this second!" Lina's command dashed cold water on the horses' displays of anger.

Apollo stepped silently to the side, intrigued by this new Persephone. Hands planted firmly on her shapely hips she marched from his golden mares straight to the black beast. He watched, eager to see what she would do next.

"Orion, what in the world is wrong with you?"

She positioned her body so that she could berate all of the horses together. Her back was turned to Apollo affording him an excellent view of her very shapely rear end. He mused that it looked even rounder and more pleasantly inviting than when last he'd seen it. Or perhaps he had never before looked closely enough.

"And you four! What were you going to do, pick on Orion when he is clearly outnumbered?" She shook her head in disgust.

Five horses dropped their heads and looked like repentant school children. Orion took a halting half step toward the object of his affection, stretching his muzzle out to her. She gave him one more hard look before capitulating.

"What are you doing here?" she asked, trying not to smile as he nuzzled the side of her face. Then she noticed that he had been outfitted with a bridle and an attractive saddle made of leather dyed as black as his coat. Tucked into the crownpiece of the bridle was one perfect narcissus blossom. Lina felt a little thrill of pleasure. "Did he send you to get me?"

Apollo was irritated at the obvious delight in her voice. He? Surely she didn't mean Hades.

One of the golden mares nickered. Persephone tilted her head at Apollo's horses.

"Looks like I have to get going. It was wonderful to meet all of you. I hope we see each other again soon."

The goddess moved to the black steed's side and grabbed a fistful of mane, obviously preparing to mount and leave. Apollo couldn't believe it. She'd said good-bye to his horses, but she hadn't spoken another word to him.

"Allow me to aid you, Persephone," Apollo said, moving quickly.

"How rude of me, Apollo. With all this"—she waved her delicate hands at the horses—"excitement I totally forgot about you. It was really nice to meet you, too."

"Meet me." Apollo smiled suggestively at the lovely goddess. "It is not as if we were strangers before today."

Persephone blushed an attractive pink. "Oh, of course not. I didn't mean . . . I'm just . . . discombobulated."

Apollo threw back his head and laughed. "Discombobulated? From hereafter I am going to think of you as Goddess of Surprises rather than Goddess of Spring." He touched the side of her face gently. "And I *will* think of you. Often."

Lina felt the warmth of his hand on her face. His body was so close to her that she thought she could hear his heartbeat—or maybe that was her own. His eyes were such a vibrant shade of blue, the perfect match for his sun-colored hair and his golden skin. Without realizing it, she leaned into him.

Orion snorted.

Lina jerked back.

Apollo smiled knowingly. Before she could refuse him, he took her waist in his hands and slowly lifted her onto the impatiently waiting stallion's back, being careful to brush her body firmly against his own as he did so.

"When will I see you again?" Apollo asked when she had arranged her seat and placed her feet in the stirrups.

"I don't have any idea. There's a lot I have to do." She nodded her head behind her in the direction of the entrance to the Underworld.

"You sojourn with Hades?"

Apollo's incredulous tone irritated Lina. "I am vacationing in the Underworld."

Apollo laughed again. Orion's ears flattened to his head and Lina worried that he would bite the god.

"Vacationing with the dead? I have never heard of such a thing."

"I am finding that the Underworld, as well as its god, has been vastly underrated. Have a nice day, Apollo." Lina nudged Orion. The steed spun on his back hooves and lunged forward into a gallop, eager to return home with his treasure.

"I will be here every dawn, Persephone!" Apollo shouted after her.

Lina leaned forward, grabbing two fistfuls of Orion's mane. She ignored the Sun God, concentrating instead on keeping her seat, even though Orion's gallop was smooth and a childhood in Oklahoma had taught her to be an excellent rider. Apollo was handsome, seductive, and interesting. But she—unlike Persephone—had a job to do and would not let distractions get in her way. Nor did she—again unlike Persephone—want to create a situation that might cause embarrassment for either of them when their bodies were re-exchanged.

The breeze whistling past Orion's head brought with it the enticing scent of the narcissus blossom. Without realizing it, Lina's lips turned up in a wistful smile.

CHAPTER SIXTEEN

ORION'S fluid strides covered the distance from the entrance to the Underworld to Hades' palace in what seemed like minutes. Even the ferry ride was faster and easier with the big horse beside her. As the palace came into view Orion slowed his pace to a gentle canter. Without having to be guided, the stallion carried her around the side of the palace and directly to the stables. A uniformed stableman jumped to attention at their appearance, catching Orion's bridle and holding him steady while Lina dismounted.

"Thank you," she whispered to the stallion, kissing his silky muzzle. Orion nuzzled her affectionately. "It was a wonderful ride." Before she gave a final pat to his sleek neck, Lina reached up and pulled the narcissus from his bridle. She hesitated just a second, then tucked it behind her right ear before she turned to the stableman. "Do you know where Hades is?"

"Yes, Goddess. He is at the forge. You may follow that pathway. It will take you to Hades."

Lina smiled her thanks to him and started down the path. She knew Eurydice would be waiting inside with her meal, and she was hungry, but first she wanted to thank Hades for sending Orion to her. She thought that she also might ask him if he would mind if she rode the horse occasionally. The stallion was definitely a horse-lover's dream come true.

The path curled around the stables. It was lined with a hedge of roses the color of cream. She took deep, even breaths, enjoying their fragrance as it mixed with the tangy sweetness of the narcissus behind her ear. The little path angled to her left, and Lina could see that it led toward a small building that sat a little way from the main stable. From it a rhythmic clanging drifted to her on the wind. It was metal pounding on metal, proclaiming that she was heading in the right direction.

The door to the building was slightly ajar, just enough so that Lina could slip silently into the dimly lighted interior. She blinked, trying to adjust her vision from the brightness of outside. She heard a strange *whooshing* noise, which was followed by more clanking. In the far corner of the building flames from an enormous, openmouthed furnace flared, licking the air and adding sudden bursts of light to the darkness.

A man stood before the furnace, magnificently silhouetted against the orange fire. His back was to Lina. He was almost naked, covered only by a loincloth-like wrap that fit snugly around his hard buttocks. With long, powerful strokes he hammered a flat metal object held firmly in place by an ancient looking pair of tongs. With each fluid movement his muscles tensed and released. His body was slick with a glossy sheen of sweat, highlighting the strong ridges of his well-shaped form. His hair was tied back in a thick, dark queue.

Lina felt a jolt of recognition. It was Hades. Of course she'd already thought of him as handsome, and she had definitely been attracted to him . . . but . . . but . . . *merda!* She'd had no idea just how scrumptious he was. Until then he had always been so . . . fully dressed. Her mouth felt dry. He was so . . . so . . . not dressed. And muscular. And absolutely the sexiest thing she had ever seen.

Apollo had been almost as scantily clad, but seeing Hades nearly naked was different. The God of Light was handsome, but his beauty was a tame kitten compared to Hades' wild and feral masculinity. Seeing him so gloriously sweaty and under-clothed called awake fantasies within Lina that she thought she had permanently put to sleep.

Fantasies . . . charmed like a cobra, Lina stared at the god. Fantasies . . . she felt an ache deep within her body. It had been so long. Her thoughts flew free. If only Hades would stroke her with the same intensity with which he was working metal against metal. He looked so incredibly powerful. Lina shivered and imagined hot, sweaty flesh against hot, sweaty flesh. If only . . .

When she was younger Lina had dreamed about being passionate and unrestrained in bed; she had longed for it. Instead of finding a partner who matched her desires, she had married a man who thought quantity in bed equated to quality. So they "did it" a lot, quickly, and with boring regularity. Her husband didn't have the imagination or the inclination to experiment with passion. At some point in her marriage Lina's fantasies had died in a bed of boredom, and by that time she had hardly noticed their passing. Of course she had had lovers before and after her husband, not many—but enough. Long ago she had resigned herself to the fact that she seemed only to attract men who were more cerebral than sensuous. Her love life had been a bust.

So it was with unexpected intensity that Hades' body resurrected her youthful fantasies.

Not realizing he was being watched, Hades wiped his dripping face with the back of one hand and straightened, stretching his back to first flex and then release his massive shoulders.

A little aching sound slipped from Lina's throat.

His head snapped around, and he saw her. She was standing near the doorway with a peculiar look on her beautiful face. Pleasure flushed his already heated body; she was wearing his narcissus in her hair.

Lina licked her lips and cleared her throat. "Um, I didn't mean to disturb you."

"You haven't." He set aside the tongs and wiped his hands on a piece of cloth. Her voice sounded odd, like she was having trouble breathing. Perhaps the return ride from the World of the Living had taxed her strength. Concerned and wishing to put her at ease, he made a welcoming gesture with his hand. "Please, come in."

Lina walked toward him, trying to keep from staring at his chest. His

bronzed skin was slick and inviting. Muscles . . . she wanted to moan with pleasure and run her hands up and down his sweaty torso. *Act your age!* she mentally scolded herself.

"I wanted to thank you for sending Orion after me."

She seemed breathless and maybe even a little jittery, which he found
strange. What was bothering the goddess? "He was happy to be of service to
you."

Lina's hormones shouted that they wished Hades would *service* her, but her
voice was better behaved. "If you wouldn't mind, I would love to ride Orion
again."

"I would not mind." Hades hesitated. *Keep talking, don't stand there like
a mute fool,* his mind commanded. "I am quite sure that Orion would be
pleased. Of course, there are three other steeds who will be clamoring jealously
for your attention, too," he said, wiping the back of his hand across his brow
again.

His movement caused a single bead of sweat to slide from his neck. Lina
watched as it traveled with agonizing slowness down his chest and over the
well-defined ridges of his abdomen to disappear enticingly under his loincloth.

Her mind refused to formulate a response. All she could do was stand
there, speechless, and stare at the damp path the drop left on his glistening skin,
wishing with X-rated intensity that she could follow it with her tongue.

"Persephone? I only meant to jest with you. Of course you may ride Orion,"
Hades assured her. Why was she not speaking? It was certainly not like her to
be silent.

"Th-thank you." Lina's eyes snapped up to his face. "I'm sorry. I guess my
thoughts are elsewhere."

Hades nodded with sudden understanding. "Of course, it has been a difficult day." He looked down at her sheepishly. "I asked Iapis to report to me if
Aeneas had entered Elysia."

"Really?" Hades' words pulled her interest from his body. "And what did
he say?"

"I appear to owe you a crystal chandelier. The warrior's soul is, indeed, resting in the Elysian Fields. And, just as you predicted, he has only recently entered the Underworld."

Concern wrinkled her smooth brow. "What are you going to do about
Dido?"

The god sighed and wiped another trail of sweat from his cheek. "I will not rescind my decision. I suppose I must have Iapis keep watch on her and . . ." he broke off. The goddess's instincts about Dido had been correct. Why not get her input? He gave her an appraising look. "What would you suggest I do, Persephone?"

Lina felt a little flutter of pleasure; Hades valued her opinion. "Well, I don't think it's wise to leave them in Elysia together. Dido will never get over him like that." Absently, she tugged at one long lock of hair as she considered what to do with the spirit. "I'm assuming that you don't want to send Aeneas out of Elysia?"

"No. The warrior has earned his paradise."

"And you already said you won't send her back to that lamentation place, so I think the only reasonable answer is to let her drink from," she hesitated, making sure she had the right name, "the River Lethe. You said that when they drink from Lethe, souls forget their lives, but remain essentially the same type of people. So send her back for another lifetime. Maybe she really did learn something during her lamentation, something that Aeneas' presence would overshadow, but without any memory of him—" Lina gestured abstractly with her hands. "I guess what I'm trying to say is that maybe she'll do better the second time around."

Hades' smile made his eyes dance. He wanted to throw his arms around her and shout for joy. "Persephone, how is it that a goddess who is so young is also so wise?"

Lina's heart thudded at the warmth of his expression. "You shouldn't judge me by how I look. There's a lot more to me than just a pretty young face."

Hades couldn't stop himself from reaching out and touching that lovely face. "You are correct again. Of all the gods, I should know better than to judge others on appearance and rumor."

His fingers were hot and Lina wanted to turn her face into his palm and press herself against him.

"I'm far from perfect," she said, her voice hardly above a whisper. "I made a mistake in my decision about Eurydice."

"But you were wise enough to correct your mistake. You saved the little spirit. All is as it should be now." As he spoke, his hand moved from her face to touch the moonlight-colored bloom she had tucked behind her ear. Hades glanced from her eyes to the flower. "I hoped that you would approve of Orion's decoration."

Lina sounded out of breath when she answered him. "He looked very handsome with it tucked in his bridle; it's a beautiful flower."

Speak your thoughts aloud! Hades' mind spurred him on. He drew a breath and said, "It is, indeed, a beautiful flower, but it pales in comparison to your loveliness, Persephone." Almost as if it acted on its own, his hand moved from the blossom to trail down the side of her throat, caressing her smooth skin with gentle fingers.

The goddess's breath caught and a little surprised "oh!" sound broke from her lips. Instantly, Hades stopped, his hand hovering near the curve of her neck. His eyes met hers.

"Would you rather that I did not touch you?" His voice sounded rough and foreign.

Persephone blinked twice—quickly.

Hades tightened his jaw and turned away from her. What a fool he'd been! He had read the look in her eyes. He had not seen desire or acceptance there; instead, he had clearly seen shock and confusion.

"Wait!"

Hades took another deep breath, steeling himself. He turned to face her.

"It's not that I don't want you to touch me. I'm just . . . it's just . . ." Lina forced herself to stop babbling. Then she started over in a more controlled, rational tone. "Demeter told me that you weren't interested in women, and it's a well known fact that you don't cavort with nymphs or chase after goddesses, so it's a surprise to me that you're so . . . so . . ." She sighed, frustrated at her inability to explain. "Hades, you are definitely *not* the boring, dour god that Demeter had described to me."

Hades' body became very still. His eyes met hers and held and she read good-humored surprise reflected within their expressive depths.

"The rumor *was* correct," he said slowly and distinctly, his lips curving up. "I did not cavort with nymphs or chase after goddesses because I had met none who interested me."

"Oh," Lina said, unable to look away from his penetrating gaze. Sexy—he was just so damn dark and sexy.

"Until you entered my realm," Hades said with finality.

He stepped forward, and in one swift motion, took her in his arms. Lina felt herself melt into the simmering heat of his sweat-slickened body as he bent and pressed his mouth against hers. Her lips parted and for one delicious moment the kiss deepened. Then, too soon, he released her. She felt dizzy, like she had been underwater for too long and couldn't catch her breath.

"There is more to me than appearance and rumor." Hades echoed her earlier words.

"I believe you."

Hades bent to taste her sweetness again. Lina moaned huskily against his mouth and the sound inflamed him. The full globes of her breasts burned into his chest. He felt his willpower begin to dissolve as his passion for her consumed him.

The shudder that passed through his body became her own, and Lina slid her hands up his bare chest and wrapped them around his neck.

"Don't stop," she whispered. She took his bottom lip between her teeth and bit down teasingly.

With a groan of unleashed desire, Hades cupped her buttocks and lifted her from her feet so that her softness was pressed firmly against him. In two strides he had her pinned against the wall of the forge. One hand slipped up to entrap her breast. The sweet, enticing nipple puckered against his palm and he molded and stroked it. Beneath his other searching hand he found an opening in her silky robe and his hot fingers grasped her naked skin. His pulse thundered in his ears as his world narrowed to exclude everything except his raging need for her.

Caught between the hard coolness of the stone wall and the hard heat of Hades, Lina felt that she was being consumed by him.

Eurydice burst into the forge like a Fourth of July sparkler.

"Persephone! There you are! Oh—" She broke off, her eyes widening as she took in the rumpled, flushed condition of her Goddess and the dark intensity with which Hades had her pressed against the wall.

"*What is it!*" Hades roared, causing the floor of the forge to shake in response.

"Forgive me!" Eurydice's pale face blanched, and she backed fearfully toward the door.

Fighting to catch her breath, Lina pushed firmly against Hades' chest. The god stared down at her. His eyes still burned with need.

"You're scaring Eurydice," she hissed, and, Lina added silently, he was scaring her, too. She had never witnessed the raw power of a god's desire. It definitely had the ability to excite, but it was also overwhelming.

Slowly, through the fog of his passion Hades recognized the fear that flashed through Persephone's eyes. By Zeus' beard! He didn't want her to fear him. Hades blinked, and with a sigh like a storm wind, he moved back, setting her gently to her feet as he suppressed the hot tide within him.

"The spirit may not yet depart," Hades snapped the command and the door to the forge closed before Eurydice could scuttle through it.

The little spirit turned slowly to face the god. Her voice trembled. "It was foolish of me to interrupt. Please forgive me, I . . . I . . . did not realize."

Lina thought that Eurydice looked like she was close to dissolving into tears. "Don't be silly, honey, there's nothing to forgive." She smoothed her hair and tried to ignore the heat that still tingled up from her breasts, through her neck, and into her cheeks. "I was just thanking Hades for sending Orion after me."

Beside her, Hades snorted, "I'll have to send the stallion after you more often."

Lina's gaze met Hades', which sparkled with a mischievous sense of humor, and something else, something that she thought might be tenderness. He brushed the side of her cheek with the tips of his fingers before reluctantly turning his attention to Eurydice.

"Calm yourself, child," Hades said.

Eurydice gave the god a dubious look.

He smiled reassuringly at Eurydice, his voice full of fatherly concern. "Why is it you were searching for your goddess?"

Eurydice looked from Hades to Persephone, who nodded encouragingly at her. The little spirit's expression began to relax and she smiled tentatively back at the dark god. "Iapis asked me to find Persephone. The Limoniades are calling for her."

"Are they indeed?" Although he hated the interruption, he couldn't help but be pleased that the spirits in his realm were not simply accepting the goddess, they were actively seeking her out.

Eurydice nodded enthusiastically. "Iapis said they would not begin the gathering until the goddess joined them."

Lina looked from Hades to Eurydice while she quickly accessed Persephone's memories. *Limoniades—nymph-like spirits of meadows and flowers.* So the spirits of flowers were calling her for a gathering, and Hades and Eurydice looked pleased about it. Lina tried to appear as if she knew what they were talking about. Gathering? What could they be gathering? She frantically asked her built-in memory file.

"It is only logical that they would desire the presence of the Goddess of Spring," Hades said.

In Olympus, forest nymphs are responsible for the gathering of many things: herbs for potions, grapes for wine, flowers to bedeck the palaces of the immortals—

Her internal monologue was interrupted by Hades' voice.

"It is, of course, Persephone's decision," Hades said, obviously surprised at her hesitation.

"Well, I . . ."

"Oh, please, may I watch?" Eurydice rushed forward and grasped her hand. "I have never witnessed the gathering of nectar for ambrosia. Nor have I even seen a nymph, not in the flesh or in the spirit." Eurydice beamed at her.

Lina smiled at Eurydice's infectious exuberance. "Of course you may watch." She felt a trickle of relief. Gathering nectar for ambrosia couldn't be that difficult. She'd just follow the lead of the Lemonade-whatever-their-names-were nymphs.

"Thank you, Persephone!" Eurydice danced to the door.

"May I watch, too?"

Lina looked up at Hades, surprised by his question. He was, after all, God of the Underworld. He had the power to command anyone within his realm; he certainly didn't have to ask her permission. Yet there he stood, doing just that. A little half smile played around his full lips. Sweat still beaded his bare skin, making the bronze muscles of his chest look erotic and exquisitely touchable. Lina felt a tug deep within her, an elemental response to the virile beauty of the dark god.

"No, I don't mind," she said breathlessly.

"Good. It pleases me to watch you," Hades said. Then he repeated his earlier gesture by gently touching the blossom tucked behind her ear. When he withdrew his hand, he allowed his fingers to brush the side of her face in the whisper of a caress. The goddess still shivered under his touch, but this time Hades saw only the reflection of his own desire within her eyes.

"Hurry, Persephone!" Eurydice called from the doorway without looking back at her goddess. "I can't wait to see the Limoniades."

Hades sighed again, quelling the frustration he felt at having to share Persephone. But would he really have it any other way? No, he wanted the goddess to be accepted within his realm, and with that acceptance went the responsibility of sharing her attention. Reluctantly, he moved from her side to reach for a length of dark material that hung from the wall behind him, which he wrapped, toga-like, across his body.

"I'm coming," Lina said, hurrying to catch Eurydice as she scampered through the door and along the pathway. Hades strode beside her, and Lina felt his presence like he was a live wire, humming in time to her own electricity. She was energized by his closeness and by the lingering thrill of his touch. How long had it been since a man had made her feel breathless and excited? Too long, she told herself, ignoring the little voice of reason that counseled her to think about what she was rushing into, that reminded her that she was only there to complete a job and that she didn't know anything about immortals, or the Limoniades, or nectar, or . . .

The path turned abruptly around the corner of the stable and then it opened onto the expanse of the palace's rear gardens. Lina stumbled to a halt, drawing a deep, surprised breath.

Shapes made of incandescent light filled the first tier of the trellised lawn. As Lina came into sight, the glowing forms trembled, and then with a noise that sounded very much like the coo of doves, they surged forward until they surrounded Lina, Eurydice and Hades. Lina stared at them in wonder. Naked women! Her mind registered that the lights hovering and cooing around her were fashioned in the shapes of hundreds of naked women. They were tiny and delicate, the tops of their bright heads barely reached Lina's shoulder, but each one was unique and beautiful in her own right—like flakes of snow, or petals on a flower. And sprouting from the back of each spirit was a pair of sparkling, gossamer wings that looked as fine as mist.

Eurydice giggled. "Why are none of them dressed?"

The echo of Eurydice's youthful laughter rippled through the Limoniades like water over a pebbled brook.

"Look closer, child," Hades' deep voice answered Eurydice. "They are dressed in light and laughter and the brilliance of their souls. It is the only dressing spirits of flowers and meadows require."

"I think they're perfect," Lina said.

The sound of the goddess's voice sent a wave of excitement through the group, and several of the spirits twirled and leapt in glee.

"Join us, Goddess of Spring. Bless the gathering of nectar, which will become the ambrosia of the Underworld."

They spoke with one melodic voice that was magnified magically on the soft breeze.

"Come with us, Persephone. The flowers await the Goddess of Spring."

Their voices were enchanting. Instinctively, Lina's body responded. She stepped away from Eurydice and Hades, joining the Limoniades. Musical notes and the whir of hundreds of wings engulfed her. On feet that felt like air, Lina moved with the spirits out into the flower-filled grounds.

The Limoniades began humming. It was a sound that thrummed through Lina's blood, reminding her of the feel of warm summer nights, the smell of newly cut hay and the taste of fine dark chocolate. Entranced, she watched the glowing forms separate and descend upon the listening blossoms. Wings blurring, they hovered above the ground like elusive hummingbirds, and then, as one they dipped their fingers within the open blooms.

Lina watched the nymph spirits draw beads of golden drops from the flowers. Hades was forgotten. Eurydice left her mind. The only thought that filled her body was how very much she would like to join the Limoniades.

"Yes! Call the nectar to you. Take your rightful place as Goddess of Spring amidst the Limoniades."

The whisper within Lina's mind sounded restless and impatient. It was the final goad she needed. Her heart drumming in time with the song of the Limoniades, Lina approached a cluster of milk-colored tulips. Their stems were long and thick and their blooms opened to expose the crisp yellow of their pistils.

She needed to call the nectar to her. Lina squinted her eyes, dipped her finger into one of the tulips and concentrated. The first blob of golden liquid spurted from the bloom with such force that Lina yelped in surprise as it flew into her hand and disintegrated into a sticky mess.

The deep base of Hades' chuckles framed the light, trilling sound of laughter that trickled through the watching Limoniades. Lina glanced over her shoulder at the god. His eyes sparkled at her. She tossed her long hair back and sent him a saucy look. Then, a thought drifted through her mind. . . . She felt alive and sexy and incredibly, amazingly seductive. With a wicked smile Lina caught Hades' gaze. She arched one brow up, raised her hand and let her soft, pink tongue slowly lick a trickle of the sweet, syrupy nectar from her middle finger. The Limoniades responded with appreciative coos and trills as Hades froze, slack jawed and speechless.

"Gently, Goddess, gently," the Limoniades purred. *"The nectar already desires to come to you. You need only coax it, not command it. It is not a god. . . ."*

Without looking at Hades' reaction to the nymphs' words, Lina stifled a smile and turned back to the cluster of tulips. She tickled another blossom with the tip on one slender finger and sent the gentle thought to it that she might like the nectar to come to her, please.

A pearl of gold drifted from the center of the flower to perch on the tip of her extended finger. Lina smiled triumphantly at it.

"The gathering, Goddess. Join the gathering."

Still smiling, Lina gazed around her. Each spirit nymph was creating a pile of glowing golden drops beside her as she flitted from flower to flower, calling the nectar forth.

Okay, Lina thought. She could do that. And she began weaving her own pile. Without stopping to think or understand or question, Lina used Persephone's perfect voice to harmonize with the spirits of the flowers, and when she joined the Limoniades in their song, Hades' garden seemed to inhale with a tangible sense of joy and then erupt into glorious full bloom. Every flower opened itself. Every blossom dripped golden drops of nectar, aching to be harvested.

Amidst it all, Lina shined.

Hades couldn't take his eyes from her. In his entire existence he had never desired anything as much as he desired Persephone. He was becoming consumed by her, and the thought made his immortal soul shiver.

What would happen when she left? She would, he reminded himself. She was the Goddess of Spring. She belonged to the world above. He was the dark God of the Underworld, scorned by everything living.

Everything except Persephone. But for how long?

The ache within him pulsed and took on a life of its own. And the god gave name to it, finally understanding what it was that caused him such elusive, unending pain—what it was that Persephone had awakened along with hope.

Loneliness.

Hades clenched his jaw against his inner turmoil and turned blindly away from the sight of the lovely young goddess frolicking joyously amidst the spirits of his realm.

He ran right into Eurydice. Hades stifled his groan of frustration as he caught the little spirit and kept her from tumbling to the ground. He forced his stiff face into the semblance of a smile. "I was not looking, child." He changed his path of retreat, but Eurydice's voice gave him pause.

"But, you aren't leaving? What shall I tell Persephone?" she asked in her sweet, shy voice.

"Tell her," he ground his teeth, "that I had the business of my realm to attend." Eurydice's eyes were large and round and they seemed to reach into his soul. Her disappointment was obvious, as was her concern for her goddess. The god raked a hand through his hair. "And tell your goddess that I wish her to ride with me on the morrow."

Eurydice's face lit in a smile. "Persephone will enjoy that very much."

Will she enjoy it enough to stay with me? the god wanted to rant and rage and roar. Instead he pulled the familiar mantle of sternness over his features and made certain that when he spoke his voice was free of his seething emotions.

"I will send Iapis to escort her to the stables after daybreak."

"Yes, Lord."

Hades strode away, muttering under his breath about goddesses and young girls.

As soon as he was out of sight, Iapis materialized beside Eurydice. She glanced at the daimon, her look betraying no surprise at his sudden appearance.

"How goes it?" Iapis asked her.

"I am pleased," Eurydice said, sounding wise beyond her years.

"Do you think he took my advice and thought of her as one of the dead?"

"Not for long," Eurydice said enigmatically, remembering her goddess's flushed face and the heat with which Hades' eyes followed her. "Not for long . . ."

The daimon smiled and took the little spirit's hand in his. Raising it to his lips, he kissed her gently. Eurydice's pale cheeks pinkened slightly, but her large eyes gazed steadily at him. She returned his smile.

CHAPTER SEVENTEEN

"GOOD-BYE! Thank you!" Lina waved to the Limoniades as the glowing spirits faded into the distance, taking their shining golden drops of nectar with them. Their farewell coos tumbled musically on the wind.

"That was wonderful to watch, Persephone." Eurydice was all smiles as Lina rejoined her at the edge of the gardens.

"I'm so glad they called me. It was an amazing experience," Lina gushed. She felt giddy and energized, like she'd had too many double-shot cappuccinos before breakfast. "Oh, Eurydice, this world is incredible." She grinned, slinging an arm around the spirit and hugging her. Lina glanced around them. "Hades left?" she asked, trying to sound nonchalant.

"He had to attend to the business of his realm. But," she added quickly as the goddess's shining face dimmed, "he commanded me to request your presence at the stables on the morrow."

"Riding Orion again." Lina's smile turned dreamy as she thought about the black stallion. She would definitely look forward to the morning ride—almost as much as she'd look forward to seeing Hades. Her mind skittered around, jumbling images of the god's sweat-beaded body, the sensuous song of the Limoniades and the way Hades' lips had burned against hers. Lina's young borrowed body tingled erotically.

"That horse frightens me," Eurydice said.

Lina blinked, refocusing on Eurydice's pale face. *Merda!* She needed to stop letting her mind wander.

"He's nothing to be frightened of. Really, he's like a puppy in my hands," Lina said breezily, trying not to think about Orion's master, and how *un*like a puppy he felt under her hands.

"I think I'll just stay away from him," Eurydice said.

Lina told herself that's probably the attitude she should have about Hades. He was too damn dangerously attractive. She should just stay away from him. But the low ache in her body murmured that she wouldn't.

She definitely needed to get her mind off Hades.

"Hey, how about we go find me something to drink?" Lina wiggled her eyebrows at Eurydice. "All this nectar-gathering has made me thirsty for ambrosia."

Eurydice tittered, "It has also made you sticky."

Lina glanced down at herself. Shiny speckles of golden dots were sprinkled like dew all over her body. She touched one of them and then put her finger to her mouth. It tasted like sugarcane mixed with honey mixed with something like caramel or maybe butterscotch. It was delicious. But Eurydice was right, she was a mess. And she certainly was not going to think about how it would feel to have Hades lick the sweet drops off her body.

"I need a shower. A cold one," she muttered.

"You wish to be caught in a cold rain?"

Lina laughed. "Not exactly. A shower isn't just rain from the skies. It's kind of like bathing, only you're standing up and water is being poured over you."

"Oh, that sounds like my mother's bathing ritual, although she did not like her water cold," Eurydice said.

Startled, Lina asked, "Really, what kind of bathing ritual did your mother have?"

Eurydice grinned impishly. "I could show you. It would probably be an easier way to get the nectar off of you." She touched one of the drops and it trailed long, gooey tendrils from her finger back to the goddess' skin. "They might make your bathing water a sticky mush."

"Eurydice, you are a genius. Tonight I put myself in your capable hands."

THE little spirit had turned into a mini drill sergeant. From the second they reentered the palace she had been firing orders and directing a bevy of flitting servants. She wouldn't allow Lina to do anything except sit on the edge of the vanity chair and sip ambrosia.

"The goddess would prefer to bathe on the balcony."

Mid-gulp of ambrosia, Lina sputtered. Bathe on the balcony? What was Eurydice thinking? The spirit was using the voice that Lina was rapidly coming to recognize as her formal, she's-my-goddess-you-better-mind-me tone as she tapped one slender foot thoughtfully against the marble floor. Without giving Lina a chance to speak, Eurydice barreled on.

"Yes, mother always used our inner courtyard. No! Not there!" she snapped at two male servants who were struggling to carry a large basin into the bathing room. She pointed to the door in the middle of the wall of windows. "Take it through there."

"Um, Eurydice, why are we going out on the balcony?"

"You are not to worry, Persephone. All will be perfect." She frowned at one of the servants who jostled the basin a little too roughly against the marble floor of the balcony.

"Goddess," Iapis entered the room and bowed politely to Lina before turning his attention to the spirit. "You have need of me, Eurydice?"

"Yes," Eurydice said, hooking her long, wispy hair behind her ears. "The goddess is going to bathe on her balcony, and—"

Here Lina had to interrupt. "Wait, I think it's a lovely idea for me to bathe on the balcony—I mean, the view is spectacular—but I'm really not comfortable with, well," Lina dropped her voice so that the daimon and Eurydice had to lean forward to hear her. "I don't want a bunch of guys seeing me naked." Even if they were dead guys, she added silently.

Eurydice squinted at her as if she didn't fully understand what she was saying, but Lina was relieved to see Iapis nodding his head.

"It is also true of the Goddess Artemis. She will not allow her nakedness to be glimpsed by any mortals except for her handmaidens. But that problem is easily remedied, Persephone. I shall simply command that all spirits stay away from your wing of the palace and the surrounding grounds."

Eurydice gifted the daimon with a smile filled with warmth, and Iapis looked inordinately pleased with himself. Lina felt like she had been caught in the middle of a well-meaning tornado. It was whirling her around and around, and was determined to spin her clothes off.

"I really don't want to cause any trouble," Lina said helplessly.

"It is no trouble at all," the daimon assured her.

"You are the Goddess of Spring," Eurydice said.

Apparently, that was the final word on everything.

Resigned, Lina settled back, deciding not to care if she got nectar all over the silk-lined chair. She was, after all, the Goddess of Spring. She watched the whirlwind of preparation for her bath. They appeared to like cleaning up after her. Eurydice shook her head severely at an insubstantial servant who had failed to retrieve the correct number of towels from the bathing room. Or maybe they were just scared of Eurydice. At least the little spirit didn't seem to have been traumatized by the day's events. Lina sipped her ambrosia, considering. Had it only been that morning that Orpheus had descended into the Underworld? It felt like it had happened so long ago. How could she only have known Hades for a couple of days? What was it that Demeter had said? Something about the passage of time being measured differently by the gods. Her instincts told her that Demeter's words rang true. The passage of time was different in the world of the gods, as different as her borrowed life. Her heart felt different, too. The veneer of cynicism that had muffled it the past several years didn't seem to have transcended worlds. Lina's stomach tightened. To lust after a god . . . wouldn't that be the ultimate stupidity?

"Goddess, I will leave you to Eurydice and the maiden servants. Let your mind be eased—no mortal male will gaze upon you." Iapis bowed to her.

"Iapis!" A sudden thought made Lina call him back. "You said no *mortal* male would see me, but what about Hades? Where is he?" Lina pretended that she didn't know her cheeks were blazing with hot color.

Iapis' face remained impassive. "The Lord of the Underworld has gone to the Elysian Fields. He spoke of seeking out Dido and escorting her to the River Lethe."

Even though Lina was pleased at the news that Hades had followed her advice, she frowned and pointed out the open glass doors to the balcony and beyond.

"Aren't the Elysian Fields that way?"

"Some are, Goddess." Then his eyes flashed with understanding. "I will go to my Lord and guide him back to the palace by a different route. Rest assured, Persephone, Hades would not wish to disturb your privacy."

"Oh, no, of course not," Lina said hastily.

"Enjoy your bath, Goddess." Iapis bowed again.

Eurydice followed him to the door.

"If your goddess requires anything else, you need only send one of the maidens for me, and I will see it done," Iapis said.

Eurydice tilted her head in acknowledgment. "That is most gracious of you, Iapis," she said, stepping into the hall. There she lowered her voice so that Persephone could not hear her. "Did Hades really go to Elysia?"

"Yes," Iapis whispered.

"But you will not stop him from returning through the gardens?"

Iapis answered with a slow, knowing smile and a wink. Eurydice had to clamp her pretty lips together to keep from giggling.

EURYDICE was chattering happily as she helped Lina out of her nectar-speckled robes. They were standing in the middle of the spacious balcony that looked out over the glorious rear grounds of the palace. Grounds that were decidedly empty of all spirits, male or otherwise, Lina noted. Directly in front of her was the basin Eurydice had ordered the servants to bring. Beside it was a small table covered with bottles and sponges. Sitting closer to the basin than the table was a short, fat stool. Near the edge of the balcony was a chaise lounge that Eurydice had insisted the servants drag out of Lina's bedroom. On the chaise sat an intricately carved wooden tray, which held sumptuous pomegranate fruits, their skins already opened and spilling forth their garnet-colored seeds. And, of course, there was also a crystal bottle filled to brimming with chilled ambrosia. Lina grinned. A goddess could certainly never have enough ambrosia.

The balcony itself was, like the rest of the palace, opulent and unique. It didn't just extend out and around the wall of windows. It curved gracefully, like one half of a Valentine's Day heart, until the balustrades opened to a circular marble staircase, which spilled out into a flower-lined path, which led, like spokes in a wheel, to the first tier of Hades' gardens. It was her own private entrance to paradise.

Lina gazed out on the amazing scene while Eurydice unwrapped her clothes from around her. She hadn't been exaggerating when she'd said that the view was spectacular. And there was something about the light—it had begun to change. The pastel sky was darkening and the colors were deepening from pink to coral and violet to purple. Suddenly, torches flared alive all throughout the gardens, causing Lina to jerk in surprise.

"There is no need to worry, Goddess." One of the maidens who had stayed to assist Eurydice spoke up with the voice of a child. "The torches light themselves. There is no mortal man in the gardens to look upon your nakedness."

"What is your name?" Lina asked the young spirit.

"Hersilia," she ducked her head shyly.

"Thank you, Hersilia, for reminding me not to be so silly." Lina smiled at the servant.

Eurydice unwrapped the final layer of silky fabric from around her waist and bent to help her off with her leather slippers.

"Now just step into the basin, Persephone," Eurydice directed her.

The marble basin felt cool against Lina's bare feet, and she decided that it was a little like standing in a giant cereal bowl. The lip of the bowl came up to her knees. She was about to say that she felt like a naked Fruit Loop when Eurydice climbed on top of the stool.

"You may bring me the urn."

The waiting servants formed an unlinked chain from the balcony, through the glass doors and into the bathroom. From there they began passing hourglass-shaped clay urns filled with water, which, to Lina's delight, Eurydice poured in steaming waves over her head.

More servants dripped soap onto sponges soft as cotton balls. Slowly, gently they began cleaning her skin. Lina's initial response was to stay very still, with her arms held at a rigid T away from her sides.

Then Eurydice began to sing, softly at first, but soon the other spirits joined with her and sweet, feminine voices filled the balcony.

Pale, beyond porch and portal,
crowned with hair of silk, she stands,

she who gathers all things mortal
within her soft, immortal hands.

Their song was slow and sensual, like the beat of bolero, and it stirred something deep within Lina. Intrigued, she accessed Persephone's memories. *They sing ancient praise to the beauty of the goddess. They do you great honor.* They did her great honor. . . . Suddenly it didn't matter that she was wearing a borrowed shape. She was alive and beautiful and filled with the exquisite power of a goddess. Lina let her body go loose. She drew a deep breath and exhaled all the stress and cares and inhibitions of her mortal life. Her ivory skin tingled and she began to sway gracefully with the tempo of the song.

Her languid lips are sweeter
than love who pines to greet her
no mortal man shall meet her
the goddess solitary stands.

The hot water sluiced over her naked body, a river of silk the soapy sponges traveled along. Lina turned and laughed and reveled in the sensations cascading down her skin. She felt the evening air lick her sleek sides. It was warm, but in contrast to the heat of the water it brought gooseflesh rising on her skin and caused her nipples to pucker erotically. Her laughter was infectious, and soon the maidservants joined her and the sounds of song and joy drifted through the palace and the gardens of the God of the Dead.

With slow, thoughtful steps Hades followed the snaking path that led from the forest, which separated his palace grounds from the Elysian Fields. The path took him through the third tier garden. He was glad that he had listened to Persephone's advice. Dido had been easy to find. All he had had to do was locate Aeneas. Her spirit had been nearby, pining miserably as she obsessively shadowed the warrior's every move. She hadn't wanted to drink of Lethe, such was the strength of her unrequited love, but Dido's soul belonged to Hades, and what he commanded she must do. As always happened, when she drew near Lethe, her spirit had quickened. The river's seductive voice had entranced her, making her transition a gentle one. But it was not the memory of Dido that slowed the god's steps. It was Persephone. The goddess haunted his senses.

Though he had only held her in his arms briefly, he could still feel the satin of her skin against his . . . taste the sweetness of her mouth . . . smell the scent of woman that clung to her body.

He could still hear her laughter. Hades swore under his breath. Was this what love was like? Must he be consumed with thoughts of her?

The laughter came again. Listening carefully, Hades halted. Then he drew a relieved breath. The sound wasn't coming from his imagination. It was being carried from the palace by the warm evening breeze. Now he could discern different voices along with Persephone's. Some were laughing, some were singing. All were delightfully female. When Hades began walking again, his stride was no longer slow and thoughtful.

Entering the second tier, Hades scanned the rearview of his palace. Daylight had darkened to evening and the flickering torchlight that periodically illuminated the gardens did little to aid his vision. As usual, the palace windows were gaily lit, and Hades thought he could see graceful, curving shapes outlined against the wall of windows that belonged to Persephone's chamber. He thought it odd that they appeared to be on her balcony. Hades increased his stride.

When he reached the stairs that would take him up to the first tier, he was sure that he could hear the splashing of water. Taking the stairs three at a time, he climbed quickly up to the level of his palace. Here the greenery and flowers wound around in labyrinthine twists and turns, and Hades did not have a clear view of Persephone's balcony until he was very close to the edge of the gardens. The god stepped around an ornamental hedge and stopped like he had slammed against an invisible wall.

Persephone was naked. She stood in the center of a large marble basin, looking like an exquisite statue that had come to life. The stray thought passed through Hades' numbed mind that he suddenly understood Pygmalion's obsession with Galatea. Then his mind seemed to cease functioning completely and he became nothing more than a receptacle for the desire that scorched through his blood.

Eurydice was pouring trails of steaming water over Persephone while semitransparent maidservants lathered her skin and hair. The goddess laughed and teasingly splashed water at the spirits, who were humming a slow, seductive tune between breathless, girlish giggles. The evening light was muted, but Persephone's body was silhouetted against the wall of glowing windows. Hades could see the flush that swept her ivory skin. His eyes ravished her body. His fingers tingled as he remembered how the delicate curve of her neck had felt under his too-brief caress. Hades' gaze lowered to her breasts. The soft globes were full and heavy. Their blush-colored nipples were taut, begging for the touch of his lips and tongue. His loins tightened and throbbed achingly with the heat of his lust. He ground his teeth together to keep from giving voice to the moan of frustrated desire that was building within him. But he did not turn away, he did not stop gazing at her. He could not.

Persephone's waist curved in, and then swelled to flare into well-rounded hips. Her legs were long and shapely. Hades' eyes were drawn to the inviting V of dark hair that formed at their junction. The curling triangle glistened with water, which dripped down her inner thighs.

As if sensing him, Persephone's chin went up and her gaze shifted from the laughing servants to rove over the distant gardens. Hades was sure he would be discovered, but his dark cloak blended like night with the shadow of the hedge and the goddess's eyes passed unseeing over him.

Eurydice poured a final stream of water over Persephone and then the little spirit called for a maidservant to bring her towels. They helped the smiling goddess step from the basin and began drying her body.

Now was the time for him to turn away. Persephone's laughter floated to him and his eyes refused to leave her as they sought glimpses of her nakedness. His conscience told him he should go, but the voice of newly awakened desire and longing and loneliness drowned it out.

The servants finished drying Persephone's body. Her hair drifted around her in long, damp tendrils, which Eurydice gathered and piled loosely atop her head. Then the spirit poured a thick liquid from a tall glass bottle into her hand and began gently massaging the oil into her skin. Two other maidservants joined her. Hades watched Persephone's eyes close. A sensuous smile curved her lips as the slick hands of the maidens anointed her body. Hades' breathing quickened. The glistening oil caught the flickering lights that shined through the windows of her bedchamber, and soon the goddess's body glowed with a wet, luminous invitation.

The throbbing ache in his loins was unbearable and Hades' hand sought his engorged flesh. His breathing turned ragged as he stroked himself, quick and hard, never taking his eyes from Persephone's body. His focus narrowed until she was all that existed in his world. He imagined that it was his hands that were slick with oil caressing her breasts, cupping her luscious buttocks, traveling up her ivory thighs to find her moist core. There he wanted to bury himself, to pump his need into her and to be surrounded by her velvet heat. His orgasm ripped from his body, exploding with such hot intensity that it drove him to his knees. There he remained, knelt within shadow, alone, struggling to regain his breath. And, still, his longing eyes locked on the goddess.

"Persephone . . ." Her name was a harsh whisper on his lips.

CHAPTER EIGHTEEN

LINA felt like a well-fed kitten. Her body was in that wonderful place between relax and replete. Every bit of stress had been massaged from her muscles. Her skin was so incredibly smooth that as she lounged across the chaise and nibbled pomegranate seeds she absently stroked her fingers across her body, which seemed to hum with pleasure.

"Youth, beauty, and the power of a goddess—Persephone has it all," she said, and then looked guiltily around. No, she was totally alone. Just as she'd asked. After her shower and fabulous oil massage, Eurydice had dressed her in the shimmering narcissus nightdress and Lina had curled up on the chaise. When the little spirit asked if there was anything else she required, Lina had drowsily told her that the only thing she wanted was to lie on the chaise, drink ambrosia and eat pomegranates. Then she was going to go to sleep.

Eurydice had clapped her hands together like the bossy headmistress of an all girls school and hastily shooed the maidservants from the balcony, announcing that Persephone required privacy. And then, to Lina's surprise, Eurydice had actually followed the servants from the chamber, saying that she had an appointment with Iapis to go over her preliminary sketches of the palace, but she promised to bring by what she completed for the goddess's approval in the morning.

Iapis and Eurydice again. Lina tugged at a lock of long hair and twirled it around her finger. If she wasn't mistaken, the daimon's interest in Eurydice was more than friendly. Maybe she should speak to Hades about it.

Hades . . . thinking of the god brought the restlessness that was simmering just below her skin to the surface. She poured herself another glass of ambrosia. What was up with him? Why had he suddenly disappeared? He'd told her very clearly that he was interested in her, then he'd kissed her. Kissed her, hell! He'd pinned her against the wall and ravished her thoroughly. Remembering his passion made her shiver. Hades was the personification of dark and dangerous—a living, breathing Batman. She licked her lips and swore she could still taste him, or maybe that was just the ambrosia? Both were certainly delicious.

Lina closed her eyes, letting her fingers trail from her throat down, brushing over her already aroused nipples. She breathed a moan. *Merda!* Persephone's body was young and responsive and . . .

Lina's eyes snapped open. "And very, very horny," she said in a frustrated voice. "Or maybe it's more me than her. Or a combination of what happens when a forty-three-year-old woman who hasn't had sex in"—she stopped and counted back in her mind—"who hasn't had sex in almost three years is put into the body of a nubile young goddess and then is tempted by a handsome, Batman look-alike. Up! Time to get up and walk it off."

She stood, too fast, and felt all bubbly and slack-kneed. The ambrosia had definitely gone to her head . . . as well as to other sensitive spots. Her lips twisted in chagrin and a pretty pink flush heated her cheeks. Jeesh, she had it bad. Well, she'd tried the cold shower, and it definitely hadn't worked the way she'd planned. She sighed and trailed her finger across the smooth marble railing of the balcony, thinking of Eurydice's idea of a shower. It had been a heavenly experience. But it had done nothing to dispel her fantasies about Hades. Actually, it had accomplished the opposite. Her body had been bathed and massaged, pampered and preened. She felt like a royal concubine who had been prepared for her sultan.

So where the hell was her sultan? Pun definitely intended.

Lina shook her head and rolled her eyes. "You've had entirely too much ambrosia." With finality she set her half-empty glass on the flat top of the railing and started purposefully, if a little wobbly, for the circular staircase that wrapped down to the palace grounds. She'd take a nice brisk walk in the garden. That would clear her head and make her sleepy enough that she would remember that bed was a place in which one slept more often than one had hot, sweaty sex with a dark, handsome god.

In an ambrosial mist, Lina followed her private path to the first tier of the palace gardens. When she reached the entrance she stood very still, soaking in the magical view of the torch lit grounds. The Underworld was such an incredibly lovely place. The sky had continued to darken, but it was not black, as was the night sky in the world above. Instead, it was slate gray, illuminated by several brilliantly lit stars, each haloed with iridescent color that reminded Lina of the pearlized belly of a seashell. The unusual sky caused everything to be bathed in soft darkness, as if this part of the Underworld was a sweet dream.

"Those stars are the most beautiful things I have ever seen," Lina said to the silent sky.

"They are the Hyades."

Hades seemed to materialize from the shadows of the garden.

Lina's hand flew to her throat. She could feel her heart pounding there. "You scared me!"

"I did not mean to startle you, but I was just thinking of you and when I heard your voice I wanted very much to join you."

Lina bit her bottom lip and tried to clear her wine-fogged mind. He was wearing that damn cape again. And, even more dangerously, he had traded in the voluminous length of material he usually wrapped around his body for a much more revealing outfit. He had again chosen to wear black, but that night it was in the form of a short, black leather chiton that appeared to have been molded to his chest. It ended in panels just over his hips. Beneath, he wore a fine, pleated tunic, the color of thunderclouds, which left almost all of his muscular legs exposed. Lina wrenched her eyes up to meet his. He was watching her with a dark intensity she felt tingle through her blood.

"You've been on my mind, too. I'm glad you're here," she said, and reminded herself to breathe as he moved with feral intensity closer to her.

His body was like a furnace; she could feel the heat that radiated from him. Hades took her hand and raised it slowly to his mouth. His lips seemed to burn a brand into her skin. He didn't release her hand. Instead, he traced a circular path across it with his thumb. The cooling wind brought his scent to her. He smelled of the night and of leather mingled with man. It was an erotic, dangerous scent that made her stomach tighten and shiver. It made her think of sweat-slicked, naked skin. Without conscious thought, she breathed more deeply and leaned toward him. His eyes flashed and the teasing breeze caught his cape so that it rose behind him like wings. She was submerged within the intensity of his gaze. She could feel his passion ignite. This Hades was not the smart, sexy god she had been getting to know. Once again he was the being who had possessed her in the forge. He loomed before her, an infinitely powerful immortal—seductive, alluring, overwhelming, and a little frightening. She still wanted him. His presence was magnetic, but her mortal soul was struggling to maintain some semblance of control. Lina forced her mind to work, grasping at something, anything she could say to him.

"You said the stars are Hyades. I don't understand," she finally managed.

Hades lifted his eyes from hers to gaze at the night sky.

"You don't understand because you know them only as the bright nymphs they are in the world above. What most immortals do not know is that a group of forest Hyades tired of their earthly duties. They begged Zeus to allow them to become mortal so that they could die and be relieved of the burden of immortality."

His voice was as deep and as hypnotic as his eyes. Entranced, Lina stared at him as he wove the tale. He was a dark flame that drew her soul inexorably to him. Batman. Definitely Batman. And, ambrosia or no ambrosia, what sane woman would *not* be into Batman fantasies?

"Zeus granted the Hyades their wish and that same night they entered my realm. I was so moved by the iridescence of their souls that I proclaimed that their great beauty could light all of Elysia. The nymphs were intrigued by the idea and they came as one to petition me. As Zeus before me, I, too, granted their wish, and they have illuminated the night sky of the Underworld ever since."

Lina forced her eyes from the magnetic god to look up at the stars that were really the spirit of nymphs.

"What are you doing here, Persephone?"

The raw emotion in the god's voice stopped Lina's breath, and her gaze flew back to his. What had happened to him tonight? And how could he be so powerful and yet look so vulnerable at the same time? She shook her head and gave him the only answer she could.

"I drank too much ambrosia and I thought a walk in the garden would help sober me up."

Hades stared at her a moment longer, then he blinked, raked one hand through his hair and expelled one long breath. Slowly, the tense lines of his face began to relax. "Too much ambrosia? I understand that feeling all too well. It makes your head cloudy and your knees weak."

Relieved that he seemed more normal, Lina smiled. "Glad to hear I'm not the only one it's happened to."

"A walk does help." He returned her smile, and bowed gallantly to her. "I would be honored if you allowed me to escort you."

He was her dashing Hades again, and she grinned, curtsied and realized that she was wearing nothing but a thin silk nightgown. She cleared her throat.

"I, uh, seem to be underdressed for an evening stroll."

Hades' eyes glinted darkly as they roamed from her flushed face down to her silk-draped body. In one graceful movement he unclasped his cape, and with a swirling motion that reminded her of a matador, wrapped it around her shoulders.

"Better?"

Encased in his warmth and scent, she could only nod.

"Then I may escort you?"

"Absolutely," she said.

He smiled and pulled her arm through his. Hades led her slowly into the night-shrouded grounds. They didn't speak; they just accustomed themselves to the feel of one another. Hades chose a wide path that bisected the gardens. Lina gazed around her in awe. The unusual gentleness of the Underworld's night cast a magical glow over the sleeping flowers and hedges, so that even though many of the blossoms had closed, the flowers still dotted the landscape with splashes of snowy color.

"I can't decide whether I think they're more beautiful during the day while they're in full bloom, or like this, looking like sleepy children," Lina said, reaching out to trail one finger gently over the closed blossom of a milk-colored day lily. At her touch, the folded flower burst into full bloom. Lina bit back a startled cry. She had to remember that she was Goddess of Spring. Obviously, she shouldn't be surprised when she made a flower bloom.

"Now you can have both beauties together," Hades said.

Lina's brow furrowed. "No, I don't want to wear them out." She thought for a moment before waving her fingers at the flower. "Go back to sleep," she told it. With a sound that was very much like a sigh, the lily closed.

She turned back to Hades to find him watching her with an expression she couldn't read. Before she could ask him what was wrong, he took her hand, the one that had touched the flower, and turned it so that it rested, palm up, in his own, then he raised the tips of her fingers to his mouth.

The touch of his lips made her stomach shiver. She wanted him to kiss much more than her hands.

Too soon, he released her hand and said, "You are a very kind goddess."

She wasn't really Persephone, but Hades made her feel like she truly was a goddess. Instead of wrapping her arm through his again, Lina slid her fingers down his arm so that she could hold his hand. His lips quivered, then turned up in a pleased smile. He squeezed her hand, and they resumed their walk.

"I would like to show you something," Hades said suddenly. "Something that is very important to me."

Lina glanced up at him and their eyes met briefly. Then he looked away, and Lina could see the tense line of his jaw.

"If it's important to you, I would love to see it."

His jaw unclenched and he squeezed her hand again. "It is this way."

The first tier ended and Hades led her down the stairs to the second level. Earlier that day when she had been collecting nectar she really hadn't been able to pay attention to anything except calling forth the sticky liquid, and Lina would have liked to have stopped to take a closer look at the fountains and statuary, but the god's pace quickened. Obviously, he was anxious to get to whatever he wanted to show her. Curiosity piqued, she lengthened her stride to match his.

On the third level Hades chose a path that branched to their right. It wound in little S curves down the side of that tier. Gradually, the well-tended gardens gave way to large pine trees. Their sharp scent reminded Lina of holidays and home.

"I love the way pine trees smell," Lina said.

Instead of answering, Hades pressed his finger against her lips. "Ssssh," he whispered. "We do not want them to know we are here."

Before Lina could ask who he meant, Hades pointed to a cluster of large stones.

"We must wait behind those."

Intrigued, but completely confused, Lina let him pull her down next to him as they crouched behind the jagged rocks.

"What's going on?" Lina whispered.

Hades changed position so that he could see over the top of the nearest boulder. He gestured for her to do the same. She peeked over the rock.

On the other side of the cluster of rocks the land angled sharply down until it met the bank of a river. Lina blinked several times to make sure her eyes weren't fooling her, but the water remained the same, sparkling like liquid diamonds in the magical light of the Underworld night. Everything was very quiet around them, and Lina could hear the sound of the river. Its voice laughed and sang the words of a strange language. She didn't understand the words, but the sound was compelling, and she felt a sudden desire to rush down the bank and wade into the water so that she could be immersed in its bright laughter.

Hades' firm hand enveloped her shoulder. His lips almost touched her ear as he spoke quietly to her. "Do not listen to the river's call."

Lina focused on his voice and almost instantly she felt the river's allure slide away.

"I should have warned you. The call of Lethe can be very strong." Hades' breath was warm and Lina leaned into him. He shifted his position, put his arm around her shoulders and drew her in front of him so that she was half resting intimately across his lap. She leaned back against his chest and tilted her head toward him so that he could catch the whisper of her words.

"This is Lethe, the River of Forgetfulness?"

Lina felt him nod and she stared at it, unbelieving. So this was the famous river that caused souls to forget their lives and readied them to be born anew.

"Is that what is so important to you?"

"In a way," he whispered, "but there is more."

"Why do we have to be so quiet?"

"We do not want the souls to know that we are here. Our presence would be a distraction. For this the dead do not need us."

Lina felt a rush of excitement and she searched the banks of the river. "I don't see any dead."

"Watch and wait" was all he would say.

Lina settled back against him. Hades wrapped his arms tightly around her. It felt incredibly good to be so close to him. The bite of pine lingered in the air, mixing with the heady male scent of Hades. Once she tuned out its compelling call, the river's voice was lilting and melodic. Lina felt immersed in an experience of the senses. Her entire body felt aroused and ultra-sensitive. The god's hand rested on her forearm and his thumb was tracing lazy circles over her skin. She shivered under his touch.

"Is my cloak not warm enough?" he murmured, his breath licking against her ear. "Are you cold?"

She shook her head no, and turned in his arms so that she could see his face. He surrounded her. His body was hard and strong and he radiated heat through the leather of his breastplate. His bare arms encircled her. She opened her mouth to tell him that it was his touch that made her tremble and that . . .

"There." His whisper was urgent. He leaned forward, moving her with him. Hades pointed and Lina's eyes followed his finger.

Two figures were approaching the river from the opposite side. As they drew closer Lina could see that they were holding hands. The bright water reflected off their bodies, showing them to be an ancient-looking man and woman. They moved slowly, allowing their shoulders and hips to brush against one another. Every step or two the man would raise the woman's wrinkled hand to his lips and hold it there while she gazed tenderly at him.

Lina felt a little uncomfortable spying on them, but she was also mesmerized by the obvious adoration the two felt for one another. Finally, the couple reached the river's edge. They turned to face each other. The man rested his hands on the woman's shoulders.

"Are you quite certain?" His voice was cracked with age and emotion, but it carried clearly across the river.

"Yes, my love. I am certain. It is time, and we will find each other again," she answered him.

"I have always trusted you. I cannot doubt you now," he said.

As the old man drew the woman gently into his arms and kissed her, Lina felt her eyes fill with tears. She blinked quickly to keep her vision clear. The couple ended their embrace, and then with their hands still joined, they knelt beside the river, bent down and drank the crystal water. Instantly, their bodies began to shine. Their hair and clothes whipped wildly around them as if they had been caught in a fierce wind. Then they began to change. Lina gasped as she watched years fall away from the couple. Their images shifted from old age, to middle age, then young adulthood, and finally they glowed with the vibrancy of teenagers. There the metamorphosis paused. Stunned, the two gazed at each other. Then the man threw back his head and shouted with joy. Again, he pulled the woman into his arms and she wrapped herself around him, laughing and crying at the same time.

Tears spilled from Lina's eyes—that must have been how they had looked when they had first fallen in love. While they were embracing their bodies became brighter and brighter, until Lina had to use her hand to shield her eyes against the light. Then they exploded, as if two stars had just burst, raining a shower of sparks into the water. From the center of each of the explosions twin dots of fist-sized lights were formed. They hovered over the water, acclimating themselves to their new senses. Then they began to float downstream, carried by their own special breeze. Lina stared after them. The two globes of light remained close together, so close that, as they moved farther away, there appeared to be no visible distinction between them. The river curved to the left and the lights followed it, disappearing from sight.

Lina wiped at her eyes and sniffled. "What will happen to them?" she asked in a broken voice.

"What you saw them become is how the soul appears after all memories and all links to the body are removed. Their souls will follow Lethe to its beginning. There they will be reborn as infants to live new lives," Hades said.

Lina swiveled in his lap so that she was facing him. "But will they be together again? If they're reborn as new people with no memory of their previous lives, how can they find each other?"

"Soul mates will always find each other. Do not weep on their behalf. The woman spoke the truth; they will be together again."

"Do you promise?" Lina's voice trembled with emotion.

"I promise, sweet one. I promise."

Slowly, warring against eons of solitude, he cupped her face in his hands. Hades made his decision. He had to try. He would be lost if he didn't. Hades gazed at her while his pulse beat erratically. Taking a deep breath, he let his thumbs wipe away her remaining tears.

"This is what I wanted to show you—to share with you—the bond of soul mates. Once you have seen it, it is something that you will remember always. It may even change you. It has surely changed me."

Gently, Hades bent to her. First he kissed the closed lid of each of her eyes, then he placed his lips over hers. The kiss began as sweet and hesitant, but when Lina's arms slid up around his shoulders and she opened her lips to accept him, Hades automatically deepened the kiss. She was there, a reality in his arms. This time he did not have to imagine that he touched and tasted her. His desire for her, which had not truly been sated, surged through his blood. With a moan of pleasure, he met her tongue with his own. She was soft and she tasted of ambrosia and heat. His hands slipped inside the covering cape and found her waist. Hades caressed the curve of her hip, following the path his fantasy had taken. He buried one hand in the silk of her hair and he felt her breath quicken as his other hand roamed up and down the length of her thigh. The silky slip of a nightdress offered little barrier. She shifted in his lap, so that the hard flesh of his erection pressed firmly against the curve of her buttocks.

The sound deep in his throat was low and feral. How had he lived so long without her? He desired her with a fire that was burning him alive.

His hand traveled back to the luscious curve of her waist and continued up. He could feel the round fullness of the side of her breast, and in his mind he again saw the puckered nipples glistening wet with water and oil. His fingertips found the hard bud and he rolled it gently through the thin silk.

Persephone made a choked gasping noise against his mouth.

The sound penetrated the red haze of lust that fogged his brain and he wrenched himself back from her. His cape had been pushed aside and Persephone's body lay across him, trembling and exposed. Her hair was disheveled and her lips were red and swollen. By all the gods, what was wrong with him! Had he lost total control of himself? He hadn't wanted it to happen like this, even a callow fool knew better than to maul a goddess in the middle of a forest. Uttering a curse he stood, lifting her abruptly to her feet. She had dried pine needles and smudges of dirt on her nightdress and she looked achingly young and alluring as she gazed up at him, a confused smile tilting her sensuous lips.

Hades was filled with shame. He still wanted to press her to the ground and take her right there. He brushed frantically at the pine needles that clung to her robe, muttering nearly incoherent apologies.

The force of the god's passion stirred a desire in Lina so intense, so fierce, that it was a little frightening. But as she watched the lust that drained from Hades' face being replaced by an expression that could have been either anger or embarrassment, she brought her breathing under control and commanded her mind to function again. She'd never had a god for a lover, but she was certainly no virgin, and she shouldn't be reacting like one.

"I did not mean to bring you here to . . . to . . ." He shook his head miserably and continued to wipe at her dress. "To rut you like a beast."

He wasn't angry, she realized with relief. He was mortified. Lina grabbed his hand and tugged on it until he met her eyes. "Hades, stop. I'm fine. What is this all about?"

"A goddess deserves more than a tussle on the bare ground."

Her smile was slow and sensuous. "I can't speak for other goddesses, but I was enjoying that tussle." She slid her hands up to rest against his leather breastplate. She could still feel the furnace-like heat radiating from him. "And I wasn't sitting on the bare ground. I was sitting on your lap."

Hades expelled his breath in an audible sigh. The haunted expression in his eyes made him look decades older. Gently, he touched the side of her face. His voice was thick with restrained emotions. "Truly, I did not bring you here to seduce you, but I find that I cannot keep my thoughts away from you . . . nor my hands. I desire you above all things, Persephone, may the gods help me," he finished in a rush.

"Then may the gods help both of us, Hades," Lina said. And when his lips met hers she refused to think of Demeter and tomorrows.

Hades broke the kiss gently, while he was still able to control himself. She was so soft and so open to him. That she desired him was obvious, but Hades wanted more than to possess her body. He wanted her soul. With a gesture that was incredibly tender, he straightened his cloak around her shoulders and wrapped her arm through his.

"The night grows cold. We should return to the palace." He brushed a long lock of hair from her face, noting the disappointment that flashed through her eyes. Good, he thought. He wanted her to desire him and yearn for him, until it was more than his body that she craved.

He led her back to the path that would take them to the palace. Lina's thoughts were spinning. Her body still felt overheated, and her heightened physical sensitivity somehow merged with the incredible beauty of the scene she had witnessed between the soul mates. The poignancy of the lovers' devotion stayed with her. Under her hand she could feel the pulse of Hades' blood, which was steady and strong. He had brought her there to witness the rebirth of the soul mates, but he hadn't used it as a seduction device—if that had been his intention, he could have taken her right there on the ground. But he hadn't. Hades obviously wanted more from her than sex. Her soul quickened even as alarm bells rang within her mind. Love—he had shown her his idea of love. Hadn't he already said that he believed mortals understood love better than the gods? Did the gods have soul mates? She had no idea. All she knew about the immortals was what she had inattentively read decades ago. What she did remember was that the ancient gods were fickle, that they discarded lovers at their whim. That didn't fit with what she was learning about the god who walked by her side.

She glanced up at his dark profile. Who would ever believe that she had found such desire and romance in the Land of the Dead? As if he felt her gaze he looked down at her. Hades' lips twitched and then curved up.

"You look as if you have many questions playing through your mind. You know I have already given you leave to ask me anything, and I promise you that this time I will remember my manners and not insult you as my guest."

Lina felt herself blush and she hoped that the dreamy darkness hid her suddenly pink cheeks. She had completely forgotten about snapping at him and his instant withdrawal from her. It seemed like it had happened an age ago, and that they had been two totally different people then. She leaned into him, loving the strong feel of his arm and the way he bent attentively over her.

"It was a magical thing we watched tonight," she said.

"Yes, it was the most perfect type of magic—that which is created naturally by the soul and not contrived by the gods."

"The gods don't bring soul mates together?"

Hades snorted. "No. Mortal souls find their own match; they do not require the meddling hands of the gods."

His words brought another question to her mind.

"Can the dead fall in love?" she asked, thinking of the shy looks Eurydice had begun giving Iapis. "Or is it only soul mates that have the ability to love after death?"

"You can answer that question yourself, Persephone."

Lina glanced sharply up at him, but his tone was instructional and not patronizing.

"Think, Goddess. What is it that loves? The body or the soul?" he prodded.

"If you're asking about real love, and not just lust or infatuation, I'd have to say the soul."

Hades nodded. "The body is just a mantle, a temporary covering for our true visage."

"So that means that the souls that exist in Elysia, or even in your palace, can fall in love?"

"Any of the unnumbered dead who are capable of it may find new love." Hades frowned. "But you should know that not all souls are capable of that emotion."

"Are you talking about mortal souls, or do you mean the souls of the gods?"

Hades stopped walking and turned to face her. They were standing very close and her hand still rested on his arm. The god hesitated before answering her. Then his fingers brushed her cheek in a familiar caress.

"I cannot speak for the other gods, only for myself. My soul longs for its eternal mate." He bent and brushed his lips against hers. He gestured to the space behind her. "It seems we are back where we began."

Lina looked over her shoulder and blinked in surprise. They had stopped at the mouth of the little path that led to her balcony.

Without speaking, Hades cupped her face in his hands in such a gentle gesture that Lina expected the kiss to be sweet and brief. When his lips met hers she realized that she had been very mistaken. The god took his time tasting her, splaying his fingers into the thickness of her hair until he was caressing the sensitive nape of her neck. Lina ran her hands up his arms, thrilled anew by their muscular strength. He nibbled at her bottom lip before ending the kiss. Still holding her he spoke against her mouth, "Will you ride with me tomorrow?" His voice was husky with desire.

Heart fluttering, Lina nodded.

"Yes."

"Until tomorrow then." He released her reluctantly, brushing a strand of hair from her face. Then he bowed to her, turned and strode away.

Lina climbed the steps to her balcony and entered her room on shaky legs. As she sagged onto the bed she caught a reflection of herself in the mirror situated over the vanity across the room. Her cheeks were flushed and her hair looked wild. Hades' cape had fallen down around her waist and her sheer nightdress was smudged, a couple of pine needles clung to the side of her hem. And even from across the room she could see the clear outline of her aroused nipples.

"*Misericordioso madre di Dio!*" she said, using her Grandmother's most potent exclamation. "You're forty-three years old," she told her reflection. "And you haven't felt like this since . . . since . . ." She shook her head at her strange, youthful image. "Since never. No man has ever made you feel like he does. And he wants eternal love." She squeezed her eyes shut. "Oh, Demeter. What am I going to do?"

CHAPTER NINETEEN

"HONEY, I think you have the makings of a real artist." Lina studied the charcoal sketch on the parchment. She had expected Eurydice's map to be a crude little drawing, but when the spirit unrolled the parchment Lina had immediately been impressed by the quality of her work. The palace blueprint was laid out with strong, clear lines, each section labeled in a flowing script, but what impressed Lina the most was the meticulous detail with which Eurydice had symbolized each section of the palace. To mark the main dining room she had reproduced in miniature the ornate table, complete with candelabrum. The Great Hall had been labeled with a dais on which she had drawn Hades' throne. She had even sketched in the flower-filled courtyard and outlined the massive fountain in its center.

"Do you really like it?" Eurydice asked breathlessly. "It is not completed yet. There are still many finishing touches I should add."

"I love it. Have you always been an artist?"

Eurydice's face was animated with excitement. "Yes! I mean, no, not actually an artist. My father did not believe drawing was a proper pastime for a young lady—even as a hobby. But I used to draw things in secret. I sketched pictures of flowers on dry patches of ground with a sharpened stick. I dipped a bird's quill in my mother's dye and drew animals on old rags." She grinned impishly at Lina. "My father would have been very upset if he had known."

"Well, I think being an artist is the perfect pastime for a lady, and I give you wholehearted permission to draw and draw and draw," Lina said.

"Thank you so much, Persephone!" Eurydice did a happy skip-step. "I cannot wait to tell Iapis. He said he thought that I drew very well, and that he could find more supplies for me if I wished to keep sketching."

"Did he?" Lina raised her eyebrows suggestively.

Eurydice's face, already luminous, took on a decidedly pink hue. "Yes, he did. I thought he was just being kind, because he is always so kind, but if you agree with him then I know it must be true."

"Tell Iapis I said to load you up with supplies. You are now officially Personal Artist to the Goddess of Spring." Lina raised her arm regally to punctuate the proclamation.

Eurydice's eyes grew round with wonder. Impulsively she threw her arms around Lina, hugging her tightly. "You are the most wonderful goddess in all the world!"

Lina laughed. "That is exactly the opinion I expect from my Personal Artist."

"You must task me with a commission. What shall I draw for you?"

"Shouldn't you finish the map first?"

"That will be done soon. Then what would you like me to draw?" she demanded eagerly.

Lina thought for a moment. Then she smiled. "The narcissus is quickly becoming my favorite flower. Why don't you draw me a big, beautiful picture of a narcissus?"

Eurydice's face glowed as she curtsied deeply to her goddess. "Your artist will do your bidding, Goddess of Spring."

Lina inclined her head in her best goddess-like gesture, pleased at how happy she had made Eurydice. "I will try to wait patiently for your first commission."

The little spirit popped up from the curtsy. "Oh! My first commission!"

Two firm knocks sounded against the door to Lina's room. Eurydice danced to open the door.

"Iapis!" she gushed. "Persephone has declared that I am her Personal Artist!"

Lina observed the daimon closely. His expression was warm and open as he congratulated Eurydice, and his eyes never left the girl's face. Lina's grandma would say that he looked very much like a man who was on his way to being well and truly smitten. Lina noticed that Eurydice touched the daimon's arm twice during her excited recitation. The girl's body language definitely said she was returning his interest—no, Lina corrected herself—she was going to have to stop thinking of her as a girl or a child. Eurydice was a young woman who had already been unhappily married once. In actuality the body Lina currently possessed didn't look to be much older.

"Goddess, may I commend you on your excellent taste in artists?" Iapis said gallantly.

Grinning, Eurydice hovered at his side.

"Thank you, Iapis. I think we are just beginning to discover Eurydice's talents."

Iapis smiled fondly at Eurydice. "I must agree with you, Goddess." Then he bowed to Lina. "Hades awaits you at the stables. He asks that I relay to you that Orion is growing impatient."

Lina's stomach gave a jolt at the mention of the god. "Well, then, it's a good thing I'm ready. I wouldn't want to keep a dread steed waiting."

"They scare me," Eurydice said.

"Remember, just think of them as big dogs," Lina told her. The spirit and the daimon hurried after her as she walked briskly down the hallway and through the courtyard, fully aware that now she was the one who felt like dancing happily.

"Was your bath satisfactory last night, Goddess?" Iapis asked.

Lina was glad that she was walking ahead of him. She knew the expression on her face would give away just how satisfactory last night had become.

"Yes, it was lovely. Thank you."

"Persephone said she slept very well," Eurydice added.

Lina smiled. She had slept wrapped in Hades' cape, falling in and out of teasingly erotic dreams.

"It pleases me to hear it," Iapis said to Eurydice. "Especially after the restless night my Lord spent. I do not believe Hades slept at all."

"Perhaps you should try bathing him as I did Persephone," Eurydice said.

Lina quickened her pace, letting the soft breeze that drifted through the courtyard cool her flushed skin. Her body already felt like a spring that had been tightly wound. She definitely didn't need to start visualizing Hades' naked body being bathed and covered in oil. Lina hurried past the central fountain and the lovely sculptures, relieved when she finally reached the wrought iron gates.

"I think I will stay here, Persephone," Eurydice called from behind her. The little spirit pointed to a cluster of narcissus flowers. "I can begin some preliminary sketches while you are riding with Hades."

"And I must procure the proper supplies for your artist," Iapis said, but his eyes never left Eurydice.

"Behave yourselves. I'll be back soon," Lina said.

The pair waved her away and she hadn't taken more than a couple of steps from them when she looked back to see that they already had their heads together. Eurydice's girlish giggle was followed by the deep sound of the daimon's laughter. She was going to have to remember to talk to Hades about them. Iapis seemed like a good guy—if guy was the right word to use when referring to a semi-deity—but what exactly were his intentions? Eurydice was recovering from a bad relationship, not to mention the fact that she was newly dead. That had to make her doubly vulnerable. Didn't it? No matter what, Lina was definitely responsible for her and she didn't want to see her hurt. Iapis should be told to take it slow. Eurydice needed to be treated carefully and with respect.

An ear-splitting neigh brought Lina up short and she stopped her inner tirade. Orion was standing outside the stable. His mane had been combed and braided with ribbons the color of moonlight, which was the exact color of the narcissus tucked under the crownpiece of his bridle. He caught her eye, arched his neck and snorted, taking a few frisky side steps to show off. Beside him stood another stallion that could have been his twin, except that the other horse's night-colored coat was broken by a single white splotch on his forehead in the shape of a lopsided star. The two steeds were almost as magnificent as the god who held their reins. Hades was scowling impressively at his lead stallion.

"Settle down you great foolish beast!" Hades told Orion. "You see that Dorado is not making such a fuss."

Lina hurried to join them, trying not to be obvious about staring at the way the god's arms and shoulders bulged as he pulled Orion to order. He was wearing another short tunic which exposed an excellent amount of his arm muscle as well as most of his legs. His black cloak billowed around him. Batman. A delectable, ancient version of Bruce Wayne. Lina fought the urge to fan herself.

"Don't scold him. I've decided that he's incorrigible, but loveable," she said, heart fluttering. Laying her cheek against Orion's soft muzzle when he nuzzled her in greeting, she averted her eyes from Hades. "You're just glad to see me, aren't you, handsome boy?"

Hades thought he knew exactly how the stallion felt; he had the ridiculous urge to strut and shout at the sight of her. Persephone was swathed in a long length of fine linen with a skirt that was full enough so that she could ride comfortably. When the breeze stirred it pressed the semisheer fabric against her body, outlining the swell of her breasts and the delectable curve of her waist, making Hades wish that he had thought to call up more wind. He watched jealously as she caressed Orion, even though he felt like a shallow clod for being jealous of a horse.

Dorado nickered at the goddess and looked bereft. Instead of doing the same Hades said, "Persephone, I do not believe that you have been formally introduced to Dorado. He does not lead as well as your Orion, but he is the swiftest of the four." He patted the horse's glossy neck affectionately.

Lina rubbed Dorado's head. "It's nice to meet you, Dorado. Faster than Orion, huh?" She slanted a sassy look at Hades. "I guess that means that we won't be able to run away from you."

Hades swallowed past the sudden thickness in his throat. Just being close to her made him feel powerful and helpless, hot and cold, all at the same time. He was probably going mad—and he didn't care. Moving close to her so that the sides of their bodies pressed against each other, Hades caught her teasing gaze with his own. "No, you will not be able to escape me."

Lina felt like she was falling into his eyes. Escape from him? Not likely. She wanted to climb under his skin.

Orion butted her back and snorted. She laughed, breaking the spell between them.

"Okay, impatient boy!"

"The beast is not impatient. He is jealous," Hades said, sending the stallion a black look, which Orion pointedly ignored and lipped innocently at his goddess's shoulder.

"Jealous?" Lina pretended to be taken aback. "Just because I petted Dorado? That's very silly of you," she cooed to the horse.

"You have no idea how silly," he muttered, but he wasn't talking about Orion. "Come." He took her elbow, guiding her to the horse's left side and helping her mount. "The Elysian Fields await the presence of the Goddess of Spring."

THEY rode side by side, following the black marble road. The steady clip of the horses' hooves mingled with the lyrical sound of songbirds calling to one another from the boughs of the imposing cypress trees that lined their pathway. The fragrance of narcissus blooms perfumed the air. Every so often they would pass spirits, sometimes in groups, sometimes a solitary soul walking alone. But all of the reactions were the same. First, the spirits would step off the road, giving the dread steeds a wide berth. Then the realization of who was riding the steeds would hit them. The dead bowed solemnly to their dark god, all the while keeping wide eyes fixed on Persephone. The men would smile at the goddess and bow to her, some of them even called greetings to her, but it was the women whose reactions moved Lina the most. When women recognized that they were in the presence of the Goddess of Spring, their faces became alight with joy. Many of them addressed her by name and asked for her blessing, which Lina readily gave. Some even dared to approach Orion so that they could touch the hem of the goddess's robe.

Lina couldn't believe what a difference her presence seemed to make to them. She had to admit that Demeter had been right—for whatever reason, the spirits of the dead needed to know that a goddess still cared for them. It was an awesome responsibility, but it made Lina feel needed and cherished. If, just by being visible in the Underworld, she could spread happiness and hope, then Lina was very glad to be there.

At first she worried that Hades would be upset, or even threatened by all the attention she was receiving. But though he said little in words, his pleased, relaxed expression spoke volumes. The dark god was obviously glad that the dead responded so joyously to her.

Eventually, the road climbed sharply uphill. They topped a rise and Lina pulled Orion to a halt.

"It's like someone divided it in two, and then painted it—one side dark, the other light." She shook her head in disbelief, even though she knew her eyes didn't lie. The road they were on stretched in front of them as the dividing line in a radically different landscape. It was the most bizarre thing Lina had ever seen.

"Painted different colors, dark and light, that is an apt description of it," Hades said. He pointed to their left where the land reached down into a vast darkness ringed by a distant red line of fire. "That is the flaming River Phlegethon, which borders Tartarus, where darkness reigns." With his other hand he gestured to the brightness to their right. "And there you see Elysia, where light and happiness exist perfectly together and the only darkness that is there is what is required for the spirits to rest peacefully."

Quickly, Lina accessed Persephone's ghostly memory. *Tartarus,* the voice whispered within her mind, *the region of the Underworld where eternal punishment is meted out. It is a place of hopelessness and agony. Only evil dwells there.*

It was Hell. Lina couldn't take her eyes from the dark abyss. Suddenly she felt chilled. The darkness seemed to reach for her, like tendrils from a malevolent creature.

"Persephone!" The sharpness in Hades' voice drew her attention from the void of Tartarus. She met his intense gaze. "You may roam anywhere within my realm, with or without me at your side—except for Tartarus. There, you may not enter, nor may you travel near its boundaries. The realm itself has been tainted by the corrosive nature of its tenants."

"It's awful there, isn't it?" Her face felt bloodless.

"It must be. You know that there is great evil in the world. Would you have it go unpunished?"

Lina thought about her mortal world. Snippets of news stories flashed in her memory like nightmares: the Oklahoma City bombing; the horrors of grown men and women who abused and killed defenseless children; and, of course, 9/11 and the cowardice of terrorists.

"No. I would not have it go unpunished," she said firmly.

"Neither would I. That is why I command that you do not enter its borders."

Lina shivered. "I don't want to go there."

Hades relaxed his stern expression. He nodded toward the brightness that illuminated the right side of the road. "What I would like to show you is a little of the beauty of Elysia."

With a conscious effort, Lina turned her back on the horrors of Tartarus, smiled at Hades and patted Orion's warm neck. "All you have to do is lead the way. We'll follow you."

Eyes sparkling, the god gathered Dorado's reins in his hand. "It is well that you follow me. You ride the slower steed."

Lina narrowed her eyes at him and she drew out her words in her best John Wayne imitation. "You shouldn't talk about my horse, pilgrim." Then she pointed down the hill. "See the big pine at the edge of that field down there?"

Hades grinned at her and nodded. "Dorado and I will reach it first. He is the faster horse."

"He may be the faster horse, but he's certainly carrying more dead weight," Lina quipped. "Oops, that's probably a bad pun to use in the Underworld, but— YAHH!" She yelled, catching the grinning god off guard. Orion responded instantly by leaping forward and lunging past Dorado to fly down the embankment. The wind whistled past her cheeks as the stallion ran. Lina leaned into his neck and he increased his speed until the world blurred by her. Close behind, she could hear Dorado gaining on them. "Don't let them catch us!" she shouted into the stallion's flattened ears and Lina felt him respond with another burst of speed. Then they were past a tall, green shape that was the pine tree and Lina straightened in the saddle, whooping with victory as Orion slowed to a snorting, prancing trot before he stopped. Breathing hard, Dorado slid to a halt beside them.

Lina laughed aloud at the expression on Hades' face.

"The fastest horse, huh? Don't ever underestimate the power of a resourceful woman."

"I believe you cheated," Hades said in mock seriousness, trying unsuccessfully to hide his smile.

"I like to think of it more as using all my resources to win than actually cheating."

"I had no idea you were so competitive."

"There's a lot you don't know about me, Lord of the Underworld," Lina said, still stroking the stallion's neck. "I am not your typical goddess."

Hades snorted. Orion snorted back at him. Dorado tossed his head.

The god gave his horse a couple quick pats. "Don't feel bad, old steed. We will have our day of victory." Adding in a staged whisper, "We must keep a close eye on her—the goddess is wily," Hades said, more to himself than Dorado.

"Uh-huh," Lina agreed and they both laughed.

"Persephone!" a young voice called. Lina turned to see who had spoken.

"Oh, it is the Goddess of Spring! I knew it!" A lithe figure broke from the grove of pines that ringed the lovely little meadow in which the horses stood. She was followed quickly by several others who skipped and danced with excitement toward Lina. The entire group was made up of young, beautiful women. Their flowing wraps were draped alluringly around their strong, young bodies. If they hadn't had the semi-substantial look that marked them as spirits of the Underworld, Lina could have believed that she had stumbled into a sorority toga party.

Hades kneed Dorado so that he was close to her, speaking in a low voice for her ears alone. "They are maidens who died before they could marry. They tend to frolic a great deal before choosing to drink of Lethe."

When the group got close to the two horses, they slowed, making an obvious effort to contain their excitement so as not to get too close to the fearsome steeds. The spirit who had called her name dropped into a deep, graceful curtsy, which the rest of the maidens mimicked. When she rose she was the first to speak. "I heard that you had been seen, and with all my heart I wanted to believe it. Oh, Goddess! It is so wonderful to have you with us."

A chorus of "Yes! We are so pleased!" followed her little speech.

"Well, thank you. I am having a wonderful visit," Lina said.

The first maiden frowned. "You only visit? You mean to leave us?"

The meadow was silent as if every blade of grass and leaf on each tree listened for her answer.

She didn't know what to say.

"Persephone may stay in the Underworld for as long as she wills it." Hades' voice, rich with feeling, broke the silence.

Lina's breath caught at the sudden rush of pleasure his words brought to her. She pushed aside the oh-so-serious-and-responsible thought that reminded her that she could not stay, that she was there for only six months. Instead she smiled at the god, and thought how very much she would like to kiss him again.

"Then you have no reason to rush on. Come dance with us, Goddess!" the maiden called.

Lina tore her eyes from Hades. "Dance with you? But there isn't any music," she told the young spirit.

"That small detail is easily remedied," Hades said. "Our goddess requires music!" he commanded with a flourish. The breeze took his words and swirled around them with an odd whistling noise that grew to a crescendo that melted unexpectedly into the melodic sound of musical instruments. The god inclined his head graciously to her. "Now you have music."

"So it seems." Lina's heart was beating so loudly she was sure everyone could hear it over the music. Dance? She didn't know how to dance with those girls.

"Yes! Oh, please."

"Now you can dance with us!"

"Come frolic to the music of the god, Persephone!"

"But . . . I . . . well . . ." Lina looked around helplessly. "What will I do with Orion?" she floundered.

"You will leave him here with Dorado and me," Hades said, already dismounting. He strode to Orion's side and lifted his arms so that she had little choice but to slide down into them. Hades held her close for a moment, and then he whispered, "Please dance for me here in Elysia. No goddess has ever done so."

Lina looked up into his eyes, saw the desire as well as the vulnerability that he was feeling, and she knew she had no choice. She had to dance for him.

"I would be happy to dance for you," she said.

"My dread steeds and I will await you." He paused, and then added, "eagerly."

"Okay. Well." She brushed at her robes, pretending to straighten that which was already straight. "I won't be long."

"Persephone! We already have the circle formed!" a maiden called to her.

"Oh, good," Lina said, starting toward the waiting group. Sure enough, they had formed a loose circle in the middle of the meadow. Lina was so nervous that she felt vaguely nauseous. Dance with a group of dead maidens? It was just something that her life experiences had not prepared her for. Her hands felt sweaty. This wasn't like the nectar gathering; she didn't have an example to follow. They were expecting her to show them. Should she break into an imitation of one of John Travolta's disco solos from *Saturday Night Fever*? She was going to mess up. She was going to make a fool out of herself. Hades and everyone would know that she wasn't a goddess. She'd be found out as a fraud.

Cease this nonsense!

The echo within her mind startled her so much that she almost cried aloud.

Your body knows the dance. Relax and trust it.

Lina glanced down at herself. She had forgotten that she wasn't wearing her forty-three-year-old skin. She was young and lithe and in such amazing shape that she could probably eat Godiva chocolate nonstop for days and not have to worry about zipping her jeans.

"Goddess?"

Lina looked up to see all the maidens watching her with openly curious expressions on their pretty faces. She probably looked like a moron standing there staring down at herself.

Lina smiled, straightened her shoulders, and let her legs begin walking again. "I was just admiring the . . . uh . . ." She looked down again, "clover in this meadow. It's lovely, don't you think?"

All of the heads nodded energetically, reminding Lina of dashboard ornaments.

"It is our special meadow. We like clover and green, growing things, so it has arranged itself to please us," the first maiden said.

"Well, I like it, too," Lina said, joining the circle.

You begin in the center. Her internal voice directed.

Lina took a deep breath and moved to the center of the circle. Then she did the only thing she could think of doing. She closed her eyes and concentrated. The music filled her and automatically her body began to sway. Her arms raised themselves and she spun in a slow, lazy circle. The music was wonderful. It reminded her of something wild and feminine. Her body matched itself to the music as she began to trace intricate steps with her long, supple legs. Her hips turned and swayed. Her arms painted images in the air. She wasn't a forty-three-year-old baker. She wasn't a young goddess. She was the music.

Lina opened her eyes.

Faces glowing with pleasure, the maidens circled around her, trying to match her movements. They were beautiful and many were obviously talented dancers, but the difference between their mortal dance and that of Persephone's was clear, even to Lina. Persephone moved with the inhuman grace of a goddess. Lina's heart swelled with joy at the power she felt within her. This must be how a prima ballerina felt at the peak of her career. She leapt and twirled and shouted with joy.

She could have danced forever, but one of the maidens stumbled and then collapsed into a laughing heap in the middle of a bed of clover. Soon after, several of the other girls were obviously struggling to keep up the dance. Lina quelled her disappointment, and with a glorious final twist and flourish she brought the dance to an end. While the girls cheered and clapped, she sank into the deep curtsy of a prima ballerina. Then the spirits surrounded her, gushing their thanks and asking when she would return to frolic with them again.

As they giggled and talked, Lina tried to unobtrusively search the background for Hades. She found Orion and Dorado first. They were grazing contentedly not far from the pine tree that had served as their finish line. Her eyes traveled back. Hades was standing under the tree. He was leaning against it, his arms crossed nonchalantly and his body relaxed. But his eyes were bright and his hot gaze was locked on her. His lips were tilted up in just the hint of a smile. When he saw that she was watching him, he slowly raised his hand to his lips and then gestured toward her, as if sending her a kiss.

It was the most unabashedly romantic thing that a man had ever done for her.

"Well, ladies, it has been wonderful to dance with all of you. We'll have to do it again very soon, but Hades and I must move on," Lina said, extricating herself from her circle of admirers.

Several of them shot shy glances at the waiting god, and then there was much whispering, of which Lina could only catch the words *Persephone* and *Hades* linked together. Giggling and waving good-bye, the maidens disappeared into the pines.

Hades walked away from the tree to meet her in the middle of the meadow. For a moment neither of them spoke. Then, he reached out and brushed a damp strand of hair from her face.

"I have never watched anything as graceful as your dance," Hades said.

Lina suddenly felt more breathless than she had been while she was twirling and leaping to the music.

"You must be thirsty," he said.

Until then Lina hadn't realized that she had been thirsty or sweaty, but in actuality she was both.

"Very."

"There should be a spring near here." He took her hand and started toward the opposite side of the meadow. "Things never stay completely the same in Elysia, but they do tend to reflect the same elements."

"So it's kind of like a changeable fantasy?" Lina asked, letting her hand trail over the clover that was knee-deep at that end of the meadow. Instantly, tufts of white flowers sprang from between the shamrock-shaped leaves, emitting a perfume that smelled of summer and freshly mowed lawns.

"Yes, a little." Hades smiled at her. "Elysia is divided into different parts, but those parts can mingle and change, according to the desires of the spirits."

"Different parts? You mean like there's one place for people who have been really, really good, another for people who have been mostly good, and another for people who were just ordinarily nice?"

Hades' laughter filled the meadow. "You say the most unexpected things, Persephone. No, Elysia is divided into different realms. One is for warriors. One is here"—he gestured around them—"for maidens to come and frolic. And there are several others. Royalty exists in one. Another is for shepherds." His smile turned lopsided and Lina thought he looked twelve years old. "Oddly enough, shepherds do not like to mingle with others."

"Who would have guessed?"

"Exactly."

"So they can't mix? What if a warrior wants to court a maiden? I'd think even the most dedicated warrior would get tired of only doing manly things after awhile."

"They may mix, but it is rather difficult." Hades paused, considering. "But perhaps it should not be difficult. Perhaps they do not realize what they are missing because they have been so long without." The god stared off into the distance, deep in thought.

"Can you make Elysia rearrange itself according to your will?" Lina asked.

Hades' gaze returned to her. "Yes."

"Then have the meadow of the dancing maidens placed next to the warriors' practice field. The rest should work itself out."

Hades barked a laugh. "I think you are correct."

They entered the forest of pines and after some searching, Hades found a small path. They followed it until it crossed a stream that bubbled and tumbled over smooth rocks. Hades left the path and led Lina downstream and around a bend where the water pooled into a little sandy-bottomed basin before continuing its trek by splashing noisily over one side of the rocky ledge.

"For you, Goddess, only the best in drink and dining," Hades said with a rakish smile.

"You may be kidding," she said, hurrying to crouch at the edge of the pool, "but all that dancing has made me incredibly thirsty, and right now water looks better to me than ambrosia."

She cupped her hand and drank of the clear liquid. It was so cold that it made her teeth hurt. She sighed happily and slurped another handful. After she drank her fill, Lina kicked off her soft leather slippers and let her legs dangle into the icy pool. Hades reclined next to her, leaning against a fallen log. The wind sloughed in the trees above them, surrounding them in the scent of pine and sap. The mystical Underworld sky cast an opaque glow over everything. Rose-colored glasses, Lina thought dreamily, so this is what the old cliché meant.

"Demeter told me that the Underworld was a magical place, but I would never have believed that it held so much beauty," Lina said softly. "If the gods really knew how wonderful it was down here, you'd have a constant stream of visitors."

Hades shrugged his shoulders and looked uncomfortable.

Lina studied him, and almost didn't press him further. Then she remembered his words from the night before. He wanted more than simple sex from her. She knew that, and in order for there to be more between them, they would have to be able to talk. About everything and anything. And, quite frankly, she was too old to play college dating games with all the silences and misunderstandings that went with them. She was a grown woman, and she needed to be able to say what was on her mind.

"If you didn't want visitors, why did you build such a huge palace with all those empty rooms just waiting to be filled?"

He considered the question. How much should he admit to her? He certainly didn't want to tell her that he had never before been involved with a goddess, sexual or otherwise, that he had spent an eternity longing for something more than the frivolity that satisfied the rest of the immortals. He remembered the last time he had visited Mount Olympus. Aphrodite had teased him with an open sexual invitation, and he had not responded to her offer. Later he had heard her smirking with Athena as the two goddesses discussed what part of his body must be dead—along with his realm. Thinking about their cutting words he felt a rush of anger. His body was not dead. It was simply attached to his soul, and his soul required more than the insincere attentions of a self-serving goddess.

What could he say that wouldn't make her bolt away from him? He glanced at her. She appeared to be waiting attentively for his answer. He had to be as honest with her as possible. He couldn't lie or dissemble. A lasting relationship could not be based on falsehoods. He released a long sigh.

"Sometimes I have wondered myself why I built it. Perhaps I was hoping that some day I would learn to overcome my"—he struggled, trying to find the right word—"my difference."

"Difference? What do you mean?"

"I have always found it difficult to interact with other immortals," Hades said slowly. "You must know that I am shunned because I am Lord of the Dead."

Lina began to deny it. Then she remembered the look on Demeter's face when she spoke of Hades, and the offhanded way she discarded him as unimportant . . . uninteresting. The memory made her suddenly very angry.

"They just don't know what you're really like."

"And what is it that I'm really like, Persephone?"

Lina smiled at him and said exactly what was on her mind. "You're interesting and funny, sexy and powerful."

Hades shook his head, staring at her. "You are a constant surprise."

"Is that a good or a bad thing?"

"It is a miraculously good thing."

She was a goner. She couldn't resist him, and she didn't want to. "I'm glad."

"You are not like any of the other immortals. You know how they are . . . so filled with their own importance, constantly striving to outdo one another, never satisfied with what they have." He shook his head and leaned forward so that he could brush her cheek with his fingertips. "You are honest and real—what a goddess truly should be."

Honest and real? A true goddess? Lina wanted to crawl under a rock. She wasn't even who she was.

"I . . . you . . . I . . ." Lina babbled, not sure what she should say.

Hades didn't give her a chance to collect her thoughts. He slid forward and pulled her into his arms. Her mouth was still cold from the spring water. He wanted to drown in her. He plunged into the softness of her lips. If only he had known about her earlier. How could he have spent so much time without her? The goddess wrapped her arms around him and pressed her breasts against his chest. Hades moaned. His desire for her was a molten, throbbing need.

Lina jerked and screamed. Flailing water everywhere she scrambled to pull her long, bare legs from the little pool. Leaping up, Lina rushed around behind the god so that he was between her and the water's edge.

"Something rubbed against me." Her voice shook as Oklahoma experience flashed visions of water moccasins and snapping turtles through her mind.

Hades patted one of her hands that clutched his shoulder, trying to pull his thoughts together. He could still feel the imprint of her breasts against the supple leather that covered his chest and his body still surged with hard longing.

"Persephone, nothing in Elysia would harm you."

"There!" Lina was ashamed that the word came out as a squeal. She pointed to a dark shape that flitted under the water. "There's something in the pool."

With a sigh Hades stood and walked the few feet to the bank. He crouched down and peered into the clear water.

All of Lina's senses were on high alert. "Be careful," she said. "It might be a snake."

Hades shot her a bemused look over his shoulder. "Why would you fear a snake?"

Lina twisted a thick strand of hair around her finger. *Snakes are closely allied with Demeter. They are nothing to fear.* Her internal voice chastised her.

"I know it's silly, but I've never liked them," she said miserably.

The god's wide brow wrinkled in confusion, but a splash from the pool called his attention. Lina cringed back, not wanting to see the slithering reptilian body.

When Hades looked at her again a small smile played around his lips. "You cannot possibly fear this creature."

"I don't really like turtles, either," Lina said quickly, keeping her eyes averted from the dark shape that had just surfaced in the pool. "Especially snapping turtles."

Hades chuckled and motioned for her to join him. "Come. You like animals."

Lina didn't bulge. "I do. I like mammals. I like birds. I don't even mind fish. I do not like reptiles. I know it sounds narrow-minded, but—"

An odd barking noise came from the water. Lina peered past Hades to see a little creature floating on its back.

She gasped. "You're not a snake!"

The otter barked at her again, kicking the water with his adorably webbed paws.

Lina hurried to join Hades. She crouched next to him, leaning in against his side. "I think it's the cutest thing I've ever seen."

"Don't tell Orion," Hades said. "He believes that he is your favorite."

Lina pushed her shoulder against his before she reached across the water to tickle the otter's belly. "Orion is my favorite horse. This little guy can be my favorite otter."

At her touch, the otter went into a frenzy of puppyish yips and snuffling sounds, wriggling so much that he sprayed water all over before swimming to the ledge and disappearing down the little waterfall.

"I didn't mean to scare him."

Hades smiled at the goddess's disappointed expression and wiped beads of water from her cheek.

"You did not scare him, sweet one. The otters of Elysia are notoriously shy. Even I have never before seen one this close. I certainly have never touched one."

Lina looked wistfully after the cute creature. "Can't you get him to come back? You are a god."

Hades laughed. "As a wise god, I know when it is best not to tamper with the natural order of things. And you would have more luck than I at charming the little beast. You are the animal sorceress, not I."

"I'm not really a sorceress," Lina said. "I just like animals, and they like me, too."

"Mammals," Hades corrected her, brushing a long strand of hair back from her face.

Lina tilted her head so that her cheek nuzzled his hand.

"Perhaps it is only me you have bespelled, sorceress." Hades rubbed his thumb across her full bottom lip.

"There's no one I'd rather work magic on," Lina heard herself say as she leaned forward to meet his kiss.

When something butted her in the back, she didn't jerk around in surprise or scream. She simply reached up and patted Orion's muzzle.

"You know, the uninformed would believe that the Underworld would be the perfect place to find peace and quiet."

Hades scowled at the stallion. "They would be incorrect."

Orion snorted and tossed his head at the god, then he nuzzled Lina again, breathing warm, horsy breath on her neck and making her giggle. Lina grabbed a handful of silky mane, and Orion raised his head, pulling her to her feet.

Lina looked down at the god, who was still glaring at the horse. She bent down and took his hand and tugged at him until he rose reluctantly to his feet.

"Would you like to see more of Elysia?" Hades asked.

Lina raised up on her tiptoes and brushed his cheek with a kiss. "I would love to see more of your realm."

Her words brought Hades a surge of happiness and he bent to kiss her swiftly and possessively before he lifted her to Orion's back.

CHAPTER TWENTY

THE day passed delightfully. Elysia was an endless adventure where beauty and harmony had been melded perfectly together. And everywhere they went, souls of the dead responded to Persephone's presence. She was moved beyond words by the happiness that she saw on the faces of the spirits as word passed throughout the Underworld that there was a goddess abiding among them.

Hades stayed close to her side, often guiding Dorado close enough so that he could touch her. The reaction of the spirits to Persephone's presence filled him with a bittersweet pleasure. The dead respected and feared him. Some were even intensely loyal to him, but he had never evoked within them the love and joy Persephone's presence did. He did not feel envious of the goddess's effect on his realm. He understood it. How could he not? She had awakened the same feelings within him. Again, he wondered how he had existed so long without her. He could not bear to think what would happen to him or to his realm if she chose not to remain.

Daylight had faded and the night sky was beginning to twinkle with the souls of the Hyades when they finally neared the rear grounds of the palace. Hades nudged Dorado close to Orion and reached over to take Persephone's hand. She smiled at him. Hades' hand felt warm and strong, and she was content to lace her fingers through his and daydream about the wonders of the day as they entered the familiar pine forest. When they reached the bottom tier of the gardens, Hades pulled Dorado to a halt, causing Orion to snort and stop short.

"There is one last thing that I would like to show you today, if you are willing."

"Of course," she said.

"We must walk," he pretended to whisper.

Lina dropped her voice to a conspirator's level. "What will we do with"—

she waggled her fingers at the two stallions who had their ears cocked back, obviously listening—"them."

"Leave them to me."

He dropped athletically from Dorado's back and then held his arms out to help her dismount Orion. She slid against his body, loving the erotic feel of having muscular horseflesh on one side of her, and a hard, hot god pressing against the other. Hades leaned down and nibbled the sensitive lobe of her ear before whispering, "I believe it is time to be rid of our chaperones." Then he straightened and barked the command for them to return to the stables in a voice so powerful that the leaves on the trees surrounding them whipped wildly in response. Orion and Dorado reacted instantly by plunging into the palace grounds.

Lina raised her brows at him. "I'm impressed. I didn't think they'd go so easily."

Hades lips twisted. "They were just surprised. I rarely command them to do anything. Actually, they are rather spoiled."

"Then they'll be mad at you later."

"Probably." He laughed and linked his fingers with hers. "What I want to show you is this way." He led her to a path that skirted the edge of the gardens. They walked beside rows of ornamental hedges trimmed into curling cones. Sleeping flowers shadowed the hedges, and Lina was careful not to let her fingers pass too close to any of the closed blossoms. When Hades stepped from the path and entered the line of cypress trees that ringed that side of the gardens, she couldn't contain her curiosity any longer.

"Where are we going?"

"Not far. To a field there." He pointed ahead of them.

All Lina could see was more of the huge trees, but they were close enough to the palace that the land was still well-ordered. The ground beneath the trees was grassy and free from brambles and debris. The night forest had been emptied of the songbirds' trilling melodies, and Lina began to feel intimidated by the vast silence.

Speaking in a whisper she said, "What's in the field?"

Hades squeezed her hand. "You do not have to be quiet tonight."

"Oh," she said feeling a little embarrassed. Raising her voice to a normal level she repeated her question. "What's in the field?"

"Fireflies."

"Fireflies?"

The god nodded.

The one last thing that he had to show her of the mysteries of the Underworld was fireflies? She'd seen fireflies before. Lots of them.

Reading her expression he grinned mischievously and said, "I believe that you will find these fireflies unique."

Lina shrugged and kept her mouth shut. Maybe the real Persephone would have thought a field of fireflies was unique, but it would take a little more than summer bugs to raise the eyebrows of an Oklahoma girl, especially after the wonders she had already seen that day.

"Ah, here is the break in the trees. Watch your step, we must cross this small gully first."

Lina's attention was focused on stepping across the little ditch, so she didn't look up until she was actually standing in the field. When she did her eyes widened with surprise.

The field was filled with light, but it wasn't the familiar butter-yellow firefly light she had grown up chasing. It was light the color of moonbeams, lace, and . . .

"Narcissus flowers!" She gasped. *"Misericordioso madre di Dio!* They're making narcissus flowers."

Hades' soft chuckle sounded happily self-satisfied. "Few outside of the Underworld have witnessed their like. So, Goddess of Spring, do you approve?"

Lina stared at the field. What must have been thousands of fey fireflies were hard at work. And they were spinning flowers. From the middle of tufts of ordinary-looking green foliage a group of the tiny insects would swarm, then they would begin flying in a sparkling spiral, around and around until, like miniature comets, their glowing tails took on form and mass, leaving behind a perfect narcissus in full bloom.

"It's incredible. Is this how all of the narcissus are made?"

"All of them that exist in the Underworld. Occasionally, a group of fireflies will get confused and drift too close to the opening to the land of the mortals. Sometimes they create a flower in the world above, but I try to prevent that. As you may have noticed, the fragrance of my narcissus bloom is different than those in the World of the Living. Mortals find it too intoxicating."

Lina remembered the night she had bent to breathe in the scent of a very unusual narcissus bloom.

"I can see how that might cause problems," she said faintly.

As if the sound of her voice had just registered on their small consciousness, several of the closest groups of fireflies paused in their flower building.

Then, like they all had the same thought, in one glowing flock they flew to Lina. They hovered in front of her spinning in sparkling circles and making strange little chirping noises that Lina thought sounded a lot like soprano-singing crickets.

"What do they want?" Lina whispered out of the side of her mouth to Hades.

The god tilted his head and then smiled. "They want you to create flowers with them."

"Really?" she said, undecided about what to do.

"Really," he said. Hades let go of her hand. "Go to them. I will wait for you."

She pretty much had to. She was supposed to be Goddess of Spring. Building flowers would definitely be a part of her job description. And, as she stood there pondering what she should do, she realized that she wanted to join them, very much.

Just touch them and wish the blossom into being. They will bloom, her internal monitor told her.

Lina stepped into the field. The long grass swayed softly against her calves. The fireflies danced in dizzying circles around her, chirping happily. Lina approached a clump of green that wasn't grass and wasn't flower. Hesitantly, she stroked the wide, flat leaves with her fingertips, thinking about how much she would like it to bloom. In a burst of bright light that reminded her of a fireworks display, a brilliant white blossom exploded from the center of the plant.

She bent and inhaled the unique fragrance. Lina laughed aloud. She had created that beautiful flower. The joy of youth and new beginnings filled her. Without thinking, she followed the lead of her body and did a graceful pirouette and a little leap step to the next cluster of greenery. The fireflies haloed her body as she caressed the flower alive and then danced to another bloom.

Hades stood at the edge of the field and filled his eyes with her. How could anyone be so lovely? He felt a ferocious desire to have her, and through that act to finally gain true belonging—the kind of belonging that he had born witness to so many times as he had watched it reflected in the eyes of soul mates.

She spun and danced and called the narcissus flowers alive. And wasn't she doing the same to him? The Lord of the Dead, the god who had considered himself immune to love, had fallen in love with the Goddess of Spring. No matter how ridiculous or ironic it seemed, it had happened. And he didn't want it to end. The decision was made. He wanted to do more than to watch the ghosts of love—he wanted to experience love for himself.

He rubbed his chest automatically, anticipating the burning, but it didn't come. Even though Persephone made his body ache and his blood pound, she did not make his choler flare. His hand stilled and he tried to remember the last time he had felt the burning in his chest. Hades blinked in surprise. It had been the night he had offended her and walked out of dinner. Not since then. He smiled. She was not only the breath of spring; she was also balm for a weary soul. Perhaps his loneliness had truly come to an end.

Lina felt his eyes on her and as another narcissus burst into blossom, she looked back to where he waited. He stood at the edge of the meadow, tall and dark and silent, watching her with an intensity that sent a thrill through her blood.

But why must he always just watch? Suddenly she wanted more for him. A wonderful thought came to her. She'd been frolicking with maidens and nymphs since she'd arrived. It was definitely Hades' turn. Smiling happily, she danced up to him, trailing a mist of glittering fireflies in her wake. She grabbed his hand.

"Come on! Make flowers with me."

His eyes were shadowed with sadness. "I am the God of the Dead. I cannot create life."

"You can if I help you," she said with more confidence than she felt and tugged at his hand.

"No, I . . ." He sighed. "Persephone, I can refuse you nothing." Reluctantly, he allowed her to pull him into the meadow.

Surrounded by the sparkling fog of fireflies, Lina led Hades to a clump of not-yet-narcissus. She motioned for Hades to stand behind her, then she reached back and slid her hands down the underside of his arms until his hands enveloped hers and his arms encased her. She splayed her fingers wide, as if she had just thrown a ball.

"Lace your fingers beside mine." His nearness caused her voice to be a husky purr. "And think about how much you would like to make the narcissus blossom."

Lost in her, Hades let her guide his hands. He did wish he could make the narcissus bloom, but even more he wished that he could make this goddess his own, that she would stay beside him and relieve his loneliness for an eternity.

His fingers began to tingle as the magic within Persephone's body merged with his own. Incredulous, he watched as the brilliant narcissus burst into being beneath their joined hands.

Lina shouted with joy and turned, face blazing with joy. "We did it!"

Hades' arms wrapped around her and he looked into her glittering eyes. "Together, Persephone. I could not have done it without the Goddess of Spring. I wish I could find words to tell you what great pleasure it gives me to share my world with you."

His voice was serious, his expression earnest, and she felt completely lost in his eyes. Hades wanted more from her than a quick kiss, or even a quick affair. She knew that she should make a little joke and dance away from him. But she couldn't make herself. She burned to be with him as badly as he ached for her. She kissed him, pressing herself against the hard length of his body.

Abruptly Hades ended the kiss. Resting his forehead against hers, he concentrated on controlling his ragged breathing. He would not grope her in the woods again. Persephone deserved more than that. She deserved all that he could give her.

"It is late. We should go back to the palace now," he said, kissing her forehead gently.

She looked up at him. "I'm not tired."

"Nor am I."

"And I'm not ready for the day to end."

"Then it shall not." He took a deep breath. "You have not yet seen my private quarters. Would you like to?"

Lina saw how difficult it was for him to ask. She felt her heart pounding—a heart that was not truly her own, inside a body that didn't belong to her. But her soul did, and it wasn't simply her body that desired him. She loved his sweetness and sense of humor. She loved the sound of his laughter. She loved his power and his passion, and the care and wisdom he showed in his dealings with the spirits in his realm. Lina touched his cheek, and admitted the truth to herself. She loved him.

"Yes. I would like to very much."

Joy flashed over his face, followed quickly by desire, and he bent and kissed her again, hard and fast. Then he reluctantly released her from his arms, took her hand in his, and began to retrace their steps. Lina heard a high-pitched buzzing behind her, and she and Hades turned.

The fireflies were hovering in a huge cluster at the edge of the field. All of them were turned toward Lina.

The god laughed. "Persephone will return. She is not leaving the Underworld."

Their frantic buzzing eased a little.

"I'd love to come back and make more flowers with you," Lina assured them, and their buzzing changed to happy chirps. Smiling, Lina and Hades continued on their way. "It's nice that they like me so much."

"All of my realm adores you, Persephone," Hades said.

Lina glanced up at him. "Just your realm?"

The god's lips tilted up. "No, not just my realm."

She squeezed his hand. "Good."

It was as they stepped from the trees into the ornamental garden that Lina heard the sobbing.

"Someone's crying," Lina said. Peering around in the gentle darkness she tried to discover who it was.

"There," Hades said.

He was pointing ahead of them in the direction of the road that passed in front of the palace and led farther into Elysia. Lina could barely make out a blur of human-sized brightness near the edge of the road.

"I think we should see what's going on." Lina looked up at the god for confirmation. "Don't you?"

"Yes. It is odd that a spirit would cry in Elysia," he explained as they started toward the blotch of light. "The dead might miss family and loved ones from the Land of the Living, but by the time they are ferried across Styx and enter Elysia, their souls are filled with joy, or at the very least, peace. The ability to cease longing for the living—or at least the ability to understand that all partings are only temporary—is built into the mortal spirit. Those who have earned an eternity in Elysia find that they are content."

As they got closer to the spirit the brightness took shape. Lina could see that she was a pretty young woman with long, upswept dark hair and a plump figure. She was sitting at the edge of the road, face in her hands, weeping with such passion that she did not even notice their approach. Instinctively, Lina motioned for Hades to stay back, and she walked to the woman's side. Just before she touched her shoulder, Lina noticed that the spirit's body looked unusually dense. If she hadn't had the typically pale luminescence of the dead, Lina would have believed that she was a living woman who had somehow gotten lost and stumbled into the Underworld.

"Honey, what's wrong?" Lina asked softly.

The woman jumped, and raised a tear-stained face to peer with frantic brown eyes at Lina. Instantly she recognized the goddess, and began to bow her head. Then she caught sight of Hades, and her hand went to her mouth. She changed the direction of her bow, but ended up bobbing back and forth, not sure which of the immortals to acknowledge first.

"I did not mean to disturb the gods!" she cried, wiping her eyes. Climbing awkwardly to her feet, she began backing hastily away from Lina. "Please forgive me."

"No." Lina held out her hand in what she meant as a calming gesture. The woman jerked to a nervous halt, staring at her outstretched arm. Lina thought she looked like a frightened mouse. She sighed and modulated her voice to the tone she used to reassure young animals. "Don't go. You didn't disturb us. Hades and I were taking a walk and we heard you crying. We were concerned, not angry."

She seemed to relax a little.

"What is your name?" Hades asked in the pleasant, fatherly voice he used with Eurydice.

She glanced nervously at him. "Alcetis."

"Tell us why you were crying, Alcetis," Lina said gently.

Alcetis looked down and spoke to her feet. "I am so very lonely. I miss my husband and my family desperately." She pressed the back of her hand against her mouth, trying unsuccessfully to stifle a sob.

Lina's worried gaze found Hades. She saw that he, too, looked surprised at the spirit's words. Then she saw him tilt his head to the side and his face took on a listening expression. In a moment his eyes seemed to darken and he pressed his lips together before speaking to the spirit.

"It was not your time, Alcetis," Hades said in a voice shadowed with sadness.

The spirit drew another ragged, sobbing breath. "No, it was not. But I had to come."

Hades frowned. "You did not have to. It was your choice."

Alcetis raised her dripping face. "Do you not understand? He asked others. They would not. I had to."

Completely confused, Lina shook her head. "Wait, *I* don't understand. What are you two talking about? Has some kind of mistake been made?"

"Alcetis, tell Persephone why you have entered the Underworld," Hades said.

Alcetis took a deep breath and wiped her face with the sleeve of her burial robe. "I have only been married a short time. My husband's name is Admetus."

The spirit's damp face brightened as she said the name and she almost smiled. "Yesterday at dawn the arguers prophesized that Admetus would die before the sun set. My husband immediately petitioned Apollo, and the God of Light concurred. Indeed, the prophesy was true. The Fates had finished weaving Admetus' life, and at dusk his mortal string would be cut. But my husband has long been a favorite of the God of Light, and Apollo heard my husband's cries. He granted Admetus a new fate. He would be spared if someone would agree to die in his place. First, Admetus went to his parents, who are old and not well, but they refused. Then he went to his brothers. They, too, would not die in his stead. He asked his closest friends, assuring them that he would see their families well cared for, but the answer was always the same. No one was willing to die for him. In despair, he returned home to await his fate." Alcetis paused, looking searchingly at Lina. "I could not let him die."

Hades' jaw clenched, but when he spoke his voice betrayed no anger. "And he let you die for him."

The spirit turned wide, wet eyes to the god. "He wept and rent his garments. His sadness was great."

"But not great enough to stop you," Hades said.

"You must see that I had no choice. I had to take his place." Alcetis began weeping again.

"That is why you feel such loneliness and pain. It is not your time. Your life's thread is still spinning. Your soul knows this and you cannot find peace." Hades spoke solemnly, as if a great weight pressed down upon his words.

"Well, this can't be right," Lina said. "Look at her—she doesn't even have the same kind of body as the rest of the spirits."

"That is because she is not like the rest of the spirits. She is misplaced, outside of her allotted fate."

"Then it sounds to me like you need to fix this," Lina said firmly.

"She is here because a god meddled in a mortal's life, something that happens far too often, and for far too many selfish reasons. I do not believe in interfering with the lives of mortals."

"But she's a part of your realm now. You're not technically meddling. You're doing your job."

Hades spoke through gritted teeth. "Persephone, do you not remember what happened the last time you made a judgment about sending a spirit back to the Land of the Living?"

Lina flinched as if he had slapped her. "This is different, and I can't believe that you are heartless enough not to see that." Her voice was ice.

"Oh, please!" Alcetis threw herself on her knees between the two immortals. "I did not mean to cause strife between the King and Queen of the Underworld."

"What is it you called Persephone?" Hades said, fast and sharp. "What title did you give her?"

Trembling, the out of place spirit answered the god. "I called her Queen of the Underworld, but I did not give the title to her, Lord. I simply repeat what she has been named in the world above." She managed to smile shyly at Lina. "It is well known that she is now reigning at your side."

Lina was struck speechless. Queen of the Underworld? People were really calling her that? She looked at Hades and the dark god captured her gaze. His eyes flamed and his face seemed to burn with transparent joy. As he spoke, Lina could not look away from him, and she forgot to breathe.

"Pronounce your judgment, Persephone. I bow to your will."

And then he did, almost imperceptibly, bow his head to her.

Lina forced her eyes from him. She smiled shakily at Alcetis. "Then my judgment is that you return to the mortal world and your husband to finish living out your fate. And tell your husband that he can continue following whatever new thread the Fates have woven for him."

With a happy cry, Alcetis jumped to her feet and took Lina's hand. She kissed it, then held it to her wet cheek. Through shining eyes she beamed at Lina.

"Oh, thank you, Queen of the Underworld. My children and my children's children shall make sacrifices to you every spring until the end of time."

"That's really nice of you, but you should know that I prefer a little wine and honey scattered around the ground. I don't so much like the blood sacrifices," Lina said quickly.

Alcetis curtsied deeply. "I will always remember your kindness, Goddess."

Chapter Twenty-one

HADES had been very quiet after Alcetis disappeared back down the road that would return her to her mortal life. Lina watched him with little sideways glances. He was holding her hand, but his face was inscrutable. He was definitely making her very nervous. Were they still going to his room? Had she misunderstood his reaction to hearing her called the Queen of the Underworld? Could it have been an emotion other than fierce happiness she had thought she had seen? But then why would he have allowed her to pass a judgment that he was clearly against? Her mind felt like it was filled with fireflies.

They entered the palace through the rear courtyard, and turned to the left away from the direction of Lina's room. They walked past the entry to the dining room. Finally, Hades stopped in front of a huge door into which had been carved the rearing image of Orion and the helmet from the Great Hall.

Feeling nervous, Lina pointed at the door. "It's a good likeness of Orion. He looks very ferocious."

Hades snorted. "I think a new rendition is needed—one which shows him nickering softly to his goddess."

Relieved by his banter, Lina gave him a playful nudge with her shoulder. "Oh, he's still thought of as a dread steed. Eurydice certainly avoids him."

Hades shook his head. "I'm afraid his reputation of being a fierce, solitary creature has been forever shattered." He turned to her and took Lina's chin in his hand, tilting her face up. "But he does not mind. His gain far exceeds his loss." He kissed her gently, and murmured against her lips. "Will you join me in my chamber?"

"Yes." Her stomach tightened.

Hades opened the great door for her and she stepped into the god's private world. The first thing she noticed was the enormous bed that was centered in the room. It was canopied by a gossamer net of sheer silk that hung in luxurious folds all around it. Lina could see that the bed itself was covered with thick white linens so that the whole thing looked like it was a cloud that had lost its place in the sky. It was opulent and sexy and very, very inviting. Lina realized she was staring at the bed, and letting her imagination wander. She felt her cheeks grow warm.

Yanking her eyes away, her attention was drawn to the impressive pair of chandeliers that hung from the domed ceiling. They appeared to have been made from black glass, and flames from hundreds of candles danced and glistened in their unusual surface.

"Your chandeliers are always so beautiful. Are these really made of black glass?"

"Obsidian," Hades said. Pressing his hand intimately into the small of her back, he led her into the room. "Although when it has been cut and polished it does resemble glass."

Lina smiled at him. "What are its properties? I know they must be special if you chose this stone for your room."

"Obsidian's powers are that of protection, grounding, divination and peace." He glanced up at the winking light. "And I find it soothing."

"Well, it definitely works with your color scheme." Lina gestured at the rest of the vast chamber. The predominate colors were black, white and silver. But instead of making the room austere and cold, the dramatic differences fit well together, as if the god had found a way to comfortably wed light and dark.

"Would you like some wine?" Hades asked. He was nervous and he wondered if she could hear the pounding of his heart.

When Persephone nodded, Hades hurried over to a squat table that sat between two white satin chaises and poured two glasses of wine from a bottle that had already been opened and placed in an iced container.

Lina smiled her thanks and took the crystal glass that was filled with golden liquid. Its fragrance drifted to her and Lina's smile widened.

"Ambrosia!"

"Rumor has it that you are fond of it." His lips twitched.

"Rumor should also have it that sometimes I'm overly fond of it."

"That is our secret." He smiled. Then he cleared his throat and raised his glass to her. "To new beginnings."

"To new beginnings," Lina repeated, touching her glass against his. As they drank their eyes stayed locked together.

Then Hades placed his glass back on the table. Without hesitation, Lina placed hers next to his. The dark god took a deep breath. Then he closed the small space between them and took her in his arms.

"You are haunting me, Persephone. I cannot breathe without thinking of you."

He captured her lips in a hungry kiss. Their bodies pressed together. All she could think was, oh-thank-you-finally! His hardness pulsed against her and she responded with liquid heat. Lina's hands roamed up and across his chest, the width of his leather chiton, and Lina wanted to curse in frustration. She had no idea how to get the thing off him. While his deep kisses sizzled through her blood, she directed her fingers until she finally found the ties that laced the leather together low on his side. She tugged and pulled, and they loosened enough for her to slip her fingers within so that she could stroke the hard muscles of his waist and abdomen.

Hades moaned against her mouth. His hand moved down to cup her curved bottom as he pressed her more firmly against him. Heat flooded his body as he felt her move against him in response.

She nibbled on his bottom lip teasingly. Then she pulled back, but only far enough to meet his eyes.

"Take me to bed, Hades." She sounded breathless.

He swallowed, trying to clear the dryness in his throat, and nodded. Then he led her to his bed. Hades parted the silk curtain for her, but he did not follow her within. Lying back against his pillows, Persephone looked beautiful and ultimately desirable. At his hesitation, the goddess smiled questioningly up at him.

"I must tell you something first." Hades' voice was thick with emotion. "I have never before done this."

"You mean you have never brought a woman to your bedroom before?"

"It is true that I have never brought a mortal woman here, but that is not all that I have never before done."

Lina's eyes widened. "You have never made love?"

Hades' laughter sounded forced and nervous. "I have made love, just never with a goddess."

Lina sat up. She wished desperately that she could admit to him the irony of their situation. He was nervous for the same reason she was feeling a herd of butterflies stampeding around in her stomach.

"Truthfully, I haven't been with anyone in quite a while." She reached and touched his hand. His fingers wrapped around hers. "And I can promise you that no god has ever made me feel the way you do."

He sat next to her on the bed, looking at their joined hands.

"When Alcetis called you the Queen of the Underworld I was filled with unspeakable pride. To think that others believe that you might belong to me, that you could be content reigning at my side. I cannot conceive of anything that would bring me more joy."

She released a long sigh. "I would be proud to be called Queen of the Underworld, but I don't know . . ." She faltered, trapped between her promise to Demeter and her need to tell Hades the truth.

He cupped her face in his hands. "It is enough for now that I know that the idea is not repellent to you. Time will take care of the rest."

She placed her hands over his. "How could your wonderful realm repel me? I adore it," she said hoarsely.

His smile was dazzling, and Lina wondered how it was possible that the other immortals did not see him as she did. Then she was suddenly, fiercely glad that they did not. If they knew, then he wouldn't belong to her; he'd be like the rest of them. Hades kissed her gently, but she could feel the tension in his body through the corded muscles of his arms.

When he spoke his voice had deepened with his breathing. "Show me how to bring you pleasure. Just the thought of you, just a glimpse of your skin, makes my blood heat. But I know desire is not so simple for women." Despite his taut nerves Hades managed a chuckle. "And even with my limited experience I have learned that goddesses are, indeed, much more complex than gods. Teach me how I can flame your desire, Persephone."

Lina's mouth felt dry and she ran her tongue over her lips, feeling a shiver of pleasure as Hades' gaze became riveted on her mouth.

"You could start by undressing," she said breathlessly.

With no hesitation, Hades pulled off his already loosened chiton, unwrapped his short undertunic and the linen loincloth that Lina had found so enticing when he was dressed only in it at the forge. Tossing his clothes away he stood before her naked. He was magnificent. The rich luster of his skin gilded his muscles, making him look dark and exotic. She had never seen such a beautifully made man. Her eyes traveled down his body and her breath caught in her throat. He was already fully aroused.

Lina felt a heady rush of pleasure at the knowledge that the power of a god was hers to command. She stood, resting her palms against his bare chest. Then, slowly, she drew them across his skin, loving the feel of the hard, well-defined ridges of his chest and arms. When her hands moved down to his lower abdomen, she felt a tremor run through him.

"One thing that all women like is to believe that their touch is arousing," Lina said huskily. "It gives us pleasure to know that even though our bodies are less powerfully built, one small touch from us can make a man tremble and moan."

She took his hard flesh in her hand and stroked it caressingly. A moan that sounded almost painful came from deep within Hades' throat.

Lina's smile was a seductive tease. "Am I hurting you?"

"No!" He gasped. "Though I believe you could slay me with one touch. All I need do is to think of you . . . to see you . . . to smell you and I become engorged, aching, longing for your touch."

His words sent a bolt of heat through her body. She released him so that she could tug at the lacing on her left shoulder that held her robe together. She shrugged the top off, leaving her breasts bare. It only took her a moment to pull loose the ties over her hips, and with a small, sensuous movement she caused the material to slide from her body. Then she stepped into Hades' arms.

"Your skin is so hot. I love the way it feels against mine," she said between kisses.

"Wanting you makes me feel that I am on fire," Hades whispered against her lips as his hands explored the deep curve of her hips. Then he turned and fell back, pulling her with him onto the bed. "Show me more, Persephone. Teach me how to set you afire, too."

Lina rolled off of him, so that they were lying on their sides, facing each other. She hardly knew where to start. She already felt so hot and wet that for a moment she almost pulled him on top of her. Then she took a deep breath and stopped the impulse. No, he wasn't like her ex-husband or any of her other disinterested lovers. This time it was going to be different. Hades was different. In him she had what all women really desired—a man who honestly wanted to please her, and was willing to listen and learn so that she would, indeed, find that pleasure. All she had to do was show him what she desired.

And that was much more difficult than she had imagined. What did she desire? She closed her eyes and collected her thoughts. All of her adult life she had wanted a man who would cherish her enough to care about her pleasure as much as his own. She had to be honest with Hades, as well as with herself. She must break down the barriers her previous lovers had required her to erect. Lina shivered. She was ready. She opened her eyes.

Lightly, she touched the spot where her neck met her shoulder, and with a voice that sounded suddenly shy she said, "To me, it's the little things that matter. For instance, I like to be kissed here."

Hades propped himself up on his elbow, then he bent to the curve of her neck. Kissing and nipping her gently, he ran his tongue around the sensitive area.

"I would also like it if you caressed me while you kissed me. Let my body become accustomed to your touch," she whispered.

When her breathing deepened, he followed the seductive line of her shoulder down to her breasts, which he cupped gently in his hands.

"Oh, yes, there, too," she moaned as he rained kisses on the soft mounds.

"Will it give you pleasure if I lick and kiss your nipples?" Hades' voice was husky with desire.

"Yes," she said, burying her hands in his dark hair.

As he teased and sucked, his hand traveled down. First he caressed the length of her leg, molding his touch to her curvaceous muscles. Remembering that she desired him to pay attention to the small things, he teased the velvety area behind her knee. Then, following the unspoken cues of her body, he drew hot circles on her inner thigh. She opened to him and guided his hand to her core, showing him how to caress her sensitive bud, whispering breathless encouragement when his touch moved with her rhythm.

The wave of her orgasm came hard and fast. She gasped his name as exquisite electricity began deep within her and radiated throughout her body.

Hades held her close, his own desires temporarily forgotten in his amazement that he had been able to evoke such a passionate response from her. He wanted to shout with happiness. She knew him for who he was, and she desired him and had given herself to him.

She opened her eyes and looked up at him. He was smiling at her and stroking the hair from her face. Her breathing had not even returned to normal when she began kissing him again.

"I think that the best lovemaking is mutually satisfying," she said breathlessly, pressing him gently back against the bed. "It is a dance of give and take, where even though your partner's pleasure can become your own, it shouldn't exclude you from having your needs and desires fulfilled as well."

She stroked his muscular body, kissing and tasting the saltiness of his skin until his breathing was ragged. Sweat glistened on his body and all of his muscles strained and tensed as he fought to control his desire. Quickly, she wrapped her arms around him.

"Don't hold back anymore. I want you inside of me—and I want to feel all of your passion."

With a growl, he rolled so that he was on top of her. Holding himself up on his hands, he stared into her eyes as he plunged into her body. Her wet heat surrounded him and it took all of his force of will to hold back the explosion that raged to be released. Possessing her was better than his fantasy, better than anything he could have imagined. He held very still for a moment, trying to regain control. Then, with a whimpering sound, she thrust up to meet him and he responded, matching her passion with his own until he was lost to everything but the sensation of her. Feeling her tighten rhythmically around him, she drove him over the edge. As the spasms of pleasure coursed through him, Hades buried his face in her hair and said one word over and over.

"Persephone . . ."

A sweet, familiar scent awakened her. Hades was standing beside the bed smiling. He was naked, except for the snug loincloth wrapped low around his waist. He was holding a chilled glass of golden liquid in one hand and a silk robe in the other.

"Good morning," she said, sleepily.

"Good morning. I thought you might be thirsty." He nodded at the crystal wineglass. "Also, Eurydice brought those things for you." He gestured over his shoulder at a table that was laden with pomegranates and a mouthwatering assortment of cheeses and breads.

Lina thought he couldn't possibly have looked more adorable standing there nervously, trying to act like he was used to having a goddess in his bed.

"Thank you." She sat up and stretched. The sheet fell down around her waist, and his eyes devoured the sight of her bare breasts.

Entranced, Hades placed the glass on the table and knelt before her, taking her breasts in his hands and kissing her nipples. Although his touch was gentle, Lina couldn't help flinching. Her body was incredibly, wonderfully satiated, but also very, very sore.

The god pulled back. "I am hurting you?"

"I'm just feeling a little . . . sensitive. Seven times in one night is, well, unusual."

Hades actually blushed as he draped the silk robe over her shoulders and smoothed her hair. She did look rumpled, and she had a red bite mark on the curve of her neck. Had he been too rough with her? Last night he had thought that he had pleased her, but this morning she seemed almost disgruntled. She stood up, a little gingerly, and shrugged into the robe. By all the gods! Had he hurt her?

She gave him a distracted smile, and sat gingerly before she descended hungrily on the laden table. She did not notice how the god flinched in response at her obvious physical discomfort. Hades silently damned himself for an inexperienced fool.

As Lina ate, she felt her energy level return to normal and the aches of her well-used body dissipate. Responding to her revived good humor, Hades' nerves evaporated, and they ate breakfast like lovers, with their knees touching, feeding each other choice tidbits from their own plates. He was just explaining to her how he had fashioned the chandeliers that hung gracefully from the ceiling above them when two firm knocks sounded against the door.

"Yes! Enter," Hades called.

Iapis entered the room, holding a square, flat box in his hand. He bowed first to Hades and then to Lina.

"Good day, Hades, Persephone." His eyes danced and he tried unsuccessfully to hide a delighted smile. "I have brought that which you requested, my Lord." He handed the box to Hades.

"Excellent, thank you, Iapis."

Seeing the daimon reminded Lina that she had been neglecting Eurydice lately, and she felt a twinge of guilt.

"Iapis, could you take a message to Eurydice for me?" Lina asked.

"Of course, Goddess."

"Tell her that I would love to see what she has been sketching."

Iapis smiled. "She will be pleased, Goddess."

"Good. Have her bring her work to my room later today. And please tell her that I am looking forward to seeing her creations—and her. I've missed her lately."

Lina thought she saw a telltale flush darken the daimon's cheeks before he nodded, and, still smiling, bowed his way from the room.

"He's certainly in a good mood," Lina said, drumming her fingers against the table.

"He likes seeing me happy," Hades said, kissing her hand.

Lina felt herself grinning as foolishly as the daimon had been. Then she mentally shook herself.

"I don't think that's all there is to his jolly expression. I've been meaning to talk to you about that daimon of yours."

Hades raised an eyebrow at her.

"I think he's interested in Eurydice," Lina said.

Hades' grin reminded her of a little boy caught with his hand in the cookie jar. "I think you are correct."

"Then I need to know his intentions," she said firmly.

Hades nodded, his expression instantly sobering. "I see. Of course you would be concerned. I believe I can speak for Iapis. His intentions are honorable. He truly cares for the little spirit."

"You will see that he is careful with her? She has been through a difficult time. It's hard for a woman to love again after she has been hurt."

Hades touched her cheek gently, wondering suddenly if the goddess was speaking only about her loyal spirit.

"You may trust me. Always. I will watch out for Eurydice as if she were the Goddess of Spring herself."

"Thank you. It's not that I don't like Iapis—I do. I just worry about Eurydice."

"You are a kind goddess who cares for those who love you," Hades said. Then he looked down at the square box sitting beside his hand. He slid it across the table to Persephone.

"This is something I made the first night you were here. I could not sleep. All I could do was to think about you, about your smile and your eyes." He gestured for her to open the box.

The little clasp unlatched easily and Lina lifted the lid. Nestled in a bed of black velvet inside the box was a chain made of delicate silver links from the middle of which hung a single amethyst stone that had been carved and polished into the shape of an exquisite narcissus blossom.

Lina felt tears fill her eyes. "Oh, Hades! It's the most beautiful thing I've ever been given."

Hades stood and moved behind her, taking the necklace from its case so that he could place it around her neck. It hung perfectly, just above the swell of her breasts.

"Thank you. I will always cherish it."

The god pulled her into his arms. "The night I made it I was filled with emptiness and longing, but now you are here with me and the black hole within me exists no more. The mortals were wise; you are Queen of the Underworld.

I cannot imagine my life without you. You have brought eternal Spring to the Underworld, and to the heart of its god. I am in love with you, Persephone."

The tears that had been pooling in Lina's eyes spilled over and she couldn't speak.

He wiped her cheeks with his thumbs. "Why do you weep, beloved?"

"Things are just so complicated."

Hades' brow furrowed. "Because you are Goddess of Spring?"

"That's part of it."

"Tell me truly, Persephone. Do you weep because you cannot imagine remaining in the Underworld?"

The god tried to keep his voice neutral, but Lina could see the pain reflected in his eyes.

"I want to be with you," she said, trying not to sound too evasive.

"Then I cannot conceive of any difficulty that we cannot overcome together." He hugged her fiercely.

Resting within the strength of his arms, Lina squeezed her eyes closed, willing her tears to stop. Crying wouldn't help.

She did love him, but that was only a small piece of the truth he needed to know. She wanted to tell him everything. She had to.

But she had given her word, and first she must talk to Demeter.

CHAPTER TWENTY-TWO

"YOU say she is not in her chamber?" Hades snapped at the daimon.

"No, Lord. The goddess is gone."

"And Eurydice does not know where she is?"

"No, Lord. Eurydice has been busy with the paintings she is to show her goddess later today."

Hades paced. Persephone had told him that she needed to soak in a hot bath and then take a nap. Yes, she had appeared distracted, but he had told himself that the goddess was just tired. He had given her time to herself while he had presided, in an unusually distracted manner, over that day's petitions of the dead. Most of them had come to see Persephone, and were visibly disappointed that the goddess did not appear. His jaw tightened. He did not blame them; he wanted nothing more than to see her as well. He could still smell her scent on his skin, and when his mind wandered, he could feel her soft heat against him.

Where had she gone? And why hadn't she told him? What was she thinking? He raked his hand through his hair. After eons of solitary existence, his desire had been too fierce; he had been too rough with her. Perhaps he had hurt her. Or perhaps his lovemaking had not satisfied her. Had she compared him to her other immortal lovers and found him wanting? He clenched his fists. Just the thought of another god touching her caused him to feel ill.

"Find her, Iapis," Hades growled.

The daimon bowed and disappeared.

OKAY, Lina admitted to herself, she was worried. She chewed her bottom lip.

"*Merda!* Why does it have to be so complicated?" Orion's ears tilted back to catch her words and he whickered in soft response.

"I do love him," she said aloud. "So now what are we going to do?"

She knew what *she* had to do, which was why she'd evaded Hades and sneaked off with Orion.

"I think my cover story was excellent, though," she told Orion. "And I'm sure Iapis will only be a little annoyed when he finds out that the huge wineskin of ambrosia that Eurydice insisted he fill to the brim was for Cerberus."

At the mention of the three-headed dog, Orion snorted in disgust.

"Oh, he's not that bad. Perhaps a closet alcoholic, but at least he's loveable. Anyway, you know I like you best." She patted the horse's glistening coat. Orion arched his neck and shifted from a trot into a rolling canter. The dark road passed quickly beneath them. Lina's faithful ball of light hovered over her right shoulder, keeping pace with the stallion. In the distance, she could see the milky outline of the grove of ghost trees.

She wondered if Hades had noticed her absence yet. She hoped not, but if he looked for her, Eurydice would tell him that Persephone had wanted to bring Cerberus the treat she had promised, and the stablemen would report that she had taken Orion for a ride. Hades shouldn't worry. She didn't want him to. She didn't want to cause him any pain.

Their night together had been a new experience for her. Hades had awakened feelings in her that had, until then, just been wisps of dreams and fantasies. And it wasn't just about the sex. Lina sighed. That would have been easy to deal with. She could have a torrid, steamy affair with him, and then be satiated and pleased with herself when it was time for her to leave.

No, it hadn't just been the sex.

The memory of the soul mates haunted her, as did the look on Hades' face when he had declared his love for her. She had wanted to respond with the same words, but she wasn't free to pledge herself to him—not yet—not until she dealt with Demeter. And it had broken her heart.

Lina hadn't meant to love him. She had gone to the Underworld with the best intentions; she'd had a job to do. Period. She hadn't been interested in romance or love or sex. And, quite frankly, the Underworld was the last place she had expected to find any of those things. *Merda!* Demeter had described Hades as an asexual bore. Lina had been totally unprepared for the truth.

She twirled a strand of Orion's satiny mane around her finger as the stallion navigated quickly through the grove of ghost trees. She was definitely in the middle of a mess. She loved him—that Lina was sure of—but a nagging thought wouldn't leave her alone. While she was with him, while she could touch him and look into his eyes, it was easy to believe that he loved her, too. *Her*—Carolina Francesca Santoro—and not some flighty young goddess. And hadn't he been the one to point out that true love had more to do with the soul than the body? So why should it make any difference to him that her real body was that of a forty-three-year-old mortal? In theory it shouldn't.

Orion shot through the dark tunnel toward the broadening speck of light spilling from the world above.

It was undeniable that she had been lying to Hades. Even though she hadn't meant to deceive him into loving her, would he believe that when he learned the truth? Would he understand?

And, most importantly, would he still love her?

Orion galloped out of the tunnel and into the soft light of a cool early morning. She pulled the stallion to a halt, got her bearings and then guided him toward the marble basin which held Demeter's ball-shaped oracle. She slid from his back.

"Just hang around and be good. Hopefully, this won't take too long."

*   *   *

"SHE has ridden Orion to feed a treat to Cerberus?"

The daimon nodded, looking slightly annoyed. "I filled the wineskin myself. She brought that great brute ambrosia!"

At any other time that would have made Hades laugh. Now doubts stabbed him in the heart. "But she told me she was exhausted. She was going to bathe and rest. Why would she go for a ride instead?"

"Only Persephone can answer that, Lord."

The growing sense of unease that had been gnawing at him since that morning blossomed. He must have hurt her. Had he frightened her? Or had he declared his love for her too soon? His chest tightened. She had not proclaimed her love in return. He remembered her tears. Silently cursing himself for his inexperience, he turned to the daimon.

"Bring me the Helmet of Invisibility!" he commanded.

LINA studied the oracle. It rested, still and benign, a simple milky-colored glass ball. But it was a conduit to a goddess who had the power to shape her future. Lina closed her eyes, admitting to herself that she wasn't just worried, she was scared. How could it work? She was a mortal, from another time and place. He was an ancient god. She felt tears of frustration well in her closed eyes.

Stop it! Pull yourself together! She had to tell Demeter everything. She couldn't avoid it any longer.

PERSEPHONE wasn't with the dog, although Cerberus had been happily licking at the well-mauled wineskin she'd fed him. She hadn't passed him returning to the palace, so Hades continued down the road. When he reached the boatman, Charon reported that he had ferried the goddess and her steed across Styx.

Hades admitted the worst to himself. Persephone was definitely returning to the Land of the Living. Hades felt a familiar burning begin in his chest. She was leaving him without saying good-bye? He did not want to believe it. He wouldn't believe it until he confronted her and she told him herself. With the speed of a god, Hades followed the dark path that would lead him to the world above and the Goddess of Spring.

* * *

LINA took a deep breath, and opened her eyes. Concentrating on the goddess, she passed her hands three times over the oracle.

"Demeter, we need to talk," she said.

The orb began to swirl and almost instantly Demeter's handsome features swam into focus.

"When a daughter calls upon her mother, the tone of her voice should be more welcoming than grim," Demeter said, softening the reprimand with a small, motherly smile.

"I didn't mean any disrespect, but I do feel rather grim," Lina said.

Demeter frowned. "What is troubling you, Daughter? I have heard only positive reports about your work. The spirits are pleased that the Goddess of Spring is sojourning in the Underworld." And that was quite true. Since the arrival of the goddess everyone believed to be Persephone in the Underworld, the unceasing, annoying petitions to Demeter from relatives of the dead had ended. Instead, sacrifices of thanksgiving had increased. The mortal must be making her presence known and doing an excellent job of impersonating a goddess. Demeter couldn't imagine what could be bothering her.

"Things have taken an unexpected turn."

Demeter's frown deepened. "Do not tell me you have been discovered."

"No! Everyone still thinks that I'm Persephone." Lina paused, chewing on her bottom lip. "But my problem does have to do with that."

"Explain yourself," Demeter said.

"I've fallen in love with Hades, and he loves me too, and I need to tell him who I really am and figure out how to fix this mess," Lina said in a rush.

Demeter's eyes turned to stone. "This is not some kind of mortal jest you make?"

Lina sighed. "No, this is absolutely not funny."

"You are truly telling me that you and Hades have become lovers?"

"Yes."

"Then a god has dallied with your affections." Demeter shook her head sadly. "I am to blame for this. I exposed a mortal to the whims of a god. Forgive me, Carolina Francesca Santoro, my intention was not to cause you pain."

"No," Lina protested. "It's not like that. He wasn't taking advantage of me. *We* fell in love—with each other."

"Fell in love? With each other?" Demeter's voice went hard. "How could that be? Hades believes that you are Persephone, Goddess of Spring. He has no idea that he has been making love to a mortal woman. Think, Carolina! How could you believe that it is you he loves?" She made a rude noise and her handsome face twisted. "Love! Are you really so naive? Immortals *love* differently than mortals. Surely even in your world you have heard tales of the excesses of immortal *love*."

Lina lifted her chin and narrowed her eyes. "I am not a child. Do not talk to me like I have the fickle emotions of an inexperienced girl. I know the difference between love and lust. I know when a man is using me, just as I know when he is treating me honestly. The lessons were hard, but experience taught me the difference."

"Then you should know better," Demeter said.

Lina's face burned as if Demeter's softly spoken words had struck her. "You don't know him. He's not like the rest of you."

"Not like the rest of the immortals? This is naive nonsense. He is a god. The only difference between Hades and the rest of the gods is that he is reclusive and has chosen to place the dead above the living."

"And that's part of what makes him so different." Lina took a deep breath; she didn't want to betray Hades' confidence, but she had to convince Demeter. "I am the only goddess he's loved."

Demeter's eyes narrowed. "Is that what he told you? Then here is your first lesson in immortal love. Never believe anything a god says when he is trying to gain access to the bed of a goddess. What he told you was only what he thought you needed to hear so that you would give yourself to him."

Refusing to believe Demeter's words Lina shook her head from side to side, but the goddess ignored her and continued her barrage.

"What did you believe? That you and he would be together for eternity? Forget that you are a mortal. Forget that you are from another world. Even if you were truly the Goddess of Spring, did you honestly believe that Hades and Persephone would be mated, that their names would be linked for eternity? The idea is absurd! How could Spring exist in the Land of the Dead?"

"Then Spring doesn't have to exist there. I will. Me—the mortal, Carolina Francesca Santoro. I'll stay in the Underworld and love its god. Just re-exchange me. Give me back my body and return this"—she gestured at herself—"to your daughter."

"I cannot. You are not of this world, Carolina." The anger drained from Demeter's face. "You knew your time there was temporary. I did not pretend otherwise."

"There has to be a way."

"There is not. Both of us must abide by the oaths we have given."

"Can't I even tell him who I am?" Lina asked hopelessly.

"Use your mind, Carolina, not your heart. What would the Lord of the Dead do if he knew he had wooed, not the Goddess of Spring, but a middle-aged baker from the mortal world? Would he open his arms to your deceit?" Demeter held up a hand to silence Lina's protests. "It matters little that you did not intend to deceive him. You say that I do not know Hades, but all immortals know this much of him: the Lord of the Dead values truth above all things. How would he react to your lie?"

"But he loves me."

"If Hades loves, it is Persephone, Goddess of Spring, who has won his affection," Demeter said with finality. "And consider for a moment how the spirits of the Underworld would feel if they learned that the goddess who has brought them such joy is only a mortal in disguise."

Lina flinched. "It would hurt them."

"Yes, it would."

"I cannot tell anyone."

"No, Daughter, you cannot." Lina closed her eyes and Demeter watched the woman in her daughter's body struggle to accept the pain of her words. "Remember this, when you have returned to your rightful place, *Persephone* will just consider Hades another god with whom she dallied. And no matter what you believe has passed between you and he, Hades will eventually feel the same. Listen to the voice that is within you and you will remember that this is simply the way of immortals."

When Lina opened her eyes, her gaze was resolute.

"I'll return to the Underworld and finish my job. You said my time is almost over?"

Demeter nodded.

"Good. I'll be ready to go when you say so."

"I knew I made a wise choice in you." The goddess's image began to fade. "Return with my blessing, Daughter," she said, and she was gone.

Lina turned away from the oracle. Her eyes passed over the beauty of Lake Avernus without actually seeing. She didn't cry. She held herself very still, as if the lack of movement could protect her against further pain.

* * *

CLOAKED in invisibility, Hades had, at first, stayed within the mouth of the tunnel. His initial reaction to finding Persephone had been relief. She wasn't leaving him. She was only speaking to her mother's oracle. He could not hear what she was saying, but as he watched, his relief was rapidly replaced by concern. Persephone was visibly upset, she almost looked frightened.

Was that why she hadn't told him she meant to speak with Demeter? Was she afraid of her mother's reaction to their love? Had she been trying to protect him? Surely, she was aware that he was a powerful god in his own right. But perhaps she wasn't. Persephone was very young—she behaved with such maturity that it was easy for him to forget just how young—and he had kept himself separated from the rest of the immortals for a very long time. Did she believe that he only wielded power in his own realm?

He watched as her face paled. Demeter was wounding her. Anger surged through him. Still wearing the Helmet of Invisibility, he strode toward his beloved.

Demeter's hard voice drifted to him from the oracle.

"Remember this, when you have returned to your rightful place, Persephone will just consider Hades another god with whom she dallied. And no matter what you believe has passed between you and he, eventually Hades will feel the same. Listen to the voice that is within you and you will remember that this is simply the way of the immortals."

Hades stopped short. Had he heard her correctly? He was just another god with whom she had dallied? Incredulous, he listened to Persephone's reply.

"I'll return to the Underworld and finish my job. You said my time is almost over?"

He had only been a job to her?

"Good. I'll be ready to go when you say so."

She wanted to leave him. Invisible to her, Hades watched the goddess he loved turn from her mother's oracle and stare off into the distance. Her eyes were dry. Her face was stone. She looked like a stranger.

No! He wouldn't believe it. He had heard only part of their conversation. He must have misunderstood. He knew Persephone. His Persephone could not deceive him. As his hand lifted to remove the Helmet of Invisibility, a sound drew his attention. Together, he and Persephone turned to face the god who strode from the path that curled around Lake Avernus.

Apollo's handsome face was alight with pleasure. His lips curved in a warm smile of welcome.

"Ah, Persephone, it pleases me that you accepted my invitation. We all knew that too much time in the Underworld would cause the Flower of Spring to yearn for the sun again."

With a growing sense of numbness, Hades watched as Apollo took Persephone's unresisting body in his arms.

Unable to continue watching, the Lord of the Underworld turned his back on the two lovers and silently returned to the realm of the dead.

Chapter Twenty-three

I T didn't take Apollo long to realize that holding Persephone was like hugging a corpse. He pulled back and studied her pale face.

"What's wrong? More problems with Demeter?"

Persephone shook her head. When she blinked, two perfect teardrops fell from her eyes and made glistening tracks down her cheeks. He was just considering whether he should kiss her or materialize a drink for her when a black monster burst from around the path and thrust his body between them.

"Be gone, beast from the pit!" he yelled as he staggered back, trying not to fall.

The stallion turned and bared yellow teeth at him.

"It's okay, Orion. Apollo doesn't mean any harm."

The sadness in her voice touched the god. He peered around the black brute who was nuzzling Persephone. The goddess caressed the horse absently. Tears leaked down her face, but she took no notice of them.

"Orion! I need to speak with your mistress." Eyes blazing, the stallion turned his swiveled head to face Apollo. He held his hands out in an open gesture of peace. "I wish only to offer her aid."

Orion seemed to study the god, then he blew through his nose and lipped the goddess's cheek before moving a few feet down the path where he grazed while keeping one black eye focused on the God of Light.

Apollo took Persephone's limp arm and led her to a bench carved from bare rock. The goddess sat. He made a spinning motion with his hand and a clear goblet appeared suddenly in a shower of sparks. He offered it to Persephone.

"It is only spring water," he said when she hesitated. "I thought you might need its refreshment."

"Thank you," she said woodenly. The water was cold and sweet. She drank deeply, but it didn't begin to quench the emptiness within her.

Apollo sat next to her.

"What has caused you such pain?" he asked.

She didn't answer for so long that he thought she wasn't going to respond. Then she spoke in a voice that was filled with such hopelessness that the god felt his own chest constrict.

"My own foolishness—that is what has caused me such pain."

Apollo took her hand. "What can I do to help you?"

She looked at him then, and the god felt as if her eyes could see through to his soul.

"Answer a question for me. What is it that loves—the body or the spirit?"

Apollo smiled and began to respond with a witty reply, but he found he could not. Once again, she surprised him with her candor. Since their last meeting, the Goddess of Spring hadn't been far from his thoughts. His eyes met hers. He could not belittle her obvious pain, so he answered honestly.

"Persephone, you ask this question of the wrong god. As you know, I have had much experience with lusts of the body. I feel desire and I slake it. But love? That most elusive of emotions? I have witnessed it bring an undefeated warrior to his knees, and cause a single maiden to wield more power than Hercules, but I cannot say that I have ever truly experienced it." Wistfully, he touched her cheek. "But looking at you makes me wish otherwise."

The light was growing. It signaled the coming of dawn. His chariot had to be near, and his time was short. Apollo could see that, though he was close beside her and offering her comfort and compassion, Persephone was not even looking at him. She was staring at the mouth of the tunnel which led to Hades' domain. His hand dropped from her face.

"You love Hades!" He did not bother to hide the surprise in his voice.

Persephone's eyes snapped to his. "And why do you find that so shocking?

Because I am Spring and he is Death? Or is it because immortals don't really know how to love?"

"I just didn't think it possible," Apollo said.

"It's probably not." The temporary fire in her voice was gone, and the hopelessness had returned. She lurched to her feet. "Orion!" The stallion moved with supernatural speed to her side. Without another word, she flung herself astride the horse and dug her heels into his sides. Orion leapt forward, leaving Apollo to stare openmouthed at the dust that rose from his iron-clad hooves.

"Persephone and Hades? How could that be?" he murmured.

HADES was at his forge. He stoked the fire to a level that was almost unbearable and striped down to his loincloth. He wouldn't work on a horseshoe. That would not satisfy him. He needed something else, something larger. He would fashion a shield, wrought from the strongest of metals. Something that could protect a body, if not a soul.

He fed the coals until they screamed with the voice of searing heat. Then he thrust the naked sheet of unformed metal into them and pulled it out when it hummed with readiness. He began pounding it to his will.

On and on Hades worked. His shoulders ached and his blows coursed through his body, and still he could not pound the pain from his soul. He did not blame her. She was just a young goddess. He should have known better. He had been wise to set himself apart from the immortals. She had simply proven how wise he had been. His way had worked for age after age. He had been foolish to deviate.

He felt her presence the moment she entered the forge. Absently he wondered if he would always know when she was near him. How could his soul be linked to hers even though she did not love him? It would bear consideration. Later. When he was alone again, when he could think of her without feeling such raw yearning. Now he must end it. He must return to his old ways before he humiliated himself further. And before she caused him irreparable pain.

"I wish you knew how incredibly handsome you are when you work at your forge."

When she entered the room he had stopped pounding metal against metal, and her voice sounded too loud in the echoing silence. He could not force himself to speak.

"Hades?" She cleared her throat and continued, even when he didn't respond. "I'd love to see more of Elysia today. Would you escort me?"

Her voice. It was so young and sweet. For a moment his resolve wavered. Then he remembered how easily she had allowed Apollo to take her into his arms. When he turned slowly to face her, Persephone did not meet his eyes. Hades felt a little more of his soul dissolve.

"I am afraid our travels have come to an end. As you can see, I have work I must complete."

Lina felt her stomach roll. The man who turned from the forge to speak to her wasn't her lover. He was the cold, imperious god she had met when she had first come to the Underworld. No—she studied him more carefully and realized her initial impression had been wrong. He wasn't even that familiar.

"But, I thought you liked teaching me about your realm," she said inanely.

He laughed, but his voice held no warmth and his eyes were flat and cold.

"Persephone, let us stop this—"

"But," she interrupted him, shaking her head. "Last night . . . I don't understand."

The look of naive shock on her face sliced through him. It was all a cruel pretense! He wanted to scream his pain, and with the anger of a god he hurled the hammer across the forge. When it landed, sparks exploded and the floor beneath them shook. His eyes blazed and his voice thundered.

"Silence! I am Lord of the Dead, not a lowly teacher!"

Lina felt her face lose all color. "All this time you've just been pretending to—"

"DO NOT SPEAK TO ME OF PRETENDING!" The walls of the forge vibrated with the intensity of the dark god's rage. Before he destroyed the chamber in which they stood, Hades brought the force of his anger under control. Through tightly clenched teeth he hurled sarcasm at her. "Have you not been *vacationing* here, Persephone? Masquerading as Queen of the Dead?" His laughter was cold and cruel. "You may be young, but both of us know you are far from inexperienced. Yes, our *lessons* were amusing, but you must realize that it is time the charade end, and, as I sense your visit is also concluding, my timing is perfect. Unfortunately, I have allowed our dalliance to take me too long from my duties. If I do not find time to speak with you again before you depart, let me wish you a pleasant return trip to the Land of the Living. Perhaps you will sojourn in the Underworld another time, perhaps not."

He shrugged nonchalantly, and then turned his back to her, closed another hammer within his shaking fist and resumed his rhythmic pounding. He didn't need to see her leave, he felt it. Soon sweat poured down his face, mixing with his silent tears, and still he kept on beating against the unspeaking metal until the ache in his arms mirrored the pain in his soul.

"I don't belong here." Lina's lips felt bloodless, and she spoke her thoughts aloud to assure herself that they could still form words. It didn't do any good to tell herself that Demeter had been right, that Hades' treatment of her was the norm for one of the immortals. She wasn't really a goddess, and so it was her mortal soul that grieved, and her mortal soul that couldn't understand.

Lina fled the forge without caring where her feet led her. She just wanted to be away. She skirted the stables and passed quickly between rows of ornamental shrubbery, but instead of keeping to the paths in Hades' gardens, she plunged into the surrounding woods. Finally, through the tumult of her mind, she recognized that she was retracing the path to the firefly meadow, and instantly changed direction. Her mind cringed away from the sweet memories of that night. She couldn't bear to go there.

She didn't notice the spirits of the dead except as vague, distant images that might have whispered her name. Her eyes were too blurred with unshed tears, leaving her vision as unfocused as her thoughts. Somewhere in her mind she realized that she was grateful that none of them approached her. She couldn't be their goddess today.

As she passed, the dead paused. Something was wrong with Persephone. Her face had lost its color. Her eyes were glazed and she did not seem to be able to hear them. She moved with the numb steps of the newly dead. Concern for their goddess began to flicker throughout Elysia.

Lina kept walking. She'd be all right. She'd make it. Time would help it not to hurt so badly. The three sentences were a familiar litany. They had become her mantra when her husband had left her for a younger, more perfect woman who could bear him children. They had helped her through the shattered dreams and the sleepless nights that had followed. They had kept her strong through the series of disappointing relationships afterward. And they had soothed her when she had realized that she probably would never love again.

She'd be all right. She'd make it. Time would help it not to hurt so badly.

A mischievous breeze brought with it the intoxicating fragrance of narcissus blossoms and she winced, recoiling from a bed of flowers in front of her.

She changed direction, picking her way around the beautiful blooms, choosing her path according to which way led past fewer flowers.

Her hand rose to her chest where the amethyst narcissus dangled from its silver chain. What had his gift really meant? It wasn't a token of his love, his speech at the forge had made that painfully obvious. Lina blinked her eyes rapidly. In her mind she still heard the echo of his uncaring words. Her fingers caressed the beautifully wrought outline of the narcissus. Payment for services rendered; that's all the gift had been. Hades—a different kind of a god? Her self-mocking laughter came out like a sob. Her hand closed over the jewel and she tugged, snapping the delicate chain.

"Demeter was right. I should have known better." Lina hurled the necklace to the ground and kept walking. She didn't look back.

She'd be all right. She'd make it. Time would help it not to hurt so badly.

The only notice Lina took when the landscape began to change was to feel relief that there were no more narcissus blossoms to avoid. There were also fewer spirits of the dead hovering in the periphery of her vision, and that, too, brought her relief. Vaguely she acknowledged that it was growing darker, but the trees were very tall and dense. They could easily be shutting out the pastel light of the Underworld's day. And she had been walking for quite a while—at least she thought it had been quite a while. She didn't feel tired. Actually, she didn't feel much of anything. The thought almost made her smile. Demeter needn't have been concerned. The gods underestimated the resiliency of the mortal spirit.

She should probably start back to the palace. Eurydice would be waiting to show her the sketches. She would enjoy the upbeat company of the little spirit, and then she would take a long bath. Not a shower on the balcony—her mind skittered away from the thought—just a long, relaxing soak. For the time that remained to her in the Underworld, she would simply avoid Hades. That shouldn't be difficult. He had made it clear that he was too busy to bother with her. Instead of pining over the god, she would spend time with Eurydice, but she'd be up-front with the spirit about the temporary nature of her visit. She'd also warn her to be careful about falling in love with Iapis. He seemed trustworthy, but so had . . .

Her mind shied from the rest of her thought.

She would ride Orion into Elysia and let the spirits see the Goddess of Spring. But she would be more careful with them, too. They deserved to know that hers was only a temporary visit. She could tell them that Persephone would continue to care for them from the world above, and then all she could do was hope that the real Goddess of Spring would follow through with her word.

Deciding on her course of action felt good and she was so preoccupied with her thoughts that she did not notice that she had come to the forest edge until she stumbled from the tree line. Confused, she looked around her, trying to make sense of what she was seeing. The trees had ended, as had the grass and the ferny ground cover. The land was barren; the cinnamon-colored ground cracked and eroded. Directly in front of her flowed a river of seething flames, perfectly silhouetted against a background of inky darkness.

Lina stopped breathing. Tartarus—she had stumbled into the edge of Hell.

Turn around. Retrace your path. Her mind knew the logical thing to do, but her stunned body would not obey her.

And then she heard it, the whisperings from the blackness beyond the river of fire. Like threads of hate they called to her, weaving a net of dark remembrances: every mistake she'd ever made, every lie she'd ever told, every time her words or actions had caused others hurt. Her mortal soul cringed. Lina whimpered and staggered under the weight of her own misdeeds. She fell to her knees.

The oily darkness leaked from the bank of the blazing river. It licked at her with tendrils of hate.

She wasn't a goddess. She was a mortal woman—middle-aged, plain of appearance—a failure in relationships. No man loved her. Why would anyone? She couldn't even bear children. She was a failure as a woman and a wife. Being alone was what she deserved.

Slowly her soul began to peel away from Persephone's body and Lina felt herself begin to disintegrate.

"HADES, you must come." The daimon had to shout over the incessant pounding to gain the god's attention.

Hades straightened and wiped the sweat from his face. "Whatever it is, you must deal with it. I do not wish to be disturbed."

"It is the dead. They ask to speak with you."

Hades' expression was dark and dangerous. "Then they can petition their god when I hold court."

"I do not believe you will want to wait for court to hear what they have to say," Iapis insisted.

"Leave me in peace! What they have to say could not interest me today," Hades snarled.

Unmoved by the god's show of temper, Iapis met his eyes. "They say there is something wrong with Persephone."

Hades was pulling on his tunic when he burst from the forge. The sight before him brought him to a sudden halt. Spreading down the landscaped tiers of his formal gardens were countless spirits of the dead. They stood quietly, side by side: young girls, maidens, mothers, matrons and crones.

An ancient crone and a maiden Hades recognized as one Persephone had danced with in the meadow, detached themselves from the forefront of the group and approached him. The women curtsied deeply. The crone spoke first.

"Great God, we come to you because of our love for the Goddess of Spring. Something is amiss. The goddess is not herself."

"We saw her walking through the forest," the maiden said. "We called her name, but she did not hear us, nor did she see us."

"It was as if she were dead," the old woman said.

A dagger of fear pricked the god's heart. "Where was she last seen?"

"There," the crone and the maiden turned, raising their hands to show the direction.

They were pointing toward Tartarus.

"Saddle Orion!" Hades commanded in a voice that carried to the stables.

Then the god closed his eyes and took a deep, calming breath. He blocked out the voices of the dead and focused his entire being on Persephone. He found the link that tied their souls together, the link that had told him when she had entered his forge, and then told him when she had departed. But it was like a thread that had been cut. Their connection had been severed. Fear mushroomed within him.

"Bring Cerberus," Hades commanded Iapis. The daimon nodded and disappeared.

Hades turned back to the spirits of the women. "You did the right thing coming to me."

The crone and the maiden bowed their heads, as did the multitude behind them.

Hades' gaze searched the faces in the throng surrounding him.

"Eurydice! Bring me an article of Persephone's clothing. Something she has worn recently."

Instead of instantly obeying his bidding, the young spirit approached him. Her eyes met his and he felt the light touch of her hand on his arm.

"You must bring her back to us, Hades." Her voice was choked.

"I will," he said, and strode to the stables.

ORION plunged through the forest close on the heels of Cerberus. The three-headed dog hunted silently, following the scent of his goddess. Hades' hands were slick with sweat, and they gripped the steed's reins tightly. The stallion needed no urging to stay on the dog's trail, which led inexorably toward the dark realm of Tartarus.

His thoughts warred within his mind. He must have wounded her terribly if he had driven her to the dark realm. He hadn't meant to hurt her. His own pain and jealousy had made him forget her youth. Persephone couldn't possibly know into what she was heading. Not even being a goddess would afford her protection against the utter despair that reigned in Tartarus. Desperately he tried to remember if she had been wearing the amethyst narcissus when he had last seen her. Yes, he thought she had been. A trickle of relief cooled his panic. The amethyst would help to protect her. It was a powerful jewel that he had fashioned specifically for her. Its protective properties were vast.

Hades tried not to imagine what might be happening to Persephone. As God of the Underworld, he knew only too well the horrors of Tartarus. It was the eternal dwelling place of the damned. Only the souls of mortals who had completely embraced darkness were condemned to that region. He loathed it, but he acknowledged the necessity of a place to house immutable evil.

And that was where his beloved had gone.

Orion came to a halt beside the dog. Cerberus was snuffling through dried leaves and pawing at something that flashed silver in the dim light. Hades dismounted and picked up the object. It was Persephone's amethyst necklace. She had no talisman to protect her.

"Faster, Cerberus!" he commanded.

The dog redoubled his efforts and Orion responded in kind. They broke through the forest of trees. Cerberus had come to a halt beside the fiery bank of Phlegethon. The dog was whining piteously and all three heads were nudging what Hades thought might be the collapsed body of a dead animal. Then Orion pierced the air with a heart-wrenching scream and plunged down the bank toward the dog. As the horse slid to a halt, Hades recognized the body.

"No!"

He flung himself from Orion's back and pushed Cerberus' massive body aside. Persephone had collapsed upon the cracked earth. Her arms were wrapped around her legs so that her knees pressed into her chest and her body had formed a rigid ball. Her eyes were open, but her pupils were fully dilated and she stared unseeing into the darkness beyond the flaming river.

Hades followed her gaze. The blackness of Tartarus was leaking from its banks. He looked down. Fingers of darkness had slithered from Phlegethon and they soaked the ground around Persephone.

Fury pulsed through the god. Quickly, he bent and knotted the broken chain around Persephone's unresisting neck. The amethyst narcissus began to glow. Then he raised his arms and the air around him began to swirl. In a voice magnified by anger and love, he commanded the grasping darkness.

"Away! You have no right to harm this goddess!"

The dark tendrils shivered, but they did not loosen their hold on Persephone.

"I am Hades, Lord of the Dead, and I command you. Do not touch her!" The god roared, casting all of his formidable power against the malignant fingers of evil.

The darkness drew back and then with a sizzling sound it dissipated like a thief retreating into the night.

Hades fell to his knees beside Persephone. He grasped the goddess's shoulders and turned her rigid body to face him.

"Persephone!"

She did not respond. Instead she continued to stare unblinkingly into the darkness beyond Phlegethon. Her face was deathly pale and her skin was cool to the touch. She was gasping in short, panting breaths, like she was having difficulty breathing.

"It is gone. It cannot harm you now. Look at me, Persephone."

Still she did not acknowledge his presence.

"Persephone! You have to listen to me." He shook her until her head bobbled and Cerberus whined his distress.

The goddess's lips moved.

"Yes! Speak to me," Hades cried.

"Too many mistakes. I can't . . ." Her voice cracked, and her words became inaudible.

"You can't what?" Hades prompted, shaking her again.

"Can't find my way. My body isn't here. I've disappeared."

The emptiness in her voice terrified Hades. Her face was blank. Her eyes were glazed. The Persephone he knew was not there. It was as if an echo of her spirit was speaking through a shell.

And suddenly nothing mattered to him except bringing her back. He didn't care if she thought of him only as a job her mother had charged her to complete. He didn't care that Apollo was her lover. He didn't even care that she was going to leave him. He cared only that she was herself again.

Hades cupped her cold face in his hands. "Your way is here. You must come back to those who love you."

Persephone blinked.

"Come back to us, beloved. Come back to me."

She took one deep, rasping breath and Hades watched as her hand lifted to grasp the glowing amethyst flower. Then she blinked and struggled to focus on his face.

"Hades?" she croaked his name.

Dizzy with relief, he pulled her into his arms. "Yes, beloved. It is Hades, the foolish, arrogant god who loves you."

"Take me away from here," she sobbed, and buried her face in his chest.

CHAPTER TWENTY-FOUR

THE women watched silently as the Lord of the Dead carried their goddess into his palace. Though the god's face was grim, Persephone's arms were wrapped securely around his broad shoulders and her face was pressed into his neck. Relief passed through the spirits. She would be herself again. The god's love assured them of that. Like wind sloughing through willow branches they murmured softly to one another and departed the palace grounds.

"Eurydice!" Hades bellowed as he entered the palace. The spirit materialized instantly with Iapis at her side. "Draw the goddess a bath. Make it very hot."

"Yes, Lord," she said and disappeared.

Iapis kept pace with Hades. "What can I do?"

"Go to Bacchus. Tell him I must have his most potent wine. Something to soothe the soul of a goddess," Hades said.

"I will, Lord." Before Iapis disappeared he touched Persephone's head. "Be well, Goddess," he whispered, and was gone.

Hades carried Persephone quickly to her chamber. Fragrant steam was already escaping from the bathing room and Hades entered the moist fog to find Eurydice hurrying around, pulling thick towels from shelves and choosing soft, plump sponges.

There was a well-cushioned chair near the mirrored wall. Reluctantly, Hades placed Persephone in it. Her arms slid lifelessly from around his shoulders and she sat very still. Her eyes were closed. Hades knelt beside her.

"Persephone, you are home now," he said.

A tremor passed through her body.

"Beloved, can you hear me?"

She opened her eyes and looked at him.

"I can hear you." Her voice was flat and expressionless.

"Do you know where you are?" he asked.

"I'm at your palace."

"Yes." He smiled encouragement, ignoring the dead sound of her voice.

Iapis materialized in the room. He held a crystal bottle of ruby-colored wine and a matching goblet. He poured the wine and an intoxicating scent drifted from the glass. It smelled of grapes and meadows, of ripened wheat and summer nights under the full moon.

Iapis offered the goblet to Persephone. "Drink, Goddess. It will revive you."

She tried to hold the glass, but her hand was trembling so violently that she almost dropped it. Hades wrapped his hand around hers, guiding the wine to her lips. She drank deeply. The magic of the immortals' wine began warming her almost instantly. Soon, the trembling in her hands subsided so that she could drink without the god's help.

"Go, now," Eurydice said, taking charge. "The goddess needs her privacy to bathe."

Hades stood, but hesitated to leave the room.

"My Lord, I will call you when she is ready," Eurydice assured him.

Still Hades hesitated. "Persephone, I will not be far away."

The goddess looked up. "You don't need to worry. I'm back now," she told him.

Even though her voice was expressionless, Hades nodded and he and Iapis reluctantly left the room.

HADES paced in the hallway outside her chamber. How long did it take to bathe? Would the spirit never call him? He wanted to thrust open the door and order Eurydice from the room. Then he would make Persephone listen to him. She had to hear his apology. He was a stupid, inexperienced, jealous fool. Hades sighed. She knew him. It shouldn't be difficult to get her to believe that he had blundered into such a terrible mistake.

The door opened and Eurydice stepped into the hall. She closed the door gently behind her.

"How is she?" Hades asked.

Eurydice looked up at the god, searching his face before she answered him. When she did she sounded much older than her years.

"She is sad, Lord."

Hades raked his hand through his hair. "I have caused this."

"Yes, you have," she said simply.

Hades nodded tightly and turned to the door. Eurydice's pale hand halted him.

"Be patient. Treat her carefully. It's hard for a woman to love again after she has been hurt."

Iapis materialized beside Eurydice. He slid his arm around her and the little spirit leaned into him.

"It's hard for a woman to love again after she had been hurt, but it is possible, Lord," the daimon told his god.

Hades watched them walk slowly away. They fit well together. He turned back to the door, took a deep breath and entered Persephone's chamber.

The goddess was wearing a sheer silk chemise the color of candlelight. She was curled up on a chaise that sat in front of the wall of windows. Part of the velvet drapes had been pulled back and Persephone seemed to be studying the night-cloaked gardens while sipping Bacchus' wine.

"Your gardens really are very beautiful." She spoke without looking at him.

He crossed the room and stood beside her chaise.

"Thank you. I am glad . . ." His words faded. He didn't want to make inconsequential conversation with her. Eurydice had warned him to be patient and careful, and he would. But he must also speak his heart to her. He sat beside her on the chaise.

"Please forgive me. I am a fool," he said.

She turned to face him.

"I knew you were going to leave me, so I wanted to break with you first. I thought it might save me pain. I thought I could go back to how it was before I loved you. I was wrong. I was selfish. I did not think of your feelings. Like an aging, solitary monster, I thought only of myself."

Lina put up her hand to stop his words. "Don't say any more. You're a god. You were simply acting like a god."

Hades clutched her hand. "No! I am not like the others. Everything I said to you in the forge was a lie. I was angry. I was hurt. It is hard for me to understand that you can be with me, and share yourself with Apollo, too. I . . ." he faltered. "It is I who am not accustomed to the way immortals choose and then discard their lovers."

"Hades, Apollo is not my lover."

The god studied her face. "I saw him take you into his arms."

Lina blinked in surprise. "You were there?"

"I followed you. I heard Demeter remind you of the way immortals love, then I watched Apollo hold you."

"If you had watched a little longer, you would have seen that that's all that happened. I don't want Apollo, Hades. If what Demeter had said to me hadn't upset me so badly, I would never have let him touch me at all."

Hades wiped his hand across his brow. "You don't desire Apollo, too?"

"No."

He bowed his head. "Then the pain I caused you was truly for no reason. I do not know if you can forgive me, but please believe me when I say that I do love you, Persephone."

She turned her face away from him. "You don't love me, Hades. You love what you think I am. You don't really know me at all."

"How can you say that to me?" He grasped her chin and forced her to look at him.

"You just love the goddess, not the woman inside her soul."

"You are wrong, Persephone, but let me tell you what I love and then you may decide for yourself. I love your curiosity about everything. I love how you see my realm with new, wondering eyes. I love your sense of humor. I love your kindness and your honesty. I love your unbridled passion. I love the way you bespell animals. I love your loyalty. I especially love your stubbornness, because it was your stubbornness that did not let an ancient god remain trapped within his own denial and loneliness." Tears fell from Persephone's eyes and Hades brushed them gently away. "Now you tell me, what is it that I love—the goddess or her soul?"

"But you don't know . . . you can't really know," she said brokenly.

"I know that I feel your presence before I see you. Something has happened to me, and it has little to do with anything physical. For the first time in an eternity, I understand why soul mates cannot be separated, even after death. It is because their hearts beat in tandem. While I was waiting outside your door, I could feel your heart breaking within. Let me heal it, Persephone, and in the mending of your heart, I will save myself."

"Is it possible that you really do love my soul?" Lina whispered.

Hades smiled at her as he felt the fear inside him begin to thaw. "Death is completely enamored with Spring. If that is possible, then anything is possible, beloved."

She melted into his arms and their lips met. Hades meant for the kiss to be soft and reassuring, but Persephone opened her mouth and pressed herself against him, demanding more. His desire for her flared and he moaned her name as he crushed her barely clad body against his chest.

"Make love to me," she gasped. "I need to feel you inside me."

He lifted her in his arms and carried her to the bed, but as he began to strip the clothes from his body, she stopped him.

"Let me," she said.

She sat on the edge of the bed and Hades stood in front of her, forcing his hands to remain at his sides while she undressed him. He was wearing a shorter version of his voluminous robes, and she slowly unwound the linen from his muscular body. She slid her hands down his chest; his skin felt hot and slick to her touch. At his abdomen she bent forward and replaced her teasing hands with her mouth. He sucked in his breath as her tongue feathered sensation over his skin. She couldn't get enough of him. She felt like she had been awakened from the dead, and she needed his passion and his love and his touch to keep her anchored there with him. She loosened his loincloth and slid it from his hips. Then she stroked his hardness in her cool hands, all the while moving her mouth slowly lower. When she swallowed him his body spasmed and swayed.

"Your mouth is like a silken trap that has captured me," he moaned. He thought his knees might buckle.

She drew back and met his eyes. "Do you want to be free?"

He lifted her into his arms and held her tightly against his body. "Never," he breathed into her hair. "Never, beloved."

She led him to her bed. While she stroked him he explored her body. The chemise was so thin that it felt like she had been wrapped in mist. He found her nipple, teasing and suckling it through the transparent material. He remembered the touches that brought her pleasure, and he did not need her to guide his hand. She responded to him as if they had been lovers for centuries.

Suddenly she sat up and pulled the chemise from her body. When he moved to take her back into his arms, she stopped him.

"What is it, beloved?"

"I want you to do something for me."

"Anything," he said.

"I want you to make love to me with your eyes closed. Pretend you cannot see my body." She peered into his face as if she were searching for an answer written there. "Can you make love to me without looking at me?"

He smiled and closed his eyes. Blind, he opened his arms to her and she fell into his embrace.

Surrounded by her scent and touch, Hades existed in a world of Persephone's sensations. Without seeing her, he had to pay more attention to her small sounds and follow the flow of her hips and the movement of her body. When her breathing quickened and his name sighed from her lips he did not need to see her flushed face to know he was bringing her pleasure. In his soul he felt her need and Hades responded with caress after caress. And then he filled her body and they rocked together in an ancient rhythm that needed no sight or sound—only feelings.

LATER she nestled against him, her head resting on his shoulder. He didn't know it yet, but he had helped her to make her decision, and now that she had made it, she felt at peace. Whatever happened next, she would survive it. Nothing could ever be as terrible as the black nothingness of Tartarus. With Hades' help, she had found her way free of that ultimate nightmare, and now she must be free of all the lies remaining in her life. She wasn't willing to hide the truth from him any longer. Demeter's anger be damned, she would tell him. He deserved to know everything. He loved her soul.

"Hades, I have to tell you something."

The god smiled. "May I keep my eyes open?"

Lina laughed softly. "Yes."

She sat up so that she was facing him, the silk sheet wrapped around her naked body. Hades grabbed a few pillows from the disheveled bed, and propped himself comfortably against the padded headboard. He raised his dark eyebrows questioningly.

"I didn't mean to go to Tartarus. It was an accident. I was too upset to realize where I was until it was too late."

Hades frowned. Just the thought of how close she had been to losing her soul made his stomach tighten. "I know, beloved. You don't have to explain it to me. It was my fault. If I hadn't hurt you—"

"Sssh . . ." Lina leaned forward and pressed a finger against his lips. "Let me finish."

The god looked uncomfortable, but he remained silent.

"Tartarus was," she shivered, "horrible. It called to me. It knew things about me—every bad thing I've ever done, or even ever thought about doing. Every mistake I've made. It caused me to lose myself. I could feel it capturing my soul. There was nothing I could do." She took his hand and laced her fingers with his. "Then I heard you. You called me back. *Me,* Hades. The real me—the soul inside the body."

"I had to get you back. I love you," he said.

"And I love you, too. But you need to know more than that. I am not who you think I am. I am not—"

"*Enough, Persephone!*" Demeter's voice cut through Lina's words. "Your time here is finished. You must return."

Appalled, Hades shot from Persephone's bed. Giving no thought to his nakedness, he faced the goddess who had materialized in the middle of his beloved's chamber.

"What do you mean by this intrusion, Demeter?" he challenged. "This is not your realm. You have no right to trespass here."

"You dally with my daughter, Lord of the Underworld, and I have come to reclaim her. I am her mother. That is all the right I need."

"You are not my mother." Lina enunciated the words carefully so that there could be no mistaking what she was saying. She stood next to Hades, clutching the sheet to her breasts.

Demeter sighed. "Let us not play these childish games, Daughter. Your adventure has ended. It is time you return to your own reality."

"I know I can't stay, but I won't leave without telling him the truth. He deserves to know. He loves *me*."

"You are being a young fool," Demeter said.

"As you know very well, I am not young. And let me tell you once and for all, I am not a fool, either." She faced Hades and looked into his eyes. "I'm not really Persephone. My name is Carolina Francesca Santoro, but most people call me Lina. I am a forty-three-year-old mortal woman who owns a bakery in a place called Tulsa, Oklahoma. Demeter exchanged my soul with her daughter's." She glanced at Demeter and her mouth twisted into a sardonic smile before she looked back at the god. "She said she would help me out with a problem I was having, and in exchange I needed to do a little job for her in the Underworld."

The god's eyes widened.

"Remember when you overheard her reminding me how immortals love? She wasn't *reminding* me, she was explaining it to me because I'm a mortal. The whole thing was new to me."

"You are not the Goddess of Spring?"

"No, I am definitely not the Goddess of Spring," Lina said. She was so relieved to finally be telling the truth, that she didn't notice that Hades' face had gone expressionless.

"So it has all been a lie," Hades said.

"I wanted to tell you, but I gave my word to Demeter that I would keep my real identity a secret." Lina tried to touch his arm, but Hades flinched away from her.

"The things you said to me . . . what we did together. It was all pretense?"

"No!" Lina felt her stomach knot as she watched Hades withdraw into himself. She reached out to him, but again he moved away from her. "I meant everything I said, everything I did. It's just this body that is a lie. Everything else has been real. I love you; that is real."

"How can love be based on a lie?" he said coldly.

"Please don't do this," she pleaded with him, trying to reach the man inside the god. "Don't let us part like this. We can't be together. I have to return to my own world, but let's not make hurtful words what we remember when we're apart."

"Do not beg for his love like a common mortal, Carolina," Demeter's voice interrupted Lina. "There is enough goddess within you that you should have more pride."

Lina spun to face her. "You caused this! He does love me; he just feels betrayed because of your insistence on maintaining a lie. I don't blame him—how could he feel any other way right now?"

Demeter raised on arched eyebrow. "You believe he loves you, Carolina Francesca Santoro? Then let us test your belief in this immortal's love."

With a flick of her wrist, Demeter showered Lina in golden sparks. Lina felt her body tremble and she was suddenly horribly dizzy. She closed her eyes, fighting against nausea. Then there was an odd settling feeling, like she had just stepped back into a comfortable pair of jeans. Before she opened her eyes she knew what she would see.

Across the room, the full-length mirror—the mirror she had preened in just that morning—reflected a new image. Lina's body was her own again. Gone was the lean young body of the goddess. Lina's curves were fuller, and she was older and decidedly not perfect.

"You *are* a mortal." The god sounded strangled.

Lina shifted her gaze from the mirror to Hades. He was staring at her, his face a mask of shock and disbelief.

"Yes, I am a mortal," she said. Squaring her shoulders she dropped the sheet, exposing all of herself to him. "And I am also the woman who loves you."

Hades averted his face, and refused to look at her. "How could you have lied all this time?"

"And what good would the truth have done?" Demeter broke in indignantly. "You would have shunned her as you do now." Her tone turned sarcastic. "At least you finally possessed the body of a goddess, Lord of the Dead. The irony is that you have a mortal to thank for it. No true goddess would have you."

Hades clenched his jaw. While Demeter had been speaking his face had become very pale. When his eyes met Lina's she saw only anger and rejection reflected in their darkness.

"Leave my realm," he commanded in a voice that raised the hair on Lina's arms.

"Come, Carolina. Your time here is finished." Demeter moved to Lina's side and covered her with her cloak. Without another word, the Palace of Hades faded from around them.

CHAPTER TWENTY-FIVE

THE chime over the front door of Pani Del Goddess jingled merrily, letting in another stream of customers as well as a rush of cold air.

"Brrr," Anton shivered dramatically. "Oh, poo! Winter is really coming. It's just so hard on my skin."

"The weatherman is predicting an unusually snowy season. You'd better stock up on moisturizer and get some sensible shoes," Dolores said, pointing down at Anton's feet.

"What's wrong with these?" Anton pouted, turning his feet this way and that so that the entire bakery could admire his glossy black eel-skin, pointed-toe, mock cowboy boots with their two and a half inch heels. "Lina," he called from across the room. "Do you think I need new shoes?"

Lina looked up from the cappuccino machine. She wanted to say that she didn't care about his shoes or the weather, or . . . but Anton's expectant expression reminded her that she had to pretend. She had to keep pretending, no matter how she really felt.

"Honey, I think your boots are perfect. But just remember, my insurance doesn't cover falls outside the bakery."

Laughter fluttered through Pani Del Goddess. The customers grinned and placed their orders. Everyone was happy. Business was booming. In the two weeks Lina had been back, she had been amazed at the changes Persephone had made during her six months. The Goddess of Spring had truly worked magic. Her advertisement campaign had been miraculous. New customers filled the shop day and night, most of them clamoring for anything on which they could spread the incredible new ambrosia cream cheese that was offered exclusively through Pani Del Goddess. Persephone's creation had definitely been a hit. And that wasn't all that the goddess had changed. Instead of going in the direction of catering, as Lina had been thinking they should, Persephone had steered Pani Del

Goddess into a whole new realm of business ventures, via the Internet. She packaged a wide variety of their specialty bread, gubana, added a small tin of ambrosia cream cheese and shipped it all over the United States. For an outrageously high price. Their new Internet service was booming. Persephone had even hired an additional full-time employee who did nothing but service their Net orders.

It amazed Lina. It had taken a goddess from an ancient world to see the potential in something as modern as the Internet. The IRS debt had been repaid threefold. Just as Demeter had promised. All was well.

And Lina was so miserable she thought she was going to die.

No, she couldn't think about dying, or death, or spirits, or the Lord of the Dead . . .

The bell over the door jingled again.

"Hello, handsome," Anton teased.

"Hey there, Anton. Nice boots," a deeply masculine voice said.

Anton giggled happily.

Lina ground her teeth together and readied herself, glad she had the cappuccino machine between her and him. At least he wouldn't try to kiss her hello.

"Good evening, Lina."

"Hi, Scott." She sighed and looked up at the gorgeous young man. He was tall and muscular. His blond hair was neatly cut and his deep blue eyes gazed down at her with open adoration. He was wearing a perfectly tailored business suit, complete with red power tie. The suit did nothing to camouflage his amazing body. Actually, the long Italian lines accentuated the young man's incredible physique. Not for the first time, Lina thought he could have been a young Apollo—if the God of Light had come to Earth as an up-and-coming Tulsa attorney.

It wasn't hard to understand why Persephone had been attracted to him. That didn't surprise Lina. What she didn't understand was why he was so obviously smitten with her in return.

"I still have those front row tickets to Aida. I thought I'd come by and see if you'd changed your mind. I really don't want to go without you," Scott said.

"Thank you, but no. I really can't."

"Why, Lina? I don't understand. Just two weeks ago—"

"Not here. Not now!" Lina interrupted him, mortified that the bakery had gone silent and everyone was watching their little scene while they pretended not to be.

"Then where and when, Lina? You've been avoiding me for two weeks. I deserve an explanation."

Knowing he was right didn't make her feel any less miserable, nor did it make her decision less certain. Scott was handsome and incredibly sexy. Add to that he even seemed to be an honestly nice guy. But she didn't feel anything for him. It would have been easier if she could care for him. Losing herself in his youthful infatuation had seemed, fleetingly, like a good idea. She'd even tried going out on a date with him—once. When he touched her, she felt nothing except the empty ache within her. Scott couldn't make her forget.

"Come on," she said. Rushing out from behind the counter she grabbed his arm and led him to the door. As she stepped out of the bakery, she could hear Anton sighing mournfully and saying, "What a waste . . ."

The evening was chilly, and Lina should have already put up the little café tables and chairs that sat on the sidewalk outside the bakery, but as she struggled to find some barrier she could erect between them, she was glad she hadn't. She sat down at one table, and Scott took the chair across from her. Before she could say anything, he slid it around so that they were sitting close together. Seeing her shiver, he took off his jacket and wrapped it around her shoulders. It was warm, and it smelled faintly like expensive aftershave and virile young man. He would have taken her hand, but she kept it out of reach in her lap.

"Scott," she began, honestly wishing that the sexy way his muscular chest looked in his dress shirt could make her feel more than an aesthetic appreciation for his well-toned physique. "I told you before. It's over between us. I wish you would respect that and just let it alone."

Scott shook his head. "I can't. There's no reason for it. Just two weeks ago everything was fine. Everything was better than fine. And then one day I wake up and, *wham!* It's all over. No explanation. After almost six months, you dump me and you won't even tell me how I screwed up."

"That's because *you* didn't screw up. *Merda!* I told you before—it's me, not you." He's perfect, Lina added silently. Young and handsome and successful and attentive. He needed to go find a nice young woman and settle down in the suburbs with a big mortgage, 2.5 kids and a dog.

"Tell me again. I don't understand how you can suddenly be so different. What is it?"

"You're too young for me, Scott," Lina said earnestly.

"Would you please stop it with that crap! I'm twenty-five, not fifteen. I'm not too young."

"So let's say it's not that you're too young. Let's say the problem is that I'm too old."

"You are not." He leaned forward and pulled her hand from her lap, holding it in both of his. "I don't care that you're forty-three. You're beautiful and sexy, but it's more than that. Your heart is young. You sparkle, Lina. When we were together, you made me feel like I was a god."

Lina smiled sadly. "Not anymore. I'm not like that inside anymore." She stood up and pulled her hand from his. Then she slipped his jacket from her shoulders and gave it back to him. "I can't give you what you need. I don't have it inside of me anymore. Please, just leave me alone."

He shook his head. "I can't. I'm in love with you."

"Okay, here's the truth, Scott. I'm in love with someone else."

Scott straightened in his chair and the skin on his face tightened. "Someone else?"

"Yes. I didn't mean for it to happen, but it did. I'm sorry. I didn't want to hurt you."

His handsome young face flushed and Lina watched as he erected a barrier of pride between them. Scott stood up. His jaw was set, but his eyes were sad.

"I hadn't realized there was someone else, but I guess I should have known. You're too amazing to be alone. I apologize for bothering you. Good-bye, Lina."

"Good-bye, Scott," she said to his retreating figure as he walked away from the bakery.

Feeling seventy-three instead of forty-three, Lina slowly reentered the bakery.

Anton, Dolores, and just about every other face in the store looked up at her expectantly, but when they saw that she was alone, they looked quickly away.

"I think I'll call it quits early today," Lina said.

"Oh, no problem, boss lady." Anton smiled at her and gave her arm a motherly pat.

"Yeah, we can take care of locking up," Dolores said. "You need some time off. You've been working really hard."

Anton nodded. "Why don't you sleep in tomorrow, and then go for a nice massage and a facial. You know, from that place you found a few months ago. Remember, you said that they knew how to treat you like a goddess."

"Want me to call and set up an appointment for you?" Dolores asked.

"No, I'll be fine," Lina said, grabbing her purse and her jacket. "But you're right. I think I need to sleep in tomorrow." She tried to smile at them, but her lips didn't form much more than a grimace.

"Oh, by the way, we're almost out of the ambrosia cream cheese. You better make some more soon. Or . . . you could let us in on your secret recipe," Dolores said, waggling her eyebrows at her boss.

"Yeah, we've already promised not to sell it to terrorists, or to Hostess, even though it would breathe new life into their dreadful Twinkies." Anton shuddered dramatically.

Lina rallied her sense of humor. "A girl has to have some secrets of her own." She winked at Anton and slung her purse over her shoulder. "I'll see you tomorrow afternoon, and I'll have a new tub of ambrosia cream cheese with me." She tried to swing jauntily through the door.

Her employees watched her go. As soon as she was out of sight, they met behind the counter and put their heads together.

"Something's wrong with her," Dolores said.

"Well, of course there is, she broke up with that young stud," Anton said.

"It's more than that." Dolores sighed. "She liked Scott, but I never got the feeling that he meant more to her than a good time. Breaking up with him shouldn't make her this sad."

Anton thought about it and nodded. "You're right. It is something else. She's not herself—again. Remember how weird she acted last spring?"

"Of course I remember, but she was worried about losing the bakery."

"Well, she saved Pani Del Goddess, and it did her good. She changed her whole image. She bought different clothes, started roller skating along the river. I swear she lost ten pounds."

Dolores nodded. "She even changed her hair."

"*And* she started dating young men. Adorable young men," Anton said.

"So, what's the point? That's all old news. What does that have to do with what's going on with her now?" Dolores asked.

Anton shrugged his shoulders. "Could be some kind of delayed stress reaction. Or maybe a tragic split-personality syndrome that is manifesting in her middle-age."

Dolores rolled her eyes at him. "You've got to stop watching so much Discovery Health Channel. How about this: it could be that she worked herself too hard and now she needs a vacation."

"Oh, poo! You always spoil the dramatic effect," Anton said.

"Let's just agree to keep an eye on her and take as much work off her shoulders as we can. Okay?"

"Okay."

CHAPTER TWENTY-SIX

"YES! Yes! Yes! I know—I love you, too." Lina struggled to get in the door, past her over-enthusiastic, slobbering bulldog. "Edith Anne, will you behave? Let me take off my coat and put down my purse." The bulldog backed off half a step, still whining and wriggling. Patchy Poo the Pud jumped down from his perch on the chaise and was rubbing himself against her legs, complaining in indignant meows that she wasn't giving him enough attention, either.

"Crazy animals," she muttered, hanging up her coat. "Okay, come here." She sat in the middle of the hall and let Edith climb into her lap while she scratched Patch under his chin. The bulldog licked her happily. The cat purred. Lina sighed. "Well, at least the two of you missed the real me." Her pets looked as well-fed and healthy as they had the night before Demeter had transported her away, but from the moment she'd reappeared in the middle of her living room, the two of them hadn't wanted to let her out of their sight. They followed her from room to room. Patchy Poo the Pud had even gone as far as to sit outside of the bathroom and yowl if she didn't let him in with her. "You two need to relax," she told the adoring creatures.

But secretly she liked it that they were so pleased that she was back. At least she wasn't a disappointment to them. Everyone else kept looking at her like she'd suddenly grown a third eye. No, that wasn't it. People didn't treat her like she was doing anything weird, they were treating her like she *wasn't* doing something, like they kept expecting more from her.

How had Persephone been more like Lina than Lina was like herself? She sighed and gently pushed Edith Anne off her lap. Persephone was a goddess. Of course people wanted Lina to be like her. Who wouldn't rather be around a goddess?

Hades . . . Her thoughts whispered his name before she could stop herself. Hades had liked being with her more than he had liked being with any goddess.

She shook her head.

"No," she reminded herself. "That's not true. He only wanted to be with me as long as he thought I was Persephone." She remembered the look on his face when he had seen who she really was.

"No!" Lina stopped herself, she wouldn't think about that.

She had to pull herself together. She'd been moping around like a jilted schoolgirl for two weeks. She'd been hurt before, why should this time be any different? It wasn't like she was going through another divorce.

Lina stared, unseeing, down the hall. It wasn't like a divorce. It was worse. Why did she feel like part of her—the best part of her—was missing?

Lina remembered the night she and Hades had watched the soul mates drink from the River Lethe. He had told her that soul mates would always find each other again. But what happened if they were separated by time and worlds? Did their hearts turn into wastelands? Did their capacity for happiness erode until they were just walking shells, going through the motions of daily living but not really feeling alive?

That wasn't what was happening to her. Hades couldn't be her soul mate. He had rejected her. She'd just done something she should have been too old to have allowed herself to do. She'd fallen in love with someone she couldn't ever have. She'd made a mistake. She was simply going to have to get over him and get on with her life.

She'd be all right. She'd make it. Time would help it not to hurt so badly.

Edith Anne whined while Patchy Poo the Pud rubbed a worried circle around her legs.

Lina pushed the sadness away from her heart and straightened her shoulders. "Okay, you two. Let's make some ambrosia cream cheese."

IT didn't matter how many times she read it, it still gave her a weird feeling. The paper that the note and the recipe had been written on was from her private stationary that had CFS printed across the top in the Copperplate Gothic Bold she liked so well. The words were written in her favorite blue pen, and the handwriting was identical to her own. But she hadn't written it. She'd found it taped to Edith Anne's dog food bin the day Demeter had brought her back. She'd almost ignored it. After all, it had been in her own handwriting. She'd thought it was just an old note she'd written to herself reminding her to get more dog food, or dog treats, or other items of dog paraphernalia. Then the salutation registered in her mind, *Dear Lina,* and her eyes had moved quickly to the closing, *Here's wishing you joy and magic, Persephone.*

Lina had taken the note into the living room and read it. Then, just as she did now, she thought how bizarre it was that she and Persephone's handwriting was identical.

Dear Lina,

Six months is almost completed. It feels to me that I have been here so much longer—time passes differently in your world. Mother will call for me soon and I want to be certain that you have the recipe for the ambrosia. Our customers love it, and I would not want them to be disappointed.

How odd! I just realized that I called them "our" customers, but I do think of them as that. Your mortals are good people. I shall miss them.

I shall not miss your wretched cat or that horrid slobbering dog, although the black-and-white beast has finally deigned to sleep with me, and yesterday the dog did bark protectively at a stranger who tried to accost me while I was frolicking beside the river.

Perhaps I shall miss them after all.

Remember to have fun with your life, Lina. You have been richly blessed.

Here's wishing you joy and magic,
Persephone

The cream cheese recipe was written neatly on the back of the note. Lina studied it one more time. She didn't want to follow it, but Persephone had been right, their customers did love it, and she didn't want to disappoint them either.

She refilled her glass of pinot grigio, leaving the bottle on the counter next to the crock that she'd already filled with softened cream cheese. She didn't need to double check the calendar to see if there was a full moon. All she had to do was to glance out the kitchen window. There was no escaping it. A round white moon was hanging brightly in the clear night sky.

"Just get it over with. It's not like you're a stranger to magic." She grabbed a measuring cup from the cabinet. "And stop talking to yourself."

She put the recipe on the counter and began the steps it would take to make ambrosia cream cheese.

Persephone's recipe was wordy. Lina sipped from her glass of wine while she read it.

> *Fill that pretty yellow pot—the one that is the exact color of wild honeysuckles—with cream cheese. Let the cheese soften. (And Lina, do not use that atrocious low fat concoction others use. Its taste borders on blasphemy.)*

Lina couldn't help smiling. She and Persephone had the same attitude about cooking with low fat ingredients.

> *Next add one cup of your favorite white wine to the cream cheese and mix thoroughly. The specific type of wine is not important, as long as it is not too sweet. (Lina, I have grown quite fond of the lovely Santa Margherita Pinot Grigio I found in your cooler. I certainly hope Mother gives me time to replenish your supply before she exchanges us. If not, I offer my apology for depleting your supply.)*

Lina chuckled. "Apology accepted." She had been totally out of white wine when she returned.

> *After adding the wine to the cream cheese, drink what remains in the rest of the bottle yourself. (Lina, don't underestimate the importance of this step.)*

She poured herself another glass of wine after she added the cup to the cream cheese. She tried not to gulp, but she was in a hurry to get done.

The more she drank, the easier it was for her to admit it, Persephone did sound like fun. Lina read the rest of the recipe with a wine-induced smile.

> *During the night of a full moon, take the mixture and place it under the old oak tree. You know the one. It is in the courtyard next to the fountain. I sprinkled a little of the magic of Spring there (do not be surprised if you see a nymph or two, although they seem to be very shy about showing themselves in your world). Before you leave the mixture there, you must dance three complete*

circles around the tree while you focus your thoughts on the sweet beauty of the night. (Lina, there are no particular dance steps you must complete. Simply listen to your soul and frolic! I think your body may surprise you. . . . It has certainly surprised me.)

Lina groaned and re-read the line. *It has certainly surprised me.* She didn't even want to guess what Persephone meant by that, but the searing looks Scott had given her, and the fact that he had a hard time keeping his hands off her, gave her a pretty good idea.

Well, it wasn't like she'd been particularly chaste in Persephone's body, either. She didn't want to think about that, though. She returned her attention to the end of the recipe.

Retrieve the finished mixture the next morning. You must dilute it ten times for mortal consumption. (Lina, be careful. I can only imagine what would happen if Anton sampled some of it while it was full strength.)

"No kidding," Lina muttered. "Talk about a nymph. He'd probably sprout wings and fly." She laughed.

Then she caught herself. Persephone had just made her laugh— twice. And she wasn't even there. No wonder everyone loved her so much.

"Well, kids," she said to Patchy Poo the Pud and Edith Anne. "I'm going to finish up this last glass of wine, then I'm going to take this honeysuckle-colored crock, put it under an old tree, do some quick frolicking before I pour myself into bed." She hiccupped and her pets stared at her with accusatory eyes. They always seemed to know when she'd had too much to drink.

Lina wrapped an arm around the crock and started blearily for the door. Edith Anne, of course, stood directly in her way.

"Don't fret, old girl. I'm not going anywhere without you." That was one good thing about her dog being so umbilically tied to her—she didn't have to bother with a leash anymore. "We'll be back soon. I promise," Lina told Patchy Poo the Pud, who was watching her with eyes that were somehow disdainful and worried at the same time.

The night had gotten colder, and Lina wished she had grabbed her coat, but the cashmere turtleneck Persephone had added to her wardrobe was snug and warm—even if it was a delicate pink color that Lina thought would look better on a teenager than a middle-aged woman, no matter how many compliments she got whenever she wore it.

Forget it, she told herself. She didn't have the energy to worry about her wardrobe, and if she didn't want to go on a major shopping spree, there wasn't much she could do about it. In six months Persephone had replaced every single item in her closet. Everything. From shoes to jackets to a whole new line of sexy silk panties and matching bras.

"Where did the girl find the time?" she asked Edith Anne. The dog made a snuffling noise while she kept pace at Lina's side.

Lina shook her head. "I don't know either. I think she needs to be renamed the Goddess of Shopping instead of the Goddess of Spring."

Lina giggled. Quite frankly, she was a little drunk. She needed to be for where she was headed.

She followed the little brick path that led from her condo to the centrally located courtyard. She heard the fountain before she saw it. Six months and two weeks ago, it had had a calming effect on her. Now as she came closer to the courtyard, her stomach clenched.

Thankfully, the area was deserted. Lina glanced at her watch, twisting her wrist so that the dials could be illuminated by the light from the full moon. 10:45 pm. How had it gotten so late? Steeling herself, she approached the old oak—the same oak under which she had discovered the beautiful narcissus.

It looked much as it had six months before. Then the branches had been bare except for buds of new growth waiting to open. Now the branches were almost bare again. There were just a few leaves the color of paper grocery bags clinging to its boughs. Lina cast her eyes down. Thick, gnarled roots criss-crossed the ground at its base. Slowly, Lina walked its circumference, studying the shadows.

Except for dirt and roots, the area around the tree's base was empty. There was no hidden flower that smelled of first kisses, moonlight and springtime. What had she expected? Frowning at herself, she tucked the crock of cream cheese and wine in a semi-flat niche between two roots near the trunk of the tree. Then she stepped back.

In her mind she could see Persephone's directions. *Before you leave the mixture there, you must dance three complete circles around the tree while you focus your thoughts on the sweet beauty of the night.* Okay, she rubbed her hands together. I'll think about how pretty the night is—I'll dance around the tree—and I'll be done.

She looked around her. Except for Edith Anne, who sat a few feet away from her watching attentively, the courtyard was still deserted.

"Good," Lina muttered. "They'd think I was crazy."

Edith huffed at her.

"Don't worry, this won't take long."

Think about the beauty of the night, Lina told herself. She looked up. The moon really did look pretty, sitting up there like a glowing silver disc lit from within.

Lina took a tentative step, lifting her arms over her head she half turned. Moonlight filtered through the branches of the tree and stroked the cashmere that covered her arms, making them glow a silvery blush color that reminded Lina of the breast of a dove. She skipped over a root, surprised at how gracefully her body responded.

She passed once around the tree.

A soft breeze blew through the branches of the old oak, and the dry leaves whispered an autumn melody. Lina lifted her arms and twirled. She raised her face to the sky, letting the moon caress her skin. The night felt rich and beautiful and magic-filled.

She passed twice around the tree.

Lina pointed her toe and swung her leg forward. It seemed that she heard the humming of women's voices in harmony with the sound of the leaves. From the corner of her eye she saw familiar shapes join her in the dancing circle. They glittered and glowed and their wings made a melodic humming noise. Arms spread Lina leapt and twirled and reveled in the beauty of the night.

She passed a third time around the tree.

Lina stopped. She was breathing hard and her breath showed in the cool air like little puffs of magic smoke. She looked around, but the nymphs that had danced with her had disappeared. Edith Anne waddled past her, sniffing curiously around the base of the tree. Cocking her ears forward, she peered up into the oak's branches.

"They're gone," Lina told her. "Come on, old girl. It's time for us to go, too."

The dance had left her body feeling more alive than it had in two weeks. Maybe she should dance more. Anton and Dolores had questioned her several times about why she had suddenly stopped rollerblading along the river. Lina thought about it. *She'd* never rollerbladed—ever. But Persephone obviously had quite often. And she hadn't needed Anton and Dolores to tell her that. Her body was a full dress size smaller. Her legs were fit and her butt was firmer than it had been when she was twenty.

Lina let herself back in her condo. Before she could change her mind, she walked straight back to her bathroom, kicking off her shoes and stripping off her clothes until she stood totally naked in front of her full-length mirror.

She looked good, and not just for a woman in her forties. Except for the dark smudges under her eyes, her skin looked firm and healthy. She still wore her hair as Persephone had worn it—shoulder length with loose, messy curls. Her breasts weren't perfect and perky, but they were full and womanly. Her waist curved in nicely and her hips swelled down to tight thighs and well-defined calves.

She smiled at her reflection. She was pretty and smart and sexy and successful—everything a man should want.

"It's past time you got over him, Lina," she told herself.

With a sense of finality, she clicked off the bathroom light and tucked herself into bed. She felt the mattress sag as Patchy Poo the Pud curled into his place near her hip. She heard Edith Anne sigh as she turned twice and then flopped down in her doggie bed. Lina closed her eyes and before she fell asleep she made a promise to herself. Beginning tomorrow she would start over. Persephone had been right—she was richly blessed.

PERSEPHONE had been brooding when she felt the stirring of her magic being used. As nonchalantly as possible, she excused herself from Hermes and Aphrodite's tiresome conversation. The immortals waved her aside and continued their argument about whether the Limoniades, nymphs of the meadows of flowers, or the Napaeae, nymphs of the glens, were the most beautiful. They didn't mind that the young Goddess of Spring was leaving the conversation. She was an expert on forest nymphs, yet she had been uncharacteristically reticent and had had nothing amusing to say on the subject. They hardly noticed her absence.

Demeter did.

"Daughter, where are you going?"

Persephone paused and schooled her face into an aspect of innocent boredom before she turned to face her mother.

"Oh, Mother, you know I cannot bear to be indoors while the flowers are blooming. The meadows call me."

"Very well, child. I expect to see you tonight at the Festival of Chloaia."

"Of course, Mother." Persephone bowed and left her mother's throne room.

Demeter watched her daughter depart with a mother's sharp eyes. The Great Goddess was ready to admit to herself that exchanging the mortal for her daughter had been a mistake. Oh, her plan had had the desired effect. Persephone had matured. To Demeter's surprise she was even being called the Queen of the Underworld, and the relatives of the dead had quit their ceaseless petitioning. But at what price? Since her daughter's return the Goddess of Spring had behaved in a more sober manner. She rarely hosted feasts and had stopped consorting with semi-deities. But she was also moody and distracted. Much of the young goddess's sparkle had dimmed. Demeter worried about her. And she also worried about the mortal woman.

Carolina Francesca Santoro seemed to have taken up permanent residence as a nettle within the goddess's conscious, and it was not a comfortable arrangement. Demeter could not forget the look of raw pain on the mortal's face when Hades rejected her. She had caused Carolina a great hurt, and that had not been her intention.

Then there were the disturbing rumors. The immortals whispered that Hades had gone mad. He would see no one. It was even said that he had refused to grant Zeus an audience when the god had entered his dark realm.

"Eirene," she called her old friend to her side. "Something must be done about Hades."

"Again?" Eirene asked.

"Again," Demeter said.

THROUGH her mother's oracle Persephone watched Lina dance around the oak tree. She smiled when the little nymphs joined her. Lina's body twirled and leapt with a grace that Persephone recognized as not completely mortal.

"Her body remembers," the Goddess of Spring whispered to the oracle. "It has been touched by the presence of a goddess, and it will never be the same. . . ."

Just as she would never be the same, Persephone finished the thought silently. Carolina had departed her body, but she had left behind an essence of herself. Absently, Persephone stroked the amethyst narcissus that hung between her breasts. The chain had been broken, but the goddess had left it knotted around her neck. She could remove it and command it repaired, but she had been loath to part with it. In some way, its touch soothed her.

Lina finished the dance and returned to her home. Persephone watched as she stood naked before the mirror. Her smile echoed the mortal's. She was proud of the changes she had wrought in Lina. Persephone still remembered the burn of tired muscles and the satisfaction it had given her to watch Lina's body grow more fit and flexible. She had molded it into a vessel fit for a goddess. When Lina slid into bed, Persephone could almost feel the warm, soft body of the cat pressed familiarly against her own hip.

The oracle swirled and went blank.

"What is it, Daughter? Why do you and the mortal seem so unhappy?" Demeter's voice caused Persephone to jump guiltily. "No," Demeter continued before her daughter could answer with a ready excuse. "I do not want empty words meant to salve my feelings. I want truth."

Persephone met her mother's eyes. If Demeter wanted the truth, she would give it to her. "I miss it, Mother. I did not intend to, but I fell in love with Lina's world. It is so vibrant and messy and *alive*. And they did not know I was a goddess. They did not know I was your daughter, yet they embraced me."

"Was it not Carolina that they embraced?" Demeter asked gently.

"No. I wore her body, but the soul was mine."

Demeter shook her head sadly. "Carolina said the same thing to me, only I did not listen to her. I believe that was a mistake."

"What if there was a way to correct your mistake?"

"This time I would listen."

Persephone smiled fondly at her mother. "Good. I have an idea."

Chapter Twenty-seven

"ARE you sure you want me to leave early? I really don't mind staying," Dolores said.

"No, honey." Lina waved a linen napkin at her. "I insist. It's not busy and we're going to close in thirty minutes. Anton and I can handle it."

"Well, if you're sure . . ." Dolores said dubiously.

"Oh, go on! Lina and I will be fine alone. Who do you think I am, Mr. Incompetent?" Anton huffed.

"I have never called you Mr. Incontinent—at least not within your hearing." Dolores dissolved into snorting giggles at her own joke.

Anton drew himself up into his full Southern belle glory. "Ah'll nevah be niiice to you again!" he said, raising his fist in the air.

Lina laughed. "I don't think Scarlett would have worn those boots."

"She would have if she had been gay," Anton said smugly.

"Okay, ya'll, I'm leaving." Dolores opened the door and then hesitated, smiling back at Lina as she said, "It's nice to hear you laugh again, boss." Then she hurried out into the Oklahoma evening.

Surprised by Dolores' words, Lina stared at the closed door.

"It is, you know," Anton said, touching her arm.

"Thanks." Lina patted his hand. "It feels good to laugh again." They smiled at each other. "I'll take care of closing up out here. Why don't you finish the dough in the back? It should be ready to be separated and put into the bread pans."

Anton nodded and scampered through the French doors separating the kitchen from the café. Lina was taking the pizza del giorno sign from the wall so that she could change it to read the next day's special, when the front door jangled open.

"I'll be with you in just a moment!" she called without turning around. "You're in luck; I still have one pizza of the day left. It's a lovely three cheese blend with garlic, basil and sun dried tomatoes."

"It is one of my favorites, but I have been dreaming of a thick slice of warm gubana with butter spread over it."

Lina froze. That voice. She knew that woman's voice as well as her own. Lina turned and was struck anew by the goddess's beauty. She was wearing jeans and a snug knit sweater, and she had her long hair pulled back into a thick ponytail, but her casual clothes did nothing to dispel her unique loveliness.

"Hello, Lina."

"Hello, Persephone."

Persephone smiled. "That is one thing we can count on—we would recognize each other in the middle of a teeming crowd."

"I—" Lina ran her hand across her brow as if she was trying to wipe away her confusion. "I didn't expect to see you. This is a surprise."

Before Persephone could respond, the door chimed again. A tall, handsome woman stepped regally into the bakery.

Persephone sighed and glanced over her shoulder.

The woman chose a table near the front window. She sat as if readying herself to hold court.

"I had a feeling Mother would follow me," Persephone said.

Anton breezed from the kitchen.

"Ohmygod, who knew we would get a rush right before closing?" Like a feather, he fluttered up to Demeter. "May I bring you something?"

The goddess raised one eyebrow at him. "Wine. Red."

Anton tilted his head, considering. "Is the house Chianti okay?"

"If Carolina has chosen it, I will abide by her will."

"Oh, sweetheart, you are right about that. Our Lina knows her wines," he cooed. "Anything else?"

"Anton!" Lina suddenly found her voice. "You can go back to the dough. I'll take care of both of these ladies."

Demeter raised her hand to silence her. "No. I am enjoying this"—she returned Anton's considering gaze—"young male. You two must talk. He shall attend me."

Anton shot Lina a *so there* look.

"Can't I tempt you with something more than wine? We have an ab fab pizza today. I promise to heat it for you with my own lily white hands."

"Pizza?" The goddess spoke the word as if it was a foreign language.

"Cheese, tomatoes, garlic, basil—it's to die for."

"Create it for me," Demeter said with an imperious waft of her hands.

Anton smiled smugly. Before he turned away he said, "Sweetheart, what is your name? I don't think I've ever seen you in here before."

Lina opened her mouth, but Persephone shook her head, motioning for her to keep quiet.

"You may call me Robin Greentree."

"Well, Ms. Greentree, may I just say that on anyone else that outfit would look like a silk muumuu, but on you it looks like something a goddess would wear. You are perfectly majestic."

"Of course I am," Demeter said.

"I'll have your wine right out." Anton hurried back to the kitchen. As he passed Lina and Persephone he said, sotto voce, "I can't resist an old queen."

Persephone covered her laugh with a polite cough. Lina scowled at him.

"Robin Greentree?" Lina whispered after Anton had disappeared back into the kitchen.

"Mother has a rather eccentric sense of humor, especially about names. Do you know in some languages my name sounds just like 'corn'?"

"I am across the room, but I am not deaf."

"Of course, Mother," Persephone said.

"Sorry, Demeter," Lina said.

The two women shared knowing looks that turned into smiles.

Persephone studied the bakery with keen eyes. "Dolores isn't here?"

"I let her go early."

Persephone nodded. "She works hard. She deserves time off."

"It's hard to get her to take time for herself." Lina and Persephone spoke the words together.

They stared at each other.

"Yes . . ." Persephone said.

"Yes," Lina echoed.

"Here's your Chianti and some bread with spiced olive oil." Anton placed the red wine goblet and a bread basket in front of Demeter. "Your pizza will be out in a jiff." He swished past Lina humming "Shall We Dance" from *The King and I* and fluttered his fingers amiably at Persephone.

Persephone laughed. "I've missed Anton."

"Well, he certainly grows on you."

"Stop wasting time!" Demeter snapped.

"Mother! Please. Drink your wine. Your pizza has to cook. Try to be a little patient." Persephone sighed and turned back to Lina. "Being the daughter of a goddess is not easy."

"I know," Lina said.

"Yes, you do." Persephone looked down at the counter and took a deep, cleansing breath. "I needed to come back."

Lina's face was a question mark. "Why?"

The goddess met her eyes. "I am not happy. I miss my bakery—our bakery—your world," she stuttered.

Lina glanced at Demeter, expecting her to react to her daughter's words, but the goddess continued to sip her wine silently.

"I don't understand."

"Is there nothing you miss about the Underworld?" she asked imploringly.

Lina felt her spine straighten. "What do you mean?"

Persephone searched the mortal's eyes. "We cannot lie to each other."

"I'm not trying to lie to you," Lina said. "It's just that it . . ."

"It hurts," Persephone finished for her. "I know. I tried not to think about everything I missed, too. I thought it would be easier if I chose not to remember."

Lina nodded, struggling to keep her emotions under control.

"I will begin." Persephone's smile was wistful. "I miss the bakery—its busy efficiency, the way it smells and sounds, and how it is a gathering place for so many different types of mortals. And I miss little things, like how Tess Miller has to have her glass of white wine precisely at the same time every day. I miss her little dog, even though he shocked Tess so badly when he snubbed me that she threatened to take him to the pet psychic. Animals do not react to me as they do to you." Persephone wrinkled her brow at Lina. "You know, the connection you have with animals is very odd."

"Yes, I know."

"I think what I miss most is the way everyone looked to me to solve problems. They did not see me as a younger, incompetent version of my mother. No one ran to her after I made a decision to double check that I was being wise. They respected me and trusted my judgment."

"You showed excellent judgment, Persephone," Lina assured her. "The bakery is thriving. Everyone is happy. *Merda!* You even managed to get me into shape."

Persephone gave her an assessing look. "Your body was a comfortable place to live, Lina. Do not underestimate your own beauty." The goddess grinned and Lina was reminded of a cat regarding a bowl of cream. "That is another thing I miss. Mortal men are so very *appreciative.*"

"Scott," Lina said dryly.

"Scott," Persephone purred. "I found him to be an interesting dalliance."

"He fell in love with you."

"Of course he did." Persephone shrugged her shoulders. "He will recover and be a better man for the experience. Knowing how to please a goddess is something all men should learn."

The idea made Lina smile.

"I even miss those two creatures who live with you, especially the cat," Persephone admitted.

That made Lina laugh. "Patchy Poo the Pud is awful, but loveable."

"Horrid beast," Persephone teased.

Lina nodded.

"Now it is your turn to remember. What is it you miss about the Underworld?"

"I miss Eurydice," she said with only a slight hesitation. "The little spirit was like a daughter to me. I worry about her."

"What else?"

"I miss Orion. I know he's supposed to be a dread steed, but he reminded me more of an overgrown black lab puppy."

"And?"

"I miss the way the sky looked. Daylight was like a watercolor painting that someone had breathed into life. I realize that sounds ironic because I'm talking about the Land of the Dead, but it wasn't dark and gloomy there, at least not after you got to Elysia. Actually, it was the most incredible place I've ever been, ever even imagined." Lina let her mind wander. Now that she had started talking she didn't want to stop. "Did you know that the night sky is lit by the souls of the Hyades so that when evening comes to Elysia everything looks like a beautiful forgotten dream?"

"No, I did not know that," Persephone said.

"And the souls of the dead aren't scary or disgusting. They are just people whose bodies have become less important. They still have the ability to love and laugh and cry."

Persephone took Lina's hand. "What is it that you miss most?"

Lina's eyes filled with tears. "Hades," she whispered. "You fell in love with my world, but I fell in love with the Lord of the Underworld."

"Good!" Persephone said happily, squeezing Lina's hand.

"How can that be good? I love Hades, but he loves you."

Persephone's laughter was a joyous noise that seemed to make the lights in the bakery glow brighter. "If he loves *me*, then why is he refusing to see me?"

"You've tried to see Hades?"

"Of course. I was miserable with missing your world. Then I started hearing rumors of Hades having gone mad and the spirits in the Underworld being in disarray, et cetera, et cetera, because the Queen of the Underworld had left her realm."

"Wait! Hades has gone mad?" Lina felt the color drain from her face.

"Oh, it is nothing. He is simply sulking." She made a careless gesture with her slender hands. "But the rumors made me think that perhaps I was not alone in my unhappiness. So I visited the Underworld."

"And?" Lina had the sudden urge to shake her.

"And the first thing that happened was that awful three-headed dog refused to allow me to pass." She shivered. "Edith Anne has much better manners."

"Cerberus gave you a hard time?"

"Hard time? He blocked the road, growling and slobbering. I was afraid to get near him. I actually had to call for help." Persephone shook her head in disgust.

"And Hades didn't come to you?"

The goddess frowned. "His daimon appeared instead. With that hateful black horse."

"Orion was mean to you?"

"He laid back his pointed ears and bared his teeth at me."

"I'm sorry about that. I have spoken to Orion about his attitude. He probably just thought you were me, and when he realized you weren't, well, he should have behaved better," Lina said.

"Yes, he should have. Anyway, I told the daimon that I wanted to speak with Hades. The daimon asked me if I was the Goddess of Spring, or the mortal woman, Carolina." Persephone looked annoyed. "As if he did not already know! Even the spirits of the dead knew. The whole time I was traveling down that gloomy black road they watched me. At first they seemed happy, then when I spoke to them—simply trying to be polite—they drew away from me. I even heard them whispering things like 'Someone is masquerading as Queen of the Underworld.'" Irritably, she brushed aside a strand of hair that had escaped from her ponytail. "I can tell you, it was certainly a disturbing experience."

She paused before continuing and studied her well-manicured fingernails. Lina wanted to shake her again.

"Well, I assured the daimon that my body and my soul were the same. He disappeared, and when he returned he said that his Lord refused to see *Persephone,* and he commanded that I leave his realm and stop bothering him."

"And how does that prove that he doesn't love you? Hades is very stubborn." Lina glanced at Demeter, who was pretending to study her wine. She leaned forward and lowered her voice. "Sometimes it takes a lot of work to get him to relax and talk. Actually, he's romantic and passionate. You should try again. He will probably see you next time." Lina's stomach clenched and she hated herself as soon as she said the words. She didn't want Hades to see Persephone. She didn't want him to see anyone except her.

"I think *you* should try," Persephone said firmly.

"Me?" Lina blinked in surprise. "How can I?"

"We could exchange bodies again." Persephone gestured at Demeter. "Mother will aid us. She recognizes that her plan did not work exactly as she had expected."

Lina looked at Demeter. The goddess inclined her head in a small, regal bow. "I acknowledge the truth of my daughter's words. I was mistaken in how I handled the situation."

The awful bedroom scene flashed through Lina's memory. "I'm glad to hear you say it, but it doesn't change anything."

"Do you remember, Carolina, when you came to my oracle distraught because you had made an error in judgment?" Demeter said.

"Yes, I almost caused Eurydice a lot of pain because I made a decision without thinking it through."

"Do you remember what I told you then?"

"You told me to learn from my mistake," Lina said.

"Yes, and I have taken my own advice. I, too, did not fully consider my decision. What I have learned from my mistake is that even a goddess can be surprised by her daughters." Demeter gifted the two women with one of her rare smiles. Then she returned her full attention to Lina. "Hades was being truthful with you. He has always been different from the rest of the immortals. I believe the Lord of the Underworld did fall in love with you, Carolina."

"And I have a proposal for you," Persephone said. "You love Hades. I love your bakery and your world. Why must we live forever without our loves?"

"But Hades—" Lina began.

"Hear me out," Persephone interrupted. "As Goddess of Spring, I must be in my world for six months, then, as you would say, my 'job' is completed until the next spring. I could come here during that interlude. And while I am here, you could return to the Underworld as Queen."

Lina's head was spinning. "I would pretend to be you again?"

"No." Persephone's smile was enigmatic. "*You* would not have to pretend. Everything from the animals to the spirits knew I was not you. You will not be pretending, Carolina, you are their Queen. You will simply be housed temporarily in my body because I need yours here. I will be the one who must masquerade as another."

"No," Lina said.

"Why not?" Persephone gave a long-suffering sigh. "Oh, I give you my word that I will neatly discard any 'Scotts' before you return."

"It's not that," Lina said.

"Then what is it?"

"He doesn't want me, Persephone. He told me he loved my soul, and then when he saw the real me, he rejected me."

"Lina, he was just surprised," Persephone said.

"You didn't see his face."

"I saw his face," Demeter interjected. "And what I read there was, indeed, surprise and hurt. I did not see disdain or rejection."

"Then you saw something I didn't," Lina said.

"Perhaps you are simply making a mistake, Carolina," Demeter said.

"Maybe, but what if I'm not?" Lina felt the sick wave of pain that remembering Hades' rejection evoked. She blinked furiously. "I can't bear it if he looks at me like that again. And what if he doesn't? That might actually be worse. How would I ever know that it's not just your body he desires?"

"Can you bear to live an eternity without him?" Persephone asked softly.

Tears spilled from Lina's eyes and left shining trails down her cheeks. "What I can't bear is what it would do to my soul to have him turn away from me again—or to have him accept me only because he wanted me to be something that I'm not."

"Do not make a decision before you have pondered it properly," Demeter said.

"Yes, promise me that you will consider my proposition. Fall has just begun here. You have until the first days of spring, then I will return for your final decision."

Persephone wiped a tear from Lina's face. Then the goddess's smile became bittersweet. She reached under her sweater where a silver chain lay hidden. Without speaking, she pulled it over her head. The amethyst narcissus caught the bakery lights and sparkled.

"This belongs to you," she said, placing it carefully over Lina's head. "The chain had been broken, and then knotted. I did not have it replaced. It is just as you left it."

"Oh," Lina said with a sob. She wrapped her fingers around the bloom that had been so lovingly carved for her. "I didn't think I'd ever see this again. Thank you for returning it to me."

Anton burst from the French doors whistling a show tune from *Gypsy* and carrying a round tray which held a fragrant, steaming pizza. He glanced at Lina and came to an abrupt halt.

"Why are you crying?" His eyes flashed and he turned on Persephone. "Little Miss Cute Thing, if you made her cry, I'll—"

"No, Anton, it's nothing bad." Lina smiled through her tears, wiping her face with the back of her hand. "Persephone gave me this necklace, and it is so beautiful that it made me cry."

Anton's body relaxed. "Persephone? You mean like the goddess?"

"Exactly like the goddess," Persephone said.

"I haven't seen you here before, either. How do you know our Lina?" Anton said.

Persephone smiled. "Lina helped me grow up."

Anton looked confused.

"Persephone," Demeter called from across the room. "We should depart."

"Anton, we will need that pizza in a 'To Go' box. And could you please add a big slice of gubana, too?"

"Of course," Anton said. "Anything else I can get for Her Majesty?" He nodded his head at Demeter.

Persephone laughed. "Just the check."

"I shall pay," Demeter said. With a great sense of dignity she stood and then strode to where Anton waited at the cash register.

"With what?" Lina whispered.

Persephone shrugged her shoulders.

"Anton!" Lina said.

He looked at her.

"With these ladies we accept barter. Just be sure you drive a hard bargain."

Anton's eyes widened. "Whatever you say, boss." He faced the approaching goddess. "Well, Queen Greentree, what are you offering for pizza, gubana and wine?"

Demeter raised her haughty chin. "I prefer the title goddess. Queens have realms that are entirely too limited."

"Fine, *Goddess* Greentree. What are you offering?"

Demeter's smile was sly. "Do you have any need for a talking bird?"

"No, honey." Anton rolled his eyes. "We have way too many animals that hang around this place. Try again."

Persephone pulled on Lina's sleeve. "Leave them to their bargaining. I have one more question to ask you."

"What is it?"

"What did you do to Apollo?"

"Nothing," Lina said, surprised.

"Nothing?" Persephone asked.

"Not a thing."

"You refused the God of Light?" Persephone wasn't sure she had heard her correctly.

"Of course. I'm only interested in one god at a time," Lina said.

"Really?" Persephone tapped her perfect chin thoughtfully. "What an interesting concept."

"Sold! For one gold crown that is probably fake but I just *adore* it!" Anton squealed.

CHAPTER TWENTY-EIGHT

HADES brooded, and he couldn't stop staring at the sketch the little spirit had given him.

"Do you like it?" Eurydice asked.

"How did you know?" Hades' voice sounded rough and foreign to his own ears. How long had it been since he had carried on a real conversation with anyone? He couldn't remember.

"I have been thinking a lot about her. I even started dreaming of her. Only, when I see her in my dreams, she does not look like she did when she was here. But how she looks—it's hard to describe—how she looks in my dreams *feels* right. So I drew her that way. When I showed Iapis, he told me that I should bring it to you."

"I hope I did not overstep myself, Lord," Iapis said.

Hades could not take his eyes from the sketch. "No, old friend, you did not overstep yourself. You were right to show me." He made himself take his eyes from the sketch and look at Eurydice. "Thank you. May I keep it?"

"Of course, Lord. Anything I create is yours."

"No, little one," Hades said sadly. "Anything you create still belongs to her."

"Will she return to us?" Eurydice asked.

Hades looked back at the sketch of Carolina. Her mortal features were sweet and kind, her body full and womanly. He felt a stirring within him just looking at the likeness of her, and he closed his eyes, blocking her picture from his mind. He had lacked the strength to trust her, and because of that she had almost lost her soul to Tartarus. But she had battled back from the abyss only to be betrayed and wounded by his rash, thoughtless words. He did not deserve the gift of her love.

"No," Hades said. "I do not believe she will return to us."

Eurydice made a small, sad noise, and Hades opened his eyes to see Iapis taking the spirit into his arms.

"Hush, now," the daimon soothed. "Wherever she is, she has not forgotten you. She loved you."

"Please leave me," Hades rasped.

Iapis motioned for Eurydice to go, but he stayed in his Lord's chamber. His concern for the god gnawed at him. Hades did not pace back and forth in frustration. He did not work out his anger at the forge. He refused to eat and he rarely slept. He held court, passing judgment over the somber dead as if he belonged among their ranks and had been condemned to eternally wander the banks of Cocytus, the River of Lamentation.

When Persephone tried to see the god, Iapis had felt a stirring of hope at Hades' display of anger. But it was short-lived. As soon as the Goddess of Spring left the Underworld, Hades had withdrawn within himself again. The god could not continue as he was, yet Iapis saw no respite ahead. Time seemed to fester the dark god's wound instead of allowing him to heal.

"Iapis, do you know what happens when one soul mate is separated from the other?" Hades asked suddenly. He was standing in front of the window that looked out on the area of his gardens that joined the Elysia forest and eventually led to the River Lethe.

"Soul mates always find each other," Iapis said. "You know that already, Lord."

"But what happens if they cannot find each other because one of them has done something inexcusable?" Hades turned his head and looked blankly at Iapis.

"Can you not forgive her, Hades?"

Hades blinked and focused on the daimon's face. "Forgive her? Of course I have. She was only keeping her oath to Demeter. Carolina's sense of honor would not allow her to betray her word, not even for love. It is myself that I cannot forgive."

"Yourself? How, Lord?"

"Carolina Francesca Santoro is a mortal woman with the courage of a goddess, and I hurt her for the most empty of reasons, to salve my own pride. I cannot forgive that in myself. How can I expect her to?"

"Perhaps it is much like the night you insulted her," Iapis said slowly. "You have only to ask, and then be willing to remain and hear the answer."

Hades shook his head and turned back to the window. "She bared her soul to me and I betrayed her. Now she is beyond my reach."

"But if you would agree to see Persephone—"

"No!" Hades snarled. "I will not see a frivolous shell who mocks the soul that once resided within her body."

"Hades, you do not know that the goddess mocks Carolina."

"Cerberus rejected her. Orion loathed her. The dead called her a charlatan. That is knowledge enough for me," Hades said.

"She is a very young goddess," Iapis reminded him.

"She is not Carolina."

"No, she is not," the daimon said sadly.

"Leave me now, Iapis," Hades said.

"First let me draw a bath and set out fresh clothes for you." When Hades started to protest, Iapis blurted, "I cannot remember the last time you bathed or changed your clothing! You look worse than the newly dead."

Hades' powerful shoulders slumped. Without looking at the daimon he said, "If I bathe and change my clothing, will you leave me in peace?"

"For a time, Lord."

Hades almost smiled. "Then so be it, my friend."

HADES settled back into the steaming water. The black marble pool was built into the floor of his bathing room. He rested against a wide ledge that had been carved from the side of the pool. A goblet of red wine and a silver platter filled with pomegranates and cheese had been left within reach of his hand. The few candles that were lit glowed softly through the rising steam like moonlight through mist. Hades drank deeply from the goblet of wine. He had no appetite and he ignored the food, but the wine left a satisfying wooziness in his head. Perhaps, for just one night, he would drink himself into oblivion. Then he might sleep without dreaming of her. In one gulp he upended the goblet and looked around for more. Iapis had left a pitcher close enough that he did not have to leave the soothing heat of the pool to refill his cup.

"That daimon thinks of everything," he muttered.

"Not quite everything."

Hades jerked at the sound of her voice, and dropped the goblet. It clanged as it bounced against the marble floor.

Persephone blew on the steam. It parted and suddenly she was visible to Hades. She lounged on the ledge opposite him, and though she was submerged in water up to her shoulders, her naked body was as fully exposed to him as his was to her. The goddess's eyes rounded in surprise. Carolina was certainly no fool. She had had no idea the dour Lord of the Underworld was so delectable.

"Hello, Hades. I do not believe you and I have been formally introduced. I am Persephone, Goddess of Spring."

He averted his eyes from her and lurched from the pool, quickly wrapping himself in a robe. She could see his jaw clenching and when he spoke it sounded like he was forcing his words through gritted teeth.

"Leave my presence! I refused to see you."

"I know you did, but I have a problem, and you are the only god who can help me solve it, though Apollo is definitely more hospitable, and would be very willing to aid me in this particular venture." She ran her fingers playfully through the hot water. "But after talking to Lina, you appear to be my only recourse."

"Apollo!" Hades said fiercely. "What has he to do with Carolina?"

"Nothing, even though he wishes otherwise."

The rest of what she had said broke through his shock. "You have spoken to Carolina?"

"Yes, I have. Actually, I just left her bakery," Persephone said smugly.

Hades drew in a ragged breath. "She is well?"

"Her body is in excellent shape and her business is thriving."

Hades studied the drops of wine that had splattered from the goblet to the floor. "Good. I am pleased that she has—"

"I was not finished," Persephone interrupted. Flicking her fingers across the top of the pool, she rained water on him.

He glared at her. "Then finish."

"What I was going to say is that her body is good, her business is fine, but *she* is miserable."

"I . . . she . . ." Hades began and then stopped. He raked his hand through his damp hair.

"I—she—what?" Persephone prompted. "Lina told me that sometimes it was difficult to get you to relax, but if I was stubborn enough, I could get you to talk."

Hades felt his face flush. Then his gaze sharpened on hers. "She wanted you to talk with me? Why?"

"Oh, I do not believe she really wanted me to talk to you. She just said it because she thinks that you're in love with me."

Hades snorted. "That is ridiculous."

"Thank you, kind god."

"I did not mean any offense," Hades said quickly.

"Oh, I know, I know," Persephone said.

She brushed her hair back from her face and one of her breasts broke free of the surface of the pool, its taut mauve nipple pointed directly at Hades. The god cleared his throat and turned his head, focusing on the platter of fruit and cheese.

"I think it would be easier to talk with you if you joined me in the other room." He pointed to a cabinet near him. "There are robes there in which you may cover yourself."

"Wait!" Persephone said before he could leave the room. "First there is something that Lina and I need to know."

Hades looked at her, careful to keep his eyes focused on her face.

"Just stay where you are, and believe that this is very important—to all three of us."

"What is it you need to know?" Hades asked.

"This," Persephone said. She stood up.

The hot water flushed her slick skin. The nipples of her breasts were puckered and looked as if they had just been caressed. Her body was long and lean and as exquisite as Hades remembered it. He stared at her as she stepped slowly and gracefully from the pool and walked with an enticing sway toward him. When she reached him, she stopped. Lifting her arms she draped them around his shoulders. Then she pressed her naked body against him and pulled him down to meet her mouth.

Hades' lips touched hers and his arms instinctively went around her. But there was nothing there. Oh, he could certainly feel the familiarity of her body, and her mouth was warm and soft, but she did not move him. It was as if he held a malleable statue. Gently, but firmly, he pulled away from her.

Persephone stepped out of his arms.

"Then it truly is not this body that you desire."

"What I desire has not changed, nor will it. I desire only one woman. It matters little what body she inhabits."

For a moment, Hades thought he saw sadness in the goddess's eyes, but the look was fleeting and when she smiled, her air of youthful nonchalance was firmly in place.

"Well, thank you for answering that question for us."

"You are most welcome." Hades took a robe from the cabinet and Persephone slipped into it. He retrieved the goblet from the floor and picked up the pitcher of wine.

"Now all we have to do is to find a way to make Lina believe it," Persephone said.

They walked into Hades' bedchamber.

Persephone stared. "Hades, this is a beautiful room."

"Thank you," he said. "Make yourself comfortable while I find another goblet."

Persephone walked to a velvet-swathed window. She pulled aside the drape and gazed out on a fantastic view of tiered gardens filled with statuary, well-tended greenery, and thousands upon thousands of white flowers, all of which were bathed in a soft, unusual light.

"Your wine," Hades said.

Persephone turned from the window. "Lina was right—it does look like a beautiful forgotten dream."

Her words made Hades' heart ache.

"Why are you here, Persephone?"

The goddess tossed her hair back and smiled. "I have a proposition for you. . . ."

"I still do not understand what I can do! Carolina refused your proposition. You cannot force her into this exchange," Hades said as he paced across the floor in front of her.

She raised one eyebrow at him. "I cannot?"

"You will not force her." Hades' words were firm, but he felt his resolve wavering. Carolina could return! He could touch her and talk to her again. Surely he could convince her of his love. He shook himself. No! She had been through enough. He would not allow her to be forced into something she did not believe she could bear.

"The two of you are mirrors of stubbornness. You refuse to force her; she refuses to go of her own will." Persephone sighed. "Then you must find a way to convince her to return without being forced."

"How?" Hades bit the word.

"I don't know that you can," Persephone said sadly. She walked to Hades and placed a hand on his arm. "If you need me, you can call me through Mother's oracle." On impulse, she kissed his cheek.

He patted her hand and gave her an endearingly paternal smile. "Forgive my rudeness to you. Old gods sometimes have cantankerous ways."

Persephone smiled back at the god who was so obviously deeply in love with Carolina. "You are forgiven," she said and disappeared.

THE forge glowed with an otherworldly heat. Sweat flew from the god's body in time with the pounding of metal against metal. Hades was hardly aware of his surroundings.

She still loved him.

He had to find a way to repair the damage he had done so that she could allow herself to trust him again. But how?

"You remind me of a foolish old spinster, Lord of the Dead."

Hades whirled around to face the sarcastic voice, and squinted against the glaring light.

"Apollo! You and your garish sun are not needed here," Hades roared.

"Oh, yes, I tend to forget." Apollo passed his hand in front of his face and the brightness of his visage faded. "Better?"

"I do not recall inviting you within my realm."

"I simply had to come and glimpse what the other half of wasted love looks like."

Hades swelled with rage. "Do not presume—"

"And what I see here," the Sun God's voice broke through Hades' tirade, "is much less attractive than the mortal version."

"Of what mortal do you speak?" Hades demanded.

"Carolina, of course. Do you know that she actually spurned me? She was honestly more interested in my mares than she was me." Apollo chuckled. "When I thought she was Persephone, her actions confused me. When I found out she was a mortal clothed in the goddess's body, I was astounded. And then to learn that she chose you over me? Truly amazing."

Hades narrowed his eyes at Apollo. "I do not think it so amazing."

Apollo grinned. "You should. Mortal women find me irresistible."

"Carolina is more discerning than most mortal women."

"And more faithful, too. She has refused the suite of at least one man since returning to her world." Apollo looked at Hades appraisingly. "And though he is only a mortal, he is definitely younger than you."

"You have been watching her?" Hades growled.

"Is that not what I already said?"

"No!"

"I think perhaps your dreary lamentation for your lost love has affected your hearing. I distinctly remember saying—"

In two strides Hades reached Apollo. He grabbed the god by the throat and lifted him off his feet.

"Tell me how you can see her!" he snarled.

"Through Demeter's oracle," Apollo squeaked.

Hades dropped the God of Light and rushed from the forge. "Saddle Orion!" he bellowed.

Inside the forge Apollo rubbed his throat and rearranged his rumpled robes. "Good deed accomplished. You owe me, Demeter," he muttered before disappearing.

CHAPTER TWENTY-NINE

"IT's February, but it feels like April." Lina sighed happily. "I love it when Oklahoma weather does this," she told Edith Anne, who trotted contentedly by her side.

Rollerblades had taken some getting used to. It wasn't that her body didn't know what to do, it was Lina's mind that kept repeating thoughts like *yes, that pavement is hard* and *slow down, we're going to fall and break something.* So, even after several months of practice, Lina still took it slow, stroking the wide cement walkway that ran along the Arkansas River with controlled, careful strides.

"On your left!" someone shouted behind her and Lina moved closer to the right side of the pavement.

"Thanks," she yelled as a racing bike streaked past.

"No problem," the rider called back.

"I really appreciate it when they do that," she said to Edith Anne, who continued to keep pace with her in the grass that was just beginning to hint about future green off the side of the walkway.

Edith snorted.

"Well, you know it scares me when someone just busts past us without any warning. That big yellow-bike guy almost knocked me over last week." Lina reached down and flipped Edith's ear. The bulldog huffed at her and licked her hand. "I guess I should pay better attention, especially when it's quiet like it is this evening, but sometimes it's just so beautiful . . ."

Lina smiled. Evening was her favorite time of the day to rollerblade. Oklahoma sunsets were glorious, and sometimes, just as the sun was falling beneath the Arkansas River, the light would glint off the water, mixing pink and orange with blue and gray—and she would be reminded of the magic of Elysia. It didn't make her sad. Time had helped her with that. She liked the remembrance, in little doses. It helped to keep the emptiness at bay.

Edith Anne stopped to sniff at a particularly interesting clump of weeds.

"Hey, keep up with me! If you get mud or thistles on you, expect to get a bath when we get home."

Edith snorted a couple of times at the weeds before galloping after Lina. Lina slowed to let her catch up. She thought she heard the clop of a horse's hooves in the distance. *Interesting,* she thought, *the weather must be nice enough for the riverside stable to have opened early.* Horseback rides along the river were big business during good weather, but the business didn't usually open until April. She wondered how she'd missed the notice in the paper. Usually she liked to post things like that in the bakery. She made a mental note to check on it the next day.

The bulldog by her side again, Lina picked up her pace. She had already gone four miles, and her breath was still coming easily. Her legs felt strong. Lina was glad she had added rollerblading as a regular part of her weekly routine. Not only did it keep her body in shape, it helped her think.

And she'd had a lot to think about since Persephone's visit.

Merda! She'd been tempted by the goddess's offer. How could she not have been? To return to the Underworld as its queen . . . she would like nothing more. No, Lina corrected herself. What she would like more was what was keeping her from taking Persephone up on her offer. She'd wrestled with it over and over in her mind during the long winter months. She'd even wished she could call her grandmother and ask her advice—without her grandmother thinking she needed to be committed.

Sometimes she thought that maybe Demeter had been right and she had just made a mistake. Then all she had to do was to remember how Hades had turned away from her when she had revealed herself to him. *"Leave my realm"* had been his response to seeing the real Carolina. Time had helped to heal her, but remembering his words still caused her soul to ache.

And it was almost spring. Persephone would return soon for an answer. Lina breathed deeply and kept a steady pace while she considered, for what must have been the thousandth time, her answer. Unconsciously, Lina's hand found the amethyst narcissus that always hung around her neck.

She couldn't return. She wanted to. She even dreamed about it. But she couldn't do it. Maybe she was a coward, but she couldn't take the chance. It had taken her so long to heal. Lina couldn't break the wound open again. She would tell Persephone no. Maybe Persephone could find another mortal to exchange places with. Dolores was active in the Society for Creative Anachronisms. She'd probably be very interested in hanging around Mount Olympus and frolicking with nymphs while Persephone baked bread. The thought made Lina laugh. She could even plan a long vacation and leave the bakery in Dolores/Persephone's capable hands. Italy was nice in the spring . . .

Lina was preoccupied with planning her Italian vacation when she noticed that the clomp of horse's hooves had gotten closer and faster. She was moving to the edge of the walkway when a joyous neigh of greeting sliced the air. Lina's heart jumped in recognition.

She spun around as a large black shape overtook her. A dark muzzle was shoved in her face. Orion alternated between nickering and snorting while he nuzzled and lipped her hair and shoulders. In shock, Lina could only cling to the horse's tack and hope that in his exuberance he didn't knock her over.

"Who dares touch the dread steed of Hades?"

His words mimicked those he had spoken to her long ago, but his tone was completely altered. His voice was filled with love and longing. Lina looked up at Orion's back. He sat in a glossy Western saddle. He had replaced his archaic clothes with a black Western-cut shirt, the sleeves of which were rolled up to expose his muscular forearms, jeans and Oklahoma cowboy boots. His hair was pulled back and his eyes were bright.

Lina stared at him without speaking. The sight of him tugged at the newly healed wound in her heart. All those dark winter months he had left her to hurt alone. All that time. All that pain. The fierce surge of anger she felt surprised her.

He tried to smile, but his lips only quivered.

"You asked who dares to touch your steed, Hades." Lina's words were clipped. "Allow me to reintroduce myself to you. I am Carolina Francesca Santoro, a middle-aged mortal woman from Tulsa, Oklahoma, who owns a bakery. And I didn't dare to touch your dread steed—he stuck his face in my hands. Again."

Hades felt her words like knives. He didn't blame her for her anger. He understood it, but he wouldn't allow it to make him give up. He kicked his leg over the saddle and dismounted. He wanted to approach her, to take her into his arms, but she was staring at him with a cold, unblinking gaze that was anything but welcoming.

"You left one title from your introduction, Carolina." His voice made her name a prayer.

"I don't think so. I know exactly who I am," she said. He hadn't come any closer to her, but she still moved a step back from him.

"You are Carolina Francesca Santoro, a middle-aged mortal woman from Tulsa, Oklahoma, who owns a bakery. You are also Queen of the Underworld," Hades said.

Lina felt a tremor pass through her and she clutched her anger, afraid if she let it go, her heart would tear into tiny pieces.

"I'm sorry, Lord. You must be confused. The Goddess Persephone is Queen of the Underworld. I was just a temporary stand-in, and I wasn't up to the job."

"Your subjects feel differently, Carolina." He looked pointedly at Orion, who had stretched out his neck so that he could nibble her shoulder while she stroked his muzzle.

"Animals like me," she said. As if to prove her words, Edith Anne butted against her legs, wriggling for attention. Orion snorted and bent to blow at the bulldog.

"He reminds me a little of Cerberus." Hades nodded at the squatty dog, trying again unsuccessfully to smile.

"He is a she. And I hear she has better manners than Cerberus has been exhibiting," Lina said, and then bit her lip. She shouldn't converse with him.

"No doubt Cerberus' manners are lacking because he is feeling the absence of his Queen, as is the rest of the Underworld."

"A dog and a horse aren't anyone's subjects. And I'm not a queen. I'm a mortal woman. I do not have any subjects."

Hades turned back to Orion's saddle and pulled out the rolled-up canvas he had lodged under the pommel. "I have something for you. Eurydice tried to give it to me, but I reminded her that her work belonged to you. She still thinks of herself as Personal Artist to the Goddess of Spring, though she misses her mistress very much."

"I'm not . . . no, I don't want . . ." Lina stammered, feeling a wave of home-sickness at the thought of Eurydice. Then, Hades stepped close to her. In the months they had been apart she had forgotten about his size. He seemed to surround her. Even in modern clothes he was dark and rakishly handsome. Her Batman . . .

"The little spirit drew this from a dream she had of you. She said that it felt right."

Hades was so close to her that she could feel the heat of his body.

Wordlessly, Lina took the canvas from Hades. She unrolled it and gasped. "It's me!"

It was her—the mortal woman, Carolina Francesca Santoro—her body, her face, her smile. Not Persephone. As she gazed at the image Eurydice had drawn from a dream, her fingers began to tingle and suddenly a current of emotion traveled through the canvas and into her soul. Within the current she could hear the unnumbered voices of the dead. They were all calling to her, begging their queen to return.

Her hands trembled and she felt the knot of anger within her begin to dissolve.

"Your subjects recognize you and call for you, Carolina," Hades said gently.

"It's too bad that their god did not recognize me," she said without looking up at him.

"There is no god here now, nor any lord." Hades' voice broke, and he had to pause before he could continue. He took Lina's chin in his hand and brought her face up so that she must look into his eyes. "Tonight I am only a man who is desperately seeking his soul mate. You see, she was separated from me because of my foolishness, and I had to forgive myself before I could find her and ask that she—"

Tears began spilling from Lina's eyes.

"Do not weep, beloved."

"You turned away from me," she whispered through broken sobs. "When you saw who I really was, you didn't want me."

"No!" He pulled her into his arms and crushed her against him. "It was never you I turned from. It was pride that goaded my words and actions."

"Because you didn't want to love a middle-aged mortal," she said into his chest.

His laugh came out as a sob. "No, because I was terrified that I had lost my soul to a woman who wanted nothing more than a dalliance with an inexperienced god about which she could brag."

Lina looked up at him. "I only told Demeter about you not being with any other goddess because I was trying to convince her that you were different."

"I know, beloved. Forgive the pride of an old, solitary god." His lips were finally able to form a smile. "And please come home."

In answer, Lina pulled him down to her.

"Carolina." Hades breathed her name against her lips. "My soul has ached for you, my eternal beloved."

Before he could kiss her again, Orion bumped him from behind. The short, stout dog was sniffing around his feet. Hades glanced down to see streams of saliva on his boots.

"Orion, stop that," Lina said, pushing the big, black head aside. "Oh, Edith Anne, don't do that. You're messing up his boots."

Hades threw back his head and laughed. He swept his queen off her feet, tossed her up onto Orion's back, and then he swung up behind her with a strength that clearly said he was no mortal man.

"Hades! What are you doing?"

"Taking you out of the reach of those beasts." He wrapped his arms around Carolina and pulled her firmly back against him.

"But, Edith Anne—"

"Do not fret. Orion will go slowly. We will not lose your dog." Holding her securely, he clucked at the stallion. Orion turned his head and snorted, but he began walking, slowly, so that the bulldog had no trouble trotting by his side. Then the god returned his attention to Carolina.

"We have a short time before spring returns to your world. Perhaps you would like to show me some of this kingdom you call Tulsa," Hades said, stroking the soft brown curls that formed at the nape of her neck. He was having a difficult time restraining himself from ravishing her right there. He thought the new body she wore was seductive and womanly. She was soft and fragrant and delectably inviting.

Lina twisted around and smiled at him. "You know about Persephone's plan?"

"Who does not?" he said good-naturedly.

"I'm beginning to think that it could work," she said.

"As am I." He bent to claim her lips.

Lina pushed back from him. "Wait, you shouldn't be here; you certainly can't stay very long. You don't have anyone taking your place in the Underworld."

"No, I do not." He smiled at his queen and his soul felt light and young. "But sometimes even Death must take a holiday."

As their lips met the sun touched the bank of the river. It paused there and shone one brief, winking beam on the lovers before falling from the sky.

Today Tulsa mourns the passing of a local matriarch, Carolina Francesca Santoro. Ms. Santoro was a restaurateur, philanthropist and renowned animal lover. Ms. Santoro is not survived by any biological children, but she will be greatly missed by many who felt they were her family. For decades her chain of Pani Del Goddess bakeries have been a vital part of many Oklahoma communities. The bakeries are best known for their specialty, ambrosia cream cheese. The recipe for this delectable cheese has been a closely guarded secret for more than half a century. But do not fear, loyal Pani Del Goddess patrons. Before her death, Ms. Santoro shared the recipe with an Italian relative, her great-niece, Persephone Libera Santoro, who will be assuming the position of major stockholder of the Pani Del Goddess Corporation. The new Miss Santoro has announced that she will be dividing her time between Oklahoma and Italy. As is only appropriate considering her name, she will spend each spring and summer with us in Tulsa. To honor the memory of her great aunt, let us give her a warm Oklahoma hello!

—The Tulsa World,
21 March 2055

EPILOGUE

LINA was feeling a little breathless and displaced, which was truly ironic. She was, after all, finally wearing her own skin.

"It probably has something to do with being one of the newly dead," she muttered, holding out her arms and looking in amazement at her glowing body. She was more substantial than the dead she was so used to seeing, and she was pleased that it appeared that her body had taken on a form that was much younger than she had been at her death. With a start, Lina realized that she had materialized within her forty-three-year-old body. She laughed. "The exact age I was when I met him," she said.

The tunnel stretched before her, black and unending, but its darkness didn't intimidate her. Lina walked forward with confidence without once looking back at the last light she would ever glimpse from the mortal world.

Suddenly, a little ball of brilliance burst into being at her shoulder, and she laughed in surprise. "What are you doing here?" The globe bobbled around, wiggling like a puppy. But she didn't really need to ask—she knew who had sent the light. "Thank you, Persephone," she called to the listening air.

She walked quickly through the cluster of beautiful ghost trees that had come to be known as Persephone's Grove. As always, she enjoyed the sparkling facets that were their leaves. Lina left the grove, and blinked in surprise. Before her, the onyx road that led to her lover's palace stretched as usual to the gates of pearl, but this time the gates had been flung wide open, and behind them were multitudes of glowing, semi-substantial shapes. At the head of the teeming mass stood Hades, flanked on one side by Orion and on the other by Eurydice and Iapis.

As the stallion caught sight of her he screamed a shrill neigh of joyous welcome. Eurydice clamped one hand against her pale mouth, and with the other she waved gaily at her mistress while tears of happiness streamed down her cheeks.

But when Hades began to move toward her, Lina's entire world narrowed to hold only him. He strode to her, his eyes dancing with emotion. When he finally stood before her, he reached out, and with a gesture that was as familiar to her as was her own heart, he caressed her cheek.

"Welcome home, beloved," he whispered.

She smiled at her soul mate.

Hades spun around to face the mob. Cloak swirling, he raised his arms victoriously over his head.

"She has come!" he thundered in the voice of a god.

A shout rose from the unnumbered dead that echoed from the Underworld up and spread throughout all of Olympus. *"Rejoice! Our queen is come and she shall leave us nevermore!"*

On her throne in Olympus, Demeter raised her goblet and touched it against Persephone's as they smiled at each other in acknowledgment of Carolina's happy ending.

"Well done, my daughters," Demeter said. "Well done."

TURN THE PAGE FOR A PREVIEW OF
P. C. CAST'S STORY
"CANDY COX AND THE BIG BAD (WERE) WOLF"
FROM HER ANTHOLOGY

Accidental Magic

NOW AVAILABLE FROM BERKLEY SENSATION!

"Godiva! Wait—wait—wait. Did you just say that you and your sisters called forth the dead two nights ago?" Candice said, rubbing her forehead where it was beginning to ache.

"Yeah, but you missed the important part. Romeo was . . . *spectacular,*" Godiva said breathlessly into the phone. "Who knew that poor, wounded wolf would turn into something—I mean, some*one*—so delectable."

"So he actually did more than hump your leg this time?"

"Candy Cox—I swear you haven't been listening."

"You know I hate it when you call me that."

"Fine. *Candice*, you haven't been listening," Godiva said. "He's not just a wolf. He's a *were*wolf, which means he has an excellent tongue and he humps a lot more than my leg."

Candice kept muttering as if Godiva hadn't spoken. "It's not like I don't get enough of that name crap at school. Why I ever decided to attempt to teach high school morons I'll never know." She cringed inwardly, remembering the countless times some hormone-impaired sixteen-year-old boy had made a wiseass remark (usually replete with sophomoric clichés) about her name. God, she was truly sick and tired of Mysteria High School—Home of the Fighting Fairies.

"You could have kept one of your ex-husbands' names," Godiva said helpfully.

"Oh, please," Candice scoffed. "I'd rather sound like a porn star than keep any reminders of ex-husbands number one through five. No. My solution is to change careers. As soon as I finish my online master's in creative writing I can dump the fucking Fighting Fairies and snag that job in Denver as assistant editor for Full Moon Press."

"Honey, have I told you lately that you have a very nasty mouth for a school-teacher?"

"Yes. And I do believe I've told you that I *have* said nasty mouth *because* I'm a schoolteacher. Uh, please. Shall we take a moment to recall the one and only day you subbed for me?"

Godiva shuddered. "Ack! Do not remind me. I take back any form of criticism for your coarse language. Those teenagers are worse than a whole assortment of wraiths, demons, and undead. I mean, really, some of them even smell worse!" Just remembering had her making an automatic retching sound. "But Candice, seriously, I don't want you to move!"

"Denver's not that far away—we shop till we drop there several times a year. You know I need a change. The teenage monsters are wearing on me."

"I know," Godiva sighed. Then she brightened. "Hey! I could work on a spell that might help shut those boys up whenever they try to speak your name. Maybe something to do with testicles and tiny brains . . ."

"That's really sweet of you, but you know that magic doesn't work on or around me, so it probably wouldn't work on my name, either." Candice sighed. It was true. As a descendant of one of the few nonmagical founders of the town (his name was, appropriately, John Smith), Candice had No Magic at All. Yes, sadly, she lived in a town full of witches, warlocks, vampires, fairies, werewolves, et cetera, et cetera, and her magic was nonmagic. It figured. Her magic worked like her marriages. Not at all. "Men are such a pain in the ass."

Without losing a beat at her friend's sudden change in subjects, Godiva giggled. "I agree completely, which is why I know exactly what you need—a werewolf lover."

"Godiva Tawdry! I'm too damn old to roll around the woods with a dog."

"A werewolf is not a dog. And forty is not old. Plus, you look ten years younger. Why do you think high school boys still get crushes on you, *Ms. Candy Cox*?"

"Put boobs on a snake and high school boys would chase after it. And don't call me Candy."

Godiva laughed. "True, but that doesn't make you any less attractive. You've got a killer body, Ms. Cox."

"I'm fat."

"You're curvy."

"I'm old."

"You're ripe."

"Godiva! Do you not remember what happened last time I let myself commit matrimony?"

"Clearly," Godiva said. "It took ex-husband number five less than six months to almost bore you to death. And he seemed like such a nice guy."

"Yes, I admit he did seem nice. They all did at first." Candice sighed. "Who knew that he would literally almost kill me? And after my brush with death, I decided that I. Am. Done."

"Okay, look. You accidentally took an unhealthy mixture of Zoloft, Xanax, and pinot grigio. It could happen to anyone, especially when she's being bored to death by a man scratching himself while he incessantly flips from the History Channel to CNN—"

"—And pops Viagra like they're M&Ms and thinks that the telltale oh-so-attractive capillary flush constitutes foreplay," Candice interrupted. "Yeesh. I'm going to just say no from here on out. Truly. I've sworn off men."

"No, I remember exactly what you said. 'Godiva'—here you raised your fist to the sky like Scarlett O'Hara—'I will never marry again.' So you've sworn off marriage, not men. And anyway, a werewolf is not technically a man. Or at least if he is, it's only for part of the time. The rest of the time he is the most adorably cuddly sweet furry—"

"Fine." Candice cut off Godiva's gushing. "I'll think about it."

"Really?"

"Yes." *No*, she thought. She hurried on before Godiva could press the point. "I've really gotta go. I'm deep in the middle of Homework Hell. I have to turn in my poetry collection to the online creative writing professor next week, and I still haven't figured out a theme for the damn thing. I'm totally screwed if I can't get rid of this writer's block."

"Well . . ." Godiva giggled mischievously. "I don't know how it'd work on writer's block, but Romeo sure unclogged me last night."

"You're not helping."

"I'm just saying—a little werewolf action might fix you right up."

"You're still not helping."

"Sorry. I'll let you get back to your writing. Remember, you said you'd think about a werewolf lover."

"Yeah, I'll think about it right after I think about my poetry theme. Uh, shouldn't you and your sisters be frolicking about the graveyard checking on the dead or whatnot?"

"Oh, don't worry about it. Our little screwup actually ended up being a good thing, what with those horrid demons on the prowl; the town could use the extra protection. And anyway, it's only temporary and the dead have already quieted down. Uh, but since you mentioned it . . . are you planning on going jogging today?"

"Yes."

"Do you think you could take a spin through the graveyard and keep your eyes open for my broom? I must have forgotten it in all the excitement that night, between Genevieve scampering off into the woods with Hunter—whose eyes, by the way, were glowing bright red—and my Romeo morphing from wolf to man rather unexpectedly. Anyway, if you see it would you please grab it before somebody flies off with it? You know a good broom is hard to find."

"Yeah, sure. If I see it, I'll get it for you. But wait, isn't Hunter Knight supposed to be dead?" Candice said.

"Well, kinda. Actually, he's a little undead."

"Isn't that like being a little pregnant?"

"Don't be a smart-ass. It's embarrassing enough for me to admit that my sister's getting some vampire action. God, I wish the girl had better taste in men, alive or dead."

Candice sighed. "Hey—don't be such a prude. If I'd chosen one of the undead I might not be unmarried."

"Candice, honey, I love you, but you are a hopeless piece of work. Now be a doll and go find my broom. Bye."

Godiva hung up the phone and sat tapping her chin with one long, slender finger. Candy was getting old before her time. Goddess knew, she really did need a lover. A young lover. A young werewolf lover. A hot, naughty affair would be the perfect thing to keep her from moving to Denver. Her fingers itched to swirl up a little love spell, but magic wouldn't work on her friend. Godiva's eyes widened and her full, pink lips tilted up. Magic wouldn't work on Candy, but it definitely would work on a werewolf. . . .

ABOUT THE AUTHOR

P. C. Cast, writing with her daughter, is the #1 *New York Times* bestselling author of the House of Night Novels: *Marked, Betrayed, Chosen, Untamed, Hunted, Tempted, Burned, Awakened, Destined* and *Hidden*.